EXTRAORDINARY EXPERIENCES

of JAKE VAN YORK

CLAUDE PETERSON JR

outskirtspress
DENVER, COLORADO

Extraordinary Experiences of Jake Van York
All Rights Reserved.
Copyright © 2014 Claude Peterson Jr
v3.0

Outskirts Press, Inc.
http://www.outskirtspress.com

ISBN: 978-1-4787-0202-3

Outskirts Press and the "OP" logo are trademarks belonging to Outskirts Press, Inc.

PRINTED IN THE UNITED STATES OF AMERICA

Table of Contents

Preface

This book is dedicated to the loving memory of my wonderful mother and father. It is also dedicated to my warm and caring grandmother, who stood at my side for all of my childhood days. I shall forever cherish my memories of each them, for from the day of my birth, they gave me their devoted love. They also educated and guided me, while protecting me from the evils of this world. Moreover, they provided me with the tools which I would need to lead a productive, fruitful, and active life in this old world of ours!

First, I pay tribute to my mother, a self-respecting, highly competent lady who loved and protected her child, as she cared for her family. Even under the most adverse conditions, she never once complained, but continued her routine as if all was normal. This was a person who, although her body (in the end) had been eaten away by cancer, never required any type of pain medication! Not only was mom a loving person, – she was also an unusually strong person!

Second, to my great father, a self-respecting, dedicated, and highly disciplined man who always ensured that the needs of his family remained his first priority! This was a man who would do whatever was necessary to provide an honest living for his family. And, even though times were austere, and life extremely challenging, I believe I can truly say of my father, he never once considered leaving my mother and me. Yes, he remained with us until the very end, when my strong mother sat while holding his head in her lap, as he breathed his very last dying breath. This was, and shall always be, my one true hero!

Finally, I pay tribute to my warm, caring grandmother (dad's mom). She was the glue that held our family together! If either of us stumbled, she steadied us. If either of us fell, she would pick us up and dust us off. If either of us seemed to lose our way, she was there to guide us out of the darkness. She augmented our small family in every conceivable way, particularly spiritually, physically, and monetarily. In fact, she was so very dedicated and helpful she continued working in our fields with my mom and dad, until just two hours before her lengthy life ended at the ripe old age of one hundred and two years! To say the least, she was much more than just great – she was miraculous!

To them I say "I TOAST YOU – EACH OF YOU! I shall cherish your memories for as long as I shall live. I am forever indebted to the three of you!

This section has been specifically reserved for one of the all-time greats: Her name was Paraskivi, and she was born ninety-five years ago, on a small Greek island. Her life had been an unusually difficult one from an early age, where as a young girl she began work on commercial fishing boats owned by her parents. As just a teenager, she would remain at sea throughout the night, even during cold winter months. While there, she would work side by side with the other men on the boat, raising heavy nets laden with fish. (This was not a task suited for a young girl)! Nevertheless, she continued doing this for many years. Finally, she grew into womanhood, and later accepted matrimony. She married a handsome young gentleman named John. Their lives were great for the first ten years. John was a wonderful husband and father. He was dedicated to his loving wife and his four very young daughters. Unfortunately, John's life was brought to an early end, due to illness. This left his wife Paraskivi as the sole provider for their four young daughters. She had been devastated by his sudden loss, but her faith in The Father provided her with the strength needed to continue their lives together. As the days and months passed their situation continued to worsen! Paraskivi soon found herself without food for herself or children. Even worse, she had no money with which to purchase food, so she reluctantly began selling what few belongings John had acquired, to support her children.

Living on faith alone, they persevered. Her four daughters eventually became attractive and respectable ladies. Each married a young man who strived to prove his love to his dear wife. Today, each of Paraskivi's daughters leads a productive and happy life! As for Paraskivi herself, she chose to remain a widow for another sixty-five years after John's death. Her daughters had moved away, leaving the appearance that Paraskivi now lived all alone. But, Paraskivi was never really alone! Our Lord and Savior Jesus Christ had walked with her every step she had taken during each of her remaining days on earth. Paraskivi is gone now; her days of tribulation are ended. But, she left behind many who knew and loved her. I personally am proud to consider myself a member of this group. I shall now speak for our entire group. Our Dear Paraskivi: We shall forever cherish our loving memories of times spent with you. And, if any soul should hereafter be elevated to sainthood, we are confident that it shall be the soul of Paraskivi Triviza! WE LOVE YOU!

Introduction

The names of those persons mentioned in this unusual story have been purposely changed. These steps were taken in order to protect their anonymity and privacy. Also, the names of certain geographical locations have been omitted for legal and political reasons. (This autobiography was written as narrated by Mr. Van York himself).

I begin my rare story by relating to you my early childhood years. I was born shortly before the beginning of World War II, in a small town in the eastern area of South Carolina, and was raised by two very caring parents. My sweet, dear grandmother (dad's mom) was also at my side during those eighteen years. My adolescent years were virtually uneventful, as I was never involved in any juvenile disciplinary matters. I always obeyed both parents, so daily I would try doing any little thing to make them a bit more proud of me. In fact I tried so desperately, I even succeeded in maintaining total sexual abstinence until after I had enlisted in the United States Air Force! Might I also add that while I'd strived so hard in remaining a model child, many teenagers in my neck of the woods were having sex, even before they had reached fourteen years of age!

Prior to joining the military, I had never traveled more than seventy-two miles (in any direction) from my hometown. Thusly, one might say that while growing up, my life was simply one of pure boredom. But not to worry, because after military basic training, my life took a complete one-hundred-eighty degree turn. It was at this point that my most unforgettable experiences in life would begin!

I am Jake Van York, a patriot. I shall not reveal to you each personal covert operation because of the unique nature of my work, which was done primarily in secrecy, but often boldly and in plain view. Long before the occurrence of 9/11, and the subsequent development of the Department of Homeland Security, I roamed these lands, while secretly performing reconnaissance missions for my country. Although, I regrettably find myself prohibited from revealing certain information concerning those special covert operations in which I participated. I remain convinced that such indiscretion would undoubtedly produce some negative effect on the outcome of certain ongoing national defense programs!

My qualifications for such duties were my excellent health, a unique style of self-defense, and proficiency in several foreign languages. Fortunately, I never seemed to need a doctor except during annual physical examinations. I acquired proficiency in Arabic, Greek, Japanese, Thai, and Vietnamese. Also, my self-defense skills throughout enabled me to survive even the most difficult of situations. But most significant of all these attributes is – through most of my adult years I've remained in sole possession of one mysterious, but magnificent, acoustic instrument which was known to me only as the "Elm".

This strange, tiny object was given to me on the day of

my departure for induction into the military by my grandmother, who resided in our modest household. On that warm summer morning she called me to her side while sitting in her old rocking chair. "Son, I want to give you something". I slowly walked over to her, saying, "Yes Mama"? She then reached into the pocket of her old apron, withdrawing a paper napkin. Ever so carefully she unwrapped the plain napkin, holding up to me what I had thought to be just a bead. (I could not have been more mistaken)! She then said, "I want you to have this, but you absolutely must promise me that you will safeguard it for as long as you may live". "Please, I beg you – do not let this fall into the wrong hands". "I am told that this little thing that you see here comes from a site in old Mesopotamia". When my dying father gave this to me, he told me that this little Elm was believed to have been accidentally left behind by an ancient group of superior beings (called gods) who inhabited this planet many thousands of years ago". She added, "It has certain powers and can allow you to hear sounds from great distances". Little did I know at the time, that when used properly, this tiny instrument would allow me to listen to activities and voice communications from distances of slightly more than two miles, which was amazing! But, grandmother had made me promise to never use the Elm for personal gain! Nor, could I use it for any form of evil. Ultimately, I could only use this tiny object while serving the good of all humankind!

The Elm was extremely small in size, measuring only one-half inch in length, and one-quarter inch in diameter. Its color was that of pale green. Also, the Elm was oval in shape, and slightly transparent. A small round opening had been reamed through its center. Though upon close inspection, I noticed that this opening was tapered, measuring 1/16 inch at the small end and 1/8 inch at its opposite outer end. Also, around its outer upper edge, it held a small ring-like part which was movable. On this tiny ring were twelve pin-point dots. After several weeks of becoming familiar with this little Elm, I discovered that its ring was a distance calibration and fine-tuning device! Each little dot measured the distance of .02 kilometer. By rotating this ring, I could initially adjust my listening range from just a few feet, to slightly more than one mile! This allowed me to listen in on any conversations of my choosing. Imagine the significance and advantage of possessing such a powerful little tool as I currently held!

In using the Elm, I would insert it into either ear (whichever was the most convenient for the task at hand). I would then aim that ear in the direction I wanted to listen, and set for distance. At first, I was fascinated by much of what I overheard! However, on frequent occasions I would overhear dreadful, alarming, and even shocking conversations and activities (i.e., robberies, rape, and even worse)!

I usually operated in plain sight. For example, you may have seen me standing on some street corner. I was probably holding a sign bearing the words "Will work for food". You may even have seen me on some sidewalk holding a cup up to you. But then on occasion I am sure you've seen me driving down some street in a shiny police patrol car. I might even have waved to you, but if I did so, then my friend – you may have had yourself a major problem!

I regrettably have no siblings; hence, for a long period my social life consisted of mere casual encounters. However,

I now have a very special lady in my life! For the purposes of this story, I shall refer to her only as Lora. Fortunately, I also have a dozen or more friends, most of whom are in their mid-forties. I am hesitant to mention my two chromed .45cal Colt automatics, an assortment of certain chemicals, and my highly accurate miniature crossbow. Although, I am extremely proud to mention my very special black Doberman Pinscher (Mac). When at home in the U. S., Mac guarded me as I slept. Though whenever I was away on some mission, I mostly relied upon my defensive skills, various chemicals, and my trusted miniature crossbow. These were the special tools with which I succeeded in surviving for over twenty-five years!

Occasionally, I would call upon the services of my good friend Bill. Those services which Bill provided included (but were not limited to) the rapid health deterioration of officials of certain unfriendly nations and/or organizations. In some instances, this even involved the mysterious disappearance of certain officials, including members of governments plus a number of high-value crime figures. Bill's methods of operating usually precluded the necessity for political assassination of individuals. To the contrary, they merely rendered those persons incompetent; and, thereby incapable of continued performance in their current position (notwithstanding official status). Hopefully, I've provided you with information sufficient to give you a clear picture of what this was really about – the continued safety and security of our great nation!

Chapter 1

My Childhood Years

For more than thirty years I have pondered the issue of whether or not I should publish this story. Only when I could procrastinate no longer, did I finally decide upon proceeding with this project. So here now is just a peek into my life as a young child. My grand entrance onto this world stage (commonly referred to as *life*) was marred with extensive adversity. Consequently, during my first eighteen years of life, I remained in direct opposition to opposing forces such as austerity, deprivation, and semi-isolation from society. Remarkably though, it would be these very same conditions which would prepare me for the prosperous life which lay ahead!

I was born in a respectable and quiet little town on the eastern seaboard of the United States. At the time of my birth, the population of this little town numbered less than twenty thousand. The year was 1936, in the midst of winter. December 27th was the fateful day. I am told that the temperature hovered around zero degrees for several days surrounding this period. Fortunately though, I naturally don't remember any of this. I am also told that I was delivered by midwife as a reasonably healthy baby, and that my mother had experienced no complications from this childbirth.

Of course I am unable to recall any of the events associated with my first year on earth. But, as later stated to me by my parents, my first year passed smoothly and free of any problems. The second and third years, however, were quite different and difficult. It seems that during each of those two winters, I was afflicted with severe pneumonia. That first case of illness had kept me in bed for three weeks, and as I had not yet fully recovered, the second case nearly aborted my young life. By this time I'd reached three years of age, thusly I vaguely remember that bout. I vividly recall my dear mother having sat at my bedside throughout each critical night.

Luckily for me, my resourceful father had been able to secure the services of one of the very best doctors in our town. I feel certain that this great doctor, who just happened to be a family friend, was the primary reason for my surviving my second pneumonia attack. He diligently visited me each day and evening in our home, providing care and expert instruction to my exhausted mother. Might I also add, my dear elderly grandmother played a major role by assisting and supporting my young and inexperienced mother in my treatment and subsequent slow recovery.

Finally, after five long weeks this dreaded illness passed, and I had gained sufficient strength to delicately move about our old house. I was not allowed outside though for two more months. It seemed that with each passing day I became a little stronger. But my doctor still visited us, checking on me for the next full month. He stopped by at least three times each week. During one of his evening visits, after my father had arrived home from work, I remember overhearing him say to my father, "Mr. Van York, I strongly advise that you buy a young cow, so that little Jake might have fresh milk each day to drink". My father did not question our doctor's wisdom or advice, so the very next evening when he arrived home from work, he brought along a young female cow. I was thrilled to see and touch this docile young animal. My parents named her Fannie and I quickly adopted her as my pet. As strange as this may seem, at the tender age of only three years old, I was even then a bit older than our young female cow Fannie.

Each morning and afternoon, my mother would take me by my little hand and lead me to our new 'family member'. There, she would draw from Fannie a pitcher of milk. She would then feed me the fresh, warm and tasty, unpasteurized milk as I stood there beside her. The natural vitamins contained in the milk strengthened me as the months passed, and I began to grow at a normal rate. Also, I became healthy and strong enough to run and play with the other kids in our neighborhood. I soon began making friends and leading a normal childhood life.

Years four and five passed virtually unnoticed, as I continued drinking my fresh, warm cow's milk several times throughout each day and gaining strength. For my fourth birthday my father brought me a young male goat. I appropriately named him Billy and we soon became friends. I now had a pet to play with! Having no brothers or sisters caused me to depend on Billy for much of the companionship that I received. He grew rapidly and soon I was able to ride him as I would have the pony that I'd never had. Then, seeing how attached I had become to my little goat, my father located and brought me one cute little spotted male puppy, which I appropriately named Spot. Now, though I still had no siblings, I was happy because I had Fannie, Billy, and Spot in my daily life. They gave me companionship at times when there were no children to play with. Oh, I failed to mention that we lived just a short distance outside the established city limits of our town. Accordingly, having these animals in the neighborhood posed no problem. Thusly, time moved on.

I did not attend preschool simply because in those days, none existed. When I reached age five though, I expected to commence kindergarten, but sadly this did not happen. After consultation with my doctor, my mom and dad decided it best to keep me at home for at least one more full year. So, I stayed at home while all the other children of my age attended kindergarten. I was unusually fortunate though to have had a very nice lady (6th grade teacher) living directly across the street from us. She was also a close family friend, and she had agreed to provide tutoring services to me several evenings throughout each week. My mom and dad had factored this consideration into the equation when they'd decided to keep me at home. This solution worked exceptionally well in that my tutor was extremely competent and dedicated. She was also very patient and taught me well. During these tutoring sessions, I learned many of the basic and essential elements of our language. She taught me to write my name in both upper and lower-case lettering. She taught me to spell short words and read nursery rhyme materials. And, finally she taught me to count into the thousands, so by the time I started school at age six, I was further advanced than most of the other children who had already completed kindergarten. This kind lady's actions were highly beneficial to me; and, gave me a significant advantage in beginning my life in society. I shall be forever indebted to this wonderful teacher.

During the following year I commenced what was known as public primary school. I had long anticipated starting school; nevertheless, my first day of attendance was absolutely traumatic! There was no school bus transportation and we did not own a car. Even had we owned one, my mom could not drive, and dad was at work providing for our family. So on that very special first day of school, mom awoke me earlier than usual. I was now six years old; nonetheless, while mom was preparing for our departure, she would constantly check on me to make sure that I had properly washed, brushed my teeth, and combed my hair. Then she personally supervised my dressing, ensuring that my clothing was all in order. Though I was not hungry at such an early hour (6:30AM), mom prepared ham and eggs with buttered toast. Naturally, she'd also placed on our table my glass of fresh, warm milk. I quickly ate my breakfast and finished my milk. At that time, I did not understand why I felt such uneasiness in the pit of my stomach. Much later, I would learn that this condition or sensation which I felt is called "butterflies" or nervous stomach. Finally, it was time for mom and me to depart for school.

Mom took me by the hand and off we went, walking the three-quarter-mile distance to the schoolhouse. The month was September, the hour 7:00AM, and the sun had risen. It was early autumn, but we both were certain that this would be a warm, sunny day. And, except for the fact that I would be inside a classroom, we knew that this would be a beautiful day. The trek to school took us about forty-five minutes. We could have made it a bit quicker, but all along our route, people who knew us would come out from their homes to greet us and wish me well on my first day of school. We would exchange pleasantries and I would thank each of them for their well-wishes as we continued to walk along the quiet, tree-lined streets.

We arrived at my school at about 7:45AM. This would normally have been considered a bit early, but it was my mother's desire to reach the school yard a little early. Mom wanted to observe the behavior of the other children playing and milling about the school grounds. This was so that if any of the children there had, in any way, indicated harmful intent toward me, she would have instantly been on the scene to control the situation. I was quite shy among so many strangers for the first time. So, for a short while mom remained alone in a corner at the edge of the school yard. Soon though, some children whom I knew came toward me and we began to run and play. Meanwhile, mom was standing just a few yards away observing, and I could see that she seemed happy at this. Finally, the bell rang and we entered the building, being escorted and guided like herded cattle.

Each respective teacher received her class (no male teachers). Once inside our classroom, our teacher introduced herself as Mrs. Smith. She then proceeded to orientate the class as to rules, requirements, and procedures. During Mrs. Smith's briefing, she also made clear to each of us her demands and expectations. I had on several previous occasions seen and briefly spoken to her in passing her home and on the streets of our little town. So, I at least felt a bit more comfortable, as I wanted to feel that we knew each other. This way, I felt much more secure. As the morning progressed, she asked each of us to stand and introduce ourselves to the class. Then she read to us, following up with a session of basic arithmetic. The time seemed to pass quite rapidly and soon the bell rang, signaling time for lunch. Our school hosted a mediocre lunch room, and the food it served (canned pork & beans) had not been seasoned or properly heated. I tried to eat but found it to be so bland, any pig would have probably tasted this and walked (or run) away! I finished eating and rushed outside, hoping to play for a few short minutes. But, as soon as I was outside, I began feeling a slight queasiness in the pit of my stomach. Our lunch period was forty-five minutes in duration and I knew that about one-half hour had already passed. So, at that point I decided that I had better pay a visit to the restroom. I barely made it! I guess the excitement or maybe those awful beans had really gotten to me. I was physically unable to leave that old restroom for what seemed to be about twenty minutes. The bell had already sounded, but I could not venture outside! Finally, I was able to stand and arrange my clothing, so I quickly washed my hands before rushing to class, not knowing how late I actually was since I had no watch.

I literally ran to my classroom! Upon nearing the room, I could hear Mrs. Smith reading to the class. Cautiously and apprehensively, I approached the door and peered inside the classroom. Mrs. Smith glared at me briefly but continued reading, so I quietly entered the room and went directly to my seat. A few minutes passed before she reached the end of that chapter. Then, she abruptly closed the book and took her seat at her desk. During this time I had quietly sat wondering if or when she might mention my tardiness.

Then, it happened "Van York, come up here!" she snarled. My heart skipped a beat as I arose and walked slowly toward her desk. As I approached her she asked me in a very harsh tone, "Where have you been"? But at that moment, I did not know exactly how to answer her. I knew exactly where I had been, but I could not repeat such before the class; hence, I hesitated - and this annoyed her immensely! "Hold out your hand!" she shouted at me. As I complied with her command, she reached into her upper left-side desk drawer, withdrawing a large brown leather belt. My mind raced as I franticly searched for a suitable answer to her question. Alas, the words simply would not form in my young and inexperienced mind. All the while I had stood there with my hand outstretched. KARAACK! was the sound of the heavy belt as it struck my hand with powerful force! That sound had been frightening, but the ensuing pain was even worse! She continued delivering a series of equally strong blows! I could see and feel that my hand had begun to rapidly swell. But, Mrs. Smith seemed to enjoy this, so she continued whipping me. The pain was unbearable, and I could feel my hand becoming numb! I wondered when she would stop - but she did not stop! I then blurted, "I had to doo-doo"! With this, she paused. Then, she said, "Give me your other hand"! By now, I was approaching a state of shock, so I pleaded of her, "Why, Mrs. Smith? – I have answered your question". She replied, "We don't use such language in this class!" and began whipping my left hand. At that point I seemed to hear my mind speaking to me, saying "The pneumonia did not kill you, but this will"! I was convinced that this was, in fact, the case. Then finally she stopped. What a relief! I had amazingly survived that ordeal. My teacher then ordered me to take seat, and I quickly complied.

I took my seat and sat quietly while suffering painfully! I'd once possessed the petite hands of a weak and skinny six year old boy. Today though this was quite different, for each of my little hands had now swollen to twice their normal size. At this point, I really wanted weep myself into oblivion! But back in those days boys were taught not to cry, so I just sat and continued to suffer. Mrs. Smith had managed to ignore me that whole time. Finally, I could no longer bear the pain, so I raised my hand and asked for permission to speak. At first, she did not acknowledge me. But then, after a couple of minutes, she asked, "Yes, what is it"? I responded, "I hurt so much – may I be excused"? My request further annoyed her, so she abruptly arose and rushed to my desk, whereupon she grabbed me by my right ear and walked me out of the classroom and down the hallway to the office of the principal. The school's principal instructed me to sit and await his summons. I sat there anxiously alone, wondering what was next.

Mrs. Smith had briefed our principal, so he already knew the facts. However, when he finally called me into his office, he asked me for my version of the story. Naturally, I was more than happy to provide him with my version, to which he quietly listened. He seemed to have sympathized with me, but told me to try harder at following the rules. I assured him that I would comply, although I felt that my tardiness had been unavoidable. He then ended my visit before instructing me to sit in the hallway for the next hour or more until the end of the school day. Again, I complied – and suffered!

Finally, the end-of-day bell rang and my mother arrived immediately to pick me up. She was happy to see me and I was overcome with joy at seeing her. This had been our first day apart in six years, so we both missed each other dearly. Right away, she wanted to know how my day had gone. I showed mom my badly swollen and reddened palms, explaining to her both how and why this had happened. She instantly became furious! Now, I was in a state of confusion and shock. Mom then said to me, "Wait here, Jake" and had me again take my seat there in the hallway. I watched as she walked the short distance down the hall to Mrs. Smith's room.

Mother was a lady in every respect, and a very attractive one at that. She stood nearly six feet tall, and without an ounce of fat. At that time, she was only twenty-seven years of age and in great health. To say the least, she was physically fit to face any confrontation. I remained in my seat as I overheard her talking to my teacher. Then, after several comments had been exchanged, I heard mom say to Mrs. Smith, "If you ever whip my child that way again, I'll make you wish that you had never been born"! And at that point mom reappeared in the hallway, walking toward me. She approached me and gently clasped my shoulder (not hand), as together we walked away from the schoolhouse toward home. I was so relieved at leaving that old schoolhouse that day!

We walked briskly all the way to our house, stopping only momentarily a couple of times. When we arrived home, my mother immediately and ever so delicately washed my hands in cool water. Then, she reached for a bottle of skin lotion and gently massaged my aching hands.

But that was not good enough it seemed, because upon seeing my mother at work on me, my sweet aging grandmother inquired of mother, "What is wrong, Lee"? Mother then told her about the severe whipping I had received from my teacher earlier that day at school. Then grandmother came over to me, saying "Let me see your hands, son". I held them out to her and she carefully examined them. Next, she said to my mother, "Lee, I think the boy needs more than just skin lotion". If you don't mind, I'd like to prepare a special solution for him". My mother was satisfied at the recommendation, and agreed. Grandmother then went into our kitchen and began arranging several ingredients upon our kitchen table. I could clearly see what she was doing from where I sat. I watched as she heated a pot of water. As the water heated, she squeezed lemon juice into a cup. After this, she reached into our icebox (we had no refrigerator) and removed a stick of butter. She sliced off two regular-sized pieces, which she dropped into the warm water. Next, she went to our small medicine cabinet and returned with a bottle of Cod Liver Oil. She also poured a small amount of the oil into the warm water. But she was still not finished. She added two tablespoons of salt. At this point, she began to rapidly stir the mixture. When she was done she came back to where I sat, and said, "Now, let's fix those little hands". "I want you to sit here and soak them for a half hour". When that amount of time had passed, she returned and sat directly before me. She alternated the gentle massage of each hand at about two-minute intervals. The massage phase lasted for about ten minutes. By now, she had finished her work so she said to me, "There, you should start feeling much better in no time at all". Then mom led me to my bed, where she lay me down to rest and recuperate. Mom placed a large towel over my lap and told me to remain faced up and keep my hands atop the towel. She then kissed me on my forehead, telling me to get some rest. I lay there and I rested—but I could not sleep. I kept thinking over and over, "*How could such a terrible thing have happened to me*"? I received no suitable answer, so I stayed there on my bed—content that this ordeal was over!

At 6:15PM that evening, my father arrived at home on his bicycle. He had become accustomed to my sitting on our front porch, and seeing me joyfully run down the street to greet him. But this day was different, for I was nowhere in sight. This gave dad cause for concern, so as soon as he entered the house, I heard him ask mother, "Where is the old man?"(meaning me). This was the pet name he had given me. My mother called me "Stick" because I was so very skinny. Mother answered him by saying, "He is not feeling so well, so I have him lying down". "His teacher gave him a bad whipping, so his hands are really swollen, and he feels so badly about it". When my father inquired as to what I had done wrong, mother gave him the complete details. Although I was only six years of age, I had come to know both of my parents quite well. Thus, I sensed that dad was extremely unhappy with this news. He walked into my small bedroom and greeted me, saying, "Hey, old man, how are you doing"? "I'm doing pretty good" I answered. "I hear you've had a rough day" said dad. "Yes sir, I did" I replied. "Well, try not to worry too much for, things will bee better tomorrow". Dad appeared calm while speaking to me. He then bent over me as he touched my shoulder, saying "Stay strong". All the while, dad had remained standing. Finally, he turned and walked out of my room. Once he had left my room, I heard him say to mother, "Don't fix my plate yet – I'll eat when I return". "Where are you going?" she asked. "To the principal's house" answered dad. This seemed to worry mom, so she said to him "Clay, please don't do anything bad to him". Dad calmly responded "If he behaves, I won't". I listened quietly as I heard him leave the house. I knew he had ridden his bicycle because that was our only form of transportation at that particular time.

Soon mother and grandmother returned to my room to check my current condition. I was very happy to see them. Mother asked "Are you hungry Stick"? I had not eaten since lunchtime at the school. But with all the turmoil I had just experienced, food was the furthest thing from my mind. Just then though, I realized that I was famished. I told mom "yes," so she went into our kitchen and quickly returned with a platter of stewed chicken, along with rice and green peas. I tried to eat, but my hands still ached so badly, I simply could not hold onto my fork. Mom had already rearranged my pillows, raising me to a sitting position. But once she noticed my difficulty in holding my fork, she sat on the edge of my bed and patiently fed me. My meal was delicious—properly prepared and well-seasoned. I consumed every morsel, enjoying it immensely. Mom had also brought me a cool glass of freshly prepared lemonade (my favorite drink). When I had finished my food, in walked my grandmother with a fresh, warm slice of homemade apple pie. I loved all the special attention. Then, shortly after I had finished my dessert, grandmother returned with another pan of the solution she'd earlier prepared. She sat with me while repeating the very same gentle treatment

I had initially received. I then rested before finally falling asleep.

I was still asleep when my father returned. The sound of his and my mother's voices quietly talking together had awakened me. At this point I had rested a bit, so I felt a little better. Pretending to be a big strong man, I got up from bed and went into our living room to join them. They were all very pleased to see that I was up and moving about the house. "Atta boy" my father exclaimed upon seeing me enter the room. Both my mother and grandmother also voiced their praises. My father then said, "Son, I talked to the principal, and he has promised me that you will not have a problem such as this again". I believed dad—and was quite relieved!

Early the next morning, my mother quietly entered my room. "Are you awake?" she asked me. The sound of her footsteps had awakened me, so I said, "Yes mom, I'm awake". "How do you feel?" she asked. At this early hour, and having just awakened, I had not yet realized just how I had felt, but I said to her "I feel pretty good". Mom then said "Let's see how those little hands are doing". I sat upright and pulled my hands from beneath my covers. We could readily see that the swelling had decreased quite a bit. But the soreness still remained in each hand, though I found that I could flex my fingers, and also open and close my hands without experiencing severe pain. Next, mother asked "Do you feel well enough to go to school"? "I'm not sure" I responded, so mom called out to my grandmother, who was in our kitchen preparing breakfast. Grandmother came in, greeting me with a warm "Good morning, son". "morning Mama" I replied (which was the manner in which

I'd always addressed her). Grandmother checked my hands, and when she'd finished, she said to mother "I believe it would be best if Jake stayed at home, at least today".

Mom was in agreement, so I remained at home that day. Soon Grandmother came back into my room, carrying another pan of her special soaking solution. Again she told me to soak my hands for a half hour— which I did. After that, came the massage. She told me to rest there a bit—, and when I was ready, I could wash up and have my breakfast. At about 8:30AM that morning, I arose and washed up. Then I had a light breakfast of bacon with toast and jelly— accompanied by my regular glass of warm, fresh milk. When I had finished, I returned to bed, where I remained for most of the morning. I guess I must have slept for awhile because finally my hands felt much better. I quickly found that I could even apply small amounts of pressure to each hand without experiencing undue pain.

Nevertheless, at about 1:00PM that afternoon grandmother repeated my therapy. I continued to relax throughout the afternoon. But even though I had begun feeling a bit better, mother suggested that I take things easy. In this way, she said my hands would heal faster. The hours passed slowly. At about 2:30PM mother fed my lunch to me, though now I could comfortably handle my fork and knife. I was grateful for my rapid recovery (mostly due to grandmother's instant and very special treatment).

As usual, my father arrived home at about 6:15PM. This time, I was sitting on our front porch waiting for him. Down the street he came—, riding his bicycle. As soon as I saw him, I ran down the steps and out into the street toward him. There were no cars passing, so I knew I was safe in doing this. As we neared each other, dad stepped down from his bike and rushed toward me. I hugged dad, and he hugged me. I could readily see that he was very happy at seeing me in my greatly improved condition. Dad asked me how I was doing, and I told him that I was feeling much better now. "Wonderful," he said as we entered our yard. Whenever my family was very happy, we would usually sit around the house singing religious hymns together in praise to "The Almighty." This evening was no exception, for as soon as we had eaten we all joined together in song, being led first by grandmother— then father—then mother. I always let them lead, settling for just joining in. It was a joyous evening. Before settling in for the evening, it was agreed by all that I would attend school the next day (Wednesday). But before bedtime, grandmother once again treated my hands. I felt really great in my surroundings.

The night passed and I had slept well. On this particular morning, I was already awake when my mother entered the room. She asked how I felt, and I told her that I felt fine. I then showed her my hands. The swelling and soreness had gone away, plus I found that I could squeeze and slap them together without feeling pain. So she laid out the clothing I would wear that day, and had me wash up. When I finished washing, I dressed myself and went into our kitchen for my usual breakfast. As soon as I had finished eating, mom and I left for school.

We walked the three-quarter-mile distance to my schoolhouse without incident, arriving shortly before 7:45AM. As she had done on that first day, mother took up her position a short distance away so that she could observe me as the children and I ran and played about the small schoolyard. After a few short minutes the bell rang. We had been told where to assemble, so each of us then gathered at our respective positions. As we stood there, I felt a slight tingling in the pit of my stomach, but it was not nearly as severe as it had been on the first day. I knew then that this feeling was due to my concern over how I would be received by Mrs. Smith. Although, I need not have worried, for coming toward us was my principal, accompanied by an attractive and well-dressed young woman. They walked directly to our holding position. Then Professor "B" (our principal) said to my group, "Good morning, children, this is Ms. Wilson— your new teacher." We were all quite surprised at this change; however, as I looked about the group, I sensed that no one seemed disappointed. At this point, our principal departed. Ms. Wilson greeted us in a warm and kindly voice. "Good morning, class— shall we go?" She walked us quietly to our classroom. Once inside we were seated, and then she began telling us about herself. Also, she requested that all students introduce ourselves once again. As soon as the formalities were finished, Ms. Wilson began her first teaching session.

"Class, I don't know exactly what was already covered by Mrs. Smith, so let us start from the beginning, okay?" We all chimed in, "Yes ma'am". As she began, I saw a lady pass our classroom door. She'd paused briefly, as if listening to us. I quickly recognized her as none other than my mother. It seemed she had wanted to see how our day was shaping up (which was just fine) I felt. Upon seeing our new teacher, mom winked and smiled at me as she departed the building. Needless to say, mom's presence that morning provided me with the courage and determination needed to resume my beginning school year.

Our new teacher's format was reading, — spelling, — and arithmetic, in that order. Our morning progressed smoothly, and I could feel that the entire class was relieved and happy. Time passed quickly, and soon the bell rang, signaling lunch time. Before Ms. Wilson released us for lunch, she said, "Class, it's lunch period now." Then she added "If any of you should have a problem of a personal nature,— then by all means, attend to your problem. And, should you need help, be sure to ask someone." Her comments were both comforting and reassuring to us all. None of us had looked forward to our visit to the lunch room, but we each proceeded there anyway.

We were instructed to form a single line, whereupon we entered the dining facility. One by one, we slowly inched forward. Finally, I reached the point from which I would receive my tray. My main concern now was "What sort of goop would I be forced to eat today"? I had focused upon the food itself—not the server. Then, standing directly before me was none other than Mrs. Smith (my former teacher). I spoke to her. "Hello, Mrs. Smith, how are you?" She responded, "I'm doing well, Jake". But it seemed that she was experiencing great difficulty in maintaining eye contact with me.

I carefully picked up my food tray and moved on to a table and sat down. Once seated I paused as I eyed my food, thinking, *"How am I going to eat this again?"* I looked around the dining area and noticed that all the kids were gulping down their food. So, I sniffed mine and found that it smelled enticing. Still, I had not yet mustered the courage to taste it. I asked the boy sitting across from me, "How is this stuff"? "Good" he responded, "May I have yours"? *"Odd"*, I thought. Still, I figured that I might as well try it, for after all I was hungry! I tasted my food, finding it to be quite delicious! Though it was the same as I'd had on Monday, this had been prepared with care. It had been well-seasoned, and served at the proper temperature. I was ecstatic, and in no time at all, I had emptied my tray also! When I finished, I went outside and joined the other kids, who were running about and playing games of tag. After a few minutes, the bell again sounded and we all rushed back to our classes. This time, I would not be late!

Ms. Wilson began by reading us a short story. When she had finished, she asked each of us to take turns commenting on what she had just read. This was our first lesson in reading comprehension. After the students had made their input, she summarized, to make certain that each student in her class completely understood the material. This course had taken one hour. We had one more hour of study to complete on this first day. Our next half hour was spent on spelling. Then during the final hour of the day, she taught us basic addition and subtraction. That afternoon passed quickly, and without incident. The school bell sounded and it was again time to walk home. This had been a very good day. I thought, *"Why could Monday not have been like this"?*

As soon as I exited the door, I saw my mother waiting for me. This time she held my hand as we walked along. "Tell me about your day" she said, and I was more than happy to do so! I told mom that Ms. Wilson was a nice new teacher, and that my day had gone just great. I could see that she was very pleased at hearing this news. We soon arrived home to find grandmother also anxiously awaiting the news. When we told her, she was nearly overcome with joy. Then my father arrived home at his usual hour, and I ran out to meet him. "Hey, son— how's my boy doing"? I told him that I was fine and I'd had a good day. I also told him that my class now had a new teacher. He just smiled, saying "I know" as we went inside to wash up to eat.

Several years later, I would realize the importance of this unfortunate and unpleasant event. It is true that I had suffered severe pain in my hands. But the positive results of my suffering had been significant. My pain lasted for only three days. In return, I gained three years of greatly improved conditions at my school. The lousy cook in the dining facility had been demoted to dishwasher and helper. Mrs. Smith had been transferred to a position for which she was much better suited. So I guess I could say that overall, things had worked out pretty well for me and our school!

I remained at this particular school for three years. Ms. Wilson was my lone teacher for the first two of those three years. Our entire class respected and liked her very much. She had proven herself to be highly competent; and, her teaching methods were extremely effective. Each of us students learned quite a lot from Ms. Wilson's classroom instruction. Thus, our school year seemed to pass quickly and soon this first year ended and it was time for summer break. It had been a good first year, but each of us looked forward to our summer vacation.

Nothing spectacular occurred during that entire summer, so I shall keep this brief. I remained at home, mostly playing with the other children in our neighborhood. Once in a while, mother would take me with her to the downtown stores. We always walked whenever mom went shopping, but I looked forward to getting away from the house occasionally, so the walking was okay by me.

When I stated earlier that our only means of transportation was my father's bicycle, this was a true statement. However, parked in our backyard garage was a very nice Hudson automobile with only 32,000 miles on its odometer. This was a beautiful car, loaded with every available luxury for a car during that time period. It was both light and dark blue. It had plush carpeting with seat covering of gray velvet. Its top was vinyl in dark blue. It also had a wood-grained instrument panel, along with wood-grained spoke wheels. Any ordinary person would have been simply thrilled to have possessed this vehicle. Even with such an automobile continually parked in his garage, my father had opted to completely ignore its presence. At such a young age, I simply could not understand how this could be. It would be several years later before I would begin to comprehend this situation. I had frequently asked of my grandmother and mother, "Why does daddy never drive his car?" My mother was not certain either, although grandmother would always reply, "I guess he just got tired of driving it." This did not make sense, for "How could anyone tire of a car that nice"? However, there it sat - abandoned. So, if anyone ever searched for me, they would either find me riding my goat Billy, or inside our fine automobile, 'driving' the heck out of it. I was good at pretending, so I frequently pictured myself as a race car driver. This was the manner in which I spent my very first summer vacation away from school.

Much later, I learned that daddy had not in fact grown

tired of his car. It seems that in his earlier years he had been somewhat of a speed demon, and he'd received several tickets for speeding. So, after much deliberation, he had decided that it would be best to never drive this car again. I later learned that one traffic court judge had told him, "One more offense will mean jail time"! So, dad had made a vow to himself, and he upheld that vow. Then, over the years the car began to deteriorate— first the tires—, then the upholstery. Over the next three years it became just an old junk heap. Finally dad sold it as junk for one hundred fifty dollars as payment in full. Forty years later, I would again see this very same car (fully restored) at one classic car auto show in Anaheim, California, which I verified through its VIN number. I am told that it auctioned for forty-five thousand dollars. Sadly, I never got the chance to tell dad about this.

The summer passed quickly and soon the vacation was over. It was now back-to-school time. For the second year, we again had Ms. Wilson as our teacher. Things went smoothly that whole year. I did well again, receiving high grades. Nothing major occurred, and soon another school year had finished. I had not been ill during the entire year, and my parents (and grandmother) were very happy for my greatly improved health condition. I am certain the improvement in my health was a direct result of the fresh cow's milk that I drank each day. Again, time passed quickly, and I had now completed my second school year.

I spent my second summer vacation much as I had the first. I was now eight years old so I had become too large and heavy to ride my goat, Billy. But mother had purchased for educational purposes a few story books for me to read.

Also, the female teacher from across the street would occasionally come over and tutor me in arithmetic. Studying occupied a considerable amount of my free time, but I still managed to find the time to 'drive' the Hudson. I also found that I usually had time to play with the other children in our neighborhood. Soon this vacation was also over, and it was back to school for a third year. I knew that my upcoming year would be different because I would attend a new school.

Early one September morning, off I went along my new route to school. I was now nine years old, so mother had allowed me to walk along with a group of other children without her presence. I was now beginning to feel quite proud of myself, in not being chaperoned. Our new school facility was very nice. It was a sprawling complex of buildings that covered a large area. It also accommodated all grades from one through twelve. After seeing it I had wished that my first two years were at this location. All teachers and employees from our old school had transferred to this new site, so one of the first persons I saw was Ms. Wilson.

However, for this, (my third year), I had a new teacher. She was a middle-aged lady, and she was a very nice person whose name was Mrs. Mann. I had known of her from our church. She was our sole teacher for the year. Mrs. Mann seemed very capable and thorough in her teaching methods. My first day in her class passed smoothly, and without incident. I was always attentive in class, and I was constantly alert so that I might avoid any possible trouble. I was successful in this endeavor, and the weeks turned into months. Finally the school year finished, and I realized that

I'd gotten through the whole year without any problems, for which I was happy. This was the conclusion of my first three years of school. Overall, they were a very good three years.

Thus far, I have focused primarily on the more positive aspects of my younger life. However, I shall now visit those negative aspects. First, there was World War II, which started and lasted throughout my early years. During this time we lived under extreme conditions of austerity. Very often, there were times when we could not purchase household items such as salt, pepper, or sugar. Imagine having to prepare and eat meals without these staple ingredients. Second, since we resided outside the city limits, we had no electricity, telephone service, or running water. The absence of electricity necessitated that I study using lamp light or candles. The absence of running water meant that taking a bath was a real chore. When drawing bathwater, we manually pumped it from the ground, which took us at least twenty minutes. Then we needed to heat the water, using several large cooking pots. This took another half hour, since the source of our heating was either wood or coal. Naturally, there was no bathtub, so this necessitated that we use thirty-inch aluminum washtubs for bathing.

Also, during winter months the temperature hovered around zero degrees, which was the reason I had caught pneumonia during two consecutive years. We did not have a washer, dryer, or even refrigerator. With no telephone, communication between ourselves and others was unusually difficult. We could not call a doctor, the police, or even the local fire station. This meant that when a family member was seriously ill or injured, it was necessary that someone within our household travel on foot for help. It also meant that had our house ever caught fire, it would have simply burned to the ground. All any of us could have done was pour buckets of water onto the burning structure. But as I reflect upon our situation, I recall that no one on our street owned a car. Therefore, none of us could have gone to any of our neighbors to seek help in the form of vehicular transportation. And last, but not least, we had no bathroom in our house, due to the lack of water. This meant that each of us used an old outhouse, which was located outside and several yards away from the actual house. So, even if the temperature had fallen below zero——, even if there were two feet of snow on the ground——, and even during the pouring rains, we went outside.

These conditions would last throughout my eighteen years of living in South Carolina. Actually, I considered them awful, but each of us had accepted them simply as part of our everyday lives. And then there was the problem of the frequent and severe hurricanes! This region in which we lived consisted solely of flatlands. There was not a single nearby hill. Had there been, it possibly would have facilitated the dispersal of accumulated flood waters. But there were none, so whenever the flood-waters came, there was the constant danger of our being swept away and drowned. Even at the young age of six, it was often necessary for me to step outside and into those extremely dangerous waters. Now, as some of you read these words, you might think, "*So what? Many of us have had tough lives,—— but we're not complaining.*" Well, to you I say—— I am not complaining, I'm merely contrasting childhood against my adult life.

Chapter 2

My Childhood Years
(continued)

I had finished my first three years of school attendance, and was now nine years old. I felt comfortable in my surroundings, both at home and at school. But then things changed a bit. We moved to another location, which was one and one-half miles farther away from town. This really complicated matters, for I could no longer walk to and from my school. Also, as I have previously stated, we had no car. Further, there was no neighborhood, so there was no possibility of hitching a ride with anyone. Thus, my only form of transportation would be our bicycle. The bicycle ride (one way) would take about half an hour. There would be no one to ride along with me— I would be all alone. So even during frequent periods of inclement weather, I would be caught outside in it, riding my old bicycle. Also, by now my father's bicycle had become aged, and was no longer completely dependable. This was the predicament I now found myself enduring. I would occasionally find myself longing for my old surroundings, but I realized that they were gone now— and, gone forever! I could no longer run and play with any of the children I had known.

But to make matters even worse, my pet (and companion) goat Billy, had recently died, leaving me all alone as my dog Spot had been struck by a speeding car. This made me even more eager to attend school, for at least there, I got to see children.

I cannot refer to that old dilapidated structure we had moved into as a house. Once upon a time it had been— but that would have been many years ago. This was a depressing, old shack! It was also quite large. In fact, it contained six bedrooms, along with a living room and kitchen. It had been built long before, and was wooden throughout. It had stood abandoned for many years, and was falling apart. Its floors and doors sagged. Its windows had been broken out (possibly by young children who were now adults). Its roof had long since vacated this house, and its doors creaked loudly (even after lubrication). But to make matters even worse, it also provided none of the comforts of life. Overall, this old house was ten times worse than the one in which we had previously lived for the past nine years.

My father and mother had already made numerous repairs, but it was still uninhabitable at the time we'd moved in. So for the first three months, they'd spent their time working feverishly to make as many repairs as possible before winter arrived. But they were not builders or carpenters, so the repairs they'd made were inadequate and not of professional quality. But this was our new residence, so I struggled desperately to become accustomed to my 'new' home. We were also now semi-isolated. The nearest house stood five minutes away, and only an elderly couple lived there. So if anyone needed assistance at any time, they needed ours much more than we needed theirs. Hence, here we were—completely on our own!

My father had logical reasons for this move, but it was difficult for me to understand his reasoning at my young age. His work record at the company where he had worked was a good one. His supervisors and coworkers regretted seeing him leave the company. But he had wanted to try farming. I learned that dad had grown up on a farm, and had enjoyed farm life. He felt that he might possibly make a better living for his family by doing this type of work. He had for a long while seen this old farmland, lying unattended, and he'd decided that he would check into the possibility of renting it. It turned out that the old fellow who owned this land was eager to rent it, and thusly supplement his meager income of only social security. So, he rented to dad this small parcel of farmland which covered thirty acres of space.

It cost dad only two hundred fifty dollars per month, but this was considered a fair price. This was a substantial sum of money, considering the cost of living in those days. Back then, two hundred fifty dollars was twice dad's previous monthly income. Notwithstanding, he had calculated that even with this monthly expenditure, he would realize an increase in annual income of over two thousand dollars. In addition to these considerations, he would now have complete freedom of movement. Here he would be responsible to no company supervisors. These were his motivations for making such drastic changes in our lives. As the years passed we all came to realize that dad's decisions had been based upon sound judgment, and we had each earlier decided to comply and go along with the program he had established for us.

Soon, the summer passed. Now, it was back to school for me and into the fields for my mother, my father, and my then ninety-two year old grandmother. I feel it appropriate to add here that, in all our years of farming, I had never seen an old lady of her age, working the fields. And she would continue doing this until her final days— at the ripe old age of one hundred two. Actually, this was a very bad situation, as she should never have had the need to do this type of work at her age. But she had insisted upon doing this, to help in minimizing operating costs. So, each weekday morning at 5:00AM, dad would leave the old house, heading for the fields. He had bought used farming equipment, and an old mule for tilling the soil. Then, at 7:00AM, my mom and grandmother would also head out into the fields. I would at the same time climb onto our old bicycle and start on my long two-mile trek to school. My first day seemed as though it would take forever, as I was not at all accustomed to riding a bicycle for such long distances. I arrived at the schoolhouse that first morning at around 7:30. This gave me a half hour to play—but I was already exhausted! But since this was the first day in three months that I'd had children to play with, I celebrated by running and playing anyway.

This year I had a different teacher. Her name was Mrs. Street and I quickly found her to also be a very good teacher. That first day had gone well. There were no incidents worth mentioning, and I was glad to have found it that way. Then when the school day ended, I was initially quite happy to be heading home. As we were all leaving the school grounds, I located the children whom I had grown accustomed to walking with over the previous years. We gathered and started walking away down the street— on our way home. We had walked nearly three blocks when I suddenly realized that I could not walk this route— EVER AGAIN! This both shocked and hurt me! I abruptly stopped walking. Some of the children noticed my actions and asked, "What's wrong, Jake"?

I shrugged my shoulders, saying, "I'm going the wrong way"! Some of them burst out in loud laughter. I joined them in their laughter, but deep inside I was both hurt and embarrassed! I was even more embarrassed to see the expression on some of the children's faces. It seemed that some of them had genuinely felt pity for me. However, I bade them farewell before turning to walk away. I headed back to the schoolhouse, where my old bicycle awaited me. I unlocked it, hopped on, and quickly rode away toward home.

At home I told my folks what I had done and we all had a big laugh together. Mom then told me, "Your food is on the stove— it's covered, and it's still warm". My father then said, "Son, when you finish eating, you can rest a bit – then study your lessons for tomorrow". Next, grandmother asked, "How was your first day of riding your bicycle to school"?

I told her that my day had gone well— and also that I had a good teacher. They were all pleased to hear my news. I then proceeded to the house, where I washed up and had my meal. Afterwards, I changed out of my school clothing, and moved outside onto our porch for a moment of quiet relaxation. After about half hour had passed, I picked up my books and began my reading lesson. I read for awhile and then began studying my spelling assignment. When I had finished with that subject, I began working my arithmetic problems. I found some of the problems to be a bit difficult at first. But I kept working with them until I finally felt more comfortable with what I was doing. Incidentally, I no longer had the tutoring assistance from the teacher who once had lived across the street from us. Here, no one lived across the street. There were only fields of corn, cotton, and tobacco, which extended for miles in each direction. This was rural living! Then grandmother entered the house, washed up, and began preparing our evening meal. After about an hour had passed, mom and dad came in and washed up. Soon, we all sat at our table, where we ate what was then called supper. We talked about how my day had gone. Then, for the next hour or more, the adults discussed the problems they had encountered and the progress they had made on this day. Now came time for me to take my bath and prepare for my next school day. This was the way in which my first day of fourth grade had gone.

I had slept well throughout the night, so when I awoke the next morning I felt really good and full of energy. My father was the first to arise at 4:00AM. The rest of us arose at 5:00AM. This would become our daily routine. I washed up, while at the same time, mom and grandmother were in another part of the house doing the same. Let me repeat here, my grandmother was the mother of my father. This meant that she was only mom's mother-in-law, but they got along well together. When we were finished washing and dressing, we each went to the large kitchen/dining room for breakfast. We greeted each other cordially (as usual) and had our breakfast meal. Our cow Fannie was still with us, so each morning I was still served my full glass of fresh, warm cow's milk. When we were finished eating and washing up, we each headed to our respective destinations. I placed my books into the saddle bag of my bicycle, and bade my parents good day as I watched the two of them walk away into the fields for another thirteen hours of hard labor. As I rode away, I thought, *"What a truly sad and miserable way of making a living"!*

I'd had no way of knowing that things would get even worse! Luckily, I arrived at the school house at 7:30AM. This gave me fifteen minutes to mill about with the other kids. I could sense that we were growing up somewhat. Our usual way of running about and playing had been toned down quite a bit. Now, most of the kids were just standing around in small groups talking with each other. Only a handful of kids in fourth grade continued to run and play. I chose to associate myself with the groups that were acting all grown up, so I joined them, just standing and talking. We were chatting about the changes we anticipated for the fourth grade. I listened, and would occasionally add my two cents worth of comment. Soon, the bell rang. Now though, we were no longer escorted to our classrooms. We were on our own now, and this felt very good. We had been briefed and also cautioned the day before that we would be allowed a slight amount of greater freedom. We were also told by our teacher that this was a probationary period for us, and that it would continue only if this privilege was not abused. None of us wanted any expanded privileges vacated, so we all complied with this new program. We each entered our respective classrooms, whereupon we quietly took our seats.

Our courses of study had also been expanded— we

now had geography added to our curriculum. Geography was the last course of the day. So, we covered each class, taking approximately one hour and fifteen minutes per course. I found that I really liked geography. I soon learned that this would be my only source for discovering the wondrous world in which I lived. Remember, we had no electricity,— so, we had no television! As on the previous day, we covered a portion of each subject until the school day ended. This would become our routine for the rest of the school year. When this second day had ended, I mounted my old bicycle and took the half-hour ride home. (Note— It only took the other kids from five to fifteen minutes to walk home). At home, I was greeted by my waiting family, who immediately inquired as to "how my day had gone". But then after a brief bit of small talk, my father asked me, "Son, do you think you could lend me a hand in the fields for a couple of hours?"

Naturally, I simply could not refuse so I replied, "Yes, I can help you, dad." I returned to our old house and rushed through my meal. Afterward, I changed into some of the old clothing I once played in. I would later find that these would henceforth be my work clothes. From that day forward, I would have very little time for play. Remember, I was only ten years old at this time. But regardless of age, this would become my indefinite future— farm work and school. These two activities would occupy the vast majority of my time. Hence, it became increasingly difficult to find ample time for study of school books. Nevertheless, I would somehow manage.

Surprisingly, I would succeed in maintaining a B+ average in each of my subjects through the remainder of my school years. Each day I would attend school, and then rush home, eat, change clothes, and rush out into the fields. All this had begun while I was only ten years of age. We continued living this way (without recreation) for the next four years. Up to this point in my young life, I had only once visited a movie theater, which was during the year prior. For my ninth birthday, my mother had promised to take me to see my first movie ever. But as my birthday came during mid-winter, the weather was too severe for the two of us to make the half-mile walk to the downtown area where our two movie theaters stood. So, we'd sadly postponed my special present until springtime when the cold had departed. Then, just before we moved from our first house, we went to watch a movie *(Batman and Robin)* – Wow! That was the most memorable day of my life! I found this to be a completely new and exciting life experience! After the movie was finished, I dreamed of that movie throughout the night. This was an example of how naïve I was. I would not attend another movie until I reached age twelve. Then, when I had reached the summer (at twelve years of age), dad asked if I would like to attend a movie. All of the other children at my school had attended movies since they'd reached the age of three or four years old. This meant that I was at least five years behind in that social aspect of my life. But let's return to my current situation on the farm. The months passed and that school year finally reached its end. That's when I hit the 'jackpot'! My dad granted me permission to visit a movie theater to view a movie for only the second time in my life! I was overcome with joy, thrilled over having been granted this opportunity!

This offer had been presented to me earlier during the

week, so for the next two days I could not relax whatsoever, as anticipation overwhelmed me! Finally, Saturday morning arrived. I would always help dad with the field work each Saturday morning (from 5:00 to 1:00PM). This day was no different. At 4:00AM that morning my dad awakened me. We washed up and had a quick breakfast. When we had finished, we went out to the old barn and hitched up our old mule, Betty. Dad had taught me how to handle the mule and plow, so Saturday mornings were my days to handle the task of plowing, while dad performed a variety of other farming chores. By doing things this way, our family was more able to keep up with our large farm workload.

So, there I was, as usual, alone in a field isolated by woodlands. My dad's presence was required in a separate field, so we had no visual or voice contact between us. This situation did not pose a serious threat, as I was not in danger of being harmed by another human being. But there was the ever-present danger of being bitten by venomous snakes! Snakes were plentiful in this area, and it was necessary to be constantly on alert for their presence. Some were not poisonous, but most species were. And, snakes live underground for much of their time, so they might be right at your feet and you would not see them. But in plowing the soil I would frequently uncover them. The function of the plow was to flip the under layer of soil to the surface, bringing the soil's nutrients closer to plant roots. This provided for healthier plant life, and healthier plants fetched better prices when sold at the markets. But in tilling the soil, I always walked two feet directly behind the plow. Then, as the plow upturned the soil, had a deadly snake been in my path, it would've been instantly pitched to the surface at my feet. I found this situation to be totally unacceptable! I was fortunate though on that morning, for I had worked from 5:00AM to 1:00PM, (eight hours). During that period I'd brought to the surface a total of six snakes, successfully killing each with heavy sticks. Luckily, I was not bitten even once! Throughout that entire morning, I experienced both distraction and preoccupation. Specifically, my mind was preoccupied with thoughts of this afternoon's movie. But at the very same time I realized that in order for me to make it to the movies, I must survive the snakes. Fortunately, I was successful! Finally, 1:00PM arrived and it was time to leave the field and head for the house. Both dad and I arrived nearly at the same time. Mom had heated two large tubs of water for each of us to bathe in. After our baths, we both changed into fresh clothing before eating our noon meal. When we had finished, it was time for us to leave.

At this point, I felt 'butterflies' but could not have been happier! Dad had also decided to go into town for some shopping and a bit of relaxation. The weather was quite warm, (nearly 80 degrees). The distance was too far for walking; so, together we hopped onto our faithful old bicycle, and proceeded along the route into town. Dad peddled, so I received a free ride. People had not seen us together in more than a year. And, since most in the area knew each other, they would stop us along the way to chat. This caused our half-hour trip to last nearly an hour. Even so, we arrived in the downtown area at around 3:00PM. Dad had a half-sister who resided in the area. I had not seen her for quite some time, so we stopped at her house for a short while to rest and chat. She was a sweet lady— a few years older than dad. And though, they each were of different mothers, they appeared as twins. Her name was Emma, and she'd always shown me great affection. As soon as we had arrived at her home, she gave me a large slice of lemon cake with vanilla ice cream (my favorite), along with a tall glass of ice-cold lemonade. I felt that I was in seventh heaven. I was away from the farm— and downtown! I enjoyed my favorite dessert and beverage. Now I would soon be inside a movie theater, watching movies for only the second time in my life. What more could one ask for? After a few minutes had passed, the time had arrived for me to leave. But before leaving, I agreed to meet dad at my aunt's house before 7:00PM that evening. I knew that the walk to and from the theater would take about ten minutes, and I was determined not to be late, since this would be my first outing on my own. When that all-important hour arrived, I bade them both farewell, promising to return on time.

I arrived at the theater shortly before 4:00PM. Luck was on my side. I rushed inside to purchase my ticket. I then proceeded to the snack area, where I bought popcorn along with a soda. For my ticket, the popcorn, and soda, I had actually paid just fifty cents. Compare this to at least fifteen dollars today. I passed through the lobby of the theater and entered its seating area. Once there I felt as though I had lost total vision! I saw only the movie screen, so I stood there for a brief moment while straining my eyes to find a nearby seat. After a few seconds, my eyes began adjusting to the inside darkness. I took a seat and began to relax. I thought, *"Gee, now this is the life"*! Soon the movie began, and I sat quietly in awe as I watched Gene Autry battle bands of renegade Indians. *"This so exciting!"* I thought. But all too soon, the movie had finished. I stood up to leave, though it was still a bit early. It was at this point that I noticed I was the only one standing. So I sat back down, not knowing exactly what to do. Then another movie (serial) began, which was *The Green Hornet*. I felt like a fool and was quite embarrassed! I was so happy that it was dark inside the theater. No one in the audience would see who had been the fool standing! I would have laughed at myself, but I realized that my situation in life was actually pathetic—not at all comical. Finally though, the short version movie also reached its end. Then the lights came on, and everyone stood and began leaving the theater. This was my cue, so I also arose and walked out along with them. The distance from the theater to my aunt's house, where dad would be waiting was very short, thus I arrived just a few minutes before my curfew of 7:00PM.

When I arrived dad was already there waiting for me. After a few minutes of chatting with my Aunt Emma, the two of us hopped onto our faithful old bicycle and headed toward home. We reached our house well before nightfall. Our evening meal had already been prepared, and mom and grandmother had already eaten. Mom prepared our plates, so dad and I sat down to our warm and delicious meal. We both had acquired great appetites that evening, so we ate quite heartily. It had been a long day (at least for me), but we all sat together discussing the week's events.

The next day was Sunday— a day for church. But here we were too far away from town to walk to our church. This meant that now we only went occasionally, and only when my dad was able to locate someone to drive us for a fee. On this Sunday, this was not the case. So, we just sat around relaxing. My dear grandmother read her Bible.

Mom and dad sat around discussing issues, and I had nothing to do, so I occupied my time by studying my school books and recalling yesterday's movie. This was how we usually spent our Sundays.

Amazingly, I finished sixth grade with another B+ average. But now that school had finished, I found myself again available for daily farm work. This was how I spent my summer that year. The one exception was that I was allowed to attend a movie each Saturday afternoon. I accepted this as compensation for the daily farm work. The summer passed and soon it would be time for me to return to school. The thought of being around other kids lifted my spirits, and I found myself eagerly anticipating the start of school. I would now enter seventh grade. Wow, how time had passed!

Then, our situation worsened! Just when we thought we had adapted to this new environment, we moved for a second time. My father had realized that the income generated by this present farm had not equaled that which he had previously anticipated. The amount of available farmland was less than desirable, so dad had searched for and located a new farm. He was lucky in his search, so he'd found the size of farm he'd hoped for. Our first farm had contained only twenty acres of workable land space; however, our new farm contained a total of sixty acres. By dad's calculations, this new farm would more than double our annual income. But there was a problem within his figures. In order to realize twice our present income, we would need twice the present number of workers. Otherwise, the present number of workers would be required to work twice the number of hours. Now, considering that we were each already working from thirteen to fourteen hours daily, additional hours of production were not possible. This meant that dad would be required to hire more workers. Ultimately, we would realize less income than dad had initially estimated. Nevertheless, we proceeded with this next move as planned.

Chapter 3

My Teenage Years

I had reached the age of thirteen, and was attending seventh grade. I had not enjoyed living the past four years at our last farm, but our most recent move had provided me a completely new outlook on life. I quickly realized that our previous location had not been all bad, for this final move was even farther from town. Here we were four miles farther into the wilderness! This meant I would spend at least two hours of each day riding my old bicycle to and from school. However, here we were in our new surroundings! Oh how I longed to have remained at our previous location, for now, a ride to and from the movies also required two hours. Such rides would remove most of the enjoyment I'd derived from my visits to movie theaters.

The old house at our new location was a bit smaller than the last, having only three bedrooms. It was in better condition though, so basically all we needed to do was give it a thorough cleaning prior to move-in. The land upon which it stood was slightly elevated, but not enough to be considered a hill. It sat nearly one-half mile from the main road. (There were no highways in the area at that time—they came much later.) Although this was a farm, the surrounding area was quite scenic. This old house stood just at the edge of a wooded area, which covered fifteen acres of land. Most of the trees here had been planted within the last twenty-five years, but about one-fourth had been planted within the last five to ten years and were still quite small. The soil was quite sandy, and within the wooded area the ground was covered with layers of snow-like white sand. It was quite a beautiful area, with the appearance of year-round snowfall. Except for the greater distance from town, this was much nicer than the last place we had lived. Still, there were no conveniences such as electricity or running water. But by now we were all quite accustomed to the absence of such amenities.

We completed our move during the first two days of September that year. I would start school two days later. For the first day and a half, I helped around the house and outside in the fields, making needed repairs to our barn and mending fences, etc. Remember, one workday consist-ed of fourteen hours— so one-half day amounted to seven hours. I worked seven full hours the day prior to school commencement. Then dad allowed me to return to our old house to make preparations for the next school day. I lo-cated my school supplies, and made sure that I had placed all the necessary items into my satchel. I then laid out my clothing for the next day.

Afterwards I went outside to the old water pump, where for the next twenty minutes, I pumped water for my much-needed bath. I then checked our old bicycle to make sure that it was mechanically sound. I found that the tires needed a little air, so I corrected this, then checked and oiled its chain. Lastly, I cleaned it as best I could. By this

time I realized that I needed to rest, so I sat and tried to relax for a bit. Then at 4:00PM, I went outside behind our old
house, where in complete solitude— I took my bath. Outside was where I always bathed during the summer months.
During winter months, the weather was much too cold to
take outside baths. Soon the hour was nearing 6:00PM, as
my dear old ninety-five year old grandmother returned to
the house to start preparing our evening meal. Both mom
and dad would remain in the fields for at least one more
hour. They each had already pumped much of their bath
water earlier during the day. So when they arrived at the
house, it was already pre-heated by the sun. Soon, they arrived and bathed. Mama (grandmother) had finished cooking, so the four of us sat at our old table and had our evening meal, after which we chatted for awhile. Each night
at 9:00PM, I would retire for the evening. I would arise at
5:30AM the next morning— and each school day morning
thereafter. During summer months, on Saturdays I would
arise at 4:00AM along with dad for a day of strenuous field
work.

Next morning arrived all too soon. Sharply at 6:30AM
I mounted our old bicycle and headed down the narrow
pathway leading to the main road. My folks were already
at work in the fields, so I waved affectionately to them as I
passed from a distance. They each waved back to me, and I
felt slight sadness overcome me. I rode onward—continuing along the old unpaved road. After half an hour, I reached
the old farm house in which we had lived just four days ago.
It appeared lonely, and seemed to wave and beckon to me.
At this point, I realized that I had become attached to this
old deserted place. But there was no time for nostalgia.

Normally, I would have arrived at school by now— but I was only at the halfway point. I took my mind away from that pitiful old house—standing all alone— and refocused my thoughts on the next leg of my long journey. I continued pedaling that old single-speed bicycle. During those days, there were no multi-speed bicycles. So each one-hour ride gave me quite a physical workout; and, I received two such workouts at least five days per week.

Finally, after what seemed as an eternity, I reached my school at 7:30AM, which gave me fifteen minutes with my few friends. Just think— I was finally again in civilization! Each talked about how they had spent their summer. Some had gone over to Myrtle Beach. Others had gone north to places like Boston and New York. This was the way most of the kids had spent their summer. They would each take turns telling about their great summer vacation. I though just stood by listening— and smiling sheepishly. Then came my turn and I wanted to turn and run away. But running away was not an option; so, I simply commented, "Oh, I just stayed home and worked. I was lucky, for the students were all very kind to me in this regard, so no one teased or ridiculed me.

Soon the bell rang, signaling time to enter our first class, so I felt very relieved. This year we would have several different teachers, including one male teacher. I found each of them to be both professional and extremely knowledgeable. The number of classes had been expanded. We now had English, geography, health, history, mathematics, and science— a different teacher for each subject. Also, the subject matter was extensive and thorough. In order for any student to achieve a high grade in a particular subject, many hours of study were required. At this point, I realized that this would become a major problem for me. First, I would be required to perform farm work each day after school. Second, since we had no electricity, I would be required to study while using only the dim lighting of a kerosene lamp (which was not conducive to effective study habits). Third, if I encountered difficulty with a problem while studying at home, there was no one in our small family to whom I could turn for help, so, what to do?

Two full school days passed before I arrived at a solution. The thought occurred to me to fully utilize the forty-five minute study period that came at the end of classes each school day. This would not be enough time, but even so, no more would be made available for study. There was only one more thing that I could do. During each class, I would focus intently upon my teacher's spoken and written words. After I had completed my fourth day of school and farm work, I took a few minutes just before bedtime to write six identical notes. I addressed one note to each of my six teachers. In these notes, I explained that I would not be afforded time for after-school study. I also explained the reasons for this. I requested (as a solution) that I be allowed to sit at the rear of my classes to prevent any disruptive students from distracting me with their frequent antics. I closed by stating that should my unusual request be approved, I could fully concentrate on my teachers' presentations. I further added that I felt this would aid me in maintaining acceptable grade levels in each of my subjects. I then explained my situation to dad while asking him to sign each of the notes. After reading them, he understood and signed them. Next morning at the beginning of each class, I handed each teacher this note. I received the same reaction from each of them. They expressed extreme doubt that this practice would prove successful. Nevertheless, they immediately assigned me to a seat at the rear of the class-room. Beginning that very day, I consistently dedicated no less than ninety-nine percent of my attention to teachers' lectures. The result of this effort was I discovered I had re-tained virtually all of what was taught each day. Then, dur-ing the final study period, I would use that time to refresh my memory in what had been covered during that day. I was pleased to discover that I was able to do this. I also learned that I would retain this information throughout the school year. My teachers were amazed, and my folks were espe-cially happy. This meant that I now possessed the stamina and mental capacity to grasp and retain my lessons, without assistance from anyone. Unfortunately, it also meant that I was more available as a farm worker!

Our school year progressed steadily and successfully, but there existed one serious problem of an entirely differ-ent nature. This problem involved the riding of my bicycle past one vicious large guard dog. On my first school day, I had not seen him. But on the second through fifth days, there he was— barking wildly— and chasing after me! I had managed to out-distance this dog on each of those four mornings, because I had developed strong legs from all my years of long-distance bicycle riding. The large house where this dog stayed stood some distance away from the road, so it took him at least ninety seconds to reach me from where he had sat waiting for me to pass. Each morning as soon as he saw me, he would run out from his yard, speeding toward me! But I was a bit like Superman! I could ride my bicycle as though I were a speeding bullet! This dog never could catch me. But on each of those first four mornings after this ordeal, I would feel my heart literally pounding inside my chest! In fact, at the end of that first week, I felt as though I had just recently experienced four heart attacks (at the young age of thirteen)! I could not have been more afraid even if I had been chased by a wild lion on those mornings!

That Friday night after our meal, my folks asked how my first week of seventh grade had gone. I first told all about school. Then, I told them about my awful experiences each morning with that dreadful and ferocious dog! They listened intently, and dad said he would ask the farmer who lived there to "please tie his dog— at least at the times when I would pass by". The next day was Saturday, so the four of us worked our normal short day (eight hours). That afternoon, I just rested. I was too exhausted to think about going to a movie. During the course of that evening, dad hopped onto our bicycle and rode down to the old farmer's house to have a talk with him about his awful dog. Dad returned in about an hour, saying, "Son, I talked to the old man about his dog, but he says that his dog does not bite". "Either way, I suggest that you cut yourself a strong oak limb and tie it to the bike". "Then Monday morning, if he rushes out at you, step off your bike and wait for him". He continued "As soon as he is within ten feet of you,— side-step and crush his skull"!

Dad's advice served to ease my mind only slightly, though I immediately went out into our backyard and grabbed our old axe. I located a six feet tall oak sapling, and cut it down. I then cut off the top of the sapling, leaving a length of about four and one half feet. Next I took the hunting knife that dad had recently bought me, and shaved the bark from the thick end of the sapling. This effectively reduced the weight of my newly formed weapon. Finally, I used heavy-duty sandpaper to lightly sand the smaller end. I now had myself a formidable weapon with which to defend myself! I also took one of mom's old wire clothes hangers, and then cut two twelve-inch lengths from it. I took these two pieces of wire and formed a hook on one end of each. I then tightly wrapped each wire around the frame of my bicycle. I was careful to tuck the ends of each wire, so as not to snag or rip my clothing.

Sunday passed with each of us just sitting around the house, and it was Monday morning again. We readied ourselves (including my now ninety-six year old grandmother) and headed off to our respective destinations. I headed to school— they into the fields. I had checked, and double-checked the weapon that I had fashioned and attached to my bicycle. Dad had told me that this dog's name was Buddy. He had also suggested that when this dog came to within one hundred yards from me, I should calmly and slowly step down from my bike and wait. I should assume a humble, nonthreatening stance as the dog drew near, and as soon as it came to within one hundred feet, I should calmly greet him by calling out his name. I prepared to follow dad's instructions in detail. So, I continued the short distance along the old dirt road, to the farmhouse where this fearsome dog lurked. I was extremely nervous with anticipation. *"What if this does not work"? "What if he rushes me and I strike at him—but miss"? Also, "What if he overpowers me and takes me down"?* At this point I would've been a goner, having been ripped to pieces before anyone could've reached me! I quickly found each of these thoughts to be extremely discomforting. I continued riding onward. I did not wait very long. Within three short minutes, I had approached that dreaded area. As I had expected, as soon as the animal spotted me, he rushed from his front yard, heading toward me! My heart pounded so heavily inside my chest, I actually felt sharp pain! My mind raced! The dog had reached the street before I could pass his house! *"What do I do now?" was my dilemma.* I was out of my rehearsed position, and I still had another thirty feet to go before I reached the point where this menacing animal stood, waiting to attack! I'd not had the chance to remove the oak stick I had made for protection. I felt vulnerable and totally helpless! I had often been told that dogs can sense one's fear. If this is in fact true, then this animal would have known that I was absolutely petrified! He stood at the left side of the road awaiting my arrival. I did not remove my oak stick from its resting place, for I dared not to. My mind told me not to make any threatening motions, or he would certainly attack! I walked slowly and to the far right side of the road. I was also on the right side of my bicycle. He stood barking loudly, as I said to him, "Hey Buddy, how are you doing?" He continued barking as I drew near him, but he did not advance toward me. So, I again spoke "Good boy, Buddy." He had been standing, but at this point he sat and just observed me. I was simply bewildered! I was not at all sure what to do. I leaned across my bicycle, and with my left hand, I lowered its kick-stand. Then, I stepped to the rear of my bicycle as I bent forward facing him. I placed my hands on my knees, saying, "Come, Buddy." Then to my amazement, this dog rose up and trotted across the road toward me. His demeanor was no longer menacing. He'd approached me playfully, so I patted him on his head. He jumped about all around me, as we played together for at least five minutes.

The old farmer had noticed that his dog was no longer barking, so he came to the door to have a look-see. When he saw the two of us playing together, I could see that he was pleased. I could see that Buddy was happy also. I was simply ecstatic! It was at this point that I realized that Buddy had been toying with me. Might I add here, that our lives are directly influenced by our perceptions of situations. I had perceived that Buddy was a threat— that he was a dangerous animal, while in reality, all he had really wanted was someone to play with. It then occurred to me that this dog and I held a common bond. We were both very lonely, and we longed for companionship— someone to play with. So after that frightening first week of seventh grade, we quickly became close friends. Each morning and afternoon thereafter, Buddy would wait for me, so I would take a few minutes of my time to stop and play with him. Finally, both Buddy and I had found companionship in our lives, and were each happier in our existence.

Now that this problem had been resolved without incident, my family and I could relax a bit. I continued riding my old bicycle to and from school each day for the remainder of the school year. I focused entirely on my studies while in classrooms, and throughout that year I rarely needed to study at night in my dimly lighted room. Each month passed seemingly unnoticed, and soon another school year had reached its end. During that year though I continued working in the fields each day after school. I would rush home each afternoon and hurriedly eat my meal before rushing out into the fields, where I would then be greeted by dad and given my work assignment for the afternoon. Sometimes this involved weeding, sometimes plowing, and sometimes harvesting. As I performed these tedious duties, my classmates were mostly playing or studying the next day's lessons. So, they would arrive at school academically prepared to face their day, while I, on the other hand, would arrive at school only hoping that I was prepared! As it turned out though, I was more prepared than they. I completed this school year receiving two A's three B's and one C grade. I believe that had I been able to study for ample amounts of time, and with adequate lighting, I might have achieved even higher grades. Each of my teachers was quite pleasantly surprised, and they complimented me on my academic accomplishment for the school year. My parents were also very happy at this outcome, although I'm quite certain that neither of them fully appreciated or even understood the great amount of effort I had put forth.

Soon summer was upon us, and this school year had ended. I somewhat regretted this fact, as I was now suddenly ninety-nine percent isolated! I would not see any of my classmates for another three months. But even worse, I would only see my new friend Buddy occasionally. For the next several months I would arise at 4:00AM with mom and dad each morning, (Monday through Friday). We would wash up and have a hearty breakfast. At 5:00AM the three of us would be at work in the fields. Then, at 9:00AM my aged grandmother would arrive in the fields to work alongside my mother. The ladies did the lighter work such as hoeing and weeding. We 'men' handled the heavy work of plowing and hauling fertilizer, etc. My dad had recently purchased a second mule to help me in hauling and plowing activities. Thus, with these two mules, dad and I would work side by side mostly plowing together from 5:00AM to 8:00PM, a total of fifteen hours each day. On Saturdays we would get a slight break. On these days, we would only work from 5:00AM to 1:00PM, eight hours! This meant that each week we would spend a total of eighty-three hours working in the fields! Compare this to the forty-hour work week and you realize this work program was both unhealthy and unsustainable. Also, when the end of the year came, dad and I sat down together and calculated the year's income. Dad was surprised to learn that our bottom line income had not actually doubled. It was significantly greater than each of the previous four years though. It is true that we did end up with nearly $3,000 more than the year before. With this realization we accepted the fact that no situation was perfect, so we would settle for these results without complaint.

Having recently realized that I was all alone now and without companionship, dad bought me a horse. Naturally, it was not a thoroughbred, but this was truly a beautiful young stallion. This was a female so we chose for her the name Belle. Her features were similar to those found in the Morgan breed of horses. Her coat was very dark brown in color; also, she was a strong and muscular animal. I had always admired ponies and dad knew this. But since I would soon reach the age of fourteen, he decided that I had outgrown them. I was thrilled to have been given this young horse to ride. I found Belle to be a docile and friendly animal, for which I was happy. So, now I had a horse— but no saddle. But I was impatient so I began riding her bareback. I was still not tall enough to mount her, so whenever I wanted to ride Belle, I would lead her to a fence, where I would then position her alongside the fence. I would then climb the fence and lower myself gently onto my horse's back. I recalled having seen the Indian warriors in the movies riding their steeds bareback, so I figured that I would try this for myself. It must have worked fairly well, because I was never injured from horseback riding.

I began my riding program by having Belle only walk while I was on her back. I remind you here that I only had Saturday afternoons and Sundays on which to ride my horse so this occupied much of my time on those two days. During my riding session the following Saturday, I slightly increased our speed by letting Belle trot just a little. I found that I could ride comfortably at this greater speed without falling. I kept with the trotting gate for several more sessions. But by my second month of riding my confidence level had risen considerably. So, one Saturday afternoon, I decided to try my luck. We started out by trotting— then I relaxed the reigns slightly, and Belle sped off. I clamped my legs around her mid-section while digging my heels into her rib-cage. At first, I maintained my balance quite well. But then something went wrong and I immediately knew that I was about to take my first tumble! I tried to stop her, but did not have time to do so. As I began slipping I sort of shoved off using both hands. This allowed me to fall away and not be trampled by the horse's hoofs, which would have caused serious injury. I fell to the ground and rolled for a few feet. At that same time, I called out to Belle, "Whoa." She ran for a few feet further, then stopped. I did not feel any pain. Nor, did I feel any burning sensations, so I figured that I had not received any bruises either. I found that I was mostly embarrassed from having fallen. I had been riding in an area at least three-quarters of a mile from the nearest house. Even so, I looked around in every direction to see if anyone had seen me take my spill. I saw no one anywhere. But now one problem remained— I was nearly one mile from our old farmhouse. This meant that since I was unable to remount my horse without assistance, I would have to walk and lead her all the way back to our house. Luckily, I had received no injuries.

It was nearly 6:00PM when I arrived back at the house. I did not see anyone, so I figured (correctly) that everyone was either asleep or relaxing. No one had heard or seen me arrive. I quietly opened the barnyard gate and led Belle inside the fenced area. I removed her bridle and gave her a pat on the shoulder. She went over to her trough where she began drinking water, after which she began eating. I'd had enough riding for this day, so I went to my special tub and took a soothing bath. I changed into clean clothing, hopped onto the old bicycle, and rode one mile to the near-est store for ice cream and a soft drink. From a distance, Buddy, (my new canine friend), saw me coming. As usual, he ran out to greet me. I stopped to play with him for a while before proceeding onward to the little store. I found no children there for me to talk to. Several farmers stood around discussing farm work and progress throughout that week. I felt like an outsider, for back then children did not initiate conversations with adults, so I simply stood alone as I finished my ice cream and drink. Finally I, rode back to our old house.

The next morning was Sunday. We would have liked to attend church, but without vehicular transportation there was absolutely possibility of this happening. So, grandmother did a combination of Bible reading and snoozing. Mom and dad sat around simply talking about farm work and the area in which we now lived. I took out my tennis ball and went out to the old barn. I stood several feet away from the building and tossed my ball onto the wall— catching it on the rebound. I continued doing this for several hours. This became boring but there was not much else to do. I had turned in my school books, so I had nothing to read. I did not even have a radio to listen to. I could barely remember the last time I had attended a movie. But worst of all, I had not seen another child since school had ended. I dreaded this state of solitude in which I found myself. It was at this point I realized that in order for me to preserve my sanity, I simply must create some form of activity to occupy my Sundays (and Saturday afternoons). Then, the thought occurred to me to make a bow, arrows, and a quiver. I was anxious to get started on this project. But this was Sunday— and in South Carolina, no one worked on Sundays. This was a state different from most. All the bars (and existing few clubs) closed before midnight on Saturdays. I had heard some grown-ups say that if one wanted to purchase alcohol for the weekend, they needed to do so before 11:30PM on Saturday night. Virtually the only activity to be observed on Sundays were the throngs of people attending the many churches throughout the state. Otherwise, this entire state was quite boring. In addition to having been classified as a dry state, it was very conservative. The one exception was the occasional noisy auto races at the local the automobile race track. But such races were only held in one small town within this state. So, having been aware of these prohibitions, I knew that I could not start construction of my bow on this day. I would have to wait until the following Saturday afternoon. But I knew I could begin with the design and specifications of the bow, the arrows, and the quiver. So I grabbed my pencil and writing pad and became a designer. I drew the plans for a forty-eight-inch bow, made of oak, with leather drawstring of 3/16" diameter. Then I designed an arrow of quarter-inch aluminum piping. I would produce twelve thirty-six-inch arrows. Finally, I designed my quiver of aluminum stove piping. I would shape this aluminum and cover it with a sheet of sheep's leather. Over the next several weeks, I would complete these projects. I had just finished my sketches when mom called to me to come in and eat. After blessing the table, we ate our meal. While eating, dad discussed our work requirements for the upcoming week, which for me, took much of the enjoyment away from an otherwise very pleasant meal.

Finally it was time to take my horse Belle out for a ride. Remember, I now had a horse—but I still had no saddle. So, I picked up Belle's bridle and called to her. She quickly came over and I led her out of the fenced area, where the other two animals also stayed. I stationed her beside the fence and climbed it. Then I lowered myself onto her back and away we went. We started this time with a slow trot, and held that level of speed. We rode for several miles and traveled alongside fields and through wooded areas. I felt myself gaining in confidence because my ability to ride bareback was steadily improving. After reaching a clearance, I slackened the reigns and allowed Belle to run a bit. We ran for nearly one mile before I slowed the horse's pace. Then, we turned back and headed for home at a walking pace. It had felt good allowing Belle to run at a fast pace without having fallen from her back, so I gave myself a little praise. We arrived back at the old house shortly before 7:00PM. Once there I dismounted and returned Belle to the barnyard. By now it was time for my evening bath. My bath water was already pre-heated from having sat outside in the hot rays of sunlight. I would always use two tubs of water— (one for washing, one for rinsing). Otherwise, I would have finished my bath while using dirty water. Afterward I went inside where I spent the next two hours talking with the family about a variety of subjects. Soon, it was again time for bed. How I longed to see other humans again!

Each day across the summer would be the same. There would be no disappointments nor any surprises. However, there is one exception to my last statement; and, this was the great number of deadly snakes that dad and I unearthed while plowing each day. We learned that the local surrounding farmlands were not snake infested. Some might say that we were simply unlucky. Others might say that dad had exercised poor judgment in selecting this site for farming. Neither of these assessments is correct. The fact is that this farm, and the last, had remained unattended for several years prior to our occupying them. This had allowed the snakes to reproduce and multiply, unmolested for long periods. As a result, each of these areas had become havens for these reptiles. Other farmers in the area were aware of this problem, so this was the primary reason these two lands had been ignored for such long periods—no one had wanted them)!

I took a short break and had myself a cool glass of lemonade and a slice of grandma's apple pie. Then I just sat alone and relaxed a bit. There was no one for me to talk with since all the family was asleep, so I walked out to the barnyard and summoned my horse. I bridled Belle and led her over to the fence so that I could climb up and mount her. As soon as I had situated myself we rode quietly away. I found that with each ride I gained confidence in my riding ability. I could presently let the horse run at full pace without losing my balance. I'd finally learned that it was balance or (lack thereof) that determined whether a person was a good or poor rider, respectively. We rode a lot that afternoon. We traversed a radius of countryside, extending nearly five miles in each direction. As I rode I imagined myself as a Comanche warrior chasing covered-wagon caravans. And, as soon as I had completed my bow project, I would become an armed warrior! The thought even occurred that I could (at will) become a famous cowboy, riding my trusted black stallion!

All these thoughts were forms of mental escape. They helped me maintain my mental health during lengthy periods of isolation from the rest of society. This was the life that had been prepared for me, but I simply refused to let it control me! These were the thoughts that occupied my mind during those younger days of my existence.

It was getting a bit late in the evening, but I continued riding, though I soon decided it was time to head toward home. It was at this point that I remembered Buddy, (my lonely canine friend), so I altered my direction, and headed toward the farmhouse where he lived. As I neared his location, he spotted me and ran toward me, barking loudly. But on this day— I was not afraid of him!

Buddy and I had not seen each other for nearly three weeks, and I could tell that he was really happy to see me. I believe he sensed that I was equally thrilled by seeing him. The two of us were the lonely souls of our area. We needed each other— and we complimented each other. We rode along together for quite a distance. All along the way, we communicated with each other. I would talk to him and he would bark at me in return. If one could have understood our communication, they would have come away with this: "I'm happy to see you, Jake." "I'm happy to see you, Buddy." Don't laugh, my dear reader— just be happy this was not you!

Belle and I walked our friend back to his house, where we said our farewells. As we slowly rode away, I looked back at him only to see his sad eyes following our every move. Over my shoulder, I yelled out to him, "We'll see you next Saturday, Buddy." He replied with "Woof, woof" so, I guess he had said to me "Swell, swell." My days with Buddy and Belle were the high points of my life back then. I decided that the following Saturday, I would ask the old farmer who owned Buddy if he would let him come along with me sometimes. Then I thought, *"Why wait?"* so, I returned to his house and called out to him. The old farmer appeared on his front porch. We greeted each other and I asked my question. The old fellow was happy over my concern for his now aging dog. He welcomed my request, and gave me his approval. All the while Buddy sat as if listening to, and understanding, our conversation. I thanked the old farmer as I rode away toward our old farmhouse. It was now nearing dusk, and time for me to return Belle to her barnyard. I did this and prepared my bath. Afterwards, my family and I again sat talking about the events of the week.

During the course of our discussion dad mentioned that he had earlier that afternoon talked with, and paid, a man to come and drive us to church that next day (Sunday). Mom and I were happy to hear this, (but we'd each had our own reasons). She was happy for having had the opportunity to attend church. My reasons were twofold. First, I was happy that I would be away from the farm for a few hours. Second, I was thrilled over having the opportunity to ride in any gasoline- powered automobile (a truly rare occasion). Only mom and I would attend church that day. Grandmother was too exhausted to make the trip. Dad was a very religious person, but for some reason he rarely attended church. So mom and I laid out our clothing for the next day. Finally it was bed time, and we prepared to retire for the evening.

Sunday morning arrived and we arose at 7:00AM in anticipation of church. After washing up, the four of us had breakfast. We ate lightly on this morning as it was Sunday. Mom and I dressed. She wore a lovely white dress covered with pink roses. I wore my only suit. It was a nice suit of thin material of midnight blue. This was only my fourth time wearing it, but I had begun to slightly outgrow it. Its material was still like new as I had only been fortunate enough to wear it on just three occasions. So, we dressed and walked the quarter-mile distance to the main road where we would be picked up. It was easier this way because the narrow road leading up to our house was composed mostly of sand, and most drivers attempting to navigate their way through it were bogged down in sand.

Dad had already paid this man in advance, and to make things easier for him, we walked down to await his arrival. The gentleman had been scheduled to pick us up at 9:30AM. Mom and I left the house at 9:00AM sharp. We arrived fifteen minutes early. While waiting, we stood chatting about our lives as we saw them. Fifteen minutes passed, and it was now 9:30AM. We could see at least two miles down the old dirt road. Also, we could detect the presence of an oncoming vehicle because it would create a small dust cloud in its trail. We peered down the old narrow road, but saw no vehicle approaching—and we saw no dust cloud. Another fifteen minutes passed— and still we waited.

It was now 9:45AM. Church would begin in another fifteen minutes. So we looked at each other, as mom said, "Jake, I guess we'll be a little late today" and I agreed. We continued standing there waiting. Finally, 10:00AM arrived—but still no transportation. We decided to wait another fifteen minutes (just for safe measure). Then, at 10:15AM, we each again peered the two-mile distance down the old country road. Not one vehicle was in sight. So, we returned in great disappointment to our old house and removed our church clothing. Everyone was disappointed with this event (or lack thereof). It would be two more days before we would learn the reason why the driver had not shown up as planned. We discovered that the man had taken the money and spent it on alcohol on Saturday evening. When Sunday morning arrived, he had been much too hung over to drive out to pick us up. In fact, he had completely forgotten that dad had given him money for this purpose. But since he no longer had the money, he asked for another chance the coming Sunday. Dad wisely declined the man's deceptive offer, telling him to just keep the money. We never requested his services again. Another two months passed before we located a trustworthy individual to drive us to church. So, during that entire year we only were able to attend church on two occasions. *"What a pathetic situation!"* I thought.

The month of August was upon us, and I'd finished construction of my bow and arrow set. I found that I had done an excellent job. I had extensively sanded the bow before staining it. However, before staining I had saturated its wood with cooking oil, which added durability and flexibility. I had made a two-feet square target from the remains of a large cardboard box, and on weekends after field work, I would practice archery for hours. Usually winds were quite calm during summer months, and I soon found that my aluminum arrows would fly true to their target. Eventually, my proficiency progressed to the point that I could strike my two-inch bull's-eye from a distance of forty feet. I was very proud of my accomplishments, and happy that I now had programs and resources to occupy my small amount of leisure time. I also continued improving my riding skills. Before the end of summer I was able to ride my horse bareback at full gallop, for long distances without any problems whatsoever. This alone was quite an achievement. Hence, over the next two years I completely disregarded going to the movies on Saturday afternoons. Instead, I settled for practicing archery, knife throwing, and horseback riding. Also, I had been successful in obtaining a few yards of discarded animal hide, which I used to fabricate a makeshift saddle for riding. So, now I was organized and equipped for enjoyment of this rural region in which we lived. Still, before completing my evening rides, I would always swing by to pick up my good canine friend Buddy.

It was finally back-to-school time. Except for the long one-hour bicycle rides each morning and afternoon, school days would have been my most pleasant experiences. I was now starting eighth grade, and had added one more class. Now, I carried a total of seven subjects. Still, I progressed through that entire school year without doing any after-school studying. I kept up my practice of focusing intently during each class and using study hall period to concentrate on any assigned homework. So again this new school year, my after-school hours were kept free for helping out with the farming chores. Each day I would rush home from school, gulp down my food, grab my mule, and hurry out into the fields to wherever dad was working. We would work side by side until just before dark. But with each passing day during the autumn months, darkness would come slightly earlier, so my days of field work were rapidly growing shorter. This meant that I got to bed a little earlier each night, thereby allowing more time for sleep. I never complained but I realized that I greatly needed every extra minute of sleep I could muster. I discovered that during this time of year I seemed to have more energy, and I was more mentally alert overall. So generally, I felt considerably better about my state of austere existence. It was finally nearing the month of November, so the weather was becoming colder with each passing day. I had fine-tuned my personal daily routine and had begun to feel more comfortable and confident. Finally, I thought, *"I believe I can get through this"!*

We had completed harvesting for the year, which meant we would have a slightly reduced workload for a short while, and I would have different chores after school. For the next two months I cut down trees and hauled them to the house to be used as firewood. I must say here that all farm work is heavy; but, cutting down and hauling trees singlehandedly is certainly extremely heavy work. Some of the trees that I cut down, using only an axe, measured up to twenty feet in height. The base of a tree of this size was at least twelve inches in diameter. The process of cutting down such a tree required great amounts of muscle exertion. It also required precision and technique. This was not a simple task; and, safety was always the prime consideration. One could lose a foot or leg from the improper use of an axe. Much of the wood was knotted, and these knot formations were nearly as hard as stone. So, if I was not constantly cautious as I struck with my axe, it would frequently strike a knot and ricochet off the tree. When this occurs, the axe tends to deflect away toward one's legs. Also, had this happened, an artery might have been severed, causing imminent death. And death would have been unavoidable, since I'd worked alone deep within the woods. I was always out of hearing range, so even if I had called out for help, no one would have heard my desperate cries. My body would have been discovered several hours after my death by those searching for me, since I had not returned home. Needless to say, cutting down trees was a dangerous undertaking, especially when working alone and out of sight of others. I had not been trained in performing this task. Sure, dad had shown me how to do this work, and he had instructed me to always be careful. But I was just thirteen years old! I realized then that dad had wished for me to grow up muscularly and strong, as he himself had.

But my two consecutive bouts with severe pneumonia had robbed me of that possibility. So dad was always patient with his skinny, somewhat weakling of a son. Nevertheless, he always tried to instill in me a sense of pride, ability, and self-esteem. Dad simply would not tolerate any persons feeling sorry for themselves. I am not implying that I, in any way, felt sorrow for myself. It's just that I'd found that first year at our new location to have been overwhelming. Guess what though— I would have five long years of this new-found lifestyle. So, I knew I had better get with the program— and stick with it! Complaining or slacking off was not an option. So, day after day, I continued with my current routine.

Soon we were in the midst of winter, which would become our first at this new location. We found it easier to heat this old house than the last, as the inner walls of this old building were in somewhat better condition, and since this was a smaller house, it was considerably easier to heat. I had already managed to cut, haul, and stack a two month's supply of firewood. Still, I had another month's work ahead of me. Incidentally, this wood was not only used for heating, it was also used for cooking. So, in the evenings after we had eaten, we would often sit around the fireplace, discussing the events of the summer, and singing a few religious songs.

This was my routine throughout the winter months. I discovered that my biggest problem during this time of year was that of riding my bicycle to school each morning in the freezing cold. So in preparation for my early morning rides, I always wore especially warm clothing. I even wore long underwear, with two pairs of woolen socks inside my padded boots. I also wore eye goggles with earmuffs and a thick scarf of wool. I wore the type of thick leather, wool-lined cap that pilots wore during World War II. I also wore a knee-length leather, wool-lined heavy top coat. But added to this attire were my thick leather gloves with heavy woolen inserts! I was well equipped for the severe winter weather which existed in our part of the country. But even after having ridden for forty-five minutes, another fifteen minutes of riding time remained. These last few minutes were the absolute worst! Even though I had been well prepared to face this cold, it always won, because by now my hands (and especially my fingers) were so numb I could not feel them at all! Also, I could no longer feel my feet. Then, there was the problem of my face. My eyes watered, my ears seemed to burn and tingle, and my nostrils ached from the constant inhalation of the freezing air, even though my face was wrapped inside my thick woolen scarf. I found it necessary to coat my lips with thin layers of Vaseline each morning, to prevent breaking of the skin. Thus by the time I arrived at school each morning, I was fully aware of what it probably would have felt like had I been an Eskimo.

During the winter months, none of the kids stood around chatting before entering their classes. Instead, each student rushed directly to their classroom, where they would huddle around the heat radiators until classes began. Each had followed this practice, even though none had suffered the misfortune of commuting for one hour on a bicycle each morning. I know this because I had asked around the school how the other kids had traveled. Most walked short distances. Others, living more than a mile away from the school, were provided school bus transportation. So,

I stood apart in this situation. Oh, I failed to mention the sleet! I quite frequently experienced sleet during my morning commutes. My classmates all knew this, so they would make space for me at the radiator, for by the time I arrived each morning, I was in nearly a frozen state. Yes, these were extremely difficult times for me. But had I mentioned any of this to members of my family, I'm sure each would have wanted to tell me of their sad stories!

I looked forward to afternoon rides home from school, as usually there was sunshine and calm. The afternoon temperatures would be considerably warmer and more bearable. Each day after school, all the kids living about town would leave in small groups, chatting and laughing together. I would stand and watch— and I would envy them! Usually they would travel some distance from the school before I'd even completed preparations for my long afternoon ride. It took me at least ten to fifteen minutes just to bundle and button up. Then I would mount my faithful old bicycle and ride away into the loneliness. As always, after fifteen minutes, I would pass the old house where I was born. This was where I had lived my first nine years. Invariably, I would wave to it and blow it a kiss, for this was the location where I had left my heart—and life! I would then ride for another fifteen minutes, where I would approach the second house that we had lived in. Ironically, I found this old house no longer so distasteful. At least it stood only at the edge of civilization. I would wave to it— but I blew no kisses. Now, I was at only the halfway point to my final destination (Hell). At this point, I would quicken my pace. Although I never looked forward to reaching home, I was always anxious to complete my long journey. This was the way life had been for me throughout those four long, cold, and miserable months!

Soon we reached the end of the month of November. It was Grandmother's ninety-seventh birthday, and mom prepared a special chocolate cake, covered with coconut frosting, for this important occasion. The field work had reduced during this time of year, so they had found the time to work around the house and in our large garden. Of course, dad's work continued, but in an altered state. Our harvesting of crops had been completed. Also, we had sold our produce at nearby auctions. The money we received for our products was minimal, compared to the great amount of effort required to produce it. But dad had managed to nearly double our income over the previous four years. This significant increase in family income led us to feel much better about long hours we had contributed toward this end.

After arriving home that afternoon, I ate, changed my clothing, and immediately rushed out into the woods, to cut down trees. But darkness now came around 5:00PM, so I returned to the house, then washed before preparing for our evening meal and grandmother's birthday celebration! As soon as I had finished, dad came in from the fields and did the same. When we had finished our meal, mom brought out the lovely cake— all lit up with an unspecified number of candles. This was grandmother's only gift. But this was the first time she had ever been presented with a cake for her birthday. She was overwhelmed with joy and appreciation! I was so very happy at seeing grandmother reach this age, and still in possession of her faculties. I was equally happy for the privilege of eating delicious chocolate cake. Grandmother seemed to have still been in great health. She took no medications and had never visited a doctor in the nearly fourteen years I had known her. We all agreed that she was truly blessed! We each gave her a great big hug while telling her how much we loved her. This was the only true gift she had wanted. We then sat together as we rejoiced on this rare occasion!

Weeks passed, and it was now nearing Christmas time, a time that was very special and dear to me. I'd had several reasons for feeling this way. First, we were taught that this was the birth period of our Lord and Savior, Jesus Christ. Second, I anxiously had awaited a few Christmas gifts from my family. And this time of year meant no commuting back and forth to school each day, for two weeks. I was grateful for each of these blessings. Also, I would now have a bit of time to ride my horse and play cowboys and Indians. I also knew that Buddy would be happy to see me. Each day I would rush through my chores of chopping and stacking firewood. Only then could I relax!

My birthday always fell on the second day after Christmas. However, on this day I would never receive more than one small gift, accompanied by one homemade cake. This time my cake held fourteen candles. I was now fourteen years old,— wow! This had always been a day of vacation time for me. So, aside from Sundays, Christmas, and Easter, my birthdays were periods of leisure. All other holidays were at least partial work days in our household.

But today came a very pleasant surprise! On New Year's Day, we received a distinguished visitor— my mother's younger brother, and her only sibling. He was an unusually tall, and unbelievably handsome young man. He was charismatic and elegant. And though he was a non-commissioned-officer of the United States Army, he had succeeded in saving a considerable amount of money. He was an enviable man. Uncle had arrived by taxi. Mom, dad, and I had been outside in our yard gathering firewood, when we saw the taxi driving in our direction down the main road. Then, as this car drew near our access road, it slowed and turned, heading slowly up the incline toward our house. From the distance at which we stood, we could not discern its passenger, so the three of us stood and waited in anticipation. Mom was the first to recognize him, and she immediately began running down the sloped, narrow road to greet him. Uncle had written often, but it had been a long while since we had last seen or talked to him. He had been equally anxious to see us (especially his only sister). So as soon as he saw her coming, he stepped from the car even before it had completely stopped. They both hugged and held each other for what had seemed like a long while. Then came my turn. Uncle Abe ran toward me and scooped me up from the ground. He greeted me and held onto me, commenting on how much I had grown since we had last seen each other. It had been more than one year since his last visit. During that visit, he had helped with our move from our last location. He released me and then turned his attention to my waiting dad. They then hugged also and exchanged pleasantries. He and mom had lost both parents at the early age of ten and twelve (respectively). This devastating loss had left them with only each other. But even so, they had become separated because there were no relatives with the means to provide for these two children. So, one family had taken this twelve-year-old girl; and, another family the small ten-year-old boy. But they each continued living in the same town and would occasionally see each other. As a direct result of losing of both parents, and subsequent permanent separation, they grew much closer to each other as siblings. After all, only these two were capable of understanding their pathetic situation.

As I stood there I recalled Uncle Abe's previous visit. He had arrived by taxi on that occasion also. The very next day, he managed to hitch a ride into the downtown area, where he purchased a brand-new Mercury automobile. It was a beautiful car, bordering on luxury. Until that time, at age twelve, I had never before ridden inside a new automobile. Its color was burgundy, with a matching leather interior. Its exterior and interior had been ornamented with shining chrome. Sitting inside this shiny new car had been a wonderful and most memorable experience for me. Even more wonderful was the morning of my first ride to school in a new car. I had been told the evening before by mom that Uncle Abe would give me a lift to school and would also pick me up that afternoon. So I awakened early that next morning, filled with excitement! After I had dressed and eaten, it came time to depart for school. I was simply thrilled! As we rode along together, I quickly became mesmerized by that enchanting new-car aroma. I found that I enjoyed this scent even more than the enticing aroma of freshly cooked popcorn at the movie theater.

We did not talk much along the way. This was mainly because I had been too busy admiring this fancy new car. Finally, we reached the schoolhouse and pulled onto the grounds to park. As we did so, I found that I could barely control my emotions. I proudly waved to all the students;

even to those I did not know. I felt embarrassed because I could not stop grinning! I'm sure that as soon as my uncle returned to our house, he immediately told my mom of my behavior. I also believe that he fully understood the reasons for my newfound ecstasy. For the first time in my life— I FELT LIKE A HUMAN BEING! For the first time, I stood before others without feeling different or inferior. This was a truly wonderful feeling for me. Suddenly, I had gained at least a slight degree of respect, which replaced some of the pity and apathy I had received throughout my prior school years. Throughout that day, and for the next few days, students would approach me inquiring about the handsome stranger with the pretty new car! I would always respond, "Ah, that's just my Uncle Abe." For the following two-week period I was blessed to have received rides to and from school. That was the most blissful period of my youth.

I now recall that when Uncle Abe's visit had ended, as he prepared to leave, he had handed my mother a thick manila envelope, saying "Sis, I want you to keep this for me." She had asked "What is this"? "Its money" replied uncle. So, mom took the envelope, saying "I'll take good care of it". Mom then placed the envelope inside a stack of new towels at the bottom of her very old trunk. I was the only witness to this event. Then, after hugs and tears (from mom), he was gone.

Nearly two weeks passed. Dad had gone into town, and grandmother was asleep. Mom called me into the house, handing me the envelope. I asked her if she was giving this to me. She replied, "I wish I could, but I just need you to count it". I asked if she had counted it and she replied, "Yes, I have." I asked how much was there, and she replied, "I count five thousand dollars". My heart skipped a beat as I sat at our table, carefully counting this money. Mom's count had been accurate. The envelope contained $2,000 in U. S. government bonds, along with $3,000 actual cash. This happened during the year of 1950. This sum of money back then would have been sufficient for the cash purchase of a new custom-built three-bedroom house. I placed the cash and bonds back into the envelope before handing it to mom, whereupon she immediately returned it to her trunk for safekeeping. She and I kept this as a secret between the two of us, while never mentioning it in the presence of others.

Back to Uncle Abraham's current visit, his present stay had also been for only two weeks. By now, I had come to understand his reasons for not staying more than one or two weeks each visit. It was simply because he had become quite accustomed to the presence of electricity, running water, heating, telephone, and television. All these were still absent from our residence, so two weeks at most were all he could take of this lack of services. I had started back to school the week before his departure, but I had not received any rides this time. Uncle Abe had left his car at his military base in Germany. Before he left, mom quietly asked him, "Don't you want to take your money along with you?" He responded "What money"? "The money that I've been holding for you" mom replied. Uncle Abe then casually responded, "Oh, that was my gift to you". Mom and I were both shocked by his comments, but she calmly said to him "Abe, you know I can't accept this money". Uncle's response was "Sis, you don't have any choice". Mom then graciously thanked her lone brother, adding "It will always be here". And, even though mom's old dresses frequently required stitching and patching, she simply refused to spend even one cent of this money for her personal needs.

Uncle Abe just smiled as he walked out of the house. He had made arrangement for a taxi to pick him up, so as soon as the taxi was in sight, he said his "good-byes" to the family, and bade mom and me a special farewell. Suddenly he was gone! Mom and I were both especially saddened at the departure of this great and charming man.

I would not see Uncle Abe again over the next twenty-two years. He did not return again until after I had left home to join the U. S. Air Force. It just so happened, each time he had returned, I was away. We seemed never to be able to synchronize our visits. But each of Uncle Abe's visits had made strong impressions on me. His strong presence had opened my 'blind' eyes and awakened my 'sleeping mind'! He had demonstrated to me how life could be. Also, he had unknowingly shown me the highly elusive path away from 'Hell'! Upon observing him during this recent visit, I realized that his lifestyle was one that I would seek for myself.

Months passed as I continued in school, worked in the fields, and patiently awaited the day of my escape. My riding skills had greatly improved. My archery, marksmanship, and knife-throwing skills had equally improved. Winter had come and gone, and my family and I were once again back at 'hard labor' in those unfriendly fields. It was at this point in my life that a stranger entered. His name was simply Lim. I would always address him as Mr. Lim out of respect. Everyone else in the area had addressed him either as Lim or old man Lim. He had occupied a house on a knoll that stood one-half mile from ours. I had discovered this elderly gentleman while scanning the countryside with a new pair of binoculars I had received as a gift at Christmastime. It was on one Sunday afternoon as I sat in the shade of our front porch peering about the area. In the backyard of an old house on the slope across the way, I noticed the slight figure of an old bearded man. His long hair was the color of snow, and he appeared to have a deep sun tan. The white hair and tanned skin greatly complimented each other. As I sat watching, at first I thought that he might be practicing some sort of dance. He would assume a crouched position. Then, he would seemingly float or glide about the yard. His arms would sway around and about— and back and forth. Once in a while, he would leap high into the air, kicking with his feet. He would make frequent striking motions with his hands. I was fascinated by this! As I continued watching this graceful display of movement, I wondered *"What manner of foolishness is this?"* for I had not seen anything like it before. I put down my binoculars and went inside to ask dad about this. Dad" I said, "There's a wild-looking little man at the house across on the slope and he's doing some kind of crazy dance." Dad smiled, saying "He's okay, son — it's just old man Lim practicing his Chinese fighting style". I was relieved to learn that all was okay.

By now, several months of school attendance and field work had been completed. Things were progressing smoothly. Uncle Abe had written several times and mom had replied to each letter. For some odd reason, they never seemed to call each other on the telephone (naturally, I jest). Then, one Friday afternoon at school, a group of army recruiters came to make a presentation. Their purpose was to provide publicity to senior students, thereby encouraging them to make the U. S. Army a career after graduation. Although I was not a senior at the time, those middle school students with high grades, were permitted to attend. Naturally, I took advantage of this rare opportunity. Two recruiters gave presentations that included the use of visual aids. They displayed professionalism and respect, accompanied by a vast knowledge of their subject matter. At the conclusion of this presentation, they presented to our group a six-man team of military martial arts specialists. They then proceeded to give us a demonstration of Karate and Kung Fu. They each did a series of strikes and kicks while employing various techniques. They even broke bricks, cement blocks, and wood with their bare hands. I had never seen anything like this before, and I was highly impressed by everything they had done! This team was awesome! I went home that afternoon and told dad what I had seen at school. He responded by saying, "That sounds like the kind of fighting that old man Lim does— I hear he breaks bricks and boards with his hands also". *"Interesting"* I thought – "I *wonder if he would teach me"?*

The next day was Saturday. We did our usual field work throughout the morning. But when we had finished work for the day, I bathed and put on fresh clothing. Then, I took my horse Belle out for an early ride. I was anxious to meet Mr. Lim as I wanted to know if he would consider teaching me his odd style of fighting. Although, I suspected that mom and dad might be a bit apprehensive about my intentions. I did not wish to be obvious, so I rode in the general direction of this old man's home, taking a roundabout route. I had previously seen him train at this hour of the day, and I'd hoped to find him at least milling about outside in his garden or yard. I was lucky, for as I came to within a few hundred yards from his place, I saw him. As in the time before, he was practicing his art. I did not wish to disturb him at this time, so I made no sound.

The route I had taken, led me over a low-lying ridge. As I reached the crest of this ridge I spotted Mr. Lim in his backyard. I'd studied the habits of Indian warriors, so I decided to employ one of their scouting techniques. I calmed my horse and remained perfectly still as I sat astride her. We were among a sparse clump of trees, so he did not see me. As I sat watching him, I began to feel great admiration for this petite old gentleman. I could tell by his appearance that he had been around for a long, long time. I estimated his age to be nearly eighty, but he seemed to have retained his strength; and, he was extremely agile. I watched as he delivered a series of kicks to areas reaching his height of about five-foot-six. I do not know long he had been at this, but he continued for another half hour after my arrival. I remained in my position within the trees. When he finally stopped, I emerged from the surrounding brush. His senses were very keen, for no sooner than my horse had started to move, did he turn, looking in my direction. We had not really made any noise as my horse had been slowly and quietly walking in sand. Still, he had heard us as we began moving down the slope toward him. I did not want to keep him waiting, so I let Belle assume a slow trot down the slight slope. He stood watching our approach, so I waved to him. At this point, I realized that I too, was a bit apprehensive about this meeting. But it was already too late to turn back.

When I reached him, I greeted him cordially and with a smile. "Good afternoon, sir, how are you?" I asked. He slightly smiled in return, saying "I be okay". At this point I realized that English was not his native language, so I gave the outward impression of not having noticed his very poor language usage. I calmly said "My name s Jake – what is yours"? "My name be Lim" replied this old gentleman. I continued "Your style of fighting is awesome – what is it"? "Not be Karate – not be Kung Fu – be my style only". I asked, "How long have you done this"? "All life" responded this old gentleman. "Great" I said – "Would you teach me"? The old man paused for a moment, before asking "Why you want learn to fight"? "A few boys at school often pick on me, so I want to be able to protect myself" I answered. He pondered my comments for awhile, and then he said to me "You be skinny boy". I smiled again, saying "Yes sir, I sure am". With that, he sort of smiled, adding "Maybe I think about". "You come next week, okay"? I was happy to have received his tentative invitation, so I graciously thanked him, asking "Would this time of day be okay with you"? He replied, "This time be good". So with a broad grin on my face, I gave a slight bow as I again thanked him. Then I bade him farewell as I rode away, using the same round-about route I had taken in coming here. As I rode along, I reflected upon my visit with this kindly old gentleman. I wondered if I was making a mistake.

I had spent my first hour of leisure time observing and talking with Mr. Lim. It was still only mid-afternoon, which meant that more than two hours of riding time remained. I steered the horse away from all civilization, and for the very first time, let her run at top speed for a very long while.

This ride felt great with the cool afternoon summer breeze flowing past my face. By now my homemade leather saddle had formed its shape, finally fitting comfortably upon my horse's back. I had placed three inches of packed cotton inside the sewn saddle as padding. This made for a soft, cushioned ride for me. It also provided for ease of movement by my horse. I had used a quilted piece of fabric material of forty-eight inches square as under-padding for my saddle. This under-padding rested directly on my horse's back, reducing the friction caused by my weight. Overall, it made for a more comfortable ride for myself and for my horse. So here I was, having learned to ride well— and finally well-equipped for my rides.

It was nearing 5:00PM, so I decided to head directly toward Buddy's house. As usual, whenever he saw us approaching he would run out to meet us. This time was no different. Buddy ran to us barking and jumping about while constantly wagging his tail. I had received permission from the old farmer to take his dog along with me, so I simply said, "Come, Buddy, let's ride, old boy." And, with these words we turned and raced away from the house. I did not continue this quick pace for long, as I felt that Buddy might become overly exhausted, so after slowing a bit, we continued along the narrow pathway, which bordered a very large wooded area. I had traveled this route on several previous occasions, so I felt comfortable in being in this area. I had even entered this area on foot many times while hunting with my Daisy carbine B.B. rifle. I felt that I knew this region quite well, and may have been correct in my assessment, but on this day things would be quite different!

The wooded area was to my left, with my friend Buddy

walking at my right. Suddenly, he bolted ahead of me! He ran for a short distance— then abruptly stopped! He stood there peering into the thick underbrush. Then he began barking frantically while dancing about and pacing back and forth! I instantly stopped my horse and stepped down onto the ground. I tied Belle to a tree in a cleared area just a few feet behind me. I had instinctively known that Buddy was reacting to the presence of either a raccoon or snake. Either animal was bad news! As I had reached a distance of approximately twenty feet from where Buddy stood, I witnessed a distressing sight that I had never before seen! It had occurred with lightning speed! One moment nothing was there—the next moment, it was there and gone,— just a blurring motion! It was during this split-second that I recognized this dreaded thing. I could now hear the ominous sound of the snake's rattles! I had encountered and killed dozens of various types of snakes, but I had never before found myself in the presence of a deadly rattler! Things had quickly changed. The snake struck at Buddy, but missed, as Buddy himself was also lightening fast! His instincts were also strong and reliable. He moved in unison with the snake, thereby evading its deadly fangs. I called to Buddy to move away, but he ignored me. He continued to stand his ground, barking and growling viciously at this rattler. The snake struck for a second time! Again it missed. Buddy had timed the snake's second strike with both accuracy and great precision. At this point I was highly alarmed! Here I was in the middle of nowhere,— and with the old farmer's only dog— about to be bitten by a deadly snake! The snake would not give in— but Buddy, likewise would not give in! They continued challenging each other!

I had always ridden with my quiver of aluminum arrows strapped onto my back, so I removed my strong oak wood bow from its resting place, hooked onto my saddle. I cautiously approached the point where Buddy stood furiously barking and growling. I stopped about fifteen feet from the brushy spot where I believed the rattler to be. I peered into the brush, but I saw no snake. I figured maybe it had crawled away, but Buddy's actions told me otherwise. I advanced closer where Buddy stood, stopping approximately twelve feet away from him. I dared not distract him, since he would most certainly have become vulnerable to this rattler's attack. Still, I saw no movement within the brush, and I saw no evidence of the snake's presence. Then, I heard it once again— that distinct, terrifying rattling sound! Slowly, I withdrew an arrow from my quiver and positioned it onto the bow. Although I could not see the snake, I now knew its whereabouts. There was only one small patch of dried oak leaves resting upon the white sand. This patch of leaves had fallen to the ground directly at the base of the small oak tree standing above it. Also, this patch of leaves covered an area spanning approximately four feet in diameter. I picked up a small clump of dirt about the size of an egg, tossing it into the patch of leaves. This aggravated the already highly agitated reptile, causing it to strike at the spot where the chunk of dirt had landed. This provided me with the target I needed, so I let fly my arrow! Immediately there was wild thrashing about within the leaves! Now I could see this rattler as it writhed and tossed about, frantically trying to free itself from my lethal aluminum arrow, and ending up outside its hiding place and on the snowy white sand. Now it was totally visible to me, and one hundred percent vulnerable. I released another arrow! It too, pierced through the snake's body— in two separate locations. I knew now that its hide belonged to me! I withdrew and fired a third arrow, striking the rattler once again directly in the thick of its body. My third, and final arrow had done the trick!

I knew that this snake was still highly dangerous. It was not dead,— not by a long shot. In fact, it would live in this wounded condition for at least a couple of more hours. Buddy wanted to rush in to finish the job I had started, but I held him back, calming him. Then I snapped a six-foot branch from a nearby pine tree, stripping it of its smaller branches. I walked to where the now crippled rattler lay. I then commenced to completely pulverize its rapidly expiring form!

I finally led Buddy away from this location as I continued to calm him. I thanked him for his valued protection. I also knelt, patted, and hugged him. I truly believe he'd understood and appreciated this. The significance of Buddy's actions is this: Had Buddy not intervened, I probably would not be alive today to tell you my story. And if I hadn't stopped by to pick Buddy up, I would have unsuspectingly proceeded along that seemingly deserted pathway until I reached that rattler. Then it would have startled my horse, throwing me onto the ground, where I would most certainly have been snake bitten! Remember, I had been riding in the wilderness, miles away from the nearest house. Even if I had been able to recover and mount my horse, it would have taken me at least fifteen minutes to reach home and my family. And even if I had managed to survive that ride (which I seriously doubt), reaching home would not have saved me. Once there, I would have been stranded, and no amount of effort could have saved me, for we had no car with which to rush me to a hospital. We had no telephone with which to call a doctor. Lastly, neighbors were nonexistent; so, there would have been absolutely no possibility of survival for me! Either I would have perished before I'd reached home, or shortly thereafter. I owe my life to Buddy, a dog that only one year ago, I had been deathly afraid of!

At this point, I decided that there had been enough significant events in my young life for one day so I returned Buddy to his house. I then went directly home and never mentioned any of this! On this day, I'd had absolutely no inkling of what the future had held for me. I'd also had no way of knowing that by having initially become friends with Buddy, I had been spared to save the lives of countless others, many of whom had not yet been born!

The next day (Sunday) my family sort of relaxed and rested. Back during those days, everyone always arose early, even though there may not have been work to do, or places to visit. So by 8:00AM that Sunday morning, we had all arisen and washed up. We finished breakfast before 9:00AM. But now that we had a little spare time, there was nothing to do. Mom was tidying up around the house. Dad had mounted our old bicycle and ridden the one-mile distance to the nearest little store. Grandmother sat in her room reading her Bible. That left me all alone. The last thing I had done the day before was ride my horse, so I chose not to begin the day by riding. Plus, I had not yet fully recovered from that deadly snake incident of the previous afternoon. *"What to do?"* I thought. At that point,

I would almost have given my left hand, just to have had another young person to talk to. Back in those days, children and adults did not really talk to each other. Instead, the adults talked to the children, and the children would just listen. The children would speak only if they had been asked a question by the adult. The only exceptions to this rule were emergency situations. Today, this would be considered a form of child abuse. But back then this was the normal way things were done! "How sad" you might say. I would totally agree with you, for this was a truly sad manner in which to live. How could any youth have been expected to reach maturity, and still retain some degree of mental stability? I lived this lifestyle, but even I have been unable to find the answer to this question. Somehow though, I managed to survive all this. My proof here lies in the fact that, throughout my future adult life, I would never require any psychiatric services.

I took many drastic measures to combat my isolation and loneliness. This was but one of those measures. I located my only catcher's glove and tennis ball and went out into our old barnyard, where I stood alone and pitched my ball onto the wall of our old barn. It would rebound and I would catch it in my glove. I had learned this game of solitary baseball quite well. In fact, I had gotten so very good at this unusual game, that I could play an entire ball game without the other team members. In short, I had become a 'great ball player' at the young age of only fourteen! But I had become much more than just a 'great ball player'. I was also a lightening-fast gunslinger, a fearsome Cherokee warrior, an archer, a knife thrower, and a marksman. At age fourteen, I was simply— awesome! These many unusual roles were the primary means by which I managed to maintain my sanity while growing up.

After tiring of playing a whole ball game alone, I decided to try knife throwing for a while. After all, I'd had ample archery practice just yesterday evening. So I walked over and picked up my hunting knife and walked the few yards to the nearest large pine tree. I preferred using these trees for knife-throwing activity because of soft bark. This made for easy retrieval of an embedded knife. I had taped a one-foot square piece of cardboard onto the tree as my target. I had picked up this practice from having watched a limited number of western movies. I stood there throwing my sharpened hunting knife for nearly an hour, and managed to hit the bull's-' eye with great accuracy.

At this point in my life I was proud of my accomplishments. I could ride well (even bareback). I was a great small-game hunter. I was an archer, knife thrower, and marksman. Also, at the young age of fourteen, I was absolutely certain of the fact that I had faced and killed a greater number of deadly snakes than anyone else of my age group! Last but not least, I had succeeded in surviving the most austere of conditions, and with my faculties still intact!

Then all too soon, another school year had come to an end. Again I had managed to hold onto my high A's and B's. This time around, my lowest grade was one B-minus. My folks, teachers, and I were all quite satisfied with my academic achievements. This was very special, considering I still had not spent one single hour of study time at home. I was truly proud of myself. So once again I had won— and lost. On the plus side, I would not have the lengthy two hours of daily bicycle riding to and from school. Thus, at least my mind could soon take a well-deserved and much-needed three-month vacation. However, on the negative side, I would find myself again enduring continued isolation from my peers. Thankfully though, I had made great social progress with old Mr. Lim. He was highly impressed with the manner in which I had learned and adapted to the defense skills he had taught me over the past few months.

At this point I really wanted to treat myself to a movie. But with my current farm workload, my training program, along with the archery, marksmanship, and knife-throwing practices, I realized I must again sacrifice the movies. Additionally, but equally important was the consideration of exercising my horse. So, my summer schedule would be even more activity packed than in the past. I had often heard the old adage "An idle mind is the devil's playhouse." It occurred to me that since the age of nine, I had not been confronted with the problem of the idle mind. I had always been busy either at work or with special programs I had initiated. Either way I was always kept busy.

My entire summer passed without any accidents or incidents. We harvested our crops and sold them on the auction market, receiving moderate sums of money. I continued improving my skills in each of my special activity programs. Again this summer, mom and I would not be lucky in our desire to spend at least a couple of Sundays in church. But we each had accepted this as simply a condition of our existence. Grandmother was rapidly approaching the 'tender' age of ninety-eight, but she was still going strong— and with no medications or doctors. Finally, our summer was gone.

It was back to school once again, a day that I had

anxiously awaited (except for the bicycle rides each day). Although, I would gladly make those long and uncomfortable daily rides, just for the opportunity of companionship. In retrospect, I believe that the word "companion" had become foremost in my limited vocabulary! So, I now resumed my in-school study habits as I proceeded through my ninth year of school. Naturally, we were assigned different teachers, along with one added class. Other than these minor changes, all remained pretty much the same. Now many of the boys and girls were just starting to socialize on a more intimate basis. This, however, excluded me! Though I was really interested, there simply was not time. Each day after school boys would walk girls to their homes, laughing and joking, while holding hands, etc. Then, evenings after completing their homework, they would go out into the town and visit with these girls. The next day at school, some of the boys would gather in small groups, discussing their progress of the past evening. I was now approaching the age of fifteen, and I'd greatly wanted to be a part of this newfound social activity. But my wishes would not be granted, and my desires not fulfilled. This served to further isolate me from my classmates and others. Occasionally, I would become fortunate during afternoons after school. Quite frequently I would receive smiles from some of the girls. Noticing this, some of the boys would urge me on, saying "Go over and talk to her." I wanted nothing more than to do just that— but what would I say? Once in a while I would work up the courage to strike up a conversation with some cute girl. But invariably, in reaching the end of our brief chat, I would sense that she'd stood waiting for me to ask, "May I walk you home this afternoon?" But I could not ask these words, because immediately after school, I was forced to rush home for field work. So in realizing that I in no way wished to find myself in trouble with my parents, I would simply end up saying something like "See you tomorrow?" Then grudgingly, I would just turn and walk away, knowing that this was no way to begin a casual relationship.

Having celebrated my grandmother's ninety-seventh birthday, we found ourselves preparing for Christmas-time and my fifteenth birthday. My work assignments around the house remained unchanged. I knew what was expected of me, so I proudly went about completing my chores, such as field work and wood cutting, without being instructed by either of my parents. I repeat, I still harbored such strong desires to satisfy my parents and make them proud of me.

Christmas finally came and we were anxious for its arrival. Each of us did our part in making this another comfortable and festive occasion. Dad had done most of the shopping, with mom having done a bit also. Grandmother even managed to reach town to make a few purchases (mainly for me). I chopped, hauled, and stacked chords of firewood for cooking and heating. I also gathered lots of pecans and walnuts from the numerous trees in our yard. As usual, dear grandmother baked her customary batch of delicious cakes and pies. Mom also added a few of her own. So Christmas was again a most enjoyable event for our family. We celebrated, but with gratitude and humility. Then as usual, after our grand meal we each sat around the fireplace singing hymns and giving praise to our Lord. We had no visitors this time since Uncle Abe was overseas in Europe. Then came my birthday two days later, along with more cake and tea. At this point in my young life, I no longer received toys. But I did receive a few shirts, pants, a couple of pairs of shoes, and a jacket, which were the gifts I really wanted. I felt that clothes would help me attract and impress the girls! So, we all had another wonderful holiday season. Oh yes, (almost forgot) my parents and grandmother also exchanged a few gifts! These rare combined gestures served to make the season even more memorable. But what I most failed to realize at the time was that they were not interested in gifts from the stores. They were each simply grateful to have their one and only child/grandchild alive and healthy. Their feelings arose primarily from the fact that, during my early years, they had seriously doubted that I would survive my two consecutive bouts with pneumonia. But added to this, they were so thankful for our overall good health (especially that of my elderly grandmother). This had been a good year.

The holiday season passed and my two-week vacation had ended. Today was a very cold and rainy Monday morning. This was the first day back to school, and I needed to attend, mainly to ensure that I would not miss any note-taking. My notes were the only sure means of a successful school year. It was just before 7:00AM, and still dark outside due to the heavy rainfall. But regardless of severe weather conditions, I had to trek to school. So, I dressed for the occasion by putting on warm wool clothing along with a thick pair gloves. I also donned my bright yellow rubber rain suit, which was accompanied by a rubber rain hat and plastic goggles. Whenever I wore those goggles I discovered that I could only see three to four feet ahead of myself. This meant that I was required to ride my bicycle cautiously and slowly, lest I hit some unintended stationary object. I was aided immensely this morning by being thoroughly familiar with the condition of the roads I traveled. So, I was able to successfully navigate my way through the semi-darkness for the entire distance to school. I arrived about five minutes before the bell rang. I barely had time to secure my old bicycle before rushing to my classroom.

My first period teacher and all of the students in class seemed happy at seeing me again. I was especially happy to see each of them! My day progressed well as I had fully optimized my skills in note-taking. I could now speedily take accurate notes simultaneously with the teacher's speaking. I could consistently do this even in the presence of occasional distractions. Don't forget— I had no machine with which to record my teachers' comments, and speed was of the essence. Our last class of the day had been designated as study period. This worked especially well for me, as I would use this period to review all of the notes I had made throughout the school day. In this way, I would be free to do any required field work with my dad. I would also be then prepared for the next day's classes. Finally, our study period arrived and all the students proceeded to their designated location for study. After another forty-five minutes, our school day ended and we headed once again toward our respective homes.

I bade farewell to the group that I mostly associated with, and bade a special farewell to one certain cute girl. I truly hurt inside for not ever being able to walk her home. And, it seemed that she had reserved this time especially for me each afternoon. I actually witnessed this by watching her over my shoulder as I rode away on my bicycle. Each afternoon I would watch in pain as she walked away all alone. This soon became one miserable daily routine! I was aware that many of the other boys in my class would have deviated from my strict regimen. Many of them simply would have walked the poor girl home, and taken their chances with their parents. I must note here that beginning in ninth grade, if any girl did not have a nice boy to escort her home each afternoon, then she was seen as having something drastically wrong with her! This was the general consensus of all the kids. This was particularly the position of the young girl in question. At this age (fifteen) all the girls always dressed to attract the boys, and all the boys dressed accordingly. This was the way things were (even way back in the fifties). There were just a few major differences between then and now. First, there were no drugs. Second, there were no gangs. And third, crime was virtually nonexistent! One might say that we lived in an era of paradise.

My second day after the holidays would become another very good day for learning. I had arrived at school at my usual time (shortly before 8:00AM). We made good progress as we proceeded from classroom to classroom. Our daily class routine was fairly constant, so there was very little change. Lunchtime came and the boys socialized with the girls as we ate. This had become the most pleasant time of my day— a time I particularly looked forward to, though not much of any significance ever occurred. There was always just small talk happening between us. But I realized even then that this was the beginning of a very important phase in our young lives. It provided us with the opportunity to familiarize ourselves with the likes and dislikes of the opposite sex. It was at this point that I first experienced the pleasant sensation known as "butterflies". I was sitting at a table with two cute girls and one other boy. Our conversations were both casual and low-keyed. My relationship with the young lady of my choosing had not begun to advance. I could sense that she liked me, and I really liked her. My problem was time, for I had no time to spend with her except during lunch period. Thusly, I believe we both knew that she should've moved on. I don't know how she had felt about our situation, but it made me very sad. Here I was having just recently met a very nice young lady, but I could not spend time with her. I thought *"What a pity"*. Although, this was not the cause of my "butterflies", for while sitting there that day, I happened to notice the most beautiful girl I had ever seen during my entire fifteen years of life on earth!

She was sitting at the table situated diagonally to the left of me. Her beauty was absolutely stunning! During that time period, I experienced great difficulty in conversing with any girl. But today I was completely speechless! The girl sitting with me asked, "What's wrong, Jake"? I just gestured by placing my hand to my throat. She then assumed that I might be choking. She was right, for I was choking— but not from food or drink! Meanwhile, the source of my new problem continued glancing my way. She would smile whenever she caught my eye. At this point I knew that if there was ever any such thing as true love— this was definitely it! Still, I had to remain a complete gentleman and not cause embarrassment to the young lady at my table, or myself. So, I was cool! I remained outwardly calm— although inside, I was in complete turmoil! Then the bell sounded, signaling the end of lunch period and our return to our respective classes. What a relief (I thought) as we arose and proceeded to return our food trays to the wash area.

The two girls who had been sitting with us had not seen any of the eye communication between the new girl and myself. However, my classroom buddy had seen it all. So, on our way to class, he gave me a slight nudge in the ribcage. I asked, "What's that for?" and he answered, "You know"! The girls had just left us to go their separate ways, so he and I were free to talk. Right away, I asked him, "Who was that?" referring to the new beauty. He said, "Isn't she something"? "Her name is Jeanne". And, with this— we reentered our classroom. While in class, I became acutely aware of the extreme difficulty I experienced in the area of concentration. I found myself making errors in my note-taking activities, which was totally unacceptable. Thus, I forced myself to remove Jeanne from my thoughts. I found this to be one of my most difficult undertakings up to this point in my life. It might be better if I explained things this way. You see, the first girl I had met, (Carol), had a very pleasing personality, and I felt good in her presence. Also, on a scale of one to ten, she would have been considered at least an eight. However, though I had not met Jeanne, she excited me! And, on the same measuring scale, she would have been a twelve!

I was already beginning to feel that I might be about to step into dangerous and uncontrollable territory. Our caring teacher continued with her lecturing and I continued struggling with my note-taking practices. I found that as the afternoon progressed, this became increasingly more difficult to accomplish. A couple of more hours passed and our school day finally ended. We each gathered our books and other materials and left the school grounds. As we were leaving, I saw Carol walking a short distance away. She happened to look my way, and we both waved our farewells to each other. This time she was in the company of two other girls, which made me feel a little better about the fact that I was unable to walk with her. I then mounted my bicycle and started to pedal away toward home. Remember, this was still in the dead of winter, so all the kids were all bundled up in heavy clothing, and most had their heads covered also.

I had only gotten a few yards down the street when I passed two girls walking alone. No sooner than I had passed them did I hear a voice call out, "Hey you—wait up"! I stopped momentarily as I looked over my shoulder and in their direction. To my utter shock, I saw that one of the two girls was Jeanne! It was she who had called out to me. I pointed my fingertips toward my chest, which in those days, meant "Are you talking to me"? My heart palpitated as she responded "Yes, I'm talking to you". I calmly stepped down from my bicycle as they approached. Jean introduced the girl standing next to her, saying "This is Gwen". She then smiled and said, "I'm Jeanne".

I tried being cool by addressing Gwen first. "Hi Gwen" and she greeted me with a warm smile. I did not wish to appear over anxious or unaccustomed to being around girls. So, I then turned my attention to Jeanne saying "I already know who you are". "Oh, and how is this?" she responded. I replied smilingly, "Word gets around". I sensed we had broken the ice in positive fashion, and I had met her approval. I asked where she lived and she told me that she lived only a couple of more blocks up the street on which we were traveling. So, I walked along with the two of them as we chatted and made small talk. We had gone only a short distance when Gwen reached her house, saying "Well, see you guys tomorrow--nice meeting you Jake". Then Jeanne and I were suddenly alone together, walking side by side along the quiet, peaceful street. I felt as though I were a king accompanied by my queen. This was only the second high point of my entire young life. The first had been two years earlier while riding in Uncle Abe's shiny new car. But this present occasion completely out-measured the previous. We continued along our route and I knew that we would regretfully soon reach Jeanne's house. I decided I would become a bit bold, so I jokingly asked her, "Why don't you drop your books off at your house, then ride home with me"? She did not appear the least bit annoyed by my brazen comments. She immediately responded, "And what will we do once we get to your house"? I replied, "Oh, I'm sure that we'll find something nice to do". "But won't your parents be at home"? I replied, "No, they'll be out working"—which was true. But naturally, even had she accepted, I could not have ever taken her to my house. And, I'm sure that this would have applied even years later. Then, all too soon, she smiled, saying "Well, this is it— guess I'll see you tomorrow". Suddenly, I felt that I was nearing tears, but I had to hide this feeling at all cost. So, I smiled at her and said, "I'll be waiting". With these words she was gone! I knew for certain this had not been a dream, but it sure seemed so. She was completely out of my sight now, but in my mind, I could picture her as though she were still at my side. I did a little dance step, and then mounted my old bicycle as I rode away toward my old house in the distant wilderness.

But today would be quite different. It would not have mattered whatsoever even if I'd had to ride this entire distance in a snowstorm (which was not the case). For the first time in my life I was truly happy! I had previously heard my Uncle Abe sing a song entitled "At Last" which was a beautiful love song, and I had learned the words because I liked it. So, while riding along those old country dirt roads, I chose this song to sing. And, I sang it with a passion, the entire distance to my house! The lyrics began, "At last— my love has come along, now my lonely days are over, and my life is but a song." *"How appropriate"*, I thought as I rode along. I reached our old house at the usual hour. Only this time, I was a totally new person— I was happy!

Next morning I arose in an unusually happy mood, fighting the urge to sing loudly even as I bathed. On this morning, I paid special attention to my grooming and clothing. For some reason I wanted to look my absolute best! (I make this last statement in jest. Of course I knew the reason why I wanted to look good). I quietly breezed through my early morning preparations, finishing up slightly ahead of schedule. I then quickly finished my breakfast and grabbed my hat, coat, and gloves. It was only 6:45AM as mom asked, "Jake, aren't you leaving a little early today"? I simply told her that I'd not seen my canine friend (Buddy) lately, so I planned to stop by his house for a couple of minutes. Mom seemed satisfied with my answer, and questioned me no further. But actually Buddy was the furthest thing from my mind that morning. I wanted to reach Jeanne's street in time to walk her to school. I failed, for she had already left for school before I arrived. I was some-what disappointed that all my special efforts this morning had been in vain. Now, the only thing I looked forward to was the opportunity to see her after school. I intended to spend lunch period with Carol and my regular small group of friends. Although I had met Jeanne and was blown away by her, I simply would not abandon Carol in this manner. I was determined to continue behaving as a complete gentle-man, regardless of whom I may have just met.

Our morning seemed to progress more slowly than usual, but I knew that this was not really the case. In fact, things only seemed this way because of my impatient desire for the true object of my affection. I found that I was able to take accurate notes. This small and seemingly unimportant fact made me a little happier, because as of yesterday after-noon, I had felt that I might never be able to successfully take notes again! And if this had actually happened, I would have failed all of my classes. Failure would have meant that either I would've needed to repeat the full school year, or drop out of school. This was the significance of my note-taking ability. The morning eventually passed, and the bell sounded for lunch.

My class quietly but quickly departed our classroom and headed for the cafeteria. At this point I realized that those 'butterflies' had returned. I so very badly wanted to see Jeanne. But as we entered the dining area, I looked around the cafeteria and saw she had arrived before me and was already seated. Making matters even worse, there were no vacant tables near her. My heart sank; however, I man-aged to keep my extreme disappointment well hidden. My group, which included Carol, located an empty table and took our seats. We held our usual low-keyed conversations. We mainly talked about any comical incidents that had occurred throughout the morning. Occasionally, we would discuss a few of our teachers, but always in a positive light. While sitting there with my group, I would ever so casually glance about the area. During one such glance, I saw Jeanne looking our way. The moment our eyes met, she smiled and waved. I felt my heart as it instantly began pounding away inside my chest. And, if I'd not fallen in love with her yesterday, I truly had at this moment! I found the sensations racing through my mind and body to be so very incredible! In short, my feelings were indescribable! I concealed all my emotions though and finished my meal along with the others. The bell again sounded and we all headed back to our classes. Unfortunately, Jeanne and I had not actually had the opportunity to speak with each other.

Back in class my mind lingered on her for a short while. Then, I managed to bring my thoughts back into focus. The next two periods finally passed, and it was again time to reluctantly head for home. I anxiously grabbed my belongings and hurriedly left the school campus. I wanted to reach the street before Jeanne so that I could wait for her. This time I was in luck, for she had not yet reached the street as far as I could see. Carol and the others had already gone in their direction. Then I saw her! She was walking in my direction with her friend Gwen. When she spotted me, I'm sure I detected her pace quicken ever so slightly. It may have been just my imagination, but I felt better already. I stood there beside my bicycle as I watched her approach me. When the two of them had reached the point where I stood, the three of us greeted each other warmly. It felt so very good being a 'king' again— and in the presence of my lovely 'queen'. Jeanne said, "Hi Jake— I missed you today". I smiled at her and said, "Yes, and that nearly ruined my day". She seemed happy with my answer. Then Gwen chimed in "Ah shucks, you two act like this must be some kind of love at first sight"! I responded, "Well, I don't know about Jeanne, but for me, it most certainly is".

The three of us then had a good laugh together. I had much earlier learned that once I had made a girl laugh, things seemed to become more relaxed and smooth after the laughter. We had been just standing there in that one spot, so then we began walking along together. I took up position at the edge of the street, with Jeanne next to me, and Gwen at the far curb side. We chatted and joked happily as we walked together. Nothing of any particular importance was said, but I was happy. Shortly, Gwen reached her home and we said our "bye byes" to each other. Now, I felt as though I were in heaven, with just my 'queen and I together! We continued walking along while making small talk. This was only our second time together, but I'd wanted her to know exactly how I felt at this early point in our relationship. I asked her if she had a boyfriend, and she told me that she did not. Then, she asked me if I had a girlfriend, and I said no. She smiled saying "I'm glad". I said, "I know it's much too soon to say this, but I feel like I'm falling in love with you already". She smiled again as she said "Jake, you're sweet". The term "sheer exhilaration" would barely describe the happiness I felt at that enchanted moment. Soon we reached Jeanne's house, where we said our "farewells".

As soon as she had entered her house, I hopped onto

the old bicycle and sped away. I knew that I was now about ten minutes behind schedule, but I also knew that I would make up my lost time during my first mile of riding. Then I could slow my pace so as to not be winded upon arriving at home. I sang love songs along my entire route home, arriving at my normal hour, and in high spirits. My evening of field work continued in its usual fashion. We each followed our routines once we had finished in the fields. I had another very cold night under my covers, but I felt great about the present state of affairs!

I'd slept well through the entire night, and now it was Wednesday morning. This would become the third day of my new and exhilarating relationship. At this point, I learned that life really did have meaning and purpose. I had finally discovered these two very important elements of life. As I had on the previous morning, I completed all my preparations (including breakfast) and was ready for my 6:45AM departure. Mom coyly asked me, "Buddy again?" "Yes" I replied, adding "He misses me". Mom did not comment further. I said my farewells and rode away down the path leading away from our lonely old house. I waved to dad, as he worked quite a distance from my location. He waved in return. As soon as I reached the main road, I sped away! My bicycle was only a single speed, so in order for me to travel faster, I simply pedaled faster. Here on this beautiful morning, I felt that I definitely had good reason to pedal fast. The morning was sunny but cold. But even if it had been rainy and cold, I would still have seen it as beautiful. This was my new mood. I rode quickly and reached Jeanne's house as she stepped out her door. She saw me instantly and began smiling as we waved to each other without speaking.

I'd hoped that neither her mom nor grandmother would be peering out at her through their living room window, but I was not in luck this time. Her grandmother had been peering— so I smiled and waved to her also. I'm not sure whether she waved back, but this was okay— I just wanted to make a good impression on this old lady. I could smell Jeanne's sweet perfume as she drew near me, and it tantalized my senses. I instantly became as Sampson with his hair clipped. Though I could barely function at this point, I struggled to project at least some semblance of calm. I just smiled slightly and said, "How are you this morning"? "I'm just fine—and you, Jake?" replied Jeanne. "Just great" I answered as we walked toward school. I was so indescribably happy at this moment in my young life! Then all too soon, we reached our school house, where we parted company. We both said in unison "See you". Then she was gone! I quickly returned to reality as I secured my bicycle before rushing to class.

This was a truly beautiful morning, and even though it was in the dead of winter, I could swear that I'd heard robins singing in the distance! I would also swear that I'd seen lovely red roses blossoming. This is how I had become in just two short days. I shuddered to think what I would be like within another year. But how was I to know at that moment, that I would have absolutely no reason for concern? Later, in classes that morning I was comforted in knowing that I had not lost my efficiency in note-taking ability. Time slowly ticked on as we moved from classroom to classroom, and soon lunchtime was again at hand. We entered our school cafeteria, where I was confronted with the exact same situation as the day prior. This time, I was somewhat prepared for such an eventuality. Also, I realized that I had survived our previous day's separation, so I would likely survive this. As had happened yesterday, we'd at least made eye contact, and even exchanged several smiles. I sat with my small group, casually chatting with them. Jeanne sat with her group, chatting and laughing with them. I had already discovered that she loved to laugh, and I liked this quality in her. I too, liked very much to laugh. My situation was very different though, for I usually had no one to laugh with— and no one to make me laugh. I found this to be one of the main reasons for my appreciation of school days. While in school, I always had many other kids of my age with whom to laugh and joke.

Then the bell sounded, signaling time to return to our classes. The next two classes seemed to literally drag past. I found this to be most challenging, as my ability to concentrate had all but deserted me. I struggled to overcome this difficulty, only finally succeeding. Two more hours crept past as we moved between classrooms, as we watched and listened to our teachers lecture and scribble on blackboards. Then, after what seemed an eternity, our study period ended and it was once again time to head homeward.

I bade farewell to Carol and my other small group of friends before heading to the street. Once there, I peered down the street to see if Jeanne was in front of me. She was not, so I stood there in that spot, pretending to rearrange my books in their satchels. Then, after about three minutes, I spotted her along with Gwen walking in my direction. My heart skipped a few beats! I was so absolutely overjoyed at the thought of being near her again, after the past very long twenty-hour period. As the two of them approached me, we greeted each other warmly. We made small talk by laughing and joking about the events of our day. By now, I had begun feeling comfortable in their presence. I had also gained confidence in my ability to communicate with members of the opposite sex. This served to provide me with an improved attitude about myself and my dreaded situation. We continued chatting jovially as we walked along together. But now, it was again time for Gwen to say farewell. I did not really wish to see her part company with us, but I so very much looked forward to having only Jeanne at my side. The two of us enjoyed a joyous walk together. Finally, I worked up the courage to ask her what I considered a very important question. I had intended to ask her if she had made any special plans for the weekend. It was my every hope that she would say no to my question. I wanted to ask her if she would go to a movie with me this coming Saturday afternoon. I wanted this so very much! But luck would not be on my side, for just as I was about to ask that all-important question, we heard Gwen's voice calling out to us. She ran up to us and asked if either of us had an extra ballpoint pen that she could borrow. I did not, but Jeanne said, "I have one at the house that you can borrow". Gwen was very happy with this, so she continued walking along with us to Jeanne's house. Since I did not feel comfortable asking my question in Gwen's presence, I decided to wait until tomorrow.

In short order, we had reached Jeanne's house— and there we bade farewell to each other. I was quite disappointed by not having had the opportunity to voice my desires. Thus, I would exercise patience and wait another twenty-four hours for my opportunity. Now, I'm fully aware that I could have actually gone ahead and asked my question, but what if Jeanne had rejected me? I would have been doubly embarrassed by having Gwen as a witness. But this was behind me now so I hopped onto my old cycle and disappeared into the distance. After all, tomorrow would be another day.

Night had come and gone, and this was Thursday morning. I did my usual early morning routine as quickly as possible. Then as soon as I had finished my breakfast, I bundled myself up in my heavy winter clothing. I bade "good day" to my parents and grand mom, then hurriedly headed away down that very cold dirt road. It would be a long and hard ride but this was okay because I would be highly compensated, for I would get to see my Jeanne. After all, this would be a very important day in my young life. I would get to ask my all-important question. And like it or not I would receive my answer. If she answered me with a yes— then I would become as an instant millionaire! But if she answered me by saying no, then no amount of money in the whole world would aid me. This was my predicament. I felt that this quite possibly might become the most important moment of my life. Alas, much concern over naught!

After nearly an hour of hard riding, I finally reached the neighborhood where Jeanne lived. I slowed my riding pace to scan the street ahead of me. She was not in sight. I figured that either she had already gone ahead or she would be a bit late. However, my assumption was wrong in both cases. I proceeded onward to school. Classes progressed as usual, but I found myself somewhat distracted in my note-taking. Though I struggled desperately to maintain focus, my mind continually drifted from the classroom work at hand, coming to rest on thoughts of Jeanne. This would be a very unsettling morning for me. I wondered and worried about her all morning. My thoughts centered on whether she was well or ill— and whether she was at school or absent. I did not have the courage to ask any of my fellow students if they had seen her. I wanted no one to know how I had come to feel about her in such a short period of time— (three days).

Then the lunch bell sounded and the students headed over to the school cafeteria. As we walked along in our respective groups, I discreetly scanned the crowd for any sign of Jeanne. I could not see her anywhere. Then we reached the cafeteria. I'd wished to see her so badly, I wanted to break out in a full speed run toward the cafeteria. But I tried hard and was at least somewhat able to conceal my emotions. Inside, I picked up my food tray and proceeded to the serving line. I then moved on to our regular table; though before sitting, I briefly looked at the table where Jeanne usually sat. Her seat was vacant! This greatly distressed me, and the butterflies in my stomach began to flutter even more franticly. I struggled to maintain some outward control over my inner despair, as I sat down to eat and chat with my three friends. My meal was well prepared and delicious, but I had completely lost my appetite. I simply was not hungry. It is very difficult to eat a meal when butterflies are fluttering throughout one's body (which was my condition at this moment). Even so, I tried to eat and act normal.

My friends and I chatted together and laughed and joked a bit as we sat at our table eating. At one point, however, I subconsciously looked in the direction of the table where

Jeanne usually sat. I should not have done this though, for Carol had been quietly observing my strained behavior. When she caught me looking toward that certain table, she softly said, "Isn't that sweet? —Jake's looking for his Queen Jeanne." And with that comment my three friends burst out in uncontrollable laughter. I was so embarrassed I wanted to crawl through the floor beneath us! I tried to laugh with them, but my heart just was not in it. I tried covering my error by saying, "It's just that I borrowed a pen from her yesterday afternoon, and I promised to give it back today." At this point I dropped the subject. My little group seemed satisfied with my statement, so no more was said about the matter. But I still felt quite a bit shaken. No sooner than we had finished our food did the bell ring. So we arose, returned our trays, and left the cafeteria. I struggled desperately to maintain self-control as we headed back to our classes.

The afternoon seemed to drag along, as I went from classroom to classroom, listening to our teachers lecture, and taking notes. Finally after what seemed like several hours, our school day again reached its end. I bade my classmates "farewell" before heading off down the asphalt street toward Jeanne's house. Then as I drew near her place, I dismounted from my bicycle and walked for several yards past her home. I had really hoped to at least get a glimpse of her, but no such luck, so I continued walking, feeling totally dejected! I had now gone past her house, and with every passing second, I thought that I might hear her call out to me, but this did not happen. My wishes were simply not to be granted on this day. I grudgingly mounted my old bicycle and rode away down the street leading to the dusty dirt road that took me home. I did not sing on this day, nor did I even think of song. For me, this would be a day that I would always remember—a day without Jeanne! As I rode along that cold afternoon, I wondered "How could I have gotten along these past fifteen years without her". It was a long and very lonely ride that afternoon. But I did not notice the cold temperatures or the distance. I did not even concern myself about the tedious field work that awaited me once I arrived at home. Jeanne was the only thought on my mind that afternoon. At one point I seemed to hear a voice saying to me, "You're acting like an idiot"! "What if you never see her again"? I realized that I absolutely must control myself and my emotions.

Finally, I arrived at home, where I greeted my family and promptly proceeded with my evening routine of field work. After one hour of work, it was again time to retire for the evening. In the presence of my family, I strived to act normal and present a positive persona, which seemed to work, because our evening went well as usual. But then came bedtime, for which I was happy. I managed to sleep well through the night, and now it was Friday morning! I arose energetically, washed up, and then dressed for school. After breakfast, I was back out on the road again. The temperature outside was extremely cold on this January morning. But this did not impair my thinking or interfere with my feelings as I rode with gusto toward my school! For some reason, I felt good about this day. I wanted to believe that Jeanne would be at school today. Then, if I were a bit lucky I would see her and even get the chance to ask her out to the movies tomorrow. I felt that this just might be my lucky day! So after riding for fifty-five minutes, I approached her house. I was in luck! As I neared the house, I saw Jeanne as she exited her front door and started down the steps.

As soon as she saw me she began waving. Heck, I'd already begun waving to her. I quickened my pace as I felt my heart once again pound inside my chest cavity! As I drew near her she gave me her usual great smile while saying, "I missed you yesterday". I replied, "I missed you twice as much". I was walking along and pushing my bicycle, as we walked together. Jeanne stated that she and her mom had gone out of town on Thursday for some shopping. I told her I was happy to hear that her absence had been due to shopping, and not illness. We continued walking, and soon we reached our school grounds. At that point, she went toward her classroom, and I toward mine. *"This will be a very good day,"* I thought as I proceeded to my classroom. The day progressed as usual and soon it was lunchtime. In the cafeteria, we took our regular tables. Once we were seated, my group made light conversation as we ate our meal. I discreetly greeted Jeanne as she sat two tables away, and she gave me that sweet smile of hers. I felt just wonderful, for this was truly shaping up to be a great day! Carol casually said to me, "I see Jeanne's here today, Jake—did you give back her pen"? I replied that I'd done so while en route to school this morning. No more was said of the subject. My friends and I continued talking while enjoying our food. Soon the bell rang, signaling the end of our lunch period. We headed back to our classes and commenced our afternoon lessons. Eventually the end-of-day bell rang, at which time anxiety reared its ugly head!

I hurriedly gathered my books and garb before saying

farewell to my classmates. I then rushed out to the street, where I hoped to meet up with Jeanne. I felt that special moment in my life was fast approaching. I had to ask that all-important question, and I was over-anxious for the answer. I stopped just a few yards from the school grounds to wait for her. Then, after what seemed to be hours (but was only three minutes) I saw her walking toward me. I squinted and scanned the entire immediate area around her, but I did not see Gwen or anyone else walking with her. *"I'm really in luck!"* I thought. I would have her all to myself for the full short distance to her house. As Jeanne approached, we greeted each other with smiles and a few warm words. She walked at my side, but very close to me. I could feel her hips gently brushing against me as we walked along together. My heart pounded, and I also seemed to have something inside my throat, making it difficult for me to speak. I struggled to conceal my emotions, as I so desperately wanted these next few minutes to go well. I did not, in any way, wish to mess things up at this point. For several days now I had rehearsed for this very special moment, so I wasted no time in broaching the subject. "Jeanne" I said "I know that it's only been five days of our knowing each other, but I like you so very much". She responded, "Thank you, Jake". At that moment, I could no longer contain myself— so I blurted, "May I take you to the movies tomorrow afternoon"? A look of bewilderment and mild disappointment appeared upon Jeanne's face. She hesitated before saying, "Jake, I like you a lot too, and I would really love to go to a movie with you". I quickly interrupted her, saying "Great, shall I pick you up tomorrow afternoon around 2:30"? But she had not yet finished speaking, so she raised her hand slightly to silence me. Then she completely devastated me by saying "I thought you knew that I'm leaving tomorrow evening." "Oh no" I blurted! She said, "Yes— mom and I are boarding the train tomorrow evening at 7:00".I found myself speechless! But then I heard myself softly ask, "Where are you going?" Jeanne then looked directly into my eyes as she said "We're going back home to Connecticut". A feeling of total despair overcame me as I feebly asked, "Does this mean that I won't see you again"? She softly sighed, saying "I guess that's what it means".

This was the very first time in my young life that I actually considered dying (which was exactly what I'd wanted to do at that moment). It seemed that the whole world had just stopped spinning! I wanted to stand right there in front of Jeanne and start hysterically bawling, but for fifteen years, dad had taught me that 'real men' don't cry. I struggled desperately to enforce and adhere to this principle. Then, after a brief speechless moment between us, she began to speak again. She said, "Jake, all the other kids at school knew I would only be here for a short while until grandmother recovered from her surgery". I felt like a total idiot! All the kids knew—but I did not! I attributed this to my isolated lifestyle. But I also realized the other kids naturally had assumed that I too had known of her situation— so I blamed no one. I said to her, "Jeanne, it really doesn't matter now, but I'll say this anyway— I think I'm in love with you". She responded, "I hope you know that I have very strong feelings for you also— but maybe this is not meant to be."

I could not disagree with her reasoning, but I simply refused to like it. Without realizing it, we had completely stopped walking, and were just standing there on the street talking. I sensed at this point it did not matter to either of us if anyone overheard our conversation. The facts were I felt that I was irreversibly in love with Jeanne and more importantly, she herself surely felt (something) for me! We both agreed at this point that our situation was overwhelming. This was simply too powerful an energy for two young and inexperienced individuals to face. I tried to joke, so I then asked her if she would consider eloping with me. Her response tore at my heart. She said, "I'm considering it right at this moment, but where would we go— and how would we live"? I had no suitable answer to either of her honest questions. So, we ever-so-reluctantly resigned ourselves to the fact that this was it— the end of our wonderful world!

Then, with tears in my eyes (I think hers also), we sadly but briefly hugged each other as we said our "goodbyes". Many years would pass before I would again feel such deep sadness. Softly she said, "Well, I'd better go in, and you'd better be going also". Then, with a quick peck on my cheek—she vanished into her house! I stood there watching her as she went inside. It was then that I noticed both her mom and grand mom watching us through their living room window. They were both smiling, so I smiled too and waved to the two of them. They waved back to me as though they had understood my sad situation. Then, as I mounted my bicycle to ride away, Jeanne also appeared at their window. She waved, smiled, and blew me kisses! This was the high point of my otherwise dreadful day! I would not see Jeanne again in my lifetime! *"How will I live?"* I thought. But worse yet, *"Why would I even want to do so"?* The term "miserable" does not even begin to describe my pathetic feelings on that dreadful afternoon! The end of the world had come and I was just now fifteen! Fortunately though, I had at least experienced five days of happiness and meaningful life!

Sadly, I lowered my head and held it this way all the way home. I did not wish to see the world around me, nor did I wish to know of its existence! I rode nearly the entire four miles without seeing a single human being— which was good! Upon nearing home, however, I was fortunate in having seen Buddy. We played together for a couple of minutes, which made me feel just slightly better. Then for- lornly, onward to our old house I rode.

I was only ten minutes late in arriving home. I had nev- er ever been late before, so naturally my parents and grand mom were just a bit concerned. They were each relieved to see that I was okay. I worked very hard at hiding my feelings of sadness simply by busying myself with the field work. So the next hours seemingly passed without my even noticing. Soon darkness set upon us and we retired to the house for the evening, for tomorrow would be another day of the same.

Having miraculously survived that most unbearable weekend, I entered another Monday morning. It was ex- tremely frigid on this day so I felt every frost-biting bit of cold that struck my body. I no longer had Jeanne on whom to focus my thoughts. Then, after fifty-five minutes of riding in this cold, I reached Jeanne's old house. I had begun sing- ing my little happy song, but soon I raised my voice another octave as I rode along. When I was directly in front of her house, I waved (even though I saw no one). Even the win- dow shades were lowered. It was as though the place was deserted! I rode quietly onward for the next three minutes, finally reaching my school. I was a few minutes early, but I quickly secured my bicycle before rushing inside the school building. I went directly to the steam-heated radiator, then squeezed in as close as humanly possible. I was the first of the students to reach my classroom, and for this I was thankful. This meant that I had this old radiator all to myself. I continued to silently sing my little happy song, fortifying my mind for this most difficult day that awaited me. Finally a few students began arriving. Then, more came and soon our entire class was present. We greeted and talked about our weekend. Naturally though, I lied a bit.

Surprisingly, I survived the morning's activities and teachings. I even managed to focus on the lessons, while taking accurate and valuable notes. As I'd anticipated this was a very difficult task to accomplish. When lunchtime arrived my situation became even more difficult. As we entered the school cafeteria, I fought desperately against looking at the table and chair where Jeanne usually sat. At one point while in the serving line, I did momentarily weaken so I took a very quick little glance at that table. I had actually hoped against hope that her plans might have changed, and that she had remained at our school. But my wishes were in vain—for she was nowhere in sight! This, in itself, was final confirmation that she was actually gone! As I sat quietly at our table with Carol and my other two close friends, I concentrated on their presence there with me. I was particularly conscious of the fact that as we sat there that day, Carol was discreetly monitoring my behavior. This did not annoy me, because I'd fully realized that her actions were completely normal. I sensed that both Donnie and

Wilton were also paying particular attention to me on this day. But they were both real cool and acted as though everything was completely normal. I tried very hard at being as cool as they were, so during the full forty-five minutes that the four of us sat there, none of us ever mentioned Jeanne.

Finally the bell rang, signaling the end of our lunch period. Beginning on this day, the school had extended our lunch period to one full hour. We now had an extra fifteen minutes of free time to spend relaxing, or whatever. So after leaving the cafeteria, Donnie and Wilton went off to toss a football, which was a favorite pastime of boys my age. I did not join them because Carol had quietly suggested that the two of us move to the outer edge of the park so we could sit and just talk for awhile. This was an all-new experience for me— being alone with a girl. Although we were not really alone, as other couples stood or sat talking nearby. I enjoyed this free time with Carol very much. But for a brief moment, my mind drifted away to Jeanne. It seemed that Carol sensed my distraction, for she commented mildly, "I guess you really miss Jeanne, huh"?

I smiled at her as I calmly responded, "How on earth could I miss Jeanne, when I'm sitting here with you"? Carol seemed to like my response, and she snuggled a little closer to me. Then she asked me a very difficult question. I say this because of my inexperience with girls. She had asked "Jake, do you like me even half as much as you do Jeanne"? I lied through my teeth by saying to her "Carol, I like you twice as much as I do Jeanne". I continued "Jeanne's just a flirt— but you're a true lady". I concluded by saying "plus I can relax with you". Carol then plainly showed that she was very happy with my answers. But just as she'd started to speak again, the darn bell rang. The two of us immediately arose and headed back toward our respective classrooms. She walked very close to me. I remember asking myself, *"I wonder if she likes me as much as I like Jeanne"*? I would eventually realize that Carol actually liked me a whole lot more.

Back in class my afternoon progressed smoothly, and I found that I did not feel so awfully sad anymore. In reality though I was only trying to fool myself, for I would not fully free myself from fond memories of Jeanne for many years into the future. So, there I sat with so much emotion, at only age fifteen! At last, the school bell rang, ending the school day. But now came another great test. I bade farewell to my classmates and proceeded outside to my bicycle. I saw Carol and we both waved to each other as we each went our separate ways. I purposely rode slowly as I passed Jeanne's house, but this time I did not wave, although, I did steal a quick glance at the place. Then I simply sat upright on my old bicycle as I rode past. Then as I rode on, I again began singing my little happy song. Naturally the pain was still with me, but that song seemed to help. I continued singing as I rode onward toward the old remote place that I had so reluctantly called home. This was otherwise, a beautiful afternoon— with lots of sunshine, and not too very cold.

I realized that I would need to begin my life anew, even though it had only begun seven days ago! But it also occurred to me that I would have not one, but two very attractive young ladies, upon whom to focus my attention. Up to this point I've not mentioned my lovely, young health teacher. Her name was Miss Cunnings, and she too, was breathtakingly beautiful! Prior to meeting Jeanne, I had constantly dreamed of Miss Cunnings both day and night. But she was my teacher and there simply was no fraternization between teacher and student! Compounding this situation was the fact that she was now twenty-two and I had just turned fifteen. Plus, I had not yet developed a great desire for 'older women'. Nevertheless, I found myself drawn to her. And given the opportunity, I believe I would have chosen her over young Carol. But I fully realized that my thoughts of Miss Cunnings were just fantasy— and nothing more! I had no way of knowing then that time would change all of this, and I would really get to know this very beautiful young teacher. Though at the time, I did suspect that I would eventually get to know Carol. But all of these possibilities were ahead of me. For now, I needed to concentrate on overcoming my problem of acute loneliness, which had resulted from Jeanne's departure. I managed to make it through the week, and all the way to Friday. Now under the circumstances, I would say that these had been a good five days. I'd succeeded in at least two areas— concentrating on my school work, and keeping my sanity intact!

Soon it was Monday morning again, and the beginning of the last week of January. I arose energetically, washed up, and brushed my teeth. Then after paying special attention to my personal grooming, I proceeded to the breakfast table. Again, dad was already out in the fields working alone. While eating, mom and I (along with grandmother) made small talk mostly about my upcoming school day. Then came time to head out again, into the cold. As I rode away from the house on my bicycle, I again struck up my little happy tune. I sang this little tune along most of my route to school. As I neared the little house where Jeanne had recently lived, I only gave one brief look.

I finally arrived at school, where I secured my bicycle before rushing inside, so I could begin my thawing process prior to my first class. Then I remembered how badly I had felt last Monday (without Jeanne), but I realized that I felt quite good on this day. I began saying to myself, *"Jake, old boy—I think you're being healed"*. Finally a few students began arriving, and I found myself thrilled at the prospect of having someone to talk to.

We then began our first school day of that week. We got through the first four days smoothly, without any problems whatsoever. Friday was slightly different however, as throughout the week Donnie and Wilton had been paying special attention to Miss Cunnings, and making little smart comments about her. So as we each walked to her class after lunch that Friday afternoon, Wilton commented, "Hey Jake, why don't you write her a little love note just to let her know how you feel about her"? The three of us got a laugh from that thought. But then once in class, I became a bit bold and foolish. While Miss Cunnings was lecturing about health and hygiene, I got the urge to actually write such a note. Here, my brains did function— although only slightly; so, I wrote this 'love' note but without addressing it. It stated, "My darling, roses are red and violets are blue. I nearly lose my mind each time I look at you"! Now admittedly, these opening lines were not so very disrespectful, but my words progressively worsened! In fact they'd worsened to the point that they are unmentionable! It so happened that one very mischievous boy named Willie, sat directly behind me in class this day. Unfortunately, he had been watching me as I wrote my note. So as soon as I'd finished writing, he quickly reached forward, snatching this note from my desk. I frantically tried persuading him to return it to me, but he simply would not. Miss Cunnings had not noticed any of this. Then, he sat quietly while reading this note. At this point I hoped that he would return the note to me, but no such luck! Instead, he quickly passed it to another boy sitting in the row next to us. This boy also read the note, and then both he and Willie had a quiet little chuckle together. I was beginning to feel reason for concern, and rightfully so! Several boys then began passing this note until it was given to a girl who sat near the front of the class. This particular girl was the teacher's pet. I was truly embarrassed as I sat helplessly watching her also read my note. Miss Cunnings was writing on the blackboard, so she still had not seen any of this. This girl, (Marge), folded the note, then arose and placed it upon Miss Cunnings' desk! I cringed as I sat there contemplating the unfavorable consequences of my actions.

Shortly thereafter our teacher finished writing on the blackboard and took her seat at her desk. At this time, she began discussing the information she had just written on the board. She spoke to us for about ten minutes and then looked over at the corner of her desk, seeing the note! I wanted to shrink myself and slide underneath my desk! But naturally since this was totally impossible, I was forced to sit there anxiously awaiting the outcome. Slowly, Miss Cunnings picked up the folded piece of paper. She calmly inspected its outer surfaces before unfolding it. My heart suddenly raced as she did so! She immediately recognized my handwriting style as she read. When she had finished, she showed no expression on her face, but she called to me, "Jake, will you come up here please"? I was truly embarrassed at this point, but I quietly arose and walked up to her desk. Then in a calm voice, she asked, "Did you write this"? I answered "Yes ma'am". "Well, I would like you to read it to the class". I could have died right there on the spot— but I didn't. Instead, I began reading aloud, and when I had finished she commented, "Shame on you"! Now when I'd written this note, I had no intention of giving it to anyone. I merely intended to show it to Donnie and Wilton (strictly for laughs)! But the actions of that mischievous Willie Jayes caused all my troubles! Though as my teacher spoke those words to me, I'm certain that I saw a slight smile, and a twinkle in her eyes. Then she sternly admonished me, "Take your seat!" which I gladly did. She did not resort to any type of punishment stemming from this incident, but I shall forever remember it! Might I mention here that after reading my note, I got the feeling that this young teacher might not have been desirous of punishing me. But had I completed my obscene statement, she would have had no alternative. Following her class came study period. After this, our school week was over. Though from this point forward, the girls in my class would begin teasing me. They would even assign to me the title of 'lover boy'. I must admit that I sort of enjoyed my new-found attention. Fortunately, our school week had just ended!

For the first time in years, I was happy to be heading home from school! I even looked forward to my forthcoming field work, and this also was another first! Presently, we said our farewells to each other as we headed off toward our homes. But then, as I neared Jeanne's former residence, I gave the place the once-over. I had been hoping against hope that I might see her peering out through her window. But she failed to appear, so I focused my gaze straight ahead, and struck up my little happy song as I began to pedal faster and faster toward home. I vowed that I would never again write notes of any type while in class! I also vowed that somehow and somewhere, I would avenge myself for the dastardly prank Willie Jayes had committed against me!

Today was February 1st, and another Monday morning. I arose as usual and readied myself for my long and cold ride to school. On this morning, I discovered that I was able to ride along without the need to sing. I had finally begun healing myself from the 'love wounds' I'd recently received. This first week of February was relatively uneventful, both at school and at home. The only activity of significance was my flourishing relationship with Carol. But I was still unable to spend any time with her, other than during lunch period. And, walking her home was completely out of the question!

So, the week had passed and another weekend was upon us. Dad and I worked together in the fields as usual. Then 2:30PM finally arrived, and it was now time for us to call it a week. Again, we both went through our ritual of washing up. Having finished, we sat at our table enjoying our noontime meal. Dad mentioned that he needed to ride our old bicycle into town to pick up a few supplies and asked if I would like to ride along with him. I eagerly accepted his offer! I was so very happy for the opportunity to leave this old farm, even if only for a couple of hours. Thus, we dressed ourselves appropriately for the cold temperatures outside.

We rode away from the house on our trusted old bicycle, with dad pedaling. I sat behind him on the passenger's rack. As we rode along, the cold winds would whip across our faces. I soon discovered that I was slightly shielded from the winds by sitting directly behind dad, so I lowered my head and pressed my face against his back in an effort to keep warm. This time, dad took a completely different route— a shortcut that had been previously unknown to me! This special route would immensely improve the quality of my lonely life! Although I had not realized it, I had always taken the long route to school. Dad had all the while been aware of the route that I took each day, which totaled one full hour of riding time. This shortcut reduced our riding time by fifty percent. This meant that I could ride to school or to town in only one-half hour! *"This is amazing!"* I thought. After riding for just twenty-five minutes, we were now passing in front of Carol's house. I knew where Carol lived because I remember having accompanied my parents during a few visits to her place. It was then that I recalled that her parents and mine were family friends. But as dad and I rode past, I kept silent and made no mention whatsoever about Carol. I'd had no way of knowing that he already knew about Carol and me. Plus, I was too ashamed to let him know that I was now interested in girls. However in retrospect, I believe that both he and mom would have been relieved to learn that it was girls I was interested in. But unfortunately in my family we did not discuss such matters. Dad and I kept riding for another five minutes, and into the downtown area.

Soon it was 4:00PM (I did at least have a cheap watch, by the way). We secured the bicycle to a bike rack, and proceeded to walk through the streets from store to store. We still had a couple of hours of daylight remaining. Now being a small town, many of the area's residents knew each other (many were even related to each other). So, as we walked along these streets and inside the stores, people would greet us and stop to chat briefly. It felt wonderful, being away from that lonely old farm. We went about selecting and making our purchases. At one point, dad took me into a nice shoe store where he bought me a very nice pair of shoes. Now even though dad never had lots of money, he was the type of person who would never buy cheap stuff. Also, he would always say, "Son, never put any cheap shoes on your feet". And, dad always stood by his words and principles. Whenever he was visiting, or out on business, dad always wore attractive attire. Even his shirts were of silk. But even more importantly, he made certain each member of his family was equally well-dressed. My entire family (including grandmother) was of this mind-set, and each of them followed these high standards. Grandmother would frequently say to me, "Son, always make sure that you are as clean underneath as you are on the outside". She especially instilled in me the practice of never wearing unclean underclothing. I adopted these high standards of personal hygiene and grooming, and I have consistently maintained them throughout my lifetime.

Now that I had my new pair of shoes, dad asked me, "What else do you need, son?" I wanted a lot of things but I meekly said, to him "Thank you for the shoes— I'm okay". I said those words in hopes that they would soften him a bit, which might lead him to buying me something else. My tactic worked quite well, for dad ended up buying me two pairs of pants and a couple of very nice sweaters. Both mom and grandmother had managed to get into town earlier in the week, and each had bought me a few shirts and pairs of socks. So now I was set and it really felt great, but my day was not yet over! I still had another treat coming! We walked out onto the street, where we bumped into none other than my teacher, Miss Cunnings! She was accompanied by female teacher who was also an acquaintance of my family's. I sensed that Miss Cunnings was as surprised to see me as I was at seeing her. As soon as she saw me, she called out my name. The four of us stopped on the sidewalk and chatted for a few minutes. Since she was relatively new at this school, dad did not know her, so I introduced them. I remembered my shocking love note! I naturally became quite apprehensive about what my teacher might say to dad about this incident. But surprisingly, she failed to mention any of this, although, I'm sure that the matter remained vivid in her thoughts. Instead, she began praising me in the presence of dad and the other teacher.

I was glad to hear my teacher's praise. She was a total lady in every regard, and now I loved her even more! But it was getting a little late in the day, and we still had a few more stops to make. So, dad politely excused us and we went along our way. But as we walked along, I seemed to hear some little voice in my mind asking, "Jake, remember Jeanne"? I also remember answering, asking, "Jeanne who"? I smiled briefly as we walked along. This had been a very good day, but it would soon be time to head back to our remote retreat. So, we finished our shopping and retrieved our old bicycle before heading off toward home. As we were leaving I asked dad if he wanted me to pedal for awhile? He responded, "Thank you, son, but I've got it." Then with these words of reassurance—, we were off and riding into the wilderness.

Darkness soon set upon us, but we were fine because we had a strong night-riding light on the bicycle, so riding in darkness posed no problem for us. Plus, during that time period and in the region where we lived, violent crime was virtually non-existent! So we'd had no reason for concern during my newly discovered half-hour ride home. After fifteen minutes, we reached the dense wooded area, which was the heart of our shortcut. But I knew that dad was not afraid of any man (or men), and this gave me both comfort and reassurance. But upon entering that dark and dense forest, I did experience a few brief moments of anxiety. Hearing the eerie hooting of an owl somewhere nearby did not help matters much. But then, in recalling dad's gallantry, and my self-defense training from Mr. Lim, I began feeling a bit more courageous. I soon found that my concerns were unfounded, for we rode through the forest without encountering another person or any wild animals. I suddenly realized that if we could ride through this area at nighttime without any problem, surely I could do so in daylight hours, while equally as safely. Yes, this new route held much promise for me. This route would open up a whole new world for me! It would provide me with social opportunity that before now I simply could not conceive of.

I considered my newfound benefits. First, I would cut my one-hour school ride by half. Second, I could ride my bicycle to and from movies occasionally on Saturday afternoons. And third, but most important of all, I could walk Carol home from school each afternoon! This was simply fantastic! Finally, I could begin living at least somewhat as an ordinary human being. I found all these great new possibilities parading before me, to be totally mind-boggling! Many years would pass before I would learn the real reason why dad had chosen to show me this new and very special route. Later, I lay awake for a very long period that night, considering the opportunities before me.

The weekend had come and gone, and now it was the beginning of the second week of the month. I was ready for my new and comparatively pleasant new ride. Naturally, I wore some of my new clothes. Now, after three long and hard years of riding for two hours each day, I simply could not believe that I would make it to school in only one-half hour. Oh, but I did! I had left home fifteen minutes later than usual, but I arrived fifteen minutes earlier. *"This is absolutely wonderful!"* (I thought). Also, I realized that this much shorter ride had prevented me from becoming as cold as I usually did.

My morning went extremely well, and I firmly believe that I even began taking better notes than in the past. This was quite possibly because previously, I had remained partially frozen during my first class of each morning. But on this particular morning, I could even feel my fingers,— as now they were not so very numb. I remember thinking, *"Wow, this feels almost like being a real human being"*. The morning seemed to pass quickly, and soon it was lunchtime. We walked across the school grounds to the cafeteria, and gathered at our usual table. As we sat eating our meal, we discussed the things that we had done over the weekend, and the morning's events. And for the very first time, I found that I was able to participate in our conversations, both factually and truthfully. Frankly, it felt very good having something truthful and worthwhile to discuss with my friends. So, the four of us spent a very pleasant lunch period together. We had finished our meal, but the bell had not sounded because there'd remained another twenty minutes of our lunch period. So, we decided to spend our remaining time outside in the park. Now even though it was still winter time, this was a very beautiful and sunny day. Surprisingly, my newly discovered travel route served to make this day even more beautiful.

Then once we were outside, my friends Donnie and Wilton walked away in search of girls to chase. I already had my companion, so their departure was just fine by me. Carol and I strolled casually across the park, until we reached a vacant park bench upon which to sit. It felt truly great being with her on this wonderful day. As we searched for suitable words to say to each other, I sensed that Carol did not wish to over-extend herself with me, and thereby appear as flirtatious. In this regard, I found her to be the exact opposite of my lovely Jeanne. This young lady was obviously a completely different type of person, and I knew that I would need to accept and respect these qualities in her. Actually, I appreciated her just as she was. With Carol, I felt comfortable. While with Jeanne for only that one short week, I'd not feel at all relaxed.

I had not made any mention to my friends, or to Carol, about my new route to and from school. However, I found myself bursting to at least say something! So, at one point during our short conversation, I said "Carol, you know this would be the perfect day for me to walk you home". She studied my facial expression for a moment, trying to determine whether or not I was kidding. So then, she laughed as she nudged me in my ribs with her elbow, saying, "Jake, why don't you stop playing around". I did not comment further on the subject. The bell had just sounded, so we arose and navigated our way back to our separate classrooms.

Back in class, I turned my attention back to classroom subjects, following the teachers' lectures and taking notes. The history class went smoothly, but next came my health class. This was the class taught by Miss Cunnings. I was happy for the fact that I had seen and talked to her last Saturday afternoon. Otherwise, I truly believe I would have been too ashamed to enter her class. But her comments that afternoon had put my mind at ease— even if just a little. So, when the time came for me to proceed to her classroom, I entered her doorway quietly and took my seat. Old Willie Jayes just sort of grinned at me as I walked facing him, toward my desk. I did not acknowledge him whatsoever. Instead I pretended that I had not even noticed him sitting there. I sensed that he did not like my indifferent behavior toward him.

Miss Cunnings greeted the class in her usual warm manner. "Good afternoon, class, I do hope each of you had a nice weekend." The class responded in unison, "Good afternoon, Miss Cunnings." Then she immediately proceeded with the lesson for the day. The note that I had written remained fresh in my mind throughout her lecture. Even so, I could not help but notice her rare beauty. Heck, I'll just get right to the point— although I was just fifteen,— she really turned me on!

Her class finally ended and it was now study period.

Outside in the hallway, I purposely turned in the opposite direction of my class group. I walked for a few paces, and as soon as I noticed the last student exit the building, I doubled back to her room. Now, don't get me wrong here—I merely had wanted to apologize for that awful note on last Friday afternoon. She was readying herself to leave the room. But as she looked up and saw me, she invited me inside. She looked at me inquisitively, asking, "Yes, Jake"? I felt quite awkward at that moment, but I spoke up saying "Miss Cunnings, I'd just like to say I'm very sorry about that awful note I wrote last Friday".

In a somewhat stern voice, she said to me, "That's okay, Jake— just don't let it happen again". I assured her that it would not. I then thanked her as I turned to walk away. But as I neared her doorway on my way out of her room, she called out, "Jake, come here for a moment". She was still standing beside her desk as I approached her, wondering *"What now"?* When I was right in front of her, she softly said to me, "If, or when, you decide to write another such note, to me or anyone else— please don't do it in class— okay"? Those words blew my young mind! Then she smiled at me, and I returned her smile as I exited her door. Once out in the hallway, I thought, *"Wow, what a day"!* I proceeded on to my study period room, but I could not concentrate nor could I focus on my studies, for I'd just been demolished, but in a most pleasing manner! But the day was not over. In fact, it was only beginning because I would soon be walking along the streets with my dear Carol. Then, the final bell rang, which signaled the end of this school day.

Once outside, I said farewell to my friends. Then I saw Carol as she was walking away. As I was about to call out to her, she turned and looked my way. I waved to her, and she waved back. She then continued walking northward towards town, and her house. I hopped onto my bicycle and headed south as usual. But my actions were only a ruse, because this would no longer be my route home. I only did this to achieve maximum effect with Carol. So, I rode south for about one minute to where Jeanne had lived. Then I turned around and headed north to the point where Carol was now walking. As usual, she was walking along with her friend and classmate, Patricia. I took her totally by surprise. I simply rode up beside her, dismounted from my bike, and began walking along beside her. Carol had been walking on the street side of the sidewalk, which allowed me to take my place at her side. I grinned at her, saying, "Hi, would you girls like some company"? I could readily see that she was completely taken aback!

She smiled at me, although at first, she seemed speechless! Then, she asked, "Aw Jake, why don't you stop playing around, and take yourself home"? "But I had hoped that you would let me walk you home." I said. Then she asked "Jake, are you really serious"? "I'm serious" I told her. I could easily see that this was a very wonderful moment for her, and it made me feel just great. Actually, I fully realized that this was as great for me as it was for her. So now, we celebrated our long-awaited occasion by walking, talking and joking together! Naturally, this also included Patricia, but we had a really great walk that afternoon. During that first walk with Carol I got to know her much better. At school she was refined and self-controlled. But now, she was a much different person— much more relaxed. I was very pleased to discover this side of her. At school I had found her to be somewhat of a bore, but now she had shown me that she was really a fun-type of girl. I felt we would really hit it off!

The walk to Carol's house took us only fifteen minutes. But Patricia lived on a different street and had left us about ten minutes earlier, so we had a full ten minutes to enjoy each other's company. We had carried on a very nice and friendly, but respectful conversation. But now we had reached her home. So as we both paused for a moment in front of her house, she asked, "Can I expect the same treatment again tomorrow"? I responded, "You sure can"! "Great!" she exclaimed. Then, we said a warm "bye bye" to each other, as I mounted my bicycle and sped away happily. Now, I knew for certain that this had been a wonderful day!

I rode away, looking forward to (instead of dreading) my ride home. I purposely paced myself so as not to reach home too early. I reached home exactly forty-five minutes after having left school. Had I taken my old route, I still would have had another fifteen minutes of riding time remaining. I had passed through the forest without having seen a single person or animal. Now, regarding my travel through this particular forest, I believe I should elaborate just a bit. This was back in the early 1950s, in one rural region of the country where most residents were at least slightly acquainted with each other. There were no serial killers here and luckily there were no drug dealers in our area; hence, violent crime was minimal. Our only concern was of inmates who might have escaped from some nearby prison. Also, there were occasionally moonshiners, processing homemade liquor in a few of the forests. Now, the moonshiners were not considered inherently dangerous, but inmates who had escaped prison, were known to be both desperate and dangerous. However, I had previously hunted in this very same forest during ages eleven through thirteen, so I was quite familiar with this area. I had even seen this small trail which I had today just used, only it had never occurred to me that this trail might actually extend through this entire forest. But finally I knew, and what a difference it would make in my young life!

I finished my meal and rushed out into the fields to help dad ready land for planting. Dad welcomed me, and we energetically went about our work until it again came quitting time. I felt that dad sensed my new-found passion for field work. But I was not aware that he actually had known the true reason for my increased interest in my work, my life, and in all things around me. If only parents would have talked to their children about the facts of life back in those days, what a wonderful world that might have been. But unfortunately, such was not the case. As teenagers we learned the facts of life from other older kids around us (which included brothers, sisters, cousins, and friends). Sadly, I had none of these. So, the question remained— how on earth could I possibly have become enlightened? The answer was— I simply could not have! Thus, naivety became my first name—and ignorance my last. Miraculously though, I would somehow manage!

February had now come and gone, and it had been a great month for me. In the first days of March, the extreme cold had begun to dissipate. So there I was— with my riding time to and from school cut by half. I now had a nice girl in my life. And to make matters even better, the weather had begun to warm a bit. This meant that for the next six months, I would not freeze my butt off whenever taking my baths! Things were going just great for me— or so I'd thought. There was still the unresolved matter of the bully Willie Jayes. I'd not been aware of just how serious the situation was regarding this individual, nor had I given it any thought. But this would soon change!

Everything else at school was going well. I was receiving good grades from my daily school work, and from quizzes and exams. My friendship with Carol improved with each passing day, so I felt that I should have absolutely no reason for complaint. But then one day at school during lunch period, I received some unwelcomed news. This occurred on a day when Carol was absent from school. While sitting in our cafeteria eating, Wilton said to me, "Jake, seems you and Carol are getting kind of close to each other". I replied, "Sort of" to which, he responded, "Well, be careful, because she's Willie Jayes' girl— or at least he thinks so". I was somewhat shocked by this bit of news. I had never seen them together. And if Carol were his girlfriend, he should have at least been walking her home from school every day. But this had never happened. So, I thanked my buddy for his warning, although deep inside I hoped that no serious problems would arise from my being around Carol. Actually, I had hoped against hope that if there were a problem, it might go away. Luck would prove not to have been on my side.

The following day, Carol returned to school. During our lunch period, she told me that she'd awakened on the previous morning with a slight headache, so her mom had decided to keep her inside for the day. Though, she was here with me now, so today I carefully chose my words in questioning her relationship with old Willie. Carol reassured me that there was absolutely nothing between Willie and herself. This relieved me quite a bit. But she advised me that he lived nearby, and tried talking to her. She also said that she disliked him because she considered him mean and disrespectful. She added that each time he would come around, her mom would chase him away. Carol had not told her dad about Willie. I was a bit uncomfortable with what she had told me, but I would continue hoping for the best possible outcome.

I continued focusing upon my lessons at school. I also kept walking Carol home each afternoon. And other than seeing old Willie in classes, it was as though he had become invisible. But I later found that he had begun stalking the two of us. I discovered that while Carol and I were outside on the school grounds, he would always position himself in a manner that allowed him to easily observe our behavior together. Then as I walked her home each afternoon, he would follow us, but at a distance. For some reason, he'd chosen not to approach us. I knew for certain that he was not afraid of me, for I had on many school days, watched him as he fought with other boys. He was a ferocious fighter (much like a bull dog)! It seemed that his first love was that of fighting. All else seemed secondary to him. In retrospect, he was not a friendly person and he did not seem to have any friends. None of the students at school knew anything about him— other than he was a fighter. Also, he was muscular and very powerfully built. I sensed that Willie was considerably older than the rest of the boys in our class. But because he had not confronted me about Carol, I continued with my daily routine while at school.

Days and weeks passed, and it was now the beginning of April— my favorite time of the year. I say this mainly because in my part of the country, this was a time when the birds began singing, and the sweet-smelling flowers began blossoming. Presently the weather was no longer cold, but neither had it become unusually hot. In my region, the average temperature during this time in the year, hovered in the seventy-degree range. This was the perfect time for working in the fields on the farm. It was an even more perfect time for romancing some young lady. I know whereof I speak because I did both. I did these things even though I never lost focus and interest in my daily assigned school work.

But now that the weather had warmed up, I could start again regularly riding my horse. I also, resumed my self-defense training with good old Mr. Lim. So for the next two months, I would have a full and heavy schedule. During weekdays, there was school, then Carol, then field work. During weekends, there was field work and Carol on Saturdays, then Mr. Lim and riding on Sundays. But I certainly preferred this current schedule over the one that would commence in early June, once school had ended. So, I rode and trained diligently. I even resumed picking up my old pal Buddy, during my periods of riding. Also, my time spent with Mr. Lim had really progressed well. I had now learned defense timing, physical kinetics, and a wide range of attack and defense techniques. Mr. Lim had been so pleased with my progress, he'd bestowed upon me my third skill level promotion. I was finally a fourth degree (expert) street fighter. At this point in my training, he told me that it would take another two years, to reach the level of master. I felt very good about myself and my achievements. I should add here that I'd had a premonition that I just might someday soon, need every bit of training I could muster, to face the feared Willie Jayes! Finally, I made it through the week, at which point, I executed my weekend programs.

After finishing up in the fields, I cleaned up before asking dad if we were riding into town this afternoon? He advised me that he would remain at the house for some much needed rest. But he also told me that I could ride the bicycle into town if I wished. These were the words that I had really wanted to hear, so I jumped at the opportunity. I did not wish to appear so very over-anxious, so I sort of took my time in leaving the house. But when it was finally time for me to leave, dad asked if I had needed a little pocket change. I told him that I could use a little, so he gave me one dollar. Back then, a movie only cost twenty-five cents. Popcorn was fifteen cents, and a soda— ten cents. This meant that I could watch a movie, with all the trimmings, for just fifty cents. I would have another fifty cents remaining, and with this money, I could take Carol along with me. However, what dad didn't know was— mom had already secretly given me a dollar. And what the both of them did not know was— on my way out the door, grand mom quietly beckoned me to her, and she too had given me another dollar. So, now I had a total of three dollars in my pocket and was rich! Away I went— riding and singing! I had not yet mentioned to Carol about a movie, so I was a bit apprehensive about my new situation. I did not know if she would be at home. But even had she been, I had no idea whether or not her parents would allow me to escort her to a movie, but I rode onward— hoping for the best. After just twenty-five minutes of riding time, I neared Carol's house. From a distance, I could see her mom working around the flowers in their front yard. I felt a pang of anxiety surge through my young body as I approached the front of their house, where I greeted Carol's mom. Her mother straightened up as she peered at me over the rim of her glasses. She immediately recognized me. I sensed that she was a bit surprised at seeing me there. Carol's mom asked me how my parents (and in particular— my grandmother) were doing? I told her that they were all doing well. She seemed happy upon hearing my words. Then she asked where I was headed? I told her I had finally gotten a little free time, so I was headed to the movies. Then I asked her if she would allow me to take Carol. She did not answer me directly, but instead called out to Carol. In a flash, Carol appeared in the doorway! As soon as she saw me, a heartwarming smile swept across her face. "Hi Jake, what are you doing here?" she asked. I responded, "I'm out here begging your mother to let me take you to a movie". I could see that Carol was thrilled at the thought as she looked questioningly at her mom. Her mom said, "Ask your dad". Carol replied, "But dad's asleep". So, her mom said to us, "Okay— but you two had better be good,—you hear me"? I nodded as I assured her that we would most certainly behave. Then, Carol disappeared from the doorway, saying, "I'll be right out"! She soon rushed out from her house and hopped onto the back of my old bicycle. I thanked her mother as the two of us rode away. Her mom yelled to me, "Have her back here before dark"! I assured Carol's mom that I would comply with her stern directive.

We arrived at the movie theater in just five minutes. I secured the bicycle to a bicycle stand and then the two of us strode into the theater's lobby, where I purchased two tickets, one popcorn, along with two sodas. Carol had said that she would settle for sharing my popcorn. I later learned that she had actually wanted popcorn also, but she had not wished to appear expensive on our very first 'date'. I appreciated this quality in her. After being seated, she snuggled close to me. I could smell her light perfume, and I could feel her warm body touching mine. I must admit— it really felt great, being there with her for the very first time! But it felt even greater being there with her in semi-darkness. So as soon as we were comfortable, I leaned slightly over to her, kissing her on the cheek. And in return, she squeezed my hand tightly. The warm feeling running through my body at that moment was indescribable! We watched several cartoons, and then the featured movie came onto the screen. The movie was called "*Mole Men*", which was about a society of subterranean fellows who only surfaced late at night. This was a scary little movie, and it caused Carol to frequently grab onto my arm, or press herself tightly against me. I found myself deeply appreciative of the fact that this was the type of movie the theater staff had chosen to show. We sat quietly through this movie, and enjoyed it in its entirety. Then after what seemed as only a very short period of time, the lights came on. It was now time for us to leave, so we reluctantly stood up and exited the theater at nearly 5:55PM.

My plan was to have Carol back at her house by 6:00PM. I was successful; however, midway to her house, we ran into none other than old Willie Jayes. He had been walking down the street, heading in our direction. When we were abreast of each other, Carol spoke to him, "Hi Willie". I believe that she was afraid not to speak to him. Willie only growled, "Hey" as he brushed past us. Now I'm certain that he was only speaking to her, which was okay by me. I say this because I had not spoken to him either. I had simply walked past him as if he'd not been there on the street. We rode on toward Carol's house, where I dropped her off at exactly 6:00PM as planned. But now, both her mom and dad were sitting on their front porch, so I greeted each of them as we rode up, and jokingly asked her mom if we were early enough? Carol's mom smiled, saying "You're right on time". I did not linger, but thanked them as I said "bye" to Carol just as she was entering her house. She waved and gave me a bright smile. The sun was still high in the sky at this time of evening, so I figured that I would ride quickly to my home and grab my horse for another short ride.

After a brief chat with my parents, I changed clothing before hurrying out to the old barn to fetch my horse. I had not told them that I'd taken a girl along with me to the movies, as I was not sure just how they might react to this. I placed my old homemade saddle onto my horse's back, and tightened its cinch. Then, we trotted off down the narrow roadway toward Buddy's house. Today as usual, he showed us that he was both eager and happy to see us, by his frenzied display of affection and excitement! His actions were fully justified because six months had passed since we had last ridden together. We headed straight toward Mr. Lim's house, for I wanted to say hello, and confirm that tomorrow would be a good day for training. He also was happy for our brief visit. At this point, I realized that nearly everything in my personal life was at its best.

Nevertheless, constant thoughts of old Willie Jayes lurked in my mind; and, these thoughts would frequently surface, reminding me of an uncertain future. I sensed an impending danger, although I had no idea how or when it might surface. It then occurred to me that I should place even greater emphasis on my training beginning tomorrow. Thusly, after a few moments of friendly conversation with this old gentleman, I bade him "Good evening" and we rode quickly across the fields, and through the forests. There was no reason for caution at this time of year, because no snakes were currently moving about. It was still too early in the year, and local temperatures had not warmed enough. So, Buddy relaxed as we moved along a maze of different forest trails. I felt good,— riding again. Belle had been out, but I had not. Occasionally across the winter, I would release her from our barn and let her run freely across the large fields. Belle had enjoyed running at times without a rider, but she would always immediately return once she was summoned. After forty-five minutes, we finally turned back, since it was now beginning dusk. Then, after dropping Buddy off at his house, we headed for home. Overall, this had been another great day and one that I would remember.

Sunday was again upon us. Church was still not a possibility, so the four of us sat around for most of the morning. But near noon time dad decided to take the old bicycle for a ride to one small, but very nice, store about a mile from our house. This was one of the few gathering places in the area where local farmers could meet and talk together. They usually only discussed farming. Such conversations focused on recently encountered problems (such as plant diseases), and remedies for these problems. Everyone was welcome, and race was not of concern. Although, back in those days, there were only blacks and whites— and of course Mr. Lim. Mr. Lim was not a farmer, so he had absolutely no interest in such gatherings anyway.

Now came time for me to head over to Mr. Lim's house to receive my weekly training. I rode my horse to his old place, where we would train for more than one hour. I had recently attained a level of expertise that allowed me to begin repeating, and refining those techniques and tactics I'd already learned. I was fully aware that this was necessary, because their successful execution depended primarily on the precision with which they were executed. Naturally, timing fell within the range of precision. I was happy to begin refresher training, because I knew that at some point in the near future, I would most likely need every bit of precision I could summon. This repeat training would go a long way in boosting my confidence level, when it came time for me to face the highly feared Willie Jayes. Consequently, I would put both Jeanne and Carol completely out of my mind as I proceeded with my refresher training over the next several weeks.

Today was Monday again and time for my ride to school, though these were rides which I no longer dreaded. In fact, I looked forward to them. I also looked forward to seeing Carol and my friends. I must say though that I was a bit apprehensive, for I had no idea what this new week held in store for me. In considering Willie, I was not yet confident that I could take him. I knew that my training had gone extremely well, but training does not equal the real thing. In training my opponent actually protected me, but in a real fist-fight, Willie would have every intention of doing me serious bodily harm! My main concern was that I had never had the need to fight any boy, so fighting experience was absent from my arsenal. I felt that I would be awesome in any street fight, but I only hoped that this would not be proven to the contrary. First of all, I certainly did not wish to be injured. Second, I was equally emphatic about not wishing to be embarrassed, so I became a virtual training machine! Strangely though, this entire week passed without Willie confronting me. He had continued to sit directly behind me in health class. In other classes, he would sit at various locations within the classroom. I did not feel comfortable sitting directly in front of him, but I would write no more notes! Also, I was determined not to give any indication whatsoever, that I felt any fear or respect for him.

The week passed with Carol and I hanging out at lunch time. Also, we were seemingly glued together each afternoon, on our way to her house. But old Willie always kept his distance. Today was Friday again, so after lunch Carol and I sat at our regular little spot. I told her that we would have to skip the movies tomorrow as I would need to work for a couple of extra hours, helping dad in the fields. She jokingly said, "For a moment, I thought you were going to say that you just didn't want to take me". I replied "You know better," as we both chuckled. Our school day soon ended, so I again walked Carol home that afternoon—without interference from Willie.

The days were becoming a bit longer now, so I spent an extra hour helping dad in the fields that Friday afternoon.

We also extended our workday on Saturday for an extra hour. But I did not mind one bit, for I was a happy young boy. Mom and grandmother had managed to get into town on Friday morning, and they had brought me some candies and other goodies such as nuts. Mom also had bought me a very nice baseball cap, made of silk. It was bright green in color. I instantly fell in love with that cap! However, this was the weekend and since I wasn't going anywhere, I had no place to wear it. Thus, I would be patient and await the arrival of Monday morning, so I could wear my cap to school. I sat around the house for most of the morning while waiting for noontime.

Finally noon arrived, so I rushed out and saddled up before riding over to Mr. Lim's old place. He had been awaiting me, so we immediately resumed my training program. But this time he made a slight modification in my training. He had wisely added weight training to my program early last fall, so now he felt it was time that I be tested in this area. I'd practiced lifting heavy objects that weighed fifty to one hundred pounds, and over the past seven months, I'd become quite effective in handling them. I had begun my weight program by lifting and simultaneously tossing two twenty-five pound sandbags. But after only one month of such training, I advanced to handling one single hundred-pound bag filled with sand. I found this to be fairly easy, since for the past three years I had daily lifted (along with dad), hundred-pound bags of grain. But now, at age fifteen, I had begun lifting this amount of weight without assistance. Mr. Lim tested me in this weight category, and I even surpassed his expectations! He began showing me how to not only lift, but also toss such weight for distances of up to twelve feet. I was amazed that I was able to accomplish this feat, but he explained how this was possible. This technique involved proper timing, body positioning, and leveraging, along with the use of kinetic energy. The amount of synergism derived from this unusual skill was truly awesome! I was highly impressed. So there I was at only age fifteen, able to toss a one-hundred bag to a distance of twelve feet. But what was even more impressive, was that although Mr. Lim was slightly smaller, and weighed less than I, he was able to toss that old bag even further. I was thrilled to have reached my level of accomplishment. Then upon completion of my testing, we proceeded with refresher training. After another half hour had passed, it was time to cease my training until next weekend. I thanked Mr. Lim for his valuable teachings, bade him farewell for the week, and rode away toward home.

It was time to swing by and pick up my pal Buddy. After our usual greetings, I rode away across the fields and into the forests. This was a perfect afternoon for riding. The current temperature hovered around seventy degrees. There was not a cloud in the sky; and to make matters even better, those damned snakes were still hibernating. So we traveled into the depths of these forests, appreciating and enjoying the beauty and serenity of our surroundings. I rode for nearly two hours, at which time we turned and headed back toward our homes.

Our return trip would take us at least one and one-half hours. I eventually emerged from the forest and was able to see far into the distance, which was where I was headed. Finally, we reached Buddy's house and I dropped him off. Then Belle and I raced toward home, as if we were being chased by Indians (a favorite pretense of mine). As soon as we reached home, I watered and curried Belle. Next, I released her into the barnyard and prepared to take my bath. I had already hand-pumped a full tub of water in which to bathe. I dipped my hand into the small round tub, finding it to be sufficiently sun-heated to bathe in. I had positioned my tub on the back side of our old house so that my family would not see me. At the edge of our backyard, was the forest, so I felt that no one would be watching from there. It was nearing 6:00PM, so I finished my bath and put on fresh clean clothing. It was also time for my evening meal. This had been a great day, but it was time to relax and spend a little time with my parents and grandmother. Dad had also returned, so the four of us sat around just talking. Naturally, they did the talking as I sat listening to them. Unfortunately, this was the way things were back then.

Once again Monday morning was before us. This was a new day, and the beginning of a new week. As I prepared for school, I wondered what lay ahead of me. I sensed a strong feeling of foreboding, though I felt that with the exception of old Willie Jayes, this should be a good day and a great week. After all, my grades were good, I had a much shorter ride to and from school, and I had Carol in my life. What more could a young boy have asked for? But even so, I felt a certain uneasiness in the air about me. I knew though that I must face whatever lurked around the corner, lying in wait for me. After washing up and dressing, I had a good breakfast before climbing onto my old bicycle. Naturally, I wore my nice new baseball cap! The now one-half hour ride to school was a very good one.

I had left the house about fifteen minutes early, so I also

arrived at school fifteen minutes early. But now that the weather had warmed a bit, there was no need to rush into the classroom. I parked and secured my bike, and then stood around outside on the school grounds, chatting with other students. Many of them verbally admired my cap. I must say here that this was one of the very nicest baseball caps that I would ever own, and I really liked it a lot! Finally when lunchtime arrived, we gathered in the school cafeteria at our usual tables. My usual group of friends were present. We discussed mostly the events of the recent weekend. We had gotten into the habit of talking less and eating a little faster. This would give us more time to mill around after lunch on the school grounds. So after lunch was finished, we moved to the grounds outside. There now seemed to be three separate and distinct groups on the grounds. There were the boy and girl couples, who either sat or stood around talking. Then there were two separate groups of boys— each passing around footballs. I also would soon begin occasionally participating in this sport. At this point in my life I had discovered that I enjoyed sports. But for now Carol was my main focus in life, so on this particular day, I sat talking with her. I enjoyed this form of relaxation and socialization very much. We spent nearly twenty minutes talking about life in general, but then the bell sounded, signaling the end of our cherished lunch period.

During the entire time that Carol and I had sat in the park, I had not seen Willie Jayes even once. But as we walked back toward our classrooms he paid me an unpleasant surprise visit! We were just walking along together, joking and laughing, when I suddenly felt my nice baseball cap being snatched from my head! I quickly turned to see what had just happened, and to my dismay, I saw old Willie running away through the throngs of students who were walking along. My cap was now on his head! I couldn't believe that this had happened to me! But at the same time I did not feel strong reason for alarm. I simply thought that he had been taunting me, and once we were in class, I would retrieve my cap. But I had greatly erred in my assessment; for, when I arrived in our classroom and asked Willie for my cap, he completely ignored me. To make matters even worse, I did not see my cap anywhere nearby. This quite alarmed me! But since we were now inside the classroom, talking was not allowed. So, I just sat there furiously, seated directly in front of Willie. I figured that as soon as this class was over, I would approach him and ask for my cap. And this was exactly what I did. I exited our classroom before Willie and waited just outside the door. This meant that he would pass my way as he exited the classroom. There, I waited quite impatiently!

Finally Willie boldly emerged, strolling past me somewhat as would have a game-cock rooster. I quickly caught up to him, and asked him for my cap. I said to him "Willie, may I have my cap back"? He responded, "I don't have your cap". "Then, where is it?" I asked? "I threw it away!" replied Willie. "*So, this is his answer*" I thought. At this point, I began to get a very bad feeling inside. I had not anticipated that he would come at me in such a bold manner— but he had! I so badly wanted my cap back, but in no way did I want to start a fight with the feared Willie Jayes! So, I decided to let the matter rest for awhile. I then proceeded to my study period to do my homework for the next day. I found it difficult to concentrate though, because my mind kept drifting to my cap and what to do. I figured I would wait until the school day ended, and then I would try applying Willie's tactic. I would try sneaking up behind him and grabbing my hat!

I waited patiently for the school day to end. Finally, my moment of reckoning had arrived. The bell sounded and I quickly rushed outside. I hoped that I would not have to fight Willie in order to retrieve my cap, though I need not have worried. I scanned the schoolyard in all directions for several minutes, but Willie was nowhere in sight. Now I was really upset, because this meant going home to my mom and dad without my cap! But then Carol showed up, so we started walking down the street toward her house. Along the way I told her what had transpired between Willie and me. She sighed, saying "I really wish that I had an older brother to help you fight him". Then she said words to me that I did not wish to hear: "Of course you know that now you will have to fight him".

Now as I have stated earlier, until today I had never fought anyone! So, I found myself about to enter unchartered waters. I had observed Willie on many occasions, fighting other boys at school. He was a fearsome warrior in every respect, and he'd never lost a single battle! It was this knowledge alone that nearly psychologically defeated me, even before the battle had begun. We finally reached Carol's house, where we reluctantly said our "Bye byes" to each other. All along the half hour ride home, I kept thinking about my situation. I now knew that retrieving my cap was out of the question. I also knew that in order for me to show my face around school, I would have absolutely no choice but to face-off with Willie Jayes! Otherwise, I would become the laughing stock and wimp of our entire school.

After all, many of the other boys had faced him gallantly. Some of them even managed to give him a good fight— at least for the first few minutes. But he was so very ferocious, even the best of them soon gave in to his devastating and relentless attacks! Frankly, I found myself quite intimidated by Willie. But I took solace in remembering words that my great and fearless father had often said to me, "Son, no matter how tough a man appears to be— there's always someone who is tougher". If only I were as fearless and capable as my father. But my problem was twofold. How would I tell my dear mother some boy at school had taken my coveted cap? I decided to tell her that someone at school had stolen it. That way I felt I might save face. Now, if I had told dad that a boy had taken my cap, he would have said, "Son, when you go to school tomorrow, take your cap back— no matter what it takes"! "And if he doesn't have your cap with him— take his hide"! Sadly, dad would have meant each of these words, because this is exactly what he would have done.

At home mom immediately asked, "Son, where's your cap?" I gave her my concocted version that someone at school had stolen it. I felt badly about lying to her, but I simply could not face up to the truth. Then she said, "Well, I hope you find it tomorrow, because I went to great lengths to get it for you. It was such a nice cap, and I liked it so much". At this point, I must tell you that I loved my mother more than anyone I had ever known, and there was nothing that I would not have done for her. In retrospect, if she'd said to me, "Son, I want you to take this girl Jeanne and dump her into a fast flowing river", I would have strongly considered her words. Needless to say, it hurt me deeply to see mom saddened by the loss of my new baseball cap! I knew that I would need to take some sort of action! Meanwhile, I would simply sit at our old table and enjoy a peanut butter sandwich and a glass of lemonade. When I had finished, I changed into my work clothing before rushing out into the fields to help dad.

Afterward I cleaned up and had a good meal. Then I tried to sleep, but sleep did not come easily to my deeply troubled mind. And now, it was Tuesday. I prepared for school, but all the while, I could not rid myself of the feeling of sickness in the pit of my stomach. I washed up though and found that I was actually able to eat breakfast. To be truthful, I forced my breakfast down because I felt that on this day, I would need every bit of nourishment I could possibly consume. This would be my day of battle! It would also be a day that I did not look forward to. I bade my folks "Good day" as I rode away down our narrow road to face my destiny.

Since I was again a bit early, I lingered on the school grounds chatting with other kids while I waited for Carol. But mostly, I was on the lookout for the dreaded Willie Jayes! Finally I saw him, but I did not see my cap anywhere. He walked onto the school grounds, passing each of us without even saying good morning to anyone. This told me that this would in fact be the big day! But at this point, I found myself actually looking forward to the big moment! After all, it was for times such as this I had trained so diligently with Mr. Lim. Finally, I began to relax just a bit. I considered my possibilities, and examined my position in all this. I now realized that I had a unique advantage over Willie. I had seen him fight many times, and I knew quite well all of his bag of tricks. I had studied his attack methods, and I understood them. I also knew that he would not hesitate to dash a handful of sand into my eyes in an attempt to temporarily blind me. I knew too that he had never before seen me fight. This meant that he had no knowledge of my abilities or styles. And finally, he certainly was not aware of Mr. Lim and the special training I had received from him over the past twenty months. Each of these considerations served to provide me with the element of surprise! I would never underestimate Willie, but soon I felt my level of confidence begin rising. Then the bell sounded for our first class of the morning. During morning hours Willie was in different classrooms, so I would not see him until at least noontime. I went through all four classes of the morning, but with extreme anxiety. Then, finally lunchtime was upon us. My three friends and I did our normal routine while in the cafeteria. Then came the moment when lunch was finished!

As we exited the cafeteria, Carol and I walked casually over to our favorite park bench. It was vacant, so we took our seat there. I began briefing her about what to expect from old Willie. I sensed that she was very nervous about our situation, so I asked, "Are you okay"? She replied, "I just wish that this did not have to happen— because I really don't want to see you get hurt." I was sitting there with Carol, holding my head in a slightly lowered position. I figured this would give old Willie the false impression that I might be somehow submitting to him. I felt he would misinterpret my posture as an indication that I was afraid to fight him. After all, I had allowed him to take my cap yesterday, but without any form of confrontation. For had

I been another boy, the fight would have started the moment he'd told me that he had thrown my cap away! I sat there with my head still lowered, considering these factors, although I would not be allowed to sit for long. I had suspected all along that Willie would be observing me from some nearby vantage point, and I was correct! Suddenly he appeared from amidst the crowds of kids! But most important of these considerations, was the fact he was presently headed in my direction! He walked rather slowly but deliberately, and there was absolutely no question as to where he was headed! He was now only fifty yards away, and Carol also had seen him. "Jake, he's coming!" she exclaimed, as she excitedly clutched my arm! I tried comforting her by saying, "Don't worry," as I squeezed her hand. I had already given her my watch for safekeeping. I had also already removed my thin jacket, so now I was as ready as I would ever be! But I found that I was still apprehensive. I had not yet looked up at Willie. I continued sitting there with my head lowered, so I believe this may have confused him. However, he kept advancing at a steady pace.

When Willie was nearly twenty feet away from us, I suddenly arose, taking two quick steps in his direction! Immediately upon seeing me standing, old Willie did exactly as I had anticipated. He instantly ducked low to the ground, as he rushed forward toward me. I knew beyond a doubt that he intended to grab me below the knees and scoop me up from the ground, while still rushing forward. He would then slam me with full force, onto the hard ground! As soon as I'd had fallen he would've jumped down onto my chest and pounded my face into a pulp! But I'd had other plans!

So, just as he'd reached the point where I stood, I quickly took one wide side-step to my left! In that very same instant, I spun around. This maneuver served dual purposes. First, it removed me from Willie's line of attack, preventing him from scooping me up. Second, it quickly placed me at his side, with the two us now rushing in unison toward the heavy-duty steel wire fence that stood directly in our path! I instantly grabbed firmly onto his wrist, as we raced forward, extending it forward as we rushed toward the nearby steel fence! Now, I was pulling him along, while not allowing him to slow down. Then just as we were only four feet from this fence, I performed a lightning-fast 180-degree turn of his body. Presently he faced away from the fence, as I abruptly brought him to an upright position! Suddenly, old Willie was completely off balance and rapidly stumbling backwards!

As we reached the fence I stepped directly in front him, lunging forward with all my might! His body slammed with the force of a raging bull, into the steel fencepost that I had selected especially for him! I had employed the principle of kinetic energy. I had also taken his forward motion and used his own movement against him. The force of his impact was so great, the entire steel fence seemed to shake and reverberate! But I wasn't finished! Willie appeared dazed as he stumbled away from the fence. I timed him perfectly. With one lightening-quick reverse side-kick, I spun to my right, burying the heel of my right foot deeply into Willie's midsection! He made a sort of grunting sound, (similar to that of a wounded pig), as the air rushed from his lungs! He then bent forward, clutching his belly. But, I still wasn't finished! As Willie stood bent forward, I backed away from him a distance of three feet. I then sprang forward, raising one foot from the ground as I reached him. Again, I buried my foot into his belly! I'm quite sure that it was his spinal column the toe of my shoe had impacted against! My last attack had done the trick!

Old Willie fell onto the ground, immediately assuming a fetal position, all the while grimacing and groaning as he clutched his aching belly, but I still was not finished! Actually, from the very beginning my strategy had been not only to defeat Willie physically, but also mentally! I knew that unless I defeated him mentally, I would always need to watch my back, and I simply wasn't prepared to move around each day, looking over my shoulder as I did so! With these thoughts racing through my mind, I stepped over to him and then violently jerked the hand away from his belly. He did not struggle, but lay completely dormant. I then dragged him along the ground to a distance of nearly twenty feet from the fence. Once there, I quickly stomped him again in his now extremely sore and painful belly! Each of my four attacks had served specific purposes, designed mainly to: (1) remove all confidence in Willie's ability as a fighter, (2) so totally demolish him, the return of even the least bit of will to fight, would have been highly unlikely, and (3) simply embarrass the heck out of him before all the kids here at our school. Thus, I knew that I had one final step to take. So, as Willie lay with his body contorted and still clutching his belly, I attacked him both physically and psychologically! I turned and walked a few feet away from him. But I had walked to a point where I was certain that he could not observe my actions. I scooped a handful of sand from the ground and walked back to where he lay. By now, large crowds of kids had gathered around to watch Willie's surprising defeat. I returned to him, placing the heel of my foot onto his shoulder. I then gave a strong shove, rolling him over onto his back. Immediately, he drew both knees upward and again began clutching his belly! I casually observed him, but without speaking. I looked over at Carol and saw that she was beaming! So too, were the many kids here in these large crowds. None seemed dissatisfied except old Willie himself!

I knew that our lunch period was rapidly coming to an end, so I sped up my action. I placed my foot upon his chest, bending slightly forward. Then I said, "I've really enjoyed this. In fact, we can do this again tomorrow. I'll be right here— same time— same place". Willie was still lying face-up, so I decided to take advantage of this position. Before he could bring his hand up to his face, I held my fist directly above it, as I released the combination of sand and dirt. It splattered into his eyes, his nostrils, and even into his mouth and throat! Adding insult to injury, I sifted the remaining sand onto his face. He lay sputtering, gagging, coughing, and clawing at his eyes! Lastly, I turned to the crowd as I said, "Behold— the bad Willie Jayes"! The crowds began roaring and chanting! Just then the bell began ringing, telling us to return to classes. It had been a great lunch period, and I was especially pleased with my impressive performance. I retrieved my watch from Carol and then walked over to old Willie, roughly jerking him to his feet! He did not struggle or protest, as I walked along behind him toward our classroom. However, before reaching the classroom I took the pleasure of escorting Willie into a nearby lavatory facility. I ordered him, "Now wash your filthy face"! He surprisingly complied. When he had finished, I escorted him from the lavatory, walking slightly behind him. We entered our classroom in this same manner; but this time, I instructed him to sit at my desk. He did so, again without protest. I then picked up my books and seated myself directly behind him, at his former desk. I would keep Willie's desk for the remainder of this school year.

Soon Miss Cunnings began the lesson of the day in her usual manner—"Good afternoon, class". The class responded in its usual manner—"Good afternoon, Miss Cunnings". She always dressed well, and she kept her grooming at its best. I sat there behind old Willie, watching her as she spoke to us. I found myself so very attracted to her, I nearly forgot about Willie— my enemy. So I focused on him, paying particular attention to his posture, as he sat at his newly appointed desk. He sat hunched forward, which was a departure from his normal sitting position. Normally, he would slouch backward at his desk each day. This told me that he must have been presently experiencing considerable discomfort in his stomach area. There was no visible evidence that he'd been in a fight. Remember, I had purposefully not struck him to the face.

Miss Cunnings had noticed this change in Willie's demeanor, so she asked, "Are you alright, Willie"? He hesitated slightly before answering, but then replied with a nearly inaudible "I'm alright, Miss Cunnings". At this point, several of the boys— and a few of the girls— began snickering lightly. She chided them, and then added, "Class, if there's a problem— I want to know about it". None of the class commented, and she returned to the task of teaching the class. I sat there quietly taking notes, and the class period proceeded without further disruption. Finally it ended, so we gathered our books and departed her classroom. I walked directly behind Willie as we left the room. I had intended to taunt him even further, as I needed to know whether or not he'd still had any fight left in himself. But Miss Cunnings noticed this and called out, "Jake, may I see you for a moment"? I dropped my role of escorting my nemesis, and walked to her desk. She was standing as I approached her, so I was afforded a full view of her rare beauty. Even at only fifteen years of age, I wanted so desperately to reach out and touch her. But she interrupted my lascivious thoughts by asking, "Jake, is there something wrong between you and Willie Jayes"? I decided I would be perfectly candid with her, so I began recounting the events of the past two days. I first told her about how he had taken my brand-new cap yesterday. I also told her of his rude response when I asked him to return it. At this point, she commented, "You poor dear". Then she completely surprised me by giving me a warm hug. Without even thinking about what I was doing, I hugged her in return. But when she finally released me, I still held her in my arms. She quickly returned me to reality by saying simply, "Jake". At that time, I believe that she'd felt those strong emotions racing through my young and inexperienced body! But she did not appear offended by my actions so I did not apologize. I wanted her to know how I felt about her, even though there was no possibility of a future between us. She then said, "Tomorrow, I'm going to make sure that Willie returns your cap to you immediately". I replied, "Never mind— I don't want it back – he probably has head lice anyway". When I made this comment, I'd been totally serious. But she had taken my words comically, so we both just laughed it off.

Then I told my teacher about what had happened during lunch period today. At first, she seemed shocked by my revelation, but the expression of shock quickly disappeared and in its place, I saw what I am certain was an expression of sheer delight. Her eyes were wide and she had a big smile on her face, as she said, "You're telling me that you defeated Willie Jayes"? "That's right," I said. She then said "But I didn't see any bruises or marks on him at all". "I was careful not to mark up his face." I answered. "Unbelievable!" she exclaimed. "I know" I said. "But always be very careful— because he is a very mean and dangerous boy!" she added. I thanked my teacher for her genuine concern, as I proceeded to study period. I did not see old Willie anymore that day. In fact, I would not see him again for another two days—which was still much too soon!

Finally our end-of-day bell sounded so I gathered my belongings and exited the building. Once outside, I looked carefully about the school grounds for any sight of old Willie, but I saw him nowhere. I figured that even though he might still be in pain, he would most likely attack me at the very first opportunity. I stood on the grounds for about three more minutes, waiting for Carol. In that short period of time, more than a dozen kids approached me. Each had wanted to thank and compliment me on facing and defeating that terrible boy. I politely thanked each of them.

Soon Carol showed up. I told her that I would give her a lift on my old bicycle today, because I needed to rush downtown to buy a new baseball cap. She, in particular, was thrilled by the fact that I had apparently so easily defeated Willie. As we mounted my bicycle, she placed her arms around my waistline to steady herself. Then, the first thing she said was, "Maybe now, he'll leave us alone".

This had been a very stressful day for me, but I reveled in the fact that it had turned out so well. I also took great pleasure in receiving all the attention from the students. But I was mostly pleased to receive attention and compliments from Miss Cunnings. Our bicycle ride to Carol's house took us less than ten minutes, but I did not linger. I immediately rushed the short distance to the downtown store where mom had told me that she'd bought my hat. I was fortunate in that the store only had one remaining cap, of my size and color. Now if you recall, two weeks earlier I had been given $3.00 to defray my cost of going to the movies. But I had only spent one of those dollars, having saved and stashed the other two at home. Today I would spend one of my remaining two dollars to purchase my replacement baseball cap. I picked up the cap from the rack and proceeded to the cashier. I advised the kindly middle-aged lady that I would not need a bag. I then asked her if she would remove the price tag for me, which she did. Then after paying it, I put the new cap on my head and left the store for home.

My ride to and from the downtown area took me directly past old Willie's house. I recalled that I had not seen him while en route from school. Now I'd passed his house again, but still there was no sight of him. This suited me just fine, because I'd had absolutely no desire to see him. I rode onward toward our old farm. Along the way though, I gave much thought to this eventful day. Suppose I had not been successful in the execution of my self-defense efforts? I would have been physically demolished by Willie! I certainly would have been seriously injured by him. Even worse, if I had replaced my cap, I'm certain he would have taken that one also. But the most unacceptable of all these considerations, was I might not have been hugged by my teacher, Miss Cunnings.

I arrived home at my usual hour. But on this day, I arrived wearing my new cap. Mom was very happy to see that I had 'retrieved' it. As soon as she saw me she said, "Son, I thought that you might never see your cap again". I just smiled, but did not speak. Then she asked, "Where did you find it"? I told her, "One of the kids had been playing a little joke on me, but gave it back". "I'm glad." replied mom. Both dad and grand mom were also happy to see that I had recovered my cap. But most of all, I was the happiest! This had turned out to be a great and constructive day. In defeating Willie, I had gained much-needed confidence in myself and my abilities. I had also gained recognition and respect from my fellow students. These factors served to greatly elevate my self-esteem.

I then rushed through a light snack, before hurrying into the fields to help dad for a couple of hours before darkness arrived. We had begun setting small plants, such as potatoes, tomatoes, and tobacco. We had already finished planting cotton, corn, and peas. We were now in the third week of April, and the weather had improved considerably. As we worked side by side, our conversation focused mainly on the planting we were now doing. Those were the simple times. I will not say, "Those were the good old days." for although crime (at least in our area) was minimal, there existed a number of other problems which I shall not allude to. At best, I shall simply say that life back then was not nearly as complicated as it is today. We finished work for the day and retired to the house to bathe and change clothing. After our meal, I excused myself as I went into my room to do a little brushing up on some of my subjects. I knew that we would soon commence taking a series of quizzes, before our final exams began.

Prior to this year, I had not felt the need to review my subjects. But some were now considerably more difficult (especially math), so I was not taking any chances. I would not settle for more than one 'C' grade on my report card. I maintained the position that grades below 'B' were an embarrassment, and I did not wish to become embarrassed. After a couple of hours of note review, it was time for bed. As I lay in my bed, I wondered what tomorrow would bring. I also recounted the events of the day, and I realized that this had been a great day!

Another Wednesday morning had arrived. I arose and prepared myself for a new day at school. The apprehension, which I had felt the morning before had subsided. I felt relaxed and generally good about myself and my situation, although I would not lower my guard. I would remain constantly on the alert for some form of surprise attack by old Willie. I had my breakfast and prepared for my ride to school. I felt particularly good on this fine morning. I paid special attention to the blossoming flowers and trees. I also noticed the birds chirping and flying about the area. I quickly saw that this was a good morning, and I hoped that it would also be a good day for me. However, I mentally prepared myself for whatever the day might hold in store.

EXTRAORDINARY EXPERIENCES OF JAKE VAN YORK

As always, there were large numbers of kids standing about here and there in the school yard, but this morning was different. The moment I rode onto the campus, they all stopped whatever they were doing and began applauding and chanting! Many called out my name. I was completely taken aback by all of this new-found attention. Some of these applauding kids did not even know my name. But even they were shouting my name— "Jake!, Jake!, Jake"! This really made me feel great! So after securing my bicycle, I joined them. They immediately began asking me all sorts of questions. What they had wanted to know was "How was it possible that I had seemingly so easily defeated old Willie Jayes"? I just sort of shrugged my shoulders, as I smiled and said, "I guess I just got lucky". Suddenly, I was a hero— their hero! Two days ago, less than a handful of these students had even known I existed. I tried hard not to show my exuberance. Although, I must admit— this was truly a wonderful feeling! I had not seen Willie so I wondered if he'd slipped past me.

The first morning bell now sounded, so we all proceeded to our classrooms. The morning went well for me, as usual. We went through the first five classes of the day. And now, it was lunch time. At the sound of the bell, we deposited our books and other belongings into our lockers, and then went to the lunch cafeteria. But before sitting down at our regular table, I scanned the area where Willie normally sat. His seat was empty. I figured he may have relocated himself, thereby making it easier for him to mount a surprise attack. I scanned the entire cafeteria, but Willie was nowhere in sight. At this point, I was a bit perplexed— although not alarmed. As my group of four students sat chatting and eating, my friend Wilton commented, "I see old Willie's not here today". Donnie joked, "Maybe he died last night" so we all had ourselves a big laugh. This was an example of the amount of love the students generally felt for Willie.

But Willie had brought all this negative sentiment upon himself. At this point, I began to realize just how lonely he must have felt at our school. At the time, I did not know that his behavior had caused him to be here at our school. I would later discover that he had been permanently barred from entering the grounds of his previous school, where he had committed a series of violent offenses. I would later discover that on more than three occasions he had personally caused hospitalization, and serious injury to several of the students there. I would also learn that his latest incident caused severe loss of vision to one of Willie's victims, resulting in his being permanently expelled. He'd normally have been jailed for that offense; however, he escaped the region and ended up at our school, nearly one thousand miles away. I was determined that I would not allow myself to become another of his victims.

We finished our lunch and then went outside. As soon as I reached the grounds area, I stood for a moment with Carol as she asked, "Are you looking for him"? "I'm just checking— to make certain." I answered. Then we both walked toward the area where the 'famous battle' had occurred just yesterday. I remained on keen alert the entire period that we sat outside. Sitting on our bench, Carol began recounting the excitement of yesterday's action— even her voice assumed a higher pitch, evidencing her excitement. Over and over she thanked me, telling me how happy and proud she was to have me as a dear friend. Though, she did emphasize the fact that I should not, for even one moment, relax or lower my guard. I assured her that I would never become careless at any time. Finally, the bell sounded our return to class. As we stood up I again scanned the area, continually looking about as we walked together.

I arrived at Miss Cunnings' classroom at my normally appointed time. Nowhere along my path had I seen Willie Jayes. So upon entering the room I looked about, only to find that he was not present. I sat at Willie's former desk at the very back of the classroom, as our lovely teacher began her afternoon lesson to our class. I followed my usual routine of attentive note-taking. At one point during that class, I realized how relaxed the whole class seemed. Even Miss Cunnings seemed more at ease. As I sat there, I pondered this new classroom atmosphere and concluded it was because of Willie's welcomed absence. At the end of Miss Cunning's class, we all arose to leave the room. As we were leaving she looked directly at me, beckoning me to her desk. The last kid had exited the room. Now, she and I were there alone together! Unfortunately, this was as far as things went. She merely asked me if I'd seen Willie, and I told her that I had not. Then she warned me to please be extremely careful this afternoon. She added that I should be alert each day hereafter. I thanked her for her concern, saying I would be. As I was about to leave, she said, "I don't want anything to happen to you, Jake". Her words were very soft and warm, and they were uttered with a very warm smile. I wondered if I was imagining things. I decided to take a big chance, so I asked her, "No hug today"? She smiled as she stepped forward, with her arms opened and extended toward me. Now even at only fifteen, I was becoming keenly aware that boys were always supposed to be 'cool', so I feigned calmness as I stepped toward her, closing my eager arms about her soft, warm body. A myriad of erotic thoughts coursed through my young and inexperienced mind, as I held her close. Our building was totally vacated by the students, so no one saw us standing there clinging to each other (teacher and student). More than a full minute had passed, but we continued standing there while clinging to each other. This moment quickly became the most exhilarating period in my young life! In fact, those two short minutes far surpassed any of the sensations I'd experienced with my beloved Jeanne. But all too soon she released her grip on me, so I reluctantly did likewise. I did not turn and walk away though. I backed away, taking in her enchanting beauty. We both just sort of gazed hungrily at each other, as I continued to back away toward her door. I so very much wanted to blurt, "I'm madly in love with you"! But I dared not go this far. After all, there was absolutely no fraternization permitted between teacher and student! And, there was no exception whatsoever to this rigid policy! But at that moment I was confident that she knew what I'd felt for her. I also believed that she knew I had sensed her feelings toward me. So as I reached the door of her classroom, I said, "Hope you have a good evening, Miss Cunnings". She smiled in return, saying "You too, Jake".

After school, I quickly gathered all of my materials and rushed outside to await my dear Carol. As I stood there waiting, I constantly peered through the small groups moving about. I also carefully scanned the entire school grounds for any sign of Willie, but he was nowhere in sight. Still though, I needed a sentry at my rear who would serve as 'lookout' to protect my back. So, I asked my buddy Wilton if he would do this favor for me. He willingly accepted this very important challenge. Our plan was that he would lag at least fifty feet behind me, and casually stroll along as though all was normal. Then, if Willie passed him by, he would immediately commence singing our National Anthem. This would serve as my emergency notification of Willie's presence. I now felt protected.

Soon Carol showed up and we walked away from the grounds, with me pushing along my old bicycle. As we walked along chatting, I realized that I actually felt comfortable in this peculiar situation. I felt that I was in control and capable of handling whatever old Willie might throw my way. But for safe measure, I chose to look around (in particular behind me) to make sure Wilton was there and all was well. I repeated this at three-minute intervals during our brief walk to Carol's house. Each time I had looked backward, my friend Wilton was there. But old Willie never appeared. For this, I was both relieved and happy— and so was Carol. This had been a good day, and I hoped that the next day would be equally pleasant and peaceful.

At Carol's house we stood chatting in her front yard for just a few brief moments. Then I said "bye-bye" and rode away toward our old farm. As soon as I was out of view of her house, I quickened my riding pace. I knew that by walking her home, I would be five minutes late in reaching home. I got home exactly at 4:00PM. I followed my daily routine of greeting and chatting with mom and grandmother, and rushed through a light snack before heading out into the fields to work with dad. We were now nearing the end of the third week of the month of April, and the weather was perfect. Working conditions in the fields were excellent as it was not yet hot, so there were no snakes about. I was quite pleased that my day had passed free of any unpleasant incidents.

The hours of daylight had already begun to lengthen. And while I was totally appreciative for the great improvement in weather conditions, I was also a bit saddened, for this change meant that my evenings in the fields would be extended to three hours, instead of only two. It also meant that soon the dreaded multitudes of wide varieties of snakes would surface. We had managed to decimate them, but new eggs had hatched and produced replacements. Thus, we would soon be required to carry a flashlight each time we ventured outside our house in darkness. Otherwise, our chances of being bitten by some poisonous snake at night would be increased to one hundred percent. These were unfavorable odds that none of us could afford, as most snake bites would have meant almost certain death. And, since synergy played a major role within the structure of our small family, the well-being of each member was essential. Nighttime arrived, so dad and I retreated to our old house for the evening. We took turns with dad first to wash up, after which, we had our evening meal (supper) before retiring. As usual, grandmother and I retired first. This left mom and dad to themselves, to discuss the day's events and problems. I slept well through the whole night, and do not recall having had any dreams. However, had I dreamed at all, I'm certain I would have dreamed of my dear Miss Cunnings!

Now I found myself at the beginning of a new day. The morning was sunny and only mildly cool, but Buddy was outside already. When he saw me, he began running in my direction while barking frantically! Buddy ran up to me, with his shaggy tail wagging. It was obvious that he was very happy to see me. I, too, was happy to see him— since it had been awhile. We played together for about three minutes, and then I instructed him to return to his yard. He immediately obeyed my order. As Buddy trotted away from me, I yelled out to him, "I'll come by for you tomorrow". Then as if he were human, Buddy briefly turned toward me while making his distinct barking sounds. This assured me that he had clearly understood my words. I happily mounted my bicycle and rode onward to my school.

I passed Carol's house, but as we had never discussed my picking her up during morning hours, she had already left her house on foot. I rode on alone, and in another few minutes I reached my schoolyard. I secured my bicycle, and stood around mingling and conversing with the kids outside on the school grounds. Then, I saw both Donnie and Wilton chatting with Carol and two other girls, so I walked over to them. Many of the other kids there had already warmly greeted me on this special morning. Now, my three close friends also warmly greeted me. We exchanged a few pleasantries, as I thanked Wilton for his much-needed assistance yesterday afternoon. He replied, "We can do it again today", so I unhesitatingly accepted his offer!

Soon, the first bell of the morning sounded, so we all headed off to our classrooms. I still had not seen or received any comment on Willie Jayes. In fact, I had nearly forgotten that he existed. I silently admonished myself to not become lax or careless, because I knew this was not yet over! At lunch time, while standing in the serving line awaiting my food tray, I spotted Willie standing in line just a few feet ahead of me. I don't think he had seen me yet. But as we advanced through the serving line, he turned and looked in my direction. He looked directly at me, but his was a cold (even icy) stare! In return, I stood there emotionlessly as I glared back at him! We both continued our exchange of menacing stares and glares until he had received his food tray. Then he moved on to his usual table.

My three friends and I sat at our usual table and made small talk, laughing and joking. I sat facing away from old Willie, so I could not observe his actions. I considered this a psychological ploy. I wanted him to feel that I'd totally disregarded his existence. But all the while, both Donnie and Wilton kept him in their line of vision. They constantly advised me as to each move he made. Thusly, it was as though I had been all the while looking directly at him myself. Willie continued sitting there not saying much, just eating his meal. I inwardly struggled to control my thoughts and emotions. Then when my friends and I finished our meal, we prepared to move outside onto the school grounds.

Once outside, Carol and I headed for our regular bench. Donnie and Wilton remained several yards behind us while keeping an eye open for Willie. He had not chosen to approach us as of yet, so we took our seats, trying to act normal. I carefully searched the school grounds visually, but I saw Willie nowhere. Although I had not seen him leave the cafeteria, I felt certain that he must have been sneaking around somewhere outside at this very moment. Less than five minutes had passed, when I noticed a crowd of students gathered about fifty yards from where we both sat. The crowd was so dense, I could not see what was going on, but I knew that something had gone wrong! I decided to walk over to check out the action, so I walked cautiously in the direction of the commotion. As soon as I neared the gathering, I saw Willie wrestling with another boy who was slightly larger than he. I immediately called out Willie's name! Then while still holding the boy down, he looked briefly in my direction. The boy continued to struggle, but to no avail. I said to Willie, "If you fight him, you're gonna have to fight me also". This seemed to enrage him! I had been speaking to him from a distance of about twelve feet, as he quickly released his grip on the other boy and jumped to his feet. He immediately lunged toward me—but it was already too late! He had succeeded in taking only two forward steps, but I had already prepared for his attack! This time, I did not side-step. Instead, I sprang straight forward and into old Willie. At a distance of three feet away, I lifted slightly from the ground, burying the toe of my right shoe again into his already very sore midsection! I had aimed my strike for the exact same belly location of two days before. I felt certain that his belly would have still been extremely sensitive from my previous attack. I had been correct! Willie immediately fell onto one knee, his face contorted, while groaning loudly! He did not attempt to stand, but instead toppled to the ground! This all had happened in a flash, but it was over before it had even gotten started. All the students crowded about us, and again began wildly applauding and chanting. Willie lay there in the dirt, but not a single student offered to help him up from the ground.

I decided to become the good guy for a change, so I

walked over to him and extended my hand. Willie did not grasp my extended hand; he merely looked up at me with bewilderment, as pain showed upon his face. I backed away to a point about ten feet from where he lay. Then, in a cold and calculated voice, I said, "If you don't get up right now, I'm gonna kick your sorry ass until you can't get up"! Upon hearing my threatening comments, Willie slowly began struggling to his feet. Still, no one offered to help— but neither did I.

The bell had sounded so we all began walking toward our classrooms. I maintained a short distance behind Willie (for safe measure). Today, I escorted him directly to the classroom. We entered Miss Cunnings' room, with me on his heels. She took note of this, but did not comment. When we had reached the desk I had given him, he obediently sat down. This time, it was not necessary for me to direct him to sit. *"Maybe this clown is trainable after all!"* I thought. I was proud of my second successful battle with this abhorrent individual! As I sat there behind Willie, I silently thanked good old Mr. Lim for his kindness and patience with me. I also remembered my vow to Carol, Miss Cunnings, and myself, that I would not become careless in this most volatile situation involving Willie Jayes.

Miss Cunnings greeted us, "Good afternoon, class". For some reason, she seemed to have looked directly at Willie as she spoke. As usual, all of the students (with the exception of Willie) chimed in "Good afternoon, Miss Cunnings". She noticed Willie's lack of response, so she addressed him directly, "Good afternoon, Willie". At this point, he sort of mumbled, "Good afternoon, Miss Cunnings". But then, just as she'd begun the lesson of the day, our school principal appeared in her doorway. He made one slight gesture with his hand, summoning her to him. She immediately stopped the lesson, and walked briskly toward him. The two walked out into the long hallway where they began talking inaudibly. After a couple of minutes, Miss Cunnings peered into our classroom, beckoning me to her. I thought, *"Aw shucks, I must really be in serious trouble now"!* I knew that I was being summoned as a result of today's incident with Willie. Although, they had not summoned him— only me. I found this to be quite strange.

As soon as I reached the hallway, Miss Cunnings calmly remarked, "Jake, our principal would like for you to accompany him to his office." She did not seem overly concerned, so I walked with him from our building to the next building where his office stood. I did not sense any degree of tension. The two of us simply walked along, chatting about our upcoming May Day event. Soon we reached his office, where he offered me a seat. As I sat down, he said to me, "Young man, I've been advised that you were recently involved in two altercations with student Willie Jayes". I began to defend my actions, but he raised his hand to silence me. Our principal was a huge man, 6'4" and weighing 265 pounds, so I felt slightly intimidated in his presence. I believe he must have felt my apprehension, because he continued speaking softly to me. "I'm also advised that you are one of my few model students," and with these words, he smiled at me. I felt a bit more at ease at this point. He added, "Relax, you're not in any trouble". I was now very much relieved!

My principal continued. "I've just learned that this Willie Jayes is a very dangerous individual". "So, I am going to tell you what I've learned about him, but you must promise me that you'll keep this just between the two of us". I agreed to his terms, because I was curious and concerned about Willie. Then our principal began relating to me the information contained in a newly released bulletin issued by the police department of New York City. He said, "Of course you realize that I am not at liberty to show this document to you— however, I will read it to you". He read the details of four separate incidents of violence. Each incident had been initiated by Willie himself, and each of these incidents had ended very badly for his victims. It seems that his last offense had ended with the near-death of one student. At the time of this incident, Willie was sixteen years of age. Ordinarily, he would have been placed in juvenile detention somewhere within the state of New York. But he had secretly and quickly left that state, seeking refuge in South Carolina with his grand mom. He had an outstanding warrant issued against him. Our principal finished by saying, "So there— you have it— this is the type of person we're dealing with". "I feel that it's my personal responsibility to appraise you of the situation here, to warn you". "I know that it's my duty to turn him in to the authorities". "But I know that in doing so, I would be killing his poor grandmother— and I don't want that on my conscience". "I really wish that there were some other way of ridding ourselves of this problem". Our principal then arose from his seat, so I followed his lead by standing also. "Be careful," he warned! I graciously thanked our principal for his concern, assuring him that I would definitely keep my guard up. I was excused and allowed return to class. My meeting with the principal had lasted nearly twenty minutes, which meant that I would need to work quickly to make up the notes I had already missed.

As I entered my classroom, all eyes were upon me—especially the eyes of old Willie Jayes. Without looking directly at him, I walked past his desk and took my seat immediately behind him. I then promptly began copying down the notes Miss Cunnings had placed upon the board. At the time, I did not realize that she had written these notes particularly for my benefit. While I sat there hurriedly copying my notes, I occasionally glanced up at old Willie. I wanted to keep myself fully abreast of his actions and demeanor. I noticed that he'd sat there like a statue. But this was his usual manner of sitting while in class, so I simply could not read anything into this particular situation. I would simply apply my 'wait and see' tactics.

When the bell rang, I was one of the last to leave the room. As I began to walk forward (behind Willie), I looked in Miss Cunnings' direction. She was sitting at her desk, but she'd made eye contact with me. So, I purposely lingered behind the other students. Then when the last student had departed the room, I approached her desk. She look up at me saying, "Yes, Jake"? I responded, "Is there anything that you'd like to say to me, Miss Cunnings"? She answered, "We've already talked about this, but I will say it again— be careful"! "I just have this strong premonition that he intends to mount some sort of vicious attack against you". "Miss Cunnings, I'm being as cautious as possible— so try not to worry about me." I replied. "Just don't forget to do so," she admonished.

I thanked her for her concern before turning to walk away. But before I had reached her door she called out to me. I turned around to find that she had arisen from her desk and was now walking slowly toward me. I continued to maintain my position, and did not move toward her. I considered my actions as being 'cool'. Now, she stood directly in front of me! I felt my heart rate quicken, as I stood there before her. Then she smiled and said, "What— no hug today"? Of course, I did not need further encouragement! I encircled my arms about her body, pulling her close to me. She responded in kind, and we stood there for a brief, but precious moment! Then, we simultaneously released our grip on each other. "Take good care of yourself," she quietly said to me as I walked from her classroom. I wanted so very badly to blow her a kiss as I left. But even at only age fifteen, I fully realized that I simply could not afford to allow myself to become presumptuous, in my interaction with my irresistible young teacher!

Once outside, I located both Donnie and Wilton. I then partially briefed the both of them as to the seriousness of this situation with Willie Jayes. They were each shocked at this news, and wanted to know how they could help me. I told them the best way they could help would be to keep a close watch over those areas behind my back. I also told them this information was highly sensitive, and that we would be in serious trouble if we ever mentioned any of this to anyone. They each assured me of their silence. Soon Carol showed up, and she and I began to walk away from the school grounds. I tried to remain low-keyed as I voiced concern over Willie. She wholeheartedly agreed that I should remain constantly on guard, for any potential attack by him. Both dad and Mr. Lim had trained me to always remain prepared for any contingency, so as usual, I positioned Carol to my right side. I always walked next to her, keeping my bicycle to my left as I guided with my left hand. Donnie and Wilton followed inconspicuously several yards behind.

It was a sunny and mildly warm afternoon. The asphalt street was virtually free of all vehicular traffic, so the street seemingly belonged to us students. Our school accommodated nearly 1,000 students. One-fourth of those walked this street twice daily. So on this particular afternoon, there were well over 200 students walking together in small groups. There were rarely any fights or disturbances because neither the school nor the parents, would tolerate such behavior. So on the surface all seemed quite peaceful. Unfortunately, this obviously peaceful environment was soon to change!

We had walked only one block, but I had already looked over my shoulder four separate times in search of Willie. Each time I checked, all was quiet, and Donnie and Wilton were both there behind us. Still, I did not feel comfortable with this situation. I felt that something dreadful was about to occur! A few feet ahead of us sat a middle-aged lady on her front porch. She had been knitting, but she peered down the street behind us and suddenly stood up, yelling, "Watch out"! At that very same moment, Donnie and Wilton yelled, "Jake"! Without even looking around, I quickly ducked low as I lunged to my right, and shoved Carol to safety. At the same instant I released my bicycle, letting it fall to my left. But during the time this was happening, I felt a strong rush of air pass just inches above my now lowered head! While still in this bent position, I strained to see the street ahead in an effort to learn what had just happened.

There, about twenty feet directly in front of me, was Willie! He sat upon a bicycle, holding a length of steel piping in his right hand! He appeared both disappointed, and angry at himself for having failed in his latest attempt!

I realized the rush of air I'd felt had been caused by the steel pipe! Willie had aimed this pipe for my head, and had I not quickly ducked, he would have connected! I would now have been lying upon the street before him, unconscious, or maybe even in worse condition! I immediately saw that he had begun to dismount from his stolen bicycle. I knew that he intended to attack me with that eighteen-inch piece of steel pipe that he held in his right hand! But I would not allow him the needed time! I rushed straight toward him, reaching him just as he'd managed to plant both feet onto the ground! I knew that he expected me to begin punching him, but this was not my plan. Willie started to raise the pipe, but as he did so I grabbed his right wrist, forcing it into a vertical position! Immediately, I then pivoted to my left, effectively twisting his arm forty-five degrees to his right. He was now off-balance, which was exactly what I'd wanted.

Mr. Lim had taught me a number of ways to keep my opponent off-balance, and this technique was merely one of many. The theory of this principle was –that an off-balanced opponent is an ineffective one! I positioned Willie's arm so that—when parallel to the ground,— the palm was up and the elbow downward. This was precisely what I wanted! He was unable to extricate himself from the bicycle. In this way, I had kept him off-balance, and unable to move freely. This was my moment! I took one quick step backward! As I did so, I quickly slammed downward his outstretched arm! Then halfway through this maneuver I lifted slightly into the air, but in a split-second, I had returned to the ground! This maneuver proved most unpleasant for Willie! It was also one that he would most likely never forget! For in my rapid descent, I'd completely disconnected his arm at the elbow, having slammed his inverted arm forcefully onto the wishbone frame of his stolen bicycle. The steel pipe dropped from his limp hand onto the street below. He immediately began to yell and scream! His body began to convulse and writhe with pain! He presently was probably more helpless than ever before in his wretched lifetime! Comparatively speaking, old Willie was now in round ten of a ten-round fight. However, I was only at the beginning of round one of this very same fight!

I recalled the somber message of my principal: We were all in constant danger with fugitive Willie present. It was quite obvious that our student body would be much safer with Willie's removal. Therefore, my plan was to execute our principal's desire. I could see that Willie was in no condition to mount any form of attack. In fact, he was now completely defenseless, but I would show him no mercy! I momentarily released his arm. He stood bent forward, attempting to steady himself by placing his only functioning hand onto his left knee. I shall never know exactly what coursed through his mind at that moment— but neither did I care. I shoved the bicycle from between us. A throng of students had quickly crowded around us. All were chanting, "Get him, Jake"! The poor lady stood on her porch, yelling, "Y'all stop that— you hear me"! I paused to look at her, saying "Ma'am, he just tried to kill me— you saw it"! She shrugged her shoulders, threw up her hands, and returned into her small house, closing the door behind herself.

It was still too early for the teachers to begin passing by, and no cars were in this area. I peered in both directions up and down the street, but I only saw crowds of students. Most had not discovered what was happening. I thought about my poor family, in case I had been struck by Willie. It would have been an unbearable situation. I thought about the poor student back in New York, realizing that he would never know a normal life! Finally, I thought about my cherished new silk baseball cap, which old Willie had so brazenly taken from me. Lastly, I remembered Willie's attitude when I had asked that he return it to me. I looked at his contorted form, as he stood there groaning. I picked up the steel pipe he had recently wielded at me. I struggled not to become enraged toward him for his actions. But even so, I'd felt incensed! I then took three short steps to where Willie stood. He remained bent forward, as I surveyed his facial expression. Needless to say, I did not like what I saw. Then without speaking, I stepped to his rear. I raised the steel pipe high into the air, and brought it crushing down onto his curved back! He yelled loudly, as he tried to move away! But two of the students in the crowd shoved him backward towards me. He groaned and writhed in pain even more— and with good reason! I knew that he would not be able to stand upright. Presently, he was no longer a menace— and I wanted to keep it this way. I began talking to him as the crowd continued chanting, "Get him"! I said, "Look around, Willie, everyone here wants you dead, so why should I let you live"?

While still bent forward, Willie raised his head to look

up at me, but he did not speak. I was not sure that I had understood the expression on his face. At that moment, I recalled my policy concerning battling poisonous snakes—. Basically, any snake remains deadly until it is dead! I had no intention of killing Willie, but I wanted him to believe that I did. Then I remembered more of Mr. Lim's teaching philosophy. "Strike a brick wall in the exact same spot continuously, and eventually it will begin to crumble and fall". He'd taught me to use this same philosophy with an opponent. I said to him again, "Willie, tell me why I should let you live". Still, he did not respond to my comment. For a second time, I stepped to his rear and raised the steel pipe, though he did not utter a word. I aimed the pipe for the very same spot, midway along his back. This time, I brought it down with even greater force! Once again, he yelled loudly! But this time, he stumbled forward a bit. Now, I instinctively knew that his tormented body was beginning to weaken. His groans became more frequent and pronounced. Still clutching the pipe, I walked back to the left of his head. He still refused to speak, so I bent slightly over him as I spoke once more. "Willie, you don't have to answer me— I'll just stand here and beat you until you speak or die!" I said. I then placed my left hand beneath his chin, raising his head. "Do you understand me?" I growled. Still, I received no answer from Willie, so I abruptly released his chin, allowing his head to drop forward. The crowd continued chanting, "Get him"! Ten minutes had passed, and I was running short of time. Again, I walked around behind him. I raised the steel pipe once more, but paused. I tried scaring him by saying, "Okay, Willie— this was your choice. When I start beating you this time, I won't stop until your sorry ass is dead"! I know the police are searching you, so when I kill you, I'll be doing them a big favor"! I stepped forward, feigning another strike. This time he responded! Willie's response was weak and barely audible, but I was certain that I had heard him speak. I paused and then asked, "What did you say?" "Please"! "Please what?" I asked. "Please don't kill me!" he pleaded.

I repeat—I had absolutely no intention of killing Willie. I simply wanted him to feel that I would not hesitate to do so. I also wanted him to know that we were all aware of his fugitive status, and now we were all harboring him. Then I gently helped him to stand upright. I guided and aided him, and even helped him to sit. But his left arm was still removed from its joint. The crowd of chanters suddenly became quiet. I then said to one of the boys, "Go across the street and ask the lady there if she would give us a glass of water for our friend Willie." The boy looked at me as if I were crazy! "Go!" I shouted to him, so he scampered away. Shortly, he returned with the water, which I gave to Willie to drink. Now, I too was in round nine of this ten-round fight. While Willie sat there gulping the water, I took the stolen bicycle across the street to the same lady's house for safekeeping. The kids started to disburse because the action had subsided.

Round ten: I had Donnie and Wilton place Willie onto the back of my bicycle and I rode with him the short distance to the office of our family doctor. Twenty minutes had passed since I had left the school grounds. I asked Wilton to walk Carol the rest of the way home. Luckily for us, the doctor was in his office. This was the same great doctor Johnson who had treated me from infancy. He promptly and expertly checked and reset Willie's dislocated arm. Then, he began to check for other injuries. It was now 3:30PM, and I needed to be at home by 4:00. I inquired about Willie's condition. Dr. Johnson responded "I'm sure that he'll be just fine in a few days. His answer made me feel a bit better. I then asked Willie if he would be able to walk the four-block distance to his home. Finally, the two of us were on minimal speaking terms. Willie answered "Yes," so I said to him, "I hope you feel better real soon". Then surprisingly, he thanked me for helping him reach the doctor's office. I then bade both Dr. Johnson and Willie good afternoon. In a sense, this had been anything but a good afternoon. But on the other hand, it had turned out surprisingly well! But I was out of time! I would need to be at home in less than thirty minutes. So I quickly hopped onto my old bicycle and then rode at full speed for the next twenty-five minutes!

I was presently in full view of our old house, so I slowed to a normal riding pace. I did not want to arouse the suspicion of my parents, by allowing them to see me riding at such a high rate of speed. I realized that I had completely made up for my lost time, so I rode the rest of the distance at my normal speed. I checked my watch as I rode into our yard. The time was exactly 3:58PM. I found that I was not tired— or even winded. Neither, was I bruised or injured in any way. This had really been a great day! I gulped down a quick snack, accompanied by large amounts of water along with a glass of cool lemonade. (Notice that I did not say cold lemonade). Remember, we had no ice or refrigerator. But even so, my lemonade was delicious and soothing!

Having finished my snack, I rushed out into the fields.

Dad and I accomplished a lot of work that afternoon. But we each worked in separate fields, so this was somewhat of a blessing for me. By working alone, I was free to express my emotions without creating undue attention. So as I continued to work that warm afternoon, I reflected upon the events of the day. First, I had successfully defeated my great enemy twice on the same day. Second, I had done this without receiving the slightest injury. Third, and probably most important of all, I had at least neutralized my foe! I pondered this last consideration; and as I did so, the thought occurred to me: *'Why not try to make Willie a friend'?* At this point, I began formulating a simple plan based on the words of my wise old grandmother, who had often said to me, "Son, always treat others as you would have them treat you".

Accordingly, I decided I would try this philosophy on Willie and await its results. Slowly though these thoughts faded from my mind, as I mentally returned to the fields. Surprisingly even as I worked, these thoughts of kindness and consideration continually resurfaced in my young mind. Finally, the end of our work day arrived and for that I was very thankful. This had been a busy day! Dad and I retired to the house to begin our difficult clean-up process. When this was finished, we sat down to eat.

In those days, ordinary working folk did not talk much while at the table. Instead, we would wait until after we had finished eating to engage in conversation. So afterward, we sat around discussing the highlights and progress of our week. Grandmother spoke first. "I weeded half of the south field, and I finished sewing my new dress". Now don't forget, we're talking about an old lady who had now reached the ripe old age of ninety-eight! As I sat there listening to her I thought, *"What an accomplishment"!* Then mom took her turn "I finally finished the last of the four fields this evening". Next, dad chimed in with a long list of field work that he had completed. Now, came my turn to speak. I thought about what I would say about my week. I then said, "I learned a lot at school this week, and it all ended well". Mom added, "I see that nobody took your hat this week". Then with a slight smile on my face, I replied, "No, not a soul". Shortly afterward, I excused myself and retired to bed. I had begun to feel a bit tired so I slept soundly throughout the entire night. When morning arrived I realized I had not had a single dream— not even a nightmare. This had been a good week, but I was glad to see its end!

Another Saturday morning was upon us. Dad was always the first to reach the fields, but on this morning, I had awakened along with him. Today I could have lain in bed for an extra hour, but I'd felt so rejuvenated, I sprang out of bed and quickly washed up also. Soon, I joined dad, reaching the fields at the very same time. He was quite surprised by my early rise, and it showed on his face, but he made no comment. I suppose he figured that I must have wanted something special. I figured that he was playing a waiting game with me. We worked from 5:00AM to 10:00AM, then took a thirty-minute break. We reentered the fields at 10:30AM, working continuously until 2:00PM that afternoon. During this time period, I purposely did not ask about dad's plans for the late afternoon. Though I must say that during this time, anxiety had nearly gotten the best of me. Actually, I had been dying to ask dad if I might use the bicycle this afternoon. I supposed he must have read my mind, because as the two of us were washing up, he asked, "Son, are you riding into town today"?

I so desperately wanted to say yes to his question, but I answered him indifferently, "If you don't need the bike, I'd like to". He then generously answered, "Then, might I hitch a ride with you"? I had been flattered by his calm answer, so I said, "Certainly you may". I recalled that I had not mentioned anything to my dear Carol about going to the movies today. I realized that I did not have any idea as to whether she even wished to see a movie. I figured that she probably would, but this presented a slight problem. For at only age fifteen, I could not afford to have dad learn that I had taken a girl to the movies (how truly naïve I had been). I knew I would need to juggle my schedule, in case Carol wanted to accompany me. So I asked dad if we might leave for downtown about thirty minutes earlier than usual. He agreed with my unusual request. Then at the agreed-upon time, he and I hopped onto 'Old Faithful' and rode toward town.

This time, I pedaled— but only after my strong insistence that I be allowed to do so. I won him by saying, "Dad, you could use the rest— so sit back and relax"? Dad wholeheartedly agreed with my position. We were now nearing the end of April, and this was a typically warm and sunny day. As I pedaled along, I realized that I would need to slightly alter my route to avoid Carol's house. I successfully made my route change before dropping dad off at my Aunt Emma's house. I remained with them for about fifteen minutes, while we chatted and drank cold lemonade. Aunt Emma was fortunate to have had a refrigerator with ice. She also had electricity, running water, and a bathroom. I could not help thinking, *"How could their two lives be so absolutely different and apart"?* Though they were not, she and dad appeared to be identical twins. Other than the fact that she was a woman, they each possessed similar features. My aunt's house was comfortable and well-maintained. It was also in a very nice neighborhood. I must state here though, that most of the neighborhoods in my hometown were decent and peaceful. Naturally, there were absolutely no gangs present! Loitering was not tolerated, so no one stood about holding signs reading "WILL WORK FOR FOOD". And, to make matters even better, whenever we would exit a store, there was no one standing outside asking, "Got some change"? There definitely were some serious problems back then; but, many of those very same problems still exist today.

I prepared to make my exit, and thanked Aunt Emma for her hospitality, before asking dad about our departure time for our ride home. He surprised me by saying, "You go ahead, son—I'll hitch a ride home". I asked, "Are you sure, dad"? He replied, "Yes, you go on home when you're ready— I'll be there soon too." I'd thought this was quite strange, but I did not comment further. In fact, I was somewhat relieved to learn that I would not need to juggle my return ride home.

As the hour neared 3:45PM I quickly hopped onto my bicycle, speeding away toward Carol's house. I knew that if we were going to make it to the movies, we would need to hurry. But I still did not know if we were even going to a movie. As I rounded the corner to Carol's house, I saw her sitting on her front porch, peering down the street, which was in the opposite direction of my current approach. She had, in fact, been peering in the direction from which I usually arrived, so she had not seen me riding down the street. I rode quietly as I did not wish to alert her. I wanted to surprise her—and I really achieved my goal! The expression on her face was one of shock, joy, and relief! I had really given her a big surprise! Carol excitedly exclaimed, "Jake"! I could see that she was happy to see me, even though she tried had to conceal her emotions. Heck, I was happy to see her too! She had already dressed, but I asked anyway— "Are we going"? "I'm ready," she said, as she ran down her steps. Then she yelled to her mother, who was inside their house. "Mom, I'm leaving now!" to which, her mother replied, "You all be careful, you hear"? This was the way many in the south talked back then. We reached the movie theater just in time to purchase our popcorn and sodas.

We sat through the cartoons, holding hands and stealing glances at each other. I already knew that many of the older boys had followed the custom of marrying their childhood sweet-hearts after graduating from high school. I began wondering where this casual, but warm relationship with Carol was heading. Then, the main feature flashed onto the screen, which shocked me back to my senses. We continued holding hands as we sat enjoying the movie together. I found I was very happy with having Carol at my side. I knew that this was a very nice girl, in every aspect of her character. She was very cute, sweet, intelligent, poised, and very much a lady! What more could any young boy have wished for in a companion? As inexperienced as I was at the time, I realized even then she was the near perfect mate. I also realized how truly fortunate I was by having known her.

Our movie had ended, and we were again outside the theater. But before leaving, I asked Carol if she would like to accompany me to Willie's house to check on him. Naturally she declined. But she showed considerable surprise at my statement, by asking "Jake, you would do that"? I told her I felt that this might be a good thing to do. She did not disagree, so I took her by the hand as we briefly returned to the theater. I walked to the counter, where I purchased a bag of popcorn, along with a soda. Then we left the theater, and rode to her house on my bicycle. I remained there with her for a few minutes and then said "bye-bye before riding the short distance to Willie's house. I saw no one as I rode into his yard, so I dismounted from my bicycle and walked up onto the porch. The inner front door stood open, with only the outer screen closed. I stood there momentarily listening for sounds. I heard no movement or sound from inside, so I called out, "Anyone home"? At first, there was no response. I repeated my call, but this time just a bit louder. Then after some slight hesitation, I heard Willie's voice calling out from the rear room of their house. "Yeah" was all he said. "Willie, this is Jake – may I come in?" I asked. "The door's not locked," he responded.

I then cautiously entered the house, not knowing what to expect. I was certain that he would be physically unable to attack me. I also felt confident that his dear old grandmother (a friend of my grandmother's) would not have any allowed guns inside her home. However, still there was another possibility. Willie may have quickly grabbed a baseball bat, and was now holding it with his left hand. I knew that he was right handed, so wielding a bat with his left hand would have been quite awkward for him. So

I decided to 'feel him out' by talking to him, as I slowly walked toward his room. "Where're you at?" I asked. He responded immediately, saying "I'm here in my bed". I felt a bit comforted by his seemingly reasonable response, but I still remained alert. Presently, I stood at Willie's door — peering inside. There he lay, perched upon his plain single bed. His right arm had been placed into a cast-like, specially designed sling. I stepped into his room, and to his bed. "How are you feeling today?" I asked. "I feel pretty good," he answered. Willie then eyed the bag of popcorn, as a big grin appeared on his face. "I brought you a little something," I said, handing him the bag. Still grinning, he graciously took the bag. I held onto the soft drink because I realized that he could not handle both at the same time. Willie opened the bag of popcorn and instantly began munching on it. I then removed the top from the plastic cup before placing it upon his nightstand. "Thank you, Jake," he said. "Grab yourself a chair" he added. I accepted his offer, so I fetched myself a chair from their small kitchen. Upon returning I asked, "Where is your grandmother"? "She's next door — I think she got tired of me." he said. I smiled, saying "Shame on you, Willie — you know that your sweet grandmother would never become tired of you, for she loves you so very much"! Those words seemed to cheer him up, as his grin instantly became even broader. I then changed the subject by asking him, "How long will you need to wear this sling"? "The doctor says I might have to wear it for at least two weeks" he replied. "That's a long time," I said. "Yes, it is" he answered. "Does your arm hurt?" I asked. "It only hurts when I try to move it," he answered. "I'm glad to hear that — I'm just sorry it happened", I said. "I'm sorry too, Jake." said Willie.

I did not perceive that his words were meant as an apology. At that moment, I interpreted his words to merely mean— he regretted having ended up with his arm in a sling! So, I asked pointedly, "Just what is it that you're sorry about, Willie"? "I'm sorry about the whole thing," he answered. "Then why did you do that – do you know you could have killed me," I asked. "I know – but I don't know why I did it," he replied, adding, "I guess I was just real angry". "But, until you started this, I had never done anything to harm you," I said. "And until you started this, I had never done anything to irk you," I added. "I know," he said. Now even at my young age, I had begun to apply the principle of psychology here. I said "We know about your past, at your last school. And we know about your terrible behavior here at our school. You must know that if you keep this up, somebody really is going to kill you." He sat pensively for a moment, and then added, "I want to do good— but I've got a lot of bad stuff on my mind." "What sort of stuff?" I queried him. "Just some bad stuff." he answered. I realized that he did not wish to discuss his personal problems with me, so I did not press the issue any further. I decided to change the subject. "Willie, do you play any sports?" I asked. His eyes seemed to light up, as he said, "I play baseball and softball, but football is my favorite game". Willie seemed to feel a twinge of excitement, as he spoke those words. I recalled having seen him throwing football passes during lunch period. I also recalled that he really threw an awesome pass! So I asked, "Were you on any of the teams at your last school"? Willie answered "Well, I played shortstop in baseball – outfield in softball. I also played quarterback on our football team, and I played well." "That's great," I said. "Are you going to play here at our school?" I asked. "If my arm heals okay, I'm going to try out for football and baseball" Willie responded. "I'm sure your arm will be just great, long before next season," I added. "I certainly hope so" he replied. I had been sitting with Willie for nearly a half-hour, and it was nearing time for me to get out of there and head home. I had quite a bit of riding to do, so I excused myself.

I briefly stopped by Carol's house to let her know that my visit had gone well. She was happy to hear the good news! She also complimented me for having the courage and personal interest to do so. I thanked Carol for her kind words, as I climbed onto my old bicycle. I arrived home at exactly 6:30PM. Then after chatting briefly with mom and grand mom, I went out to the barn, where I bridled and saddled my horse. I knew that I would only have about an hour and a half of riding time, before darkness set in, so I headed straight for my pal Buddy's house. It seemed that he was able to understand time, because he had been sitting in his yard waiting for me. We said our greetings before heading off toward the forests. I put my horse Belle through her paces by letting her run at will. I had become a skilled rider, so I was no longer concerned about the possibility of a spill. But Buddy was unable to keep pace with us, so it was necessary for me to frequently turn back to fetch him. I even rode past Mr. Lim's little house. I wanted to show him that my concern for his well-being was founded in more than just what he could do for me. I spent about fifteen minutes conversing with him. I'd found that he was always happy to see me. Maybe, this was partly because I meant companionship to him. On the other hand, maybe he was simply a lonely and aging man. But no matter what his reasons, we had always gotten along well together. I believe this was primarily because I had always shown him proper respect. I also had shown a personal interest in him as a person. And in return, he had always treated me (a kid) kindly. But now my riding time was rapidly drawing near its end. So I bade farewell to Mr. Lim after confirming my training schedule for the next day. As I rode toward home I dropped Buddy off at his place, arriving home at 8:00PM.

Grandmother had already eaten, but mom had been waiting to eat with me. So I quickly changed into more casual dress and we sat down to eat. We mostly discussed rapidly improving weather conditions; but, we also talked about the way our week had gone. Mom focused on the great amount of field work that she had personally accomplished. Then she expressed her hopes for fruitful crops, during this approaching summer. Now, came my time to speak. My week had been filled with danger and excitement; but I could only comment on school, so this was what I talked to her about. At the end of my brief report, mom complimented me on my excellent academic achievement.

Darkness had just set upon us, but both mom and I continued on our front porch talking. So there we were— one middle-aged lady, and one teenaged boy— sitting outside in total darkness. But neither of us was the least bit afraid. Though there was no dog present, we felt completely comfortable in our serene surroundings. We felt no need for apprehension. As we continued sitting there in darkness on our old rickety porch, we detected the sound of some mechanical engine in the far distance. It sounded like an approaching tractor. Here, most families in the area operated at least two tractors (although, this latter statement does not apply to my family). We only utilized two mules in accomplishing our necessary farm work. Anyway, mom and I both felt that this somewhat obnoxious sound was being caused by some old farmer in the area, moving from one location to another, so we continued to sit there and relaxing. The sound of this machine continued its advance toward our location, but still there was no reason for concern. Finally, we began to discern what appeared to be a faint pair of headlights in close proximity to each other, very similar to those of a tractor. We knew though that this was a bit strange, for tractors never passed our house on Saturday nights. The faint yellow lights continued slowly moving in our direction, and the sound grew louder, but we remained sitting on our old porch. We paid no particular attention to this abnormality, but still sat talking about trivial matters— while laughing and joking. Now when we had first heard this sound, we estimated it to be about one mile away. But when we finally saw these lights, we instantly knew that this old 'tractor' was slightly more than three-quarters of a mile away.

Farmers are able to judge long distances simply through visualization, and similarly, they are able to determine the time of day merely by peering up at the sun. Nearly any person can develop these skills by having lived in some remote, sparsely populated area for extended periods of time. My entire family possessed these skills. We were accomplished natural judges of distance. Those lights were still faint; although, the sound of this 'tractor' had become highly audible (to say the least). Then as it approached the long and narrow little access road up to our house, it slowed a bit. It had been traveling at about fifteen miles per hour, so deceleration was not necessary, for it to execute ninety-degree turns. The vehicle turned onto the little road that led up to our old farmhouse, which stood on one slightly elevated parcel of land. But even though this elevation was ever so slight, this old 'tractor' struggled desperately to navigate this nearly imperceptible incline. It coughed and sputtered as it slowly ascended the narrow dirt road. Mom was the first to speak. "Jake, I wonder what in the world is that thing?" she exclaimed. "Well, judging by its lights and sound, it's got to be somebody coming by on a tractor" I said. After a few minutes, the vehicle finally conquered its great obstacle by reaching our yard. There was no moonlight at this time, so it was totally dark outside (with the exception of this machine's faint headlights). Surprisingly, it honked at us as it drove through our front yard and around to the side of our old house. Finally, mom and I discovered that this 'thing' was not a tractor! But if this was not a tractor, then just what in the heck was it?

Then, dad called out to us. We immediately recognized the sound of his voice, so we relaxed a bit. But now, curiosity had gotten the better of us. We stepped from our porch, and rushed around the side of our old house to where dad awaited us. Mom had always called dad "Clay," and he had called her "Sis"— as had my Uncle Abe. So mom said to dad, "Clay, what is this"? Dad just laughed, saying, "I brought you and young Jake a little present." There was complete darkness about our yard, so dad fetched a flashlight. He then shined his light upon this old machine. Both mom and I stood there peering at it, but we were still uncertain as to exactly what this old contraption was. I took a very bold step by asking, dad "Is this a car"? "Yep, son – it's a car" he answered"! "Wow" I said, feigning excitement. Fifteen years earlier this had been a new 1939 Chevrolet, four-door sedan. But, that had been a very long time ago.

As I stood viewing this machine, I began to earnestly wonder "How much worse my life could become?" for, this was really the pits! Then dad said, "We really can't see it out here in the dark, so why don't we go inside, and I'll take you all for a ride tomorrow". We agreed, so we went inside. Grandmother had already gone to bed, and I prepared to do likewise. I excused myself and lay down to read comic books, in the semi-darkness of my old kerosene lamp-lighted small room. During those days, I rarely experienced nightmares. But on this particular night, I would have several of them. Each of my bad dreams that night was about being chased by some great angry monster! When I awoke next morning, I was truly relieved to have awakened.

Early on Sunday morning (about 7:00AM) I found myself startled awake! In my state of semi- sleep, I thought I had heard the sound of army tanks and loud gunfire! At first, I wondered if we were being invaded by some enemy nation! The noise was almost deafening, and the sound of 'gunfire' was very frightening! This was especially true, considering that our Sunday mornings were always quiet and peaceful. I hurriedly threw on an old pair of pants, and rushed out of my small bedroom. Dad had always kept a .12 gauge shotgun in his room, so I grabbed the gun, along with a few shells. I quickly loaded it and rushed outside. But as soon as I stepped out onto our rear porch, I became both relieved and embarrassed. There was dad inside this old machine, that only he would consider a car. As soon as he saw me, he waved and gave me a big grin. I quickly unloaded the shotgun and returned it to dad's room. Then I washed up and went outside to observe the 'show'.

I soon discovered that dad been testing this old contraption. I've searched extensively for a suitable adjective to describe this old machine, but unfortunately, all have eluded me. What I can say here is— this old piece of metal totally failed to meet the criteria for an automobile. But dad had bought this old jalopy— and now we were stuck with it. Truthfully speaking, I found this to be an embarrassment. Though, I most certainly could not say these words to dad. Hence, we would all just have to grin— and bear it!

I had not yet learned to drive, though as a young child I had experienced the feel of a good automobile. But in listening to this old machine, I knew beyond a doubt that this heap was ready for the graveyard! Then a thought occurred to me— maybe dad had, in fact, retrieved it from some 'automobile graveyard'. I would soon learn the true condition of this very old 'car' (a term I use loosely). First, it had no brakes. So when it was in motion, and the brake pedal depressed, the pedal lowered to the floor— but the 'car' kept rolling. Second, its steering mechanism had been wired together with coat hangers. This meant that this old 'car' was completely unsafe! Third, its old engine was so badly worn it had lost more than fifty percent of its compression. Fourth, its electrical wiring was faulty— making this a serious fire hazard and, the list goes on! Ironically, grandmother, mom, and I all felt the need to compliment dad on his very bold purchase! At least, now there was the slightest of possibilities that our family might be able to ride to church. This latter comment was the absolute best to be said about dad's recent acquisition! Soon breakfast was on the table, so we all went inside to eat. Mom would occasionally look at me with a coy smile on her face. I would give her a discreet coy smile in return. Without speaking, we knew exactly what caused our smiles. We wanted so very badly to just burst out in wild laughter, but laughter of this type was not an option (at least not in our household). For had we laughed, our actions would have been perceived as disrespectful.

Dad volunteered to take us all for a ride when we had finished eating, and we accepted his generous offer. So as soon as we were finished, mom cleaned the table and washed the dishes. Then since this was Sunday, we each put on decent clothing. Now came our moment of truth! We all went outside and climbed into our new chariot! Strangely, I felt none of the excitement that I'd felt upon entering Uncle Abe's new Mercury. Anyway, the old vehicle had ample seating space. Dad and I rode in the front, and mom and grandmother rode in the rear seat. Then the all-important moment arrived! Dad inserted the key into the ignition. With his left foot, dad pressed the starter switch, which was installed in the floorboard. The old 'car's' engine was still warm, so it started up without great difficulty. We all realized that its engine was alarmingly noisy! In fact, the noise level was hazardous to one's eardrums. Dad then turned the old 'car' around, and it slowly sputtered and chattered down our narrow little trail and onto the main road. None of the rural roads here were asphalted or paved back then, so they were all only of dirt. Consequently, any vehicle traveling at thirty miles per hour, kicked up a great amount of dust. Pedestrians moved out into the fields in order to avoid this dust. Also, these old vehicles were not equipped with air-conditioning, which meant that during summer months, passengers rode along with all windows rolled down, and much of this stirred-up road dust entered the vehicle. As a result, when one reached his or her destination, their clothes probably needed cleaning. This was our lot!

Dad headed southwest once we had reached the main road. We'd lived in this area for slightly more than two years, but only dad had ever traveled the region we were now entering. We soon were two miles from our house, but we were in some strange new land. I had often ridden my horse Belle nearly to this point, but I had never actually come this far. The region we had just entered was even less populated than ours. The houses here were spaced three to four miles apart. Now, I began to develop a slightly greater appreciation for our location. The countryside was serene, and as far as the human eye could see, no human beings were in sight. But I knew that this absence of people was due to the fact that today was Sunday. On any given work day, these expansive fields would have been filled with farm workers. I was a bit disappointed that there was not much to see. I had seen fields each day of my young life and had grown weary of them. Here, there were large areas of woodlands, but I had also traveled through wooded areas, while riding my horse. So there was nothing new except for a few rural churches. Albeit, mom and grandmother enjoyed the scenery. I also pretended to enjoy the new sights. I sensed that dad was quite pleased, at seeing our satisfaction in viewing this different part of the countryside.

When we were ten miles from our house, dad decided to turn back. I would later learn that this was due to his lack of confidence in our new 'car'.

Dad parked the old vehicle and the three of us began to thank and compliment him for his generosity. I truly believe that he'd thought our compliments were sincere. But nothing could have been farther from the truth! Mom and I realized that now we owned a 'car', but although we could ride around in it, we were ashamed to be seen in this old junk heap! My parents and grand mom then prepared for relaxation for the remainder of the day. I, on the other hand,— saddled my horse.

It was still a bit too early to visit Mr. Lim, so I picked up Buddy, and the three of us rode for an hour. This was a warm and sunny day. The flowers and trees had blossomed and grown leaves. As I rode along, I began to realize that though my life was one of poverty and austerity, I still had many blessings for which to be thankful. Most of all, everyone in my household was healthy. And though we had very little money, we had lots of good food and a roof over our heads. Also, I now had my dear Carol in my life. Then I recalled Willie, with whom I was finally on speaking terms. I was doing excellent in school, receiving consistently high grades. And then I recalled the lovely Miss Cunnings— wow! I asked myself *"Jake, what more could you possibly ask for"*?

When I finally reached Mr. Lim's place, I found him sitting alone in his back yard enjoying the warm sunshine of springtime. We greeted each other, as I tied my horse's rein to a nearby tree limb, and Buddy lay down in the shaded area of another nearby oak tree. I knew I had arrived a bit early, so I sat on an old chair that had been placed there for me. We sat talking for a short while about how our week had gone. I really wanted to tell him about the three serious attacks by Willie, but I reconsidered and chose not to mention any of this. I simply told him that I'd had a very good week at school. I had told him the truth— it had been a good week! But now came time to begin my training. He began by telling me that I had progressed exceptionally well in all areas of my training program. Then he added that although I had made great progress, there was still room for improvement, and we would begin by focusing on making improvements in my technique. I realized that Mr. Lim was correct in his assessment of me, for even though I had successfully defended myself against Willie, I still lacked confidence in my ability. So I welcomed this new phase in my program.

We began refresher training in timing, balance, and speed. When I speak of balance, I refer to balance of both myself and my opponent. Mr. Lim had taught me that balance of my opponent was equally important in hand-to-hand combat. He had specifically focused upon the importance of influencing and controlling the balance of one's attacker. I realized that balance and timing, were two key elements that had enabled me to defeat Willie. Naturally, speed continued to be an integral part of my personal training program. It was speed that had served as the platform, from which to launch my other important tactics. I knew beyond a doubt that when merged, these three skills were an awesome combination. I trained throughout the hour, executing a variety of attack and defense tactics. Finally it was time to 'call it a day'. I thanked Mr. Lim as usual before leaving. I awakened Buddy, and gave him water. I then mounted my horse and away we rode.

It was just 1:00PM, so I decided to ride for one more hour before returning home for our noontime meal. I rode slowly along a series of narrow, winding trails before entering the forests and covered much space. The month of April would end in just two more days, and the weather was simply beautiful. This was truly a day for which to be grateful. I escorted Buddy home, and then raced at top speed towards our old farmhouse. It occurred to me that my horse could probably outrun the old 'car' that dad had brought home.

My family had gathered around our meager dinner table for our afternoon meal. As soon as we had finished, dad offered to take us into our little town. Back then, all the stores and shops remained completely closed on Sundays. The only facility open on Sundays was one of our three pharmacies, which rotated each weekend. The only reason for any person to enter our downtown area was for social visitation. Dad wanted to take us for a visit to his sister Emma's house. Aunt Emma was grandmother's step-daughter. She was the youngest of three sisters, and only a couple of years older than dad. Both mom and grandmother had agreed that it would be nice to get away from the farm for at least a short while. So after dressing, we all piled into our new mode of transportation. Mom sat in front alongside dad. I chose to sit beside grandmother in the back seat. But I had an ulterior motive. I realized that it would be much more difficult for any person along our route to recognize me. Plus, I had anticipated that I might need to scoot down lower in my seat, to avoid being noticed. I simply could not allow any of my schoolmates to see me riding in an old contraption such as this.

Our normal route into town was a four-mile ride. We could not take my recently discovered shortcut, as there were no roads through the forest. After driving along for two miles, we reached the previous old house in which we had lived. Today, it just stood there in total loneliness and abandonment. Grass and weeds had again engulfed the large yard area that surrounded this old house. But oh how I wished that we still lived there. I'd had five kids of my age group within five minutes' walking distance. There were another two kids only fifteen minutes away. So in comparison to where we presently lived, this area had been nearly paradise. At least, it stood on the fringes of civilization! We continued riding for one more mile, at which point we reached the house where I had spent my first nine years of life. Here, I felt that I was truly in paradise! As we drove along slowly, I gazed longingly at the long string of neat and cozy homes that lined this quiet street. Kids here were playing and walking all along this narrow but well-kept street. *"If only I could have remained here,"* I thought. But now, I was acutely aware of my new problem. Most of the kids along this street were my schoolmates! I could not allow them to see me this way, so I slid just a little lower in my seat. I was not wearing a hat, so I discreetly lowered my head. Neither mom nor dad could see me from their position up front, though I'm certain that my wise old grandmother had noticed and fully understood my actions. However, she remained silent and made no gestures. I was very happy to have had her on my side, for I did not wish to in any way embarrass or offend dad.

We continued riding along increasingly densely populated streets. As we rode along, we saw an increasing number of adults and children moving about. We finally reached the residential uptown area, approaching the home of my Aunt Emma. Dad boldly drove our old jalopy right into her driveway and parked there. I would not have had the audacity to do such a thing! I'm sure that she must have heard us coming long before we reached her house, because she was standing on her front porch and peering down the street in our direction. We filed onto her porch. Aunt Emma was so happy to see us all together. She had just seen dad and me yesterday, but she had not seen mom or her step-mother in nearly a year. Since we had moved so very far into the wilderness, visits had become virtually impossible. The only times she was able to visit us was whenever one of her two sons was in town. She literally welcomed us with opened arms. Both mom and grandmother did likewise.

I soon asked to be excused from the small assembly of adults. After all, the conversation would be conducted by the adults, and they would be cautious of the words they used in my presence. Mom and dad asked where I would go— since all stores were closed, including the two movie theaters. I told them that one of my fellow classmates had been a bit ill and I wanted to check on him. Naturally, there was no way I could tell them that a boy had tried to kill me just two days ago, so now I was going to visit him. My parents excused me from their small group, so I politely disappeared from their view.

I first walked the three blocks to Carol's house. I found that they had attended church earlier in the day, but had just returned home. Carol had not expected to see me, so she was in her room doing homework. I had already finished my homework at school on Friday. I did not go inside, but took a seat on her front porch. Soon she came out to join me. Her parents then joined us also. I had just escaped from one group of adults, but here I again sat, surrounded by two more. I told Carol I was just passing by on my way to Willie's house. She agreed to accompany me (with the blessings of her parents), so we casually walked down the street toward Willie's place. As we approached, I saw his grandmother sitting alone on her front porch. Carol and I walked into her yard and warmly greeted her. She knew both our parents, and especially my grandmother, so she inquired about each of them. I told her that grandmother was down the street visiting her daughter Emma. She responded, "I'm going to walk down there to see her right now". Then she said, "I guess you've come to see my grandson". "We did," I answered. She then called out to Willie, saying "Willie, you've got company". Momentarily, he emerged from inside his house. I closely observed his mannerisms, but found that he genuinely seemed happy to see both Carol and me. He smiled and spoke to us cordially, (which was a first,) for Willie had never smiled or spoken cordially to any human being!

At this point, his dear grandmother left the house to visit my aunt. Now we were alone—just the three of us. I asked how his arm and back felt. He replied, "My back feels worse than my arm". I said, "I'm sure you'll feel much better in a couple of days". "I hope so," he said. I noticed that he did not appear resentful of the fact that Carol and I were together. Then I said to Carol, "Did you know that Willie was a star football player at his last school"? "No,

I did not," she replied. I turned to my new 'friend' Willie, saying, "Tell us about some of your games". His eyes seemed to brighten, as a wide grin appeared on his face. "You guys really want to hear about my games?" he asked. "We sure do," I said.

Willie began relating a long series of recollections of some of his favorite past games. Soon, the words were flowing from his mouth. I would never have imagined that this was the Willie of the past several months. But here we sat— listening to this highly animated young man talk to us about his favorite pastime of football. I recalled how in class he never spoke more than one or two words at any given time, and those were only spoken in answer to some particular question from our teachers. Right at this moment, he seemed truly happy and at peace. I could not help thinking, *"I wonder what could have gone so drastically wrong in this young boy's life"?* For presently, he was a totally different person—and a seemingly normal person at that. Finally after a long string of dissertations he paused, saying, "There, you have it." I said, "If you wish, Willie, we will try to make you an even bigger star here at our school". His eyes lit up with genuine excitement! But it was time to go, so we said farewell to Willie.

Carol and I walked back to her place and sat outside in their neat, well-maintained front yard. It was lined with an assortment of beautiful, sweet-smelling flowers and completely free of any debris. The hedges surrounding this very neat yard seemed to have been professionally manicured. But it was Carol's mother who pampered this well-kept yard. While sitting there admiring these surroundings, I recalled that this was exactly how the yards of our first house had been. However, my grandmother had maintained our yard, and mom had always done her share.

I had now been away from Aunt Emma's for nearly two hours, so it was time that I return. When I reached Aunt Emma's, I found everyone there eating lemon cake, topped with vanilla ice cream. This was complemented by tall glasses of cold lemonade. As soon as I stepped onto her porch, Aunt Emma said, "Jake, yours is in the refrigerator". I thanked her for holding mine for me. I then took the great pleasure of washing my hands in her very neat little bathroom. This was a luxury that I had never known at home— for there was no bathroom. Then I removed my refreshments from the refrigerator and returned to the porch to feast upon them. They were delicious! It was finally nearing 5:00PM, so dad said "Son, when you finish eating, we'll be heading home". I had visited Carol. I had also visited Willie, plus I had revisited Carol. So, I too, was ready to return to the wilderness. I still had time to do more riding, so I finished my dish before returning the utensils to the kitchen sink. I took great pleasure in doing this— because at home, there was no sink.

Finally, my family stood up and said their "farewells" to Aunt Emma. At this point, I began to feel a bit of pity for her. Her husband had died years ago. And to make matters worse, each of her five children had moved far away. So now this poor aging lady lived all alone, and while she'd had electricity and city water, she did not have a telephone. Thus, in the event of some personal emergency, she would have been totally helpless. Auntie would continue living this way for another twenty-five years. So, before leaving her little house that Sunday, I promised that I would stop by at least a few times during each week to check on her, (for which she was grateful). We then piled into the 'car' and traveled slowly, never exceeding speeds of thirty miles per hour. I would later learn that this was this vehicle's maximum speed, and all this old engine could endure. Its valves and pistons had long since ceased functioning properly, and it had lost more than fifty percent of its normal compression. Notwithstanding, we made it all the way to our house without encountering any mechanical problems.

At home, I quickly changed into my riding clothes and saddled my horse. I rode past and summoned Buddy. We covered great distance, even venturing into the remote area that dad had driven us through earlier in the day. We rode slowly, moderately, and quickly. I alternated our speeds to allow Buddy to keep pace with us. As I rode along, I recounted the events of the day. This had been a very busy and important day for me. I had visited an area that I had never before ventured into. I had ridden in a vehicle with my family— which I had never before done. I had visited two schoolmates as a group, which was also a first. I had entered into a new and advanced phase of self-defense training with Mr. Lim. I had revisited each of the homes in which we had previously lived. Finally, I had visited my dear Aunt Emma on two consecutive days. I realized the only thing missing today was a visit to church.

It was time to head back toward our old house for the evening meal. I should mention that we never ate leftovers except during winter months, because of our lack of refrigeration. Mom had quickly prepared a meal consisting of rice, green vegetables, and honey-cured ham. Our meal was simple, but wholesome and delicious. Afterward, we sat together and discussed our day. Dad asked about our feelings about the old 'car' which he had just purchased. Each of us searched for suitable and complimentary words, though none of us succeeded. Grandmother was the first to speak up, saying "Clayton, where did you find that old thing"? Dad replied, "I bought it from John". Mom said, "Well, at least it took us into town and back". I commented, "I liked the Hudson better". "I liked the Hudson too, son," dad responded,— "but we'll just have to make do with this for now". We had given him our candid opinions and he had accepted them. Grandmother was the first to say "Good night" and I followed closely behind.

Now as I lay quietly in my bedroom, I began to realize just how fortunate I had been over the past week. I had survived three attacks from Willie— one of which had been vicious! But I'd seemingly managed to smooth things over. I realized now that I had never liked fighting, so I began hoping the worst of such situations had passed. At least I was currently on talking terms with Willie. Also, I felt that if I handled this situation properly, all of the animosity between us might come to an end. I vowed inwardly to do everything within my power to make this happen. I recalled that dad often had referred to me as the 'old man' because, he said, "You're wise like your dear old grandmother". My grandmother had always tried to instill in me much of the wisdom she had acquired over her long lifetime. I greatly appreciated her efforts, and tried to absorb as much of this as I possibly could. This imparted wisdom had helped me to endure my lonely life. I would now use this wisdom to try nurturing relations between Willie and the many students at our school. I began formulating a plan to make this all happen. I realized that this would be a huge endeavor, but I also knew things definitely should not remain as unpleasant as they had been in past months.

The night passed rather quickly, so this was the beginning of a new week at school. Tomorrow would be the very first day of May (also one of my favorite months). I left home fifteen minutes earlier than usual so I could talk to some of the students about Willie, and the incidents of last Friday. I reached Carol's house as she was leaving. She was quite surprised to see me there, as I had not done this in the past. I asked, "Can I give you a lift?" and she accepted. We reached our school grounds twenty-five minutes before classes would begin. As soon as we arrived, the throngs of students began applauding and chanting my name. Some were chanting "Judo Jake, Judo Jake"! Their attention gave me a sense of achievement and pride. But at the very same time, it gave me a sense of doubt and uneasiness.

"Hey everybody— isn't this a beautiful day?" I said. The students started to applaud and cheer even more loudly. I raised my hands to silence them. Even at age fifteen, I had begun to feel that I was in charge of the situation. I said, "I'd like to talk to each of you for just a moment". A sudden state of calm emerged within the crowd. I continued, "As all of you know, last Friday began as a bad day— but then, it became much worse! But before the day was over, it had changed for the better". Then there came some applause, but I calmly silenced it with another gesture of my hand. I continued, "Some of you may know that I took Willie to the doctor's office Friday afternoon". I quickly added "Then I went to his house and visited with him on Saturday afternoon. I also went to see him yesterday". "Carol and

I have talked with him, and we believe that he is finally a changed person". "Naturally, only time will tell, but Willie has promised me that he is finished fighting with the students". "I hope that he keeps his promise". Then my friend Wilton stepped forward and asked, "Why are you doing this, Jake"? – "He tried to kill you"! "My grandmother always taught me to turn the other cheek— so that's what I'm trying to do here now" I replied. There was murmuring among a few of the students. "We sure can't continue as we have been, so let's try to make this better for all of us— including Willie". "Can I count on you to help me?" I asked. The crowd then began to applaud and cheer loudly, being silenced only by the bell to enter classes. Carol thought that I had really given an impressive little speech. I hoped that I had given an effective speech. Such intense involvement— at the tender age of fifteen!

We had just entered our English classroom, which was always the first subject of the day. But no sooner than we had taken our seats, did our teacher, (Mrs. Mann) call me to her desk. I approached her inquisitively as she calmly said, "Jake, Professor Thomas would like to see you in his office." *"Not again"*, I thought. I had just been in his office this past Friday afternoon. Even so, I went directly to the principal's office. Once we had greeted each other, he said, "Jake, I want you to tell me exactly what happened on the street last Friday afternoon after school." I tried to minimize the seriousness of the situation by saying, "It was nothing much, sir". He responded in a relaxed tone, saying "That's not the way I heard it". "Willie snuck up behind me and tried to hit me" I answered. I quickly added, "He missed me, so it was really nothing". Our principal paused briefly before saying, "Jake, I'm counting upon you to tell me the truth— so I want all of the details concerning this matter". I sat there thinking, *"Shucks, here we go"*. I had no choice, except to provide my principal with the information which he sought, so I summarized the events of the second incident. I then quickly informed him that all had turned out well. My principal pondered my input for a moment. Then he commented, "Well, he has just ended his stay at our school".

Now as of Friday afternoon, I would have been thrilled to hear such words. However, after visiting with Willie on both Saturday and Sunday, I had somewhat changed my thinking. I no longer wanted to see him expelled from school. I thought of the devastation such action would cause Willie's grandmother. I also considered his future, and realized that he would not have one. He would probably end up either in prison, or some graveyard. I knew then that in no way, did I wish to influence such an unfortunate outcome. So I said, "Sir, Willie is not a bad kid— he is just troubled". "He's assured me that he will cause no more problems while attending our school". "If we would just give him one more chance, I believe that he would prove to all of us that he is sincere." I added. Professor Thomas sat quietly for a moment. Then he said, "Well, I can't figure out why you are standing up for him, but I certainly admire your concern". Then just for safe measure, I followed up by saying "Plus, he plays baseball, softball, and football—and is a great player of all three of these games". Professor Thomas had previously coached football, so I knew that there existed a soft spot in his heart for this sport. I also knew that this happened to be Willie's first love. The principal said, "Let me confer with my vice principal to see what he thinks of your idea". I thanked him and arose to leave. But on my way out of his office, I added, "I do believe that he won't fight anymore— and I believe that he'll win us some ballgames." "We shall see." was all my principal had said. I thanked him graciously, as I left his office— happy to be out of there!

Twenty minutes of my first class had passed. I would have to really rush to take notes, so I asked my teacher for a single sheet of carbon paper. "Why do you need carbon paper?" she asked. "I need to make copies of my notes for a very ill student," I replied. She reached into a desk drawer and removed two sheets of carbon paper. She handed them to me, saying, "You may need more than one sheet". I thanked her and returned to my desk. I stored one sheet of the paper inside my notebook. Then, I placed the remaining sheet between the two first pages of my notepad and I began rapidly scribbling down notes from our blackboard. I would follow this new procedure for the next two weeks, while Willie was out of school. I'd barely managed to finish copying notes when the bell rang, sounding the end of this first class. So we moved from classroom to classroom for the remainder of the morning. And while in each of these classes, I ensured that I took concise and legible notes. I would deliver the carbon copy of my notes to Willie at the end of our school day. I would continue this practice for the next two weeks while Willie was absent.

Finally, lunchtime was again upon us, so we all rushed out of our classrooms and to the cafeteria. I occasionally looked about the cafeteria area as I stood in the serving line. Things were different on this day though, for today I had no need for concern over Willie's whereabouts. Today I knew exactly where he was— at home nursing his injured arm and back. I then took great comfort in feeling that the threat he had posed, had most likely ended. I picked up my tray and moved toward my table. All around me, I noticed that many students were noticing me. Most of them would wave as I looked in their direction. I smiled and greeted them in return. I promptly seated myself with my friends. I soon felt strong excitement at our table, and throughout the cafeteria. Donnie and Wilton began recounting the wild events of the past Friday afternoon. Donnie excitedly stated, "Jake, from now on we're going to call you Superman"! I grinned while thanking him for his kind flattery, adding "But I could not have done it without you guys". Wilton commented, "But I still can't imagine how you fight the way you do"! Carol asked, "Jake, do you really know judo"? "No Carol," I said, "I don't know judo or jujitsu". "Then, what style of fighting is that?" she asked. "Oh, that's just my own style that I've developed". Wilton said, "Well, you sure did develop it well". I then said to them, "I visited Willie both Saturday and Sunday afternoons, and he seems to be a changed person". "He's also promised me that there will be no more fighting— at least, not by him". Everybody at the table chimed in, "Well, we'll just have to see that to believe it"!

We finished our food and then moved to the outside area. On this day though I requested that the three of them remain with me for the remainder of our lunch period. They were perplexed by my strange request, since Willie no longer posed a threat to any of us. I told them I'd hoped to speak to the students outside about the new situation concerning Willie. Wilton quipped, "Let's forget Willie." I responded "What Willie really needs is our friendship". "I believe we can help him—let's try".

We walked together to the center of the park. I asked Donnie and Wilton to issue shrill whistling sounds to get the attention of the students. They complied and all the students began to look in our direction. We waved and summoned them over. "Everybody please listen" I said. "We don't have much time, so I'll be quick with this". "You all know about last Friday". "I visited with Willie on both Saturday and yesterday afternoon". "We got to know each other and became friends". Now there was some applause— and some silence. I continued "Willie has sworn to me that there will be absolutely no more fighting"! Now, there came the sound of roaring applause. I continued "After talking to Willie, I found out that he feels disliked and rejected by us here at this school". "And, I believe that if we show that we do care about him, we'll find that he will become a good friend". "On Saturday afternoon, I took him popcorn and a Coke". "He was so happy and thankful". "So let's all be friends— shall we"? There came a huge round of applause! I was very happy about their willingness to join me, and I hoped that I would not disappoint them. The bell then sounded for our return to our classes. On our way back to class, Carol volunteered, "When I get home, I'm going to ask mom to bake poor Willie a nice pound cake". "That's very nice of you," I said.

Soon I was again seated in my favorite classroom. I had not feasted my eyes upon my dear Miss Cunnings since last Friday. I was thrilled to be once again in her classroom. She greeted the class in her usual warm manner, with a special "And, how are you, Jake?" for me. I felt confident that none of the students were aware of our special 'relationship'. But I'm certain that I'd understood her personal message to me. Now, admittedly— in no way did I consider myself an angel. To the contrary, while in Miss Cunnings' presence I was constantly keenly aware of the existence of my 'invisible horns'!

As I sat there taking notes, I thought of what Willie was missing and I noticed that Miss Cunnings had not inquired into his absence. This suggested that she was aware of Friday's after-school incident. After class, I purposely lingered behind the rest of the students. As I neared the door, I briefly looked over my shoulder. I was not surprised to see her watching me. She motioned me to her desk and said, "Jake, I heard about Friday afternoon's second incident". I told her that all had turned out well and that I did not anticipate any future problems from Willie. She asked, "But how are you doing?" – I mean, how are you *really* doing"? "I'm doing great," I said. "I'm really happy to see that you're okay," she said. She continued "Our principal has reversed his decision to permanently expel Willie, so I truly hope that this works out well". "I'm not concerned about Willie himself, but I am concerned about you." she added.

Now, I fully realized that she may have made her last statement in total innocence, but it would have been very easy for me to have become vain in my assessment of her last comment. However, I did not wish to make a fool of myself by making the wrong assumption, so I simply thanked her for her concern. "I had better be running along now," I said. But instead of stepping backward and away from her, I stepped forward and toward her. In that very same instant, she had taken one step toward me. We were now inches apart, as she passionately threw her arms around me! This time I completely abandoned all caution, as I squeezed her warm body tightly against mine. I abruptly released her when I heard footsteps walking down the hallway outside her door. At that moment, I did not understand exactly what was happening between us, but I knew for certain that I could not allow our actions to be noticed by the school's staff, or the students. I quickly bent forward and kissed her lightly on her left cheek. Before she could respond in any way, I turned and walked quietly out of her room. As I reached her doorway, I looked back at her— only to find that she was looking affectionately at me! We smiled briefly at each other, and away I went down that long, nearly deserted hallway. Right then, I wanted to commence singing my little 'happy song', but there was no time. I quickly rushed to my history class. History was my least favored subject, and as a result, I'd averaged grades of C+ in history. Oddly, this class always seemed to pass much more slowly than the others. Afterward came our study period. Soon, the end-of-day bell sounded. It was once again time for us to head homeward.

I was curious about our principal's decision, so I walked quickly to his office. I asked, "Have you reached a decision about Willie, sir"? "I have," he answered. "I have decided to let him stay". "However, I'm placing Willie on probationary status for the remainder of this year— and all of next year". "And if he's still with us at that time, we'll review his case again". "Thank you very much, sir— I believe this will help us all". "I hope so," he replied. I felt both relieved and happy over this outcome.

When I reached the bicycle rack outside, my three

special friends were waiting there for me. There was also one more boy standing there with them whose name was Horace. I had casually known him throughout my years at school, and had known him to be a good kid. Carol was the first to speak, asking "What did the principal decide"? I knew they were all curious, so I said, "He's going to let Willie stay— but on probation". "How long is his probation?" Donnie asked. "From now until the end of next school year," I said. "Good—his butt needs to be on probation," said Wilton. Horace still had not spoken, but then he began to speak to me, saying "Jake, can I join you guys"? "What do you mean?" I asked. "I'd like to become part of your group," he answered. "I didn't know that we were a group— we're just friends," I said. "But you guys are special" he said. "Are you including Carol?" I asked. "Of course," he responded. I extended my hand to him, saying, "Welcome." I saw that my friends seemed happy with my decision. Horace appeared happiest of all. But he would not walk to and from school with us, because his house was only a minute away. I had often watched Horace as he left our school each afternoon, and each day I found myself thinking, *"How lucky can you get"?* He would never be cold walking to and from school. And even on days of heavy rain, he would not get very wet. Then I recalled how in the past, kids at school referred to Donnie, Wilton, and me as the "Three Musketeers". "What would they call us from this day forward"?

After escorting Carol to her house, I immediately hopped onto my bicycle and headed to Willie's place. I found him again in his bedroom. "Hey, Willie, how're you doing?" I asked. "I'm doing a little better," he answered. I wasted no time,— "I spoke to our principal today, and he has agreed to let you remain at our school." I said. His eyes lit up as a wide grin covered his entire face! His expression of joy was unbelievable! I quickly added, "But he says you can cause no more trouble whatsoever"! Willie accepted those terms wholeheartedly! I discovered that he had expected to be permanently expelled— which would have been only fair. I told him, "I've got to rush home now— but here are the notes from today's lessons". "Jake, I can't believe that you would do all this for me" said Willie. Then he extended to me his only good arm and hand. We shook hands— and at that moment, there began a true friendship! I quickly added, "I'll bring you my notes from our classes each day until you return". Now, I've got to run" I said to him. Willie thanked me graciously, as I hastily departed his room. I said "Good day, ma'am" to Willie's grandmother, who was sitting outside on her old front porch. I then rode like the 'dickens' toward home, reaching our old place at precisely 3:58PM. At the house, I quickly gulped down a snack that mom had left for me. Then I changed into work clothing and hurried out into the fields to plow a mule for another three hours. Those hours seemed to pass rather quickly. Dad and I quit the plowing and returned the mules to the barnyard. Then we bathed outside in small washtubs. Soon we ate supper, and retired in anticipation of the day ahead. I slept soundly throughout the entire night.

Now, it was another Tuesday morning, and the first day of May (my favorite day of the month). I followed my usual routine throughout the school day, and then had lunch with my three regular friends. There was not space for Horace at our table, but the table next to us held a vacant seat, so he sat next to us. We soon realized that Willie's absence had created a pleasant void. At the same time we looked forward to his return. After lunch, Carol and I moved to our bench at the edge of the school's park. Horace joined the boys who were passing footballs around. Carol told me that her mom had baked the cake for Willie and, that she would take it to his grandmother after school. In those days girls simply did not visit boys regardless of the circumstances. She knew that I would be unable to accompany her, because I would need to hurry home.

Our day had passed uneventfully, but I had quickly developed a craving for my daily hug, and I was determined not to leave school without it! So at the end of Miss Cunnings' class, the two of us briefly indulged ourselves with another 'thrilling moment' in our lives. At this point, I became acutely aware of one simple but true fact – I did not even know her first name! but I would not be so brazen as to ask her to tell me. After all, I was her student and had I in any way misinterpreted her actions, I might have found myself facing serious embarrassment and trouble. So I opted to settle for only the hugs— for the time being.

Finally, another week of school had ended. There had been no fights or other incidents of any kind. I had made an extra copy of my notes for Willie and each afternoon after school, I would drop them off at his house. I knew that his grades were poor, so I advised him to carefully study them. I also volunteered to stop by on Saturday afternoons to help Willie with his studies. I knew that I would be able to keep this promise because dad would no longer need our bicycle.

This had been another surprisingly productive week for me. First, I had stood next to the 'object of my affection'.

Second, a new friend had entered my somewhat lonely life. Third, I had nurtured my friendship with my dear Carol. Fourth, I felt that I had truly helped another human being who was in distress. And last but not least, my family had received the benefit of 'vehicular transportation'.

I had decided to visit Willie the next day. As I neared his house, I saw him sitting out front along with his grandmother. I could see that she was very happy to see me as she now realized that her precious grandson did have at least one friend. He also seemed happy to see me. The old lady offered me a seat along with a cold glass of iced tea. Willie kept eyeing my packaged cake. "How are you feeling?" I asked. "Much better— my pain is gone," he replied. "That's great," I said. At that point though, what I really wanted to say was "I certainly hope I won't have to kick your butt again", but since I was a gentleman I would not speak such words to him. I had kept him in suspense long enough, so I handed him the cake, saying, "This is from Carol's mom" I said. Now, Willie's eyes really seemed to light up. I handed him the chocolate cake, which even had his name across its vanilla icing top. He appeared truly thrilled at the sight of it! "Wow, it's been a really long time since anybody's given me a cake," he said. He handed it to his grandmother, asking her to cut it for us. She went into her small kitchen and soon returned with dishes, utensils, and napkins. Then when she had cut only pieces for Willie and me, we asked her to cut a piece for herself. She hesitatingly cut a thin slice for herself also, saying, "I don't eat sweets". The cake was so very delicious Willie and I both ate two pieces each. I realized I'd had only a little time, so I got right to the point by asking "Willie, do you need me to help you with any of your studies"? He replied, "Well, I could use a little help with the math work". "Get your books and note pad," I said. He quickly fetched them and we began solving fractions. I helped him with math for the next half hour, and we made considerable progress. But then I had to get home, so I bade farewell to his grandmother and him. They both thanked me for my assistance, as I prepared to leave them.

Mom and grandmother were sitting on our front porch when I got home. After chatting briefly with them, I changed into field clothing. Normally I would have grabbed my horse, but on this evening I intended to do an hour of quail hunting. We were nearing the end of bird hunting season, so I wanted to bag just a few quail for my family. I grabbed my Daisy carbine and started walking away from the house. As I was leaving our yard, mom called out to me, "Jake, you be back here by seven-thirty— you hear"? It was 6:45, so she had allowed me only forty-five minutes hunting time. Now, a few of you may know about hunting quail— though most of you will not. First of all, one needs a bird dog and light gauge shotgun for quail hunting. I had neither— only a BB rifle. Ordinarily, no hunter or marksman can strike a quail with one simple BB rifle. Quail are unique birds, in that they remain secluded in grass until startled, and at this point, they startle you (the hunter)! The hunter has almost no response time in which to take aim, and fire a shot. It is virtually impossible to down a flying quail with a BB rifle. However, I managed to bag four quail that evening by knowing the terrain around me— the 'hot spots' for finding quail. So as I neared these locations, I would be on full alert and ready to fire. Then whenever these birds suddenly fluttered up and flew away, I would immediately fire into their heavily concentrated flock. This was by no means an effective tactic for quail hunting, but this was the best available to me at that time.

Finally, it was time for me to return home. I had walked for about five minutes, when I saw mom leave our yard, heading in my direction. This seemed to be not quite right. She seemed to have not been in any kind of distress, thus "Why is she coming to meet me?" I thought. Deep inside, I'd already known my answer and it was not one that I would have wished upon any young boy. Mom was much closer, so now I could clearly see the skinny five-foot oak branch she carried partially concealed behind her back. My heart skipped a beat! I knew fully well what her intentions were. Mom intended to severely whip my back side with that slender oak branch!

Mom was approximately fifty feet away and heading directly for me. I didn't want any whipping, so I held up my tiny burlap bag of quail, saying, "I got us some quail". Mom's response was "I told you to be home by seven-thirty"! "But I'm right here—there's the house—, just a few feet away." "That's right—it's there,— and you're out here," she admonished! Then before I could say another word, the oak switch swished past my back! Normally it would have struck the center of my back, leaving a sharp burning sensation! But thanks to Mr. Lim, I had mastered several maneuvers not before seen by her. Immediately she swung the oak switch at me again. Again, she missed. During each of mom's first two attempts, I had not moved more than one foot away from her, so her arms had extended past me. Now we were facing each other, as she swung the switch once again, attempting to strike me across my chest, but again she failed miserably! I'd accurately timed her swing, as I took one step toward her. Again, the switch extended past my body. Now, mom was really frustrated— and somewhat confused. All the while, I had not dropped either the quail or my BB rifle, which really baffled her. Then as she prepared to take another swing at me, I performed what Mr. Lim referred to as a 'double pivot" maneuver. In unison with her swing of the switch, I ended up immediately behind her. At this point, I'm aware that many boys would have struck or shoved her, and I'm sure that these very same thoughts had occurred to her. She abruptly spun around to face me. But as she did so, I gracefully repeated my pivot move. Suddenly mom whirled about once more as she prepared to swing the switch. I just stood there— unmoving. Once more, she raised her arm to strike me. But as she did so, I stepped closer to her while encircling her in my arms. Then before she could react, I said, "I love you, mom". Now my loving mom was totally undone! She was completely bewildered, and wondering what to do next. I held out the quail to her, asking, "Do you still want these"? I believe that mom truly was embarrassed at that moment, but she would not admit it. Then, she did a surprising thing. Standing there before me, she broke her switch into four separate pieces and tossed them several feet away onto the ground. Then she took my hand, and the two of us walked together back to our old house. This was the very last time that my dear loving mother ever attempted whipping me!

We reached the house within five minutes after that incident. But once we arrived, mom cleaned and seasoned the quail. Then she immediately placed them in a frying pan, on our old wood-burning stove. Grandmother was still up, but she had not seen any of the 'action'. Dad came home shortly afterward, and the four of sat down to a delicious meal of rice with green peas and quail. The quail was absolutely delicious, and the three of them continuously praised this hard-earned meal. Mom did not mention our little incident to dad, and neither did I. In fact, twenty-seven years would pass before it would be jokingly mentioned.

My weekend had passed rather eventfully, so I presently found myself once again headed for school. The first half of my ride was lonely, for it ran partly through the forest. But as soon as I emerged from the forest, houses began to appear. A few dozen school-aged kids lived along this stretch of dirt road. There was no school bus service along this route, because it only extended for a distance of one mile, so the kids here walked to and from school each day. I knew many of them quite well. Others, I knew only fairly well. But since the incidents with Willie, they all had begun speaking to me as I rode past them.

When I reached the asphalted main street to our school, I found it quite crowded with children. As I passed them, they greeted me. Suddenly, I had become somewhat of a celebrity! Now for the sake of honesty, I must tell you that I really did enjoy all of my newfound attention. I rode onward to school and secured my bicycle. Then I joined my friends and some of the other kids who were standing about the school grounds. Prior to my incidents with Willie, we usually just stood around discussing our weekend. But today, the focus had shifted to Willie. The kids were increasingly dismayed by my three successful defenses against him. I found that they were even more dismayed by the relative ease with which I had defeated him each time.

Several of the boys even approached me, asking if I would teach them my skills. In response, I would always say to them, "Guys, I just got lucky— that's all". Then I would add "But Willie's finished fighting now, so you don't need to worry about him". Here, I attempted to set the stage for his peaceful return to our school. My four close friends asked why I was defending him"? "He needs our help and friendship— and he'll be okay" I responded. I could easily see that they doubted me.

Two weeks had passed, during which time I'd continued my daily routine of note-taking, teacher visitation, horseback riding, self-defense training, and field work. I had kept in touch with Willie by daily providing him with copies of my notes from school. I had also agreed to escort and assist Willie upon his eventual return to school. Today though was Monday morning— a day of action! I arose and washed up. Then I dressed and had my breakfast. But today, I noticed one distinct difference in myself. Those 'butterflies' that had haunted me as a younger child, seemed to have vanished. I had begun to feel that if any situation occurred, I would handle it!

Again this morning, the kids all along my route waved and spoke to me. This gave me a really great feeling as I rode onward. When I reached Willie's house, I found him standing at his front gate waiting for me. "How are you doing?" I asked, as I rode up to his yard. "I'm fine Jake," he responded. "Hop on, and we'll ride," I said. He climbed onto the passenger rack on the back of my bicycle, and away we rode. The five minute ride to our school had gone smoothly and without incident. As we rode onto the schoolyard, many of the kids began applauding. Others just stood around, looking on. *"They're probably wondering what's next."* I thought. I secured my bicycle, and Willie and I walked onto the school grounds together. Just as we'd walked onto the grounds, I saw the looming figure of our principal standing at the top of the steps of our auditorium. He had not done this before; so, I knew that he was there specifically to observe us. I pretended to not have noticed him. Then together with Willie, I walked to the center of the grounds directly in front of our auditorium. Willie had not spoken one word so I asked him "Are you okay"? "I'm okay," he said. I walked with him to the nearest group of kids and greeted them, saying "I'd like to introduce you all to our new friend Willie"! "It would really be nice if we could begin this new friendship with a round of handshakes". We then began moving about the area, shaking hands with every kid we approached. I murmured to Willie to follow my lead— which he did. One by one, each kid on the grounds heartily returned both, my handshakes and Willie's. *"This morning is beginning beautifully"*, I thought as we mingled with the crowd. "We don't have the time now, but we would like to talk with each of you in the park at lunchtime." I said. At this there came slight applause.

Our principal still stood at the top of the stairs. I said to Willie, "Let's walk over and say good morning to Professor Thomas". Without argument, Willie walked at my side to the point where our principal stood. I detected a nearly imperceptible smile on our principal's strong face, as we walked toward him. "Good morning, professor," I said to him as we approached. Willie echoed my words, so our principal responded, "Good morning boys, how are you today"? We each answered by saying that we were doing well.

"I'm very happy to see this," he replied. Then as the first morning bell sounded, our principal said to us in a calm but authoritative manner "I want you boys to accompany me to my office". I wondered if he was about to spring some sort of surprise on us.

In his office, he picked up a manila folder from atop his large desk. He removed a single document from this folder, and read to us its contents. He looked directly at Willie, saying, "This is to you". Then he began quoting the letter. "Effective immediately, you are hereby permanently expelled from Butterfield High School". "From this day forward, you shall not enter onto these grounds for any reason whatsoever". I stole a glance at poor Willie, who had by now, slumped far downward in his seat. His head was lowered into a humbled position, and on his face was an expression of despair and disbelief. Our principal continued reading the letter in its entirety. When he had finished, he looked squarely at Willie as he shoved the letter forward to him. "Here—would you like to read it for yourself?" he said. Willie did not speak, but instead just sat there in a stupor with his head lowered, as our principal sat awaiting his response. But then for some reason, I spoke up. "Professor Thomas, is this your final position in this matter?" I asked. A slight smile appeared on his face. "For awhile, I'd begun to think you both had become mute." he said. Then he looked at Willie as he asked "Do you find this decision to be at all unfair"? "No sir, I do not," Willie answered.

"Good." was the principal's response. He still had not answered me, but I remained silent simply because I could not think of any more appropriate comment to make. After all, I didn't want to turn him against me too. But then he did a strange thing by placing the letter back into its folder. He then said to Willie, "This just happens to be a very special day for you, son— you get a reprieve"! "This letter is contingent upon your future behavior here at our school". "But if you should cause any more incidents while you're here, I will not hesitate to administer it"! "Do you understand?" he asked. Willie could not believe that he was being given another chance! He sat upright and squared his shoulders. A wide grin covered his whole face! He then stood up and approached the principal's desk, reaching out for the principal's hand. They shook hands for nearly one full minute. Then Willie said, "Sir, I will not let you down"! "I hope not, because I'm counting on you," responded our principal. Then with these comments, he excused us.

We'd spent fifteen minutes in our principal's office, so I would have to really rush while taking notes from my first class. But at least today, I would not need to take notes for Willie also. He could take his own notes now. This meant that I could even scribble, but still read what I had written. Willie had gone on to his first class, so I would not meet with him until lunchtime. Incidentally, this was my first time being late in entering a class, since my very first school day. Now even at my current age, I still vividly remembered that stinging whipping I received from my terrible teacher on that first day of school.

This morning we had begun review of the material covered during the current quarter. This would be easy for me, because I had retained my notes from each day of school. At the very same time, studying became much more difficult for the other students because they had not taken and retained their notes in the detailed manner I had. We managed to get through all our morning classes without encountering any problems. Finally, it was lunchtime so we hastily headed to the cafeteria.

While standing in the serving line, I looked about the area as I usually did. Then for the first time in two weeks, there stood Willie just a few feet ahead of me. We looked at each other and waved. Today for the very first time since he had arrived here at our school, I no longer felt any tension between the two of us, which was a truly wonderful feeling! Willie picked up his food tray and moved toward his table. As I stood there watching, I noticed something distinctly different about him. As he'd walked toward his table, he actually greeted a number of kids! They had each warmly returned his greetings. I hoped that this positive atmosphere would continue.

Now I too picked up my tray and moved toward my table. Many of the kids also smiled and waved to me as I moved through the cafeteria. I seated myself with my four friends, and we enjoyed our meal together. While seated there, Wilton in particular voiced his disbelief at the apparent transformation of Willie! I then advised my friends that I would continue to watch him. I also told them that I believed he had finally reached a turning point in his life. They all agreed with me in hoping that this was, in fact, a turning point. Soon we finished our meal and then moved outside.

Willie had left slightly ahead of us, but I found him standing just outside the door and waiting for me. "What do we do now?" he asked. I said, "Let's just take a little walk around the park, so we can greet all the kids," I answered; and, this was precisely what we did. My four friends also accompanied us, so now we were a small group of six students. I found this to be a large enough group to draw attention. So we went about the school's park, shaking hands and cracking jokes with the majority of students. We waved and smiled to those standing in the distance. They returned our smiles and waves. I began to feel that we were, in fact, making progress in student relations. Then as we neared one of our bleachers, I noticed Professor Thomas sitting high up, along with two other teachers. "Let's go up and greet them," I said to my little group. Willie and I walked side by side, with my four friends immediately behind us. We approached our principal and teachers, greeting them warmly. They returned our gesture of respect and kindness. Our coach was one of the three sitting there. He asked Willie, "Are you ready to play ball"? "I sure am." Willie grinned.

"Good— I'll be calling you," our coach responded. We then excused ourselves and soon, the bell sounded for our return to classes. Carol and I had not gotten the chance to sit alone together. Also, the boys had not gotten the chance to pass the football around. But this was okay— for tomorrow would be another day. It then occurred to me that I had never before seen my principal sitting in bleachers. They had actually been monitoring our behavior! I truly hoped that we had passed their test.

We returned to our classes with Willie walking at my side, and closely followed by my four friends. He and I entered Miss Cunnings' room together. This time, I chose to walk in front of him. In this way, I would reach my rear seat first, which would allow me to be last in departing the room. As soon as we'd all taken our seats, our young teacher greeted the class. But this time, her greeting was more enthusiastic than in the past. "Good afternoon, class! - How is everyone today"? The class responded in kind. She then continued "Glad to have you back with us, Willie— How are you"? "I'm doing fine, Miss Cunnings," he responded. "I'm happy to hear this," she said. This time Willie had not sat slouched down into his seat, but had assumed an upright sitting position, which in itself was a major improvement! But he had also responded warmly to our teacher, which was a first for him! Today she began our review of course material covered throughout the semester. Naturally, I sat attentively taking notes. Willie also began taking notes— which was something he had never before done. Miss Cunnings noticed this, and I could clearly see the expression of satisfaction showing on her young face. She glided gracefully through the lecture. Then at the end she opened up this session to questions from the students. I rarely asked questions, for I'd always felt that I understood the material. Willie had never asked a question, but today he asked two. Miss Cunnings was completely taken aback at this great new transformation! Then the bell sounded, ending today's class session, so we gathered our materials and quietly left the classroom.

This time, I actually exited the room. But once outside in the hallway, I turned in the opposite direction of the other students. I counted off three steps before abruptly reversing my direction, which returned me directly to the door of my beloved teacher's classroom. "What have you done to Willie?" she asked. "Well, I've talked to him a lot— and I've tried to give him hope," I said. "It seems to be working," she replied, "I just hope that it lasts". "I do too" I replied. Then without warning I stepped away from her and to the doorway. I carefully scanned both directions of the hallway, but saw no one. I quickly returned to her, taking her into my arms! She did not resist my advances, but drew herself close to me. Now I had gotten a whiff of her sweet perfume. The scent of it and the closeness of her were almost more than I could bear! But then, a 'voice' in my head seemed to say, "She's your teacher"! So, I reluctantly released her. Neither of us had spoken a single word. After all, what could either have said? I then bade her a pleasant afternoon before promptly departing her classroom.

I sat quietly through history class, anxiously awaiting the sound of the bell for study period. Even though I did not care much for history, I still took comprehensive notes. I found this particular teacher to be extremely competent in her field, but I did not find her even remotely as exciting and interesting as Miss Cunnings. They were both approximately the same age and size. But while this lady did possess a certain attractiveness, she did not possess the allure of Miss Cunnings. I viewed these two ladies as I had Jeanne and Carol. I found Carol to be very special; however, I had found Jeanne to be simply indescribable! Miss Coates was really very nice— but there was absolutely no comparison between the two.

But I was only here to learn, I reminded myself. The long-awaited bell had now sounded for study period. I sat there reviewing my notes from the day and preparing myself for our upcoming final examinations. Now even though I had never studied at home, I fully realized that I felt both comfortable and confident about these upcoming tests. This was during the very same time that most of the other kids were 'pulling their hair out' in, trying to prepare themselves. Then the last bell of the day sounded, ending a highly productive day at school!

Outside, Wilton and Donnie approached me, inquiring whether or not I wanted them to remain on the look-out for Willie. But I had already spotted him up ahead, so I told them, "He's in front of us so we can relax." I felt comfortable in saying this to them because my vision was perfect, and I had trained my eyes, as had the Indian warriors of the past. As long as Willie was in front of me, I would be able to spot him long before he could mount any form of attack. I then left the grounds with my dear Carol at my side. She and I really did enjoy our walk together that afternoon. As we passed the house of the middle-aged lady who had warned me of Willie's imminent attack, we waved to her. She gave us a warm greeting in return. I later learned that this poor lady had lived alone for many years. And as such, the kids walking to and from school were her only companionship. *"How sad"*, I thought. Now we had reached Willie's street. He had stopped and actually stood talking with two other boys. One of these boys had on a daily basis been a previous victim of his. I interpreted this as a positive sign. *"If he continues making friends with his prior victims, then our problems should be resolved"*, I thought as I watched them. As Carol and I approached, Willie turned and cordially greeted us. We naturally returned his greeting. "I see that you and Spunky have finally made friends," I said to him. "Yep, we sure have" he grinned". "Well, that's great—keep it up," I said. "Don't worry, I will," he responded. Then he surprised us by saying "Carol, please tell your mother I really thank her for the cake". This was another first, for Willie had never said please or thank you to anyone! We walked past them and onward to Carol's house. "I can't believe this!" she exclaimed. "What do you mean?" I asked. "I can't believe he's changed so much – it's as if he's a completely new person." she said. "Let's hope he sticks with his new personality," I responded.

We found Carol's mom trimming flowers in their front yard. At this moment, I thought of my poor mother. My mother was also a very attractive lady, but she was not fortunate enough to trim flowers at this hour of the day. Instead, she would be far out into the fields and digging in the soil. (What a real waste of one human life this was). "Mom, Willie says thanks for the cake," Carol called out. "Really? – I'm surprised," her mother responded. "He's changed a lot—you should see him!" Carol exclaimed. "We'll see." said her mom. I said "Good afternoon" to them before quickly riding away into the distant wilderness.

After supper, I retired to my room to reflect upon the events of this day. I was fully aware that this had been a truly great day. First, I had seemingly put an end to the long string of violence Willie had caused at our school. Second, I had managed to secure for him continued attendance at this school. Third, I had set the stage for harmonious relationships between the students and himself. Lastly, I had positioned Willie to become a social contributor to our school. I felt that these actions would make it possible for this boy to reach adulthood! Then once Willie had achieved this great feat, I hoped he would begin leading a productive life. I soon fell asleep. I must have been really exhausted, because I slept soundly that night.

Soon Tuesday morning was upon us. I arose and

attended to my needs. Mom and dad were both already in the fields. It would have been nice if they could have worked in close proximity to each other, but this was not the case. The distance between them was at least one quarter mile. If either needed the other, they were forced to communicate using hand signals. *"Poor mom,* I thought, *she's out there all alone— and soon the snakes will start moving all around".* But this was the life that dad had given her, so she stuck by him and never complained!

I left the house at my usual hour, and rode directly to the schoolhouse. I would not escort Willie today, for I had intended to test him. I was quite concerned as to how well he might behave with the other students. I felt that if he was going to fail, then he may as well do so early on. In this way, we could get rid of him and get on with our lives. I spent a couple of minutes each with different groups of kids, outlining my hopes for our future with Willie. Then after about fifteen minutes of this, the subject of our discussion arrived. I saw him before he reached the school. On all previous days, he had walked alone; but, today he walked in the company of three girls and two other boys. *"Now this is quite an improvement!"* I thought as I watched them. Willie was actually laughing and joking with them, and for the very first time he seemed happy! As soon as he reached the school grounds, he began greeting students with a smile. I found this overture to be truly miraculous! Finally he spotted me, quickly turning in my direction. "Hey, Jake!" he shouted as he approached me. "How am I doing?" he asked. "You're doing just great, Willie." I answerwed. I could clearly see that for once— he had begun to feel good about life! "Now you're doing the things that you need to be doing— just keep it up! "How's your arm?" I asked. "It feels okay, but the doctor said I should not throw any balls before he sees me again". "When do you see him next?" I asked. "This coming Friday evening." Willie responded. "Good—then maybe we can throw a few passes next week," I reassured him. "I hope so," he replied.

The bell rang for our first classes of the day. Again, all the students moved from classroom to classroom, listening to teachers as they reviewed the subjects. I cleared my mind of all other thoughts and focused entirely on my teachers. Even though studying at home was not practical, I was determined to keep my grades high. This would take great effort on my part, but I would succeed nevertheless. Finally it was lunchtime. I was happy for the chance to sit and converse with my four friends. As we sat eating and chatting, we suddenly realized that the stressful feelings we had all experienced had recently begun to dissipate. Of course, each of us fully realized that this new peaceful situation could quickly reverse itself at any given moment. We agreed to keep our fingers crossed and hope for the best. As soon as we'd finished our meal, we moved outside.

We had all spent our leisure time yesterday by talking to students. Today, we would relax and simply enjoy the short amount of time we would have together. Naturally, we greeted a few curious students. Some voiced concerns but I tried to assure them that things were under control. At one point, I saw Willie running across the school park catching football passes. He seemed to be enjoying himself for the very first time at our school. At that moment, I actually forgave him for having taken my baseball cap. I also forgave him for having attempted three assaults against my person! I now felt as though some great invisible weight had been lifted from my shoulders! It was a wonderful feeling of peace and tranquility. I turned to Carol as we sat on our bench, saying to her "I really feel great today". "I do too!" she responded. As I sat there on our bench I looked about the school's park, seeing all the kids milling around together. Everyone seemed completely relaxed. I really liked this new and amazingly pleasant atmosphere!

The bell sounded, and we all began moving toward our classrooms. I saw that Willie was far ahead of me, but this was okay. My concern was that he would arrive at Miss Cunnings' classroom ahead of me and take back his original seat. And since I could not cause a scene, I would be forced to take my original seat, directly in front of him. This gave me reason for concern. It would mean that possibly we had not made the progress I had hoped for. I did not mention any of my concerns to Carol, as I did not wish to alarm her.

I felt a slight twinge of apprehension as I approached Miss Cunnings' door. "Where would Willie choose to sit?" I wondered. But to my surprise, he had opted to sit at the desk I had personally assigned him. I breathed a great (but imperceptible) sigh of relief. I had, in fact, made progress with him, it seemed. He even looked up smilingly at me as I approached the point where he now sat. I returned his smile as I walked past him, to take my seat. Then Miss Cunnings again greeted our class, and each of us (including Willie himself) returned her warm greeting. She too seemed encouraged by the display of cooperation she had just witnessed. But we would cover a great amount of material this day, so she began immediately writing information onto the blackboard. I watched Willie as he sat upright and began taking notes. As I sat there watching him, it occurred to me that this person could actually become likeable. *"Amazing!"* I thought. But then I shook myself and began concentrating upon the subject matter. As I sat there taking notes, I silently asked "Why couldn't this lady be my sole teacher for each of my subjects"? I also wondered if I would have been able to withstand the constant pressure of being near her for such great amounts of time! I realized then that things were better for me just as they were. Suddenly, an alarming thought entered my young mind. "Just how many more boys at this school were similarly interested in her"? And, even more alarming, "How many of these boys did she hold an affinity for"? I considered this latter concern particularly disconcerting! I realized though that I would have to put each of these considerations on hold, for now was not time for such distractions!

The sounding of the bell played a strong role in shocking me back to normal. I played my deceptive role in allowing the students to leave the room. I also repeated my tactics from the previous day. I stepped out into the hallway, but then quickly doubled back. Miss Cunnings had been awaiting my return. We embraced, and then quickly stepped away from each other. Then she began to behave as teacher to student. "Jake, I can't begin to imagine what you said or did to Willie to cause such a great change in him." "But whatever it was— I congratulate you"! I thanked her, adding, "Oh, I just showed him that no one here is afraid of him— and we care about him". "You did a really great job." she exclaimed. But even though she tried to act and speak professionally, I'm certain that I felt her emotions flowing through my body. I now knew for certain that I would have to find some way to have at least a brief conversation with this lady. We said our "Good afternoons" to each other as I left her room.

We had just completed our history class review, and some of us headed to our study period class. However, our school staff had commenced work on the many floats that were to be presented in our upcoming May Day parade. So, half of the students had gone off to work on decorating floats. I really wanted help, but I needed to complete my homework, so I would miss out on the joy and excitement of decorating floats. I felt a little sorry for myself. All the other kids were fortunate enough to play ball on one or more of our four teams. Others were fortunate enough to attend the many games played here. And now, they were spending their time decorating school floats. I had been deprived of each of these activities and felt as though I were only a part-time student! Worst of all, I did not foresee any opportunity to improve my situation. This was my life at age fifteen!

It was again 4:30PM, and I had become my other self— a virtual nobody— suffering behind one smelly old mule! Somewhere during this time I discovered the ability to fantasize, so I began to employ this technique each day while I worked in the fields. As I plowed the long rows of corn, cotton, and tobacco, I would imagine myself in some far-away, exotic location. I had seen some of these places during my recent visits to the movie theaters with Carol, so my mind became my new escape mechanism. I found that by employing this technique, the hours I spent in these hot and dusty (or cold and wet) fields were much more bearable! Thus, for the next three years this would be the manner in which I would survive.

The end of the day arrived, and I 'returned' to my current physical predicament. But during those past three hours, I had spent a wonderful brief period 'wandering throughout the orient'! On past days, I would find myself a bit exhausted at the end of the workday. But on this day, I actually felt refreshed! This was a direct result of my long and exciting 'tour of the orient'. I knew that over the coming three years, this new day-dreaming process would become my primary method of survival. At day's end I returned my old mule to the barnyard, then watered and fed the animals. This had been a truly productive day and an absolute first for me, for I had even 'visited' the Far East!

As I lay alone in my quiet room, I reflected upon the day which had just past. I knew that I had further improved relations at my school. Not only had I succeeded in improving conditions for Willie, I had also gotten many kids who were former strangers, to begin communicating with each other! This I felt was quite an accomplishment. I was aware of no other student (not even seniors) who had realized such an achievement. Suddenly I had become someone special here at school. I wished that my dear Jeanne was still with us to witness this greatly improved environment here on campus. I finally felt very proud of myself. I would very much have liked to inform my parents of my recent accomplishments, along with my new and significantly improved personal status. But this was completely out of the question! They did not even know that I had been undergoing self-defense training. Neither had they learned of the serious problems I'd recently encountered with this formerly terrible boy named Willie. Now, it was not that they did not care. In fact, they cared too much about my safety and well-being, and I was fully aware of this. But how could either of them have known of my activities— being separated from the rest of civilization!

Once more Wednesday morning had arrived. I had been awakened by the loud ringing sound of our old 'wind-up alarm clock. I immediately hopped from my bed, and began washing up. At 6:15AM, I sat at our table, downing my breakfast. Then fifteen minutes later, I rode away down the narrow bicycle trail leading from our old house. The morning temperature had already reached seventy degrees. No winds were present, so riding my old bicycle along these country roads and through the forest was a real pleasure. I realized that for some strange reason, I was full of energy. For the first half of my route I even struck up a little song, since there were no people in the area. But I soon began the second half of my thirty-minute ride. Along this portion of roadway, kids were out and walking to school. As I passed them each would speak to me, and I made certain that I returned their greetings. I arrived at school at my usual early hour of 7:30 and after securing my bicycle, I returned to the large yard area in front of our auditorium.

I had only finished greeting the first group of students when my new 'friend' Willie arrived. He again joined me in greeting and cracking jokes with the many students there. As we moved together through the crowds, we seemed to pick up a following. Suddenly we had become quite a sizeable group of greeters, moving about and greeting each person standing! This included our principal, along with many of our teachers, making this a truly jovial and most memorable moment! Now, every student here appeared both relaxed and happy. Accordingly, our kind principal and his staff of teachers seemed much happier. As for myself, I felt just great! Naturally, I remained somewhat cautious, but I'd felt great optimism about this new and fresh attitude at our school. Our principal and teachers remained outside with us until the morning bell had sounded. He then promptly returned to his office while the teachers returned to their classrooms, accompanied by their students. This morning had begun on a surprisingly positive note!

There was more to come. No sooner than I had taken my seat in my first class of the morning , did our principal again summon me to his office. As I entered, he immediately arose from his desk to greet me. With a broad smile on his face, he reached forward as he grasped my hand in a firm handshake. "Young man, I just want to thank you for the great job with the students," he said. He added "I know you need to be in class now, so I won't keep you". "I'm with you in this endeavor, so if you need my help— don't hesitate to call upon me". "Thank you very much, sir" I said. With these words I was excused. The concern and personal involvement of my principal left me with a really positive feeling.

At lunch, the mood in the cafeteria was jovial. Even our food handlers moved about with smiles on their faces. I don't recall having ever before seen them smile. We had just entered into a new era—one of cooperation and companionship! Presently, everyone marveled at this new emerging attitude of fellowship among our students. When I received my food tray, I discovered that I had been given an extra portion of beef, and I attributed this rare act of generosity to the new mood I had helped create. My friends all seemed somewhat awestruck. Even Wilton had begun to see things my way. "Jake, I don't know how this is going to end up— but it sure feels good now," he said, "I never dreamed that we could make this much difference"! I thanked him, adding, "Each of you sitting here with me has helped to make this possible". "But it's still a bit too early to begin rejoicing— let's just see how it goes." I concluded. We finished our meals and moved to the outside grounds.

As we walked across the park, several boys (and girls) walked right up to me just to say hello. I very much enjoyed this new feeling of popularity, but I maintained humility. The last thing I wanted was for the students to sense that I had now begun to feel important. I was that same young country farm boy who just three weeks ago these students hadn't known existed. Carol and I again parted from the boys who were tossing footballs around. Then as we sat peacefully on our bench, she said, "Jake, I guess now that you're popular around school, you'll forget about me". We had refrained from touching while on the school grounds, but I took her hand into mine as I said to her, "Carol, no matter what happens here, I will never forget about you". My words seemed to bring her great comfort. She smiled sweetly at me as she gently squeezed my hand. Then one of the boys called out my name, and signaled me to run for a football pass interception. I accepted his offer and immediately began running to receive the ball. It was a long pass, but I caught it gracefully. The students in the area had been watching the action, and they began to applaud and cheer for me. At that moment, I really felt great! Then Willie called out for me to pass the ball to him. I signaled for him to run 'long'. I timed his speed and location. I timed his before releasing a long, smooth, arching pass that landed precisely into his waiting arms. He also caught the ball with precision and grace! Now the students really began to applaud and cheer loudly! He waved to them and did a little dance step. They loved his little 'show' and cheered him even more. Sadly, at this point the bell sounded. Our lunch period had ended.

Normally this would have been a regretful moment for me, but I looked forward to this moment with considerable anticipation. "Why?" you might ask. The answer is quite simple, for I would soon get the chance to be near the true object of my affection. By this, I mean my dear Miss Cunnings! I did not take great joy in leaving Carol; but, I most certainly looked forward to this very special moment in my day! Miss Cunnings resumed review of material for upcoming final examinations. I noticed that Willie had again busied himself in note-taking. Although we were nearing the end of our school year, he seemed intent on passing the ninth grade. I silently wished him well as I sat taking my own personal notes. Our finals would begin the coming Monday morning, so I would need to study as much as possible. Albeit, I would set aside just a little time on Saturday afternoon to tutor Willie.

This class period passed much too quickly. My heart raced as I anticipated my approaching brief encounter with my teacher. But today, I would be disappointed. As I lagged behind in my exit, I noticed that two girl students had approached her desk. Immediately, my previously high level of morale began rapidly dropping. I imagined the very worst possible scenario. *"What if I don't get to talk to her today?"*–

"How will I survive"? It then occurred to me that – in less than ten more days— I would not see her all! I was shattered! Until this very moment, my day had been unimaginable. But now all seemed lost, though I tried to be strong. I strolled nonchalantly down the long hallway, all the while hoping those visiting girls would emerge from her room. But it seemed that my luck had just ended, for they had not yet left her class. But to make matters worse, I'd run out of time. I could wait no longer so, I decided to acknowledge my fate and proceed to my next class.

I sat taking notes in history, my mind kept drifting to amorous thoughts of Miss Cunnings. I knew that I desperately needed to focus, so I purposefully pinched myself so hard, it actually hurt! On my way to study period, I knew that somehow I just had to see her, so I decided to make one more attempt. I proceeded slowly down the long and dimly lit hallway toward her classroom. I strained my ears for sounds, but all seemed quiet. *"Maybe I'm in luck"* I thought as I neared her door, so I chanced just a bit of boldness! For only a split-second I peered into her room. No other person was inside! I had not made a sound and because she was not expecting me, she had not seen me. She sat with her back turned slightly toward me. No one else was in sight! "Ma'am, do you have the time?" I asked, catching her completely off guard. Instantly, she recognized the sound of my voice, and immediately sprang up from her desk rushing straight for me! "I was so afraid that I would not see you today," she whispered as she threw her arms around me. "I was dying to see you, so I could not let that happen," I said as I drew her close. We squeezed each other passionately before stepping apart! Then she said, "I was worried that you would return while the girls were here". "I would not have done that to you," I reassured her. She did the unexpected by quickly drawing me to her again, and planting a warm kiss on my left cheek! I reciprocated by holding her tightly and kissing her on the forehead! (Now many of you reading this will say, "forehead— how romantic"! (Remember, I was only a student)! We said "byes" to each other and I abruptly left her room. Now I had become alive again! I no longer wondered how I would survive the remainder of this day. Also, I had learned something! This beautiful young lady actually did care something for me— (exactly what, I was not sure). I could finally move on to my study period. But most important, I could again concentrate. For the first few minutes of my study period I could only think of her, for I was in love again! I knew that this afternoon while riding home— I would once again sing my little 'happy song'! I had felt great beginning early this morning, but now I felt absolutely ecstatic!

After school I saw Willie again walking ahead of me. This was the way I'd wanted things. Soon my friends reached me and together we left the school grounds. Horace walked directly across the street to his house. He would reach his home in less than two minutes. How could one be so very lucky? The rest of us continued walking together. And though I recently had been thrilled by my sweet teacher, walking with Carol also felt really great. *Too bad— all this will end in less than two more weeks*", I thought. We reached Carol's house, where we stood talking for just a few more minutes. Then I climbed onto my old but faithful bicycle and rode away for home. My spirits remained high, so along my route I began singing my little 'happy song' from months earlier. At home, I completed my daily work routine. Today, even this work seemed to have become a bit more bearable. This had been the best day of my young life!

My next two days at school passed uneventfully. There were no incidents at school and morale remained high. My relationship with my favorite teacher continued to flourish. So overall, this had been a great week! Once again Saturday was upon us. I completed my usual eight-hour work day, then prepared myself for a bit of socializing. Dad also prepared for his usual trek into town. Once more, he asked me to join him, but I knew that his schedule conflicted with mine. So, I ever so politely explained my situation. "Dad, I would really love to ride along with you," I said. "But after the movie I have promised to stop by old lady Jayes' home to help her grandson with his school work". Dad accepted my explanation, and complimented me for getting involved. So we left our house separately. He drove and I rode my bicycle, but we reached the downtown area at the very same time. This time however, a thought had entered my mind. Specifically, dad had seen me riding through this dense forest shortcut on Saturday afternoons. But he had never questioned whether I traveled this route to and from school. Although, it would seem likely that since I had taken this route on Saturdays, I had probably also taken it throughout the week. But if I had, then why had I not arrived at home at least one half hour earlier each day? Something seemed slightly unusual in this situation!

I knew that although dad had only completed sixth grade, he had a very keen mind. So he must have known something about my recent activities. But what— and how much—was the question. Then an even more alarming thought struck me! "What if he (and maybe mom) were aware of my weekend visits with my friend Carol"? If this were in fact the case though, I did not feel that I would've actually been in trouble. However, I also did not feel that I was ready to face teasing from either,— or possibly the both. Even worse, I certainly did not wish to face counseling from them. Although if dad already knew of my activities, then why had he not said something? One full year would pass before I would receive my answer to this most perplexing question. I rode onward to Carol's house.

As usual Carol was waiting for me, so after ten minutes of casual conversation with her mom, we left their house. As I had done on each of the previous Saturdays, I kept my eyes peeled for dad. But again today, we walked the entire distance to the theater without being discovered. After purchasing our refreshments, we entered the darkened theater. Carol and I strongly desired at least a slight amount of privacy for ourselves, so we chose seats apart from the masses sitting in the audience. I felt more secure this way. At least if Carol wanted to kiss me on the cheek (or I her) we would not be easily seen. Then at school, we would not be teased by any of the students. This was a common practice of the students every Monday morning. They would gossip about the events of the weekend. Naturally, I never had anything to contribute, but I was acutely aware of this practice. In this remote corner of the theater, we were safe from scrutiny by others. Today's main feature was a heartwarming love story. Though I felt a little cheated, in that there was no opportunity for Carol to pretend to be frightened. Even so, she frequently squeezed herself as close to me as possible.

I had a full appreciation for this wonderful young lady. I realized that it was she (and not Miss Cunnings) I might have a future with. Nevertheless, I had become completely addicted to my young teacher. Unfortunately, I merely liked Carol very much, but I was determined never to do anything that would harm her or hurt her sensitive feelings. Carol was truly a kind and sincere young lady who deserved the best in life. Now I'm not inferring that I looked forward to (or cherished) a lifelong future with this person. Such thoughts would not enter into my mind for many years to come. We enjoyed our movie, but still, there had been no kisses on the cheek (or elsewhere). Finally, our movie ended.

I had already told Carol of my plans to visit Willie, so I took her home before proceeding directly to Willie's house. Again today, he was sitting on his front porch along with his elderly grandmother. They seemed genuinely happy to see me. After a brief conversational exchange with this old lady, I instructed Willie to grab his books so that we could begin our work. Today I would spend one full hour helping him with his school work. This meant I would only be afforded only half hour of horseback riding time this evening. But since this was a singular occurrence, I would accept these terms. I would do this great favor for this person who had less than one month earlier tried to take my life, even though many would have called me foolish! We concentrated mostly on mathematics and English, although at the end of the hour there was still work to be done. So I opted to forfeit my entire riding period just to help Willie complete this ninth grade. I continued by reviewing math formulas with him. Luckily for the whole period I spent with him, he remained diligently attentive. I concluded our session by reviewing history.

With the weekend ended, another Monday was upon us— (my final week of school this semester). For the most part, I felt really great on this particular morning. However, I realized that I was a bit saddened in that these were my final days of ninth grade education. I was even more saddened by the fact that I would not see my friends for three months. But as I had done over the past week, I began my school day by moving among, and greeting the other students on campus. Soon afterwards my four friends joined me. Five minutes later, Willie also joined us. We moved about the large groups of students, voicing well wishes and encouragement for this morning's rigid exams. I made a special point of encouraging Willie himself. But my main message to the students was "Concentrate— and remember what you were taught throughout this year". As we continued through the crowds I incidentally turned toward our main school building and for a brief moment, I'm certain that I saw our principal standing there. I waved in his direction, and he'd waved back at us. He then quickly vanished back into the building. Soon the bell rang and each student proceeded to his or her classroom. I felt that this had been a very good beginning. When the morning had finished, I had completed exams in English, mathematics, science, and geography. I found that I was comfortable and confident while taking each of these four tests.

Finally our lunch period arrived. It was time to quench our thirst and hunger, so we quickly gathered inside our modest cafeteria. As I looked about, it seemed as though there were more smiling faces than usual in the building.

I picked up my tray and moved to my special table. My friends were waiting for me. In fact, they did not begin eating until after I'd seated myself. This was another first for me, and I greatly appreciated their consideration. Each of them indicated that they felt generally good over their performance with this morning's exams. As usual, we all moved outside as soon as we'd finished our meals. Naturally Carol and I went directly to our special park bench. I discovered that she' been particularly impressed over the great improvement in student relations at school. I also had been both surprised and impressed. Even the students themselves seemed to have been impressed, for again today, my former foe and I had continued an unspoken partnership. Together, we demonstrated compassion, harmony, and teamwork as a duo! This demonstrated to the whole school that virtually anything could be accomplished, with just a tiny bit of group cohesiveness. No longer were there the pockets of students standing around together, ignoring others. As Carol and I sat there together, we each expressed our deep regret that this semester was at its end. Then hesitatingly, she squeezed my hand, asking, "Will you still take me to the movies on Saturdays"? "Of course," I reassured her. Now this was not just an empty promise, but one I would keep!

At last our lunch period ended, so we readied ourselves for three more exams. This was health class. Willie had entered ahead of me and had taken his 'assigned' desk. I winked at him as I walked past. By winking, I had sent a signal to Willie that all would be well with this exam. Our teacher and class greeted each other. Then she said, "I wish each of you well". This young lady was exceptional. No other teacher had expressed such concern for our success. Then she started around the room, passing out the exam to each student. When she had finished she gave us the rules for taking the exam. Specifically, there would be absolutely no communication between any students. Any violation would result in automatic failure. I had no problem in adhering to these rules. I'd felt that I knew the answers even before viewing the questions. Now I don't wish to appear cocky, but I had mentally retained nearly all of the information I had received throughout the year. I took the examination, and felt that I had completed it with ease. As each student finished his or her exam, that student would place the exam face down on their desk. Then they were required to sit quietly through the remainder of the class period. This is what I had done. Finally the bell sounded and each of us prepared to leave the room. But today, I would alter my routine. I would not wait around, or double back for the purpose of seeking a hug. Instead, I departed the room along with all the other students. I would not risk being discovered with my teacher at this special time. Thus far we had been very fortunate, and I wanted this to continue unnoticed, so I braced myself and then proceeded directly to my next class.

I was again in history class, and as I've stated previously this was also a young female teacher. Though I had found this young lady to be distinctly different in personality from my dear Miss Cunnings. She greeted the class, and then gave us the rules for taking the exam. Here, there were no well wishes, although I had paid particular attention to the obvious absence of such. Unfortunately, I experienced greater difficulty in completing this exam. I'd always had problems remembering dates of certain events; although, I'd experienced no problems in remembering names of geographical locations or the names of those persons involved. Hence, I struggled slightly in completing this particular exam. When results were released, I would receive only a C+ in this subject. This would conclude our exams for this year.

Incidentally, when test results were released, my grades were as follows: English=A+, math=B, science=A, geography=A-, health=A, and history=C+. I viewed these grades as 'not too shabby'. Actually, I was quite proud of my accomplishments, considering I had managed this without having done any home study during the year. "*Not bad*", I thought as I read my report card. One of my many regrets here was the absence of electricity at home. For without electricity, home study was virtually impossible. Additionally, the need for me to work in the fields had eliminated any possible study time while at home. So overall, I felt that I had done quite well!

At last, our final week of this school year had ended, leaving me with just one more requirement. So with some degree of apprehension, I approached the door of her classroom as I peered inside. She stood facing away from me, and since I had made no sound, she was not yet aware of my presence. "Good afternoon, Miss Cunnings," I said. She instantly spun around and rushed toward me! I sensed some urgency in her stride, as I moved toward her. Then she threw her arms around me! Naturally, I acted accordingly! I stood pressing her youthful body tightly against mine— all the while listening for footsteps in the hallway outside. I'd heard no footsteps, so I continued squeezing her tightly against me. "It's been three days since I've seen you," she whispered. "Seems longer than that to me," I said.

At that point when she could no longer restrain herself, she kissed me— on my left cheek! I found myself wanting more, but I settled for just a kiss on the cheek. In return, I kissed her on each cheek, squeezing her gently as I did so. My heart beat rapidly as I held her. I seemed to develop a lump inside my throat, as I'd stood there wondering what to do next. So I did the most sensible thing I could think of—I released her! She then said, "I was wondering if you'd possibly forgotten to stop by". "That would never happen," I responded. "I'm glad to hear that," she answered. We were now standing apart from each other, (in case someone had poked their head inside her door). I then said, "Do you realize, I like you so very much— but I don't even know your first name."! She quickly stepped forward, whispering into my left ear, "Catherine". "I'm pleased to meet you, Catherine." I stammered. "Likewise" was her warm response. But now we were out of time! So we gave each other "Best wishes" for the summer, and I then quietly (but sadly) left her classroom.

It was time to depart for home, when I suddenly realized that I had not yet picked up my report card. I asked my friends to wait for a moment, while I ran to the school's office. The nice lady at the office handed me my report card, and I immediately rushed outside to meet my friends. They were aware that I never studied at home, so they were quite curious about my final grades. I had not yet reviewed my card, so I took a moment to open it. Upon seeing it, they expressed dismay at my final grades. As I stood there reviewing them, I also found myself pleasantly surprised.

Without any home study whatsoever, my grades were as follows— English; A, geography; A+, health; A+, history; B, math; B+, science; A. I was quite pleased! Had I been able to study at home, I'm quite sure that I could have improved my history and math grades. But even so, the grades I'd just received ranged within the top five percent of my class. Needless to say, I was generally well pleased with my academic achievement, during this past school year!

We finally left the school grounds, and were heading toward our homes. Although today was special and somewhat different. Instead of my usual group of four friends, Willie also joined us. As we walked along together, I failed to detect any degree of tension between us. Everyone seemed totally happy and fully relaxed. Incidentally, Willie voluntarily showed us his report card. I was the first to review it. He'd managed to achieve an average grade of C+. And according to Willie himself, this was the highest overall grade he had received in recent years. My average grade was an A-, and Carol had received an A as her overall grade. Donnie and Wilton had received grades of B+ and B, respectively. So as a group, each of us was quite satisfied with our performance.

Summer painfully dragged past, but it was back-to-school time for which I was most appreciative. Upon resumption of high school I was pleasantly surprised to find that student attitudes and behavior had remained constant. My recently acquired friend (Willie) had been assigned the position of substitute quarterback on our school's football team. In coming years he would become our primary quarterback, where he would prove himself as an invaluable football player. Amazingly, my platonic relationships with Carol and Catherine would flourish even beyond my greatest expectations!

I began this current school year as a proud sophomore, and from the very first day I realized an elevated level of respect and admiration from those students who were junior to our grade level. I substituted my geography class with industrial arts, which would provide me with a viable trade upon graduation from high school. During the following two years I would also include brick masonry in my curriculum, thereby increasing my opportunities for a suitable lifetime career.

With my busy schedule, time seemingly passed rather quickly, so in just a short period of time, my parents and I were once again joyfully celebrating grandmother's ninety-ninth birthday. Then one month later I found myself celebrating my own birthday—, at the tender age of sixteen! *"Wow"*, I thought as I eagerly blew out the candles on my cake. This birthday was accompanied by dual significance. First, I had finally reached the age of permissive dating. Second, I was also eligible to test for my driver's license. These two very special privileges would significantly change my life. Unfortunately though there were no gifts for me, but by now I'd become quite accustomed to the absence of presents on my birthday. I really wished that my friends could have been present for this special occasion. But due to the great distance at which I lived from town, none of them knew how to reach my house. There was one upside to this situation, which was— I would get to enjoy my whole cake all by myself!

It seemed only yesterday that our current school year had begun. But here we were once again only one month away from its end. Things had gone exceptionally well throughout this year, and I found myself deeply regretting this impending event. There were several reasons for my feelings of remorse, but most important, was the fact that I would not see my friends for another three full months. Heck, even Carol and my lovely Catherine would be absent from my life during this time.

We finally entered the third week of May, and were commencing final examinations. Each written test would be completed within less than one hour. However, my industrial arts project would take three class periods for completion. Now due to the nature of this skill, there were no girls in this class. So each boy had randomly drawn his test project from a brown paper bag. It was now my time to reach into this bag. I carefully reached inside and removed one small slip of folded paper. I quickly unfolded the paper but was nearly floored, as it revealed the nature of my exam project. I (of all people) had been tasked to produce a fully functional electric lamp! Can you imagine that? Also, I would do this from scratch— and without instruction! *"What irony"*, I thought as I contemplated how to begin my project. Our instructor had already informed us that we would be allowed to keep our completed products as mementos of this class. As I sat there that day, I wished that I could have drawn any project other than this. For, although I would dedicate considerable effort to the construction of my lamp, I would most likely never use it. I certainly could not use it at home— for there, electricity was nonexistent. But regardless of my situation, I decided I would give this project my very best effort. So I dedicated those final three class periods to producing an item worthy of desire and admiration. And in the end, my project would receive a final grade of A+. But it would never be used by me or my family. Incidentally, I would receive the following grades in each of my other subjects: English- A; math- B+; health- A; history- B; and science- A+. I had slightly improved my grades over those of the previous year. Again, it wasn't that I had grown any smarter; it was merely that I'd had even more time for study and preparation. Still though, I was proud of these grades.

Then suddenly I found myself entering into my final week of tenth grade. The difficult school work had ended. With today's work completed and this school year finished, it was definitely party time! But before heading to the near-by lounge, I would pay one final social visit to my dear and lovely Catherine. I found her once again anxiously awaiting my arrival. As I'd hoped, she was alone. Upon seeing me she rushed forward and embraced me. But more accurately stated, we fervently embraced each other! She then wisely stepped back and away from me so as to present a respect-able appearance. And although I had really wanted to hold her in my arms for a much longer period of time, I released her without protest. If any faculty member or student had passed or entered her room, all would have seemed nor-mal. I knew that neither of us could afford to become lax in our 'relationship' but I longed to see her at some point during the summer. So, I said, "I'd really like to see you across the summer, will you be around"? She answered "Jake, I'd love to see you as often as possible—but I'll be in San Francisco across the summer". My heart sank! "Then I don't know how I will survive this summer," I said to her. "I'll miss you also, but I'm sure you'll manage without me," she softly answered. "But I don't want to manage without you, for you see I love you so much!" I blurted. There— I'd said those endearing words and my secret was now known! Immediately I regretted it, fearing that I might have over-stepped my boundaries. But I need not have worried, for upon hearing my words, she immediately threw herself into my waiting arms. She abandoned caution and began passionately pressing her warm body against mine while kissing me! I vainly struggled to control my pent-up emo-tions— for I was a young male, and as such, I was supposed to be cool! But 'cool' wasn't within my grasp at this partic-ular moment. This was not so much because her body had seemingly become welded to mine; but, because she had also forced her tongue into my mouth! Now this was an act of passion that until now I had only fantasized about! And this act, while coupled with her sighs and body movements, instantly lifted me to a whole new level of awareness in-volving the immeasurable pleasures of the female anatomy! We soon reluctantly released each other while attempting to regain some degree of self-composure. Fortunately for us, no one had witnessed our wild display of affection, or all would have been lost!

During the month of June I'd spend a fair amount of my weekend leisure time with Carol. It so happened that another new lounge (The Lantern) had recently opened in our little town. Carol and I would spend as much time as reasonably possible at this very nice new facility. We were quite fortunate in that this lounge also catered to teenagers, and it was located only three blocks from Carol's residence. But all too soon, the month of June had passed and I suddenly found myself quite alone. Despite

Carol's absence, there still existed my dear friend, Mr. Lim. Thus the combination of this old gentleman, my horse, and Buddy, I had no reason for complaint. But even in the absence of these three companions, there was also my former nemesis, (Willie). So, had I felt the need for an extra person as companionship, I could always have paid a visit to Willie's house!

Finally, with the arrival of September, I happily and proudly returned to school as an eleventh grader. Again this year I juggled my subjects to include industrial arts and brick masonry. I quickly discovered that my friend Willie had already established himself as a football star and a respectable individual. He had even acquired his very own following (including a large number of female students). I watched him as he flirted with the girls and interacted positively with the boys, and I marveled at his unbelievable transformation. Even my friends had recently begun to like and respect him. So now, things could not have been better here at school. And while observing the large numbers of students milling around, I realized that this school campus had become their sanctuary. Once again I walked Carol to the spot where we usually sat together. We felt that this would truly be a good year. But as we sat holding hands, I decided to comment on the subject of our relationship. I had absolutely no idea how she would respond, because my words would not be exactly flattering. Even so, I knew this would be the proper time for such a discussion.

So hesitatingly, I began "Carol, there's a small matter that I believe we should discuss". "Yes, Jake?" she said, looking at me questioningly. I had opened this conversation, so now I needed to finish it. "Of course you know that we're both of dating age". "You are a lovely young lady, so I know that many boys here would just love to have you as their girlfriend". I concluded, "I would love to have you as my girl— but I don't have anything to offer you". At this point she abruptly stopped me by turning to face me with her hands placed upon her hips. At first I had viewed her reaction as possibly confrontational. But as she began speaking, I found myself somewhat at a loss for words. "Jake Van York, I find you to be the nicest boy I have ever met". "So, I'll wait for you until the day that you actually do have something to offer me". I was so taken aback by her kind and understanding words. I did not speak— but I hugged her tightly. In return, she squeezed me even tighter. I then inwardly vowed not to mention this subject ever again. But I was bothered by the fact that upon graduation from high school, I would soon be leaving to join the United States Air Force. I would be unable to take her along with me.

I was rescued by the sounding of the bell, signaling our return to class. So I proceeded to my new class, which was where I would learn to become a brick mason. Back in those days, this was a respected and well-paying career. So, if for some reason my plan to join the Air Force failed to materialize, I would have become a brick mason. I would have then married my dear Carol, and we probably would have ended up with a large number of children. And in this situation I would never have had the wonderful opportunity of continuously traveling around the world.

Back inside the classroom, our teacher introduced himself and outlined the program we would follow. Now here,— out of respect and admiration, I shall use his real name, (Primus) for he was truly a great man! Over the coming two years he would teach me and others, much of what we would need to learn while becoming master brick masons. He used a combination of lecturing and actual demonstration, and I quickly concluded that I would really like this class.

This day had just ended, so after a brief (but passionate) visit with Catherine, I grabbed my bicycle and headed for my waiting friends. Carol was the first to greet me, asking "How was your day, Jake"? I told her that my day had been good and inquired about hers. Now the five of us headed directly for the recently opened lounge called "Hattie's". Inside, Carol cuddled against me, but she quickly sniffed, saying, "Jake, I smell perfume". I played down the matter by telling her that one of my teachers had just hugged me. My answer seemed to satisfy her and no more was mentioned about the subject. Then for the next half hour we danced and partied like crazy! When my time was up I placed Carol onto my bicycle and rode swiftly to her place. I spent another five minutes with her before heading home.

It had been awhile since I'd sung my 'happy song' but I did so on this day! My reasons were I'd known for sure that I truly did have two very strong reasons for singing. Though I must admit I did experience slightly perplexing feelings. As I've said before, Carol was one very fine young lady and I truly did have feelings for her. But on the other hand, Catherine was an exceptionally fine young adult lady. The difference here was— although Carol was quite attractive, Catherine was totally irresistible!

I would spend the next four weeks working in the fields, but at the end of this period our annual harvest would be completed. I would not revisit the fields until

January of the following year. But I would escort Carol to movies each Saturday afternoon and then party at the Lantern lounge for nearly an hour. Then each Sunday I would train in archery and knife-throwing skills. Without fail, I would participate in self-defense training with my friend Mr. Lim. Lastly I would usually do my four hours of horseback riding each Sunday.

Back in school, I would intently study my lessons (including my new brick masonry studies). Then at the end of each school day, I would visit Catherine for a few minutes before partying at Hattie's. These activities would actually become my routine for the remainder of this year. I've often heard the phrase "Time flies when you're having fun". And while I realize that this is not actually true, for me time seemingly had lately begun to fly! Soon, three full months had passed and my family and I were once again enjoying our Thanksgiving dinner. Then four days later we celebrated a once-in-a-lifetime milestone— my dear grandmother's 100th birthday! Mom prepared well for this and even ordered a slightly expensive and specially designed candle for this occasion. Poor grandmother was overwhelmed, and she even shed a few tears of joy. We all rejoiced with her! Now summer had gone and the green leaves on the trees had once again turned golden. Soon these golden leaves would completely disappear, and we would be left with only a great number of bare trees. I must say, this was my second favorite time of the year.

We had celebrated Thanksgiving and grandmother's birthday, and we'd now just entered the month of December (my favorite month). I would celebrate two separate occasions during this month: Christmas with my wonderful family, when naturally I would receive a few items of clothing in the form of Christmas gifts, and two days later I would celebrate my birthday with a modest vanilla-coconut cake. But I would once again celebrate alone, because of the remote location of our house. Finally Christmas arrived and we had ourselves another joyous occasion. Two days later my favorite day of the year arrived— December 27th (my birthday). Mom prepared my special cake that afternoon. Then in the early evening, she presented me with my special delight. I received no gifts, although I had expected none. As I prepared to blow out my candles, I silently wished for the companionship of my four close friends. But this was not possible, so I basically enjoyed my cake in solitude. Even so, life for me had greatly improved—and wow, I was finally seventeen! Incidentally, during my celebration, I was pleasantly surprised by having been granted permission by dad, to accept a recent part-time job offer at one of our town's leading department stores. This was my greatest Christmas gift ever!

A new year had arrived and I soon found myself back in school— studying hard and enjoying the companionship of my friends. Each day, I would steal a few minutes of my study period to briefly visit Catherine. Our 'relationship' continued flourishing, and soon I found myself actually falling in love for the very first time! At last, I no longer longed for the presence of my 'first love' (Jeanne). Sure, I still vividly remembered her— but the pain and loneliness caused by her sudden departure had finally completely disappeared. I know many of you ladies are thinking, *"Gee, what a dog this young man was"*. I fully accept and understand your judgment, and in taking this just a step further— I might even agree with you. Though from my personal perspective, I was simply investigating the experiences of teenage life. In no way did I wish to lose Carol, for she was my guiding light!

Over the next eighteen months I intently focused upon maintaining grades at school. I also ensured that my (still platonic) relationships with both Carol and Catherine continually flourished. I'd successfully completed my personal self-defense training program, and even rather miraculously secured myself a part-time job. Then having celebrated my long-awaited eighteenth birthday, I finally (gleefully) celebrated graduation from high school! Just four days later I would board one large Greyhound bus destined for the nearest Air Force Induction Center.

I have often heard the phrase "Be careful what you wish for"! This wise statement certainly applied on my departure date. On that fateful summer morning I arose a bit later than usual. I then painstakingly prepared myself for my four-mile trip into town with my close friend Donnie. After I had dressed and eaten I quietly knocked at my dear grandmother's door. "Is that you, Jake?" she immediately responded. "Yes Mama" I replied. "Then come in here and let me get a look at you" she said. I immediately entered her small room. "I suppose you'll be leaving now," she said with deep sadness in her voice. "Yes, I'll be leaving soon" I responded, struggling to conceal the great sadness I also felt.

"Come here, son, I want to give you something," she said softly to me. She slowly reached into her old apron, removing a folded plain white paper napkin. Slowly and carefully, she unwrapped the tiny item this napkin held. She then said "Son, I want you to have this— but you must promise to protect it for as long as you may live". She handed me a tiny object that appeared to be either a sea shell or some form of hearing aid. This was the mysterious tiny Elm that I fully briefed you on in my introduction. I thanked 'Mama' while promising that I would make every possible effort to protect this little item for the rest of my life. She then stood as we lovingly hugged each other for at least five minutes, amidst another flood of tears. At this time I heard mom calling out to me, so I excused myself to go out to meet her. Both she and dad had returned to the house to bid me farewell. Dad asked, "Have you got everything together, son"? "I have, dad," I replied.

Mom then gave me a quick hug before going into our old house. But while she was inside, dad handed me five twenty-dollar bills. When mom returned, she handed me another two twenties and a ten. So my departing gift amounted to a total of $210. However, I'd also saved $200 of my own, so now my wallet contained the grand total of $410! I would not need any of this money where I was headed. Then the four of us stood together on our old side entrance porch, taking turns hugging each other.

At last my long-awaited special moment had arrived. My friend Donnie was now parking his car next to Old Betsy. Mom and dad then said one final "good-bye" to me before returning to the fields. I hugged grandmother once more before entering my friend's car. I had already said "farewell" to each of my friends, (including Willie, and Mr. Lim. I had also said "farewell" to each of the farm workers who were helping mom and dad to carry on with their work. Naturally, I'd said "bye" to my horse Belle and to my canine friend Buddy. The only remaining person was my dear Aunt Emma, so we would briefly stop by her place while making our way to the down- town bus station. We arrived at my aunt's house to find her waiting for me. She warmly hugged and squeezed me for what seemed like hours, but was only a few short minutes. She then wished me her blessings, before sending me along my way.

I soon arrived at the bus station at precisely 11:30AM, thirty minutes prior to the arrival of my bus. I knew that my friend Donnie needed to get back to helping his grandfather on their farm so I bade one final "farewell" to him also. So now (and for only the second time in my life) I found myself all alone! I sat down on a hard wooden bench as I awaited the arrival of my bus. The hour of noon arrived, but without any sighting of the bus. Then came the loudspeaker's announcement that the bus would be a bit late. I waited— and waited. At 2:15PM our bus finally arrived. There had been some sort of mishap along its route, which had caused this delay. At 2:30PM we departed the bus station, heading for the Induction Center located on Fort Jackson, just outside our capital city of Columbia, South Carolina.

The distance was only approximately seventy miles, but the duration was just over one hour and thirty minutes. Along my route, I managed to control my sadness by staring out through the windows of our bus. As I stared continuously through this window, I finally realized that it had never been my wish to move away from my parents and grandmother. However, had I remained with them I would most likely have suffered the very same fate as they had. The very most that I could have hoped for was to become either a brick mason or carpenter. Granted, each of these fields was respectful, and each would provide me with adequate income. I could have married my loving Carol, and subsequently become the proud father of an undetermined number of children. This, though, was not the lifestyle I had envisioned for myself (or Carol). Thus, I found myself all alone here on this spacious Greyhound bus, which was presently nearing the sizeable city of Columbia. This was only the second time I had traveled this highway, so each and every sight was strange to me. Every new sight interested and even excited me! Finally we passed through the entrance of that historical site known to many as Fort Jackson. Field work for me had finally ended, and now I would be afforded the opportunity to forge a completely new life for myself!

Chapter 4

Maturity in the Military

We had just passed through the front entrance gate to this massive military training and Air Force Induction Center, situated just outside the small city of Columbia. It was rapidly approaching 4:00PM. Many of the base's permanently assigned military members had ended their day's work, and were now departing the base. The main road, which extended through the expansive drill training areas, was lined with a long string of cars. By sitting in my elevated position inside the bus, I had the perfect vantage point from which to clearly view these soldiers as they drove by. I was highly impressed by the professional appearance of every soldier I saw. Each person was immaculately dressed. Their uniforms appeared as if they had just been picked up from the laundry or cleaners. I also noticed that each soldier and officer appeared to recently have come from the barber shop. Even their cars were mostly new ones. Those that were not new appeared to be in excellent condition. I saw no slouches as soldiers, and no jalopies as cars. I then noticed the base itself, which was meticulously maintained. Its grounds were completely free of debris. Even its buildings (without exception) were all properly maintained.

Overall, I found myself totally in awe of my new environment— and I liked what I had seen thus far.

There were approximately one hundred fifty new inductees within my in-processing group, and we were all taken to our temporary living quarters. Each building housed approximately one hundred personnel and was well-kept, but simple in construction, erected without inner walls. These were commonly referred to as open-bay barracks. The only sources of privacy within these buildings were the few existing toilet stalls. I did not particularly care for being forced to sleep among a bunch of total strangers, but I really couldn't complain, for I could at least shower and use toilet facilities without venturing outside in the dark. Inside our barracks I was given a number on a small slip of paper. This number corresponded with the bunk bed upon which I would sleep. Each bed already had fresh, clean linens. Naturally, we were each required to make our own beds, which was another first for me. For back at home, my dear loving mom had always made my bed for me. However, I would watch a few of the other newcomers as they made their beds, and hopefully pick up a few tips.

We made our beds and then sat around watching TV until 9:00PM (bedtime). We had already been advised that all lights would be extinguished at this hour. At 8:55, our assigned military barracks guard made his rounds, reminding us, "Lights out in five minutes". We immediately proceeded to our bunk beds and quickly tucked ourselves in. Our guard then returned to his post at the entrance of our building. He would remain there until 6:00AM the next morning, at which time his shift ended. No talking was allowed within these walls.

We were awakened at 5:30AM the next morning
(Thursday) whereupon we rushed through washing up and
preparing for breakfast. Even though we had not yet been
officially inducted into the Air Force, we were marched to
the dining hall for breakfast. The dining hall was immaculate. Everything was exceptionally clean and properly arranged. My breakfast was wholesome, but not as tasty as
mom's. This was my very first morning of awakening and
not seeing my caring family around me, so I naturally felt
strange and very lonely. But I concealed my loneliness and
tried to act natural. At one point as I sat at my table of four
persons, someone made a light joke and I forced myself to
laugh.

By 8:00AM my entire group of new recruits had assembled in our appropriate testing rooms. Here we would
all be tested for suitability as members of the United States
Air Force. We would be administered a battery of tests, and
would be here in testing for the whole day. Also, during the
morning I would take a series of four academic examinations. I completed test after test, and when I'd finished the
morning's session, I felt that I had done quite well. But it
was finally noon— and lunchtime. We marched as a group
to the dining hall. We were allowed forty-five minutes in
which to eat, for at 1:00PM we would again be seated inside our testing rooms. I hurriedly consumed my meal, but
I did not particularly enjoy the food. I found it somewhat
bland and not very tasty. Anyway, I finished my meal and
promptly picked up my tray. I then proceeded directly to
the long line of arranged fifty-gallon garbage cans. I scraped
the left-over food from my tray into the first can and, then
deposited my tray onto the stack of nearby trays waiting

to be washed. I walked away, intending to exit the dining hall. But I'd taken no more than five steps when I heard one unusually loud and ominous-sounding male voice from behind me, yelling, "HEY YOU, GET BACK HERE"! I quickly looked to my left and right, but no one walked along with me. I slowly turned in the direction of the voice, only to find a burly sergeant scowling at me. "Are you speaking to me, sergeant?" I asked. "YES, I'M SPEAKING TO YOU— YOU GET YOUR ASS BACK HERE RIGHT NOW"! By now I'd become a bit confused, for I felt that I'd done nothing wrong. But this old sergeant was acting as though I'd just killed someone. I cautiously returned to the point where he stood. "What's wrong, sergeant?" I asked. "Do you see this mess in this can?" he yelled. I stared into the can, but saw only garbage. So I again turned questioningly back to him. At this point he seemed to lose patience with me. "PICK UP THIS STUFF!" he yelled once more! Becoming a bit frustrated myself, I questioned, "What stuff"? Now he really became highly irritated, saying, "TAKE YOUR CABBAGE AND BREAD OUT OF THIS CAN"! I still did not comprehend the reason for his obnoxious behavior and silly order. However, I grimaced as I bent forward over the (very smelly) can and began removing the particles of leftover bread. My slow response served to annoy him even further, so he yelled one last time, "MOVE OUT OF THE WAY, I'LL GET IT MYSELF"! I stepped aside as he reached down into the garbage can and removed the bread and cabbage I had deposited there. Next he placed the bread into one can, and the cabbage into another. I had not a clue, for prior to this time, any garbage can was simply that. I had not been made aware of the need for separating the various types of discarded food, but I quickly learned of this most important practice! Finally with these food items properly placed, the grumpy old sergeant dismissed me.

But what the old sergeant had not known was that— as a result of his constant yelling, I had become much more irritated than he; and at this point, I wanted nothing more to do with the military! I had just decided that laying bricks for the rest of my life would be preferable over life in the military. So when I returned to my first afternoon testing session, I had absolutely no intention of completing the remainder of my exams. So, I accepted my first test sheet of the afternoon, then filled in my name and other personal information. But instead of answering the questions, I drew a single diagonal line downward across the entire length of my test sheet. I then immediately deposited it onto the desk of my testing official. This session was just now getting underway, but I had already finished. The testing official scanned my test sheet and then squinted at me, asking "What is this"? "This is my answer," I calmly replied. I did not fear reprisal because I had not yet been inducted. I was still just a lowly civilian, so I would exercise my option to return home! The testing sergeant then commented, "Well, if this is your answer, then walk your little self over to the out-processing center, and get yourself a one-way ticket out of here"! I smiled as I thanked the sergeant for his generosity.

I retrieved my few belongings from our barracks, and by 2:00PM, I sat in the downtown Columbia bus station— headed for home. I left Columbia at 2:45 and arrived back in my hometown at exactly 4:00 o'clock. I had again enjoyed the scenery along my return route, but my greatest thrill came as the large Greyhound Express entered our little town's city limits. This was a truly wonderful moment for me. I disembarked from the bus and immediately walked the short distance to my recruiter's office. I was quite fortunate, for I found him in his office and unoccupied. He was quite surprised to see me, so I quickly explained to him what had transpired, and why I'd returned home. He indicated his understanding of my situation, commenting that he probably would have done the same under those circumstances. I was happy that he had not openly faulted me for my unusual behavior. But at the same time, I knew that he needed my enlistment to help meet his current quotas. I then showed him my very impressive test scores from this morning's testing session, and requested rescheduling for induction. He checked his calendar of induction appointments. When he had finished he turned to me, saying, "Jake, the earliest that I can get you in is six weeks away". "That'll be just fine," I said. "Great" he replied as he filled in my new appointment form. When he had finished, he handed me my copy of the induction form, and I thanked him before promptly leaving his office.

Next, I paid a brief visit to my former place of employment. Everyone at the store seemed genuinely happy to see me. The store manager soon poked his head out from his office to investigate the commotion and also rushed out to greet me. "We thought we'd lost you, Jake" he said, with a big grin on his face. "I missed all of you so much, I thought I'd return at least for a short visit," I replied. "I'm glad you did, for we could use your help on a full-time basis," he said. "I'll be more than happy to help out, but I'll be gone again in six weeks," I said to him. "Great, can you start tomorrow?" he asked. "I'll try my best to be here," I replied. We then ended our brief conversation and he returned to his office. I visited with just a few more sales staff before leaving the store. I'd been back in town for just over an hour, but already I had secured a new appointment for enlistment, and gotten myself a new full-time job.

It was not yet 6:00PM so I would have about ten minutes to hitch a ride to our old farm site, miles outside of town. It so happened that one of the four sons of Buddy's owner worked less than one block away, so I walked quickly to the store where he worked. Again I was in luck, for he was still at work. I'd seen his car parked in back of the store, so I entered and asked if I might hitch a ride home with him. "I'll be more than happy to give you a ride, Jake," he replied. He then gave me the keys to his car, allowing me to wait there for him. I sat pondering my good fortune. First, I'd been allowed to return home, but without reprisal. Second, I had secured a new enlistment date without difficulty. Third, I now had been given brief, but full-time employment at a higher pay rate. And although I was not yet aware, I would be provided full transportation to and from work each day for the duration of my stay. The only problem would be dad's request that I help him with the farm work. And naturally, if he should ask this of me, I would have no choice but to say, "Okay, dad." But I would keep my fingers crossed that such would not be asked of me.

A few minutes passed, and Dave (my ride) exited the store heading to his car. As we drove along toward home, he asked, "Are you home for good, Jake"? I advised my friend that I had been rescheduled to return six weeks from today. "Well, I know your dad will be happy to have you back on the old farm." he said. "I hope not, for I've just been given my job back— but as a full-time employee." I said to him. "Great" he said, "I'll be happy to give you a lift each day while you're here". "Thank you very much Dave, that would be a big help to me," I replied. Then we agreed that I would walk to his house each morning. We reached his house and he dropped me off, saying "See you tomorrow morning". I thanked Dave before quickly walking away.

It was only 6:30 and although I desperately wanted to see my parents and grandmother, I felt that it would wise to slightly delay my return to our house. Otherwise dear old dad would most likely have invited me to join him in the fields—but such an invitation, I could do without! So I walked the short distance to Mr. Lim's place. As usual, I found him relaxing outside in his backyard. He had heard me as I'd approached, so I had not surprised him. "Hello, Jake, why you here?" he questioned. We greeted each other and I informed him that I had been rescheduled for a later date. He quickly fetched me a cold glass of water and we sat talking for the next forty-five minutes. Then at 7:15 I bade him "Good evening" and promised that I would return often, during my current stay. I then picked up my small suitcase and began the fifteen-minute walk to my old house.

At exactly 7:30, I reached the field where dad and the workers were assembled. They were all greatly shocked at seeing me— but especially dad. We warmly greeted each other and I gave everyone a hug. Dad immediately asked, "What happened, son?" so I informed him I'd been rescheduled. Now though he made a strong effort to conceal his happiness, I easily saw through his facade. He then said "I know your mother and Mama will both be very happy to see you". I excused myself and then walked the short distance to our house.

As I neared our house I struck up my little 'happy song'. Mom was in our kitchen preparing their supper, but no sooner than she'd heard my voice did she rush forth from the house and toward me. At the same time grandmother had also heard my singing and was now limping spryly in my direction. Mom had already reached me and the two of us were locked in a 'bear hug'. "I can't believe you're back!" she exclaimed excitedly. "Just for a few weeks," I said to her. "A few weeks will be a whole lot better than nothing," she replied. Now grandmother had reached me, and I quickly found myself enjoying one more 'bear hug'. Grandmother asked, "Are you okay, son"? "I'm just fine, I said, adding I've been rescheduled for late July". They were both overjoyed by my brief return. "Are you hungry?" mom asked. "I could eat something," I answered. "Then come into the house and let me fix a plate for you" she replied. "I'm okay, mom— we can wait for dad and all eat together." I said. "It's up to you," she responded. I went into my room and unpacked the few items of clothing I'd carried.

Soon dad arrived and then washed up, whereupon we gathered once again together to eat. Dad always said grace before our meal, but this time he out-did himself. I could feel the happiness within those old walls, but no one was happier than I. We would enjoy this meal more than ever, for each of us had fully realized just how blessed we were by having been joined together once more. Finally when we'd finished eating, we gathered out front in our usual spot. I'd felt certain that dad was anxious to make mention of my continuing to help out with the field work, but I was determined to avoid any such discussion if at all possible. So as soon as we'd seated ourselves, I stated, "Dad, I know that this may come as a surprise, but Mr. Beatty has offered me my old job, but as a full-time employee". At first he did not respond— but I knew exactly what he was thinking at that moment. When he did speak, he simply said, "You have my blessings, son". I was so very relieved, for this could have turned out quite unfavorably for me. I thanked dad several times over. I sat with them until 10:30 that night. Even dear grandmother remained with us for an extra half hour past her bedtime. And for the very first time, I was allowed to participate in their conversations as an adult, which felt really wonderful! Eventually, grandmother said "Good night" before moving into her little room. Finally, I too said "Good night" and entered my room. It felt really great, sleeping in my bed again!

Next morning I arose at 6:30AM and prepared for my first full day on the job. Might I explain here, this job was nothing special. I mainly performed custodial-type duties. I mopped, waxed and buffed floors. I washed windows and took out the trash. I even cleaned the store's restroom facilities. But in my spare time, I assisted with inventories and did lots of gift wrapping (which I'd learned earlier on this job). But my favorite part was running errands around our town. And in so doing, I often got to drive my store manager's fine luxury automobile (all by myself). So day after day and for the next six weeks, this was my job. And believe this (or not), I really enjoyed working at that store. But I also realized a special benefit by working there. It so happened that our head custodian (a fellow in his early fifties) was what is known today as a sex addict. Throughout each day, he would spend his idle time discussing the subject of sex with me. So, during my first six months of part-time work, he had provided me an extensive second-hand knowledge of this subject. But now that I had returned, he would finish the job he had started. This middle-aged fellow, (Roy) was very thorough and even graphic in his teachings. Thus, by the end of my tenure, I would walk away carrying a substantial amount of carnal knowledge. And naturally, this served to boost my level of confidence, for whenever my very special moment finally arrived!

I got through the day without incident, and I found myself once again riding in Dave's car toward home. Walking from Dave's house to mine caused me to arrive at home just shortly after 7:00PM, (which was perfect timing. As usual, mom was already cooking. Dear grandmother was reclining in her room. So after a few kind words to each of them, I prepared to once again take my outside bath. Shortly after I'd finished, dad also arrived to take his bath. Then we sat together over our supper. Afterwards we gathered outside to chat. It was now Friday evening and I was quite anxious to get into town for a bit of socializing. So, I chanced asking dad if I might use our car, (Old Betsy) to drive into town, and without protest, he gave me his "Okay son".

He said, "Be careful," and I promised that I would. I began wondering "Why exactly was he being so kind to me?", but I would soon learn the reason. It so happened dad was very pleased with the substantial improvement in field work production—a direct result of my having injected the practice of singing together while at work. This increased level of kindness was his way of saying "Thank you, son".

With all potential obstacles removed from my path,

I dressed and prepared for my drive into town, where I hoped to at least meet up with my friend Donnie. It was nearly 9:00PM and I would need to return home by midnight. As I stepped from the rear side door of our old house I immediately noticed the lowered headlights of an approaching car. It was now dark outside, so I was unable to actually see the car itself. Soon it reached our yard, and I recognized Donnie's car. I approached the car just as he'd switched off its engine. He was as thrilled to see me as I was at seeing him. He said, "I heard that you were back, so I thought I'd drop by to see for myself". I told him that I'd returned home because of a scheduling conflict. "Well then, are we ready to party?" he asked excitedly. "We sure are," I replied, with equal excitement. But before driving away I returned the keys to Old Betsy back to the house. I called out, "Dad, I'm riding with Donnie". Again came his "Be careful, son". I didn't bother answering,— for we were gone! For the next several weeks we partied like crazy!

The weeks passed quickly, so on the morning of July 18th 1955, I again struggled to hold back the tears as I prepared to make the return trip to Induction Center at Fort Jackson, S.C. After washing up and eating, I went to my grandmother's room to once again say good-bye. I found her as usual, rocking in her old chair. "I'm getting ready to leave again, Mama" I said. "I know son, I was just sitting here thinking about you," she responded. I told her how deeply I would miss her. "I'll miss you too, son— and I'll pray for you," she said. "I'll do the same, Mama" I said to her. Then she asked, "Do you have the Elm, son"? "I do, Mama, I've wrapped and tucked it into the lining of my suitcase." I answered. "That's good, son, now come here and let me give you a big hug," she commanded.

I did not hesitate in complying with her request, for I strongly felt that this might be the last time we would see each other. Time would prove me correct. Mom and dad returned from the fields for just a few moments to say farewell. We rarely used the term "good-bye" for it sounded so absolutely permanent. So even this time around, I found saying "farewell" to mom to be excruciatingly painful. There was a strong possibility that I might not see any of my family ever again, and this concerned me a lot. As we said our final "farewells" dad asked, "Do you need any money, son"? "I'm fine, dad". "Don't forget— I've been working every day." I said. My words elicited a slight chuckle from him. Then mom also tried to give me two twenty-dollar bills, which I politely refused. Shortly before 11:00AM, I spotted Donnie's car moving along the main road. So one final time, I said "farewell" to those three precious members of my family. Mom and dad then returned to the fields. I had just grabbed my small suitcase as Donnie drove into our yard. I tossed it into the back seat of his car and we quickly drove away towards town. I decided to stop at my dear aunt's house, just to say one final "farewell", so we stopped by for fifteen minutes (long enough for cake and lemonade). My aunt was also saddened by my final departure, but such was life. Then shortly before noon, we left her home and drove around the corner to the nearby bus station. I had just finished the purchase of my ticket as the bus arrived. Now even though this was my second time in making such a departure, on this day it hurt equally as much!

My dear friend (Donnie) and I hugged and shook

hands— not knowing that this would be the very last time we would see each other. I boarded the bus and sat watching him as he drove slowly away from the station. But as I watched him, I felt a slight bit of pity for him because until now— he and I had been inseparable. Sure, there was Wilton and Horace— but Donnie and I just naturally had gelled together; though alas, this great friendship was lost forever!

At 3:00 we drove through the main entrance gate of the historic Fort Jackson at Columbia. This time though I was not quite as apprehensive, as on my first visit here. I felt a bit more comfortable this time around. We disembarked and were met by a young sergeant from our induction center. Once again we were escorted to our temporary living quarters. Once there we received our 'in-briefing,' which outlined rules and regulations of the base. Next we were given a set of blank personal information forms for completion. Then at 4:00PM we were marched (as a group) to the nearby dining hall. But while en route, I realized that I was concerned over the probable presence of that grumpy old dining hall sergeant. So as soon as we entered the dining facility, I scanned the area. This time though I did not see him anywhere nearby, and I kept my fingers crossed that I would not see him this time around. Either way, I would not make that same (near fatal) mistake in dumping my food remains.

The meat portion of my meal consisted of prime rib. But at that point in my young life, I had never even heard of prime rib. As I sat there eating, I could not keep from wondering if I was eating buffalo (or even grizzly bear). Nevertheless, I was hungry and found this dish to be quite delicious, so I ate— and enjoyed it. I finished my meal and proceeded towards the exit, where I would dump and scrape my tray. I once again looked about in search of 'Old Grumpy' but I was in luck, for he was nowhere in sight. I then read the posted signs above each of the garbage cans, and made certain that I had fully complied with instructions. When I'd finished, I scraped my tray into the can labeled 'miscellaneous garbage'. Then I breathed a strong sigh of relief before exiting the dining hall.

I was again outside but we were not free to roam about unescorted, so we waited as a group in our pre-designated staging area. Our group leader arrived to walk us back to our dormitory, where we were informed that we would be allowed to attend the 6:00PM movie, if we so desired. Well, I certainly did not care to just sit around the dorm, so I chose to attend the movie. At least, I could have popcorn and a soda. It really didn't matter what the movie was about, for I would attend anyway. It so happened that the movie was a western (my favorite). But as I sat there in the semi-darkness, I remembered my dear and loving Carol. I sat munching my popcorn and sipping my soda,— but with no one at my side. Then it struck me— this was how I would view movies for the foreseeable future! I quickly removed this highly depressing thought from my mind by concentrating upon the movie.

At 6:00 the next morning, I was awakened by the sound of a shrill whistle, accompanied by the interior lights being turned on. I sprang up from my bed and rushed to the bath room to wash up. Sharply at 6:30AM we were all herded outside and marched to the dining hall for breakfast. We were allowed forty-five minutes in which to finish eating. At exactly 7:00 my group of fifty inductees marched across the large base to the official testing center. Our test sergeant was a different individual this time around, so I was not required to face the previous one. We had already been advised that we would be here for most of the day, completing a series of tests. This time I felt more comfortable, and was therefore more prepared. Also, I was determined that I would do well on this battery of examinations. At precisely 8:00 we began our testing. I would be allowed one hour in which to complete each test. For the next four hours, I carefully read and answered questions involving general knowledge. When I'd finished the final test of the morning, I felt that I had done quite well.

At noon we once again marched to the dining hall, and were given thirty minutes to complete our meal. As soon as I'd finished, I carried my tray to the garbage disposal area. I again carefully scanned the area for the mean old sergeant from my first visit. At first there was no sight of him, but the very instant I began scraping my tray, I spotted him walking rapidly in my direction. He seemed to have recognized me. When I'd finished scraping away food particles, he began a close inspection of each can. But this time I had read and followed posted instructions. He held up the line of inductees who stood behind him just so he would have ample time for his inspection. I walked slowly away, but with each step I took, I expected to be called back. This time I was lucky, for he did not yell out to me. Then as I reached the door of the dining hall, I turned to briefly look at him. I was quite surprised to see him smile at me— which I returned in kind. I had succeeded in escaping 'Old Grumpy' this time around.

At 1:00PM we resumed testing. These would consist of specialized tests in the subjects of English, math, science, and history. I would draw no diagonal lines today— I would answer each question properly. As the afternoon progressed I completed test after test, ending up with the subject of history. At this point I felt certain that I had done well on my first three afternoon tests, and I even felt I'd done well on the history exam. We were then told we would receive today's grades within the hour, so we would return here at 6:00PM.

Meanwhile, we again marched to the dining hall for our last meal of the day. Here we rushed through our meal before returning outside to begin our march back to the testing facility. The center had used a group of office staffers to manually score our test sheets, and they had completed the scoring by the time we returned. Then the names of every inductee were called to receive their test scores. I was pleasantly surprised to find that I had received an overall grade of ninety-five percentile. I scored in the eighty-five to ninety-five range on each test. We were then immediately officially sworn in as enlisted members of the United States Air Force! Needless to say, this was an extremely proud moment for me!

Next, we were marched back to our temporary quarters and instructed to immediately turn-in our linens, and prepare for 7:00PM departure to our training base in Texas. We complied and even cleaned the area around our bunk beds. Finally, at 6:50 I found myself strapped into the seat of what I would later discover was a modified midsized cargo plane. This was a C-54 twin engine turbo- jet/propeller-driven aircraft. This was also the very first large airplane I'd ever been near, and it so happened that I had been given a window seat, situated just aft the right wing. I struggled to act normal and conceal my extreme excitement. After all, I'd heard none of the other members of my group make any comments about being on an airplane, so I decided to sit quiet and keep my mouth shut.

Within a few minutes our plane began to taxi, and soon we were airborne. I felt a great rush of adrenaline as it coursed its way through my body, but I remained outwardly calm. Our plane banked left and assumed a south westward heading. I made myself as comfortable as possible and began peering through the window at the cities, towns, and countryside below. *"Wow, I can't believe I'm actually flying on an airplane"*, I thought as we flew along our route. After about an hour into our flight, the sun began to fade from sight and I discovered that we were now flying through twilight. And that's when I noticed the flames!

There were only two females on our flight and both were airline stewardesses. I quickly raised my hand, shouting, "Stewardess"! Both immediately turned their attention to me. I beckoned them to come forward, and they complied. By this time I could clearly see blue flames as they spurted from the engine near me. I realized that I was now in a state of maximum panic, for when I tried to speak,— only a whisper ushered forth. I faintly uttered, "fire," as I pointed out the window and to the aircraft's right engine. The stewardess nearest to me quickly bent forward over me, peering out the window at the flames. She then withdrew and turned to her companion, who'd also leaned over me to peer out the window. When the second stewardess had satisfied her curiosity, she stood upright, taking one step backward. Then they began laughing almost uncontrollably, as I sat dumbfounded. Then the stewardess nearest me bent forward, whispering in my ear, "Don't be alarmed, dear, those are only the plane's exhaust flames." adding, "We're not on fire". Right then I felt so absolutely stupid, all I wanted to do was crawl through that window and plummet to the ground below! I have never been more embarrassed in my entire life!

We flew for several hours, although I stayed wide awake for the duration of our flight. Then at some point, I felt our plane begin its descent. But we continued along our route for another half hour before finally banking and turning for our final approach. I peered once more out my window, and was astonished to see a massive city filled with bright lights! I figured that this was undoubtedly the famous city of San Antonio, and in just a few minutes more, my thoughts would be confirmed. Soon I felt and heard the wheels of our plane touch the runway's surface with brief screeching sounds. We had arrived on Lackland Air Force Base, which stood just outside the city of San Antonio. As we disembarked from the plane, the stewardesses standing at its exit doorway gave me a quick wink and smile, saying, "Watch out for those fires now, ya hear"? I lowered my head as I squeezed my way past them.

It was shortly past midnight as four military busses arrived to transport us to our barracks. There were approximately one hundred fifty young men in our entire group, so we were divided into four separate groups (which would become known as flights). Each group was then herded onto one of the four waiting busses. As soon as we had taken our seats, we were given our initial in-briefing (orientation) to

Lackland Air Force Base. However, I must stipulate here that this was not, by any means, a welcoming. To the contrary, this orientation was more akin to the in-processing of prisoners of war. In fact, I strongly believe that prisoners of war would have been treated much better than we were that night. It was as if our trainers regretted the fact that we had shown up on their base. Our assigned tactical trainer began his 'welcome speech' by loudly yelling, "Listen up, you sorry bunch of assholes! I'm your trainer, Airman Wilson— so you will obey me at all times! Whenever I tell you to jump—YOU WILL JUMP! And If I should tell you not to breathe—YOU WILL NOT BREATHE! This is because, starting this day—and for the next three months— I OWN YOUR SORRY ASSES! Now remain in your seats UNTIL I SAY OTHERWISE— BECAUSE YOU'RE A SORRY BUNCH— AND I HATE YOU ALREADY"! This commentary had constituted our welcoming process, and it had made me feel really great! I then thought *"Fool, you've successfully escaped the frying pan— only to land directly into the fire"!* We rode for the next fifteen minutes in complete silence before reaching our assigned barracks. Once there, we were issued three pairs of fatigues plus a duffle bag.

Now we were hurriedly forced into our barracks accompanied by more yelling. But up to this point, our treatment by Airman Wilson had been mild— compared to what was about to happen. Inside the barracks we were assigned to specific bunks, and ordered to stand at attention until told otherwise. We did as we were told, and held our assumed position of attention for nearly fifteen minutes. No consideration was given to those new airmen who may have been in desperate need of restroom facilities.

Then suddenly in the doorway, there appeared the most awesome non-commissioned-officer I'd ever seen! He stood approximately 6'4" and I estimated his weight at 240 pounds. He was quite muscular, with broad shoulders and washboard mid-section. He wore his hair short-cropped and in crew-cut style. But most impressive of these attributes were his steel grayish-green eyes. Those fearsome eyes seemed to penetrate right through each of us. We stood mesmerized by his presence. He began to speak and walk slowly forward as he spoke to us. He did not look at us—he actually glared at us! His first words were "I'M STAFF SERGEANT DYKES"! I will be your Tactical Training NCO for the duration of your stay here". "However, none of you should ever wish to see me, for if you do— you will regret that mistake for the rest of your miserable life"! "HAVE I MADE MYSELF CLEAR?" he growled. Each of us was unsure as to whether or not we should answer him, so we remained silent. Our lack of response seemed to have infuriated him, for he immediately ordered Airman Wilson (our tactical trainer) to run us for ten laps around our block. It was now 1:30AM as we assembled outside in darkness to begin our hour-long run. We finally finished at 2:30 and everyone scrambled for the latrines. Then at exactly 3:00AM, we were allowed to crash for a bit of shut-eye. There would be no time allocated for dreaming on this night.

It seemed as if I'd just closed my eyes, when I heard a shrill whistle accompanied by someone yelling, "FALL OUT"! My initial thought was *"Am I dreaming"*? But this was not a dream— everyone was up and scampering toward the latrines to quickly wash up. I closely checked my watch to find that the hour was 5:00AM. Then by 5:30, each group had assembled outside and was awaiting further orders. Our instructor, Airman Wilson arrived and hustled us into drill formation (which was a first for each of us). We then marched to the nearest dining hall and was allowed twenty minutes for breakfast.

At 6:00AM, we began in earnest— our first day of continuous marching. We marched through the entire morning with only three five-minute breaks (for latrine purposes). At noon we returned to the dining hall for our mid-day meal. It so happened that I'd entered the chow hall at the end of my flight, thinking I would have at least a half hour in which to eat. I would soon learn though that I'd been badly mistaken, for I'd only taken three bites of my food when our trainer yelled to us "FALL IN"! This meant that we were each to assemble outside immediately. So although I was very hungry, I arose and promptly dumped the uneaten food from my tray. I then immediately began walking in the direction of the outside assembly (staging) area. But as I rushed out, something inside my brain seemed to snap! I recall reaching the staging area, but all else is a total blank. I saw people around me, but recognized no one! I heard their voices, but seemed to not understand their words! I struggled frantically to recall my name—but could not! At this point, I inwardly panicked! I did not know what to do— or where to go. I just wandered around until one of the trainees grabbed my arm and shook me. Only then did I return to my senses and rush to take my assigned position in my flight. The afternoon temperature had already climbed to 112 degrees (F), and this was my very first time experiencing such high temperatures. Surprisingly, though, I would survive the afternoon without further difficulty.

We marched until 4:00PM, at which time we paused for dinner. This time I made sure that I was among the very first to enter the chow line, for to say that I was famished would have been a gross understatement. I quickly wolfed down my food, fearing that we might suddenly be rustled again from the chow hall. So even though I may have harmed my digestive system, I at least managed to finish all my food and even return for seconds.

We had been allowed the whole of forty-five minutes for our last meal, so I hoped that this would be end of our first day of basic training. However, at 5:00 our day of marching resumed and would last until 8:00PM. Finally, we'd completed our first day of training. But still no one had greeted me during this entire day— and no one had inquired as to how I might be doing. This is when it really struck me, *"Heck, no one here even cares about me"*. I then seemed to have heard a voice saying, *"You wanted to leave home—SO DEAL WITH IT"*! So at that very moment, I began formulating a strategy to survive this harsh treatment over the coming three months. First, I would recall the extremely harsh conditions I'd survived over the past nine years. Second, I would pretend that I was now a prisoner of war— and this base would serve as my prison camp. I would force myself to believe that this was just a rugged game we were playing—AND ONE WHICH I WOULD NOT LOSE! As the third and final element of my survival program, I would keep in mind that each passing day would bring me closer to my target date of departure from this location. Then with these thoughts in mind, I prepared to take a nice soothing shower, which was something I could never do back at home. As soon as I had finished, I heard the announcement "Lights out" sounding. From this day forward, this would become my favorite part of the day while in training.

I slept soundly throughout the night, but now it was 5:00AM Friday morning. We were again rousted from our bunks and ordered to expedite our washing up. We each did as we were told and hurriedly finished bathing. Then at 5:30 we found our-selves once again outside, scrambling to locate our position in this military formation. I imme-diately noticed that I felt a bit more alert and energetic. I soon realized that we'd been allowed to sleep through the entire night without interruption. We marched to our des-ignated dining facility, where we had our usual breakfast, consisting of eggs with either bacon or ham. I made sure that I completely consumed my meal—just in case I might miss a meal sometime during the day. Then we were once again herded outside and into military drill formation.

The hour was 6:30AM, and over the next three hours temperatures would climb to well above 100 degrees. Nevertheless, we would march for nearly six hours before breaking for lunch. As on the previous day, we were allowed only three five-minute breaks and were continuously yelled at throughout the morning. Then at around 11:00, it occurred to me that all this yelling was an inherent component of our basic training program, so this was to be expected— and as such, I would not allow this to either intimidate or annoy me. I would simply go along with the military's training methods! We followed the very same routine and endured the same intense level of harassment and intimidation for the next ninety days. But on each of those unbearably hot and sunny days, our proficiency in military drill practices improved. By the time we had reached the sixty-day point, we had each become highly skilled in the art of precision drill activity, having marched seven full days per week without any time off. Now we only had thirty days remaining time in basic training. We had successfully completed the 'easy' portion of our training program.

On September 18, 1955, we were given our very first time-off. We had marched throughout the morning, and when we'd finished our noon meal, we were marched back to our barracks and dismissed for the remainder of the day. Needless to say, each of us was in a state of shock— and simply did not know what to do with our free time. So I inquired of our barracks guard, "Sir, are we free to go and see a movie"? "Go wherever you'd like— just be back here before 9:00PM," he said. I couldn't believe my ears! These were the kindest words I'd heard in the past two months. I showered and then relaxed until 2:45, at which time I walked alone to the nearest movie theater.

Back at the barracks, I relaxed for the next several hours until bed time. During this time I managed to write two letters (one to my mother and another to my dear Carol). In my letter to mom, I told her not to worry about me— for I was doing just fine. Nothing could have been farther from the truth, for I was dying inside to see my beloved family. In my letter to Carol, I stated how much I sincerely liked her. I also told her how I longed to spend more time with her. My letters would be mailed next day by our mail clerk, and would reach home by the next weekend.

Finally "lights out" sounded and we all crashed, exhaustedly, upon our bunks.

We were taken by surprise at being awakened at 3:00AM. But there was no questioning of authority, so we scampered from our beds and rushed to wash up. At 3:30 we were marched to our dining hall for an early breakfast. Then at 4:00, my flight was herded onto one of the four waiting military busses, and driven to a densely wooded area thirty minutes away from our base. Once we arrived at our destination, we were told by our instructor, "Okay, you miserable bunch of dirt bags— this is where you will spend your next twenty-one days"! We were then herded from the busses and into the waiting darkness.

During this process we were ordered to follow the voices of our respective training instructors. Now although we'd closely followed our instructions, I still do not know how we succeeded in maneuvering in complete darkness without receiving serious injury. We were now in the heart of rattlesnake territory! Most likely the great commotion we made scared away any snakes lurking in the area. We had not received any prior briefings concerning this phase of training, so many of us were somewhat confused. Then someone shouted over a loudspeaker, "Welcome, you rookies, to bivouac training". We huddled together there in the cool morning darkness, as we listened to the continuous string of orders being barked over the loudspeaker. We were informed that we had successfully completed both the beginning and middle phases of our training program. The speaker continued by saying "This is your true test—for here, we shall test your metal"! This came as a big surprise to me because I'd thought that my metal had been tested for the past sixty days.

Slowly the darkness began fading and we were finally able to visibly discern our surroundings. And as I looked around, I realized that we were in the 'middle of nowhere'. But what I had not realized was the fact that there would be no prepared food here at this isolated location. Also there would be no bunk upon which to sleep. Plus, this place bore a strong similarity to our farmlands back home— for there were no toilet facilities. This meant that (1) We would subsist by consuming three four-ounce cans of "C-rations" daily for the next twenty-one days. (2) We would sleep on the bare ground among the many crawling animals such as snakes, scorpions, tarantulas, and centipedes. (3) We would collect our only drinking water from a small near-by brook. And 4) We would take our baths in one murky man-made mud hole—the very same mud hole where the snakes would gather for a drink. Suddenly I realized that basic training had just been elevated to a whole new level of intensity! Up to this point, our flight had retained all of its trainees. But over the coming three-week period, we would lose six members of our flight to the rigors of this special training program. However, I strongly suspect that a few of our losses could be attributed to the absence of television.

Notwithstanding, at 5:30AM we began our advanced program of calisthenics. This program consisted of an extensive variety of physical fitness activities such as jogging, chin-ups, push-ups, sit-ups, etc. We would perform these rigid physical conditioning activities for one hour every morning for the next twenty-one days. We underwent this training each morning even before our breakfast of "C-rations". Then immediately afterward, we would commence war games for the remainder of each day, until darkness set upon us. In this phase of virtual combat training, we used real weapons. Specifically, we trained in the firing and maintenance of the .45 caliber handgun, the M-1 carbine rifle, and the standard-issue bayonet. However, for our first two weeks of this particular training we used rubber bullets, so whenever we were struck by 'enemy fire' we survived the attack. We were taught to dismantle and reassemble these weapons in a matter of seconds. We were also taught to crawl along on our bellies for extended periods of time. Finally, we were taught to accept the presence of a scorpion, tarantula, or snake without overreaction. So day after day, we subsisted on a mere twelve ounces of concentrated canned food, as we learned to become effective ground combatants. After what seemed like several months, our three weeks of bivouac training ended. Miraculously there had been no serious injuries.

It was nearing 8:00PM, October 8th, as we mounted our busses and returned to our military base. The opportunity to take a regular shower was a welcomed event, but by the time we'd finished showering it was once again "lights out" time. This was okay though, for each of us had realized that we really wanted this time for much-needed rest. Plus, for the very first time while here we would have two consecutive days off. I wondered just how I would use such a 'great' amount of leisure time. But when Sunday morning arrived, I played lazy and just slept in. Then that afternoon I attended another movie, before walking around the base (just to observe the sights). Now even though there was no one to accompany me, I thoroughly enjoyed my free time. The next day (Monday) I arose early enough to have breakfast at our base dining hall. At 10:00, I walked alone to the base chapel, where I attended church services. I then returned to the dining hall for the noon meal. Afterwards, I climbed onto a shuttle bus and rode into the historic city of San Antonio. Although I was eighteen years of age, this was my very first visit to any major (or small) city. Naturally I made certain that I remained within one centralized area so I wouldn't get lost. I was able to visit the famous Alamo before returning to the base. So overall, this had been a very good day for me.

Tuesday arrived and we began another battery of final examinations, designed to determine for which career field we were better suited. Each test was lengthy and time-consuming, but we all would undergo testing for a full three days (taking us into Thursday afternoon). At 2:00PM on Thursday, I received my official career field classification of AIRBORNE RADIO OPERATOR. I was thrilled beyond belief, for this was what I'd truly wanted since there was no possibility of my becoming a pilot. At least now, I would be placed on flying status. I would also receive a substantial amount of tax-free income in the form of flight pay. But most important was the fact that this was a highly respected career field. So at this point I'd come to feel that all of the unusually harsh treatment I had endured had finally paid off for me. We had now successfully completed each training phase, and there would be no more marching, so I happily returned to my barracks for a bit of relaxing.

On Friday morning, we anxiously began our initial phase of out-processing. This meant the activation of a complete set of military records for each graduating trainee. These records would include separate physical, dental, and medical sets. We had all been given maps of on-base units having responsibility for our mandatory out-processing, so our very first stop was the Military Personnel (Human Resource Office). I walked in proudly and took myself a sequence number.

Soon my number was called, so I quickly approached the desk of the young sergeant who would initiate my processing. I had absolutely no idea of the great disappointment that awaited me. The sergeant motioned for me to take the vacant seat at the corner of his desk. So I seated myself and awaited the commencement of my out-processing to technical training school. But instead the sergeant asked for my identification card and then commented, "So you're Airman Van York?"

"Yes I am," I replied. "Then you will need to go to room six for processing" he stated. The tone of his voice concerned me, though I did not question him further. I simply thanked him and walked to room six. Once there I found two sergeants, awaiting my arrival. The senior sergeant was the only person to speak. He began by saying, "I take it, you're Airman Van York". "Yes, I am, sergeant" I said to him. "Then, I have some slightly disappointing news for you," he said. My thoughts immediately shifted to my folks back home, so I asked, "Has something happened to my family"? "No, nothing like that," he replied. I breathed a sigh of relief at that point. Then he continued by saying "There's been a fire at the Technical Training School at Keesler AFB". "And as a result, all Airborne Radio Training has been temporarily suspended". "This means that we must reassign you into a different career field; so, we're placing you in the medical field" he said. My heart immediately sank to its lowest point since leaving home, but I tried desperately to maintain my composure. "Are there any other choices available?" I asked. "Not at this level—so prepare yourself to become a medic!" he snarled at me. "Then, I need to speak to someone at a higher level," I said, deep frustration sounding in my voice.

At this point he became a bit agitated, so he quickly picked up his phone and dialed a number. He then spoke into the phone, saying "Vickie, please tell the colonel that I have an Airman Van York here who wishes to speak with him". He hesitated briefly before saying, "Thank you," as he hung up the telephone. Then he said to me, "Go upstairs to room twenty-five and our commander will see you". I thanked him for his assistance, and then walked upstairs. I walked along the long corridor, which was heavily decorated with portraits of famous aviators and paintings of historic aircraft. I reached room twenty-five with (heart pounding) and I knocked twice (per military protocol).

A secretary welcomed me to this spacious office and then motioned me to the commander's door. I approached and knocked only once— as was military custom. "Enter" came the sound of the heavy male voice. I promptly entered the unusually large office and reported to the middle-aged but trim colonel, sitting at an over-sized desk. "Sir, Airman Van York reporting as ordered," I stated, standing at attention and rendering a rigid hand salute. The colonel issued the command "At ease, airman," so I quickly assumed the military position known as "parade rest". "What can I do for you?" the colonel asked. "Sir, I've just been informed that I am re-classified into the medical field, from airborne radio operator". "So I respectfully ask— are there any alternative fields to which I might be assigned?" I asked. "What's wrong with the medical field?" asked the colonel. I replied "Sir, I can do many things—but I simply cannot become a medic". Before the colonel could speak, I added, "If medical is the only available field,— then you may either throw me into the base stockade, or discharge me and send me home". I immediately knew that my last statement was inappropriate and out of bounds, but my words were out there now—and I could not retract them. But for some reason, the colonel seemed patient with me. So after a moment of silence, he called out to his secretary, "Vickie, call down to TSgt Adkins and tell him to find a more suitable field for Airman Van York". "Will do, sir" came Vickie's prompt response. The colonel then dismissed me, saying "I'm sure things will work out for you—but if not, then come back and see me". I saluted and thanked him deeply as I prepared to depart his office. The secretary then directed me to return to room six and resume my out-processing actions.

Back at the desk of the technical sergeant in room six, I sat anxiously awaiting some favorable response from him regarding career field selection. He shuffled through a batch of papers and produced a document showing a total of four non-related career fields. Then he presented me the list, saying, "Other than medical, these are the only other available fields". I quickly, but carefully reviewed this listing, but nothing on the list attracted my attention. There was one field of which I was not familiar, so I asked, "Sergeant, what is an administrative specialist"? "Oh, that's office work," he informed me. "Then if possible, I'd like to choose this field," I said. "No problem," he replied. He then cancelled my written orders, assigning me to technical training school at Keesler AFB, MS. Next he prepared a new set of orders, assigning me as an apprentice administrative specialist at Harlingen AFB, TX. At this point I was extremely disappointed over the loss of my original assignment; but, I was determined to excel in my newly assigned career field. Unfortunately, I was not fully aware of the significant loss in income and promotion that would be caused by this change of career field. Also, a total of thirty-five years would pass before I would discover that I had been completely misinformed regarding the suspension of my Airborne Radio Operator's training program. In monetary terms, this arbitrary career change would cost me in excess of $100,000 in income during my military career. The sergeant finished assembling my out-processing package before releasing me for the remainder of the afternoon.

I returned to my barracks, where I began preparing my living area for final inspection. This meant a thorough cleansing of every visible surface. Before 5:00PM I had finished with my cleaning chores, so I took a quick shower and walked over to the dining hall. I realized just how wonderful it felt, finally being permitted to move freely about as would have been expected for a normal human being. I was finally able to make at least some decisions on my own, so I decided to attend the 6:00PM movie. After the movie I chose an indirect route back to my barracks, allowing myself to view portions of the base I'd not yet seen.

Upon the successful completion of training, each member of my flight had been promoted to the grade airman third class (E-2), meaning I currently wore one stripe on my sleeves. However, we were not given a graduation ceremony— only our final weekend free from duty requirements. So for the next two days I opted to hop onto military busses for the sole purpose of riding around the famous city of San Antonio. These would be only my second and third visits into this city. I immensely enjoyed my final weekend at this historic location.

Chapter 5

Harlot of Harlingen

After completing basic military training at Lackland
AFB, TX, I proceeded by bus directly to Harlingen AFB, TX,
which was located twenty-eight miles north of the Mexican
border. I arrived at my new base at 3:30PM, Monday,
October 31st. Then as required by Air Force regulations, I
located and reported to the first sergeant of my new organization. He welcomed me to the base and briefed me on
organizational procedures. Next, he had his assistant escort
me to my new living quarters (which were quite modest).
I learned that I would have one roommate (a two striper
airman), which was okay by me. As I began to unpack and
arrange my belongings, my new roommate entered the
room. This was a tall and lean fellow of slightly over six
feet in height. He seemed nice, though I soon learned that
he was thirty years of age and had already served twelve
years in the Air Force. I had found this a bit odd because
he should have been a technical sergeant at this point in his
career. I would soon discover that this airman lacked discipline and was frequently in trouble with military authorities
here. But he had been kind enough to offer me a ride into
Mexico that evening, so I quickly forgot to further question

his character and military record. This would prove a costly mistake on my part, for I would soon discover that I would be viewed by the other airmen as 'guilty by association'. I would also find this airman (whose name was Manny) to be of questionable character.

Harlingen AFB was relatively small, but was a well-maintained installation that was used as a training site for Air Force Officer Cadets, who, upon completion of training, would become United States Air Force pilots. Its neat streets were lined with flourishing palm trees, and its grounds were covered with well-manicured lawns. This entire base was completely free of litter (as was Fort Jackson), and I immediately took a strong liking to my new home. I was quite hungry, so my new roommate and I walked to the dining hall. Inside, I observed that its interior had been conservatively decorated with a wide assortment of potted plants. The environment here was noticeably better than back at Lackland. Namely, the GIs here were friendly toward each other—so I quite possibly might make a few friends here. My roommate, Manny, wasted no time in introducing me to a number of other young GIs who were sitting at nearby tables—which made me feel a bit like being back at home—and we laughed and joked freely with each other as we ate. Then after finishing our meal Manny and I along with two other young GIs walked back to our dormitory, where I found that he had parked his car. I learned that he had only recently purchased this 1949 Ford automobile at a near giveaway. I quickly discovered the real reason he'd been able to pick up this vehicle at such a seemingly reasonable price. This old car had not been well maintained—and was only fractionally in better condition than Old Betsy back home. But this was our only means of transportation, so we piled into Manny's old vehicle and away we went—heading for Mexico.

It was customary for the airmen of the base to visit Mexico nearly each night after work. So for the very first time, I stood upon the streets of Matamoros (not the nicest places to begin with). I had heard from the time of my arrival, that this was a corrupt and dangerous little town. Even upon entering it, I sensed a certain uneasiness begin to course through my body. But, I excepted this feeling of apprehension, as I proceeded along this dirty street, because this would be the night I would eventually achieve manhood! In its business district, the streets of this little town were lined on either side with a wide variety of stores and shops, although none were elaborate or fancy. Compared to prices just two miles to the north in Texas, I found the prices here to generally be much lower than those stateside. Lots of really cheap whiskey was readily available here, but most Americans would never even consider drinking the stuff sold in these bottles. Actually, whenever GIs ventured into Mexico, they carried their own alcohol with them. So whenever you saw them sitting in a bar, they would have one drink on the bar in front of them and another drink off to their side, which was the one from which they drank (after filling it from the trunk of their car parked out front).

My story now shifts to those narrow, dusty, wind-swept (unpaved) streets of Matamoros, Mexico. For those of you unfamiliar with the geography of this region, Matamoros lies just two miles south of Brownsville, which is located in the Rio Grande Valley of Texas. I had arrived in Matamoros shortly before 7:00 on Monday evening, along with three other airmen from my new base. I had placed twenty dollars (in one dollar bills) inside my wallet. I also had placed another twenty dollars (of same denomination) inside my left side pocket. I would use this second batch of bills for 'educational' purposes in the form of services rendered by certain of this town's female populace. The other three guys had already gone about town in different directions. We had all agreed to meet at a pre-designated nearby bar. So, I was at last free to pursue my long-awaited goal of an intimate relationship with members of the opposite sex. I was quite surprised by the large number of young 'ladies' lounging about in this part of the town.

Only four months earlier, I had been that extremely naïve young fellow walking through the Carolina corn fields, and very little had changed in these recent months. So please bear with me when I say to you that I was completely caught off guard by the 'warm and friendly' manner in which so many of these lovely young 'ladies' received me. For within less than two hours I had visited ten different 'ladies'. Each was very hospitable toward me, though each would ask for a couple of dollars during my visit with them. I did not object to helping them since none had asked for much. But after my tenth and final visit of the evening, I realized that I had dispensed with the twenty bucks I'd tucked away in my side pocket. This was okay by me because I had just learned more in two hours, than in all my eighteen years on earth! I felt really great! Now, whenever the other guys would get together and start telling their tall tales, I could join in and participate in their conversation. "*Wow*", I thought, "*Now I've really grown up!*

I decided to take a little walk— just to reflect and clear

my head. It was just after 9:00PM and darkness was settling in. I headed down a narrow street of shops and away from the party part of town. I wanted to see what the rest of this little town was like. But, after slowly strolling along for about fifteen minutes, the street dead-ended, leaving me with a choice of turning left or right. I chose the right turn because I knew this would take me back toward the area where the bars lined the streets, and where I would meet the guys. But as I approached the next corner, I looked all around, left and right, and ahead and behind me. Something caught my eye. There, on my right, stood a drab four-story building. Its ground floor covered an area of approximately ten thousand square feet. Behind this old building and nearest to me, stood an open area spanning about the same amount of space. That's when I saw it! Crouched near the barbed wire fencing of the far wall was the hideous figure of some sort of two-legged creature. It did not appear to be a gorilla or any other type of ape, but it possessed all the unusual characteristics of a caveman. Its hair was long and shaggy, and its skin was undistinguishable. It sat on its haunches, while unmoving. As I stood there silently watching, I wondered if this creature was awake— or even alive. It made no sounds whatsoever. Then suddenly it arose, but only onto its knees. I watched curiously as the 'caveman' assumed and held this position— as if waiting for some special event. Then, one of the rear doors of the building burst open! The creature waited.

Abruptly, one mustached and heavy set armed guard appeared. The guard glared at the creature for a brief moment, then stepped away from the door momentarily. After about ten seconds the guard returned to the door. This time he held what appeared to be a five-gallon can that had been modified and equipped with a flip-top. I watched the anxiously awaiting creature, still in his upright kneeling position. Then without speaking, the guard raised the large metal can and gave a strong heave. The can's lid flipped open, and from within came a large live rattlesnake, hurtling through the air directly towards the kneeling creature!

In a flash the kneeling creature reached forward with his left hand, grasping the rattler just inches just below its head, and swiftly snatching it from the air, just two feet from his face! I continued watching in a mesmerized state, as the creature then shook the violently writhing body of the angry rattler! Its body extended briefly, giving the creature ample time to deliver two well-placed crushing karate-like blows to its body! The creature's first blow landed at the snake's mid-section. The second blow struck the rattler just inches below its head. I sensed by the snake's diminished movement, that its spine had been severed in at least two separate locations. The creature had not noticed me standing here, and the guard had gone back inside. I watched in shock and disbelief as the creature drew the now limp snake to his face. Then, he finally knelt and sat back down on his haunches. Once comfortable, he bit into the snake's neck while violently shaking his head from left to right! The rattler's head separated from its body, and the creature tossed the lifeless head onto a large pile of other snake carcasses. He then bit into the neck several times. I did not understand. But I soon learned that he had ripped the skin around the rattler's neck. Once he had done this, he began peeling away the skin with only his bare fingers.

After he'd cleared away about a foot of skin, he greedily began his feast. Then for the very first time, I heard him make a sound. I could have sworn that I heard him growling as he slurped down the snake's raw red flesh! The 'cave creature' downed the first parcel of snake meat, then he repeated the process by peeling another section, which he also quickly consumed. The rattler had been about four feet in length, but when the creature was done, he had consumed the entire snake's body! This was the creature's daily meal. This had taken only fifteen minutes, so I still stood there. It was at this point that the creature finally saw me. I just looked at him as I did not know what else to do. He glared at me, so I decided it best to depart this area. Feeling quite shaken by this event, I quickly walked back to the downtown bar district.

I stopped at the very first bar along my route, and ordered for myself a mixed vodka with lemon. I sat at the bar for only a short while before a very cute young senorita took a bar stool next to me. I felt that quite possibly she was accompanied by a male companion, so I did not speak to her. I need not have concerned myself though, for she soon turned to me, saying "Hello, Americano". But this was my first visit to Mexico, and having been forewarned I was a bit cautious in returning her warm greeting. I simply said, "Hello senorita". Her smile slightly brightened and she asked if I wanted to sit outside. I wasn't sure if she'd merely wanted to move to the outside area— OR POSSIBLY LURE ME INTO SOME SORT OF TRAP! Still, I decided to chance moving to the outside area and thereby avoid inhaling unwanted cigarette smoke. So together, we relocated ourselves onto the patio and sat at a corner table.

I soon found that she spoke nearly perfect English, so I asked, "Where did you learn to speak English so well"? She informed me that she was born and raised across the border in Brownsville. So out of curiosity, I asked, "What are you doing here in Matamoros"? She advised me that she had several family members still residing here, and frequently visited them. This was one such visit. She seemed to have told me truth, but still I was somewhat leery of her. Even so, I asked if I might see her again. She responded, "I'm only going to be here for another three days before returning home to Brownsville". I asked, "Will you meet me here again tomorrow night"? "I can't promise but I'll try to be here," she said. On the surface, she seemed quite nice so, I asked her name and gave her mine. I learned that her name was Juanita, and she worked in a Brownsville jewelry store. We then agreed to meet again here at 9:00 next evening. We finished our drinks and she left me sitting there quite alone.

I checked my watch and saw that it read 11:00PM. Thus, I left the club and walked the short distance to where we had parked. Once there, I soon located the other two passengers of Manny's vehicle. They invited me to join them, so I wasted no time in doing so. As soon as I'd seated myself, the elder of the two ordered three shots of tequila. Oddly when the tequila arrived, neither could seem to locate the money they had placed inside their pockets. So as they 'frantically' searched for their money, I produced two one dollar bills and handed them to the waitress. Then as we tipped our glasses, the younger of the two spoke, "The next round is on us," (all the while knowing— there would be no next round). We sat cracking jokes and sipping our drinks, a slightly disturbing thought entered my mind. Namely, I had purchased the gasoline for this short trip, and now I'd been arbitrarily chosen to also purchase their drinks. *"These guys think you're some dumb hick simply because you're from the south."* I thought. Right then, I decided "I would not be made a fool of by any of these clowns". But, I was not aware that my devious new roommate (Manny) was quite the con artist. He had already formulated a slick plan whereby he would purchase for himself a newer car, using my meager earnings to pay for it!

At 11:30PM Manny arrived and we prepared for our return trip to Harlingen. Along our route, I could not erase from memory the sight of that hideous caged creature I'd recently witnessed. I decided to mention my recent sighting to my new 'friends'. I began by casually stating, "Guys, you won't believe what I saw a bit earlier tonight". Manny quickly quipped, "Oh, so you met the toothless babe." (one particular local prostitute). Everybody laughed, but I did not consider this a joking matter. "I saw a real caveman!" I responded. At this point, they all began laughing. Manny then commented, "Ah, that wasn't any caveman— that was just California Cal". "Who's California Cal?" I asked. "Oh, he's just some guy who was here going through Cadet Officer Training School." replied Manny. "What happened to him?" I asked. He answered, "He tried to fight off two muggers, but wound up being thrown in Mexican prison." he said. "That's awful," I said. "Why hasn't our government gotten him released?" I asked. "Base officials, our embassy, and even congress have all tried, but they all failed." Manny said. Feeling quite disturbed by what I'd just been told, I discontinued our discussion regarding this sensitive subject.

By midnight we had safely arrived back on base. I returned to my room, showered, and hopped into bed. I
was once again alone now, as my roommate had gone next
door to shoot dice in the hopes of winning a little money
from other GIs. Naturally, he had quite cordially invited
me along. But, gambling had not yet become one of my
vices,— so I'd politely declined his offer. As I lay there
in the quiet peacefulness of my new living quarters, I reflected upon the more positive events of my evening. First,
my thoughts centered upon the ten very friendly 'ladies' I'd
visited earlier in the evening. I then realized that I would
most likely remember this evening for as long as I might
live. Next, my mind drifted onto that poor former American cadet officer, who at this very moment, was probably
forced to sleep outside on the dirt— while in his very own
urine and excrement. I found this particular thought to be
most repulsive and depressing. Thus, I quickly shifted my
focus to Juanita— the young senorita I had met earlier in
the evening. At some point, I fell asleep.

At 6:00AM Tuesday, I was awakened to the sound of
my newly purchased alarm clock. I checked my roommate and saw that he was still asleep, so I quickly jumped
out of bed and washed up. When I'd finished I found him
still asleep, so I shook him awake. I dressed and proceeded
alone to our nearby dining hall. There, I had myself a hearty
breakfast. Today, and for the next three days, I would initiate and complete military in-processing actions. This would
include visits to my Military Personnel Office (HRO), base
chapel, and a large number of other military organizations.
Naturally computers did not exist back then, which necessitated that I personally visit all pertinent military units. So,

with the assistance of a base map, I would locate and visit each unit. This slow process would take me to the end of the week.

I painstakingly completed each of my required actions. Incidentally, you may recall that I had initially been assigned the career field of airborne radio operator, but this initial classification had been revised to that of administrative specialist. However, at in-processing I was once again reclassified. Now, I suddenly found myself reassigned into the postal field as an apprentice postal specialist. Imagine that—I'd received three separate and distinct career assignments before ever reporting to duty. This was another huge let down for me; but, I was determined to succeed in whatever position I might be assigned. Thus for the remainder of this week, I would in-process during normal daytime duty hours, and party nightly across the border in Mexico each night. This latter issue was that in which I was most interested.

Incidentally, this day (Tuesday) was the first of the month, (payday for those assigned military personnel). So beginning this evening, I would closely monitor the spending habits of Manny and friends. I spent my entire morning at CBPO/HRO (Military Personnel Office). Then at noon, I proceeded alone to our dining hall. There, I found the food both tasty and well prepared. After lunch I resumed in-processing, walking from office to office where I completed numerous forms. Finally, the long-awaited hour of 4:00PM arrived. My first full day at my permanent duty station had ended. For the very first time, I found myself completely free to roam about the base. However, I would be rushed this afternoon, for I needed to visit both the cleaners/laundry, along with our local Base Exchange store. So with these considerations in mind, I would postpone my tour of my new base. My first stop would be a return visit to our dining hall.

Upon entering the dining facility, the first persons I saw were Manny and his two buddies. All three waved to me to join them. So after receiving my tray of food, I joined them at their table. Their morale seemed unusually high today! Initially, I figured that they were in high spirits because this was payday for them. I would soon learn though that I had erred grossly. Luckily, I soon discovered that these three had not focused upon their pay— but upon mine!

It so happened, I returned to the serving line for another glass of tea. But as I stood filling my glass, one of the food service staff approached me saying, "Be careful of those guys you're with; they'll take all your money"! His words came as quite a shock; so, I thanked him sincerely. I returned to my table as though all was normal, so we once again sat laughing and joking together. But now that I'd been somewhat enlightened, I would discreetly watch these guys closely. While at the table with them, we again decided we would leave the base tonight at 7:00PM, heading into Mexico.

I left them sitting there so that I might make my necessary stops. So after dropping off two uniforms at the laundry, I proceeded to the BX (Base Exchange Store). From there, I purchased several items, including cigarettes. Now that I had suddenly become an adult, I felt the need to impress others by smoking (how stupid of me)! With my recent purchases, I returned to my room, where I was again shocked to find my roommate along with four other

GIs—all shooting dice on a blanket. This activity alarmed me greatly, but I held my peace and kept my mouth shut. I knew that this practice was illegal, and I should have reported it. But I had already learned that I should keep my mouth shut, so I remained silent and prepared to take my shower. My roommate invited me to join their game, but I respectfully declined, saying, "Guys, I don't mess with dice". "Ah, come on," they commented. "Nope" I responded, as I stepped inside the shower. I had secured my belongings (especially the Elm and my money) and taken my key into the shower along with me. After showering, I quickly changed into casual evening dress before heading to our nearby TV room. There, I relaxed as I entertained myself with this newfound activity of television viewing!

After forty-five minutes, my roommate and his friends arrived as previously planned. So once again the four of us climbed into his old vehicle, heading for the nearest gas pump. But once there, Manny asked each of us to contribute a dollar toward the purchase of gasoline. His two other passengers 'fished' in their pockets for money, and I sat as if mute. Each then presented Manny with their dollar bill. He accepted their money, but then peered over at me sitting next to him. So I casually asked, "Why are you looking at me, Manny"? "Fork over one dollar," he quickly responded. I had anticipated such a request from him, so I replied, "I nearly filled your tank last night— and you're asking me for money"? At this point, the winner of the crap shoot handed him another dollar bill. No more was said of the matter, as we filled the car and headed for Mexico.

Along the highway heading south, I slightly turned to my left to more freely converse with our back seat passengers. There, before my very eyes, sat this GI who was carefully rolling a homemade cigarette. I had heard of marijuana, but I had never before found myself in its presence. My vastly restricted past had just dramatically changed! I knew this substance was commonly referred to as "weed" so in my masquerade of 'cool' I calmly asked, "Is that weed you're rolling"? "What else?" came his instant response. No one else in the car spoke, as we sped along.

Then when this fellow was finished rolling, he lit this cigarette, immediately producing one of the most obnoxious odors I had ever smelled. He quickly took a long drag of this substance, before passing it to me. "*The audacity of this guy*", I thought as I wasted no time in refusing his unwelcomed offer. "That's okay, Jake" he said, adding "This leaves more for us". Then as we rode along, they passed this awful-smelling weed among themselves, and I thought, *"Jake, you just got here— and already, you're in the wrong crowd"*!

We soon arrived in Mexico, where we once again established our departure time as 11:00 PM. Immediately thereafter, I slipped away from them to increase my state of enlightenment regarding the subject of sex. Although I would take no written notes, I was quite determined to rapidly become a model student. On this evening though, I would reduce my number of female contacts to only three. I also decided that I would maintain this limit during future visits. So during my first hour, I casually walked these streets to determine exactly what was available to me. I was constantly greeted by many of this area's local female inhabitants. I shall be candid here by confessing to you— I warmly returned many of the greetings I received. But since I naturally had always greeted others in my presence,— this was no big deal.

I walked around for nearly a half hour before finally spotting a young woman I deemed fanciful. I approached her and began casual conversation. I soon discovered though that she seemed mostly interested in the amount of 'tip' she would receive for services rendered. Now, I had completely forgotten that today was payday for the GIs stationed at Harlingen, and local prices had been raised by one-third of the regular going rate. Nevertheless, we reached an agreement and began preparations for my first 'lesson' of the evening. She was an expert teacher within her field of expertise, and I gained a considerable amount of knowledge in less than one hour. Then after this first session, I took a short break by taking in a bit more of this small town's scenery. However, on this particular evening there seemed an over-abundance of both activity and scenery, of which to partake.

Soon I discovered my second (very cute) teacher. This time we covered the very same single subject (sex) but from a variety of perspectives. Needless to say, I enjoyed very much this most recent visit. At this point, I felt I was gaining required knowledge at quite an acceptable pace. Soon, I would become quite skilled in this most favored subject! I left the 'residence' of this young 'lady' and proceeded along the streets toward the cantina where I'd previously met Juanita.

It was 9:00PM, and as this was payday, this little town was bustling. I entered the cantina and casually searched through the crowds for her. But after a few minutes, I decided that she was not present. However, I would remain here for awhile in hopes that she would show up. I then located a nearby vacant bar stool and seated myself. When the one available bartender approached me to take my order, I simply asked for a Coke. Until last night, I had successfully refrained from consuming alcohol of any type, but alcohol consumption had suddenly become another new experience for me. Thus, currently in my arsenal of vices there existed alcohol, sex, and smoking. I was rapidly' moving up' in this old world!

Now from my present vantage point, I could clearly see all who entered or exited this bar. So after just fifteen minutes of waiting, I was quite pleasantly surprised to see young Juanita enter the facility. The moment she'd cleared the doorway, her eyes fell upon me. A bright smile appeared on her cute face as she walked toward me. I stood (as was customary back then) as she reached me. There happened to be one vacant stool next to me, so while greeting each other, she quickly hopped onto it. The bartender approached and she ordered a margarita. Then when it arrived, I naturally paid for her drink. We then made small talk about how hectic her day had been. As she sat talking to me, I noticed a vacant table on the patio so we quickly moved outside. Once there we began casual discussion of a wide range of subjects (with the exception of sex). But this was okay by me, for I'd just wanted someone to talk to. We talked and danced together as the evening progressed. We had so much fun, we'd completely lost track of time. Then she suddenly peered at her watch, exclaiming, "Oh my goodness— I have to run now"! I checked my watch to find the time closing in upon 11:00PM. Before leaving me though, Juanita quickly scribbled down her Brownsville home phone number, saying, "I'm leaving tomorrow morning, but call me". I assured her I that would. Unfortunately though, I procrastinated and never called. I would fondly remember her.

I had spent an unusually pleasant last evening. However, 6:00AM Wednesday morning had all too quickly arrived. Once again, I was the first to wash up and leave our two-man room. Before leaving, I made sure to awaken Manny. After breakfast, I resumed in-processing. I would spend my next three days completing this necessary action. Then, each evening I would venture into Mexico and would spend the vast majority of my time partying with the 'ladies'. However, each evening I would dedicate at least fifteen minutes of my time toward monitoring the current condition of this 'caveman creature'. After my first and most unpleasant sighting of this poor fellow, I simply could not erase those terrible memories of him from my mind. Then a fresh thought struck me. I was scheduled for an orientation briefing appointment this afternoon at 1:00PM. I would use a portion of this briefing to discuss the plight of this unfortunate soul "California Cal". I felt certain that this fellow would not last through the winter in his present condition. I found this sad situation to be both deplorable and intolerable! In short, I strongly felt a personal need to attempt rectifying this situation. So upon completing hours of morning in-processing, I organized and rehearsed my thoughts for this afternoon's meeting with our base chaplain. Then after lunch, I proceeded directly to his office.

Once there, I was ushered into the office of a mild-mannered and soft-spoken young major. My chaplain welcomed me, and attempted to make me feel comfortable.

We began our dialogue by discussing my religious prefer-ence and family background. At first, I found myself a bit tense. However, as the minutes ticked past I began feeling more comfortable while discussing such matters. So I mus-tered my confidence and shifted our subject of discussion to the unbelievable sight, I had witnessed in Matamoros two nights earlier.

The chaplain suddenly became quite somber. He be-gan by saying "Airman Van York, I've spent many a sleep-less night mulling over this situation." He continued, "Our government and base officials have done all we can to se-cure the release of Cadet Officer Vincent Callen". "Sadly though, all our efforts have failed miserably." he added. At this point he paused, so I very politely asked, "Well sir, at this stage, how do you view his chances for release". "Slim, to none" was his reply. "That's very sad," I replied. "I couldn't agree with you more," our chaplain sighed. Our visitation was drawing near its end, so I asked, "May I drop by for a visit sometime, sir"? "You're welcome at any time," he responded. I then arose, shook his hand, and thanked him for his valued time. The chaplain then dismissed me, and I resumed in-processing.

Throughout the afternoon my thoughts kept returning to Cadet Callen. I simply could not believe, and would not accept the premise that this was a completely hopeless case. At this point though, I decided to remove this issue from my thoughts, and focus upon completing my in-processing requirements. Thus for the remainder of the week, I simply concentrated upon getting settled onto this military base. Naturally, I would visit Mexico evenings after work for the purpose of furthering my 'education'. Finally, I completed all in-processing actions. Then as required, I reported to my assigned duty section, (Base Post Office).

Once there, I somewhat timidly entered the building. I immediately noticed that the main postal operation was located at the rear of this building. I noticed also a solid wall of mail boxes to my left. To my right stood two separate offices. In the first (outer) office sat a fairly young, but powerfully built staff sergeant. He wore his hair in crew-cut style, which to me meant that this was a real 'bad-ass'. I cautiously knocked at his door, momentarily drawing his attention. "Yes, airman?" he responded. I struggled desperately to maintain at least some semblance of calm in my voice as I softly asked, "Sgt Storke"? "Next door," he answered. I walked ten feet to that office entrance. Once again, I peeked through the doorway. This time I saw one of the most impressive non-commissioned officers I would ever meet. He wore six gleaming stripes on each sleeve. Now in those days, this number of stripes meant the person wearing them was often looked upon as a god! But this wasn't all, for his sleeves were also covered with coveted hash markings, and his chest was completely covered by rows of shining ribbons and medals. I would soon learn this "super sergeant" was the envy of each enlisted member on this entire base. He sat intently reading a document. I gathered my courage and knocked once (as was military custom). Immediately, he looked up and in my direction. Then before I could speak, he said, "Airman Van York, I presume". I quietly entered his office, and he offered me a nearby seat. Before seating myself, I bent forward while reaching for his hand. We briefly shook hands and formerly introduced ourselves.

"Relax and take a load off," he said. "I know you must be thirsty, so what kind of soda would you like?" he asked. The cordial manner in which my supervisor had welcomed me, made me feel really good about my current situation. "I could use a Pepsi, if you have one," I said. "No problem," he quickly answered as he stood to fetch our sodas. I thought, *"Heck, not even my chaplain offered me a soda"*. Soon the sergeant returned, accompanied by his assistant, SSgt Pruitt. The staff sergeant and I shook hands. Then together they began my orientation of the Base Post Office. I learned that I would work directly for MSgt Storke, but in his absence, SSgt Pruitt would become my supervisor. I was advised about unit operating procedures, safety, and duty hours. Upon completion of my briefing, SSgt Pruitt then escorted me about the post office as he introduced me to each assigned airman. This was a far cry from my initial assignment of airborne radio operator. Even worse though, this assignment bore absolutely no similarity to that of administrative specialist. But since this was the duty I'd ultimately been given, I decided I would make the most of this assignment. Finally, the two sergeants released me with clear instructions to report for duty at 7:00AM sharp on Monday morning.

Later that evening, I found myself once again in Mexico. Again, I roamed these streets alone. I exercised patience in selecting young women as intimate partners. So by 10:00PM I had only visited two 'ladies', but this was okay, for I'd only spent four dollars. At this point, I decided to take a short break and stroll past the prison where Cadet Callen was being held. I arrived at the intersection where this dreadful old building stood. It had been two evenings since I'd visited this area, but the hideous figure remained at the very same location as on two evenings prior. The only difference I noticed was that— he was at this moment finishing up his delicacy of a meal. I stood silently watching as he noisily slurped this 'treat' of raw rattlesnake flesh. He still had not seen me, and no guards were visible, so I stood motionless for a bit longer. Then only when he had finished downing his last morsel, did he look at me. Neither he nor I made any gesture of greeting to each other. Naturally, I was unable to determine whether or not he had recognized me from two evenings earlier. Though now I strongly felt that I should leave this miserable location, and I immediately followed my instincts. Nonetheless, as I prepared to walk away, I gestured toward him in the form of a 'thumbs-up'. Instantly, his upper body appeared to have become more erect. So I then gave him a slight smile. Though he failed to return my smile, his eyes remained focused directly upon me until I'd rounded this corner and moved from his line of vision. As I walked slowly back toward the 'hot' part of town, I wondered what thoughts might now be coursing through his mind.

I proceeded to my favorite cantina in the hope that Juanita might show up. I took a seat at the bar, which provided me with a vantage point. I ordered myself a Coca-Cola and then sipped from it as one would from a glass of bourbon. I sat waiting for thirty minutes but still, there was no sighting of Juanita. Momentarily, I felt a pang of despair, for I realized then just how badly I'd wanted some decent lady with whom to hold a conversation. It was rapidly approaching 11:00PM, so I decided to return to our rendez-vous point. Manny and his cronies were a full hour late in returning to the car, which caused me to sit nearby while awaiting their return. I found that I really did not care for waiting, so while sitting there I decided I would soon purchase my very own car. Finally Manny showed up and we returned to the base.

At 5:00AM I arose, and after a quick shower, I prepared my half of our room for stand-by inspection by our squadron commander and first sergeant. I was not accustomed to staying up past midnight, so this particular morning was a little difficult for me. Luckily, I had not indulged in alcohol the evening before. Manny and I had just finished preparing our room, when our first sergeant called the room to attention. This meant we would assume and hold an upright rigid posture until advised otherwise. Each of my possessions had been immaculately cleaned and painstakingly arranged in accordance with military standards. I had not yet met our squadron commander, so upon entering our room he paid particular attention to my area and person. He carefully inspected each of my uniforms before focusing upon smaller items, such as cigarettes and razor blades. On the top shelf of my locker, I had placed the special candle containing the tiny listening device (Elm) grandmother had given me. He noticed the candle and immediately picked it up, while hefting it. He turned the candle all directions, scrutinizing every inch. He then turned to me, asking "Does this have religious significance"? "Sir, this is a gift from my dear old grandmother." I said. "How old is she?" he inquired. "She just reached one hundred one last week," I said. "How wonderful." he said, placing the candle back in its original position. "Where do you work, airman?" he asked. "Base Post Office, sir." I answered. "Great, then give my regards to MSgt Storke." said my commander. "I will, sir," I said. I noticed that he had held absolutely no dialog with my roommate,— but I did not comment.

After inspection many of the GIs headed downtown to begin their day of early partying. I was among them, having accompanied Manny and his two buddies. Our first stop was a nice family-owned Mexican restaurant, where we had breakfast of enchiladas along with cold Texas beer. This was my very first exposure to beer, and I quickly found it totally unpalatable. As I sat there struggling to swallow this most unpleasant liquid, I wondered, *"How in the world do you guys drink this mess"*? Unfortunately my taste buds would gradually begin to accept this very strange new taste.

We spent the rest of the morning wandering between bars and restaurants. When it was over, I must say that this had been a very pleasant morning. I had begun to feel that I already liked this neat little city. The streets here were lined with a considerable number of bars, cafes, and restaurants, which was totally opposite the layout back home. We walked these palm tree-lined streets while taking in the city's natural beauty. The temperature here hovered near the mid-seventies, which was a vast improvement over November months back home. *"I really like it here"*, I thought as the four of us went about the town.

Shortly after 1:00PM, Manny asked, "Jake, have you seen enough of this side of town"? "I guess so," I replied. "Good, then let's take a ride over to the other side," he said. We returned to the car and drove for about ten minutes. When we parked I exited the car while looking around in all directions. I found this section of town to be mostly residential, with neat streets and manicured lawns. In contrast, over ninety percent of homes in my neck of the woods had no lawns at all. Soon I began to like this city even more. We had parked near a moderate-sized building complex. Upon entering, I immediately became even more impressed with this small city. This entire complex was owned and operated by a single family. Inside, it contained a fully complemented snack bar at its rear, equipped with bar stools and dining tables. I was happy to note that this area was maintained with utmost cleanliness. Adjacent, stood a large lounge area with booths for seating, and music for dancing and socializing. Next to the lounge stood a huge billiards parlor, which was equipped with quality pool tables. There was also a very neat barber shop with six individual chairs. Needless to say, this was quite an establishment. It was also one of the leading social gathering locations within this city. But most importantly, this entire facility was owned solely by one retired USAF senior non-commissioned officer and wife. His target markets were fifty percent of Harlingen AFB, along with fifty percent of the city of Harlingen. Many of the GIs from the base had made this spot their home away from home. In short, this was the main hangout of many of the city's citizens. Naturally, it goes without saying—this family generated excellent income from this operation. I decided then and there, that I would make this facility my main hangout.

Accordingly, on my first visit to this complex I purposely introduced myself to the husband and wife team who were its owners. I also met their children, (and we would become lifelong friends). Unfortunately though, I'd had absolutely no inkling of the soon-to-emerge life-threatening conspiracy that lurked nearby. Thus, I along with Manny and 'friends' partied the entire afternoon there at this complex known simply as the "The Corner". While there, I met a very nice girl named Mindy. We seemed to have connected the very moment we met. So after spending much of the afternoon together, at her request I walked her home, which stood nearby. We then climbed back into Manny's old vehicle and returned to the base. During our return drive, I sat thinking *"This has been a very good day, so I believe I'm going to like this place called Harlingen"*. Upon returning to the base, we rushed to the dining hall where we had ourselves a really hearty meal. This would be our final meal of the evening, although we intended to party through much of the night. The four of us returned to our rooms for a bit of relaxation, and I naturally proceeded directly to our nearby TV room. We already had agreed upon departing the base at 9:00, heading into Mexico.

Suddenly, Manny poked his head through the door, yelling "Come on Jake, we've gotta go"! Without comment, I immediately followed him out into the long barracks hallway. "What's the matter, Manny?" I asked. "We're going to kick some ass!" was his sharp response. I was baffled by his strange behavior, but I was new here, so I very much wanted to become 'one of the guys'. So when Manny ordered "Follow me," I followed. He knocked upon several doors, rounding up a total of eight more GIs. Evidently this had been done before, for each person joined him without question. Soon our group totaled ten able-bodied young men. When we reached a certain room, he opened its door, quickly summoning us inside. I was instantly alarmed by the sight of a severely battered and bloodied young GI sitting meekly upon his bed, delicately dabbing blood from both his face and head. He couldn't have weighed more than 120 pounds. Manny was the first to speak, "Stevie, tell the guys here what just happened to you". Then slowly and painfully, little Steve began relating to us the events of the past hour. I discovered that as I had been watching TV, Stevie was getting the crap beat out of him just outside Harlingen, by a group of four burly and ruthless thugs! As I listened to him, I thought "*This could have been me*". These thoughts stimulated my already simmering anger. Stevie then told us how he had been refused service at a nearby dance hall. I felt deep empathy for him as he told us of the absolute rejection and subsequent vicious attack upon his person.

"It was about 8:00PM as I walked down this side street. As I neared a large barn-like building, I heard the sound of music so I entered and walked to the bar. I took a bar seat and waited. All I'd wanted was a soda to quench my thirst. The bartender stood at the far end of the bar, chatting with another fellow. I'm certain he'd seen me, because he looked directly at me as I took my seat. Still, he ignored me and just left me sitting there. So finally, I called to him— but he took his sweet time in coming over. When he finally approached me, he just growled "Yeah"! I calmly asked, "May I have a Coke, please"? "Hell no," he again growled at me as he walked away. I continued sitting there, but soon four big goons walked over. Then they grabbed me by each arm and forced me onto the floor. I couldn't believe this was happening. But then they began stomping my head and face, while two others began kicking me in the ribs! All I'd wanted was a cold soda." Stevie softly concluded. Manny then said "Stevie, show these guys your ribs". This poor little fellow then stood and raised his sweater. We all stood in near shock as we saw the extensive injuries Stevie had suffered at the hands of these four gangsters! Manny again spoke, saying "Guys, let's go and kick some ass"! "Let's go— we're with you!" shouted the gathered group of angry young GIs. I remained silent, although no one had noticed.

Manny took us outside, where he quickly unlocked a large metal container. Inside this container stood a large quantity of baseball equipment. He quickly handed each of us a baseball bat. I stood somewhat in a stupor as I was issued my bat. Next, we piled into two separate vehicles, heading for our dreadful destination. As I rode along with them, I kept thinking, *"My career is over—though it hasn't even gotten started"*. We arrived at the dance hall under the cover of total darkness. We parked half a block past the building, and Manny briefly left us to survey this situation. Within five minutes, he returned to provide us with attack instructions! He divided us into two groups. Manny and his sidekick, (Speed), would move quickly to the upstairs area, where they suspected there may have awaited several armed men. Team '1' would attack the dining area and its clientele. Team '2' would immediately attack the four bouncers and bartender. It was then unanimously agreed upon that no mercy would be shown to any persons inside this building!

At precisely 8:00PM, we stormed the dance hall, wearing dark glasses with baseball caps! I conveniently allowed myself to be the very last to enter the building. As I entered, I saw utter chaos! Customers were screaming as they scampered in all directions! I caught a brief glimpse of

Manny as he and Speed disappeared from view at the top of the stairs. I quickly looked to my right— only to see five huge (but cowering) figures, struggling about on the floor near the bar. I then saw four GIs (including little Stevie) forcefully swinging baseball bats to every part of these fellows' bodies! I moved freely further into the dining area, but was challenged not even by a single soul. Everyone here had crawled and huddled together beneath the many standing dining tables. As I strolled calmly among these tables, I inwardly resolved that unless attacked, I would not strike anyone. However, since all the other guys here had transformed themselves into human demolition teams, I knew that I must at least put on a bit of a show. So, I immediately began cursing and yelling loudly as I proceeded to literally smash each item of glass standing inside this facility! As I walked between tables in my moment of glory, I even several times feinted with my bat at some of the customers who were desperately attempting to shield themselves from blows by these wild GIs. But through all this commotion, I struck absolutely no other human being!

Then as suddenly as this attack had begun,— it was over! Upon hearing our predetermined signal from Manny, we rushed from the building. Outside, we strolled casually to our waiting cars. Manny then collected our eleven baseball bats, placing them inside an old woolen blanket inside the trunk of his car. We had spent only five minutes here, but in this brief span of time, we had successfully affected the lives of every person in this building. I'm certain they would not forget this night for as long as they might live. As we drove back towards the base, I asked, "Manny, don't you think the civilian and military police might be searching for us"? "Don't worry, they won't be calling the cops." he responded. "What do you mean?" I asked. "I'll explain later," he said. Then without further comment, Manny drove to a friend's house, where he deposited our baseball bats for safe keeping through the night.

Unchallenged, we then returned to the base. Once there we showered and readied our-selves for another evening of partying in Mexico. This had been quite a day—but it wasn't over yet. We arrived in Mexico at 9:15, and would remain there until 2:00 Sunday morning. I should note here—this was my very first time staying out far past midnight, so this was a pivotal moment in my young life. I had learned early on that I preferred walking these streets alone, so I departed company from Manny and his crew.

Now I found myself completely free to pursue and satisfy my personal desires. Over the course of this evening, I would visit at least three different 'ladies'. However, I had not forgotten the poor 'creature' who had unfortunately found himself incarcerated in this miserable prison. By 11:00PM I had already visited my first two 'ladies'. Naturally, I fully enjoyed myself with each of them. And, I gained a considerable amount of additional carnal knowledge from those two. At this time I decided to take a short break, so I walked casually through the narrow streets, heading in the general direction of that dreadful prison facility.

I walked quietly and cautiously as I drew nearer. This time he lay quiet and unmoving, as if asleep (or worse). I stopped briefly to observe this figure. After three minutes had passed, he still had not moved or made any sounds whatsoever. I hoped for the best, (meaning I sincerely hoped that he was alive). No guards were in sight; but, I perceived that they were watching me from some vantage point. Finally, this previously inert figure slightly shifted its body, and rolled onto a wet spot on the ground. I would learn that this wet spot was urine. Now, there was more than just urine present, but I find elaborating simply too repulsive. I feel certain you understand my meaning. The mere viewing of this awful situation completely erased the fun I'd had earlier. At least though, I'd been able to determine that he was alive. Then although he had not seen me, I quickly walked away from this most unpleasant sight!

Back at a nearby cantina, I sat alone, sipping on a tall and very cold glass of Coca-Cola. There would be no Juanita on this night, with whom to socialize. This was when a disturbing thought struck me. Namely, although I sat in the center of a buzzing city, it was as if I was completely nonexistent. No one here cared one bit about me as a person. I found this situation to be somewhat unsettling. I longed to be back at home in my little hick town. I finished my soda and moved back out into the streets once more. Once there, I quickly resumed the furthering of my 'special education'. At 1:30AM, I walked to another cantina nearest our parked car. I then sat waiting for Manny and crew to show up. After a relatively short time, they arrived and we returned (unchallenged) across the border, and onward onto the base. Once back in my room, I took one last soothing shower before dragging myself into bed. I slept soundly that night!

At 9:30 Sunday morning, Manny and I had washed up and were heading for our nearby Base Recreation Center. This was completely new to me, but this was where many of the airmen here spent much of their free time. This facility had been provided by the base for the morale and welfare of its enlisted troops. It provided entertainment in the form of dances and other social events each Saturday night, but of course we were absent. Each Sunday it provided refreshments, such as coffee and tea, sodas, and a wide variety of fresh doughnuts. This was another first for me, so naturally I made a glutton of myself. Also, this special facility provided a variety of board and table games, such as chess, checkers, ping pong, and pocket billiards. I instantly became fascinated by the game of pocket billiards. And from this very first exposure, I would dedicate a vast amount of my free time toward learning and mastering this game. I quickly discovered that Manny himself was quite the expert at this game of billiards. Unfortunately, he usually played for money. However, he did agree to teach me the basics of the game. So for the remainder of the morning, we hung out at the Rec Center.

At noontime, we crowded the dining hall. One hour later, we were all (except little Stevie) once again downtown Harlingen. Poor Stevie remained mostly inside his room while nursing his numerous injuries. Now by this hour of day, I had expected to see a number of local police moving about the base, searching for a certain bunch of GIs. But there had been none. Manny seated the four of us together at an outside patio table, which was partly shaded by two fairly large palm trees. Immediately, he ordered two quarts of ice-cold beer. At this time, I was not a beer drinker, but he filled my empty glass anyway. Reluctantly, I picked up my glass and took a light sip. "Ah, this is good," I lied. I did not (even for a moment) want them to suspect that I was not accustomed to drinking beer. Each quickly agreed with my compliment.

Moments later Manny commented, "Guys, I've got some news for you". *"What now?"* I thought. Speed then said, "Give it to us". Manny continued, "In case any of you guys are expecting a line-up tomorrow morning, don't worry— there won't be one". I was quite relieved at hearing Manny's comforting words; but, I also doubted their validity. "How can you be so sure?" I asked. "That place we hit last night is filled with tons of marijuana and other illegal merchandise." said Manny. I was shocked at hearing this revelation, but I remained silent for lack of a better response. Manny continued "In fact guys, we've each been offered good-paying jobs there by management". *"My new roommate, Manny, is full of surprises"*, I thought. The silent fellow, (Will) then spoke, asking "What kind of pay are we talking about"? Manny then answered, "You guys will each start at a thousand dollars per month". "Of course I'll get a bit more because I'm the senior member of our group." he added. "Wow, a thousand dollars per month starting pay?" exclaimed Speed. "That's right, a cool grand," answered Manny. "Guys, this is ten times more than I make now," I said. I then added "This is a generous offer, but I'm going to stick with the Air Force and try making something of myself". Manny quickly responded, "Jake, opportunity usually only knocks once". "You're right—but I don't trust these people," I said. "Then, let's vote on this," said Manny, displaying a slight bit of irritation at my attitude. We immediately voted upon our offer. The instantaneous response of our vote was: three yea's along with only one nay. Now in case you're wondering about the single nay— I was that person. Seemingly a bit disappointed over my decision, Manny then stated, "We need four guys total, but I know one fellow who is getting discharged next week— so I'll talk to him". I would later learn that this fellow had eagerly accepted Manny's offer. At the conclusion of our discussion, Manny informed us that he and his two buddies would at 3:00PM meet with management of the facility, we'd only last evening attacked. At 2:45 Manny (and friends) dropped me off at The Corner club, which we had visited on the previous afternoon. They drove quickly away with wide grins across their faces.

At this point I found myself completely alone and wondering what to do with myself. It was also at this precise moment, I found myself thinking of my family— and wondering just what my dear friend Donnie might be doing now. So with a feeling of deep uncertainty, I entered the delicatessen area and sat upon a vacant bar stool. The wife of this owning couple smilingly approached to take my order. Then (in memory of home) I ordered a slice of coconut cake and a tall glass of lemonade. Momentarily, she placed my order before me. She then took a seat directly across from me as she said, "You're new here, aren't you, son"? "Yes ma'am, I just arrived a few days ago." I replied. "Well, I hope you will enjoy your stay in our little town," she said. "I really like what I've seen so far," I replied. We sat chatting about the area and local warm weather. Now although this was early November, the local temperature was nearly seventy degrees. I really appreciated this, for temperatures back home would hover around zero degrees on this day.

At about 3:30, my high level of loneliness remained with me, so I walked outside and to the building's front area. Here, lounging about, were about one dozen GIs who were casually chatting mainly about sports. I introduced myself to them, and asked, "Are any of you guys going back to the base anytime soon"? Luckily, one fellow answered, "I'm leaving right now". He then pointed to his sporty new convertible automobile, saying, "Hop in". I wasted no time in complying and complimenting him on his excellent choice of cars (1955 black Corvette). As we rode along with the top lowered, I couldn't help thinking, *This even tops Uncle Abe*.

Then in just minutes, we'd reached the base. This driver dropped me off near my barracks, so I walked directly to my lonely room. Once there, I took advantage of the solitude to sit down and write a comforting letter to my dear mother. In my letter, I naturally explained how very much I loved and missed the three of them. I also stretched the truth somewhat by telling her, "Mom, I am just fine and am truly enjoying life". By saying these things I would at least put their minds at ease, thereby preventing them from needlessly worrying about me. I would mail my letter tomorrow. Unfortunately, she would receive it nearly four days later. This meant that I could expect an answer from her approximately two weeks from this day. Now you young folk have not fully realized how truly fortunate you are by living in current times! Dinner hour arrived, so I proceeded all alone to the nearby dining hall. I would spend the next two hours alone inside the movie theater, after which, I would return to my room where I would prepare my uniform and shoes, for my first day of active duty in the United States Air Force!

The long anticipated hour of 6:00AM Monday morning had arrived. I had set my alarm clock for this hour and it was presently ringing away at me. I quickly hopped out of bed and washed up. Sometime during the early morning hours, my roommate had quietly entered the room and climbed into bed. So now that I'd finished washing up, he followed my lead. While he washed we talked as I dressed. "Jake, you really should have been at our meeting yesterday," he said. "It went well?" I asked. "Quite well," he replied excitedly. "I'm happy for you all," I said. He then shocked me by stating, "This morning, we're going to declare ourselves as undesirables"! "And, I guarantee you we'll be outta here in less than two weeks." he concluded. His comments stunned me, but I remained outwardly indifferent. "I wish you guys the best of luck," I said as I finished dressing. As I prepared to leave the room I said to him "See you in the dining hall". "Right," he commented. I proceeded to the dining hall, but had breakfast alone. Neither Manny, nor his buddies showed up.

My new work day would commence sharply at 7:30AM. As I walked the short distance to my work place, I realized what a truly beautiful morning this was. Skies were clear, the temperature mild, with just a slight balmy breeze. *"I really like this"*, I thought as I walked along. I arrived at the post office at 7:15. Of course, my very first act was that of depositing mom's letter into the mail drop box. Having completed this most essential action, I was at last— READY TO COMMENCE WORK!

Staff Sergeant Pruitt again introduced me to the work crew of mail handlers. He also appointed a special on-the-job trainer to get me started and help me along in learning my duties. We began by off-loading the recently arrived two-ton specially designed mail truck. Then throughout the early morning hours, we sorted both letters and parcels by office of destination. I quickly found this type of work to be quite simple (possibly even boring). When this first phase was completed, we then used two assigned pick-up trucks to transport and deliver this mail to its final destination. The morning passed quite quickly and without accident or incident. At noon I was allowed to take my lunch hour. At the dining hall I was joined by Manny. He seemed to be in high spirits, as he related to me the exciting work he would soon be doing. But even more importantly, he was absolutely thrilled over the money he and his cohorts would soon earn. Manny advised me that he and friends had already initiated Undesirable Discharge processing, and would be gone by week's end. But as he sat rambling on about his prospective situation, I sat thinking *"I've just met a friend— but now he too is gone"*. At this point though, I seemed to hear my grandmother speaking to me, and saying "You've just completed nine years of isolation on the farm— so surely you will survive this". As I sat there pondering these words, I gradually began to realize my capabilities. No longer would I allow myself to become saddened by the absence of SO-CALLED-FRIENDS! Sure, this situation would occasionally burden me, but I'd already repeatedly proven—I could handle this. From this day forward, if I should find a friend— good. Though if not, then still good. This was now my newly adopted attitude— and one I would not abandon.

At 1:00 I found myself once again inside the post office, repeating the morning's process. I spent my entire afternoon assisting with the sorting, routing, and delivery of official and personal mail. Finally, the hour of 4:30PM arrived and my first day on the job came to an end. I had just completed the first day of my official military career! I walked to the dining hall and enjoyed my evening meal. But so that I would not eat alone, I squeezed myself into a vacant seat at an already occupied table. As it happened, I found myself in the presence of three other new arrivals. Each was assigned duty as an administrative specialist, which was contrary to my situation. I learned also that each of these new airmen was from my home state. As we talked, I wondered how could they have been placed in their career field, while I ended up mal-assigned. I learned though that these airmen were originally classified as administrative specialists. However, my original classification was that of airborne radio operator; thus, I subsequently surmised that since I had strongly protested reassignment into the medical field, this postal assignment served as punishment for my adamant objection. I would accept this postal duty without further protest. I finished my meal and proceeded to my room, only to find it already vacated by my former roommate. Now I would have this entire room all to myself— at least for awhile.

The departure of my roommate presented an unanticipated problem for me, in that I no longer would have transportation into Mexico. Although, getting to and from town was facilitated by local bus transportation. So for the next several days (at least) I would divide my off-duty time between downtown and on-base. Thus, for the next four days I concentrated on increasing my knowledge of my military job and the postal career field. Each evening after work I would visit the base recreation center, where I would observe many of the airmen as they played pocket billiards. Wherever possible, I would also try my hand at this game, which was very new and fascinating to me. Finally Friday afternoon arrived. By now, I had extensively familiarized myself with my postal duties. I'd even succeeded in achieving limited beginner's skill in the game of pocket billiards.

Overall, I found myself beginning to feel at least a bit comfortable in my new surroundings. At this point, my good fortune improved ever so slightly. During a short break period I walked outside and onto the rear loading dock of the post office. While there I happened to see a really sharp 1952 luxury model Buick Road Master which was parked. As I admired this car I noticed a "FOR SALE" sign posted in its rearview window. I decided I would take a closer look, so I walked outside for a visual inspection. Now even though this car was slightly more than three years old, its appearance was that of a new vehicle. Even its tires were nearly new. I really liked this car, but I felt $750 was more than I could afford. Just then I heard a lady's voice ask, "In the market for a nice car"? I turned to see a middle aged, and somewhat graying, lady approaching me. "It's very nice, but I shouldn't waste your time," I responded. "Well, I'm getting ready to leave Harlingen, and I really need to sell this car before I depart," she said. She then quickly added "So make me an offer". "Ma'am, I only have six hundred dollars to spend on a car," I said. "I'll take it," she exclaimed excitedly, handing me the car keys. "Let's take it for a quick drive." she suggested. "Are you sure?" I asked. "I'm sure," she said. "I'll need to check with my supervisor," I said. "I'll wait here." she replied. I then rushed back inside the post office, where I asked, "Sergeant Storke, may I take off for just a few minutes to test-drive a car"? "You've worked hard all week, Jake, so take the rest of the afternoon off— see you Monday morning," he said. I thanked him and rushed back outside to the waiting car owner.

The powerful Road Master's engine purred quietly as I navigated through the base. This was a car I could really enjoy. Each of its mechanical systems functioned properly. I drove off base for a short distance and found this car even more impressive. "Ma'am, this is one very nice car," I said to the owner. "I agree— it's been very good to me," she replied, adding. "I hope you're not paying by check though". "No ma'am— cash," I informed her. She then instructed me to drive to our Base Legal Office in order to complete a binding purchase contract. I complied with her instructions. However, upon exiting the vehicle I checked under its hood and underneath the entire car. It appeared to be in excellent condition throughout. Naturally, I could not afford to get 'stung' as dad had in purchasing Old Betsy. Satisfied that this purchase was a wise choice for me, we proceeded inside the office to complete the purchase agreement. While the necessary paperwork was in process, I rushed to my room to retrieve the money. Back at the Legal Office, we each signed our contract, which finalized this agreement. I then counted out for the seller, the total amount owed. We shook hands and at her request, I drove this kind lady downtown to her residence. Before leaving her, I inquired whether she had other means of transportation. She advised me that she had recently purchased a new car, which was parked inside her garage. We then thanked each other once more as I prepared to leave.

The hour had just reached 3:30PM, as I cruised the short distance along the highway and back onto the base. At this moment, I felt really great! Not only did I now have a car, but a really nice one! I resolved then and there that I would (at all times) take expert care of my newly purchased fine automobile. At this time I would partake in another recently gained luxury— (a shower). As I showered, I reflected upon the week past. I had gotten through my very first week of career-related active duty. I had also gotten rid of my roommate. Lastly, I had myself an impressive automobile in which to drive myself around. After showering I visited the nearby Recreation Center and located a vacant pool table. Although, at this point I was still less than a novice at this sport, I would work diligently correcting and eliminating each existing deficiency I currently possessed. However, I must tell you I really felt awkward while engaging in this new found activity called billiards.

At 4:00 I walked to the dining hall, where I had another excellent meal. After eating I drove directly into town and to The Corner. Upon arriving I made certain I greeted and exchanged pleasantries with the couple who owned the place. As I sat in the deli section, the gentleman's friendly wife treated me to a delicious dish of ice cream and cake. I thanked her as I devoured my treat. Afterward I ventured into the billiards parlor to watch a few pool games. Actually, my primary purpose was to pick up a few tips on how to best play this game. I was fortunate in that the owner immediately paired me against his teenage son. Now, it goes without saying— I really got myself spanked! But this was okay by me, for I was slowly gaining the knowledge and skills I needed. After about an hour of playing pool, I moved into the lounge area to hopefully socialize with a few of the young ladies.

Again luck was with me, for no sooner had I entered this

area, did I meet a very cute girl named Myra. Mindy had not yet arrived, so I decided to spend a little time with this new girl. Soon we were behaving as though we had known each other for ages. Fortunately I had kept our conversation controlled so as not to infer any desire for intimacy. Fortunately, I had employed this tact for very soon Mindy also showed up. I learned that she and Myra were next-door neighbors. But my casual manner of relating to Myra had precluded the probability of conflict between these two girls. After spending an hour with them, I bade each "good evening" before once again heading into Matamoros.

I arrived in this small town shortly after 10:00PM. However, this time I would alter my routine. So instead of at first visiting the 'ladies', I decided to check on the imprisoned cadet. Two nights had passed since he had observed my presence, so I had absolutely no idea as to what to expect upon arrival at the prison site. As I approached that dreadful corner where this cadet was held, I strained my eyes and ears in an effort to assess the current situation. I heard no unusual sounds, so I continued slowly walking toward this structure of human torture. Soon I saw him. He was sitting in his usual location amidst a number of wet spots, which I assumed were urine. He was about sixty feet away and had not detected my approach, so I attracted his attention by clearing my throat. As soon as I did this, he turned to look in my direction. Naturally, neither of us spoke. However, he seemed to have perceived some special purpose for my recent visits. Then as his eyes fell upon me, I waved to him. He continued sitting, unmoving, though his eyes remained constantly upon me. I could not risk speaking and thereby drawing attention from the guards, so I merely smiled as I

stood there. He remained nonresponsive, but totally attentive. I then began to feel that we had begun to communicate. However, remaining here was unwise, so reluctantly
I gave him my usual 'thumbs-up' as I slowly walked away.
Each time I witnessed this most pathetic sight, I became
more resolved that I must make at least some effort toward
correcting this grave injustice.

I returned to the downtown 'business' district, where
I proceeded to further educate myself regarding certain
aspects of life. This was the weekend, so naturally Matamoros had become a virtual beehive of activity. This was also
my very first time coming here all alone. To put this more
bluntly— I felt a distinct uneasiness in being here. So after
just two brief 'social visits,' I quietly climbed back into my
newly purchased automobile and returned across the border into Texas. I drove directly to The Corner, where I once
again mingled with the crowd for over an hour.

After I had returned to my room, showered, and
climbed into bed. This was a strange but wonderful new
feeling for me. I had been away from home for less than
four months, but in this short span of time, I'd become a
man. I was now completely on my own, meaning—it was
I who was responsible for each decision I made. No longer
would I become influenced by the likes of Manny, my former roommate. Then as I lay alone in the dark early morning silence, I was struck by the thought, *"Jake, this is your
new life"!* I realized then and there, — I really liked this life.
I seemed to hear the voices of my parents saying to me,
"Jake, take things slow— and don't become wild"! I would
heed their thoughts and parental wishes.

I spent the weekend mostly roaming about the airbase.

But since the weather was still quite mild, I decided to drive downtown Harlingen early Saturday afternoon. Once there, I parked my car in a safe location and then simply walked all around the city. I found this small city to be both hospitable and pleasant. Naturally, I just loved its appearance—with its streets lined with lovely flowers and swaying palm trees. Also, here one could purchase alcohol past midnight and even on Sundays. After Sunday morning breakfast, I spent several hours thoroughly cleaning my car. This was a proud moment for me— cleaning my very own car! Afterward I relished in the luxury of a shower before heading once more to the dining hall. After lunch, I headed straight for the on-base billiards parlor. Then I remembered that I had not yet written mom a second letter, so I dropped my billiards practice and returned to the barracks to write to my dear mother. When I'd finished writing, it was time to return to the dining hall for evening meal. Next, I headed downtown to The Corner. There, I socialized with a few girls and guys for awhile before finally returning to the base. This was the way I'd spent my first free weekend here at my new location of military assignment.

It had been a great weekend, although this was my second Monday morning of military duty. I decided I would remain on base for much of this week. In doing so, I would use my off-duty hours to study my Career Development Course pertaining to administrative specialist. This was a six-month course, but I intended to complete it within my first sixty days on base. Ironically though, nothing within this course was related to my present duties as an apprentice postal specialist. This complicated matters for me and served to obstruct my normal rate of rank advancement.

Nonetheless, I would concurrently learn each of these non-related fields within a minimum time period.

I had worked my butt off during the first half of this week, and now it was Wednesday noon. As I prepared to head for the dining hall, my supervisor summoned me to his office. Inside, he commented "Jake, I completely forgot to tell you that you will be off duty each Wednesday afternoon." I was pleasantly taken aback by his unexpected announcement. He continued "Each of us gets an afternoon off per week— yours falls on Wednesday". "Really?" I asked. "Yes, so see you tomorrow morning— bright and early," he answered.

"Thank you," I said as I rather quickly exited his office. Then as I walked along toward the dining hall I thought, *"Jake, what are you going to do with a whole afternoon off duty"?* My first option was to simply relax in my room. The second option was to ride downtown, where I could relax and maybe shoot a few games of pool. However, my third option was to take the little listening device of my grandmother's out for some actual tests. I pondered these three options, all the while knowing which I would choose— (the latter, of course).

First, I would visit our Base Exchange Store (BX) and purchase an inexpensive portable radio along with several other miscellaneous items (one of which would be a small magnifying glass). Next, I would make a stop downtown at Harlingen's leading bank and open a small bank savings account in the amount of $250. After which, I would drive southward for five miles and onto a deserted beach area. This location would become my testing site for this magnificent little instrument, known to me only as the "Elm".

I reached the Harlingen National Bank just prior to closing hour and walked directly to the desk containing a sign that read "New Accounts". I prefer to think that the curious look I received from the slightly chubby lady sitting there, was due to my youthful appearance. "May I help you, young man?" she asked, peering up at me through horn-rimmed glasses. "Ma'am, I'd like to open a small savings account," I answered. "Fine, but I must first advise you that we have a minimum account balance of five dollars." she said. "I believe that I can spare at least five dollars," I responded. Good, then please take a seat," she ordered. I complied as she fished through a desk drawer in search of the required account paperwork. As she arranged these forms, I removed my military ID card and placed it atop the desk before her. This card provided verification of my identity, along with other essential information. It also expedited and facilitated the preparation of these forms, and reduced the need for extensive verbal communication between the two of us. I sensed that she appreciated this advantage. After ten minutes of typing, she placed before me several forms requiring my signature. Then she asked for my initial deposit. I placed before her the meager sum of $250. She appeared impressed, saying, "Young man, this is the very first time I've had someone of your young age, open an account with us". "Thank you," I responded. This pert old lady then logged my deposit into my booklet before handing it to me, and saying, "Congratulations"! I thanked her before immediately leaving the bank.

I sat for a brief moment in my car as I evaluated my current position in life. I was still only eighteen years of age, but even without the benefit of college, I had already created a sound and promising career for myself. Even better— I was the proud owner of a fine automobile, and a small bank account. And if these improvements were not enough, I now had access to electricity, running water, and yes— even television. Even a telephone booth stood just fifty feet down the hall from my room. Ultimately, I had increased my income by one hundred percent, shortened my working hours by fifty percent, and improved my living conditions also by one hundred percent. I viewed this as a major transformation in just four short months!

I started the quietly purring engine of the powerful Road Master and promptly pointed it in a southerly direction. The afternoon was beautiful— sunny and balmy. After ten minutes I reached my destination, which was a lengthy but deserted beach area just outside the (then) small town of San Benito. I turned left from the main highway, and onto a narrow access road that extended the length of this area of beach. As I had hoped, no one was in sight anywhere along this stretch of beach area. I was in luck, for here I could perform a thorough testing of this strange little device, the (Elm). I began testing preparations by installing batteries into my newly purchased radio. Next, I carefully opened the base of the stubby candle that housed this device. After I had neatly cut open the candle's base, I delicately removed the Elm from its hiding place. Initial inspection revealed it had remained undamaged while in my custody. But having strongly suspected that this object had remained idle for possibly more than one hundred years, I felt the need to take a closer look. I particularly wanted to take a close look at the hull of this device. I also wanted to ensure that its tiny rotating ring was intact and in fully operational condition.

But to do this, I would need the small magnifying glass I'd just today purchased. So I carefully extracted this glass from its packaging, and delicately wiped it clear of any dust particles. I then used a small portion of the black leather car's seat as a focal point upon which to peer. I was surprised to note the large number of fissures within the upholstery of these seats. However, by having done this I had verified the fact that my magnifying glass was sufficient for the task at hand. Now, I peered closely at the Elm's calibration ring. I detected no defects or areas requiring special attention. It was truly amazing,— and I wondered what materials this device was made of. Next, I held the Elm firmly between my thumb and index finger of my right hand and gently rotated its tiny ring with the tip of my left index finger. The ring rotated effortlessly in both right and left directions. At this point, it appeared that all was well with this little device.

Finally, I was ready to commence testing! I once again looked in all directions, but seeing no other persons in this area, I proceeded to my next step. I noticed a nearby fifty-gallon drum marked "TRASH." I walked over and checked its contents. It had been recently emptied, and was free of debris or other unsanitary matter. I then retrieved my small portable radio, turned it on, and set its volume at mid-level. Next, I inserted the radio into its brown paper bag container. Lastly, with the radio softly playing country and western music, I lowered the device into this large standing trash can. I started up my car and drove exactly one-half mile down the beach.

Here, I finally initiated my testing of the Elm. I carefully inserted it into my left ear, with the first (12 o'clock) position pointing vertically. I might note here that during my total of twelve school years, I had only received mathematical education based upon the Dewey Decimal System. Consequently, I was quite unfamiliar with the Metric (or any other) system of mathematics. Thus, I had erroneously calculated that each dot on the Elm's tiny ring represented 1/12 mile. I was quite surprised to discover that my original estimations were significantly flawed. Subsequently, since I sat at a distance of one-half mile away from my sound source, I'd set the Elm's calibration ring accordingly at its halfway point. I was completely unaware that this particular setting was in error. Here, I found myself somewhat baffled, for this should have been the proper setting— at least based upon my learned mathematics. Now I realized why grandmother could not get this device to work. I had received a signal that was recognizable as music, but it was so vastly distorted, I could not distinguish this C&W music from R&B or jazz. I adjusted the ring clockwise by one notch. Now the ring was set at position seven, although I remained stationary. The sound I now received had slightly diminished. This confirmed that I had overshot my sound source. Thus without changing location, I reversed the ring's setting by two full notches. At this setting, I hit the jackpot! At this revised (position #5) the sound was audible and crystal clear! I could clearly distinguish each word the singer used. But equally impressive was the fact that I stood a full half mile from my source. *"Amazing"*, I thought as I sat listening to the music. Naturally, I had aimed my listening ear in a straight line with the location of my radio. Now I would try slightly rotating my head in either direction. Then as suspected, even the slightest turn of my head resulted in the complete loss of my intended signal. I decided to step out of the car and slowly rotate 360 degrees. I tried this and was pleased to find that all sound at the half-mile distance was receivable. I stepped back into the car and drove to the full distance of one mile. Once there, I repeated this process and achieved the exact same results. At this distance, the signal was equally strong. I readjusted the Elm's calibration to the position of #10. Having verified the Elm's range of up to one mile, I drove a quarter mile farther, then set to position #12. At this position of one and a quarter mile, my signal remained clear but considerably weakened. This confirmed that I had reached my maximum listening range. However, I had not yet finished my testing process. Throughout high school I had been diligent and dedicated as a student in the subject of science. As such, I possessed a considerably curious mind. This prompted me to consider introducing my car's presently lowered radio antenna into this equation. I then drove half a mile farther down the beach.

The Elm's setting remained unchanged, but as I electronically began raising the car's antenna, I was pleasantly surprised— the music from my radio reemerged in full strength. Now, I was really impressed! I resumed slowly driving away from the location of my radio, but continued receiving a strong signal until I had reached a point that was two and a half miles from my sound source. I was simply astounded! However, the instant I began lowering my antenna, all radio sound suddenly disappeared. I removed the Elm from my ear, and returned to retrieve my radio.

I'd performed my initial testing of the Elm, and it had exceeded even my greatest expectations! I secured

my radio and temporarily returned the Elm to its holding location inside the candle. I then drove directly back
to the base and returned to my room. I borrowed a small
can of machine oil from an occupant next door, and used
a clean dust cloth along with one drop of lightweight oil
to wipe and polish both the interior and exterior of the
Elm. I found that although it had retained its durability,
the oil served to further improve its overall luster. I had
completed the polishing of its interior and outer hull, and
had shifted my attention to its nearly microscopic calibration ring. Ever so gently, by using back and forth motion,
I brushed the surface of this ring. I'd calculated that over-
night this light-weight oil would saturate the entire unit,
while also penetrating areas underneath the ring. I noticed
that my little homemade lubrication job had already begun
producing results. The Elm's luster had returned. Also, its
tiny ring appeared both cleaner and clearer. As I continued wiping and polishing, I noticed a nearly imperceptible
change in the ring's appearance. These twelve dots had suddenly become more prominent. I held it closer to the light
of my wonderful new electric lamp. Each little dot somehow appeared flawed. I quickly grabbed my magnifying
glass and positioned it approximately three inches directly
above the Elm's ring. Now I received my second great surprise of the day! These dots were not at all flawed. In fact,
each contained a separate and distinct image: (1) Starting at
its twelve o'clock position, were a series of three crescent
moons (each increasing in size). (2) Starting at its three
o'clock position, were a series of three progressive quarter
moons. (3) Starting at its six o'clock position, were three
progressive three-quarter moons. (4) Finally at its nine

o'clock position, there began a series of three full moon symbols. However, within each full moon there was what appeared to be the (inverted) Sea of Tranquility. Strangely, each of these regions progressively rotated right by one hundred twenty degrees.

I made this discovery during the month of November 1955. Since that day, a total of fifty-seven years have passed. However, after extensive deliberation I've yet to even slightly comprehend the significance of these symbols. Could these images have been observed by entities positioned at vantage points located at great distances from the far side of our moon? Now while I would definitely not argue this point, this remains my only plausible explanation. I finally finished my maintenance project, whereupon I secured the Elm for the evening. Upon awakening tomorrow morning, I would reseal this device inside its storage candle.

I had recently received my Career Development Course (CDC) for the Administrative Career Field (apprentice level). This was normally a three-month course, but I would complete it within just thirty days. So for the next four weeks, I would dedicate at least two hours each evening for course study. The fact that I had been assigned nonrelated postal duty served to impede my study efforts. Even so, I was determined to complete this course within my pre-designated time frame of only thirty days. Essentially, I studied two separate fields— (administrative and postal)— and I would simultaneously complete training in each of these fields. I would also concurrently appoint myself as the personal representative of confined Cadet Vincent Callen! But since I had not yet formulated any sort of plan for assisting him, I began setting forth a course of action toward this end.

I had fully realized from the very beginning that any intervention by me might quite possibly place me alongside Cadet Callen. Also, there was the strong possibility that my efforts might jeopardize his present situation. Still, I felt obligated to at least make an attempt at securing his release from this false imprisonment. I knew that I would need vital information which I currently did not possess. The question before me was "How could I best obtain this much-needed information? I desperately needed the opportunity to peek inside the prison facility where he was being held, but I felt strongly that such an act would prove unwise. Still, I simply would not allow myself to just sit by while doing absolutely nothing to alleviate this dire situation. The thought then occurred to me, *"Jake, since you're hesitant to look around inside this old building, why not simply stand nearby and listen to sounds and voices within"?* I sort of liked this idea! At least this course of action would allow me to maintain a safe distance, while gaining some idea of conditions inside this building. I decided I would begin immediately implementing my plan. So after I had successfully completed today's chapter of CDC study material, I would visit the Matamoros prison facility!

At 9:00PM that very evening, I stood across the street from the prison. Cadet Callen also sat in his customary position, at his usual location. I gestured slightly with my right hand, as a greeting to him. He sat unmoving, as would have a statue, though I felt confident that he had inwardly acknowledged my greeting. However, I also felt that his consistent lack of response was in strict compliance with instructions of these prison officials. My thoughts on this matter were reinforced by the manner in which he maintained constant eye contact with me. It was if he was pleading, "Please help me"! I'd already learned that this area's rainy season was rapidly approaching. Accordingly, I had hoped against hope that he would be relocated into an inside prison cell before the rains came. Time would prove me wrong. After three minutes had passed I gave Cadet Callen a 'thumbs-up' before moving on.

I then walked four blocks away, employing a skill I'd learned on the farm to determine the exact distance of one-quarter mile. I was fortunate to have found a small park with bench seats. The park was completely vacant—which was great for my purposes. I sat down and prepared to 'listen' to voices and sounds occurring inside the prison. After carefully adjusting my seating position, I eventually located my sound source destination. Now, although I bore the burden of severe handicap by not understanding this local language, I succeeded in achieving my objective. Primarily, I wanted to assess conditions inside this prison. So although I'd understood not a single spoken word, I did gain a sense of the environment therein. First, I listened intently for sounds of suffering and torture from within. But after thirty minutes, I'd heard no moans or groans. This served to comfort me (at least somewhat). Second, I'd heard the voices of several males. However, only one male spoke authoritatively while all others retained a level of meekness in their manner of speech. Each had spoken only Spanish. From this, I concluded that these voices were those of the prison's commandant along with several prison guards. I detected no voices or sounds from prisoners. At this point I realized that this prison's inmates had probably already been ordered to bed. Regardless though of the lack of evidence of other prisoners here, I detected no sounds of distress. I then terminated today's 'operation' before returning to the more pleasant side of town. I would to return this prison site on both Thursday and Friday evenings, for more information gathering. Once I had determined it fairly safe, I would then enter this facility to meet with its commandant.

I would spend the remainder of the week performing the duties of an apprentice postal clerk. At closing time on Friday afternoon, I was approached by my supervisor and handed my very first letter from my dear mother. Before departing, he commended me for the great job I had done throughout this first week. I thanked him before rushing directly to my barracks to read mom's letter. I was happy to hear that all was well with my family back home. In her letter, she repeatedly stated how very much they missed me. I was deeply touched by this loving first letter from mom, and was fortunate that no other person was present to witness my state of being.

I spent the majority of weekend daylight hours by hanging out on base and in downtown Harlingen. Though at 2:30 Sunday afternoon, I once again arrived in Matamoros. I then proceeded to the corner where this dreadful prison stood. As during each of my previous visits, I found Cadet Callen sitting upon the dirt. I gave my usual greeting to him, accompanied by my customary 'thumbs-up'. This time I would not linger, for I was anxious to reach my 'relaxation' point in the tiny nearby park. After again listening for nearly thirty-five minutes, I decided, *"Jake, you may as well do this"*, so I began walking toward the prison. Incidentally, I had left a handwritten note on my bunk bed advising my supervisor and commander of my whereabouts, along with an explanation of the purpose of my visit. So with the tiny Elm neatly wrapped and tucked away inside the left pocket of my lightweight jacket, I cautiously climbed the flight of wide steps leading to the prison's entrance. At this point I seriously contemplated turning around and making a hasty departure from this wretched place! But even though I'd really wanted to run away, I knew beyond a doubt that abandonment was no longer an option. I tentatively pushed open the heavy wooden door, cautiously stepping inside.

There were no guards near this door, so none had seen or heard me as I'd entered. I stood at the entranceway, calling out "Hello". Instantly, two uniformed Mexican policemen poked their heads from their office doors to glare at me. The officer nearest me began walking in my direction. I made sure that my hands remained in full view of each, as I maintained my position. Upon reaching me, the policeman inquired, "What you want, Americano"? "El Commandante," I replied. He scrutinized me briefly before saying, "Come". We walked to the far end of the hallway, where he paused, saying, "Wait here". I stood as the other officer kept his cold gaze fixed upon me. Then momentarily, the first officer returned to summon me inside. My heart raced, as it had only done on two prior occasions!

I was now inside 'the lion's den' and possibly about to be devoured! I stepped into a large office, and faced a 'monster' of a man! He was huge, (at least 6'4") and over

300 pounds. Actually, I found his appearance a bit gross when considering his thick black unkempt mustache. He did not speak a single word as I approached his desk. Finally, he asked, "What do you want, Americano"? I had rehearsed my words well. I began "Sir, I do not come as a representative of the Air Force, or the Unites States government". "I come to you only as a Christian, seeking the release of a fellow Christian". I sensed that my words and demeanor had caught him off guard. He paused for a long while before asking, "Where is this Christian you seek"? "He is out back, sir, sitting in the dirt." I answered. Without comment, he stood facing his rear view window. He nodded his head, motioning me forward. "Is this your Christian?" he asked. I peered out the window to ensure that he was referring to Cadet Callen. "Yes sir, this is the person." I responded. "Why do you want him?" he asked. I chose to play upon his sympathy (if any existed). "Sir, I have met his poor sick mother, and she begs daily for her son." I lied. I felt I had quite possibly gotten his attention. The commandant then turned from his window and again sat down in his large heavy leather chair. In so doing, he offered a nearby seat to me. "You tell sick mother—bring me three thousand American dollars; then she can take son home." he said. I answered by saying "Sir, she has spent all her money on medical bills". "Then the Americano remains here!" he replied bluntly. At this point I felt he might possibly dismiss me, so I quickly asked, "Sir, is there any other solution you might have in mind"? At this point, the commandant advised me that there were no alternative solutions. I felt that I was rapidly failing in my efforts, so I asked "Do you have children, sir"? "I have thirteen-year-

old daughter who must pay three thousand dollars to fix teeth." said the commandant.

Now I was beginning to understand! I decided that I must try a different approach, so I said "I'm sure sir, that I have no chance of raising three thousand dollars, for I'm new to the base and I don't have any friends". "So when you fix teeth, I will give you prisoner," he said. I then stood, saying, "Sir, I will do whatever I can to help your daughter. "May I visit you next Sunday, same time"? "Come," he said, adding "Bring cigarettes and some whiskey". "I will bring you cigarettes and whiskey." I answered. I then reached for his hand, and surprisingly he reached forward and we shook hands. "Good day, sir" I said, as I exited his office. As I walked past each office, I waved to the officer sitting inside. I then quite happily exited this awful building!

Next I rounded the corner to where Cadet Callen sat helplessly. He had not seen me, as I had approached from an opposite direction. I coughed to attract his attention. He looked up at me inquisitively, but without making a sound. I wanted to give him hope, so I quickly gave him a 'thumbs-up' and a warm smile. At this point, he sat upright and really looked at me. I remained for only a moment before leaving this location.

At 6:00 Monday morning, I arose and prepared for breakfast. Shortly thereafter, I began the first day of my second week on the job. I worked through the morning alongside five other airmen. By now I had gained a bit more confidence, so the hours seemingly passed quickly. Before leaving for lunch, however, I telephoned my chaplain's office and scheduled an appointment at 1:15PM. I had already discovered that taking time away from work was an acceptable practice, so long as this benefit was not abused. So before leaving for lunch, I informed my supervisor of my chaplain's appointment. He did question my reasons for doing so, and for this I was appreciative.

After lunch, I went directly to the chaplain's office. I was surprised that he'd remembered me. "Good afternoon, Airman Van York, how are things at work?" he asked. "Fine sir," I answered. "What can I do for you?" he inquired. "Sir, if you recall— we briefly discussed the situation involving Cadet Callen, who is imprisoned down in Matamoros." I began. "Yes, I do recall this," he responded. I continued "Well, he sends greetings to all". The chaplain abruptly leaned forward, asking, "You actually got to see him"? "I certainly did sir", I quickly answered. "How is he?" the chaplain asked. "Not good sir" I responded. I quickly added "I don't believe he can hold on for much longer, sir". The chaplain lowered his head and sighed, saying, "I wish there was something we could do". This was the response I had hoped for! "I believe there is some- thing we can do, sir. "Yesterday afternoon, I visited with the prison's commandant." I added, "He has assured me that for the sum of three thousand U. S. dollars, he will release Cadet Callen". "And you believe this?" he asked. I responded, "Sir, I do not wish to appear overly naïve, but I don't think I have any choice in this matter". "Well, that's a bit comforting; however, I'm sure neither of us has three thousand dollars to throw his way," he answered. "I fully agree, sir, but I believe there might be another way." I said. "Continue" he prodded. I then presented the situation with the commandant's daughter's teeth. Once I'd explained, I said, "Sir, If you have any connections at our Base Dental Clinic, I believe Cadet

Callen just might make it home for Christmas"! I could see that I had attracted my chaplain's full attention. Now he addressed me by my first name, saying "Jake, by gosh— you just might have something here"! My heart quickened at his newly acquired level of enthusiasm. Then he commented "Let me confer with a friend of mine at the clinic" adding, "I'll get back with you within the hour".

Having concluded my business at the chaplain's office, I found myself once again inside the post office busily sorting mail. One hour later my supervisor called me into his office to inform me that the chaplain wanted me to return to his office before quitting time. He then granted me the remainder of the afternoon off, saying "See you tomorrow morning, Jake". I thanked him and proceeded directly to the office of the chaplain, who had been anxiously awaiting my arrival. "Come in, Jake" he ordered. He pointed to a leather chair as I entered his office, saying "Have a seat". "I've just talked with one of our dental surgeons at the base clinic, and he has taken it upon himself to correct the problem of the commandant's daughter." he proudly exclaimed. I was dumbfounded, but I managed to say, "Sir, that's great"! He added "My dentist would like to see this young lady one late afternoon this week". "Wonderful, I will try to reach the commandant later this evening," I said. "Good" he answered, adding "Of course she must be accompanied by at least one parent". "I understand, sir" I responded. I stood and we shook hands. I was not certain when the commandant would leave work this evening, so I would need to rush! I went directly to the dining hall and rushed through my evening meal. Next, I stopped by our base beverage store, where I purchased a bottle of mediocre bourbon. I would also take along a full carton of cigarettes from my room. After a quick shower, I gathered the cigarettes and whiskey and drove into Matamoros, arriving there shortly before 5:30PM. With these items, I then walked quickly to the infamous prison.

The commandant sat reading a magazine and seemed genuinely surprised to see me return so soon. "Si, American," he commented, although today he did not glare at me. I'd felt at least slightly reassured by his minimally improved reception. "I bring cigarettes and whiskey, sir," I said, handing him the brown paper bag. He grabbed the bag, peering inside. "Bueno!" he exclaimed. He then looked directly at me as he asked "You have news"? "I do," I replied. "Yes?" he asked, somewhat impatiently. I then said "One of the priests on base has arranged for your daughter's dental work to be done at our airbase". He sat quietly. Finally, he asked, "What this cost me, American"? I played along with him, by asking "How much can you afford to pay"? "I have five hundred U. S. dollars." he replied. I answered "Well, if you will make certain that you will soon release Cadet Callen, your daughter's dental work will cost you nothing"."Not cost me any money?" he asked. "No money," I said. At this point, a wide grin appeared across his bearded face. "I like you, American." he grinned. "Thank you, sir— I like you also," I lied. "What we do now?" he inquired. "When can you release Cadet Callen?" I asked. "When work is done, I release," he said. Then in a firm but non-argumentative tone, I answered, "No good at all". Before he could speak (or toss me out of his office) I continued, "Sir, you can trust the Air Force to complete your daughter's dental work, but you must release Cadet Callen before December 15th.

"When work start?" he asked. "This coming Wednesday afternoon." I said. "I like that!" he beamed. "Then you agree to release Cadet Callen by December 15th?" I asked. "Bueno American, I release gringo!" he exclaimed! We shook hands, although I did not trust this agreement one bit. However, I acted the part of the trusting fool. So before departing his office, I said, "Sir, either you or your wife must accompany your daughter to the dentist's office on Wednesday". "No problem, I send wife with daughter," he advised me. I then arbitrarily established the hour of 2:00PM as pick up time for his wife and daughter. He then quickly scribbled a nearby address from which I would retrieve them. We'd made the arrangements, but before leaving the commandant's office I advised him, "If there is any change in schedule, I will come same time tomorrow to advise you of the change". "Bueno, American." he grinned, grasping my hand once again. I left his office and returned directly to the base.

Back inside my room, I took a moment to reflect upon recent events. I was fully aware of the potentially grave results that might arise because of my involvement in Cadet Callen's plight. First, the good intentions of my chaplain could easily end his military career. Second, the courageous dentist who had agreed to secretly perform this very sensitive dental work would face an equally detrimental and career-ending outcome. And as for yours truly, my career, which was just beginning, would also immediately end! The careers of three individuals could be completely ruined for the sake of just one. So clearly, the negatives had vastly outweighed the positives. However, I had uncapped this 'bucket of worms', so I felt why not proceed. Heck, in the worst-case scenario, I could always become a brick mason.

Once again, I found myself downtown and partying with the crowd there. Since I'd only recently been released from eighteen years of semi-isolation, I had much lost time to make up for. So without even realizing it, this was the beginning of my ever-increasing hedonistic lifestyle. The very next morning I was once again busy at work, processing incoming and outgoing mail. I enjoyed the work environment here within this postal facility. Our work was performed efficiently, but in a relaxed manner, and I was treated well. When we had finished processing the incoming mail, I took a break to place a call to my chaplain. I was quite anxious to learn whether our dentist would be able to see the Mexican commandant's daughter on Wednesday afternoon. I'd been granted unrestricted access to my chaplain, so I had taken advantage of this opportunity by telephoning him.

I briefed the chaplain on the previous evening's progress and agreement. He seemed pleased. "Jake, this is great!" he exclaimed. I then informed him that I had tentatively established Wednesday afternoon as the initial visit for the daughter of the commandant. I explained my haste by saying "Sir, I realize that the dental clinic has a heavy workload— but severe weather is just around the corner, so we need to work quickly". "I couldn't agree more," he replied, adding. "Let me see what I can do". Call me back in one hour." he said. "Will do, sir," I said before hanging up the phone. Twenty minutes later my supervisor called out to me. I had a phone call from the chaplain in his office. "Jake, we're in luck!" exclaimed the chaplain." He continued,

"Can you assure me you'll have the young lady here at 3:15 Wednesday afternoon"? I turned to my supervisor, asking "Sergeant Storke, will I be allowed tomorrow afternoon off"? He replied, "You're off each Wednesday afternoon, Jake". The chaplain said, "Jake, I overheard the sergeant—so we're on, but keep me posted".

At the end of my workday, I decided I would return into Matamoros to con-firm tomorrow's appointment. My secondary motive was to further experience driving my recently purchased, very fine automobile. I arrived at the prison just in time to once again witness the "shaggy creature" devour his daily meal of live rattlesnake flesh. The poor fellow sat busily peeling away the snake's leather-like skin. He had not noticed me, so I decided not to distract him from this precious meal. I quietly walked away and around the corner to the prison's door. This time I received a considerably warmer welcome. As I entered the commandant's office, he greeted me with a slight grin, saying "Si, amigo". Suddenly, we had seemingly become friends. "Problem?" he asked. "No sir— no problem," I answered. "Bueno" he responded, appearing somewhat relieved. I continued "Your daughter's appointment is scheduled for 3:15PM tomorrow afternoon". I added "I will pick up your wife and daughter at exactly 2:30. She will be seen by one of our leading dental surgeons." I said. "Gracias, señior, gracias," he cheerfully responded. I then politely excused myself.

Once outside I returned briefly to the corner from which I would observe Cadet Callen. He'd finished his delicacy, and was presently reclining against a nearby steel fence post. For just a moment, I stood in complete silence.

I wanted to ascertain how long it would take him to detect my presence. Then after thirty seconds, I received my answer. Without any prompting whatsoever, he turned his head in my direction. It was as though he had been awaiting my arrival. I immediately gave him two 'thumbs-up'. But as always, he remained both silent and motionless. I gave a slight nod of my head, accompanied by another 'thumbs-up'. I was certain that he perceived something might be happening on his behalf. I then immediately departed the area.

I walked back across town before stopping at one of the many cantinas for a light drink, but there were no decent young ladies with whom to socialize. I soon finished my drink, and then began touring the town. One particularly young woman caught my attention, and we spent a pleasurable two hours together. At 9:00PM I found myself once again at The Corner lounge in downtown Harlingen, where I met my two cute female friends, (Mindy and Myra).

On Wednesday, I worked as usual until noon and then drove into Mexico. I first visited the commandant's office to confirm my arrival. He seemed relieved at my presence, and even made a few jokes (a first). At 2:00PM I walked to the family's small general store, where I found his wife and young daughter awaiting my arrival. We made no stops along our route into Texas, and I drove especially carefully on this day. I simply could not afford an accident of any sort. Neither could I afford being stopped by Texas police. Luckily, we reached the base without incident. I then drove directly to our Base Dental Clinic.

Once there, I asked specifically for the dental surgeon who would perform this very special dental work. At 3:15, we were summoned into the dental surgeon's office. Both he and his assistant welcomed the commandant's wife and daughter, and attempted to make them comfortable. This was the first time either had ever visited a U. S. military base, and I could clearly see that they were impressed by the cleanliness and the high level of professionalism which existed there.

The surgeon had even secured the services of a Spanish-speaking dental assistant. First, the dentist carefully examined the young girl's teeth. He then filled those teeth containing cavities. Next, he cleaned her teeth. Lastly, he took full-mouth impressions. By 5:30PM he'd completed this initial phase of work. We would return in two weeks for braces. The daughter was quite happy, but the mother was simply thrilled! Now this young girl could find a decent husband and raise a family of her own. But without this treatment, no self-respecting young man would ever give her a second look. The dentist scheduled the next and final phase of this work. Due to the highly critical nature of this situation, he opted to complete treatment in only two visits. This was all perfectly fine by me, for I fully realized just how severely we had jeopardized our careers. But there was an even more important consideration,— we needed to secure Cadet Callen's release before the imminent arrival of this winter's heavy rains.

We graciously thanked the dentist and made the return trip into Matamoros. Highway traffic was light, but still I drove the entire distance only at moderate speeds. At 6:15PM we crossed the bridge into Mexico. I breathed a deep sigh of relief at having returned these two females to their home. We found the commandant waiting for us at their store. He immediately began speaking in Spanish to his wife and daughter. I could only stand by, observing their facial expressions and listening to the tone of their voices, but at the end of their brief conversation the commandant turned to me, saying, "Bueno amigo"! That much, I'd understood. All three were very happy! I figured now would be the perfect time to discuss the release of Cadet Callen. So as the commandant prepared to return to the prison, I accompanied him. Then as we walked the short distance to the prison, I asked, "Sir, would you consider releasing Cadet Callen next Wednesday afternoon"? I held my breath. It seemed as if hours had passed before he finally spoke. He completely stopped in his tracks. With a sullen look, he turned to face me. "For you, amigo, I do this thing—but for no one else!" he said. He then added, "At six o'clock next Wednesday, you be at prison ALONE"!

I could hardly believe my ears! Although, I'd seriously doubted the sincerity of his words. But for added assurance, I repeated his words, "Next Wednesday at six". "Si, 6:00PM" he said. "Muchos gracias, señior," I said, reaching once again for his hand. Without hesitation, he reached forward to firmly shake my hand. His seemingly genuine smile, coupled with an expression of peacefulness, told me that he was relieved that this situation was nearing closure. I thanked him, and then walked around the corner to see Cadet Callen, who sat facing me (as if anticipating my arrival). I immediately raised the thumbs of each hand and with my right index finger I pointed directly at him. I then faced northward and with my hand held at waist-level and parallel to the ground, I slowly extended it, gradually fluttering upward. Upon completing this somewhat strange gesture, I smiled as I again raised each thumb. This poor soul sat as if mesmerized! I immediately returned to my car and then returned to downtown Harlingen.

The dental appointment had caused me to miss my evening meal, so I was completely famished. This time I drove across town into an area where the streets were lined with restaurants and stores. Once there, I treated myself to one of the most delicious enchiladas meals ever! Afterward I headed for The Corner to meet Mindy and Myra. Again, we had ourselves a great time together. Somewhat later, together we walked to their homes. Then by midnight I had returned to the base, showered, and climbed into bed. This had been a very fruitful day for me and others.

The following day I arose filled with energy, enthusiasm, and hope. I'd begun to realize that time was in fact moving at a rapid pace. Next week, I would celebrate my very first Thanksgiving Day away from my beloved family. But even before this date, with a bit of luck I would secure the release of Cadet Vincent Callen. I had resolved to 'visit' him daily from my street corner vantage point to provide him much-needed moral support— lest he lose his sanity!

Then on Sunday afternoon, I once again visited the commandant, bearing gifts of cigarettes and cheap bourbon whiskey. My gifts were well received by the commandant and his entire staff. This time I presented each of the additional four officers with three packs of cigarettes. I also gave one full carton to the commandant himself. Everyone appeared quite happy. Naturally they would open the whiskey the moment I'd left them. But for now, everyone laughed and joked with each other. I felt this was the opportune moment for me to seek a special favor from the commandant himself. I began by saying "Sir, may I ask a favor of you"? "Si amigo, ask" he replied. I continued "Sir, would you possibly consider moving the American to an inside cell"? For a moment, he considered my request. When he finally spoke, I was disappointed— but he had not finished. His words were "You ask much, amigo, but the American remains outside until Wednesday morning. Then I will have him washed with hose and brought inside to wait for you". Without hesitating, I answered, "That will be just fine sir— no problem." "Bueno" he answered. I thanked him, and then departed the prison. Now, I would have preferred to have had Cadet Callen brought inside, but he had endured six long months of eating and sleeping in pure filth. Surely he would survive for just three more days. Still, I would make sure that I 'visited' with him each day until his release on the coming Wednesday.

This endeavor had significantly delayed progress in studying my Career Development Course material. So for the next two days, I would spend my off-duty hours studying. This was an in-depth, three-volume course, but I would cover much of volume one before Wednesday. This would mean suspending my evenings of partying with my two friends, Mindy and Myra. With this goal in mind, I concentrated fully on my study material each evening after work. On the job I dedicated all my energy toward increasing my knowledge of the postal field..

Finally Wednesday afternoon arrived, and suddenly those 'butterflies' had returned to the pit of my stomach. During the morning I contacted my chaplain to remind him of this evening's highly important event. I felt great apprehension all day. I wanted to believe that all would go well with Cadet Callen's release, but I was deeply concerned that something might go dreadfully wrong during or prior to the release of this desperate human being. However, at precisely 4:00PM I visited our dining hall, where I had myself a leisurely meal. After which, I returned to my room to make final preparations for my 5:00PM departure into Mexico. Before leaving for Mexico that afternoon, I took the precaution of leaving short notes to my supervisor and squadron commander, informing them of my whereabouts. This time I would take no gifts to the prison. Neither would I bring along my little listening device.

I arrived in Matamoros at exactly 5:30PM. This time I located a parking space just yards from this terrible prison. I then walked to that awful corner, where Cadet Callen had only yesterday sat while surrounded by human body waste. He was not in sight! At that moment, a most horrifying thought entered my mind. "What if Cadet Callen had been moved to another prison where no one would ever again see him"? Worse yet, "What if plans had already been formulated, whereby I too would now be apprehended and shipped to some unknown location"? At this point, I seemed to once again hear my dear grandmother saying, "Son, I've told you many times—CURIOSITY KILLS THE CAT"! Now, all I wanted was to run from this dreadful place, hop into my car, then drive like the dickens back across the border!

Nevertheless, I climbed the steps leading into this house of death and misery. As I walked briskly toward the commandant's office, I'm certain of having heard my heart, as it pounded heavily within my chest. I was scared out of my wits! This was my moment of reckoning— (at only eighteen years of age)! In the commandant's office, he motioned for me to sit. I greeted him by saying "Good evening sir". He responded by greeting me in Spanish, though I was happy to note that he had included the term 'amigo' as part of his greeting. I struggled desperately to conceal my heightened state of anxiety. At this point though, I realized I should get right to the point, so I asked "Is the American ready, sir"? "Uno momento," he responded. I sensed that he was studying me, possibly in an effort to determine my level of nervousness. Although I was in fact quite nervous, I concealed it well. I searched for words with which to fill this ominous silence. So I spoke, saying "As you can see, sir, I didn't bring any cigarettes or whiskey this time, but when I come for your daughter next Wednesday, I will bring some". Now a smile appeared upon his face. He then spoke, saying "Bueno, señior". His smile served to comfort me ever so slightly. But now I could think of no more conversational words, so I simply waited.

Momentarily, I heard the shuffling of feet along with the light jingle of chains. My heart rate quickened, as I thought, "Could this be the moment"? The shuffling/jingling sounds moved closer. Then to my surprise, there appeared before me in the doorway— a total stranger! I've used this term (stranger) for I failed to recognize this quiet young man who had just entered the room. The commandant then spoke, "The Americano, señior". My initial thought was *"Jake, these fellows have duped you— this is not the fellow from the prison yard"*. I stood and approached him, asking, "Who might you be, sir"? "I am United States Air Force Cadet Officer, Vincent L. Callen," he answered. But I was still not convinced, so I asked, "Have we met before"? He answered "You might say that we have sir". "What do you mean?" I asked. He responded "Sir, you've visited with me nearly every night over the past month". Confident that this scrawny figure was, in fact, the real Cadet Callen I turned to the commandant, asking "Sir, may we remove the cuffs and shackles"? Without answering, he personally removed these uncomfortable restraints. The commandant then commented, "He is all yours, amigo". I breathed a great sigh of relief! I then thanked the commandant for his generosity, reminding him of his daughter's next dental appointment. "May we go now?" I asked. "Si, adios," responded the commandant. Cadet Callen and I then wasted no time in departing this 'Hell on earth'!

Once outside, we walked quickly to my car. Though as we'd walked, I'd succeeding in fighting off the urge to look back at this prison. I had feared that this young fellow might emit strong body odor, so I'd taken the extra precaution of covering my front (bench) seat with a woolen blanket from the base. As we entered the car, I immediately started its engine and headed north toward the U. S. border. For the next several minutes we rode in near silence, as I continuously scanned the road (both behind and ahead of us). At any moment I'd expected that we might be surrounded by Mexican police vehicles. We were very fortunate that evening, for no police vehicles came into view along our route. Finally, after what seemed as a very long while, we reached and safely crossed the bridge spanning the short distance between Mexico and the United States. Cadet Callen was once again a free man! Only at that moment, did my high state of alert begin to subside.

We were now safely inside the United States! As soon

as we'd crossed the bridge, Cadet Callen spoke, "Sir, would you pull over please"? I immediately complied with his request, figuring he might have felt sick. I certainly did not want him throwing up inside my fancy car. The minute I'd stopped, he quickly exited the vehicle. He walked approximately thirty feet from where I had parked. Next, I witnessed a very strange sight. This cadet officer knelt, and then bent forward until his lips reached the concrete surface of the parking lot upon which we stood. He then repeatedly kissed the ground— but this was just phase one. Next, he raised up onto his knees, assuming a kneeling position, and began weeping uncontrollably. I remained silent inside the car, as I observed him. I was touched by this cadet's behavior. Remember, I had been raised believing that men did not cry, but the cadet's actions that evening had dispelled all that I'd been taught on this subject. Still, I remained completely silent while allowing him his much needed space. Fortunately for us, this parking lot was completely deserted. Finally, he apologetically returned to the car, saying, "I'm very sorry, sir". "No need to apologize," I assured him. "Would you like a Coke or something?" I asked. "I could certainly use a cold Coke, sir," he quickly responded. "Good, then let's walk together to pick them up," I offered. "Great, I could certainly afford a bit of walking," he said. As we walked along together, I became acutely aware of the extremely high level of dehydration and malnutrition suffered by this poor and desperate human being.

At 7:00PM, I drove into a vacant parking space at our Base Chapel. As we exited the vehicle, three men along with one woman rushed toward us. I immediately recognized the chaplain and dental surgeon but had never seen these other two individuals. Then, obviously in a state of hysterics, the tall, slender lady called out, "Vinnie, my son"! "Mom, Dad," blurted the cadet as he rushed toward his dear parents. This was absolutely the most emotional event I had ever witnessed! This trio hugged and cried! Then they hugged and cried some more! But they were not yet finished, for they continued this display of deep emotion until interrupted by my chaplain. I wondered how the parents had known of the cadet's possible release. I would soon learn that my chaplain had prematurely called and informed them of this potential event. Thus, they had flown here earlier in the afternoon.

Our next stop would be at our base hospital, where Cadet Callen would be given a thorough physical examination. But once we had reached the hospital, its commander determined that Cadet Callen should be immediately admitted for psychiatric and medical evaluations. This posed a problem, for tomorrow would be Thanksgiving Day. Nevertheless, the commander remained firm regarding the immediate admission of Cadet Callen. Even the chaplain had been unable to sway him. Both of the cadet's parents had already unsuccessfully pleaded with the hospital's commander, but his decision remained unchanged. Now, please allow me to fully appraise you of my position in this matter. This small group of individuals was comprised of three high-ranking military officers, plus two prominent civilians (excluding Cadet Callen himself). Everyone here, with exception of the commander, wanted the cadet free on Thanksgiving Day. I though, was only a lowly airman third class— a virtual nobody! But even so,

I would seek my opportunity to speak. I then faced the hospital commander, asking, "Sir, permission to speak"? "You may speak," replied the colonel. I chose my words very carefully, so as not to offend this high-ranking officer in any way. I began "Sir, Cadet Officer Callen has been imprisoned for more than six months. During this time he was held in isolation in an outside holding area. And even though winter has arrived, he was still kept outside in inclement weather conditions. Though to make matters even worse, he was forced to eat and sleep amidst his very own body waste"! I continued, "During all this time, no one of the base, embassy, or our government was successful in securing his release. However, even though I've only been here three weeks, Cadet Callen and I walked away from that awful Mexican prison this evening". I continued speaking "Sir, I purposely strived for Cadet Callen's release prior to Thanksgiving Day, and fortunately I succeeded. So I urge you to please reconsider your decision in this very delicate matter. I thank you, sir." I concluded. Without answering me directly, the colonel then turned to Mr. and Mrs. Callen, asking "How long will you folks be here"? "For as long as it takes, colonel," answered the cadet's father. Next, the colonel turned to Cadet Callen himself, saying, "Mr. Callen, there are a lot of people here who have gone to bat for you. So I'm going to join them by granting you the remainder of this week as leisure time with your parents". Everyone inside the office rejoiced! In closing, the hospital's commander ordered Cadet Callen to report for admission at 7:30AM on the following Monday morning. Each member of our small group then thanked the colonel, as we prepared to leave his office. I drove the Callens back to their downtown Harlingen hotel room. Cadet Callen and I then once again gave each other lengthy 'bear hugs' as he repeatedly thanked me for all I had done for him. Only now had he begun addressing me as "Jake. "I hope that one day I'll be able to return this great favor, Jake" he commented as I prepared to leave them.

Soon I found myself once again seated at a table inside The Corner's restaurant area. This time I ordered a simple meal— hamburger, fries, and soda. As I sat enjoying my burger, my thoughts turned to Cadet Callen. Tonight he would rise above the lowly consumption of raw rattlesnake meat. Tonight there would be tenderloin for this deserving young gentleman! Soon Mindy and Myra arrived, and for the next two hours I celebrated life with these two decent young ladies. I would not venture into Mexico on this evening. By midnight I was once again cuddled up under warm blankets inside my quiet room.

Next morning I awoke to my very first holiday apart from my dear family. This would be a difficult day for me; however, I would begin it with a hearty breakfast (albeit alone). I would have welcomed the presence of my former roommate and his cronies, but there was no chance. After breakfast I returned to my barracks, where I enjoyed early morning cartoons on TV. If only I'd had TV and running water back home, I would have strongly considered remaining there throughout my entire lifetime. At 10:00AM I strolled over to the Base Recreation Center to partake in refreshments and pool. My pool game had not yet begun to develop, so I sought a vacant table where I might practice. I was in luck— at least for awhile. Soon though, the 'vultures' gathered around, trying to con me into playing for money. I was still quite naïve— but not to this extent. When they realized there was no chance of conning me, one by one, they disappeared. Now while I'd enjoyed their company, I found myself happy that they were finally gone. At least I had saved my much-needed money.

At lunchtime I dined on base in the presence of strangers— but at least the turkey was tasty. Afterward I drove alone once more into Harlingen. I soon discovered that the more I saw of this city, the more I liked it. Finally, I again drifted across town to my favorite location, (The Corner lounge). This time I stood out front on the street, discussing sports, etc., with other airmen of the base. But while standing there chatting with these guys, I'd had absolutely no inkling of the evil and sinister plot that was presently being formulated against me!

Later that afternoon I returned to the base for my evening meal of left-over turkey. I had declined an offer by the Callen family to join them for dinner. I'd felt that by joining them, I would have presented myself as somewhat of a nuisance. So, I ate alone once more. I later took in a movie and then retired for the evening. This was how I had spent my first Thanksgiving Day away from home.

Alone in my room, I reflected upon the events of the past forty-eight hours. I realized I had particularly derived great satisfaction from having been successful in securing the release of Cadet Callen. At this point though, you may be asking yourselves "How was this possible without prior approval from the Mexican penal system"? The answer to this question is as follows: First, Cadet Callen had never been officially charged with a crime of any sort, so no official record existed relating to his false imprisonment. He was simply thrown into this prison under permanent solitary confinement. This was because the prison officials there had become thoroughly frustrated by him because no matter how they'd treated him, they simply could not break his spirit! The commandant had ordered, "Chain him outside and leave him to die"! Oddly, the commandant had been given full authority to operate the Matamoros prison as he deemed necessary, allowing for a wide range of unethical policies and practices within that prison facility. Ultimately, Cadet Callen had been sentenced to die there without repercussion! This posed a major problem for the cadet himself, for since neither he nor the commandant would yield, the cadet was doomed! And now the flood rains were just around the corner (which was what the commandant had waited for). Hence, in just a matter of days Cadet Callen's lifeless body would have been discovered by a prison guard. Then upon this discovery, his body would have been quietly incinerated. Consequently, all future inquiries would have been met with negative results! It was as I lay thinking of this dreadful situation, I realized the full significance of my accomplishment regarding this matter.

When I reported for duty on Friday morning, all seemed normal. We worked through the morning without incident. However, when I returned from lunch my supervisor called me into his office. He seemed a bit removed from his usual casual demeanor. As I entered his office he informed me "The squadron commander wants to see us at two o'clock this afternoon." he said. "Do you know why?" I asked. "I'm told that it has something to do with the recent release of an imprisoned officer cadet." he said. "Oh, that" I replied. "Sit down for a moment and tell me what you know about this," he ordered. Fortunately, I had retained the note I'd written to him on Wednesday afternoon, outlining my actions. I removed it from my pocket, then handed it to him to read. He took the note then carefully read it. When he had finished reading the note, he looked directly at me with one of the most serious expressions I had ever seen. "So you took it completely upon yourself to travel into Mexico in order to communicate with the Mexican authorities, concerning a matter of this severity?" he asked. "I did," I answered. "Don't you think that was kind of dumb?" he asked. "Yes, it was dumb, Sgt Storke, but Cadet Callen is a free man today." I responded. "Well, I certainly can't argue with you on that issue," he commented. He then said "Okay, grab your hat and let's go see the commander".

My supervisor and I walked the short distance to the squadron area, where our commander awaited us. I was instructed to report in customary military manner. "Sir, Airman Van York reporting as ordered," I said. "At ease, airman— why don't you and MSgt Storke here have a seat"? I then seated myself directly to the right of my supervisor. My commander spoke again, saying "This morning I received a pleasant phone call from the hospital commander". He continued "As a result, I'm not sure whether I should commend or court-martial you". He added "But before I make my decision, what do you have to say on your behalf"? At this point I'd hoped he was joking with me - but I was'nt at all convinced that this was the case. So I answered "Sir, I'll accept whatever you decide as my fate". It appeared that my answer had at least slightly impressed him. Immediately he arose and walked over to where I sat. I too arose, as was expected. Upon reaching me, he extended his hand, saying, "Airman Van York, I truly commend you for your bold and courageous actions in securing Cadet Callen's release"! We shook hands for a long while, before stepping apart and rendering the customary military hand salute. Before dismissing us he suggested to my supervisor that I at least be granted a three-day pass in recognition of unprecedented achievement!

When we returned to the post office, my supervisor once again grasped my hand while happily commending me for a job well-done! On this afternoon I found myself anxiously awaiting the arrival of 4:30PM. At that time I rushed to the dining hall for my evening meal. This time I ate lightly, for at 8:00 this evening I would dine in style with the Callen family in downtown Harlingen. Accordingly I showered, dressed, and drove into the city to meet with this family.

Our rendezvous location was at one of the several party rooms inside Harlingen's leading hotel. Normally I would never have considered visiting such a place of luxury, but this was one very special occasion, so I relaxed my thinking regarding semi-formal dinners. Fortunately I had received lessons in dining etiquette while attending high school. Tonight, I would make use of this knowledge. My civilian wardrobe here at Harlingen was extremely limited, but I had recently purchased a relatively attractive suit from our Base Exchange Store for the meager sum of $49.95. This particular suit contained year-round fabric. I had also purchased several accompanying items, such as silk shirts, silk ties, dark socks, and black shoes. I might note here that the majority of airmen here did not own a single suit, and most owned no civilian socks or shoes. So one might say that even though I was only a lowly airman— I was a very well-dressed airman. But even so, this was another first for me, so naturally I had found myself quite nervous about this whole affair.

I parked the Road Master (no valet for me), then walked across the spacious parking lot to the hotel's entrance. Upon entering the hotel, I walked directly to the desk clerk. He looked inquisitively at me as I stated (in my best voice) "I'm a guest of the Callen family". "And you would be, sir?" he asked. "My name is Van York," I nonchalantly replied. "Come right this way sir," replied the clerk. We walked past a number of private party rooms until we finally reached the Callen party. I'd thought that I would dine with just three other persons, so imagine my surprise upon seeing at least twenty other people sitting before me. I must say— I was a bit unnerved! But having observed dad and Uncle Abe over the years, served to aid immeasurably in maintaining my composure. Then immediately upon seeing me, Vincent (Cadet Callen) rushed to greet me. Once again, we hugged for what seemed as minutes. During this brief moment, he had relived the many nights of solitude where I had provided him with hope of survival. So with tears in his eyes, he led me around, introducing me to all those present. I learned that (with exception of his parents) everyone here had flown in just this afternoon. He gave me a special laudatory introduction to his younger brother and sister before all others. Next, he introduced me to a long line of relatives, which included aunts, uncles, and cousins. I was particularly impressed by the large number of close relatives, who'd dropped work and school especially for this occasion. It was these relatives who made this event the most festive I had yet to encounter. They laughed, joked, and even sang a few songs together— reminiscent of my family back home. Only here, I was seen as an adult; which in itself, was quite significant.

Finally our long-awaited meal arrived. I quickly summoned my previously untested set of table manners, as I consumed my tender sirloin and sipped from a glass of red wine. I sensed that some in this room had been discretely checking out my table manners, but I remained confident that I had met their standards. For this, I thank my wonderful teachers of my high school days. When we'd finished our meal, Vincent's father made a gracious speech in which he toasted his son and thanked me. I then summoned my remaining bit of courage, as I moved about the room, making small talk with those present. At 11:00PM, I stood and approached the Callen family to say "Good night" and thank them for my dinner invitation. "Are you leaving Jake?" they asked. "Yes, it's time that I get back to the base" I said. "Please take this as a token of our appreciation," said Mrs. Callen, as she handed me a small gift-wrapped box. "I thank you both, but you should not have done this," I responded. Vince then grabbed me with another of his lengthy 'bear-hugs'. It was an emotional moment for the Callen family. I said "Good night" to everyone as I departed. Outside in my car I quickly opened the small package I'd been given by Mrs. Callen. I was pleasantly surprised to find a beautiful diamond-studded Swiss-made gold watch! Now, one might say "Only a watch— for a human life"? But this was more than acceptable to me, for they were in no way obligated to provide me with a gift of any sort. And prior to this day, I had not owned a watch of any significant value. Thus, I was quite happy with this gift.

I started my car's engine, but was not sure of my destination. At this late hour, Mexico was out of the question. But now I was considered an adult, and was therefore free from curfew. I'd consumed only a single glass of wine, so I was alert and wide awake. I chose the simple solution and drove to The Corner lounge, which did not close until 2:00AM. Unfortunately, by the time I arrived, my friends Mindy and Myra were just leaving, so I again walked them home. I then returned to the lounge, where I found that my peer group had departed, leaving only the older and more seasoned present. But I wanted to test my ability to remain active past midnight, so I stayed and partied for awhile with this group. One particular young woman, (age nineteen), repeatedly made herself available to me, and her highly aggressive behavior quickly stimulated my male hormones. The fact that I had not visited the streets of Mexico over the past three nights, served to further weaken my ability to resist her. Also, I was aware that some here felt that I'd shunned intimate relations with members of the opposite sex. At this point, I decided I would dispel their doubting opinions! After one final slow dance with this highly aggressive young woman, I said, "Finish your drink and let's go". To my surprise, she didn't even bother asking "Where're we going"? She simply stared deeply into my eyes, as she gulped down the remainder of her drink. I had already learned of this woman's unflattering reputation, but this was okay by me. I was also aware that many eyes were upon me as I escorted her from the lounge.

Immediately upon entering my car, she attacked me

with a series of unimaginably fervent kisses! Now, I certainly had been kissed passionately before, but never in my wildest dreams did I ever imagine that such kisses existed. This was only the preliminary stage of our encounter, but already the car's windows had fogged up. But this was only a natural occurrence under the circumstances. Now I would love nothing more than to describe in detail, our ensuing activity, but this would render my story "X" rated! After a full hour of this most rigorous activity, I backed the car for several yards so that we were no longer parked under the neon lights. Now we were in complete darkness, and free to do as we pleased! This young woman quickly became even more uninhibited! Her enthusiasm regarding sex soon caused me to realize— I had wasted my time by making those numerous visits into Mexico. Although I must admit, those visits had at least slightly prepared me for that which I currently faced. So over the next hour we set out to impress and impose our will upon each other. I must say, the spacious Road Master served our purposes more than adequately. By adjusting the car's front seat, we created a virtual living room in the rear of the car.

At 2:30AM, I had impressively completed each of my assigned tests in the subject of carnal knowledge! I had even received an open-ended invitation for further exploration. Naturally, I would accept this once-in-a-lifetime invitation. I then drove this very satisfied young woman to her home. But before leaving, she made me swear that we would resume our newly discovered activity the very next evening. And of course, I would certainly not disappoint her. I returned to the base, where I took a soothing shower before hopping into my warm bed.

EXTRAORDINARY EXPERIENCES OF JAKE VAN YORK

By 6:00AM Saturday morning, I'd arisen and prepared for breakfast. After breakfast I returned to the privacy of my room, where I studied my Career Development Course (CDC) for the rest of the morning. I was determined to quickly complete this course, so that I might enter the specialist level within my career field of office administration. I would also simultaneously upgrade myself within this postal specialty to which I had been mal-assigned.

After my noon meal I devoted several hours to washing and detailing my nice automobile. Then I escorted my new friend Vincent (with mom and dad) to a very nice local Mexican restaurant. Upon returning them to their hotel, I drove over to an on-base facility, known as the Base Auto Hobby Shop. Here, assigned base personnel performed both routine and special maintenance tasks on their privately owned vehicles— completely free of charge. Thus, one could even rebuild a car's engine without spending one single penny! This service was but one of the many benefits provided to military personnel. I would spend the next several hours here washing, waxing, and vacuuming my car. I even cleaned and treated its interior leather upholstery and wood-grained paneling. When I'd completely finished I received numerous compliments from many of the GIs present.

By 4:00PM I had showered and dressed, and was seated inside a downtown restaurant, along with the five members of the Callen family. Even though we'd reached the end of November the weather here was still mild, so we sat outside beneath the Palm trees as we downed Tacos and cold beer. Naturally, the younger brother and sister drank only sodas. Today was only the third day of freedom for my new friend,

Vince. But even so, he appeared normal and in great form. Although, one could readily see that he had suffered long periods of forced abstinence from regular food. No one at the table mentioned his imprisonment. Our luncheon had gone well, and now it was time to return the Callens to their hotel. Back at the hotel we said our "farewells". With the exception of Vince,— I would not see them again.

Now that I'd found myself once again alone, I headed for my favorite spot, (The Corner) lounge, where a small group of GIs lingered out front. No sooner had I stepped from the car, did the cheering begin. For a moment I was somewhat bewildered. Then someone in the crowd commented, "Hey, quite a show last night"! Now I was no longer bewildered, but a bit embarrassed. I soon discovered that the promiscuous young woman and I had received quite an audience last night. I feigned shrugging this all off, as if it was normal and unimportant. I would soon discover that I had gained considerable social standing among my peers. Some began addressing me by name— finally, I had gained a bit of recognition among the local crowd! I would spend the next two evenings partying with Mindy and Myra, who hadn't heard. Oddly, when the weekend had ended, neither had learned of Friday evening's escapades. Quite possibly this was because the young woman I'd been with was Myra's older sister. You may be thinking, "What a dog you were, Jake". But I would beg to differ— I was merely attempting to discover but a few of life's many pleasures! And of course, I protected myself.

I would spend the next thirty days working, studying, and honing my skills in pocket billiards. Naturally, on each Wednesday afternoon I would escort the Mexican commandant's wife and daughter to our dental clinic. Finally, the week of Christmas arrived. This was a particularly lonely week for me, for I had never before even contemplated spending Christmas apart from my family. But I had already gained the necessary experience by having successfully gotten past Thanksgiving Day. I had mailed my parents and grandmother, a package containing small gifts for each. Then on Friday just before Christmas, I received my gift package. In it were several items of nearly new clothing I'd left at home. There was also a very special homemade fruitcake which had been prepared by mom and grandmother together. Underneath the cake, I found a letter from mom. In her letter she, dad, and grandmother had scribbled notes wishing me Merry Christmas, Happy Birthday, and Happy New Year! Each of their notes told me of their love and how very much each had missed me. Now had I not listened to dad as he had frequently reminded me, "Son, real men don't cry",— there's no way of telling just how I may have acted upon reading their loving notes. Miraculously, I would succeed in at least slightly enjoying each of these three special occasions.

I had safely celebrated the holidays, and begun my first workday of January 1956. Now although I'd received no forewarning, this would become my year of regret and det-riment! On the surface, events and activities in my young and unsuspecting life appeared normal. By mid-January I had completed (ahead of schedule) my Career Develop-ment Course. Now I would commence training at the skill level of specialist. I had progressed exceptionally well in my routine postal duties, and my supervisor had seem-ingly taken a liking to me. My car was holding up well, with no problems having been detected. Lastly, my skills on the billiards tables were rapidly improving. But equally as important, I had made a few friends around my base. Incidentally, the Mexican commandant's daughter had received her braces along with initial adjustments. All future adjustments would be made in Mexico. This meant that the dentist and I were finally free of this obligation. So what more could one have asked for? "To not have been singled out and targeted as the focal point of an evil conspiracy" was the answer to this otherwise innocent question.

Three months had passed, and I consistently demonstrated exceptional job performance and military bearing. We were rapidly nearing the end of March, and were enjoying the beginning of springtime in the beautiful Rio Grande Valley. My friendship with my friend Mindy had flourished. Myra had found herself a boyfriend, who was a newly assigned co-worker of mine. (Yes, I had in fact arranged the meeting of these two very deserving young people.) I had also made Mindy fully aware that my low rank prevented me from being a candidate for marriage. I had even informed her that I would never stand between her and the possibility of happy life with another young man. She accepted these terms and had thanked me for my honesty. So overall, life for me was very good!

One week later in early April, I received a much dreaded telegram: "GRANDMOTHER DECEASED— COME IMMEDIATELY". Now although I had long anticipated such news, I was devastated! I had not seen or communicated with my dear grandmother in nine long months— AND NOW SHE WAS GONE FOREVER! I could not function! I sadly walked into my supervisor's office, whereupon I presented him with this dreadful message. He immediately gave me his condolences, before instructing me to proceed to our squadron commander's office to apply for emergency leave. I followed his instructions; however, I was seen by my first sergeant, as the commander was himself on leave. The first sergeant read my emergency Red Cross message, and then asked, "Airman, did your grandmother raise you"? No sir, I was raised by my mother and father," I answered. "Then I'm sorry, but this request does not qualify you for emergency leave." he said. Now I was really devastated! There are no words to adequately describe my feelings at that moment. I was instructed to "Be strong, son" and return to duty. Days later, I would learn that my first sergeant's ruling had been erroneous. The Air Force's position in this matter was — although I was not raised by my grandmother, she had lived in our household throughout my adolescent years. Had I contacted my chaplain, he would have immediately corrected this discrepancy. But I had remained silent simply because I did not wish to make waves or be labeled as a troublemaker. Back at work my supervisor advised me that he would grant me ordinary leave. This presented a time-related problem, for ordinary leave would delay my departure by at least seven days. I accepted my supervisor's offer and submitted my leave, knowing that grandmother's body would be buried long before I reached home. The funeral was subsequently conducted in my absence. It pains me to even write these lines!

Finally, after a week I boarded a passenger train for the long trip home. This would be my very first train ride, so I was anxiously looking forward to this trip. After exchanging trains in San Antonio, I finally settled in for my long ride to my distant hometown. The weather had begun to warm a bit, so evening temperatures ranged between forty-five to fifty-five degrees. I had worn one of my casual dress uniforms, as I had learned early in my military career that young men in uniform were generally treated better than those traveling in civilian attire. I was seated in a passenger coach that contained only about twenty persons, so I was quite comfortable. I then selected a magazine from a nearby rack and began reading a short story. About an hour into my ride I began feeling that eyes were upon me. So as inconspicuously as possible, I looked about the coach and noticed a well-dressed and quite attractive young lady who'd been sitting all alone. She was smiling and looking admiringly at me. In return, I smiled back at her. But at age nineteen, I was still quite a bashful young man, so I pretended not to notice her amorous gazes. But for some unknown reason, her eyes had remained focused upon me. Finally, I summoned my courage and walked over to her. Her brown eyes remained fixed upon me as I approached. Then in my usual gentlemanly manner, I spoke to her. "Hello, may I join you"? "Please do," she answered. So I took the vacant seat beside her and we introduced ourselves. "My name is Jake" I said. "Hello Jake, I'm June" she warmly responded. As we began talking I learned that June was a college freshman, on her way home because of family illness. When she learned of my grandmother's passing, and the fact I'd been denied attendance at the funeral, she quickly warmed to me (out of sympathy, I presumed). Regardless of her reasons though, we drew unusually close from the moment of our introduction. We had dinner together, after which we returned to our passenger coach.

As the evening progressed, we found ourselves drawn even closer to each other. No alcohol was present, but none was needed. Soon the evening temperature slightly dropped, so I placed a warm blanket about her shoulders. In response, she extended the blanket across my upper body. Soon we had completely covered ourselves.

There were only a few people seated inside our coach, but none was in close proximity. Soon most of those seated began falling asleep, so by 11:00PM only the two of us had remained awake. Then under the privacy of our thick blanket, I decided to elevate our activity to another level. I began kissing her deeply and passionately, (which I had learned from watching movies). This was only my second sexual encounter with an American girl, as all others had been Mexican prostitutes. I was quite surprised by her ever-increasing advances toward me, and I soon found myself emboldened by her brazen actions. "Take off your skirt and undies," I whispered into her ear. My words seemed to inflame her passions even further, for without a single word of objection, she slowly began removing all that she wore. Having witnessed her alluring behavior, my own passion quickly skyrocketed! So I hurriedly removed my uniform, neatly folding it, and concealing it underneath another blanket. Both my mind and heart were racing, but I succeeded in removing a condom from my wallet's safety compartment. "Hurry, Jake," she whispered to me. At this point, our first of several torrid lovemaking sessions ignited itself!

Her passion was surpassed only by my high school teacher's, (Catherine), whom I'd only kissed. We made love over and over throughout the night, exhausting a total of four condoms! At one point around 2:00AM, the train's conductor performed a walk-through of the coaches. Fortunately I'd taken the extra precaution of also folding and concealing June's clothing. Our coach was now only dimly lighted, so I took advantage of the semi-darkness by feigning sleep. As the conductor entered our coach, I faked snoring, as June lay next to me quietly giggling at the novelty of our situation. The conductor did not approach us directly, but calmly strolled past us. Now until this very day, I remain confident that he had understood exactly what we were doing under the cover of our warm blanket. By 8:00AM we'd washed up, composed ourselves, and were seated together over breakfast. We then exchanged addresses, knowing all the while—we would never meet again. But I would remember this most exciting evening for many years into the future. Then at 9:30, June was gone! The remainder of my twenty-four hour train ride would prove quite lonely.

Shortly after 5:00PM I arrived once again in my little hometown. I took my lightweight suitcase and walked the short distance to the store where Dave worked. I was in luck again this time for he would soon close the store for the day. He appeared happy to see me, and wasted no time in offering condolences for grandmother's recent passing. During our drive home we mostly discussed my life in the military, for there really was not much worth mentioning about things at home. Although I did learn that my canine friend Buddy had not given up searching for me. Soon we reached Dave's house, but this time he kept driving toward our old place.

We reached our house and I'd exited Dave's car before mom and dad recognized me. Upon seeing me, they rushed forward to meet and greet me. Ours was an indescribably heartwarming reunion. Only nine months had passed, but our separation had seemingly exceeded a lifetime. This occasion was reminiscent of the recent reunion of the Callen family down in Texas. The only downside to this situation was that my dear grandmother was no longer with us. The fact that I'd not been allowed to attend her recent funeral further lowered our morale. But we were together now, and we felt confident that grandmother would be happy and content at this moment.

Dad returned to the fields for one more hour, though mom had remained at the house to prepare our supper. I recalled that I had not showered for more than twenty-four hours, and I'd had an unusually active evening. So I quickly changed into old clothing and grudgingly once more went out back to manually pump bath water. Just as I'd finished pumping water, my horse began wildly neighing, so I walked quickly out to the barn to check on her. I found her pacing back and forth alongside the fencing. Mom had noticed and called out, "Son, your horse is happy to see you—wonders where you've been". I reached through the fencing and began patting her mane, saying, "Hey Belle, how're you doing, old girl"? My horse then pranced and snorted for several minutes before calming down. I called out, "Mom, I'm going for a quick ride before I take my bath". "Okay son, be careful," mom answered.

I quickly grabbed the horse's bridle and homemade saddle, as I prepared for a short ride. I headed immediately to Buddy's house. He had heard our approach, and had run out to the road to once again greet us. This time I dismounted and took a few moments to play with him. This poor dog was so eager to see my horse and me, it was nearly unbelievable! He jumped about wagging his tail and barking frantically! This was my second heartwarming moment in this single day. "Let's ride, Buddy," I said as I mounted my horse. The old farmer had heard the commotion and came out to investigate. I waved to him as we rode away, heading for Mr. Lim's old place.

This time we took the kindly old gentleman quite by surprise. Today we found him relaxing inside his small home. We'd approached quietly, so he had not noticed our arrival. Then as I dismounted, I called out to him, "Mr. Lim, hello". Immediately upon hearing my voice he rushed outside to greet us. "Jake San, how are you?" he exclaimed. "I'm fine, Mr. Lim, how are you?" I asked. With a wide grin upon his rapidly aging face, he answered, "I be fine, Jake San". The weather had now cooled slightly, but we preferred sitting outside. "Tell me about your new life in military," he said. I answered by telling him mostly of basic training and my work. I'd spent the whole of fifteen minutes with my old friend, but now had come the time to return home for my bath. Thus, I returned Buddy once again to his home, saying, "See you tomorrow Buddy". This time he emphasized his response by answering with dual "woofs". I returned home, settled my horse, and then gave my mom one more great big hug. It was wonderful being home again, even without the existence of running water and electricity. After bathing, I sat chatting with mom as we awaited dad's arrival.

Soon dad arrived and quickly finished his bath. Then for the very first time, we three sat quietly together as we ate our evening meal. We enjoyed the meal, but grandmother's absence had created great loneliness inside these old walls. I quickly realized just how very sad and lonely these past two weeks had been for mom and dad. First, I had created a huge vacuum by having left to join the military. Then before my parents had even partially adjusted to my absence—grandmother also was gone. It then occurred to me that these past weeks must have been completely unbearable for them. I vowed then and there, that I would do all within my power to cheer them up during my short stay here. So even though I was not much of a comedian, I would crack a few clean jokes whenever possible. However, this effort presented a slight problem since the majority of my jokes were not at all clean. I tried though—even made up originals myself. And when I'd exhausted my limited supply of clean jokes, I began singing songs to them. My endeavor worked well, and soon smiles had returned to my parents' faces. When Saturday afternoon arrived, I even took them on a limited shopping spree in town. Remember though, my after-tax income was still only $80 per month. Nevertheless, I purchased two plain dresses for mom, along with two shirts for dad. Now even though there was absolutely nothing extraordinary in my gesture, this was their very first time of shopping at their only son's expense. So for mom and dad, this was a very special occasion.

While at home, we visited my Aunt Emma and Carol's parents. I also revisited my old friend, Mr. Lim. And, of course I visited the grave site of my dear grandmother. In life she had often said, "If anyone wishes to give me flowers, I hope they will do so while I'm alive". Well, even from my days as just a toddler, I had always strived to present her with flowers while she lived. Now I found myself also

taking flowers to her gravesite. She deserved them all anyway— for she was truly a wonderful person!

Time for us had passed much too quickly, so finally I
found myself once again preparing for my return trip to
Texas. I was quite disappointed in that I'd not seen any of
my friends, for they were all far away attending college.
And even though one lived only thirty-one miles away, I
had no transportation with which to visit her. But the worst
part was that I had not seen Catherine. So most reluctantly,
I again hugged mom before having dad drop me off at our
downtown bus station. At the bus station dad waited with
me for thirty minutes, at which time my express bus arrived. Saying farewell to each other was 'easy' for us— for
after all,— WE WERE MEN. So without a single tear from
either him or me, I watched him drive away before stepping onto my bus.

The hour was 9:30PM and darkness had set upon us.
I located a vacant seat and settled in. I'd already correctly
concluded that I would probably not meet any nice young
ladies with whom to spend some time. However, during
daylight hours, I would feast my eyes upon some very beautiful countryside. After a very tiring forty-hour bus ride, I
arrived back at my military base at Harlingen.

Next morning I awoke tired, hungry, and in great need
of a hot shower. So after shedding my clothing, the first
thing I did was hop into my shower. *"Ah, how soothing"*, I
thought as the tiny droplets of warm water rained down
upon me. Now I no longer felt tired— just hungry as heck.
So after donning clean clothing, I headed straight for the
dining hall, and while there, I gorged myself. This was the
last day of the work week, but I would not sign in for duty

until later in the evening. By doing things this way, I would not be required to return to duty until Monday morning. After lunch I walked over to the parking lot where I had left my car. I was happy to find it exactly as I had left it. The only difference was— it needed a slight washing. So I spent the next two hours cleaning my car and purchasing cigarettes and small items. I then returned to my room to relax for a couple of hours. Inside my quiet room, I realized just how deeply I already missed my family. But such was life (at least for me).

Hours later, I returned to the dining hall for the evening meal. Then soon afterward, I found myself once more in the presence of young girls at The Corner lounge. It was still only 7:00, but this was Friday evening— so everyone had come out early for the night. Soon my two new friends, Mindy and Myra entered the lounge and rushed over to greet me and offer their condolences. We then proceeded to have ourselves a grand old time together. At one point I offered to take them in my car to another lounge across town. Each indicated their desire for a nice ride around town; but as twelfth-graders, they were restricted to those areas within walking distance of their homes. This was fine by me, so we stayed at The Corner lounge. We would continue our level of respectable partying throughout this weekend. Each night at 11:00PM I would walk them to their homes. I would even party with these girls at this location during each Saturday and Sunday afternoon. Now I fully realized that absolutely no one could alleviate the great loneliness I felt for my family, but I also realized that these two very nice girls had gone a long way toward easing my constant pain. I enjoyed their companionship to the point that sex with either of them was totally unnecessary. Just being near them had sufficed.

Monday morning at the Base Post Office, everyone welcomed me back and offered condolences. In a sense, it felt good having returned to military duty. Soon my supervisor called me into his office, and presented me with a sympathy card bearing the return address of Cadet Officer Vincent Callen. I was quite surprised by this act of consideration and kindness. I wondered how he had known of grandmother's passing. Then seemingly having read my thoughts, my supervisor commented, "The cadet called and I gave him the sad news". Now I understood. I read the printed message of the card while focusing on the handwritten note of the cadet himself. The note read, "To you, my dear friend, I offer condolences". I thought "This was very considerate of him. He had also provided me with a phone number with which to call him at his hospital room. I would call after work today.

Wednesday noon arrived quickly, and again I was off duty for the remainder of the afternoon. After lunch I showered and changed into new civilian clothing, which I'd brought from home. Having brought my best clothing from home had provided me with an adequate wardrobe.
Now I could dress to impress, so I donned some of my finest casual clothing before going to Cadet Callen's hospital room. By wearing civilian attire, no one would know that I was just a lowly airman third class who was visiting an officer cadet at the hospital. There had existed military regulations which prohibited fraternization between officers and enlisted personnel. Therefore, it had mattered not that I had freed this cadet from prison. Now we were required

to go our separate ways. This prohibition has remained unchanged throughout military history.

I found Cadet Callen resting comfortably inside his hospital room. He was very happy to see me. We sat and talked for nearly an hour, while covering a wide range of issues. I learned that he had successfully passed his extensive physical and psychiatric examinations and evaluations. I was happy to hear that he would soon be released from hospitalization and returned to classes. He was especially pleased at the prospect of being fully reinstated as an officer cadet. This would allow him to graduate along with his regular cadet class. Before leaving him, I promised to keep in touch.

I returned to my room, where I changed into more casual dress. Next, I carefully opened the base of my very special candle. I extracted the tiny instrument I'd come to know as the Elm and pocketed it. I then grabbed my portable radio along with one steel wire clothes hanger. Next, I hopped into my car and headed once more to San Benito beach. Once again I was the only person present. By now I had become comfortable in my ability to use this small device. Today though, I would perform two specific tests. First, I would test the Elm's capability for the detection of signals originating below the earth's surface. Second, I would test the Elm's level of signal enhancement when augmented by a grounded clothes hanger.

For my first test, I securely enclosed my radio (set at half volume) inside a small brown paper bag. Next, I dug a one-foot (squared) hole in the sand. I then buried my radio in this hole and drove half a mile down the beach. I inserted the Elm into my left ear and calibrated for proper distance.

At the distance of one-half mile, I received no signal what-soever. I then moved closer, to a distance of just one-quar-ter mile, but still, I received no signal. Finally, I returned to the point where I'd buried my radio. I then stepped off the distance of one hundred feet. After accurate calibration, I still received zero amount of sound signal. This portion of my test had proven a complete failure, but I had all along anticipated this result— so I was not at all disappointed. For my next and final test, I drove two miles from the point where I'd placed my radio. At the proper distance, I parked the car with its antenna lowered, and aimed the Elm in the direction of my now above ground radio. As expected, I received no signal. I then retrieved my clothes hanger, and un-wrapped its ends, before straightening to 180 degrees. Now I was ready to conduct my final test of the day. Hold-ing the wire hanger in my left hand, I rechecked the Elm's distance calibration. Having assured myself I'd made the proper setting, I rotated my body until the Elm came into alignment with my radio. My sound signal was loud and clear! This simple clothes hanger was an effective signal en-hancement tool! Finally satisfied, I returned to the base and to my room, then immediately once again secured the Elm. There would be only one more test I would need to con-duct. This particular test would involve methods through which I might make sound recordings of signals received.

The end of April was rapidly drawing near. I had com-pleted my CDC study materials, satisfied my personal obli-gation to the Mexican prison commandant, and visited my recently deceased grandmother's grave site. In addition, I'd successfully completed the second phase of Elm testing. So beginning now, I would focus upon: (1) Completion of my mid-level Career Development Program, (2) Acquiring minimal proficiency in Spanish language, and (3) Advancing my skills in the sport of pocket billiards. Naturally I would reserve party time.

The days turned into weeks, the weeks into months, and soon the first day of June had arrived. I found the weather and scenery both pleasant and enjoyable at this time of year in this vast Rio Grande Valley. Added to this pleasantry, I would visit nearby beaches with my friends— where I would watch as they swam, as I had not yet learned to swim. So for me, life was overall going just great. On June 1ˢᵗ I received two very pleasant surprises. First, upon reporting for work that beautiful Friday morning, I was presented with a new set of stripes by my supervisor. I had begun to climb the promotion ladder, and was now Airman Second Class Van York. Along with this promotion came an after-tax pay increase of $30 per month. Now don't laugh— for with this amount, I could fill the gas tank of my car at least eight times. Or, I could attend on-base movies for sixty days. So this seemingly meager pay increase was, in fact,— quite significant!

After lunch I was once again approached by my supervisor. This time, I was offered a new job position. The supervisor informed me that effective this very moment, I was appointed as supervisor of our on-base Consolidated Mail Room (CMR), which served as the receiving location for all incoming mail of enlisted personnel (nearly 3,000 individuals). So this was a major step up for me. I had advanced ahead of five other qualified airmen in having been given this position, so naturally I was highly appreciative of such special consideration. However, this new job assignment presented a unique problem for me. Namely, this position was currently held by a non-commissioned officer in the grade of staff sergeant (E-5). My new grade happened to be two levels below that of this staff sergeant. Now in accordance with normal military protocol, this staff sergeant should have been removed from his position as supervisor. I soon learned though that our general supervisor had wanted to humiliate and punish this poor staff sergeant. Thus, he had left the sergeant in place while assigning me as the overall supervisor of this work center. Normally, no organization would function properly while operating under such an unusual staffing structure. Subordinate personnel simply could not issue orders to superiors. It so happened that this staff sergeant was superior to me by two grades, plus a total of nineteen years in actual military service. Before departing the mail room, our supervisor had briefed us and made it clear to all assigned personnel that, it was I who was presently in charge of the Consolidated Mail Room. Then at the end of this briefing he turned to me (while pointing to the sergeant), saying "Jake, if old sarge here ever gives you any guff, just pick up the phone and call me". "I'm sure we'll get along just fine, Sgt Storke," I said. Then having received my 'reassurance', he left us.

So with just six months on base, I found myself in a completely new work environment. An all-new work crew did very little in helping me cope with my mounting apprehension. But I recalled the wise words of my dear grandmother and parents: "Son, always treat others as you yourself would like to be treated". I would apply their wisdom to this situation. So while the airmen went about their duties, I sat down with this middle-aged staff sergeant and conducted my first 'heart-to-heart' talk. I'd already sensed that he was unsure as to just how he should deal with me. To be quite candid, I shared his uncertainty. Now although I'd only recently 'escaped' the corn and tobacco fields, I did actually possess some level of common sense. I would summon this attribute at this point in my young life. So in my first talk with this sergeant, I began by saying, "Joe, I want you to know that I am not at all comfortable with this situation which we both now find ourselves in". I continued, "So for as long as we remain here together, I won't try ordering you to do anything at all". He appeared to relax slightly upon hearing this statement. I continued speaking, "However, I will work with you and assist you in every possible way". "All I ask is your cooperation in return—can I count upon you for this?" I asked. "You can count on me, Jake," he assured me. We then shook hands, and each went about our duties. I would continue working with SSgt Joe G. for three full months without any problem. Next morning at work I asked SSgt Joe to show me around this expansive mail room operation. He did so without hesitation. During my tour of our facility, I noticed one mid-sized mail pouch standing partly concealed in a corner of the building. But we moved on from section to section within the facility. At the end of my orientation, I thanked Joe before returning to my desk.

Soon my supervisor called to check on us. "How are things going, Jake?" he asked. "Just fine, Sergeant Storke." I answered. "I take it old Joe's not giving you any problems?" he then said. "None whatsoever," I replied. "Good— keep me posted," he said. "Will do" I answered". Then he was gone. SSgt Joe then asked, "I guess that was the boss, check-ing up on us"? "Yep," I said. It so happened that Joe's desk and mine were within the same office space, so we were able to communicate with (and observe) each other as we worked. Thus as I busied myself reading through applicable military operating procedures, SSgt Joe performed mail directory service, which means that he rerouted mail that contained insufficient or faulty addresses. I soon noticed that he frequently struggled in reading the addresses of such mail. However, I made no immediate comment concerning this apparent personal deficiency. The morning passed and soon it was lunchtime. Now although I was the supervisor, I allowed Joe to choose his lunch period. He seemed to ap-preciate this considerate gesture from me. So he chose an early lunch period (11:00–12:00). This choice had worked just fine for me.

By 1:00PM our crew of six personnel had taken lunch and returned to work, processing mail. I resumed my fa-miliarization with local operating procedures. Our unit's operation progressed smoothly throughout the afternoon. Soon it was once again quitting time. It was at this time that I observed Sgt Joe remove two bundles of first class letter mail from his desk. I pretended not to notice as he deposited these bundles of letters into the mid-sized mail pouch that stood at the far end of our building. Now as supervisor, I should have queried him regarding his actions. However, I remained silent. Then as everyone prepared to leave the building, I went about securing the place. Soon everyone had gone— and I was alone. I took advantage of this opportunity by inspecting the contents of this odd mail pouch. I was shocked to discover that it contained first class mail dating back as far as six months earlier! Sgt Joe's hoarding of this mail was a court-martial offense! As supervisor, my initial responsibility in this most serious matter, was to have reported this offense to my supervisor. But I would once again jeopardize my newly established military career by not reporting this offense. I was thusly derelict in the performance of my assigned duties, which in itself constituted separate court-martial action. But in my manner of thinking, this problem had existed for more than six long months. Also, I felt confident that I could alleviate the problem within just three workdays, after which, I would take preventive measures.

At this early point in my career, I found myself faced by a major problem that required serious and immediate consideration. But this particular problem had been accompanied by extenuating circumstances. But don't forget— I had not been afforded any managerial or supervisory training, so I wasn't sure what to do. I'd already discovered that poor Sergeant Joe was happily married, with four young children. In addition, I'd learned that he was highly decorated while serving in the Korean conflict. I also knew that within ninety days, he would become eligible for retirement from the United States Air Force. I certainly did not wish to end his otherwise honorable career in this manner. Had I done so, he would have been undesirably discharged from the Air Force without the benefit of retirement income. I simply would not allow myself to become a part of such drastic actions! So in case you're wondering— I kept my mouth shut as I resolved this problem.

Here now are the methods through which I achieved

undetected resolution of this situation. I secured the mail room that evening and proceeded to lunch. At 5:00PM, I returned to the CMR retrieved the stashed mail pouch. My first step was to dump its entire contents onto a nearby mail sorting table. Next I began sorting through the bundles of letter mail, searching for the most predated letters. By 8:00, I had performed directory service on four of the thirty bundles of hoarded letters. I finally secured the mailroom as I prepared for a short stint on the town.

On Friday I dedicated my whole day toward further reducing this backlog of letter mail. By the end of the day at least fifty percent had been eliminated. On Monday morning I once again turned my attention toward further reducing this mail backlog. Again on this day I noticed Joe set aside bundles of letters on his desk, and he made no mention of the decreasing size of his "special" mail pouch. At mid-afternoon I walked over to Joe's desk and sat beside him. "Here, let me help you with these, Joe" I said. He sat as if momentarily stunned. I could feel his apprehension and embarrassment! I tried easing his nervousness by saying, "We've got this under control, Joe". He sighed before dropping his head and commenting, "Jake, I don't know what to say— except, thank you"! "You don't need to say anything, Joe— I understand" I said. At this point he reached forward— and for a long while just held onto my hand. When he was finally able to speak (without tearing up), he said, "Jake, I believe you're my only friend". I had not expected those words, so even I found myself deeply touched. Unfortunately, this particular situation had arisen simply because— this poor fellow could barely read English (his secondary language). So now with this great mail backlog behind us, I focused upon teaching him the basics of our language. Over his remaining three months of military service, I would help him with vocabulary and with the practice of 'sounding' out words. His career had been saved— his future secured!

On June 29th 1956, Staff Sergeant Joe G. retired with full honors. I was very happy for him and his family. I was also very relieved that this situation was finally behind us. Incidentally, I had recently completed my five-level Career Development Course, and was officially qualified as an administrative specialist. My reward for this expeditious achievement was the immediate reassignment into the administrative career field. Finally, and at long last I had been properly assigned. I had learned the postal field well, but this was all behind me. My supervisor had prepared a small reassignment celebration for me inside our post office building. At the party, I was congratulated with handshakes by all assigned members, including my supervisor, Master Sergeant John Storke. This weekend I would have strong reasons to party!

I had myself a real fun weekend, but today was Monday morning, July 2, 1956. Prior to this day, I had worn only Class C (fatigue) uniforms to work, in performing postal duties. Today however, I had graduated into Class B (semi-dress) uniforms. Also, I would finally have my very own desk and telephone— wow! My assignment was with the Base Civil Engineering Squadron. I would work directly for the squadron commander, who held the grade of captain. This position required that I dedicate one hundred percent of my energy toward learning my new field. Here, my primary work tools were the typewriter, filing cabinet, and telephone. Needless to say— each of these items were strange to me, but I would quickly learn their operation.

My first two days on the job were quite difficult. Mainly, my typing sucked. Having noticed this, my commander scheduled me for a thirty-day on-base typing course (two hours per day). I was determined to excel (or at least not make a fool of myself) in my new field, so I really applied myself in an effort toward improving my typing skills. Each day I would type in class and at the office. I found filing to be quite easy. Now if I could only learn which end of the telephone to speak into, I would become exhilarated! After one month, my typing skills had vastly improved. I had quickly became an expert at filing and retrieving documents, and finally, I succeeded in understanding this mysterious instrument known as the telephone. I attributed my success with the phone to my considerable amount of experimentation with the Elm. Incidentally, this device had remained sealed in its holding place over the past seventy-five days. There had been no time for this little instrument.

In my new duty assignment, I rather quickly progressed to the point where I had surpassed my commander's expectations of me. Now for the very first time, I had truly enjoyed the first thirty days in my new duty assignment. It had required great amounts of extra study on my part. As a result, I had even curtailed my pleasure trips into Mexico. I realized though that the potential gain far outweighed the personal sacrifice.

Soon the month of September had arrived, and I found myself enjoying my very first three-day weekend. The weather was simply perfect during this time of year, and nearly everyone crowded the nearby beaches. But since I did not swim, I visited my regular hangout during each of my three days off. It was at this point in time that my young life took its sudden but drastic downturn! Before continuing, I must tell you— writing the rest of this chapter pains me deeply. Even these words which I've chosen for use here tend to elude me. So please bear with me as I struggle through these remaining paragraphs.

At 2:00PM on Saturday afternoon (September 1st) as I sat alone at the counter of The Corner's deli section, there entered a lone young woman. I immediately found her quite attractive. She had a cute face, complemented by a perfectly proportioned figure. She stood at 5'6", with a weight of approximately 130 pounds. I really liked what I saw! She approached the counter near me, and then sat down. Neither of us had spoken. She then placed an order for a chocolate sundae. I did not wish to appear rude, so I spoke first saying "Hello, I'm Jake". Actually, I'd only followed the customs and practices of my hometown region. However, by having followed this custom, I had unwittingly brought upon myself severe and irreversible harm! This young woman calmly returned my casual greeting with a seductive smile. She then spoke, saying "Hello Jake, I'm Francine". She seemed quite nice at first sight. But this was just the bait! For behind the scenes, a sinister plot had just been placed into motion. When she'd finished her sundae she arose, saying, "It was nice meeting you, Jake". "Likewise" I answered. I then offered to walk her back to her home, but she declined my offer. So, I discreetly admired her as she walked from the deli.

On Monday afternoon, I again showed up at The Corner deli. This time I remained out front with a small group of gathered airmen. Then as I stood discussing sports and a variety of different subjects, I once again perceived the sensation that someone was watching me. I went inside the deli and immediately, this weird sensation left me. I walked back outside to discover that the sensation had returned. After five minutes I returned into the building and again, this unusual feeling quickly departed. Fifteen minutes later, Francine walked into the deli! We warmly greeted each other, and she seated herself next to me. Soft music was playing in the lounge area, so I asked her if she would like to move to a booth. Right away she took my hand and walked with me to a nearby booth. We danced a couple of times, and each time she had pressed herself tightly against me. At one point, I kissed her on the cheek. She instantly responded by placing an arm around my neck and pulling me to her. Next she planted upon my unsuspecting lips, one of the most sexually arousing kisses any young man could ever imagine! But don't forget— we'd just met! This alone should have warned me away— NOT! I was naïve, because I liked what I'd seen!

It so happened, a co-worker had noticed her seductive behavior, and had invited us to his off-base apartment along with his girlfriend. I asked Francine if she would like to take a short ride with us. "Where to?" she asked. "Tto my friend's place" I answered. Without even providing me with an answer, she picked up her purse and stood facing me. I took her by the hand, as the four of us then discreetly exited through a far side door. We drove directly to my co-worker's apartment. Upon entering, he and his girlfriend went directly to their bedroom. I entered the opposite bedroom, pulling Francine inside. In the heat of the moment we'd left each bedroom door standing completely open. This meant that each couple would perform in full view of the other. I did not feel quite comfortable with this arrangement, but since neither of them seemed to object,— I would not complain. Anyway, it was too late for complaining, for Francine had already removed every stitch of her clothing! I quickly followed suit, and for the next full hour—WE ROCKED THE HOUSE! I found it strange that Francine had made no mention of protection, but I had applied same anyway. This was truly an exciting hour!

Back at the lounge we danced a couple more times, before Francine left for her home. I decided to return to the base for a quick shower and the evening meal. At 8:00PM I drove back to the lounge. Soon my two friends arrived, and we then partied through the evening. As usual, I walked them to their homes at 11:00. Neither seemed aware of my time spent with Francine earlier this afternoon. Alone back in my room, I wondered what it might be like with these two. I would never know, for notorious Francine would make certain of that!

Two full weeks would pass before I saw Francine again. Meanwhile I'd been befriended by a slightly older airman one grade higher than myself. We had met in our dining hall, when he had taken a seat at my table— which was a normal custom. Immediately upon seating him-self, he spoke "You're the guy who owns the sharp Road Master, right?" he said. Attempting modesty, I answered, "I suppose you could say that." He then introduced himself as Airman Zilly Bain. I found his appearance and demeanor quite impressive. But when I learned that the ultra-sharp Oldsmobile parked outside belonged to him, I was even more impressed. He asked, "Where're you from, Jake?" I answered "I'm from a small hick town in South Carolina". "Wow, that makes us neighbors," he exclaimed, (somewhat gleefully), adding "I'm from Georgia myself". "So we've got quite a bit in common," I said – thinking that I may have just found a new friend. "That we do," he replied. He suggested that we check out each other's cars sometime soon. I answered by saying "I'd like that Zilly". I'd seen his car only recently, having noticed that it displayed only a temporary base permit. This suggested that he had only recently purchased this nearly new vehicle. Then after eating we walked to the nearby parking lot, where we had parked our cars. Upon reaching the parking lot, I discovered he'd parked directly next to my car. I wondered about the possible significance of his having parked in this exact spot. "Maybe this was just a gesture of friendship." I thought. My thinking could not have been more flawed! I would later discover that this was all just a great scam that had been conjured up by those unseen eyes I've previously mentioned. I refer specifically to those times where I'd sensed having been closely watched by some unseen person, while standing in front of The Corner lounge. I would also soon discover that this was only the initial stages of an inconceivable family conspiracy. So with Zilly Bain as their instrument, and I their target (mark), this most evil plan had been set into motion!

Two weeks later, my new pseudo-friend (Bain) suggested that he and I reach The Corner lounge a bit early to attend an auto show. We each arrived at noon as planned. An hour later, Francine arrived. She walked directly to me, saying "Hi Jake, I've missed you". "I've missed you too," I said, feeling myself already becoming excited. We entered the lounge and danced a couple of times. Bain and his girl-friend then joined us. At 1:30, he said, "Jake, Betty and I are going to take a quick run down to Mexico to pick up a couple of bottles for the evening". "Why don't you and Francine ride along with us?" he asked. Now being the poor, unsuspecting sucker that I was, I eagerly accepted his kind offer. However, I would need to convince Francine to join us. But before I'd even voiced the question, she said, "I'm ready"! Now I was really excited, for not only did I have a fiery young seductress at my side,— I would also take an exciting ride in a new super car! "What more could one ask for?" I thought. Then as she and I had previously done, we discreetly left the lounge by its side entrance.

We parked the Olds coupe beside of one of Mata-moros' popular liquor stores and the four of us casually strode into the store, where we picked up two bottles of whiskey. But as Bain reached for his wallet, he exclaimed, "Uh oh, left my wallet inside the car". "You guys watch the bottles— I'll be right back." he said. Without objection, we followed his instructions. Momentarily, he returned to pay for the bottles of whiskey. We left the store and returned immediately to the car.

The hour had reached 1:45PM as we entered the car. Bain then inserted the ignition key, but to no avail. He made three attempts, but each time the car's engine completely failed to respond! Now over time back home, I had become quite familiar with the problems of Old Betsy. Today those similar problems had apparently followed me here into Mexico. Bain waited for ten more minutes before retrying the car's engine. Again there was no response. At this point he pulled the car's hood latch, releasing its hood. I had sat directly behind him, which made it impossible for me to exit the car along with him. This was a two-door coupe, which necessitated that I exit after him. He had already raised the hood of the car, and was reaching underneath as I approached his side. "Think I've found the problem," he said. "What is it?" I asked. "Seems as though the distributer cap was a little loose." We reentered the car and he made one more attempt at starting it. Amazingly, the car's engine started right up!

Another fifteen minutes had passed, so the time was currently 2:00PM. We then departed Matamoros, heading directly back to Harlingen. But just three miles before Harlingen, all Hell broke loose! First, a civilian vehicle pulled alongside us and one of its female passengers yelled, out to us "THE TEXAS STATE POLICE ARE LOOKING FOR YOU GUYS"! My morale immediately sank to its lowest level ever! *"STATE POLICE— what the heck?"* I thought. Just then I spotted another car up ahead, spinning its wheels from the gravel and onto the highway. I had seen this particular car before,— and recognized it as belonging to Francine's family. I then instructed Airman Bain to head for the airbase, figuring we would find sanctuary there. He responded by quickly accelerating, and the new Oldsmobile earned its reputation as "Rocket 88"! Even so, the pursuing vehicle paced us by remaining only a few yards behind.

We entered the base, slowing only momentarily to allow the gate guard to visually check us. We then sped away, slightly exceeding the base's twenty-MPH speed limit. However, the pursuit car failed to even slightly reduce its rate of speed. Soon several military police cars had joined the chase. As soon as we reached Base Military Police Headquarters, Bain parked his car and the four of us quickly entered the building. I peered through the building's front window, only to see Francine's family rapidly approaching. Following closely behind were four armed military police-men. But what they did not know was that this family was also armed! Needless to say, this was quite an explosive situation! Now I had not expected that I would be physical-ly attacked while inside police headquarters, but I recalled my years of training with dear old Mr. Lim, and prepared myself anyway.

The building's front door sprang open, and inside rushed an angry giant of a woman who was reputed to have been a witch! She stood at least 6'2" while carrying a weight of more than 275 pounds. This was Francine's grandmother. Immediately behind this giant walked an-other female near-giant. (Francine's mother) stood at least six feet and weighed over 240 pounds. The grandmother appeared uncontrollably violent, as she stormed into the military police building! She walked to within inches of me before stopping. "Young man, I'm going to charge you with the Mann Act, so you'll spend the next ten years of your life by rotting away in some prison"! I stood dumbfounded, for she had caught me completely off guard! I had never before heard of the Mann Act. In fact, at that particular mo-ment— I couldn't even spell "Mann Act". Had I been chal-lenged to do so, I would have said or written (Man Act). This was the extent of my knowledge of this subject. During this time that she'd stood screeching at me, I had remained completely silent, fearing what might happen if I'd spoken. I was unable to clearly see her eyes, for she'd apparently had none— only two very thin slits, located where the normal human eye should be. Then to make matters even worse, she did not really speak to me— only lots of yelling! She continued "So by the time those prisoners are finished with you— NO WOMAN WILL EVER WANT YOU"! At this point, the old witch's daughter tugged her mother's sleeve, saying, "Calm down mom, before you have yourself a stroke or heart attack". Actually, at this very moment I silently wished for either or both to occur. Unfortunately neither did! Upon hearing the words of her daughter, the old witch immediately transformed herself into a seemingly normal human being. She then said to me, "You sit here and think about what I've just said to you". "I'm going outside to smoke myself a cigarette." she snarled. I sensed that even the armed police inside this room, were highly relieved at hearing this. As for me though, I was still not convinced that this was not just some nightmare.

As soon as the witch and her daughter had reached their car, I turned to the Provost Marshall (Chief Military Police Officer) asking, "Sir, what is the Mann Act"? He responded, "Airman, this is a very serious provision within our United States legal system". He added "This applies to the transporting of minors across state lines, and carries a minimum sentence of seven years". Now I truly felt as if I might soon die, for I was certain that I would never survive this ordeal.

I remained in a holding room while this weird family sat talking inside their car. At one point, I could have sworn that I'd observed both mother and daughter laughing together, as the old witch's husband had sat alone in the car's rear seat. At the time, I'd assumed that possibly my eyes were playing tricks on me. As I continued watching them, the daughter exited the car, returning toward our police headquarters building. Meanwhile, Francine and two Air Force military policemen stood at the far corner of this large holding area. The daughter then returned to me, saying, "I've talked to mother, and she's agreed to drop these charges against you— if you will agree to marry my daughter".

Now I felt as though tons of weight had suddenly been removed from my young shoulders! However, the daughter's statement had seemed quite out of the ordinary. Namely, she apparently had not given any consideration to the feelings and wishes of her very own daughter. I found this quite strange, but I quickly responded "If Francine will have me, I will marry her". (These were those magical words they had sought)! The mother then turned to her daughter, asking "Francine, do you want to marry Jake"? "I do," her daughter answered.

I was relieved, though I'd found this somewhat strange— the mother knew my first name, even though we had not been introduced. Now, I readily admit to having been naïve; but, I did not consider myself completely stupid! Therefore, I quickly concluded that this was simply some sort of elaborate scam— but one I could not elude. Francine's mother then returned to their car, where through this window, I watched as they celebrated success! Together, witch and daughter returned into the building, whereupon each congratulated me regarding my wise decision. Exactly one month later, I would become a married man— but to a complete stranger who was reportedly only fourteen years of age (but actually seventeen).

There had been no charges leveled against me regarding

this incident, so my life continued as normal. Meanwhile, I inwardly hoped that something (anything) might happen to this family, thereby resolving my current predicament. For my remaining days of freedom, I limited my visits to The Corner lounge to only weekends. On Mondays, Wednesdays, and Fridays, I visited Matamoros. On Tuesdays and Thursdays, I remained on base practicing pocket billiards. Oddly, my new "friend" Zilly Bain had vanished. At the very last moment, I explained to my two decent friends (Mindy and Myra) the circumstances of what had happened to me. They were completely shocked upon hearing this news, but each had reluctantly accepted this latest state of affairs. After all, what else could they have done? Then all too soon, my life (as I'd known it) came to a screeching halt!

After having resided on Harlingen AFB for a period of exactly one year, I found myself standing before some city official, listening as he read marriage proceedings to us. At the end of the ceremony, he stated, "I now pronounce you man and wife". His words caused an involuntary tremor to course its way through my body! At least though, I was not standing or sitting in some faraway prison. In closing, he said, "You may now kiss the bride". I then kissed Francine on the cheek. At this point, the old witch spoke, saying "The ring"? I answered with a bit of sarcasm, "Ring, what ring"? Then, displaying considerable annoyance at my comment, the old woman silently removed the wedding band from her finger and pressed it firmly into my hand. I took her ring and placed it onto Francine's finger. Now I was officially married— but to a harlot! I found it somewhat strange that even Francine's grandfather had not chosen to attend this civil marriage between myself and his granddaughter.

I had driven alone in my car to this small town near Harlingen for this most unpleasant event. But now that I was cursed with a wife's presence, she and I rode together to the home of her family's. Once there, the old witch showed me to the small bedroom which she had prepared for us to sleep in. She then announced, "This room will cost you twenty dollars per month, payable in advance". I reached into my wallet and produced a single twenty-dollar bill, and then handed it to the old woman.

I checked my watch to discover the time was nearing 5:00PM. Oddly, I still possessed an appetite for food. However, I knew instinctively that there would be no food here for me. Even had there been, I would not have eaten it and neither would I consume liquids while in this house. In fact, while in this old house I would engage in only two activities— (sleep and sex). Also, I would always sleep lightly while here. I soon excused myself from this household, having advised Francine that I would return within two hours.

Now that I was married, I would lose the rights to my on-base room. This presented a major problem, for under no circumstances would I ever consider taking my candle containing the Elm to this family's off-base residence! Instead, I'd already rented a mid-sized clothing locker inside the base gym. I would keep my few valuables secured inside this locker. In my room inside this family's home, I would only maintain a couple of changes in civilian clothing. I would even keep my uniforms on base.

But before proceeding further, please allow me to take a moment in which to fully appraise you of the truth regarding what had just happened to me. That which I reveal to you now would be revealed to me two years after the fact. First, this evil grandmother had sought to end an ongoing love affair between her granddaughter and son-in-law! So by marrying off this young woman, she'd hoped to resolve this situation. However, this urgent problem would persist. Second, she sought to provide some level of income to her granddaughter. While these first two issues might be considered normal, the next will definitely not be. Her third and final objective was to simply murder me for profit! She had known that I carried the meager sum of $10,000 in an insurance policy. What she had not known was this: In the event of my death, these insurance proceeds would have been paid only to my mother. Nevertheless, I would have ended up in a grave. And had it not been for the existence of my precious little Elm, this old witch would have succeeded in achieving each of her three sinister objectives. Incidentally, this old woman had conspired with Airman Zilly Bain to transport us into Mexico at a predetermined date and time. This was the sole reason why his new car would not start on return from Mexico. It turns out he was slightly ahead of our return schedule. So he had intentionally disconnected his distributor box (ignition system) to stall for time. Had we returned ahead of schedule, this family would not have been in position to intercept our return into Harlingen. Thus, this old witch's efforts, (along with a $500.00 payment to Bain), would have all been in vain. But she had been successful— at least until now.

After enjoying a hearty meal, I proceeded to the privacy of my room. While there I enjoyed one last shower. Next, I took a few moments to write a loving letter to my dear mom and dad. At the end of my letter, I wrote, "I just got married"! This was a statement that was made with no forewarning whatsoever, so I was certain neither of them would ever understand. Tomorrow, I would mail my letter after preparing my room for release.

I returned downtown and to my new 'prison cell'. All the while though, I fully realized that this situation could have turned out much worse for me. Therefore, I would make the most of it. I decided then and there, that I would make every effort toward becoming a good husband to this young woman. (Remember, I had not yet been informed of her lover). I asked my new wife if she'd like to go out on the town, and she quickly accepted my offer. I felt quite embarrassed by my new situation, so I was hesitant to take her to The Corner lounge/deli. Instead, we drove across town to a street that was lined with clubs and restaurants. Neither of us were consumers of alcohol, but we enjoyed ourselves anyway by sipping on Ginger Ale containing one-half ounce of alcohol each. Over the coming months, these would become our standard drinks. As we sat holding hands, talking, and sipping from our drinks, we actually began a bonding process. Then as soon as the sun had disappeared from view, I took her by the hand and drove the short distance to the San Benito beach area where I'd conducted Elm testing. Luckily this stretch of beach was deserted, because no sooner than I'd left the highway, did she begin removing all her clothing! Now I'm sure there's no need for me to tell you just how greatly her provocative behavior had excited me. As I parked the car, she had already completely unbuttoned my shirt. But this was only the beginning! Naturally, I helped her with the remainder of this task. Soon we found ourselves reclining upon the cool but spacious leather rear seat of the Road Master. This was only my second time making love while inside this car. But this time was different— for it was with my wife now. The Buick accommodated us fully on this very special evening. Over and over— and over and over— we made love! And then, we repeated our erotic behavior! Now I'd previously heard the term nymphomaniac, and this night served to verify their actual existence! Hours later, we left the beach and drove to The Corner lounge for refreshments.

We found ourselves a secluded booth, where we immediately engaged in one of the most frenzied sessions of near love-making I had ever experienced. None of the girls back home had ever performed any of the brazen acts in which Francine had now engaged! At this very moment, I had at least temporarily ceased regretting the fact that I had been forced to marry this young woman. Simply stated, this woman was the personification of sexual pleasure itself! But this night was still young!

Now this was only mid-week, meaning I would work for another two full days before getting a day off. So at 11:30, I took her home to our small room. Once there, she immediately resumed her passionate advances. So after making love several more times, we finally took a short break. But as we lay quietly talking, she said, to me "Jake, if at anytime during the night you want me— just shake me". She added "If I don't wake up, just take it anyway". Those words really sent shock waves up and down my spine, and over time she would become the only woman to ever speak such words to me. Finally, she gave me a break. Then as I lay quietly in the darkness of our room, I thought, *"Maybe this marriage thing won't be so very bad after all".* Time would prove me totally wrong in my assumption!

Early on Thursday morning, she awakened me with another wild session of passionate love- making. I sensed that this might persist throughout the day, so after about a half hour of this activity, I convinced her that I must return to the base to prepare for work. She reluctantly released me. I then rushed to the base, where I showered and again washed up before heading to the dining hall for breakfast. At work throughout the day, I would find my thoughts drifting onto my new wife and wondering just how this might turn out for us.

After lunchtime, I took the afternoon off so that I might thoroughly clean my room. I found that I would really miss the comfort and privacy I had enjoyed here over the past twelve months. I'd cleaned and surrendered my room by 3:00PM. I then decided to report to my base personnel office to initiate paperwork, requesting overseas assignment. Now of course, I would not inform Francine or her family of my actions, for I'd developed a strong feeling that I should leave Texas as quickly as possible (but without Francine)!

Luckily for me the weekend soon arrived, which allowed me time for recuperation and relaxation. This was also an opportunity for discovery. Out of pure curiosity, I had concealed the Elm inside my car because I wanted to learn what was discussed within the walls of my new household. So, on Saturday morning I suggested to my new wife that she might pay a visit to a local beauty shop. She eagerly accepted my offer and made an appointment for 11:00AM of that day. This would provide me with the opportunity for a bit of eavesdropping. It was the beginning of my third day in this household. I'd noticed that during this entire time, Lief, who was the old witch's husband, had not spoken one single word. Now since this fellow was head of household here, I found his continued silence quite unusual. I figured "Just maybe— my sudden presence here had somehow contributed to this state of strange silence".

At 10:45, I dropped Francine off at her beautician's small shop. Having ascertained that her appointment would last nearly two hours, I drove directly a nearby city park. This park (by my farmer's calculations) was one-half mile away from Francine's house. Once I'd found the properly positioned park bench, I removed the Elm from its paper napkin and inserted it into my right ear. I had already achieved directional alignment, so I only needed distance calibration. I began calibration at a distance of slightly more than a half mile, zooming slowly inward toward my seated position. In less than a minute's time, I had struck the jackpot! Now of course I would never know what had been discussed prior, to my having zoomed in on this position. However, the dialog which I then received was of utmost importance— and unusually alarming!

Here now are the sounds and words which I received. First, there was only laughter between Francine's mother and grandmother. Then the mother commented, "I want to thank you, Mama, for it seems that your great plan is working". "I hope so," replied the grandmother, adding "But even if it doesn't completely succeed, we'll still get our ten thousand dollars"! I was stunned beyond belief, but I continued listening in on their conversation. The mother spoke once more, asking "But how are you going to do this, Mama, without going to jail yourself"? "Don't you worry," the old witch answered, adding "I have my ways". She continued "There's a strong chance that he might not swim— and if he doesn't, I'm going to take him fishing". She then shocked me by saying "But if he does swim, then he'll have himself a fatal accident one night while down in Mexico". Now to say to you that I was appalled would be understatement of the decade! I could not believe I had just overheard manifestations of such great evil! The old witch then said, "Speaking of fishing, I'm going down to the gulf to catch myself a mess of fish right now". I listened to her heavy footsteps, as she walked from the house out to her car. I knew that if she were heading to the water, she would come my way, so I quickly secured the Elm before taking my short drive out to the base.

At the base, the same military policeman from two days before was on duty. He acknowledged me with a wave and smile. I returned his gesture accordingly. I went directly to the base dining hall, as it was now noontime. After eating, I proceeded to the base barber shop for a haircut. Lastly, I did a bit of miscellaneous shopping before departing the base. Upon returning to my car, I sat alone reflecting upon those deeply alarming comments made by Francine's evil grandmother. I then gave thanks to the tiny Elm for having revealed this plot to me. At least now, I was aware of this conspiracy!

Now although I'd remained quite shaken by the disturbing comments I'd recently overheard, I would keep silent but maintain constant vigilance. I picked up Francine from her beautician's appointment, then drove downtown, where I purchased for her two new dresses along with other miscellaneous items. Tonight, I would show off my new wife! After shopping, we drove to our original meeting place—The Corner lounge and deli. There, we were congratulated on our recent marriage. I still had not purchased a wedding ring, though she had made no mention of it. We were gone for the whole afternoon, and when we finally returned briefly to the house, I struggled to maintain an outward appearance of calm and ignorance.

After bathing, Francine changed into one of her new outfits, and I into a fresh outfit of my own. We then spent much of the evening together out on the town. Shortly after midnight, we found ourselves back on the beach. This time though, I had brought along a blanket plus one bottle of sweet wine. We spent the next several hours lying together under the cover of the stars. This quiet evening together would, in the future, become known as our 'honeymoon'. Shortly before sunrise, we quietly slipped back inside our small room,— where we resumed our erotic activity. This was how we spent our entire weekend together.

Over the coming six months, we would party heavily as we enjoyed this new life of ours. However, during this very same period I would discover that this 'wife' of mine was not at all trustworthy. I make this statement only after having frequently witnessed her displays of absolute promiscuity. I quickly learned that this young woman completely lacked any degree of self-respect. She also regularly demonstrated an absence of respect for others (regardless of age or gender). I recall one particular incident where while walking along the beach, she'd paraded (completely nude) before a male stranger. I'd also seen her dance brazenly and suggestively with other strange men. But worst of all, I had observed her as she touched and caressed another nude man. At this point, you are probably wondering "Why did I not speak out against these practices"? My answer is this— I wanted to determine just how far she would go while in my presence. This would serve as a strong indicator of how far she would go during my absences. When I finally confronted her over her lewd behavior, she looked innocently at me, asking, "What did I do to offend you, Jake"? This was the woman I had been forced to marry! But I'd also recently formulated my very own plan of escape!

Just six months later, I secretly received my much-anticipated reassignment to a base in Japan. I kept this assignment secret for the next fifteen days. Only then did I break the news to Francine. At first she feigned total devastation, but I sensed even then that she was simply thrilled at the prospect of my leaving. For then, she would become totally free to pursue a lifestyle of her very own choosing. At Francine's request we waited until the beginning of the following week to break this news to her family. So when I arrived from work on Monday evening, I found Francine lying across our bed. It was apparent that she had been crying. When I asked what was wrong, she responded by asking me to take her to live with my folks while I was away overseas. Now I knew from the very beginning that this was a terrible idea! But she had begged so pitifully, she'd soon touched my heart. I discovered that Francine's grandmother had informed her that since she was now married, she could not remain within their household during my absence. I would much later learn that the grandmother had been determined to end this intolerable love affair between Francine and her young step-father.

The very next day, I mailed a Special Delivery letter to mom and dad, seeking their help in allowing Francine to reside in their household during my pending eighteen-month absence. This would prove the most disastrous request of my lifetime! Meanwhile, over the next two weeks Francine's grandmother seemed to exist in a somewhat dazed condition. In fact, she seemingly moved about while not knowing exactly what to do next. This was fine by me, for I would definitely not go fishing— nor would I venture into Mexico. Plus, I would make every effort to sleep with at least one eye open at all times!

Finally on Monday, April 1, 1957, my 'magic moment' arrived! I had loaded our few belongings into the car at midnight of the prior evening. So after washing up, all that was left was to toss our toilet articles into my trunk and drive away. I had also taken the precautions of securing the Elm, and servicing the car on Friday afternoon after work. Thus, I 'tearfully' bade farewell to this strange family, and then waited in the car for Francine. I had only exchanged a mild hug with Francine's mother before leaving. On my way from the house, I waved lightly to Lief, the old witch's husband. The stepfather was at work at this time. The old witch had stood silently in a corner of their living room, as I exited the house.

At exactly 8:00AM, with my wife at my side, I drove quietly (but quickly) away from this dreadful house! I immediately headed northward and across the expansive ninety-two mile region known as King's Ranch. At the time of this trip, there were no rest facilities in this area, so a vehicle in top mechanical condition was essential. I was confident the Road Master was in excellent condition, but still grateful that weather conditions had not yet turned extremely hot. For the next thirty-six hours, I would drive nearly non-stop. All along my route through the southern states, I kept my eyes peeled for the presence of state highway patrols. Neither Francine's grandmother nor mother had offered to pack lunch for us. But this was fine by me for even had they done so,—— I would not have touched it! Thus whenever we would gas the car, we would pick up a few snacks to munch upon along our route.

At 8:00PM Tuesday evening, I arrived at home while accompanied by my stranger of a wife. I had not provided mom or dad with our estimated time of arrival, for I was myself unsure. My timing had been perfect, for we'd arrived shortly after they had left the fields. They each surprised me by their warm welcome of Francine, so for a moment I'd felt that this arrangement might work. (WRONG)!

We enjoyed supper together, but now we needed baths. So as I prepared our country-style bath for Francine, she looked curiously at me— as if to say, "What are you doing"? Luckily, I had already thoroughly explained to her about conditions here at our old house. Eventually we each completed our much-needed baths. Francine was instantly fascinated by the antiquated manner in which my parents lived. She had not experienced country living, meaning remaining here would be a great sacrifice, along with extensive personal adjustment. I had not intended to bring Francine here to my folks' place, but in trying to do the right thing, I'd gone against my own instincts. At least Francine and mom seemed to have gotten off to a good start, and this made me feel much better about the situation. We were both quite exhausted, so we climbed into bed shortly after mom and dad. This would become one of the few sexless nights we would spend together.

Next morning, we awakened to the sounds of roosters crowing. This was a new experience for Francine, for one did not hear sounds of chickens in and around Harlingen. We pretended to be asleep at the time mom and dad left for the fields. Accordingly, they did not attempt waking us before leaving. I soon discovered that this was the strangest feeling I had ever experienced while at home. Needless to say, I'd felt embarrassed beyond belief!

At about 9:00, I arose and manually pumped water with which we would wash up. Mom had also left us a large pot of heated water, which simplified matters considerably. After washing up, we had a light breakfast consisting of fruits, bread, and butter. I then walked out into the fields to greet mom, dad, and the farm workers. No mention was made of my joining them. Soon I returned to the barnyard, where I greeted my anxiously waiting horse. It seemed that she had already known of my arrival. At this point, Francine appeared in the doorway. She was completely nude! I quickly left my horse and rushed inside the house. Upon entering my bedroom I found myself being erotically attacked by this wild woman! Fortunately, I could see mom and dad from my vantage point inside the house. So for the next hour, we engaged in one of our absolutely wildest lovemaking sessions ever!

Afterwards while Francine relaxed, I grabbed my horse and quickly rode to Buddy's house. I was extremely disappointed to find the dog lying crippled in his front yard. He would never again accompany us, having been struck while playfully chasing a passing car. This discovery nearly ruined my day. Still, after petting Buddy for awhile, we rode to my friend Mr. Lim's. He was quite surprised at seeing us, but also disappointed at not seeing Buddy. After thirty minutes I returned home to Francine. We then relaxed in the cool shade of our front porch.

After our noon meal, I drove Francine around our little town. I detected that she was not highly impressed by the sights here, but this was understandable. I found myself increasingly uncomfortable over leaving this young woman here in this little hick town. But I'd already passed the point of 'no return', so all I could do now was keep my fingers crossed and hope that things would be okay. That night I located a cheap motel, and... (you know the rest)! This would become our routine for the remainder of my brief stay here.

Thursday passed quickly, and now Friday afternoon was upon us. At 4:30 this afternoon I would board the Greyhound Express, bound for San Francisco (a city I'd longed to visit). Francine and I had already said our farewells during our most recent motel stay. I found it a bit odd that she didn't seem deeply concerned over my imminent departure. Now my final hour had arrived, so I bade a special farewell to my parents, and then with a brief hug from my wife, dad and I climbed into the Road Master and drove to the bus station. While at the station I advised dad that should Francine cause any trouble within their household, I would be in complete agreement if he deemed it necessary that she return to Texas. Dad thanked me before voicing his desire that she enjoy a pleasant stay with mom and himself. I then presented to him the car keys, saying, "Dad, this is for you and mom— enjoy it". He expressed his deep gratitude for this very special gift. They would no longer need to depend upon poor Old Betsy for transportation. Plus, they would begin riding in style. It felt really great to provide this meager gift to mom and dad.

When my bus arrived, we once again said our good-byes and I boarded the bus. I located a comfortable seat and peered through the window at dad, as he drove away toward home. I relaxed in my seat as I reflected upon recent events. As I rode along, I thought of my wife and silently wished that she would, in fact, return to Texas. My wish would be fulfilled much sooner than anticipated! I tried to relax more and give less thought to this issue, for this would become one very long bus ride. For the next seventy-two hours, I covered a great amount of territory—none of which I'd seen before. Finally at 2:00PM on Monday, April 8 1957, I arrived at the sprawling Travis Air Force Base in Fairfield, California. I would be here for three full days, which would allow me to make a few visits into the fabulous city of San Francisco. Along my route I had passed a number of major cities, which I'd only before seen in movies. So I'd had myself a safe ride, along with a memorable experience. I spent my first night on the base of Travis. On Wednesday evening, I treated myself to my very first evening in the city of San Francisco. Naturally, I carried along a map of the city. I visited a few bars and generally had myself a grand old time. I really enjoyed my stay here.

On Thursday evening at 9:00PM, I boarded a large C-121 Super Constellation flight bound for Tokyo, Japan. Unfortunately, back then there were no jets— so this flight would last for twenty-four full hours. Now I challenge each of you young readers to imagine yourselves flying for twenty-four long hours. We flew— and flew— and flew some more. At just fourteen hours into our flight, we crossed the International Date Line. We'd instantly gained a full day, so now we'd magically advanced into Friday. Then after nearly ten more hours of flight, we reached our final destination.

Chapter 6

Jaunt to Japan

Shortly before the hour of 9:00PM Friday evening, we landed at one large U. S. airbase just a short distance from the city of Tokyo. There were nearly two hundred military members on our flight. Each required at least limited in-processing actions at this time, so over the next two hours this is what we accomplished. I immediately found myself extremely excited at being in this exotic region of the world— a world I'd previously only dreamed of! We finished our in-processing within the allocated time period of two hours. And now, I was anxious to get downtown to see the sights. But then, disappointment reared its ugly head. We were told that we would be taken directly to our dormitories, as there was a mid-night to 5:00AM curfew within this region. Shucks, I'd thought I might be feasting my eyes upon some very pretty Japanese girls this time of evening! But I would be forced to exercise patience.

We were promptly walked outside to our waiting busses. Upon stepping outside, I immediately detected a very strong chill in the air. In fact, within minutes I found myself shivering, as I'd traveled unprepared to meet such extremely low temperatures. I was thrilled to find a modern and well-furnished room waiting for me. It was spacious, but contained only two bunk beds. One of these bunks held a name tag at its foot board, which told me that this particular bunk was occupied, so I chose the opposite for myself (although each was presently empty). I had carried along a manually operated alarm clock, which I set for 4:00AM. Now in case you're wondering "Why so early Jake"?— this was because I intended to be one of the very first to reach the downtown area next morning.

After all, back on the farm I would routinely arise at 4:00AM— to catch only an ugly mule, so surely, I could arise at this early hour— to catch a pretty young Japanese girl! I washed up quickly, then sought directions to the nearest dining hall. Once there, I rushed through breakfast before hailing a base taxi and rushing downtown. I quickly discovered that this base was optimally located, at least from a social perspective. Each of its gates opened inside city limits, which meant vehicular transportation would never be necessary.

I had arrived at the gate by 4:55AM, necessitating that I wait there for another five minutes before being allowed to enter the city, so I stood anxiously counting each second as it crept by. Then after what had seemed as hours, the gate opened and I, along with many other GIs, rushed through. Not having a clue as to where I was heading, I simply followed the crowd. After only five minutes of brisk walking, I reached an area where the streets were lined with bars and shops. I felt that I had just reached paradise!

I entered the very first bar I'd reached. To my amazement, I found this bar already crowded by GIs and beautiful young Japanese girls. Momentarily I stood awe stricken, but quickly regained my composure— it was time for me to really be cool. I casually strolled to a nearby vacant barstool and sat down. I immediately recognized the fact that— this definitely was not Mexico, and neither was it Harlingen. This was Heaven! At least I realized exactly where I was. I ordered a watered-down mixed drink, and then sat taking in the scenery. Soon a very pretty young girl approached me, asking, "You buy me drink, GI"? Fully realizing that I was being suckered, I bought this girl a drink containing only water along with ice and pink coloring. I was in Japan, so all was okay! I found that her English was fair. At least we could laugh and joke together. This was sufficient, for in bed it would not matter what language she spoke. We danced a couple times, and soon she repeated her original question (only this time with slight modification). "You buy me another drink, GI"? "Only one more," I said to her. She received the second drink of water, but soon it was gone. She followed suit! I looked around the small bar for her, only to spot her sitting in a corner booth begging another GI for a drink. Might I mention here that even back then, each of these small glasses of water cost some poor GI the equivalent of one U. S. dollar. These bars would sell hundreds of these 'drinks' each day and evening. Imagine the huge amounts of money earned while practicing this system. I left that bar and walked from bar to bar. At each, the situation was the same. So this was my initiation into the region. Now please don't misunderstand me, for I'm not complaining. In fact, I would quickly learn to take advantage of and enjoy partying with these bar girls. I would soon discover that there were a variety of young women here with whom to socialize. First, there were street walkers (active and retired). Second, there were a large number of unattached young women who were quite anxious to find some American GI to latch onto. Finally, there was a group of married, but jilted women (American and Japanese) who desired companionship. I would quickly discover that these two latter groups were not to be found in bars, or walking the streets. Instead, they could be found in stores, clubs, and restaurants. I would seek these as companions.

I had partied through Saturday and Sunday, and on each of these days I'd experienced loads of fun along with an excessive amount of sizzling sex! But now it was Monday morning, and time to report for duty. My first stop for the day was at our Consolidated Base Personnel Office (CBPO), where I resumed in-processing onto the base. Next, I reported to my squadron to officially sign-in with my unit. By noon I'd completed a large number of personnel information files, before proceeding to the nearest of several dining facilities located on this massive airbase. I received my food tray and sat enjoying my meal. But soon the walls of the dining hall seemed to begin dancing and weaving about! My 20/20 vision became extremely blurred. My head and body felt as though some invisible person had just pounded me with a heavy sledgehammer. I tried to stand, but my strength had completely deserted me. I realized that this was all very strange, for I had felt just great throughout the whole morning. Finally and after much effort, I was able to stand and hobble back to my squadron commander's office.

Upon entering the office, I was greeted by both my commander and first sergeant. Each appeared to be in a celebratory mood as they greeted me. I blinked several times in a desperate attempt at clearing my still blurred vision. I was at least slightly successful in this effort, so now I was able to see that my new squadron commander held a pair of new stripes. "Congratulations— Airman First Class Van York!" he said, pressing the stripes into my hand. I was truly surprised by this totally unexpected promotion— though too ill to appreciate it. My first sergeant then asked "Airman, are you ill"? "I feel as if I'm about to die," I replied. "Can you make it to the hospital?" he asked. I'd seen the hospital standing two blocks down the street, so I answered, "I'll try, sergeant." "Good, then get there as fast as you can!" he ordered. I left the office, and then hobbled slowly to the nearby hospital.

At the hospital I was promptly seen by a nurse, followed by a family practitioner. The doctor advised me that I had a rare form of influenza which frequently produced blindness and paralysis in its victims. He ordered my immediate admission into private quarantine. There I would remain for a full five and a half days. During this time there was no heat in my area, and I constantly felt as though I were freezing. To make matters worse, the hospital staff kept the windows in my area standing wide open. My treatment consisted of only aspirin, orange juice, and water. During my stay, I received no visitors— for I'd been quarantined. I longed to receive some word from mom and dad, but no such luck.

After five days of hospitalization, I realized that my condition had not improved. I asked myself "How in the heck could I improve— with near freezing temperatures and all windows, standing open?" It then occurred to me that I might not improve for as long as I remained here.

So, I drafted an 'ingenious' plan (naturally, I jest). Anyway, starting on the morning of my fifth day, I began holding two ice cubes in my mouth throughout the entire day. This effectively reduced the temperature of my mouth, where the nurses always placed the thermometer. So at 7:00AM on Friday, my temperature was taken. As a result of the cubes of ice I'd just swallowed, I received a falsely lowered reading. I was thrilled to hear the nurse say, "This is very good—your temperature is back to normal". "How do you feel?" she asked. "I feel great," I lied. "May I be released now?" I asked. "I'll need to check you a few more times this morning, before I can make that determination," she answered.

For the next five hours, I consumed dozens of ice cubes. I was rechecked at 9:00AM and again at 11:00, with each reading having been normal. Still, I continued eating ice cubes. Then at 1:00PM, I was checked once more and released (although I'd felt no improvement whatsoever in my condition). On the way to my dorm, I purchased a bottle of cheap bourbon along with a couple of fresh lemons. I then covered myself with warm blankets, as I sipped toddy throughout the afternoon. Within just a few hours, my pain subsided and I felt my strength slowly returning to my body.

At 5:00PM, I found myself for the second time seated inside this new dining hall. This time I completely enjoyed my meal. After eating I returned directly to my room, where I poured myself another bourbon with squeezed lemon juice. Next I crawled back underneath my covers, and relaxed for the evening. The bourbon seemingly worked wonders for me, for by midnight all of my viral symptoms had completely disappeared. Six full months would pass before I would accidentally discover (while monitoring communist party demonstrations) that I'd not suffered influenza, but had in fact— been poisoned! Fortunately my body was youthful and strong, or I might not have survived this ordeal.

Early Saturday morning I washed up and had myself a wholesome breakfast, after which I repeated the activities of the previous Saturday. Then for two days, I partied as though there would be no tomorrow! I was quite fortunate in having found a very nice young lady to show me the sights of Tokyo and Yokohama. I quickly discovered each of these two cities to be exciting beyond belief! By now, any doubt I may have held about this country had quickly and completely disappeared. This would be a fun tour! At the end of my eighteen-month tour here, it would seem as though I had arrived just yesterday. For me this tour would serve as undeniable evidence that— time actually does fly when one is having fun. Unfortunately, my time here would be restricted to only eighteen months because of my unfortunate and unwanted marriage.

All too soon Monday had arrived, and I found myself once again inside my new command section. Upon arrival at work, I discovered that this would become my actual duty section. I would serve as the commander's assistant chief administrator. Even my duty title sounded impressive (at least to me). In this position I would prepare and process reports, correspondence, and court-martial documents up to and including general court-martial. So at least for now, post office and mail room assignments were no longer my concern. At 9:00AM I met with my commanding officer for a one-on-one interview and introduction. This officer held the grade of captain, and was by profession a fighter pilot. Unfortunately, he had been temporarily removed from flying status for reasons of physical disability. From the moment I'd met him, I found him to be both competent and highly professional. His name was Herbert J. Edwards, Capt., USAF. I've used his real name here out of pure admiration and respect, for this was truly the finest officer I would ever meet during my twenty-eight year military career! Over the following twelve-month period, I would immensely enjoy working for this outstanding Air Force officer.

After my welcoming interview I was shown my private office by my first sergeant, who over coming months, I would also discover to be an outstanding non-commissioned officer. In the next hour I met with the remaining three members of our office staff, after which I arranged my office for optimum use. I had advanced rather quickly in both grade and position, and now I found myself using an office that was even nicer than that of my former supervisor (MSgt Storke) back at Harlingen.

At noon I went to lunch and had a delicious meal, at the same dining hall in which I'd fallen gravely ill only one week before. However, on this day I would not become ill. After lunch I checked my mail, not expecting to find any letters. I was quite surprised, though, to have received a letter— from dad of all people. In my entire eighteen years of living at home, I had never before seen dad write a letter to anyone. So, I immediately sensed that something must have gone seriously wrong. I opened the letter only to find that dad had written just a short note. In it he informed me that he had regretfully kicked my wife Francine out of our household! His note further stated that the very evening I had boarded the bus bound for California, Francine had gone out on the town. Dad advised me that she had left the house at 7:00PM, but did not return until 7:00AM the following morning. She had returned with two young hoodlums. During this time he and mom had worried throughout the night about her well-being. However, at seeing her return in such a disrespectful manner, at the point of his loaded .12 gauge shotgun, he tossed her suitcase out to her, ordering her to never return! I re-read dad's brief letter (for certainty). At that moment, I'd found myself experiencing a mild state of shock. But even more so, I was totally embarrassed! *"The audacity of this piece of trash!"* I thought. So this was the ultimate manifestation of that which I had been forced to marry.

I still had twenty minutes remaining of my lunch hour, so I used this time to write a short reply to dad's note. In my letter, I thanked him for his patience and hospitality. I praised him for his prompt and courageous action. Lastly, I apologized deeply for the embarrassment which my unwise decision had brought upon mom and him. I promptly mailed my letter. Out of pure embarrassment, four long years would pass before I would muster the courage to once again show my face before my mom and dad.

At the end of my lunch hour, I resumed in-processing actions. This included a visit to the Base Education Office, where I enrolled in an off-duty course of Japanese language. I had found while at Harlingen that I really enjoyed learning foreign languages. Beginning this day, I would establish my very own personal program of self-improvement. I would:

(1) Give top priority to becoming an expert in my new position. (2) Diligently study the Japanese language. (3) Strive for continued rapid improvement in billiard skills. (4) Eradicate and obliterate my self-perceived image as that of a simple backwoods farmer! This necessitated that I take immediate action in revising and improving my verbal communicative skills. I would no longer present myself as just some country hick. To the contrary, I would create and perfect a new personality for myself. This meant that I would no longer reveal my true point of origin. Thus, only those working within my duty section would be privy to my place of birth. And even they would never learn of my many days spent behind some mule. Lastly, I would adopt a new name for myself, which I would use while off-base. Now this just might seem as a bit ridiculous to many of my readers, but the new name I chose for myself was (Eddie). I'd had no particular reason for having chosen this name, except— I liked its sound. Thus, all the girls downtown would come to know me as (Eddie San). At work though, I would remain Airman Van York— or just plain Jake.

Time for me here in Japan passed rather quickly and very soon two full months had elapsed. By this time, I had been given the opportunity to expertly perform each facet of my assigned duties. Thus I felt quite comfortable in my new position. I suppose my squadron commander was also quite satisfied with my performance, for at this point he began frequently inviting me to fly with him. I imagine he had taken along other members of our office staff, but I was never able to confirm or disaffirm this thought.

I never really discovered when he had been reinstated to flying status, but one afternoon in early June, I received my very first invitation. As I sat at my desk preparing a report, Captain Edwards approached my desk, saying, "Drop what you're doing, Jake, and let's go flying". At first I thought he might have been just kidding me. But I noticed that he was wearing his flight suit, so I asked, "Are you serious, sir"? "I'm serious" he replied, at which time I quickly put away my report and hopped up from my desk. "Of course, we'll have to pick up a flight suit for you," he said. We drove to our Base Supply activity where I receipted for one flight suit in my size. As I donned my flight suit, my heart rate quickened and I realized that excitement was rapidly mounting within me. We then proceeded onward to Base Flight Operations, where the captain checked out a two-seated propeller-driven aircraft. No one challenged him concerning my presence. We walked to the aircraft, where he performed a thorough visual inspection. Having satisfied himself with the visual condition of this small plane, we boarded and strapped ourselves in. He then contacted our control tower and requested clearance for take-off. He sat at the controls in the plane's forward cockpit, and I in the rear cockpit seated directly behind him. As he taxied, I thought, *"Why couldn't this be me at the controls"*? Naturally, I had long ago received my answer. Then he received takeoff clearance and within seconds, we were airborne! My heart rate accelerated even faster! Soon we were executing steep climbs, nose dives, barrel rolls, and inverted flying.

While executing these maneuvers, he would frequently ask, "Are you okay, Jake'? Each time I would answer, "I'm just fine— do more"! He seemed to immensely enjoy the fact that I was not at all frightened or discomforted by his aerial demonstrations. We flew over rice paddies, small towns, and large cities, and while doing so I realized "This was the very best day of my life— ever! This would be the closest I would ever come to actually flying a plane. So even though there was no similarity whatsoever between piloting the plane and being only a passenger therein, I would settle for this. After a couple of hours had passed, Captain Edwards reversed course and we headed back to our base. I would vividly remember this wonderfully exciting afternoon for the remainder of my entire life! I would accompany Captain Edwards on similar flights at least once each month, for the next ten months.

Just two months into my assignment here in Japan, I finally made the acquaintance of my highly elusive roommate. After my afternoon of flying had ended, I sat in the quiet of my room while writing a letter to mom and dad. I was bursting at the seams to tell them of my wonderful experience from earlier in the day. So as I sat excitedly jotting down line after line of my letter, I was slightly startled by the sudden and unexpected opening of my room door. Entering the room was a young man whom I estimated to be in his late twenties. I was really surprised by his apparent age because the rank indicated on his bunk read "airman third class" (one stripe). He stood approximately 5'10" with an estimated weight of 160 pounds. *"Here we go again—another (old) low-ranking airman"*, I thought. But unlike my former roommate Manny, this fellow was unusually jolly. I would discover that this was his natural personality. I would also discover the true reasons for his seemingly high morale. "You must be Van York," he said, grinning as he reached forward to shake my hand. "Yes, I'm Jake," I said, as we shook hands. "I'm Smiley," he happily responded. "Where've you been for so long?" I curiosly asked. "I live downtown." he answered. "But isn't that expensive?" I asked. "I can afford it," he responded.

Now it wouldn't take a genius to figure out that something was wrong with this situation. As the days and weeks passed, I learned more and more about my somewhat mysterious new roommate. First, this was a skilled gambler who used highly refined cheating techniques. He preyed upon those young and unsuspecting newcomers such as myself for much of his income. But even more importantly, he frequently engaged in the illegal currency trade. Specifically, he would sell the amount of $1,000 U. S. dollars to some foreign buyer. In return, he would receive the equivalent of $2,500 U. S. dollars in local currency. And with this money he would then travel to Tokyo and Yokohama, where he would purchase expensive jewelry such as diamond rings, necklaces, and fine watches. He would then (using his personal passport) fly to Hong Kong, where he would immediately transfer ownership to a local fence—for the sum of $5,000. Thus within a period of less than seven days, he would have generated a tax-free profit of $4,000. He would repeat this process on an average of four times per year! I would also discover that his monthly gambling profits averaged $500 per month. At the end of one twelve-month period, he had the huge sum of $22,000 in tax-free income (ten times his annual military income). Now to some of you young readers, this amount may seem minimal. But this was during the year of 1957, when average working income ranged far below $10,000 annually. So for Smiley, the military had merely been a sanctuary from which to execute his illegal activities. This would soon come to a screeching halt, however, for within just sixty days I would process paperwork resulting in undesirable discharge of this young man. Fortunately for him, he would leave Japan while carrying concealed valuables in the amount of $40,000— in the year 1957!

During the following two months I concentrated upon furthering my knowledge in my newly assigned position. I concurrently focused upon learning the language of Japanese, while also improving my skills on the billiards table. By the beginning of August, I had made considerable progress in each of these three primary areas of interest. Incidentally, I had also achieved exceptional progress in the area of carnal knowledge. And of course, I'd partied nightly while downtown with the many fine and friendly young ladies. Equally important was the fact that I was continuously afforded those exciting flying experiences with my commanding officer!

Then in early September 1957, I was disappointed by having received a new roommate. This fellow, whose name was Bill Houser, was of completely different character than the former hustler, (Smiley). I instantly sensed this was a person of impeccable character and integrity. He was a handsome young man, both charismatic and poised. He stood six feet tall and weighed nearly 200 pounds and was in top physical condition (such as myself). He wore three stripes (same as I). I would discover that he was twenty-five years old and had already obtained his bachelor's degree. His field was data processor, which I found most impressive. Over coming months we seemed to naturally become close friends. We began a companionship that would only be terminated by my reassignment from Japan. We would travel throughout this country together, enjoying many experiences and interesting sights.

During the next couple of months on my job, I worked toward expanding my knowledge of military court-martial procedures (my primary responsibility). Soon I had become an expert. Meanwhile, my friend Bill focused upon expanding his knowledge as a computer specialist. During slow periods in my work, I would study the Japanese language. Then again after work I would devote one more hour to the study of this language. Several times each week I would find a pool table upon which to practice. This schedule would pay off well for me. Then (with the exception of Wednesday and Friday nights) Bill and I would often hit the bars by 9:00PM. As a pair of cool GIs, we quickly became quite popular among many of the young ladies downtown. In fact, we soon became so popular, we found ourselves receiving special treatment from a large number of these young ladies.

At this point, you're probably wondering why I refer to these young women as ladies. Unlike the prostitutes of Matamoros, a large number of these bar girls actually conducted themselves as ladies. Many had earlier been decent human beings; however, life itself had dealt them losing hands. Many had lost their parents to the ravages of war, ending up all alone— with no one to care for them. Many possessed both character and integrity, along with a strong desire to improve their situation. Unfortunately, without some support from at least someone, the vast majority of these poor souls were doomed! Their only hope for escaping this unpleasant lifestyle was that of marrying some American GI. But here, there existed another problem.

Namely, any of these young women possessing a police record were eliminated from contention. Therefore, only the
most lawful survived. This was the social situation, at least
during those days. So yes— I refer to them as ladies.

But back to the story at hand, during late October
1957, my roommate and I sat together inside our room discussing our financial situation. We were each married and
with one dependent, although Bill always seemed to have
more spending cash than I did. I'd realized he had served
more years in military service, but our differences in pay
should have only been slight. When I inquired of Bill about
this pay difference, he just smiled, saying, "Jake, I have extra income". I asked him to explain, and he said, "I do bit-
part TV acting for Japan's leading TV network". I was impressed! He then surprised me by saying "If you would like,
I can bring you into our little group". "Of course I would,"
I quickly replied. "Great, then come with me to the studio
tomorrow night." he said.

The next evening, I accompanied Bill by train to the
downtown Tokyo area, where the television studios stood.
We'd arrived a bit early, so that I might be interviewed. The
manager of Bill's acting group was a friendly middle-aged
Japanese fellow. He had me stand before him while slowly
turning full circle. I had dressed well, and had given particular attention to my grooming. At the end of my demonstration, he exclaimed "Daijobu"— meaning good. I was
hired immediately. Needless to say— I was simply elated!

Imagine— this simple dirt farmer having become a TV
actor for Japan's major network! Heck, I would've willingly worked for free! But instead, I would receive the equivalent of $200 per month for doing this. This amount equaled

my monthly military pay, so I'd just hit the jackpot! Now I could breathe a sigh of relief, for I was no longer destitute. The studio's program required that we rehearse (in studio) for one hour each Wednesday evening. Then at 9:00 each Friday evening, the network's live show would air. My roles were non-speaking— but that was just fine by me. At the end of Friday evening's show, I would receive my week's pay. This extra income greatly facilitated my social life (not to mention what it did for my morale).

By the end of December 1957, I'd become a recognized television personality. I then thought back to the days (not long ago) when I'd not even seen television. I specifically recall visiting one particular fancy restaurant in downtown Tokyo. As I sat struggling to conceal my ineptness at using chopsticks, many of the customers would smile at me. At first, I thought they were pitying me for my inability to handle chopsticks. I was momentarily quite embarrassed, but I continued eating. Soon drinks began flowing to my table. I quickly summoned my waiter, for I wasn't about to pay for drinks I had not ordered. "There's been a mistake, I haven't ordered these drinks," I said. He just smiled, saying, "No mistake sir, drinks be for you". Then sensing my bewilderment, he said, "People here buy you drinks," as he pointed to two nearby tables. I looked toward the tables to find nearly one dozen people smiling and waving to me. Naturally, I smiled and waved back at them! We remained seated as we bowed to each other, raising our glasses in toasting. This was another first for me— and an unforgettably wonderful experience! Soon, my friend Bill arrived, and suddenly more drinks began flowing our way! The two very lovely young ladies at our sides were at a loss for words, for they had never before experienced Americans, seemingly being admired by Japanese. This event was our New Year's Eve celebration.

Soon we'd entered the month of January 1958. These next two months would be relatively low in activity. There would be lots of snow on the ground, accompanied by extremely cold temperatures. Though this meant there would be no flying for me during this sixty-day period. In the interim, I would spend many warm nights while snuggled between some pretty young lady, and a hibachi laden with burning red coals!

I was then afforded the opportunity to work as an administrator for two weeks in the office of our commanding general. I was pleasantly surprised that this two-star general had personally requested me. My two-week stint in the general's office would prove the turning point in my military career! It was here that I met a young and highly ambitious captain who, in time, would change my life. This officer was officially known as Captain James. Those within his inner circle often referred to him simply as Captain "J". Over time, I also would address him similarly. He was a very personable individual who exuded ability and confidence in all that he undertook. It was widely known that this officer was both dependable and highly resourceful. At the time of his assignment with the general, he also had been temporarily removed from flying status for medical reasons. During my two weeks as administrative augmentee to the general, this captain became was very helpful with information that was essential to my success in this temporary assignment. This was an assignment I would immensely enjoy! While there I mostly prepared written communications that were to be dispatched under the general's signature. After only three days in this position, the general himself approached my desk one afternoon to personally commend me for the professional quality of my work. Now to say that I was highly pleased by his unexpected praise would be an understatement. From this day forward, Captain 'J' himself appeared to have developed an even greater appreciation of my work. I noticed that he and the general would often play chess and even checkers during their spare time. After a full work week had passed, I became bold enough to request permission to briefly observe one of their chess games. "Come on in, Jake" responded the general. I timidly entered the spacious office. "Do you play, Jake?" asked the general. "Not chess sir, but I do play checkers," I answered. "Good, then maybe you could give me a few pointers on how to whip this young captain's backside." commented the general. "I'd be more than happy to do that, sir" I eagerly replied. Over coming months I would often be summoned to the general's office, where I would render tutoring services. So now, my personal unofficial program consisted of: (1) Tutoring the general in checkers. (2) Continuing my study of the Japanese language. (3) Continuing my billiards practice. (4) Partying with the ladies here!

Soon, we entered the month of March. At this time, my commander and I resumed our monthly flying sessions. But also at this time, I resumed the testing of my listening device. It had sat untouched since my arrival here. So on Saturday, March 1st as my roommate attended to personal errands, I carefully removed the Elm from its storage candle. Next, I performed a complete visual check of its condition. It appeared undamaged and fully operational. I had intended performing just one more specific test upon this device. I needed to determine its capability for recording sound transmissions. I knew that my co-worker and administrative section chief, Joe Brickman, kept a small battery-operated tape recorder inside his desk. I figured he would not object to my borrowing this recorder, so I went downstairs to the office and carried it back up to my room. My first sergeant kept a tool kit inside a closet in his office. I recalled having seen a variety of tools, along with small reels of wiring. So I proceeded directly to this closet, where I obtained one razor knife, along with three feet of light gauge wiring. I also picked up a small role of electrical tape. Next, I stripped away three inches of insulation from the ends of the wire. I had all along suspected that when properly connected, it would be possible to record sound whenever using the Elm. Thus, I cut one-half inch of tape. With this small strip of tape, I carefully secured one end of this wire to the Elm's outer shell. Then with one more half-inch strip of tape, I attached the opposite end of my wire directly above the recorder's audio input vent.

Finally, I inserted the Elm into my ear and searched for the nearest signal. Suddenly the recorder's signal input indicator began erratically bouncing back and forth! The device had picked up a signal and transferred it to the recorder! But more importantly, the recorder had picked up and recorded the signal received! This was my ultimate achievement to date, regarding my use of the Elm. This was a most significant discovery, for it meant that I could actually make recordings of any comments or conversations overheard. But the question remained, "How would I use this newly discovered capability"? At this point I recalled having observed (from a distance) several local communist party demonstrations. Each such demonstration was conducted just outside our base, so I could visually observe many of its participants from my vantage points inside my room or office. They carried signs that read, "YANKEE GO HOME"! Also, they would shout anti-American slogans and insults! Oddly, they were allowed to carry on their demonstrations without interference from our military forces or local law enforcement. I'd often wondered *"Exactly what else transpired during these demonstrations"*. Next time, I would make this discovery! I returned the Elm to its hiding place, before returning the recorder and electrical tape.

My roommate soon returned, and upon entering the room he said, "Hey Jake, come downstairs and see what I've got"! I quickly accompanied Bill to the downstairs area, to see for myself why he was so energized. He walked me over to an old German-made WWII heavy-duty motorcycle, exclaiming, "Now we can ride all over Japan"! I feigned excitement at seeing this antique. It reminded me of "Old Betsy", back home on the farm. "Very nice" I coolly commented, lying through my teeth. In my manner of thinking, this aged bike had originally been used by the old German Gestapo! And here I was, about to take a ride on it. As expected, Bill said "Hop on, and let's go for a ride". Well, ride we did! Within the next few hours, I believe we probably covered at least half of Honchu Island. But surprisingly, this ride was great fun for me— and another first! I'd never before even considered climbing onto any motorcycle. But one just month later I would purchase my very own Yamaha 350cc bike. Until then though, Bill and I would simply settle for roaming this island on his bike.

April soon arrived, and by now I'd learned to operate Bill's bike quite masterfully. At least this is what I'd thought at the time. Although, I must admit— the excessive weight of his German-made bike had initially caused me slight difficulty. I resolved this issue by purchasing a bike for myself which was lighter in weight than Bill's. Thus, we now had two bikes between us. This would allow us to take along two young and cute Japanese ladies during our many trips. But much to my regret there was a trade-off here, for this month would bring to an end those exciting monthly flights with my squadron commander. It had come time for him to return to the United States. I would compensate this great loss through more frequent use of my bike. Soon Bill and I found ourselves taking long (accompanied) rides to all of the major points of the island. For the next six months, I would experience unforgettable fun!

Finally we had entered the month of May, and my commanding officer had departed. In his place had come another captain. Unfortunately, this officer bore no similarity whatsoever to my great leader Captain Edwards. But regardless of this change in commanders, I continued my high level of professionalism while performing my duties. I worked diligently on the job, but I partied each night. So all was well (at least this is what I had thought). By mid-month though, I'd received one mild warning from my first sergeant. In it, he stated "Jake, watch out for this new captain ours, for he's a bit vindictive"! I thanked him for his advice, but failed to give proper attention to his words. It seems that my new commander had learned of my work contribution to the general's office. I would also discover that he resented my frequent contact with

Executive Officer, Captain James. I would, therefore, soon regret having ignored the warning from my first sergeant.

June soon arrived, and on the first Monday of this month, the local chapter of communist party members held their monthly anti-American demonstration. The protest demonstration had begun at 7:00AM as usual, thereby presenting a strong presence to all Americans heading for work on the base. This large group had positioned itself in plain view, just outside the north fence wall of our base. I used my farmer's instinctive skills in calculating their distance as one-half mile from where I sat inside my office. Luckily, my workload was not unusually heavy on this particular morning. I was equally lucky to have been afforded flexible working hours. This meant that whenever I requested time-off, my request was usually granted. I would exercise this option at this time, so I asked my first sergeant for the morning off. I'd been an exceptional performer on the job, so he granted my request without hesitation. I then borrowed my co-worker (Brickman's) small recorder before proceeding to my room. It so happened that the positioning of my room afforded me full view of the communist group's participants. At this point, I was finally prepared to begin monitoring the verbal communications of this group. I inserted the Elm into my left (preferable) ear, then calibrated for distance. Next, I assembled my recording apparatus as I'd previously done during testing. The recorder immediately picked up a strong audio signal, which was verified by the movement of its needle. It still quite early, so there was very little dialog at this early hour. Now after having diligently studied the Japanese language for slightly more than one year, I'd reached a point where I'd actually understood much of what I overheard. But not very much had been spoken, other than the voicing of anti-American slogans. As I sat listening to them, I began wondering if maybe this was not such a good idea after all.

It was presently 9:00AM, and my secret project had not resulted in any receipt of information. Fortunately I had not given up in my quest for information, for at this very hour I spotted a shiny (but older) American car, slowly moving through the densely gathered crowd. The demonstrators respectfully cleared the way for the car to pass. Many followed closely behind as the car crept toward the center of the crowd. Finally it stopped, and out stepped four well-dressed male local nationals. One walked ahead of the remaining three men. I figured this person to be their leader. I would soon be proven correct. This individual then mounted a small portable platform, from which he began his address to the gathered crowd.

His speech was given entirely in Japanese; however, I comprehended the vast majority of his message. He began by telling the demonstrators, "Comrades, we have made great progress since initiating our advanced program of Yankee eviction from our country. Since January, we have successfully tested our new special formula on three Yankee soldiers. Each of our tests was a total success! Each of these Yankees remained hospitalized for one full week! I am convinced that when we introduce our formula into the water of their young, we will soon see large numbers of Yankees fleeing our great country"! His speech was interrupted at this point by strong cheering from all those present. But he had not yet finished. He continued, "If for some reason this portion of our plan fails, we will escalate our efforts immediately. In the end, ALL YANKEES WILL LEAVE OUR GREAT COUNTRY"! Now the communist protesters really roared! The speaker then ended his speech, immediately departing the area.

I was absolutely stunned by what I had heard! As I sat analyzing the communist speaker's comments, I found myself struck (as if by a lightening bolt), for I was one of those Yankees to whom this speaker had referred! I was one of their three (test) guinea pigs! Military doctors had misdiagnosed this condition as a rare strain of influenza— when the facts were, this was a newly adopted form of rare low-potency poison! A physically weaker person might not have survived such an attack. I then secured the Elm along with my short conductor wire.

Back at the office I returned Joe Brickman's recorder, but minus its recording tape. I was aware that our office had recently purchased a full pack of blank tapes, so this presented no problem. At 11:00 AM, I made my usual correspondence distribution run to our Base Headquarters. This trip included visits to the offices of commanding general, and Executive Officer Captain James. As always, Captain James had expressed an interest in my personal well-being. Upon seeing me, he wasted no time in inviting me into his office for a brief chat (sports, etc). I welcomed this opportunity, for I wanted to confer with him regarding the highly alarming recording I'd made earlier during this morning.

After a moment of casual conversation inside the captain's office, I produced my recently made recording. Many offices on base had been provided with such recorders, so I knew he would have equipment with which to replay this tape. Captain James," I said, "Earlier this morning, I discreetly recorded a portion of today's communist party demonstration". "My Japanese is weak, but I believe I understood what was said." I added. His eyes widened as he looked at me, asking "Jake, you recorded this morning's session"? "I think I recorded the most important portion," I answered. "Then, let's have it," he replied quite anxiously. I produced the tape and handed it to him, whereupon he commented, "I'll get back to you on this". He then quickly added "Let's keep this just between the two of us— shall we"? "Fine sir, no problem," I said. I returned to my office carrying the incoming correspondence I'd picked up from the Base Mail Center. Back in the office, I returned to my routine daily administrative duties. That afternoon the secretary of Captain James called, saying, "The captain would like to speak with you immediately. I informed my first sergeant that I needed to return to headquarters building for a few minutes.

I found Captain James anxiously awaiting my arrival. As I entered his office, he said, "Close the door behind you, Jake". I did as he asked, then took the liberty of seating myself near his desk. He leaned forward, looking me squarely in my face, and said, "Jake, what you have here is a bombshell"! "I'd like to know— just how in the hell did you obtain this tape?" he asked. I shocked him by answering, "Sir, I spent my teenage years pretending to be some Cherokee Indian scout,— which means, I have my bag of tricks". "I am more than just impressed— in fact, I'm amazed!" he exclaimed. "Thank you sir," I responded, now feeling a bit proud of my accomplishment. The captain then asked me a curious question "Jake, do you feel you might be able to repeat similar feats upon demand"? "I believe so, sir," I answered.

"Great!" he said, asking, "Do you also believe you can keep a highly sensitive secret"? "Of course sir," I replied. "That's wonderful, for I can definitely use your abilities and skills in a highly secret organization I'm presently forming". "But you must positively assure me that you will not mention any of what I've said here to you to anyone". "Are we in agreement here?" he asked. "We're in complete agreement, sir." I answered. "Great, that's what I wanted to hear," he said. Then as I prepared to leave his office, he confirmed my accurate translation of the recorded events of earlier this morning. Before dismissing me, the captain stated, "I'm working on this from the top down— so mum is the word here". "Mum it shall be, sir," I responded. As I arose the captain firmly grasped my hand, saying, "Great job, Jake— I look forward to working with you"! "The feeling is mutual, sir— I look forward to working with you also," I eagerly responded. Now although I'd not had even a clue as to what lay ahead for me, I'd just entered into a new and exciting— secret military career!

The week passed without further incident, and soon Saturday was upon us. Throughout the week Bill and I had partied each evening after work. Then at about 9:00 Saturday evening, as Bill and I sat in a booth facing each other, we were suddenly approached by two GIs from the base. I had seen them before and considered them hoodlum types. This was because I'd previously observed them as they fought and pounded other street gangs into pulp. So to me, these two GIs were just the leaders of some stupid street gang! I'd also noticed that they always traveled as a gang of six members, which left me wondering, *"Where are the other members of this gang"*? Their young leader, (standing directly before me) stood approximately 6'2" in height, with a weight of about 220 pounds. His deputy was a huskier fellow, standing at only 5'10" but with a weight equal to that of his much taller partner. This fellow was quite muscular, and would have been a formidable opponent against any fighter!

The taller fellow then began berating both Bill and me, using the most violently menacing tone I'd ever before witnessed! The tall fellow stood just two feet away from me, spewing unending lines of vulgarity! He began "You two m----- f-----'s think you're really something, but neither of you are worth a sh-t"! We've been watching you both, and we don't like what we see! So starting tomorrow, we're gonna wipe the streets with your sorry asses!" he snarled. All the while, I'd remained completely quiet. I suppose they misinterpreted my continued silence as possibly an indication of cowardice or fear. They were badly mistaken, for I'd been merely following dad's advice. Dad would often say to me "Son, never violently argue with another man— kill him while he's arguing with you"! Now these were strong words—but dad had meant every word of his statement. So I sat quietly as I observed the posture and facial expression of my potential attacker. At this point my roommate Bill casually said, "Why don't you two guys go outside and warm up— I'll be out in one moment". I couldn't believe my ears! For here we were about to be violently attacked, and Bill had found it appropriate to crack jokes. "How absurd" I thought, so I decided that I would take matters into my own hands now.

All the while sitting there, I was prepared to strike with deadly force! However, I wanted these two to initiate an attack upon us so that I would able to claim self-defense! They'd wisely elected not to physically attack us at this time. Anyway, I finally spoke to the tall fellow, saying, "Why don't you bend down here, so that I might let you in on a little secret". The fool followed my instruction by bending forward. His face was now within striking distance. I had considered delivering a 'Cobra's Fangs' punch to the eyes. Such a punch results in instant and total permanent blindness! I would have delivered this punch from a sitting position and in the presence of several witnesses. Thus, I would have been exonerated. But had I done so, there would have followed an unwanted and extensive investigation into the incident. I did not wish to undergo investigation, so as my 'would-be' attacker lowered his face, I did not strike. Instead, I goaded him by coldly saying, "If you're trying to scare me, it's not working". I continued "I've seen you fight, and I'm not at all impressed, so as far as I'm concerned, you and your entire stupid gang can go to hell"! I prepared myself for some form of violent reaction from him, but this did not materialize. Instead, this fellow abruptly straightened up, saying to his partner, "C'mon, let's go"! I was disappointed by their odd lack of action. But as they reached the bar's exit door, the shorter of the two issued an ultimatum, saying "You two m----- f-----s had better never show your faces downtown again"! I quickly responded, "We'll be here by two o'clock tomorrow afternoon". With this verbal exchange, they disappeared. Ordinarily I would have been relieved, but this gang had just threatened our future existence. There was simply no way that I would avoid town for the remainder of my tour here in Japan!

One hour later, Bill and I left the bar. We wandered

through the streets and bars of Tachikawa, expecting to encounter this terrible street gang. I asked my roommate, "Bill, if we run into these guys, how're we going to handle them"? "Don't worry Jake, I'll handle them myself," he calmly replied. I was relieved by his confidence, but added, "That won't be necessary, because I'm taking the two who were in the bar". Bill seemed really surprised by my response. "Jake, are you some sort of martial arts expert?" he asked. "Not really, but I do have four years of oriental special self-defense training," I replied. "Are you a black belt?" he asked. "Unofficially," I answered. "That's awesome!" he said, adding, "I happen to be a fifth-degree black belt in karate". "Great, this means that together we should be able to handle these clowns." I said. "Beyond a doubt" Bill commented. Now I would never underestimate an opponent, but I had in fact, observed this particular gang as they'd fought against others. I had also noted that few had demonstrated any extraordinary fighting skills. It seemed to me, these guys just loved fighting. I thought, *"Well, guys, as of tomorrow we're going to break you out of your bad habits"!* We then found ourselves two cute girls before partying indoors for most of the night.

Bill and I returned to this very same bar on Sunday afternoon at 2:00 as I had promised. Once there, we ordered drinks for ourselves, and then we waited. We waited— and waited— and then we waited some more! I figured that at some point, they would show up. Luckily for all concerned, they never did! Next day at work, I would discover the surprising reasons why this 'gang' had failed to show.

Bill and I remained at the bar while waiting for this notorious street gang. At 5:00PM, we received a shock of a different nature. Suddenly, the double doors of the bar sprang open! Then looming in the doorway, stood my co-worker (Joe Brickman). Joe was a giant of a man who stood 6'4" and weighed 240 pounds of solid muscle! At first I was happy because I thought he had come to help Bill and me defend ourselves. I arose to approach him, but as I neared him I detected something quite unusual in his behavior. He had not acknowledged my presence as I greeted him. Instead, he growled "Where is the bastard"? "They're not here yet" I answered (referring to the street gang). Joe then repeated his question, but with even greater emphasis, commenting "I said— where is the bastard"? I had completely failed to grasp the severity of this situation, so I asked "Who are you talking about, Joe"?

"I'm going to kill him," Joe responded. At this point, he reached underneath his windbreaker jacket and removed a .45 caliber automatic handgun! Now he had gotten not only my full attention, but also the full attention of everyone in the whole bar! Even the bar owner's pet cat scampered across the floor, seeking safety! Amazingly the music even stopped playing. Now all was completely quiet! Joe had not moved from the doorway, which served to block all entering and exiting of the facility. I stood dumbfounded, for never before had I envisioned myself in such a predicament! But even in facing such danger, I did not panic. I felt it would be a mistake to turn and walk away. I also felt that I should back away— either tactic just might have further incited Joe. I also felt that by maintaining my present distance, I might place myself in even greater danger, so I took a single step forward.

Now Joe had been the person holding the gun, but it

seemed he himself had panicked! The moment I stepped toward him, he cocked the weapon by quickly jacking a round into the chamber of the deadly .45! The awful sound created by this act was more than sufficient to stop the beating of one's heart. Still, I did not panic. Now we stood just two feet apart, as he jammed the cocked and fully loaded weapon into my belly! I dared not flinch or make any movement whatsoever! I understood that movement of any degree by me would certainly result in my sudden death! When Joe had jammed the .45 into my belly, he also had simultaneously begun whimpering! Now this was really great cause for alarm! Joe kept the .45 pressed into my belly, and at any instant I was certain it would fire— even if only accidentally. This would have created an opening of baseball size through my mid-section. I could not just stand there, and I could advance no further, neither could I turn away— for any such movement would have brought upon me instant death!

Therefore in a calculated effort toward resolving this most desperate situation, I resorted to carefully chosen words. So without moving any portion of my body, I spoke to Joe saying "Joe, I don't know how things are between your wife and yourself— but I do know that you have two wonderful young daughters who need and love you very much". "Think of what it would do to them if you were to fire this weapon." I said. Comprehension registered on his face, but still he did not speak. I filled the void by saying "Now I know someone must have done something really bad to you, and I'd like to help you find them". I added "And when we find them, together we will f—k them up"! "So what do you say to this idea?" I asked. Then without speaking, but with tears still in his eyes, he pointed the .45 upward before gently releasing its hammer into the chamber. He then reversed the weapon before handing it to me by its butt. I breathed a strong sigh of relief, as I cautiously reached forward to relieve Joe of this deadly weapon. Once it had been placed into my hand, I thought, *"Thank goodness"!*

I then advised Joe that I would wipe clean and return the weapon to its holding location inside our squadron commander's safe. I also suggested that he wait for me at a nearby bar until I returned for him, to begin our search for this 'wanted' individual. Joe agreed he would wait. This was the very last time I ever saw or spoke to Airman Joe Brickman! I would soon discover he had completely lost sanity immediately upon my departure from the bar. That very evening my co-worker, Joe was air-evacuated to Walter Reed Hospital in Washington, D. C. I would never again receive word of this once super airman.

Meanwhile, that fearsome street gang that had caused much concern never showed up. Hence with the exception of a brief intermission, Bill and I enjoyed the remainder of our evening. No further incidents had occurred. But now a new Monday morning was upon us. I reported for duty at my usual hour of 7:30AM. Upon entering the office I immediately made two observations— not only was Joe Brickman missing from his office, my first sergeant was also absent from his. And there was more— the door to my commander's office remained closed. I found this highly unusual, for normally our entire military staff always greeted each other immediately upon arrival. I then knocked upon the door of the commander's office, but received no response (even more unusual). I knew then that something was dreadfully wrong! I'd heard sounds of typing emanating from within the commander's office, which had never before occurred. *"Something is really wrong here"* I thought as I went about my performing normal daily duties.

At exactly 10:00AM, the door of the commander's office opened. My first sergeant appeared and approached my desk. There was no customary "Good morning" today. Instead, the first sergeant stated in his most officially-sounding voice, "Airman Van York, the commander orders you to report to him right now"! *"I'm in big trouble"* I thought, as I quickly arose in compliance with instructions. Military protocol dictated that under such circumstances, I knock once before entering the commander's office. Immediately upon hearing my knock, in an unusually stern voice, the commander ordered "Enter." I promptly approached my commander's desk. I then saluted as per military custom, saying "Sir, Airman Van York reports as ordered". Under less severe circumstances I would have then been granted "At ease airman"— but not on this day.

In the commander's office, I was left standing at rigid attention, which was a strong indication that my troubles were greater than I'd realized. The commander then immediately commenced reading from the recently prepared statement of Court-Martial Charge Sheet (DD Form 1358). "Airman First Class Jake Van York, you are hereby advised that I propose that trial by Special Court-Martial be imposed upon you effective immediately".

Upon hearing those dreadful words, my heart sank to its lowest level ever! While standing there, I recalled that awful moment in Harlingen when I had been charged with violation of the Mann Act. Today's action was slightly secondary, for if I were found guilty, I would receive only six months imprisonment, along with reduction in grade. Then at the end of my prison sentence, I would face possible separation from service. I found such drastic measures intolerable—although I was completely helpless in this situation!

The commander continued reading the charges and specifications leveled against me. In his haste to impress our commanding general by exercising rapid response coupled with decisive action, this squadron commander had completely overlooked the most vital issues of this particular case. As he read the charges against me, my spirits gradually lifted— for he had grossly erred! The captain then continued reading "At (hour unknown) on 8 June 1958, without proper authority, you removed one each .45 caliber handgun from the locked safe of your commander's office. You proceeded by unlawfully transporting said weapon into the downtown area of the city of Tachikawa, Japan. For these violations of existing military directives, you shall face trial by military Special Court-Martial"!

Ordinarily this statement would have proven devastating to me. However, over the past fourteen months my primary duty had been that of preparing and processing such charge sheets and other court-martial related documentation. During this time I had become an expert in my work; thus, I quickly realized that my over-zealous squadron commander had somehow overlooked one very important fact! When he had finished reading my charges, the captain then shoved the document across his desk, instructing me, "Sign here"! Before signing though, I read for myself the charges against me. Then having satisfied myself of the wording of this document— without comment or hesitation, I signed the Charge Sheet! My squadron commander appeared quite pleased by the fact that he'd just hooked a fish! He concluded my visit by sternly advising me, "Effective immediately, you are hereby relieved of duty within this office, so report to Personnel and find yourself another job"! I saluted the commander, and then promptly departed his office.

I cleared all of my personal belongings from my desk, and deposited them inside my room. It was approaching lunchtime, so before reporting to Base Personnel Office I would have lunch. I sought a vacant table, for I needed time to properly appraise my situation. Sure I'd signed the Charge Sheet, acknowledging acceptance of court-martial proceedings. But in so doing, I'd been fully cognizant of the fact that— I would not undergo court-martial for those charges as stated. Mainly, these charges were totally in error, although this officer had failed to recognize this fact. There were three separate issues here. First, it was Brickman who had removed and transported this weapon. Second, there were many individuals who would testify to this fact. Third (and most important) the official security record belonging to this safe indicated— I had never been issued the combination to this safe! With this evidence in my favor, no court-martial panel would ever convict me of these charges! So at this point, it appeared the only change here would be that of a new job!

At 1:00PM I found myself at Base Personnel Office, seeking a new job assignment. By 2:00 I had reported for work at my new duty section, Base Forms Management. I had been assigned to this office in the capacity of Forms

Management Specialist (for which I'd received no previous training). Might I note here— prior to assignment to such a position, a minimum of six months in technical training is required. Notwithstanding, I'd just officially become a "specialist" in this totally non-related field. My new supervisor was a technical sergeant in his late thirties. Within this work center there was only one A1C (E4) position. This slot was presently filled by a trained forms specialist. Unfortunately, within just thirty days this airman would rotate back to the United States. I was assigned as his replacement, as there was an acute personnel shortage at this skill level. There would be no possibility of my attending any technical training school. To further compound matters, the excessively heavy workload here, prevented one-on-one training by assigned personnel. Therefore career-wise, I had once again ended up in a most precarious predicament!

After receiving my welcome and initial orientation from my new supervisor, I was presented with two four-inch-thick printed Air Force training manuals. These were the manuals used in technical training schools to train airmen in the field of Forms Management. I was told "Study these thoroughly" by my supervisor. I felt awkward and out of place here in this new work environment. But since I'd been dealt this hand, I would deal with it commensurably. I found myself a seat in one corner of our office/work area, and then proceeded to familiarize myself with my new duties and responsibilities.

At 3:00PM, my concentrated study of this newly assigned field was interrupted by a call from my squadron commander's office. He had ordered that I return to his office for further action. I promptly proceeded the commander's office. Upon arrival, I underwent the same procedure as I had earlier in the day. I quickly discovered though the reason for my return visit. On the surface it would appear that my commander had experienced a change of heart. But such was not the case, for he had simply been advised of his lack of evidence to support such drastic action as Special Court-Martial. I was thrilled to find that he still had not detected his gross error in the charges. This time though, he had reduced the level of punishment from Special to Summary Court. This meant that any punishment I received would be greatly reduced. Still this wasn't satisfactory from my perspective. After verifying the charges, I again quickly signed the Charge Sheet. The commander then dismissed me to return to my new duty section. He hadn't even bothered to inquire as to how I liked my new section, but this was okay by me.

On returning to my office, my supervisor informed me, "Don't remove your hat, Captain James wants to see you right away". I turned and walked across the court to the general's offices. As I entered the office of Captain James he greeted me, saying "We've been waiting for you, Jake, come in". "Have a seat, I'll be right back" he said to me. As I sat alone, I thought, *"At least one person has greeted me on this miserable day"*. Captain James had stepped into the hallway and disappeared from view. Soon he re-entered the office, followed closely by my roommate Bill. Directly behind Bill walked another individual, mostly blocked from my view. "I think you are acquainted with this fellow standing here," said Captain James.

"Yes sir, this is my roommate, A1C Houser," I responded. The second fellow, who had remained concealed from me, was then summoned by the captain. As this person then entered my line of vision, I received my fourth surprise of the day! Standing just four feet away from me was none other than the 'hoodlum gang leader' of two nights prior! I was truly shocked by the presence of this fellow here inside the office of Captain James. I was even more dismayed by the fact that this fellow wore the insignia of staff sergeant (E5) on his uniform. He walked directly to me as though we were friends. He then enthusiastically grasped my hand, saying, "Airman Van York, I'm very happy to finally meet you— I'm Staff Sergeant Gibbs". I concealed my lingering hostilities as we warmly shook hands. I wondered *"Just how many more surprises might there be for me on this day"*? I would soon make this important discovery. Only now did my roommate speak, saying, "Jake, this is my deputy team chief". "So you guys know each other then," I said.

"Yep, we're old buddies," answered Bill. At this point, Captain James himself walked over to where I stood. He then spoke, saying "Airman First Class Jake Van York, I proudly welcome you to our newly formed Tactical Response Force". "You passed Saturday night's test with flying colors— congratulations!" he said. "I'm honored, sir, thank you very much," I replied. He spoke again, saying "Might I remind you—Tactical Response Force does not officially exist"! "Therefore, you're not to discuss any of this with anyone except me," he said. "Are we clear on this?" he asked. Clear sir," I answered.

I returned to my new work center just in time to retrieve my personal belongings before the office closed for the day. This day would prove most eventful of my entire military career! Later in the evening Bill and I returned to the bar where we'd been previously 'attacked'. Soon SSgt Gibbs arrived, accompanied by his Deputy Team Leader, (Airman First Class Summers). It seemed that not even the bar's owner had noticed our little 'incident' of Saturday evening. We ordered ourselves a bottle of red wine, as we sat together laughing and joking about the events of that evening. At one point A1C Summers commented, "I really look forward to working with you, Van York." "Same here" I replied. We had ourselves a great time there together!

By 11:00PM Bill and I had traveled to a small nearby town, little known to the GIs stationed at Tachikawa. This little village known as "Shoamai" had become our private off-base sanctuary. Through our television acting roles, we had become quite well-known here. It even felt that we were actually welcomed here. We had rented a neat two-bedroom house that was built of paper walls and straw floors, which was adequately equipped and comfortable.

In fact, this was nicer than our old house back on the farm! I enjoyed living here in privacy. I particularly enjoyed the small but intimate parties we frequently held here. So as I lay here this night, I reflected upon the day's events. First, I'd undergone two court-martial attempts. Second, I'd been fired from a job I loved, and assigned to a new career field. Lastly, I had been officially accepted into one newly formed secret military special forces group! Unfortunately, my future there depended upon the outcome of my pending court-martial. However, these thoughts were soon aborted by movement from the pretty young woman lying next to me. Ah yes— regardless of how badly my morning had begun, all was well now!

Tuesday morning found me studying manuals and

regulations back inside my new work center. At 9:00AM, I was interrupted by another summons to the office of my squadron commander. I was quite perplexed, as this call had come much too quickly. Normally, a minimum of two weeks would pass before I would be re-called for final administrative processing. Something was definitely out of order here! I reported as I had yesterday. However, I immediately detected a distinct difference in my commander's demeanor. This time, he greeted me with "At ease, Airman Van York". My level of perplexity quickly expanded, as I assumed the military position of "Parade Rest". The commander spoke, saying "I've reconsidered this matter and have decided upon Article 15 action in lieu of court-martial". Now I understood everything! Lawyers of our Base Legal Office had advised my brilliant commander that he didn't have a case. But in his strong desire to show decisive action, he refused to drop the case. So instead of no action at all, he'd opted for this simple form of non-judicial punishment. However, the maximum allowable punishment under Article 15 was significantly less than that of any Summary Court-Martial. Although, under Article 15, I would still most likely forfeit one stripe – which also was unacceptable by me. He then passed my new punishment forms to me for signature, saying, "Would you kindly sign here please". I studied the forms, carefully reading the charges and specifications once more. I was pleased to find that they had remained unchanged. I then shocked the commander by saying, to him "Sir, I strongly suggest that you go for either of the court-martials— I'm not signing any Article 15 forms"! Suddenly his face turned crimson! He stood up as he tried to speak— but he only stammered! He appeared to be on the verge of seizure! Finally he regained at least partial composure. Then while leaning forward and shaking his finger at me, he blurted, "YOU— GET OUT OF MY OFFICE RIGHT NOW— AND DON'T COME BACK"! Now I was no longer perplexed— simply deeply amused! I politely thanked the commander before immediately returning to my work center to resume studying. The remainder of my day would pass uneventfully— and I would be pleased!

I was given the opportunity to solely develop my very first form after only a week on the job. During the short time I'd been here, I had observed my co-worker as he designed and produced a variety of forms, and I felt that I could do this work. My first product had not been one hundred percent perfect, but it had met Air Force standards. My supervisor complimented me on a "job well-done". Before this month ended, I would have personally designed, drafted, and produced nearly one-half of all local forms recently originated by this office.

On June 30th 1958, the local Communist Party Chapter held an unscheduled rally. Naturally, I created the spare time needed to listen in on their proceedings. At 8:00AM their leaders arrived to give their brief motivational speech. By agreeing to work late this evening, I was able to persuade my supervisor into granting me a few hours off on this particular morning. So without delving into minute details, I recorded much of this event. During the process I gained more valuable information! Seemingly this organization had recently experienced unexpected set-backs in the distribution of their new toxic chemical formula. They had calculated that by this date, students and teachers at twelve American schools would have fallen ill from their new serum. Oddly though, not a single American had been infected by their acts of subversion. This lack of desired results had created confusion and distrust within the organization. With my recorder, I recorded these among other comments. "Comrades, the Yankees have somehow become lucky, for our treatment has failed to achieve results". The speaker continued "We are looking into this matter, and I have confidence we shall correct this problem very soon". Then after a brief pep rally, the leader and associates departed the gathering.

By 9:30AM, I had presented my latest recording to my new Tactical Commander, Captain James, and reported for duty. Today I was assigned full responsibility for local forms production. At this point I had read through all the volumes of forms directives, and strangely I'd already begun to feel somewhat comfortable in this totally new career position. Albeit, I had personally vowed that I would exert all my energy toward increasing my proficiency as a newly assigned forms management specialist.

By mid-July I had acquired a level of confidence in my abilities and skills relative to this duty. I had also received a number of compliments from my new supervisor, regarding my rapidly improving level of competence within my new career field. But most important of these considerations, I had been lauded by my new Tactical Commander, Captain James. Moreover, I was once again climbing the ladder of progression. In short, I felt good about myself.

The month of July passed very quickly, and soon we'd reached the end of the month. Prior to my having been reassigned by my squadron commander, Bill and I had taken

Wednesday afternoons as off-duty time. When I asked my supervisor if I might resume this practice, he stated, "Jake, you're doing a great job here, so you're granted Wednesday afternoons off". I thanked him gratefully (although I should have remained at work on this sunny afternoon).

Upon discovering that I'd been given the afternoon off, Bill suggested that we visit one of the four on-base enlisted member swimming pools. So after a light lunch, we arrived at our pool of choice. Once there we just lay about relaxing for the first hour. Finally, Bill dived into the large pool and then swam across to its side. I remained at my current seated location. I noticed that Bill was an excellent swimmer, and wished I had earlier learned to swim. But back where I'd come from, few kids from my neck of the woods swam. I was no exception. Still, I'd not had the courage to say to Bill, "I can't swim." I recalled dad having said to me, "Son, I learned to swim by being thrown into the river". I then thought "If this was the way dad learned, maybe it would work for me also". I could not have been more mistaken! But I'd become somewhat of a daredevil, so I would try this thing called swimming. I felt forced to do this because laying there in the sun was simply too darned hot!

Finally I gathered my courage and cautiously stepped into the shallow end of this huge pool. I figured Bill was watching me, as I had watched him. I so badly wanted to avoid making a fool of myself while there in the water. I began trying to repeat what I'd seen others do here in the pool. (After all, I'd learned to dance and drive by observing others), so quite possibly, I might learn to swim by having observed others. I would very soon discover otherwise! Slowly, I lowered myself into nearly waist-deep water, then began stroking and kicking. Undoubtedly, I would need to quickly fine-tune my technique—which is just what I tried doing. My efforts were fruitless— but I kept trying. At one point I thought, *"Maybe I need a different pair of arms and legs"*— though I kept trying. It then occurred to me, *"Jake, maybe you need a new body"*. Still, I kept trying. I was determined to learn this thing called swimming, so I kept on moving my hands and feet. Soon I found myself floundering about in five feet of water! *"Now I'll stroke my way out of here"*, I thought. My thinking was greatly flawed! I only drifted further into deeper water, and now my toes no longer touched the pool's floor! For the very first time in my entire life, I nearly panicked! I tried with all my might to stroke and kick my way out of this dangerous situation; but, my attempts were all in vain. Gradually, I found myself sinking toward the bottom of the pool! *"This can't be happening"* I thought as I struggled to rise up through at least seven feet of water. Soon my feet touched bottom and with a powerful kick, I lifted briefly to the pool's surface! But this lasted just long enough for me to gulp much-needed oxygen. I drifted through the water, realizing I had not taken in sufficient oxygen!

At this point I became truly alarmed, although I remained conscious and fully alert. My air was rapidly expiring, so I began hoping and praying for some form of miracle! Now for some reason, I seemed to no longer be able to touch bottom. But still, I could not reach the surface! For a brief moment, I seemed to hang suspended only inches from the pool's surface! Now over time, many persons have related to us how, (when near death), they'd visualized some form of unusual and unexplained bright light. At this very moment, I too stared into the bright light! In my case though, this light was that of the sun as it shined down into the crystal blue waters of this pool. I have no way of knowing how much time had passed. However, what I did know for certain was— I HAD COMPLETELY RUN OUT OF OXYGEN! Then out of pure reflex, I consciously opened my mouth, as I gasped for air— but only took in large gulps of chlorinated water!

MY END HAD SUDDENLY ARRIVED! I had not lost consciousness, so I remained aware of my predicament. Then seemingly out of nowhere a pair of hands grabbed onto me, lifting me to the surface and towing me toward the pool's edge. I'd heard two voices during this rescue effort. I clearly recognized one voice as that of my roommate Bill. The second voice seemed vaguely familiar. I certainly should have recognized it— FOR THIS WAS THE VOICE OF MY DEAR FRIEND, VINCENT CALLEN! (Matamoros). He recognized me instantly, saying "Jake, it's so good to see you— even like this"! Bill then said, "Jake, why didn't you tell me you couldn't swim"? I clutched the hands of each, as I repeatedly thanked them for having saved my life!

We remained at the pool as we chatted and rejoiced! Now in case you're wondering, I did not return into the pool! I found it odd that (now 1st Lieutenant) Callen was present at this pool. So I asked, "Vince, why is it you're at this pool"? "What do you mean?" he asked. I answered "This happens to be an enlisted member's pool— you're an officer now". "Jake, I hadn't even noticed" he laughed. He then explained that he had not noticed the posted sign. I should point out here that Vince (whom I'd saved from Mexico) was the first to reach me as I'd reached the point of drowning. Thus, it was he who had actually saved my life! My friend Bill had been just a split second later, so had Vince not been here this day I would still have been saved. During the course of our visit, I learned that Vince was passing through and would be leaving tomorrow morning. So just for once, we decided the three of us should visit the magnificent city of Tokyo. We had ourselves a grand time that evening. A total of nine years would pass before I would again encounter my friend Vincent Callen.

On August 4th, another communist party rally was held. Again I requested, and was granted, a couple of hours off. I succeeded in recording the most important activity occurring at this particular gathering. Then at the usual hour, the organizers arrived to lecture the crowd. This time the speaker revealed a new plan of operation. Their target remained unchanged; however, their tactics had been revised. I listened as the speaker referred to plans of small groups of party members physically attacking school busses carrying American students. The speaker did not outline any details of their plan before leaving the gathered crowd. Still, the sketchy bit of information I would provide to Captain James would form a starting point for our security forces. Before reporting to work, I proceeded directly to the Captain's office and presented my new tape to him. He thanked me but added, "Jake, you must tell me your secret in obtaining this information". "Maybe someday sir," I answered. He did not press me further. Before leaving his office I requested that he provide me with the names and addresses of the VIPs of this local communist chapter. He advised me to stop by the next day for this information.

The next afternoon I took a short break from work to walk across the court to my captain's office. I was pleased to find that not only had he obtained the requested listing, he had also provided me with the actual time and date of their next private meeting. It was at these meetings that this group discussed planning strategy. As he handed me the list, the captain stated, "Jake, I've provided you with the time and date of their next meeting, though I seriously doubt that you'll have any success with this. "I must inform you this place is heavily guarded, which means that you'll not get near the place." he said. He added "I must also caution you— these people are dangerous, so you must take extreme caution"! "Don't worry sir, I shall use caution," I said as I walked from his office.

Fortunately the communists' next private meeting would be conducted after my workday's end, but before the curfew hour of midnight. The meeting was scheduled for 9:00PM at a residential structure, situated on the outskirts of Tachikawa. In preparation for this highly sensitive bit of reconnaissance, I'd already carefully surveyed the local area. On the preceding Monday evening I had parked my bike here, before walking this street while doing a bit of 'window shopping'. By the time I'd finished my 'shopping spree' I'd accurately measured the distance of one-half mile from the site of the scheduled meeting. It so happened that a restaurant and coffee shop stood at this spot, so I chose the coffee shop for my purposes. At exactly 8:45 that Wednesday evening, I sat at a far corner table at this small shop. And although I did not drink Saki, I ordered a small cup. As I sat sipping from this sizzling hot drink, I made the final preparations for my 'visit' to the communist party's little meeting. All attendees were punctual, allowing the meeting to commence sharply at 9:00PM. I sat quietly and patiently, sipping Saki— and listening to the familiar voice of the party's leader. Over the course of the next two hours I would fill four thirty-minute tapes with sensitive information. First on the speaker's agenda was reiteration of the general plan for attacks upon school busses carrying American school children. Next, he unsuspectingly provided me the minute details of this master plan. So when this meeting ended, I'd been given the locations, bus routes, dates, and exact times of planned attacks. This information would prove invaluable to Captain James in his efforts to interrupt, influence, and foil in-country communist activities. While inside this coffee shop, I had busied myself in reading from a local newspaper. Now I folded my paper, summoned my waitress, and then paid for my Saki. The polite waitress bowed sweetly as we said "Good evening" (in the language of the Japanese). Outside, I mounted my Yamaha and rode directly to my house in Shoamai.

The next morning while at work, I paid a short visit the office of Captain James. I found him anxiously awaiting my latest report. "Morning, Jake, come in," he said. "Any luck last night?" "Sorry sir, no luck," I lied. "I thought not" he said, obviously trying to conceal disappointment. He spoke again, saying "This was too much to ask of you anyway— it was an impossible task". I'd taken the precaution of concealing the four small tapes inside my hat, so he had not seen them. I then said, "Well, sir, guess I'd better be getting back to work". He stood up as he reached to shake my hand, saying "Don't worry we'll get these guys somehow". At this point, I could not hold my secret any longer. So as

I turned to leave, I turned back and presented to him the four small tapes. With a somewhat stunned look upon his face, he asked, "What are these"? Then as nonchalantly as possible, I replied, "Oh, those are the minutes from last night's meeting". His jaw nearly fell to the floor! "You're telling me you recorded their meeting?" he asked. "The whole thing sir," I said, adding, "Sorry to have pulled your leg a bit". "Well, I'll be gosh darned!" he exclaimed. He then said "Jake, you've just done the impossible"! He then gave me one unusually vigorous handshake. I returned to my office and resumed work. Needless to say, I felt really great about this accomplishment— for the well-being of large numbers of American kids could ultimately be pre-served.

I worked through the remainder of the month with no further distractions or interruptions. Soon we entered the month of September, meaning in less than sixty days I would find myself back inside the United States. Also, at the beginning of this month my office received a newly as-signed forms management specialist. This addition would dramatically reduce my current workload. The new fellow was also an A1C (E4) same as myself. For some reason he seemed to really like my bike, and asked to give it a test-drive. "Are you sure you can ride this bike?" I asked. "I used to own one exactly like this one," he answered. I reluctantly handed him the keys. He took the bike around the base for a quick spin. When he returned he asked, "How much would you take for it"? "Six hundred dollars," I exaggerated. "Give you five right now," he replied. "Five-fifty, and you've got a deal." I said. "Sold" he replied. We received permission to proceed to our nearby Base Legal Office to prepare the bill of sale. Upon completion we rode to our dorm, where he counted out the equivalent of $550. Tom (the new airman) then gave me a lift back to our duty section, riding his sharp newly purchased bike. For the remainder of the day I felt as though I'd just lost a dear friend. I called my friend Bill and informed him of the sale of my bike. Upon hearing of my loss, he commented, "I know where you can get a new one at a great price". "Great, let's check it out right after work," I replied. After work Bill and I rode his bike to the downtown cycle shop.

At the cycle shop, we checked bike after bike. Finally, I ran across one that I really loved. This was a beautiful 750cc Triumph, and totally new. After a bit of customary negotiation, I purchased this new bike for the equivalent of only $750 dollars. Now I felt whole again! With me riding my fancy new bike, Bill and I picked up our lady friends and then took ourselves a long ride through the countryside. Upon returning to our residence and bathing, I enjoyed several hours of intense sexual pleasure before finally falling asleep.

The months of September and October would become the most unforgettable periods of my lifetime! During these two months my workload dramatically lessened, allowing me lots of off-duty time in which to visit locations I would have otherwise never experienced. Also, no communist party rallies or meeting were held during either of these two months. This group had apparently become completely disorganized (at least temporarily). I had learned from Captain James that the leaders and organizers of this subversive group had all been arrested and imprisoned for indefinite periods of time. Now total distrust ranged throughout this local communist chapter! Thus as a direct result of information provided by me, vast improvement relating to the safety of American dependents was realized. Therefore, the Elm would be allowed to rest inside its holding candle for the remainder of my stay here in beautiful Japan!

Alas, the most dreaded day of my life finally arrived,— October 30th 1958! I had arrived in Japan during nighttime hours. Likewise, I also departed during nighttime hours. I had arrived during periods of heavy rainfall. I also departed during a period of heavy rainfall. A full eighteen months had passed and much had occurred. During this time I had matured considerably. When I arrived here, my level of naivety had remained constant at ninety-five percent. At the time of departure, this level had dropped to just fifty percent. (In coming months, I would work diligently at reducing this unwanted level even further)!

At 9:30PM on that unbearably sad Thursday evening, my flight took off from Tachikawa on its long twenty-three hour return flight to Travis AFB, California. Then having again crossed the International Date Line, I arrived back on Travis AFB at 8:00PM of that very same evening. I must say here— this was my once-in-a-lifetime experience in such travel. After having crossed the globe, we'd arrived in California— (at the hour of take-off from Japan)! This was a bit much for this young country dirt farmer to chew upon!

I remained at Travis AFB (Fairfield, CA) over the weekend, for I wanted to revisit San Francisco. So for the next two days, I entertained myself by riding streetcars up and down the hills of this picturesque city. At the end of two days, I decided to remain here for another two days. Then on Tuesday afternoon (Nov 4, 1958) I left the city of Fair-field heading once again to Harlingen, TX. This act alone would provide one hundred percent proof of my unusually high level of personal naivety. I'm sure no one else on earth would have made such a stupid move! Once again, I rode commercial bus over this entire trip, for I still wanted to witness the countryside. We rode for what had seemed an eternity, but I thoroughly enjoyed every waking minute of this long trip. I was quite lucky to see that spectacular site known as the Grand Canyon. Along the way we passed through famous cities such as Phoenix and Albuquerque. And as could be expected, I marveled at the wonders of each city through which we passed. My goal of seeing the world was rapidly being realized.

After having ridden for four long days, I arrived back in Harlingen shortly after 3:00PM on Friday. Before leaving Japan, I'd taken the liberty of verifying my 'wonderful wife's' current address through the monthly income allotment I'd provided for her. I had known all along that this trip would prove to be a complete waste of time and money; still, curiosity caused me to want to investigate the current situation here. I had not informed Francine of my planned trip for we never wrote to each other— even once! Now as we neared the vicinity of her current residence, I felt apprehensive. I seemed to have heard a tiny voice asking, *"Jake, what did you come here for"*? I was here now though, and there was no turning back! As my taxi rounded the corner of her street, I instantly spotted her. She was sitting on the steps of her front porch, holding a conversation with another young female next-door neighbor. Although this was the month of November, this was Harlingen, so the weather was still sunny and warm. She seemed to have been expecting me, as the very instant my taxi appeared she took notice. By this time we had parked in front of her tiny apartment.

Upon recognizing me, Francine immediately ran out to greet me. She seemed genuinely happy to see me, although nothing could have been farther from the truth. We hugged as we greeted each other. Then as soon as I'd paid my taxi, she excused herself from her neighbor before rushing me into the house. Thirty seconds later, Francine's bed was wildly bouncing about the bedroom! We kept up the frenzied action for the next two hours. After our physical encounter, we showered and went out on the town. She did not have a car and neither did I, so we used city bus transportation. We spent most of the evening in dancing and socializing at my favorite spot— (The Corner).

After returning to the apartment, we spent the remainder of the night by partying in bed. The next afternoon I made the grave mistake of taking her shopping in the downtown area. Again, we used the city bus, which took us directly past the home of her family. I thought it strange that she had made no mention of them, but I made no comment. That evening we went out again. This time though we went across town, instead of to my favorite spot. We chose a club and entered. I ordered drinks for the two of us. We then danced once. At this point I visited the restroom. As I returned toward our booth, Francine met me at the midway point. She very casually said, "Jake, I'm going to ride across town with the girls for a minute, I'll be right back". "Okay, I'll wait for you right here," I said. This was the last time I saw her— for she never returned! She'd had no intention of ever returning! At about midnight, I checked my watch. I recalled that she had left at 9:00PM. Three hours had passed, but she was nowhere in sight. Luckily, I had placed the apartment keys in my pocket, so I caught the last bus back to her place. I found no one at home when I arrived. There were no thoughts of her having gone missing, so I patiently went to bed. There would be no sexual pleasures for me this night! I lay awake in bed for several hours, finally falling asleep at about 5:00 Sunday morning. I remained in bed until noon, at which time I washed up and showered. Then I made myself a light sandwich, which I downed with fruit juice. All the while, Francine had not shown up or even called. This was the character of the woman I'd been forced to marry!

After dressing I once again took the city bus to an area near the home of a former co-worker whom I'd considered a friend. I was lucky in that I found him relaxing at home that afternoon. As we sat chatting, he brought me up to date regarding the activities of my so-called wife during my eighteen-month absence. I was shocked at the story! He informed me that Francine had returned to Harlingen within two weeks of having left. She had immediately moved into her current apartment in San Benito, but she did not live alone for very long. Within two weeks, her step-father had left his wife, (Francine's mom), and moved in with Francine. My friend told me of the many days when Francine's mom would stand on the street in front of Francine's apartment, begging her husband to come out of her daughter's bedroom! Up to this point in my young life, I'd never heard of such repulsive behavior as Francine's. But even worse, I would soon discover that this was only the resumption of previous similar behavior between these two most despicable individuals. At this point I began to comprehend the reasons for the previously baggy reddened eyes, Francine's mom constantly displayed. This poor woman had been driven to tears each and every day of her miserable middle-aged life! All the sadness had been caused primarily by her lone daughter. Francine had been the engineer and driving force of this adulterous relationship since the early age of fourteen! Her immorality had been the primary reason for her having been forced upon me! I would discover that her wretched grandmother had so desperately wanted Francine married, she had engineered our marriage. Francine had been the plaintiff— I the victim, and it had nearly worked!

After spending the afternoon at my friend's house, I rode the bus across town to the local train station. While there, I purchased a one-way ticket to Reno on tomorrow afternoon's express train. I would leave Harlingen (for the last time) at 1:00PM. At this time, I so desperately wanted-ed to travel in the opposite direction to the home of my parents. Unfortunately, I was too absolutely ashamed to even consider such a visit! While in downtown Harlingen, I made a solo visit to a nice family-owned Mexican restau-rant to kill time, for I was also too ashamed to visit The Corner lounge!

Shortly before midnight, I returned to the lonely apart-ment which had been temporarily vacated by Francine. For-tunately there was at least TV to watch, for this would be my only means of entertainment. Again this night I found it virtually impossible to sleep. I kept thinking, *"Maybe she will at least show up before I leave here tomorrow"*. My thoughts were completely off-course— for she did not show up.

At 9:00 Monday morning (November 3rd) I once more arose, washed up, and showered. This morning I dressed appropriately for my lengthy train ride to Reno, Nevada. I then sat around the apartment, hoping that Francine might still show up— but no such luck! At 11:00, I hailed a taxi cab, and then headed for the home of Francine's grandmother. I found this old woman sitting inside her car in their front driveway. She had not noticed my arrival, for she'd sat with her head lowered. I thought that she might've been asleep or even, (hopefully, worse). I was wrong in both assumptions. She had merely been pondering the current situation of her family. I could readily see that she appeared despondent, although I felt absolutely no sympathy for her. As I reached her car, only then did she detect my presence. I did not wish to even greet her, but I managed the utterance of "Morning". The old woman stared blankly at me, asking, "When did you get here"? "Friday afternoon" I answered. The old wretch remained silent, so I quickly took advantage of the moment. I spoke, saying "I just dropped by to let you know that Francine is somewhere shacked up with her boyfriend". "I haven't seen or heard from her since Saturday evening." I added. "I know where she is, and I know who she is with— her stepfather!" commented the old woman. "I just wanted to let you know," I said. I turned to walk away, but she quickly called out to me asking "Can we talk for just a minute"? "I guess," I reluctantly replied. "Then get in for a moment— I want to tell you a few things," she said. Grudgingly, I entered her car but left its door ajar. The old woman began her long awaited confession by asking "Do you have any idea how and why you ended up married to Francine"? "Not really," I replied. "Well, I will tell you" she said. "I knew long before you, that you would take Francine into Mexico that day. You see, I planned the whole thing! I knew the time you would leave and I knew the time you would return. I also knew the route you would take. So that afternoon, we waited for you. I even paid Baines money to take you down there and bring you back"!

There, she had said all these shocking things to me— but she never even once apologized. The word "angry" comes nowhere near to describing my emotions at that moment, but I exercised extreme self-discipline in my response. Without speaking, I exited her vehicle. She sat as if wondering what to say or do next. I then turned and faced as I said, "All that planning and execution— still, you failed to collect on the insurance policy". Her jaw suddenly sagged as she gazed at me, asking. "How did you know"? I did not answer. Instead, I simply returned to my waiting taxi and happily rode away! I would not see these wretches— ever again!

Chapter 7

Romance in Reno

Having once again enjoyed the magnificent scenery and sights between Texas and Nevada, I arrived in "The Biggest Little City In The World"— Reno, Nevada. I arrived here shortly before 6:00PM, Thursday afternoon. Immediately upon stepping from my train, I sensed the heavy chill in the air. As I looked about, I marveled at the majestic snow-covered mountain ranges, glistening in the distance. Although, I was somewhat disappointed by the fact that I'd not seen any mountains resembling the magnificent Mt Fuji. This was not Japan (much to my regret) but at the same time, neither was it Harlingen (much to my delight)!

I hailed a cab and took the scenic thirteen-mile ride south to Stead Air Force Base. Then after fifteen minutes of winding, weaving, climbing and dipping, my taxi arrived at the main gate of this sprawling military installation. I proceeded to the on-base transit quarters, where I was assigned a room for the next few days. Since I'd arrived here nearly twenty-five days ahead of schedule, I decided I would not sign-in for duty until the coming Monday afternoon. This would allow me to leisurely visit this especially exciting little city. The base dining facility had already closed for the day, so I sought directions to the nearby base snack bar. While there I downed a couple of burgers along with a large soda, which would sustain me through the night. I found myself quite anxious to travel into the city, but there was no taxi service or bus transportation from the base; thus, I remained on base over-night. This would be my fourth night in nearly eighteen months, sleeping alone! As I lay there in my bed, I wondered, *"How will I make it through this night"?* Albeit, I would survive!

Before proceeding, please allow me to explain exactly how I happened to end up here in Reno, Nevada. Four months prior to rotation from Japan, I was summoned to my Base Personnel Office (CBPO) and instructed to initiate forecast action. In following this procedure, I would list (in order of personal preference) five separate CONUS bases to which I cared to be assigned. However, I was the sole enlisted person on the base at Tachikawa to have declined mandatory forecast action. This was strictly out of the ordinary; however, I had succeeded in convincing the sergeant in charge of assignments, that this would be just a waste of time. I accomplished this by telling him "Sarge, you and I both know full well that no matter which bases I forecast for, — the Air Force will ultimately send me to wherever it wants me to go". After considering my comments, the sergeant said, "I have to agree with you on this point". He then allowed me to ignore forecasting requirements.

Under established procedures, I would have been forced to forecast by listing five bases of preference. Then after two months, I would have received an assignment of the Air Force's choosing. But since I'd failed to forecast, I received no such assignment. Instead, my personnel office was provided a listing of four separate and available bases. Amazingly, I was presented this listing and told, "Take your pick of these four". Now, I strongly believe that this procedure had never before, or has never since, occurred. This assignment listing read as follows: (1) Langley, VA; (2) Fort Belvoir, VA; (3) Seattle, WA; and (4) Reno, NV. I really wanted to accept the assignment to Langley (CIA headquarters), for I'd felt that such an assignment would prove both interesting and exciting. However, I had learned of the opportunities for obtaining divorce by obtaining Nevada residency. My primary concern was to free myself from the tentacles of the wretch I'd been forced to marry! I knew that by relocating to Reno, I would facilitate this endeavor. Therefore, I reluctantly skipped Langley and the next two assignments, then placed an X next to Reno, NV. I am confident that had I completed the standard forecast action, I would have been reassigned to the base located at Langley, VA.

This was the method through which I'd presently found myself here in this lonely bed on Stead Air Force Base, Nevada. This assignment would necessitate that I make major adjustments in both my lifestyle and mental state. First of all, I was no longer happily situated within some hedonistically-oriented metropolitan area! To the contrary, I was presently in the heart of the Sierra Desert. No longer were there strings of fancy bars just outside the gates. No longer were there countless cute young girls, catering to my every whim. But one of the truly most depressing considerations was— I was no longer afforded personal housekeeping services. This meant that I would return to maintaining my own shoes and living quarters. But worst of all, I would resume standing in early-morning inspection formations. I'd often heard it said, "We don't miss our water— until the well runs dry". Well, I now realized that THE WELL HAD JUST RUN DRY!

The very next day (Friday) I slept in for awhile, and at noon I went to the sole dining hall for lunch. This definitely bore no similarity to the fabulous base of Tachikawa. On that base there were four separate fine dining halls at my disposal. Here, there was only one such facility— and even this did not provide waitress service. *"What a bummer"* I thought upon entering the place. Now my loneliness and despair had suddenly returned, and I would have given my right arm to be back in Japan. As I moved slowly through the serving line, I looked about the dining hall hoping to see some familiar face. Strangely, luck was on my side!

As I walked toward a vacant table, I spotted a three-striper (E4), same as myself, whom I had on several occasions seen in downtown Tachikawa. We had never spoken to each other, although we had always acknowledged our presence with a simple nod and smile. We repeated this courtesy on this day as I walked to my vacant table. No sooner than I'd seated myself did this fellow rise and move toward my table, so I sincerely welcomed him! At this very moment, I missed my roommate and close friend Bill so very much. This virtual stranger seated himself, saying, "Hello, you must be Jake". I nearly fell to the floor! *"How could this fellow have known my name?"* I wondered. "Yes, I'm Jake" I answered, adding, "I've seen you around lots of times, but we've never gotten to speak to each other". "I'm glad to finally meet you" he said, adding "I'm Bill". *"This is unbelievable*", I thought. *"Not another Bill"!* I seemed to have heard my mind say to me. Over the next half hour, as we sat talking while eating, Bill LeGrande and I became instant friends! And over time, he would prove himself even more of a friend than my former roommate—, Bill Houser. He also would quickly reveal his character as that of a true gentleman. At the end of our meal, Bill invited me into the city of Reno so that I might get a full view of this famous location. Naturally, I eagerly accepted his offer— for otherwise, I would have been completely lost in this town. So that evening, my new friend Bill and I departed the base and took the nearly twenty- minute drive into this unique and magnificent city of Reno.

Upon arrival in the downtown area, I found Reno to be slightly reminiscent of the fabulous city of Tokyo. Both cities were highly ornamented with decorative neon lighting. But this was where the similarities abruptly ended. Here in Reno, I received no 'royal welcome' from cute young ladies. To the contrary, no one here seemed to realize or even care that I'd shown up here in this city. Still, I was totally fascinated by the glamour and glitter of this great little city. Bill parked his fancy new Lincoln automobile at the city's most popular casino. From there we walked to and visited a large number of fancy casinos, which was a completely new experience for me. I found myself in awe of the blackjack tables and crap tables. But since I had not yet been introduced to this vice of gambling, I merely stood around and watched as others played these games. Soon I too would try my luck (or lack thereof).

After having visited gaming casinos for several hours, Bill and I drove across town to an area that contained bars and nightclubs. We would spend the remainder of the evening here in these clubs. Incidentally, this would become my very first full night in roaming the streets. Unlike Japan, there was no midnight curfew here, which meant everyone remained on the streets throughout each night of every week! It would take awhile before I would become adjusted to such night life. During the evening, my friend introduced me to several charming young ladies. And before the night had ended, I had danced with each of them at least once. Unfortunately though, there would be no sex for me on this night.

At 7:00AM, and after having been on my feet throughout the night, we returned to the base to get our much-needed sleep. At 4:00 of that very same day, I found myself once again visiting casinos, bars, and clubs. Now the winter had set upon us, and temperatures hovered just above zero. Nevertheless, this in no way, restricted our movement. This time when we reached the downtown area, Bill swung by to pick up his girlfriend, (Cheryl). This was an attractive and charming young lady, in her mid-twenties. We then drove to their favorite night spot, where I decided to take control of my own destiny, by moving about and meeting available young ladies on my own. Soon Bill approached me saying, "Jake, Cheryl and I are going across town for about an hour, but we'll be back soon, okay"? "That's fine, I'll be here when you return," I answered. Now I was no longer so very naïve, so I needed not ask where these two were going, or what they would do once they'd arrived. But soon I found myself completely alone in my strange new environment.

I struggled to act natural as I moved about the club

while chatting and dancing with several of the ladies there. Then for some reason, I was invited to join two couples who were sitting together at a nearby table. So for the lack of anything better to do, I joined them. I quickly learned that the couples were married. This left me feeling like an outsider, but each of the four was friendly and hospitable toward me, so I forced myself to relax and enjoy their hospitality. At this point, I'd had absolutely no way of knowing about the nature of the kinky bet which the husbands had made concerning my orientation.

As time progressed, the two husbands informed me that they were about to return home in anticipation of a small party. They invited me to join them at the home of one couple. My instincts alerted me that I should decline their officer, so I said "My friends, I would love to join you, but I promised my buddy I would wait here for him". At this point, Jay (the senior male) said, "Come with us and we promise you will enjoy yourself". Then his buddy Crane chimed in, saying, "We'll bring you back when you're ready leave". Well, I knew that these were military couples, which meant there was little chance of their wanting to harm me; thus, I decided to join them (but just for a short while).

Across town, Crane and his wife quickly welcomed me into their modest home. Crane himself made drinks for everyone, while his wife Brenda placed an assortment of music onto their stereo. I had initially expected that some cute female neighbor might soon come over. My expectations would not be fulfilled, for no one else would visit us on this early evening. So we just sat around making small talk and occasionally dancing. It had felt great once again being in the presence of other Americans. Fifteen minutes later, Jay announced that he and Bobby Crane would return to the downtown area for just a few minutes. Abruptly both men stood and walked from the living room. I too quickly grabbed my hat, intending to accompany them. But once we reached Jay's car, both he and Bobby urged me to remain with their wives until their return. I strongly sensed that something was not quite right and tried protesting— but to no avail. Jay said, "We'll be back in an hour, so sit tight". Although his buddy Bobby quickly corrected him by saying, "We'll be back in two hours, Jake". "But what am I gonna do here for two long hours?" I asked. Then in answer to my seemingly innocent question, with a slight wink Bobby commented, "You're a man— aren't you, Jake"? At this point, and without awaiting my response, they drove away as I stood watching them.

I returned while somewhat bewildered into their house. Back inside, Christie and Brenda took turns dancing and flirting with me. Soon we had emptied our first bottle of sparkling wine. By now the ladies had become emboldened to the point each had made continuous amorous advances toward me. Christie (Jay's wife) was the first to disrobe. Her brazen act seemed to have heightened the desires of Brenda, for she also immediately followed Christie's lead. But I would remain a true gentleman, at least until they feverishly began removing my clothing also. Soon the three of us were caressing, kissing, and touching each other in the most erotic way. This was only the prelude to the ensuing sex orgy! Over and over I made love to each of these lovely ladies. Finally though common sense prevailed, causing me to at least temporarily suspend our new-found three-way love affair! Only at this point did I feel properly welcomed to this great little city known as Reno.

Shortly before 10:00PM, Jay and Bobby dropped me off back in downtown Reno, but before I left, they literally begged me to admit to having engaged in intimate activity with their wives. At first, I adamantly denied their charges. But then, they assured me that this was their kind of open lifestyle. In short, these two couples were what is commonly referred to today as swingers! I concealed my great shock at discovering their little secret. But I had not yet discovered that I would soon become the full-time lover of each of these two very attractive women. Then adding greater spice to this rare equation, I would become close friends with Christie's husband. I would also establish an ongoing friendship with Brenda's husband, Bobby.

Back at the night club, I rejoined my friend Bill and his girlfriend Cheryl. No mention was made of my recent whereabouts, or the activity in which I'd been engaged. While there at our table, there entered one particularly young couple, and the young woman instantly caused each male present to look her way, in admiration and desire. The charming young man with her achieved similar results from other women present. I soon learned that these were friends of Bill and Cheryl. They approached our table and sat with us. The young woman's name was Samantha (Sam to her friends). The young man's name was Darrell, and he too was military. Darrell had removed his top coat, but Samantha had kept hers on— and completely buttoned. I did not give this much thought though, thinking that she was probably still somewhat cold. As we sat talking and laughing together, Samantha stole frequent admiring glances at me. Might I point out here, I had dressed exceptionally well for this (or any) occasion. Also, few women would have chased me from their bedroom (based upon looks). So I had grown accustomed to having lovely women notice me. The five of us then spent an enjoyable several hours together.

On Sunday I arose, washed up, and showered. I then located the recreation center, where I knew there would be coffee, tea, and fresh doughnuts. Afterwards, I shot a few games of billiards with a few of the guys. By now, I was holding my own quite well. My new friend Bill and I had previously agreed to meet at noon at our base dining hall for lunch. We each arrived at exactly noon hour. After lunch we once again headed into Reno. Today we would visit a few different casinos. The excitement and mystique of the gaming tables served as strong lures to me, but I exercised discipline and refrained from joining the games. Thus, I simply stood by on the sidelines as I observed the action.

Later we drove across town to the Cheryl's home. Upon reaching Cheryl's apartment, I learned that she had cooked. I also learned that we would have an additional guest, although no one would inform me as to identity of this mystery guest. Then shortly, my curiosity ended with the ring of Cheryl's doorbell. When the doorbell rang, Cheryl coyly asked "Jake, would you answer the doorbell please"? Without protest, I quickly obliged. Upon opening the door, I was totally stunned! Standing there before me was none other than the beautiful and sexy Samantha from the evening before. She was just as radiant as on the day before, but today she wore a different full-length fur coat. I would soon discover that Sam possessed different fur coats for each day of the week. I would match her dress though by wearing a different tailored suit each day of the week. She greeted me warmly, brushing past me as she quickly stepped inside from the cold of this November month. I caught a strong whiff of fragrance from her expensive perfume. Her alluring presence served as an indisputable reminder that I was truly back in the USA! She surprised me by allowing me to remove her topcoat, a deviation from yesterday.

After a bit of small talk with Cheryl and Bill, who had busied themselves in their small kitchen, she joined me on the couch. I pretended to be unaffected by her beauty, but I'm sure she saw right through my defenses. I calmly poured her a glass of red (sweet) wine which she wasted no time in sipping from. The living room's lighting had been dimmed and soft and romantic music flowed from the stereo. Out of curiosity I inquired about her date of the previous evening. She assured me that she and Darrell were only casual friends. I found this hard to believe, for they seemed to have been such a loving couple. So I said to her "Samantha, I thought the two of you might even have been engaged or married". "Nothing of the sort," she quipped. She then shocked me by quickly adding "If you're wondering if he's my lover, my answer is yes— but only on a part-time basis". "Why just part-time?" I asked. "I find that he's not really my type," she answered. "So just what is your type?" I questioned. "Jake, if you're my type, we'll soon know— but if you're not, then it doesn't matter," she answered. Then there was just silence between us, as she sat staring deeply into my eyes. Without comment, I pulled her roughly into my arms, fervently kissing her full on the mouth. She did not recoil, but instead returned my embrace and kiss with even greater fervor and desire!

Evidently our silence had aroused the curiosity of both Cheryl and Bill, for they peered into the living room. By this time Samantha and I were oblivious to our surroundings, and were engaged in a heated session of petting. Upon noticing our erotic behavior, Cheryl called out, "Hey, you two, there's a free bedroom just down the hall"! Without even bothering to answer, I scooped Samantha up and carried her into the spare bedroom. Then before I'd had time to even remove my tie, Samantha had removed her dress, which was the single garment she had worn. Seeing her this way immensely heightened my desire for her, so I hurriedly removed my clothing. She immediately pounced upon me like a wild animal. In retrospect, she herself had suddenly become this wild and uncontrollable animal! But I matched her lustful attack with one of my very own. Then for the next full hour, we pleasured each other's mind and body to our fullest extent! Now please forgive me if in any way, I appear as bragging. I assure you this is not my intent, for I merely wish to appraise you of certain aspects of my younger life.

Later, we two couples sat together for our (slightly delayed) dinner of Chinese food. Samantha had suddenly become "Sam" to me, for we had just now become close friends! Cheryl and Bill were mature individuals, so neither teased us over our recent behavior. To the contrary, they congratulated Sam for having finally found herself a suitable lover! This new relationship would last for the next thirty full months. After our dinner, the four of us went out into the city for a most wonderful evening. At Bill's favorite nightclub, we ran into Darrell (Sam's former part-time lover), who joined us at our table for a short while. I suppose he had expected to leave with Sam, but she immediately advised him of our new relationship, (which he accepted) in his gentlemanly manner. I admired this young fellow because I don't believe I would have displayed his composure in this sensitive matter. Then seemingly having realized that all had ended between Sam and himself, he soon politely left our table.

At 2:00AM on Monday morning, Bill and I drove the ladies home and returned to the base. This had been a great weekend for me. I then slept for just two hours before quickly washing up and showering. After rushing my breakfast, I proceeded to my new local personnel office for two days of base in-processing actions. The young sergeant in charge advised me that since I'd arrived on base three weeks earlier than expected, there was not yet a position for me. He further advised me that I would be assigned to the work center having the greatest need. Consequently, I was assigned to the office of Base Redistribution and Marketing—*"What an impressive title"* I thought. Actually, this particular work center served as this base's junk yard!

Thus, after having served in positions up to and including that of the Commanding General's Office, here I'd ended up working in the base junk yard. So after completing in-processing, I walked to the far edge of our base, where I successfully located my new duty section. This was a rather small unit, when considering its mission (maintenance of the unwanted supplies and equipment of the base). Upon initially reporting here, I was deeply disappointed by what

I saw. Moreover, this work center was a real mess! Materials and equipment lay about in total disarray. Nothing was properly organized. But making matters worse, the civilian supervisor here was merely biding his time, as he eagerly awaited his retirement. The two assigned airmen had clearly indicated no dedication whatsoever to this organization. Hence, only the wise words of my dad provided me with the tools necessary for surviving this particular duty. I recalled those words in which he said "Son, even if you end up becoming only a digger of ditches, make sure you're the best darned ditch digger of all". I currently found it necessary to apply dad's words of wisdom. I worked my first three days at this new job mainly by assisting and observing. Specifically, I helped the other two airmen as they unloaded junk from large trucks. I thought, *"Jake Van York, this is a far cry from that of Airborne Radio Operator"*, (my original career classification). However, at the very same time I fully realized that even this menial work was far better than plowing some old mule back on the farm. Therefore, I would attempt to create vastly improved work conditions here within this work center.

Thursday morning had arrived. I reported as usual to work, but today I would attempt a new tactic. So as we three airmen huddled together in our tiny outdoor yard shack, I struck upon a new and different conversation. First, I inquired about the skills and background of each of our two airmen. Next I asked "How do you guys like working here"? I received exactly the same answer from each: "I'm just waiting for an assignment out of here"! This was the response I'd anticipated. So I said, "But do you realize we can make things a whole lot better for ourselves while we're here"? "What do you mean?" they responded. "I've noticed that we spend at least half of our time helping customers in locating items". Each fellow simply looked at me as though I might have lost it. I took advantage of their silence by saying "If we would spend the next two days properly arranging and placing this equipment, we would find our job here much easier". "So what do you suggest?" asked the oldest member of our small team. "I suggest that we spend the next few days arranging and labeling this equipment inventory" I answered. I detected no protest from either airman so I concluded, "Let's give this a try, shall we"? The least that might happen is— we'll warm ourselves up." I added.

We promptly began the major project of arranging and organizing this previously congested work center. For the next two full days, we spent the majority of our time arranging equipment. We had not informed our supervisor of this endeavor, and he had not bothered to walk outside to check on us. Neither of my two helpers possessed administrative skills, which required that I produce and place equipment identification signs throughout the area. We worked closely with each other and made rapid progress. Then by 3:00 on Friday afternoon we'd completed our project. Now we walked proudly about, as we admired our work. Only when we had finished our job, did I suggest to my team that they invite our supervisor outside to view our newly renovated work center! The older of the two airmen summoned our lead official. Soon he returned, accompanied by our supervisor. Upon entering our building the kindly old gentleman stood in shock, as he witnessed this unbelievable transformation! All equipment and shelves had been completely cleaned, rearranged, and identified by boldly printed and properly positioned signs. Now anyone desiring an equipment item would be able to locate it within seconds, as opposed to searching for hours. Needless to say, our supervisor was highly pleased by this major improvement.

My second week here began a new phase of relaxed and pleasant work. Suddenly our work center received numerous laudatory comments concerning the new and highly professional environment here at our Base Redistribution and Marketing activity. Our supervisor received compliments from many officers and non-commissioned officers of the base. Remarkably, his position and status were quickly elevated. As our reward, my team and I were afforded large amounts of time-off from work. Naturally, our innovative actions would enhance promotion opportunity for the two airmen assigned within this work center.

Two more weeks had passed, so now we'd reached Monday Nov 24th. I was released from work at noon November 26 through the 30th. My friend Bill voluntarily loaned his new Lincoln to me for use during daytime hours. So for the next four days I combed the casinos of Reno for much of each day. Of course I programmed time for visits with Christie and Brenda during each of these days. Afterwards I would return to the base, where I would eat, shower, and dress appropriately for my evening out on the city with Samantha. So at 8:00 each evening Bill and I would return to the city, where we would resume our social activities.

During the brief period of time I had known Samantha (Sam), I'd known her to be a happy and fun-loving young lady. However, during this final week of November she had become quite pensive. I'd made several unsuccessful attempts at getting her to confide in me. Each time, she became even further distant. I began feeling *"Maybe she's tired of me already"*. I would soon discover that this was not at all the case. Finally' when we were completely alone one evening, she revealed her unusual and overwhelming problem!

As Samantha began speaking to me about this most tragic of situations, her entire body began trembling. As I sat quietly listening to her story, I also quickly became distressed. She began by telling me of a charming young man, who had one year earlier befriended her. "At first, he seemed so very nice— he was charming, gentle, sweet, and warm. I felt protected and cared for when I was with him. During our first three months together, we shared blissful happiness— and soon I was madly in love. Then very quickly his personality completely changed. No longer was he this warm and caring person I once knew. All of a sudden, he turned cold, calculating, and uncaring— but I was so in love. I couldn't resist him, and he knew this. Then he became more distant, even trying to get me to prostitute myself for him. I became totally distraught and depressed. I didn't know who to turn to for help." she said. She hesitated slightly as she pondered how best to continue. Finally her young body convulsed, as she blurted, "And then the worst happened"! He forced me to have sex with two guys while he filmed us together. When it was over, I sat alone sobbing— but then he kissed me and told me that he loved me very much, and this made me feel a little better." she said. "But I had seen him pocket two one hundred-dollar bills from these guys. And though I loved him very much, I told him that I could not repeat what I had just done. This angered him deeply, even to the point where he began to beat me with his fists. But even after suffering such pain and indignity, I stayed with him." she said. She continued, "I had hoped against hope that I could talk him out of this, but the following week he brought home another two guys! I tried to protest, but he threatened to do me serious bodily harm, so what else could I do except go along with him?" she sobbingly concluded. I sat dumbfounded as I listened to her dreadful story. But she wasn't finished.

At this point, it seemed Sam was happy to have finally revealed this problem, so she continued speaking. "After this second incident I became hysterical— and this was when he violently raped me, in every imaginable way! I had sustained physical injury, so I sought prompt medical treatment. Afterwards, I reported the incident to local police. They then immediately arrested Frankie, but found that he'd had an airtight alibi. So of course, they had no choice but to release him. Now he was furious at me, and attacked once more— but even more violently this time! Again I received medical treatment before reporting him to the police. The police promptly arrested him again, and this time they held onto him— at least for a few days." she informed me.

Five days passed, so Sam felt that this time the system had worked and evil Frankie would no longer pose a threat to either Sam or her mom and dad. Ah, but things were not so simple! Sam resumed her story, saying, "On the sixth day, as Frankie sat in his downtown jail cell, he miraculously showed up at my front door! Upon seeing him there, I panicked and fainted. Mom saw me there on the floor, and being a nurse she quickly revived me. When I told her what had just happened, we went directly to the police station. This time when I tried to lodge another complaint, the desk sergeant just laughed at me! By now I was thoroughly confused, so when I asked the officer why he'd refused to take my statement, he invited me to accompany him upstairs. Once upstairs, I was shocked beyond belief— for there was Frankie lying on the cot inside his jail cell! Then it occurred to me these police think I'm making all this up. At this point, Jake, I gave up my life to Frankie— to do with as he chose." she concluded. "What happened next?" I asked. She answered "Frankie was released for the second time— and this is when I gave in to him, so we got back together. This time, Frankie promised not to force me into any more prostitution." she said. I'd thus far found Sam's story incomprehensible! My most disturbing consideration was this— "How could Frankie have visited Sam's home while sitting inside his jail cell"? I then asked Sam this very same question, to which she had absolutely no logical answer. I added, "Sam, I sincerely hope this doesn't turn you against all men". She responded, "Jake, I'm trying so very hard not to allow it to". "So where does this leave you?" I asked. I was again totally shocked by her answer! "Well, for the past eleven months, Frankie has settled for taking roughly only eighty percent of my monthly income. Plus, after each robbery— he forces himself upon me. I'm at the point where I can't take this anymore! Last month I bought myself a handgun, which I intended to use against him— but would you believe, he took my gun and my money, and then he raped me anyway"! At this point Sam completely lost all composure, falling into my arms and weeping uncontrollably. I sat speechless as I gently held her in my arms. I thought, *"How could anyone stoop so unbelievably low"?*

I'd remained fully cognizant of the fact that Sam and I had only recently met, and under such circumstances, the average young man may have simply wished her luck while walking away. But I would not abandon this poor 'damsel in distress', so I tried cheering her up. "Sam, you're a very nice person who does not deserve such treatment— so I'm going to stick with you until we clear this up." I said. The sullen expression on her sad face brightened somewhat. But with doubt showing in her eyes, she asked, "But Frankie is a very dangerous guy, so what can you do, Jake'? "We'll take care of this real soon", I assured her. The doubt remained in her eyes but at least she'd calmed a bit. In an effort to ease her immense pain, I took her into my arms!

By 1:30AM Bill and I had returned Cheryl and Sam to their homes, and were on our way to the base. As we began our short journey, I briefed my new friend Bill of Sam's current and ongoing problem of repeated robbery and rape. Bill commented, "Jake, we knew something very bad was happening in this girl's life, but she would not discuss her problem with any of us". "She was too ashamed," I replied. Bill then said, "Well, seeing as how the police can't help her, someone definitely needs to do it". "I'm considering a plan already," I said. Bill answered "That's good, but I've seen this clown (Frankie) a few times, and I know that he's very dangerous". "This means, if you get yourself involved in this situation, you'd damned sure better know what you're do-ing!" Bill warned. "I can handle this, Bill." I said. "Then tell me how you intend to do so" said Bill. "Sam's next robbery and rape is scheduled for payday, at nine this coming Friday night – I plan to be present for this event!" I said. "Then what?" asked Bill. "I'm not going to kill him if that's what you're concerned about," I answered. "My plan is to simply totally and permanently blind him." I added. "That would probably solve the problem," said Bill. Bill then shocked me by saying "My team of specialists and I would be more than happy to help you with this problem". "Specialists?" I asked. "That's right— specialists," Bill calmly responded. "Well, I would never refuse your help." I answered. "Good," said Bill, adding, "Tomorrow after work, drop by my room and we'll put together our plan of action".

That night in my room I lay awake for a long while, as I considered scenarios involving Frankie. One particular thought repeatedly presented itself. Specifically, Sam appeared both emotionally and mentally stable. Thus if my assessment was correct, how could she possibly have seen (or imagined) Frankie's standing at her door— as he'd sat in his jail cell? My mind conjured up three possible solutions. First, since Sam was not a user of drugs, she must have seen Frankie (or someone resembling him). Second, some individual within the prison had temporarily released him. Third, and most feasible, Frankie was but one-half of identical twins! This latter consideration really struck a strong note with me. Primarily, if there existed a second 'Frankie', then this problem was significantly compounded. Also, if this were true— my current solution would prove ineffective, for the remaining half of this problem would persist! In this case, I would definitely need assistance!

Next day at work we were given the afternoon off, in preparation of Thanksgiving Day (next day). I took this opportunity as an early start in the planning for Friday evening's upcoming attack upon my new girlfriend Sam. I recalled that while performing as a bit-part television personality, I often played the role of an aging karate expert. This required special make-up, including a shaggy white wig, thick mustache, and heavy white beard. I had packed and shipped these and other items (as mementos) to my new location here at Stead Air Force Base. I quickly searched through several boxes of memorabilia, finally locating the costumes. I Also removed my treasured little Elm from its hiding place. Upon close inspection, I found it to be in perfect operational condition. I would use the Elm to ascertain the existence of a second Frankie! I then sat in complete solitude as I formulated and finalized defense tactics for Friday's event.

At 6:00 PM Wednesday, I stopped by Bill's room to review strategy and tactics. I was pleased to find that he was quite anxious to engage in and conduct this most unusual operation. I first outlined my plan for this evening, which involved initial contact and neutralization of target (or targets). Next, Bill outlined his plan— that involved extraction, relocation, and containment of same. When we had merged the phases of our operation, we commended ourselves for having developed a highly viable strategy. At 8:00, Bill and I met Sam at a prearranged location in downtown Reno. From there we conducted a brief practice exercise of Friday evening's operation. Sam had informed me that Frankie always required that she present both her money ($400) and her body to him, at the door of his apartment, at exactly 9:00 on the last Friday of each month. So, the three of us drove onto the short side street where Frankie's small apartment stood. We took the very same route Sam would walk alone just forty-eight hours from now. As we approached Frankie's apartment I could actually feel the fear coursing through Sam's body! This was the perfect location for the criminal minded (such as Frankie) to commit hideous crimes such as Sam had for months suffered.

With our reconnaissance activity completed, we picked up Cheryl and then drove to a very nice Chinese restaurant for dinner. Afterwards, we walked the streets of Reno as we visited its finest casinos. Around midnight we drove to the outskirts of the city to a fancy nightclub. While there we danced often, talked and joked a lot, and even relaxed a bit. Then at 3:00AM the four of us returned to Cheryl's apartment, where Sam and I made passionate love throughout the remainder of the night! From the time I'd met her, I'd found Sam to be insatiable in the arena of sex. But for some strange reason, her desire seemed even more heightened— though this was just fine by me. One might say— she and I deserved each other!

Finally, we had reached November 27th (Thanksgiving Day). On this day, our base dining hall allowed guests throughout the entire day. Thus, after rising quite late this morning, we four drove out onto the base for our Thanksgiving Day dinner. This was another first for me— escorting a female guest to the on-base dining facility. But I quickly realized that— all I'd done over these past three years were first-time events for me. After our delicious meal the four of us attended an on-base earling evening movie. Afterwards, we dropped both Cheryl and Sam back at their respective residences, so that they might prepare for another evening of casinos and clubs. At this time Bill and I returned once again to the base, where we showered and dressed for the evening. Once downtown, we intensified the social aspect of our lives, resulting in another wonderful evening.

Soon Friday arrived, and with it came the final preparations for this evening's most dreaded event. Both Bill's team and I were off duty on this day, allowing us more than ample time in which to fine-tune our operation. As the hours passed, I found myself unexpectedly relaxed. Sure, I knew that a number of things could go wrong here, but I felt confident that all was under control. At 8:00PM Bill and I once again arrived downtown, where we immediately met up with Sam. Unfortunately, we found her as expected— biting her nails! Her first words to me were "Jake, I'm so scared"! "What if something goes wrong?" she asked. "Relax Sam, we've got this under control." I said. "I sure hope so, because I just can't take anymore of this treatment," she said. We'd not revealed our plan to Cheryl. Instead, Bill had told her that he might be a bit late this evening. This time we left Bill's fancy new Lincoln automobile on base as we headed for our destination. He and companions dropped me off just around the corner from Frankie's apartment. After having dropped me off, I donned appropriate attire before slowly limping my way around the corner to the front of Frankie's apartment. Assisted by the Elm, I then acoustically 'visited' the inside of Frankie's apartment. I initially only heard sounds emitting from a single television. But within minutes, I heard a male's voice ask, "Hey man, you sure that bitch is gonna show up on time"? Immediately I heard a second voice, identical to the first! This second voice spoke, saying "Be cool, she'll be here". This voice confirmed my suspicions that two persons were involved in this very same criminal activity. I held my right hand slightly above my head and raised my index and middle finger, signaling the number (two). My signal had been received.

At precisely 8:55, Sam rounded the corner leading onto Frankie's Street. Immediately she noticed an old, seemingly run-down black mini-van, which was parked approximately a half block from Frankie's place. There were no pedestrians or vehicular traffic at this hour on this particular street. Incidentally, she noticed one lone old (and wrinkled) homeless beggar, sitting on the curb directly in front of Frankie's apartment. As she reached the apartment, this old fellow feebly (and with trembling hands) held out his cup to her. "Little change, ma'am," he begged in his weak and scratchy voice. Without even thinking, Sam reached inside her mid-sized purse, producing several coins and depositing them into the beggar's rusting cup.

At exactly 9:00PM, Sam breathed in a strong gulp of the crisp and cold night air of Reno. She then committed the final dreaded act of ringing Frankie's doorbell. I had instructed her in detail as to what she should do next. She followed my instructions perfectly, by returning onto the sidewalk once she had rung the doorbell. Momentarily, the door of Frankie's apartment opened, and he stood framed in the doorway. "Come here bitch, and bring me my money!" he growled at Sam. We had anticipated this harsh reaction from him, having noticed that she'd hesitated in entering his apartment. Still following instructions, Sam retaliated, saying, "Here's your money Frankie, but I'm giving it all to this old beggar sitting here". She then immediately pressed the thick rolled envelope into the beggar's cup, saying to Frankie, "I'm finished with you," as she turned to walk away. This last act of courage by Sam instantly generated the desired response from Frankie. He cursed at her as he rushed down the stairs! Now we assume that at this point, his intentions were to snatch the envelope from the beggar's cup, before rushing toward Sam and forcing her into his apartment! Then under the cover of darkness, both he and his twin brother would have taken turns repeatedly raping her! The irony here is— this awful crime had been committed against her for months, but she'd never known that these were two men— instead of only one!

Instantly, Frankie had reached the sidewalk, and bent slightly forward to retrieve the envelope of (fake money). This would ultimately become his career-ending move! For as Frankie bent forward, the feeble old beggar lashed outward and upward! The sheer force of this single blow nearly crushed Frankie's larynx! Suddenly, he gasped for air as he staggered backward while clutching at his throat with both hands! Meanwhile, the old beggar quickly stood upright! In a flash, he'd stepped to Frankie's right side, where he delivered three lightening-quick blows to the right side of Frankie's neck, severely disrupting the flow of blood to his brain! This hoodlum was unconscious even before his body had struck sidewalk!

Meanwhile, the occupants of the mini-van had sat monitoring this activity; so, they quickly moved to the point where Frankie had just fallen. Then as Bill himself, along with the old beggar loaded Frankie into the van, the two other members of Bill's team sprinted up the steps and into his small apartment. Within minutes, these two uniformed men exited the apartment carrying the limp body of the second "Frankie". As Sam, Bill, and the old beggar climbed into the van, the two men loaded the second hoodlum into this van and quickly disappeared from sight! Luckily, this entire incident had lasted less than three minutes! There were no other witnesses to this incident; therefore, this clandestine operation had been a total success!

I never discovered where Bill and his team members had taken these two notorious brothers for temporary holding. However, on Saturday morning at 8:00AM, Bill's entire team of seven specialists (along with yours truly) lifted off the runway of Stead AFB via C-119 cargo aircraft, heading southward. I was unsuccessful in my efforts toward ascertaining our destination, or even the identity of the country to which we were headed. As we flew along our route, our pilot executed three separate changes of heading, causing me to lose partial directional orientation. I contemplated that these changes in heading were a routine component of our flight pattern. On the other hand though, our pilot possibly had intended to confuse me. Finally, we arrived at our destination. I glanced at my watch, noticing the hour was 2:15PM. Incidentally, I found it odd that our pilot wore no military uniform or rank insignia! Neither did our plane bear any official markings! Our team and pilot had addressed each other by name only. I would at least soon discover that my friend Bill was commander of this team! But within this group of seven men, military rank (although recognized) was non-existent. I assumed that our most capable pilot either was, or had been, an Air Force officer.

This special-purpose flight had originally transported a group of twelve prisoners. But Bill had coordinated the pick-up of two additional prisoners, (Frankie and his brother) from our base, located just outside the city of Reno. I remain confident that this entire prison group consisted of civilians. I also strongly believe that at least a few of these men were foreign nationals. I am of this opinion primarily because nearly half of this group seemed to have experienced at least some difficulty in speaking and comprehending the English language.

We landed in a clearing that had recently been specially prepared for certain types of aircraft. This temporary, make-shift runway proved highly efficient for our purposes. The forestry here was so very dense, one could not visually penetrate this jungle even ten feet. I estimated the temperature here at approximately sixty-five degrees. Our plane had parked about one hundred yards from an apparently old and abandoned warehouse. We were immediately met by two mid-sized busses, each containing two armed guards and driver. Each individual wore the same type of midnight blue work uniform. Each wore a name tag on his shirt. They quickly herded our fourteen shackled prisoners from the plane and into this seemingly very old building. Our group of nine followed closely behind. The prisoners were led through a reinforced steel door at the far west end of this lone building. Our group moved directly to a partitioned upstairs area, where we briefly rested. I was quite surprised by the fact that the inside of this 'old' building was modern and reasonably new in construction. "What is this place?" I asked my friend Bill. "Jake, this is one of our three secret correctional facilities." said Bill. "Once a prisoner comes here, he never leaves— this is the end of the line for these guys." he added. "Well, I'll be," I said. But out of curiosity, I asked "What are their chances of escape"? "Absolutely zero!" answered Bill. I was then informed that even our United States government was completely unaware of the existence of such facilities and operations! My mind then shifted onto the large number of permanent tenure prisoners who were confined here. I even felt just a slight bit of pity for some of these guys, as for all intents and purposes – this was their end! Bill then said, "Come, I'll show you around".

As we toured this facility, I noticed what appeared to be mining equipment, so I asked, "Is there a mine somewhere around here"? "You're standing on it," responded Bill, adding "Come, I'll show you." We walked to an enclosed room which stood just a few feet away. Its steel door was secured by one three-position combination lock, which Bill deftly removed. In the far corner of this room was a second steel door, which we also passed through. We had just entered a different world— one of man-made lighting! Next we boarded a small manually operated light weight rail car, with which we descended several yards into the earth. Soon we reached an underground area where there was additional lighting. As we drew nearer, I noticed several small groups of men using picks to chip away rock formations. These were miners! Even though their hands were freed so that they might perform their work, their ankles remained shackled! One armed guard was assigned to each individual work group. I learned that these prisoners worked twelve-hour shifts, six days per week. I also learned that this was a twenty-four hour per day operation. As one shift slept, the other worked. I then realized that this was the very first prison I'd had the misfortune of visiting since that awful place back in Matamoros, Mexico. But I did not wish to appear unusually curious, so I asked no further questions. I said to Bill, "I guess I've seen enough, but I sure wouldn't want to be any of these guys". We then returned to the surface and prepared for departure.

At exactly 5:00PM our plane lifted from the 'runway' once again heading north. During our return trip there were no passengers, with exception of Bill's team and myself. On our way back Bill's team mostly reclined, leaving Bill and me to discuss matters freely. So shortly into our flight, I turned to my friend, asking "How is it possible that you're involved in such secret operations"? I was totally unprepared for his reply! He answered, saying "Jake, my team and I are a test phase for what will someday become known as Commando/Special Forces teams". "As of today, there are only two teams— but more will soon form." he said. He then further shocked me by saying, "I lead Team Beta 7, but there is also Team Alpha 7, which is lead by my friend Bill Houser back in Tachikawa". "So that means you know Captain J?" I asked. "But of course – how do you think we ended up becoming friends so quickly?" replied Bill.

Now I began understanding my position in this newly formed secret paramilitary organization! These two teams were the primary tools with which the ingenious Captain James would secretly combat global communism and (later) terrorism! My specific role was that of facilitator. Granted, each member of these two teams was highly skilled as combatants; however, I possessed special ability for obtaining otherwise unobtainable information! Hence, with this information, these newly formed Special Operations teams would achieve greater effectiveness. As we flew along, I gained a new level of pride regarding my newly appointed status within this secret and essential organization. We concluded my informal briefing with Bill's saying, "Jake, whatever we've done and seen within the past twenty-four hours, we'll not mention again— agreed"? "Agreed," I answered as we shook hands. However, that which I've just mentioned began fifty-four years ago. Thus, I strongly feel the 'statute of limitations' relating to this agreement between us two, has long since expired.

The C-119 dropped off Bill and me back at our base at 11:00 that evening. By midnight we'd showered, dressed, and hooked up with our two very fine ladies in downtown Reno. "Where've you guys been?" Cheryl asked. Bill calmly answered, "Oh, we had to make a run". As soon as we were alone, Sam asked, "What happened to Frankie and his brother"? "They're both alive and well, but they will never again take advantage of you." I answered. Her large brown eyes brightened as she responded, "Jake, I sure hope not"! I reassured her by adding, "They will each reach age one hundred before either is released"!

Upon hearing my last comment, Sam relaxed a bit. In coming weeks we would discover that another seven young women had concurrently been brutalized and victimized by these two robber/rapists. Samantha had been number eight in their current group of select victims. We would also learn that these two criminals had forcefully collected $3,200 each month from these eight unfortunate, frightened young women! Let us now closely analyze this sum of money. During this time period, the minimum wage was approximately one dollar per hour. This means the average unskilled worker earned only $160 per month, from which they paid income taxes. Therefore in comparison, Frankie and brother each received (tax-free) money which was threefold the average worker's income, just for sitting at home and brutalizing innocent young women! Subsequently, yesterday's operation proved even more significant than we'd initially realized.

At 1:00AM we four sat inside one of Reno's fanciest and most expensive restaurants, where we dined on exquisite steak and lobster, complemented by a bottle of expensive French wine. *"This is even better than Tokyo"*, I thought as I sipped from my glass. Afterwards, we found a very nice nightclub for our enjoyment. When our evening ended, all expenses had been paid by Sam alone! She absolutely refused our contributions, saying, "This was money I would have given to Frankie". Several hours later, we returned to Cheryl's place for repeated sessions of wild and passionate lovemaking. I'd not before seen Samantha so very animated! Her anxiety and fear had been completely replaced by desire and passion! What a memorable night for this young former dirt farmer!

The very next afternoon we drove to that spectacular site known as Virginia City. Once we'd arrived I walked those streets in complete awe, as I witnessed real cowboys moving about town, while wearing seemingly real side arms. I was amazed to find that this tiny town had been preserved in its original state over the past one hundred years. We even visited the public grave site of the famous Belle Starr before returning to Reno. That evening we returned to fabulous Reno for more partying. Hours later we dropped the ladies at their homes, before returning to the base.

At my regular hour of 7:30AM, I again found myself back at work inside the base's junk yard. But on this day, I found my kindly old supervisor dressed in a suit with tie.

He had also brought in several dozen doughnuts, and had made an extra large pot of coffee. When I asked the reason for these treats, he answered "I expect we might receive a number of guests this morning". I did not press him for the identity of our anticipated guests. My two co-workers and I then proceeded to our work station, where I suggested that we perform a quick but thorough walk-through of our warehouse area.

As soon as we'd finished our walk-through we heard voices, walking our direction. The first to enter the area was our supervisor, closely followed by one full colonel along with several more high-ranking officers! I quickly called the area to "ATTENTION!" as per military proto-col. My co-workers and I were then presented to our wing commander and staff as the three airmen responsible for this major renovation project! We were each commended by our commanding officer for our initiative, ingenuity, and dedication to duty! The commander then handed our supervisor, a pair of airman first class (E-4) stripes, which were in-turn presented to the junior member of our work force. Our base cameraman had been summoned, and was present for picture taking. I later found that such recogni-tion was unprecedented within this work center. The other airman first class and I were each granted three-day passes, since higher promotion for us was not presently possible.

Shortly before closing time I was summoned to the of-fice by our supervisor to receive a phone call. . Upon en-tering, he pointed to the telephone and saying "telephone Jake." I picked up the receiver, answering "Airman Van York". I was pleasantly surprised to hear the friendly voice of my Tactical Commander, (Captain James) saying "Hey

Jake, how are ya"? "Fine sir", I answered. "I'm just calling to congratulate you concerning the recent tactical extraction," he said. "How did you find out?" I asked. "My Team Chief, Bill LeGrande just gave me a call." answered the captain. He continued "Just remember, Jake, we don't discuss any of our tactical operations". "Mum's the word, sir." I responded. The captain then asked "How're they treating you there"? "Just fine sir," I replied. "Great,— I'll be calling upon you for your services real soon," he said. "Okay sir, I'll be waiting" I responded, ending our conversation.

The first two weeks of December passed routinely while at work. While off duty, however, I had experienced lots of excitement along with an abundance of continuous sexual pleasure. Then in mid-December I received my recently purchased fancy Triumph motorcycle via military shipment. I was fortunate in that our transportation experts reassembled the bike for me. Two days later, I braved our extremely cold temperatures by riding the bike to work. I proudly parked out front at our work location. I immediately began receiving offers of purchase. Initially, I had absolutely no intentions of selling this excellent machine, but the offers kept growing. By week's end, I'd sold the Triumph for the sum of $1,400, which was slightly more than twice my initial purchase amount. I would apply $1,000 toward the purchase of a new automobile, while saving the remainder for partying with Sam.

On Saturday morning Bill and I made an early trip into town to shop for a car for myself. At the time I preferred Buicks, Olds, and Pontiacs. We checked the first two brands before visiting Pontiac. At the Pontiac dealership, I located a beautiful and fully loaded Pontiac Bonneville

Sports Coupe. The 1959 models were already released, but I selected one left-over 1958 model. This was one of the very finest automobiles in existence at that time! I ended up buying this car for the total sum of $2,250, financing only $1,250 of the total purchase amount. Now I no longer needed to burden my good friend Bill for transportation. But even so, we would continue riding together on most occasions, only alternating vehicles and drivers. On weekends we would take along both cars for greater freedom of movement. At this point in my life, (just shy of twenty-two), I felt I'd finally arrived! Moreover, I was the man! I would spend the remainder of the month by mostly partying in the company of Bill and Cheryl, and with Samantha at my side. Though, I feel the need to remind you that for me money was by no means in abundance. However, the $400 I'd held over from the sale of my bike would certainly enhance the quality of the rapidly approaching holidays. It would also allow me to enjoy a very pleasant birthday in the midst of these two major holidays.

The month of December had come and gone, and I had enjoyed myself immensely. But now at age 22, I'd just entered the month of January 1959. This would be the month when I would seek a good divorce lawyer. I'd been bound to this most undesirable female known as Francine for more than two years now, and I felt it high time I extricate myself from this wretched person and once again make myself whole. Unfortunately, my lawyer suggested that I postpone filing for divorce, as my application would stand a better chance with the passing of time since I had charged Francine with desertion. My lawyer felt it premature to file for divorce immediately upon attaining state residency. I followed my lawyer's advice and would allow the passing of fifteen full months. Meanwhile, I would exercise patience.

Now that I had my new car, I not only spent time with Samantha, I also resumed seeing both Christie and Brenda. Needless to say, my off-duty hours were quite active. But then, I met another extremely attractive lady whose name was Florence! This young woman was in her mid-thirties, but very exciting and sexy! I had parked the Bonneville just to the rear of a newly opened casino, and was sitting at the bar sipping Johnny Walker Black Label scotch. I was just chilling, when the small-framed young Chinese bartender slid another drink six feet down the bar to where I sat. I had not ordered another drink, so I asked, "What's this"? "The lady buys you a drink," replied the young bartender.

I suppose my perfectly tailored new suit may have attracted her attention. As I scanned the bar for my new admirer, I happened to see one very lovely lady sitting alone. Nearly twenty feet separated us, but we could see each other clearly. I gently tipped my glass in a small "Thank you" gesture. Instantly, she arose with a smile as she closed the distance. She slid herself onto the stool next to me, as we greeted each other. "Hi, I'm Florence— I've been frantically trying to catch your eye," she said, smoothing her tight-fitting, knee-length, midnight blue velvet dress. "I'm Jake," I answered as I fought to conceal the excitement in my voice. The lights surrounding this oval-shaped bar were dimmed. The soft jazz version of Poinciana played in the background. This was the perfect setting in which to form a new sizzling romance!

Fortunately Samantha had remained at home on this majestic evening. After a few minutes of small talk, I said to

Florence, "Why don't we go someplace where we can be alone"? "I was hoping you would say something like that," she quickly responded. We quickly finished our drinks and strode from the bar. As we walked toward the nearby casino exit, Florence waved to a well-dressed and very handsome young man who sat at one of the many poker tables. The fellow waved to Florence. As we walked toward the parking lot, I asked "Who was that"? Florence smiled warmly as she answered, "Oh that was just my husband". I was shocked! There I was— headed to some nearby motel with a strange married woman who had just waved to her husband! At this point I began wondering just how prevalent was this open marriage activity here in Reno. Ah, but this was just the beginning— there was more to come. Florence insisted that we ride in her new Christmas present, which was a beautiful cherry-red new Cadillac convertible. Surprisingly, she drove with the top lowered in mid-winter! Within fifteen minutes, Florence and I had become quite well-acquainted! And although I'll not elaborate further, this was one wild and exciting young woman! Amazingly, our relationship would last throughout my stay in Reno.

During the third week of January, I received my second telephone call from my Tactical Commander, Captain James at Tachikawa. The purpose of this call was two-fold. First, he wanted to inform me of his new and immediate reassignment to our Pentagon headquarters. Second, he asked that I contact a certain friend of his who worked as a detective on the local police force. He then provided me with the name and phone number of this police officer. I congratulated the captain regarding this most prestigious assignment, which would provide him with the opportunity for timely advancement to the coveted grade of four-star general. Before terminating our call, I assured the captain I would contact the police detective the very next day.

During my lunch hour the following day, I telephoned the detective. He suggested a meeting place after work this day. I advised that I would in fact be available late this afternoon. We set our meeting for 6:00PM. This would prevent me from visiting with Christie before driving into Reno, but I accepted not seeing her. At the appointed hour, I met with the highly ambitious detective at city hall. The detective wasted no time in getting right to the point. "May I call you Jake?" he asked. "Please do," I responded. "Good, you may call me Dan," he said. I soon learned that there was a vicious motorcycle gang that peddled prostitution and drugs between the Bay area and the city of Reno. It had recently been discovered that this particular gang had shown evidence of territorial expansion. The detective then said, "These guys have been a real thorn in my side; but, I can't seem to get a handle on them". "What do you need from me?" I asked. "I'm told, you have a special talent for gathering information," he calmly responded. "I can't guarantee anything, but I'll do my best," I said. "That's all I can ask of you," said the young police detective. He then produced a single manila folder containing photos and printed information relating to this gang. "These are the guys that I'm after" he firmly stated. I learned that they numbered twelve men, ranging in age from thirty to forty-five. Most were rejects that had been previously discharged from the military under less than honorable conditions. Their leader answered to "Snake" and his sidekick "Stone". There were originally twelve men in this gang, but their numbers had recently begun increasing. My job would be to conduct discreet reconnaissance into their activities, and report my findings to the police detective. "When can you get started on this?" asked Detective Dan. "Within the next two days," I replied. "Great, I'll provide you with an unmarked police car to move about in" said the detective. "That will be a good idea" I said. I then asked "When can I pick up the car?" "You can pick up the car tomorrow evening at the same time." said the detective. While sitting there, I noticed a very cute blonde secretary who'd kept watching and smiling at me. I figured that possibly she was interested in me; but, I was greatly mistaken!

The next day I arranged a ride into town with my friend Bill. It was understood that I needed to arrive at city hall by 6:00PM. I arrived at city hall as scheduled. Within five minutes the detective arrived. He had brought along an unmarked late model black four-door sedan. As he sat briefing me on the use of this car, I noticed the very same secretary eyeing me from her desk. Now I do not wish to appear vain, but I figured that maybe she really was interested in me. I accepted the car and drove to a nearby casino where I waited until darkness arrived. I had mentally prepared myself for this assignment, and looked forward to doing this particular job. I'd had no way of knowing that this would become my shortest job of all time!

At exactly 9:00PM I parked the car two blocks from the old house that this gang used as their headquarters. With the Elm in place and adjusted, I pinpointed the location of the gang's temporary quarters. From my vantage point, I could see lighting from within their house. I also heard the sound of music from their stereo. But otherwise, all was totally quiet. After an hour had passed, I changed my location. I recalibrated until I received the very same radio station, but still there were no sounds of voices. Once again I repositioned myself, but to no avail. At midnight I returned to the base, where I telephoned the police detective to brief him on initial lack of success. The detective calmly said, "Jake, this mission has been aborted, so you can return the car to me tomorrow at our same time and place". "What's happened, sir?" I asked. "It appears they've suddenly packed up and left town," he said. I would soon discover that the female clerk back at city hall was the girlfriend of this gang's leader, Snake! So all the while she'd been watching me, I'd thought she was interested. To the contrary, she'd been eaves dropping on our conversation. Thus, as soon as the detective and I departed, she'd telephoned Snake, advising him of the sting operation currently in progress. Consequently, this gang of drifters had quickly packed their limited belongings and relocated! Now I understood why there'd been no one at home as I sat for three long hours (in zero temperatures) in attempting to listen in upon their voice communications. This had been a completely wasted evening, for I had missed Christie, Samantha, and Florence. What a total waste of precious time!

As I lay there in my bed I wrestled with thoughts and images of this motorcycle street gang. Seemingly, my subconscious struggled to communicate with me— to remind me of some tiny fact I'd apparently overlooked. After several minutes of reflection, I jumped from my bed and grabbed the folder the police detective had given me. As I carefully reviewed the photos of this gang, I recalled having seen its leader and lieutenant while on my recent visit to nearby Virginia City. As my friends and I had walked along the streets of this town's west side, Snake and his lieutenant had slowly ridden past us. I had casually observed them as they rode past the end of the paved street. At that time I'd thought it a bit unusual that they had not paused while passing through town. Instead, they'd ridden onward for about two hundred yards to a point where there stood an old abandoned horse stable. Upon reaching this old stable, they rode their bikes inside and disappeared from view. Evidently they remained at this location for some time, as I never saw them leave. This strongly suggested that possibly this old stable was not abandoned after all!

I rushed to our hallway phone, where I placed another call to the police detective. As he answered my call, I immediately said "Sir, I believe this gang might be hiding out in an old abandoned stable situated at the west end of Virginia City". Before he could respond I added "There's also a strong possibility that this is the location of their cache of drugs"! I concluded by saying "If you get there right away, you just might catch them in the act"! "Thanks a lot, Jake, we'll get right on this," said the detective. I returned to my bed and slept soundly through the remainder of the early morning.

Having worked through the day, I drove the recently issued police car back to city hall. I entered the reception area where I would await the lieutenant, and I immediately observed that the female clerk was missing from her desk, but thought nothing of this. Soon the lieutenant arrived, with a wide grin upon his face! He seemed quite pleased. "Thanks, Jake— thanks to you, we got em all— plus their drugs!" he exclaimed. I never expected that you would produce such fast results— we could certainly use your skills here in the department." he added. "Thank you sir, glad I could be of help," I responded. I then returned the keys to the police car, as we proceeded outside to inspect for damages. There were no damages, so he dismissed me by saying, "Let's keep in touch". "Will do, so" I responded. The lieutenant then offered to give me a lift, but I had declined saying "I'll walk back to the downtown area— this way I can look all around as I walk". Soon I met Sam, accompanied by my friends Bill and Cheryl. We then resumed partying!

Next day at work, our organization enjoyed a pleasant and productive day as a direct result of our recent renovation project. Everyone who'd visited our site had complimented us and our supervisor. Now even though our work center was only a junk yard, working here had suddenly become pleasurable. Near closing hour I received another phone call. This time the call was from Captain James. "Hey, Jake, I just called to commend you for your contribution last night— you did great!" he said. "Thank you, sir" I modestly replied.

The days flew past, and soon we'd reached the beginning of February. This date was significant, because today I received a welcomed reassignment to a different on-base office. Now although this new assignment was nothing special, at least here I found myself once again performing administrative duties. I was afforded a desk with phone and typewriter. I would remain in this particular assignment for twelve months. My new supervisor was an Air Force master sergeant, whose last name was Soto. I quickly discovered this non-commissioned to be both competent and highly professional as a military member. This work center was supported by a total of six airmen, but we all worked harmoniously as one highly efficient team.

One month into this new assignment, I was unexpectedly offered an unofficial extra job, (which I accepted). This was a contracted custodial position— cleaning toilets, dusting, sweeping, and mopping floors. Each of the other five airmen had declined this position, for it interfered with free time for partying in downtown Reno. Some may have even felt that they were above such menial work. But don't forget, I had emerged from a life of farm work— so I could certainly do this custodial job. The position paid $400 dollars monthly. This was at a time when my monthly pay amounted to $160 dollars. After taxes, this new position allowed me to pocket $320 dollars in addition to my military pay. Suddenly, I found myself really enjoying the good life! But more importantly, I quickly discovered that with just a bit of organization, I could earn this money by contributing an average of only one hour per day! My regular duty hours were from 7:30AM to 4:30PM Mondays through Fridays. I would proceed directly to the dining hall each work day at 4:30. After rushing through my meal I would begin my custodial job at 5:00. Then by 6:00PM each evening I'd already finished the work. Also, since this extra job was performed in a partitioned area of the base, none of the other airmen ever saw me cleaning toilets or hauling out the trash. So, after showering and relaxing a bit, I would arrive downtown by 8:00 each evening. Now I say to you— "What more could any poor farm boy have asked for"?

Prior to the commencement of this new part-time job, I'd particularly admired my friend Bill for the fact that he always kept an extra $500 concealed beneath the floor mat of his Lincoln's trunk. When I first inquired about this un-usual practice, he said, "Jake, these are emergency funds, so by doing this I'll never be broke". His words made sense to me, so I also would soon begin carrying around $500 dol-lars concealed in the trunk of my Bonneville.

Beginning March 1st, I commenced thirty days of Non-Commissioned Officers Preparatory Course. This was a prerequisite for promotion to the next higher grade of (staff sergeant). Throughout this entire month I was relieved of my regular military duties for the purpose of completing this important course. However, in no way did this inter-fere with my custodial job or my social schedule. Our class contained a total of thirty airmen in grade E-4. At the be-ginning of class we were briefed that upon graduation, the student holding the highest academic score would be re-warded by immediate promotion to the grade of staff ser-geant! However, at that moment I inwardly resolved that I would not seek this promotion, for by now— I understood how the system worked. It was widely assumed that our wing commander's administrator (a student here) would receive this promotion. At the end of our course, we were proven correct. The commander's administrator received this coveted promotion, although in my personal opinion, he deserved it.

At the beginning of April, I resumed my regular admin-istrative duties. I would remain in this position for another ten full months. During this period I would consistently devote great effort toward getting myself promoted with-in the next twenty-four months. While off-duty though, I would thoroughly enjoy and appreciate the many pleasures to be found in Reno. In so doing, I would go into the city on each of my weekly afternoons off. On this particular day as I sat at the bar of my favorite casino, I noticed an unfamiliar face— an attractive lady whom I estimated as in her late thirties. She sat alone playing at a blackjack table. On the table before her, there stood stacks of chips, totaling thousands of dollars! Next to me at the bar there sat a young airman from the base. I said to him, "Wow, check out the fine lady with all those chips"! "Yeah, I have been," he replied. "She's giving this casino hell,— I count at least $75,000 in hundred-dollar chips," I said. "Yes, but don't let that thrill you because right now she's down by $25,000— she started with $100,000." he replied. "That's really something— just think $100,000 in a single sitting!" I said. "I guess she must be really loaded," replied the airman. I was captivated by her courageous action. I continued to watch this lady's huge stack of chips dwindle to just $20. At this point she played her last $20 chip, desperately hoping for some strange stroke of luck! Unfortunately, no such stroke of luck occurred. Then with great despair clearly showing on her now totally exhausted face, she arose from the blackjack table then slowly walked away.

At that moment, I truly pitied this poor lady. I'd pitied her mostly because in comparison, she had just lost a sum of money equal to fifty years of my current military pay! Heck, even with the extra income from my present part-time job, I would not earn this amount of money in twenty years! At this point I let curiosity get the better of me. I quickly finished my drink before walking toward her. As we neared each other, her eyes briefly met mine. "Cheer up, it's not the end of the world," I said to her. "You couldn't convince me of that," she quickly responded. I spoke again, saying "Hello, I'm Jake— may I walk with you"? "Where shall we walk to?" she asked.

I took her to my nearby hangout, a twenty-four hour nightclub. Once we'd ordered our drinks she immediately said, "I must advise you— if you become involved with me, you do so at your own risk". Her words of warning somewhat alarmed me, but I successfully concealed this fact from her. We discussed the various aspects of our lives. She then confided in me that she had come to Reno seeking a divorce from her husband, a Bay area syndicate boss. At this point I became quite alarmed! I wanted to jump up from our table and run far away, but pride prevented me from doing so. I once again recalled my wise old grandmother's words "Curiosity killed the cat"! It occurred to me that maybe this was the situation to which dear grandmother had referred"!

Thirty minutes later, I found myself in bed inside this lady's plush hotel room! Incidentally, her name was Joan. We also, would maintain contact through the remainder of my assignment here at Reno. But the mere fact that this was the wife of some mid-level syndicate boss would create unwanted problems for me. Joan quickly became very much attached to me, and I would not allow myself to disappoint or desert her. Therefore, over the next three months Joan would occupy much of my time. So now I would juggle my off-duty time between five different ladies! But even under these demanding circumstances, Samantha remained my number one priority. Luckily, Sam worked full-time, which served to slightly lessen the physical demands that had been placed upon me.

I soon discovered that Joan had gambled away nearly

all of her money, and only $10,000 remained. Now even
without gambling, this meager sum would sustain her for
only about two weeks. This presented a problem, for in
no way was I prepared to support her. Even so, I continued frequently seeing Joan over the next sixty days. At the
end of our first two weeks together, one afternoon Joan
placed a call to her husband in San Francisco. She asked
him for money, which he adamantly refused! Upon ending their conversation Joan shocked me by handing me the
telephone receiver. As I hesitantly took the phone from
her, I asked "What is this for"? She answered "He wants to
speak to you," she said. I was bewildered and concerned as
I thought, *"How does he even know I'm here"?* Then with a great
degree of false confidence I said, "Hello". There followed
only silence. Again I said, "Hello". This time a cold (even
icy) voice responded, "So you're the soon-to-be dead man"?
Somewhat irritated by his comments and tone of voice, I
asked flatly, "What do you want"? "What I want is your ass
lying face up in a pine box!" answered the voice at the other
end of the line. I recalled dad's teachings— "Son, never
argue with another man"— so without further comment,
I handed the phone back to Joan. She then spoke inaudibly
into the phone before hanging up. I displayed a façade of
total calm; but, inside my stomach had suddenly become
a bundle of tightly tied knots! I did not know what to say
to her— or what I should do. "Was that your husband?"
I asked. She replied, "Much to my regret— yes, it was."
She then took my hand, as we headed for the softness of
her warm and cozy hotel bed. For the next two hours, she
completely removed all thoughts of her menacing husband
from my mind! Afterwards I returned to the base for my

evening meal, and my one hour of custodial work. When this was done, I showered and then prepared for an evening out on the town with Sam, Cheryl, and Bill. Joan had indicated that she wished to remain indoors this evening, which was possibly the result of today's conversation with her crime boss of a husband! This was perfectly okay by me, for I needed time away from her to clear my mind.

As our evening progressed, Cheryl developed a splitting headache, so Bill took her home. Fortunately we had each driven our own cars, as this allowed me the freedom of taking Sam home at the reasonable hour of midnight. I dropped Sam off in front of her home at exactly 12:05AM. After waiting for a minute to ensure that she was safely inside her home, I drove the short distance to the highway leading toward the airbase. As I pulled onto the roadway heading south, I noticed a pair of headlights which were also heading in my southward direction. At first, I failed to make the connection between these trailing headlights and today's earlier threat from Joan's husband. Here, I refer specifically to his comments referring to my lying face-up in some pine box. At this early hour, few cars routinely traveled toward the airbase, which suggested that the headlights behind me were not there by coincidence! For the first three miles of this thirteen-mile drive, I maintained a steady speed of sixty-five mph. The trailing headlights maintained a constant distance between us. I decided I would gradually reduce my speed to fifty-five55. I found that as I reduced my driving speed, so did the vehicle trailing me. I did not want to alert its occupants that I was wise to then, so I held this slower speed until finally reaching the military base.

The main gate which granted access to the base was

approximately the distance of two city blocks off the main highway. As the security policeman waved me through the gate, I checked my rearview mirror only to see the mysterious headlights had just turned onto the base access road. Now if the person (or persons) following me had been crime syndicate members, then they should not have gained access to the base. However, after pausing briefly at our main gate, this vehicle proceeded onto the base. I found this quite perplexing. Normally I would have driven directly to my dormitory; but under no circumstances did I want these felonious individuals aware of my on-base residence. So I diverted to our snack bar, where I sat waiting as I sipped my cold beer.

Within minutes, three thugs entered the snack bar. None looked directly at me, but I'm certain they detected my presence. Their dress and appearance confirmed to me that these guys were definitely not members of the military! Their hair was their main give away, for each guy was simply too shaggy! But how could these guys have been allowed on base? The only plausible explanation was that they must have presented fake identification cards to the gate guard. Regardless though, they were here now and this concerned me. I was at a complete loss relative to an appropriate course of action. Had there been any security personnel nearby, I would have asked that these three be challenged for their IDs.

I finished my beer and left the snack bar; however, I walked in a direction heading away from my dormitory. As soon as I entered the parking lot, these three goons also stepped outside. This time they looked directly in my direction! I wasted no time in disappearing around the corner of the building, and into the surrounding darkness. Each took up pursuit! I realized that I had at least a slight advantage by being familiar with this rugged on-base terrain. This was the route I had traveled each day while assigned duty at our base junkyard. I walked along silently but briskly, not allowing them to close the distance between us. We were now in total darkness and could not see each other. Soon one of the three struck up a little tune, and was immediately joined by the other two thugs. This song was very uncomplimentary and quite discomforting! The lyrics told the sordid story of how they had carved up the body of Joan's former lover! They sang of how they'd then strewn these small bits of body parts across the Mojave Desert, which lies between Los Angeles and Las Vegas. Their song ended in the depiction of scavenger animals hungrily devouring those very same body parts, thus leaving the lovely (but lonely) Joan temporarily without a suitable lover! Their story scared the hell out of me!

Then in acting from wisdom and absolute concern for my personal safety, I increased the pace at which I had walked until now. I then realized that if they were to catch up to me, we would all be in total darkness; thus, the firing of weapons would probably have been their last resort. This suggested that they would resort to the use of knives (to which I harbored strong aversion). Sure, I could have probably taken down at least two of them (and possibly all three), but what if I failed? In undergoing self-defense training back at home with Mr. Lim, he'd frequently emphasized the most basic element of self-defense— (RUN)! I'd never forgotten this consideration. But had I fought these guys and survived, the ensuing repercussions would have been unending and unbearable! First and foremost, this would have constituted the commission of a crime while on federal property, which would have generated an extensive investigation by the FBI. I also had my military career to consider, so any altercation would not have been in my best interest. I therefore opted for the prudent solution!

I purposely headed directly for a slight incline, where I would then briefly become visible to these mobsters. As I topped this crest I faked a slight sneeze. "There he is— let's get him!" shouted one of their gang, as they took off running in my direction! But as I'd crossed over this hilltop, I executed a ninety-degree right turn and then ran like the dickens for the next few seconds! The three crossed over this hilltop heading southward, as from just over one hundred yards to their west, I re-crossed this crest, returning northward! I paused momentarily, listening to the sounds of their voices and footsteps heading further southward. I then quickly returned to the parking lot where the mobsters had parked their car. Then while they roamed the wastelands in search of me, I quietly punctured each of their front tires. Next I drove my car to our base's military police headquarters building, where I left it parked for the remainder of the night. I figured that once they'd given up on searching for me by foot, they would probably walk around the base in search of my car. When they discovered I'd parked at police headquarters, they might abruptly abort their search. I took an indirect route (on foot) back to my dormitory, confident that these mobsters would not even consider searching the dormitories for me, since this would have been akin to searching for the 'needle in the haystack'.

After having slept undisturbed through the night, I

awoke on Thursday fully alert and fit as a fiddle. At work
I made no mention of the unpleasant events of the prior
evening. Though while on my way to work, I did check the
parking lot of our snack bar for signs of the mobsters' vehicle. It was gone, so I figured they'd received assistance from
someone on base. Around 10:00AM I walked the short distance to Bill's duty section. "Got time for a coffee?" I asked.
We then proceeded to their outside break area, where I began briefing him regarding the events of last evening. When
I had finished, Bill commented, "Looks like I'll need to call
in the team for another little incursion". "You don't need to
do that, Bill, for I believe I have a plan for getting them off
my back." I responded. "Jake, these guys play for keeps—
and they don't scare easily. So I suggest you let me and my
team handle this." said Bill. Of course, I accepted his offer
without further protest. We then agreed we would meet
with this crime boss' ex-wife, Joan after work.

At 8:00PM Bill and I visited with Joan (over scotch)
inside her plush hotel room. While with her, Bill obtained
bits of information about her ex-husband and his current il-
licit criminal operation. In particular, he received a detailed
description of Joan's ex-husband, (including the two-carat
diamond ring which he wore on his pinkie. With this information, Bill would ensure that Team 7-B collected the right
person. At this time he excused himself, leaving Joan and
me to ourselves. So for the next two hours we sat together
while holding hands and gazing longingly into each other's
eyes – (NOT)!

After work on Friday I again met briefly with my friend
Bill. But before departing for San Francisco, he said, "Jake,
at exactly ten o'clock this evening, I want you to call this

clown's mansion and ask to speak with him". He then added "You've spoken to him once before, so I'm sure you'll recognize his voice". "I couldn't forget that voice, even if I wanted to," I said. "Good, then call this number immediately after, which will confirm his presence at home". "My team and I will then make our move," Bill concluded.

I soon found myself partying with Samantha and Cheryl at our favorite night spot. Over the eight months of Bill's assignment at Reno, he had been absent in TDY status on several occasions. Thus, Cheryl had become accustomed to his frequent periods of absenteeism. Still she had remained true to him. While observing her, I recalled how the woman I'd unfortunately married had gone out the minute I'd left home for reassignment. I realized that there was absolutely no comparison here—for Cheryl was a true lady!

At precisely 10:00PM, I placed my all-important phone call to the home of Joan's murderous husband. As he answered I instantly recognized his ominous-sounding voice. Without speaking, I quickly hung up the phone and called Bill. Then I resumed partying with Sam and Cheryl until 3:00AM, at which time I drove them home before returning to the base. This time I was not followed! Back inside my cozy room, I wondered about the current situation at the residence of Joan's ex-husband. I was fully aware that Commando Team 7-B was well-trained, well-equipped, and highly professional; however, thoughts of ill-fate plagued me throughout the remainder of the night. I would later discover that even as I lay pondering this situation, Joan's ex-husband (along with his entire crew) was already secretly escorted from these United States. None would return!

After attending to personal needs such as laundry and

dry-cleaning, plus a haircut, I drove into Reno at 3:00PM. I went directly to Joan's hotel room, where I found her relaxing and watching television. For the next couple of hours, we got to know each other even better. Later in the afternoon we found ourselves a very nice restaurant, where we enjoyed juicy steaks. During the course of our meal I frequently looked about the area for signs of mob henchmen, but saw none. For this I was very happy; but, I secured Joan's agreement that we should continuously exercise extreme caution in our relationship. Accordingly she would remain mostly inside her cozy hotel room during evening hours, lest she end up lying in some dark alley. At this time she informed me that she would return to San Francisco at the end of this month, and attempt to restore her life to some degree of normalcy. Joan made me promise that I would visit her often in San Francisco. I was thrilled by her hospitable invitation. At least I would soon have a fully qualified guide while touring this sensational city. At 10:00PM Sam and Cheryl once again accompanied me to our favorite night spot. Shortly after mid-night, Bill arrived. I must say, I was very pleased to see him. "How did things go?" I anxiously asked. "Piece of cake," Bill responded, adding "We took them all along for the ride". "I'll brief you later." "Wonderful, and thanks" I replied. Bill then joined us at our table for the evening.

The remainder of the month of April passed without further incident. However, during the first week of May a number of changes occurred. First and most important, our Tactical Commander (now Major James) had arrived at the Pentagon for duty as a strategic planner. Second, Joan returned to live with her mother in San Francisco. Third, my friend Bill Houser (of Japan) was promoted and also reported for duty at the Pentagon as Staff Sergeant Bill Houser. Fourth, my friend Bill LeGrande was also promoted to staff sergeant and moved off-base. Lastly, I also moved off base to share (at no cost) a very nice house with my former roommate.

Now that I lived off-base, I found myself enjoying greater freedom of movement. No longer would I stand periodic military room inspections. I was no longer required to prepare my living area for inspection prior to reporting for duty each morning. And of course, I could finally invite female guests into my home at anytime of my choosing. Suddenly, I was living the high life! Time passed quickly and soon we'd entered the season of summer. I had continued my sultry relationships with each of the women (including Joan) I'd previously met. But by this time I'd met two more exceptionally charming and exciting young women, each of whom equaled Samantha in the area of eroticism. Each was also a seductress in her own right. Their names were Jacqueline and Charlene. I met Charlene while visiting one of Reno's nightspots. She was accompanied by a very tall, but slender young man whom she'd introduced to me as her brother Jim. He was accompanied by two rather cute young women. They invited me to join them at their table, so I'd naturally accepted their invitation. Over the next several hours, we really enjoyed ourselves together. I discovered that they all lived in another small city just north of Reno, and were here for the weekend. As we sat making small talk, Charlene took my hand, pulling me onto the dance floor. She then immediately pressed her young body against mine, whispering into my ear, "I want you"! I responded by pulling her even closer! I felt confident that we would someday soon find ourselves together. Unfortunately, one of Jim's female companions became slightly ill and they returned to their hotel. However, in departing they obtained my address and phone number— which I had trustingly provided them. By this time I was a bit exhausted so I also returned home.

The next day (Sunday) around 1:00PM, I received my much-awaited phone call from Charlene. She advised me that she would pick me up around 2:00 this afternoon. I had already showered, so I dressed and waited. After the hour had passed she arrived in a fancy new Ford convertible, with top lowered. This car accommodated three persons in front and two persons in its rear seat. Jim and his two female companions sat up front. I joined Charlene in the backseat. We drove the short distance to the main highway, and then headed southward and away from Reno. "Thought we'd see a little of the countryside before heading into town," said Charlene's brother Jim. "That's fine by me" I replied. As we drove along in the warm sunlight with all the windows rolled up, I noticed that the young woman sitting next to Jim was apparently paying him special attention. I say this because she had suddenly disappeared from view! Any passerby would have thought that only four persons were inside this vehicle. I would remain a gentleman though, so I pretended that all was completely normal. Soon Jim pulled the car over to the roadside. The 'invisible' woman magically reappeared. They then opened their right front door, whereupon they exchanged seating positions. By now, any doubt I may have felt quickly vanished! I soon found myself envious of lover-man Jim! But I need not have been envious at all, for at this point Charlene had discretely perched herself upon my now bared lower body! We remained in this erotic position for the next full hour as we rode southward. Meanwhile, up front only one woman remained visible. During this time no one spoke or made any sounds— all was quiet. I noticed though that Jim frequently stole what I considered as affectionate glances at his sister, who'd remained sitting upon my lap. I must tell you— I've ridden inside a number of convertibles in my lifetime—, but none has ever equaled that day's ride!

But the day had just begun, for we had just arrived at a daytime house party hosted by one of Reno's highly popular female blackjack dealers. This was a relatively small party of less than twenty persons. Two were immediately announced as "Mr. and Mrs. Greene and party." I looked around in search of the Greene couple. Imagine the shock I experienced upon discovering that Mr. and Mrs. Greene were none other than Charlene and Jim! I had just made love to this guy's wife as he'd looked on! I considered it immaterial that he'd just been made love to by two other women! So here I was— already involved with three other couples engaged in practices of open marriage. I would soon discover that Charlene was an exhibitionist, who thrived upon being watched by others as she engaged in sex acts!

She had left my side and entered an open bedroom just down the hall. When she failed to return, I casually walked down the hallway to check things out. There on the bed lay Charlene! She was completely nude and beckoning me to her! Not wanting to embarrass or disappoint her, I entered the room and sat upon the bed's edge. Instantly Charlene reached out, pulling me down upon her. As we began kissing each other, we were the only two persons inside this bedroom. But suddenly the room filled with voyeurs who lined the walls on either side of the bed. They wanted to watch our little show! Now at this point in my young life, I could no longer be considered a novice regarding the subject of sex. On the other hand, I had not progressed nearly as far as had this young couple. I simply could not bring myself to put on a show for this group. But don't despair, for in this group of onlookers was a sergeant I recognized from the airbase. This fellow was reputed as being a lover of lovers! So as he stood drooling over this luscious sight, I motioned for him to join us on the bed. He pounced in a flash of motion! The two of them instantly gelled, and the show began! I was no longer needed, so I quietly removed myself from entanglement with these two frenzied human beings. Naturally I remained for the show,— which made this an unforgettable day in my life! I would party with Charlene on numerous occasions thereafter. She would even quite often visit me in Reno with her husband Jim. Each time she visited, she was successful in seducing me into sessions of public display. The mere thought by this young woman of someone watching our acts of eroticism served to elevate her to heightened levels of excitement! Heck, we even made love in the presence of police officers!

Also during this warm month of May, one voluptuous young woman named Jacqueline entered my life. From the very onset, I was uncontrollably drawn to her! Time would prove this young lady to be the ultimate seductress, for she played hard to get! Sure, she would party heavily with me several nights of each week. But at the end of our evenings together, I would find myself, in the wee hours of the morning, driving her home to her waiting husband. Granted, I behaved foolishly in my relationship with Jacqueline, but I was so into her, I was beyond the realm of the rational. All the while, I remained fully cognizant of the fact that one of these nights (as we sat kissing in her front yard at 4:00AM) her husband just might walk out from the house and begin blasting at us with a shotgun or some other automatic weapon. But still, I kept up this dangerous pattern of behavior. Meanwhile, our relationship remained platonic – which strongly suggested that I was, in fact, a fool! I would survive this relationship though, and months later the affection I'd shown Jacqueline would pay off— BIG TIME! Eventually she would overshadow the others (at least in looks). But in the arena of sex, Samantha and Charlene reigned supreme!

As time moved on, I remained professional while on duty; however, off duty I was the total party animal! My affairs with the many women with whom I associated, continually flourished. I even traveled frequently into San Francisco to visit with Joan. I found she'd made an amazing recovery in the areas of mental and physical health. This was attributable to the sudden and unexpected relocation of her ex-husband and his ring of mobsters. No longer was she sullen and depressed. Now that her morale had been lifted, she'd reduced her drinking and smoking. In fact, she had even succeeded in gaining a few needed pounds. In short, she'd become fun to be with! Prior to this time Joan had rarely displayed any sense of humor whatsoever. But this was simply because of the constant stress she'd endured at the hands of her awful ex-husband.

Samantha had also shown remarkable improvement,

although she'd not suffered from alcohol or tobacco usage. But contrary to Joan, Sam had quickly shed five pounds— so now she flaunted the perfect body (of which she was quite proud)! In August Sam moved to Phoenix, where she would complete her M.B.A degree. Also during this month of August, I reenlisted for a period of six years in our United States Air Force. As my reenlistment bonus, I received the cash sum of $1,392 (the equivalent of eight months military pay). So with this money and my extra job, I was finally somewhat financially secure.

In recent years I had received acceptable ratings from all performance evaluations. Therefore, by having recently completed Non-Commissioned-Officers Leadership School, I had rendered myself eligible for promotion to the next higher grade of staff sergeant. Unfortunately ten and one-half years would pass before I would receive this deserved promotion. We had entered the month of January, 1960. On January 4th I was reassigned to an office of higher echelon, but still within this base's Support Services Division. In my new administrative position, my immediate supervisor (NCOIC) held the grade of technical sergeant. Next in my chain of command was one second lieutenant. Above this lieutenant was our division director, holding the grade of major.

I was happy and appreciative for having been elevated to this position of chief administrator. As a result, I consistently strived for exceptional job performance. Here, I would eventually supervise a total of three airmen. However, I initially supervised only two airmen in the grade of airman second class (E-3). Thus for my first three months in this job, things progressed well for me. Unfortunately, such favorable conditions would not last. Soon another major and sinister conspiracy against me would subtly take form!

At the beginning of the month of March, I was assigned my third subordinate. This young airman held no rank whatsoever, as he had just been released from six months of military confinement. I would quickly discover that this airman was of the type commonly referred to as "spoiled brat". He was nineteen years of age, of moderate build, and seemingly mild mannered. So now I was happy to have my full work force. I initiated an in-depth training program for my new member, with the intent of accelerating his career progression. Within thirty days he had received his first stripe (E-2). I continued one-on-one training with him. In coming months his official skill level was raised, rendering him eligible for his next promotion. Then on November 1st, Airman X received his second promotion (E-3). Up to this point all had gone well within this new organization (or so I had thought).

Throughout this entire period, Lieutenant Z and A1C X had gradually become closer and closer as buddies. Strangely, Lt. Z had turned to alcoholism and gambling as his new way of life. Consequently, this young officer was always short of cash. Conversely, Airman X was blessed to have had wealthy parents; thus, he always carried lots of money on his person. But there's more— Airman X drove a new convertible Cadillac, and was quite handsome and personable. Lt. Z possessed none of these assets or qualities, for he was just a plain old country boy! To make matters even worse, I've used the lieutenant's own words here in describing him. This lack of assets and qualities in Lt. Z caused him to gravitate towards Airman X for companionship and financial support. Soon the lieutenant and airman began partying together nightly in downtown Reno. However, this was in direct violation of existing Air Force directives governing acts of fraternization. Nevertheless, these two would carry on this unauthorized social behavior for nearly two full years.

Meanwhile, my social life underwent a dramatic change. This was when I'd met a beautiful and wonderful young lady named Christal, or Chris. This young lady hailed from the great city of Sacramento, California. At the time of our meeting, she'd been visiting her older sister, who lived and worked in Reno. From the very beginning of this new relationship, Chris and I enjoyed a wonderful experience together. But Chris was different, for she had never before been with any man! I instantly discovered the great extent to which I had appreciated this rare quality in her. Resultantly, I would not pressure her to have sex with me, and she quickly expressed her gratitude for my patience. So within a matter of weeks, I converted from a program of surplus sex to one of zero sex! But of course, I did not complain. Then two months into our flourishing relationship, the platonic element was discarded! This newly added experience between us served to bring us even closer. Then in September, Chris returned to Sacramento to attend college. Soon I found myself longing to be with her and no one else. So even though we lived apart, we succeeded in seeing each other regularly.

Concurrently, during this time— I finally applied for my long-awaited divorce! My application was processed and approved in record time. The delay had seemingly paid off. Subsequently, my final divorce decree was issued by the court on August 12, 1960. At last I was freed from the tramp known as Francine! On this very special evening, I celebrated by escorting Chris to the finest restaurant in all of Reno. From there we found ourselves a quiet night-club, where we spent the next several hours. I shall not comment on what occurred afterwards (although this was a most memorable occasion)!

Soon the exciting year of 1960 had ended. The following year would not begin well for me! The conspiracy I earlier commented upon, surfaced (and in full form)! But before proceeding, please allow me to clarify and define the role of the military non-commissioned officer (NCO). The role of the NCO is that of carrying out the lawful orders of his (or her) superior officer. In so doing the NCO must apply due consideration to the operative word "(lawful)". Concurrently, the NCO must extend maximum consideration to the safety and well-being of all subordinate military members.

During this time, promotion opportunity within my career field had recently become virtually non-existent. However, Airman X (buddy of Lt Z) was now eligible for promotion to my current grade of E-4. But without the availability of a stripe, he would not receive further promotion in the near future. Thus Airman X, (the spoiled brat), had demanded that Lt. Z promote him soon— (or else)! Keep in mind, in no way did Lt. Z wish to lose the companionship and financial support Airman X provided, so he conceived an ingenious plan! (Though in retrospect, this scheme may have been the product of Airman X himself).

Within the Air Force, there existed Air Force Regulation

35-32 "Control Roster Procedures". This directive provided for administrative grade reduction of those airmen whose duty performance was considered substandard. It was intended primarily as a means of weeding out the older, marginal airmen. Specifically, these were the guys who had served nearly twenty years in the military— but who had not been promoted above the grade of E-4. This encompassed approximately three percent of all assigned E-4s. However, I was not a part of this group! To the contrary, I had worked hard at building a productive and long-lasting career for myself here in this great United States Air Force! Notwithstanding, my lieutenant would arbitrarily place me in this targeted group of airmen. After all, he needed my stripes— for his buddy and supporter, (Airman X). Up until now I've made no references to my supervisor (TSgt Y). But I've purposely overlooked him here, as until now— he'd remained dormant and derelict in his responsibilities as supervisor.

After spending Thanksgiving, Christmas, my birthday, and New Year's day apart from mom and dad,— I returned to duty on January 3rd 1961. Immediately I was summoned to the office of my OIC Lt. Z. Then in the presence of TSgt Y, the lieutenant commented, "Airman Van York, I'm sorry to say this, but last night someone broke into one of the officers' guest quarters and stole several bottles of alcohol from the bar there". "We believe that someone was you, Airman Van York". I stood dumbfounded as I pondered the lieutenant's charges against me. "Why do you think that I was the person who did this?" I asked. "We have samples of your hair, which we collected there," answered the lieutenant.

At this point, I realized that something was not quite

right here. I also realized that either of these two unscrupulous individuals could have collected my hair from right here inside our offices. Also, they could have collected samples of my hair immediately after I had returned from the barber shop. My final consideration was "How could these guys be so sure that this was even my hair"? I spoke up, saying "Sir, I wasn't in the guest quarters last night, and I'll be happy to take a lie detector test to prove it". "Good, I'll schedule a test for you right away," responded the lieutenant. In response, I quite indignantly stated, "I'm fully capable of scheduling my own test, sir". "Well, if you think you can do this— then be my guest," quipped the now somewhat irritated lieutenant. After being dismissed, I returned to my desk where I immediately placed a call to the Reno police detective whom I had assisted one year earlier. I was pleased that he remembered me. After a few pleasantries I explained my need. "I'll be glad to schedule you Jake," he said. "It so happens our examiner will be here first thing tomorrow" he added. "Great, can you schedule me for 9:00AM?" I asked. "Got you scheduled— but don't be late." he advised.

The next morning I was administered my first and only Polygraph examination! I was fortunate to have had a competent testing official, and was subsequently completely cleared of these false charges! Later that afternoon the lieutenant received my sealed report of examination via official courier. I had seen the courier arrive at 2:00PM, but neither my supervisor nor the lieutenant had summoned me to receive my notification of having been cleared. Finally, just minutes before quitting time, I was reluctantly provided the much-anticipated notification!

Next day I returned to duty as usual, and then resumed

my normal duties. I fought to conceal my disappointment in my supervisor, for throughout this time he had not uttered one single word concerning this serious matter. Might I also mention here— had I failed the Polygraph examination, I would have immediately been reduced in grade. My stripes would have then been quickly placed on the sleeves of Airman X! Fortunately for me though I had foiled their first attempt at unjustly ending my military career. Alas, this was only step one!

Two days later the lieutenant lowered an even larger boom upon my unsuspecting soul! This was his second attempt to transfer my rank to the sleeves of Airman X. At 9:00AM of the morning of Jan 5th 1961, I was ordered by my supervisor to report immediately to my squadron commander. I complied with the order and at 9:15AM of that same morning I stood at attention before my squadron commander. My reason for being here resulted from the recent submission by my supervisor and officer-in-charge, of an unjustified and substandard evaluation of my duty performance! I stood mutely and dumbfounded as my squadron commander read to me the contents of this derogatory report. My supervisor and officer-in-charge had both flatly stated I'd become a detriment to their organization! This strong, negative statement warranted my immediate placement onto the Air Force Control Roster of my organization. Might I elaborate—this was an administrative program whereby substandard performers were demoted in grade, and their stripes awarded to other more deserving airmen. Therefore as of this date, my duty performance would become specially monitored by a separate supervisor for a period of ninety days. During this entire period, the most minor of infractions on my part, would become justification for my immediate reduction in grade! What a way to begin a new year!

Then by 10:30 of this very same morning, I was assigned to a totally non-related duty section—the (Base Non-Commissioned Officers Club— as cashier. Here, I would have no desk, telephone, or typewriter. My sole duty would consist of managing cash funds, which were generated revenue of this particular organization. My former permanent supervisor had erringly assumed that by placing me in custody of large sums of money, I would at some point misappropriate at least some small amount of these cash funds! I might point out here that for some strange reason, he felt that I was desperate for money. He never even bothered to check into my part-time employment! Had he done so, he would have quickly discovered that my total monthly income exceeded that of his own. So over the next ninety days, I walked a virtual tightrope! I ensured that all funds, for which I was responsible, were present and audit-ready at all times. I treated all club patrons, associates, and superiors with the utmost respect. I also made sure I remained neatly groomed and well-dressed. Lastly, I made certain that I maintained complete punctuality during each duty day. I would allow absolutely no exceptions or deviations from my personally established regimen! I'd taken these rigid precautions primarily because— previously, ninety-five percent of all Control Roster victims ended up reduced in grade within ninety days. My survival was very much in doubt at this point! Meanwhile though, the days and weeks passed as I consistently demonstrated superior duty performance.

Finally, my seemingly eternal probationary period

reached its end! My current supervisor rendered a fair and proper evaluation of my recent duty performance and had rated my performance as EXCELLENT! This current fair rating effectively ended my Control Roster's probationary period. I was in that five percent who had survived such rigid scrutiny! Most significantly though, I would soon receive a strong laudatory letter from my division chief, (Lt. Z's boss)! Please allow me to provide you with an excerpt of this letter from Major L. F. Schmidt (our division chief):

"I would like to take this opportunity to express my sincere appreciation of the manner in which you have performed your duty during the past two years under my direct supervision. Your desire to accomplish any task in the best possible manner and your willing cooperation to work long, overtime hours when necessary, has been greatly appreciated. I consider the following word picture commensurate with your ability and makeup as an airman and a gentleman: A cooperative, neat, courteous individual who is dependable and well informed in his assigned duties. Further, I would consider myself fortunate, indeed, in having you, Airman Van York, assigned to me at anytime during my tenure in the United States Air Force".

The above comments constitute the entirety of Major Schmidt's letter to me. I remind you here that this officer was the immediate supervisor of Lt. Z and TSgt. Y, (each of whom had said, "A1C Van York has been a detriment to this organization". However, these two had somehow succeeded in concealing my performance evaluation from their boss. This act in itself constituted a separate, but direct, violation of Air Force policy! Their fate would soon be determined!

Immediately after being released from the Control Roster Program, I placed a call to my Tactical Commander, Major James. When I advised him as to that which had just happened to me, I find myself reluctant to repeat his ominous comments! During this phone call, I said to him "Sir, I need to leave Stead AFB right away"! "I agree Jake," the major responded. He then added "Give me a minute to make a phone call – I'll get right back to you on this". Within just ten minutes, Major" "J" returned my call, saying "Hey Jake, how would you like to go to Tripoli"? Now at some time in the past, I'd heard a song referring to the "Shores of Tripoli". Otherwise, my strong grasp of geography currently failed me. In short, I'd not a clue as to the location of Tripoli. So I asked the major "Sir, where's Tripoli"? To which he answered (Jake, Tripoli borders the Mediterranean Sea of North Africa". "Great, I'll take it," I exclaimed. "Good, then begin your out-processing immediately," ordered Major James. "But sir, I don't have written authority." I said. "Your reassignment authority is being transmitted as we speak." he said. "All you need to do is get yourself to the assignments section— keep me posted." he concluded. I proceeded to our local assignments section, pleased to find that my electronic "PRIORITY" reassignment authorization had already been received. At this point, I strongly believe that few (if any) other airmen have ever received such expedited actions regarding reassignment!

I had officially begun my out-processing actions even before noontime. I then took myself a well-deserved break for lunchtime. After lunch I returned to accelerated out-processing. At 4:15 that afternoon I completed all mandatory out-processing actions, including the receipt of several necessary immunizations. Throughout the afternoon I purposely avoided my former duty section, where I was certain the conspirators had anxiously awaited my return. *"Let them sweat"*, I thought as I ended the duty day.

After finishing my late afternoon meal, I hurriedly showered, dressed, and headed for the city of Sacramento, 132 miles west of Reno. This was the hometown of Chris (my wonderful young female companion). I wanted to notify her of my immediate reassignment from Reno to Tripoli. Also, on this very special evening I would shock Chris by asking her to marry me! I arrived at her parents' home shortly before 8:00PM of that evening.

I had previously visited her family on numerous occasions, so I was no longer considered a stranger, but they were surprised by my unexpected mid-week visit. I apologized for my surprise visit before breaking the sad news. Upon hearing of my rushed reassignment, tears formed in Chris' eyes, though she maintained her composure. I explained that my time was limited, so I could spend very little time with her. I then asked, "Chris, will you marry me"? I had caught her completely off-guard! But even so, she wasted no time in responding, "Yes, Mr. Van York, I will marry you"! We embraced for a long time and then I removed from my pocket the attractive (but small) engagement ring I'd purchased three hours earlier. As I placed the ring onto Chris' finger, she called out to her mom and dad, who had been watching TV in an adjoining room. "Look, mom, dad—Jake and I have just gotten engaged"! They expressed great surprise, but quickly wished us a long and happy life together. At midnight I arrived back in Reno, where I spent the next two hours saying farewell to friends (including Bill). Soon I climbed into bed inside my off-base quarters. My sexual exploitations in Reno had abruptly ended!

On Wednesday morning I arose and dressed for my 2,700-mile drive to South Carolina. At breakfast on base I stumbled across a casual friend who was also heading east at the same time as I. This airman did not own a car, so he offered to share expenses if I would drop him off in his hometown of St. Louis, Missouri. His hometown was several hundred miles north of my general southeasterly heading, but since I had not seen that region, I agreed to transport him to his home.

Before departing the base for the final time, I stopped by the office of Lt. Z to say good-bye to a couple of co-workers. I found them busily typing financial reports, but both briefly paused to shake my hand. Airman X remained at his desk with head lowered as if he was ashamed to face me, so I completely ignored him. Lt. Z stayed inside his office. I believe he may have been testing me to see if I might briefly poke my head through his door – (NOT A CHANCE)! While preparing to drive away, I noticed both TSgt. Y and Lt. Z peering out at me through the lieutenant's office window. I pretended not to have seen them! I then drove to our base service station, where I filled my car's fuel tank for the meager sum of $4.75 (nearly twenty gallons of fuel). As I drove toward the highway, I recalled my many great experiences here in Reno!

Minutes later, my passenger (Sean) and I commenced

our nonstop thirty-hour drive to his hometown of St. Louis, MO. We shared the driving, which allowed us to only
make brief refueling and rest stops. Across this vast expanse
of countryside I witnessed a number of memorable sights.
We arrived at Sean's house the next afternoon. His parents
were thrilled to see their son. They were also quite hospitable, insisting that I at least have myself a meal before
proceeding. They even provided shower facilities for me.

At 6:00PM that same afternoon, I began the final portion of my trip. This drive would course through Kentucky,
Tennessee, and North Carolina— providing me with more
great scenery! I was all alone now, with only my car's stereo
and cool air intake to help keep me awake. The Bonneville
performed magnificently, and my anxiety and anticipation
of once again seeing my parents served to help keep me
awake. Soon though I was forced to slow my rate of speed
as a result of numerous curves and hills. It felt really great,
seeing these parts of the country for the very first time! Late
Friday afternoon I reached the great and beautiful Smoky
Mountains of North Carolina. Fortunately, my car was in
excellent condition, which allowed me to navigate these
magnificent mountains without difficulty whatsoever.

At 10:30 Saturday morning, I left the highway and
turned onto the street where my parents had built their new
home. This was a truly wonderful experience for me, as my
parents had finally begun enjoying the many comforts of
their very own new home. I drove slowly along this street,
admiring the new homes that had recently been built in
this particular part of our little town. Finally, I reached the
address which mom had provided me by letter. Here at this

address was a lovely small home, which was fenced-in on a full one-acre lot. *"This is wonderful"*, I thought as I turned into the driveway. I'd been so busy admiring this home I had not seen my (now totally blind) dad manually pumping water out back. I would discover that this had become one form of exercise for him.

I eased the ultra-quiet Bonneville up to the spot where dad stood. Now even though he was unable to see, he'd heard my approach but had absolutely no idea who had entered his driveway. I considered playing a little joke on him, but four long years had passed since we had seen each other. Instead, I simply called out, "Hey dad, how are you"? My poor dad froze momentarily! When he recovered we hugged each other for a long while. At this point he called out to mom—"Hey Sis, come out here for a minute"! Mom rushed from her kitchen, thinking something had happened to him. When she saw me standing there, she nearly fainted! She rushed forward and so did I! Now mom and I took our turn in this hugging marathon! This would become my most memorable family reunion! "Why didn't you tell us that you were coming?" Mom exclaimed. "I just found out three days ago, and it takes five days for a letter to reach you," I answered. "I sent you our new phone number," she said. "I know, but I wanted to surprise you." I said. Mom then gave me another big hug! Dad followed mom's lead! I find myself unable to find suitable adjectives to describe the emotion and love generated between mom, dad, and me on that unforgettable and wonderful morning. The long drive had left me exhausted, but the reunion with my wonderful parents had quickly rejuvenated me!

Mom then led me inside our new home to show me

around (notice I've said our home). It was not elaborately fancy, but quite comfortable and cozy. Most importantly, their home was equipped with the full range of utilities, (including telephone). Naturally, I immediately took myself a much-needed shower in (my new home)! Then after chatting with my parents for nearly an hour, total exhaustion overcame me. I could no longer keep my eyes open, so mom promptly showed me to my very own bedroom. It contained all new furnishings, and even a totally new telephone rested upon one of its nightstands. I could not believe this all-new living environment, which mom and dad had created for themselves. I complimented them, and dad commented "Son, the best part of this is - it's all paid for - we don't owe anyone even one cent"! "That's really wonderful, dad" I said. He then spoke again, saying "Son, the vacant half acre of this lot belongs to you". At this point I couldn't believe my great fortune. Soon sleep overcame me, and I was immediately 'out like a light'.

After having slept for seven long hours, I awoke and drew a steaming bath. I no longer needed to hide outside in our back yard as I bathed. Heck, we even had neighbors close by now' thus, even if I'd wanted to bathe out back, there was no chance. After my soothing and stimulating bath I unpacked my clothing and other possessions (including the Elm listening device). I placed the candle containing the Elm on the nightstand opposite my telephone. As I neared completion of my unpacking chores, mom poked her head into my room, asking, "Do you need any help, Jake"? I answered that I was fine. She then noticed my special candle for the first time, asking "What's this"? "This is my personal memorial to grandmother," I answered. That's very nice of you," mom responded. She then asked "Are you ready to eat"? "I sure am," I said. "Good, I'll put your food on the table" she replied. I quickly washed up and enjoyed my meal on our new dinette set. I found myself somewhat at a loss to grasp the reality of my parents' new living environment, for everything around me was new! Previously, every possession of my family's had been over-used. *"This will require some mental adjustment on my part,"* I thought.

After finishing my meal, I joined my parents on our enclosed rear patio for conversation. We discussed Texas, Japan, and Reno; however, we did not mention the tramp (Francine). One year earlier I had advised mom of my divorce, so further comment was unnecessary at this time. I then asked dad, "How's the Road Master holding up"? "It's still doing fine, son" answered dad. He continued "Old man Jones down the street keeps begging me to sell it to him, but I won't sell it because it's been such a great car for us". "Still, it's great that you receive offers for it," I said. At this point I excused myself to prepare for my trip into town.

After quickly washing my car, I showered and dressed for my evening out. I would visit the Lantern, Hattie's, and the Hillside, respectively. At the Lantern I met a few classmates who had remained in our town. I discovered that Carol had returned and was now an art teacher at our school. I also learned that my lovely Catherine had moved to distant school. This information had both boosted and lowered my morale! My fiancée Chris and I had agreed that we were free to date whenever we chose to do so. Thus, I would take full advantage of this option while on leave here at home.

Over the next twenty days I immensely enjoyed

being at home with my parents. I visited my Aunt Emma frequently. Mom and I even drove to church each Sunday morning. We also visited family friends each weekday. While on leave I spent the vast majority of my evenings with Carol. On several occasions she and I would drive into other nearby towns for evenings of dining, dancing, and sessions of tender (but passionate) lovemaking! This fine young lady created for me three weeks of unforgettable pleasure and enjoyment! Sadly, she would also relocate to a different and far away school at the end of our current school year.

It seemed I'd arrived here only yesterday, but it was already April 29, 1961. I was to report in Tripoli, Libya, the very next day, so I began to prepare for my trip to my departure destination of Charleston AFB, S. C. This was another sad time for my parents and me, but this was the life I had chosen for myself. So at 9:00 on that very sad morning, mom and dad dropped me off at our downtown bus station. I then presented mom with the keys to the still nearly new Bonneville. To say that she was elated would have been an understatement! Upon hand-ing her the keys, I said to them, "Now you can sell the Buick to Mr. Jones". Incidentally, the loss of dad's vision had forced mom to learn to drive. "Now you can drive to church in style," I said to her. They both thanked me for the gift of the late model Pontiac. We hugged as we sadly said our farewells to each other. My heart literally ached as I watched my lonely parents drive away toward home. At least they now lived in comfort. Also, mom no longer worked the fields, so their lives were finally quite pleasing. Within minutes, my bus arrived and I wasted no time in boarding. After a three-hour ride to Charleston, I arrived at its base passenger terminal at 2:30PM. One hour later, I boarded my seven-hour flight to that far away land of Tripoli, Libya.

Chapter 8
Traversal of Tripoli

After a brief stop in Bermuda, we finally landed at that barren location of Wheelus AFB, Libya. We had arrived there at approximately 8:00AM on Sunday morning, April 30 1961. Even at this early hour, the local temperature was already well above 100 degrees. This place was by no means similar to the beautiful land of Japan. Heck, this was not even comparable to the deserts surrounding Las Vegas and Reno. At least in those areas, there flourished wide varieties of desert vegetation. But here in Tripoli, nothing seemed to flourish!

I slept through Sunday morning, having set my alarm clock for noon. Though at approximately 11:30, I was startled awake by a young male local national. In my sleep I had felt the weight of some person who had just sat themselves upon the edge of my single bunk bed. I'd instantly felt the hand of this person as it grasped one very special portion of my male anatomy. At first, I felt that I quite possibly might have been dreaming; but then, this hand began deftly squeezing me, causing me to dreamily open my eyes. This was the point at which I actually became startled! There before me sat this young male, who grinned hideously at me as he squeezed. His teeth were stained to the point where each was the color of coffee! Even worse, each of his stained teeth was broken and jagged! He did not speak, but only grinned weirdly at me. I found myself shocked and repulsed by this very strange person! Consequently, I abruptly sat upright, yelling and cursing at him, while readying myself to begin punching him! My sudden unexpected, violent behavior apparently scared this young fellow completely out of his wits! In a flash of blurred motion, he bolted from my bed and through the door leading from my room! I would remain on Wheelus Air Base for eighteen months, but I would luckily never again see this fellow! I remain of the opinion that this incident constituted my welcoming to this barren location known as Tripoli, Libya!

Now that my intruder had vanished from view, I quickly washed up and then headed for the base dining hall. I was quite surprised to discover that food quality here on base was good. After lunch I returned to the privacy of my room, locked my door, and slept throughout the afternoon. As I lay in the quiet of my room, a most alarming thought struck me, *"Jake, your days of sexual escapades have ended"!* I found this to be quite depressing.

I spent most of Monday in military in-processing. By 3:00 the very same day, I reported to my duty section, which was Base Laundry and Dry Cleaning. This operation was housed within a huge building, containing a total of one hundred local nationals (Libyans) along with three U. S. military and one U. S. Civilian manager of high grade. Here for the second time in my career, I found myself in a supervisory capacity. I was assigned responsibility for two separate work centers (Administration Office, and Cash

Sales Department). Back at Stead AFB, I had supervised personnel, but did not render performance evaluations. Here in Tripoli, I would do both. A large part of my current responsibility consisted of serving as liaison to our internal Accounting Office. This function was staffed by two female German nationals, four Libyan nationals, along with one Italian national, and managed by the two German national females. This unique staffing structure frequently led to problems caused by language barriers and cultural differences. Compounding this situation, I would soon receive the addition of one secretary, a female Greek national. This was my first assignment which involved working with and supervising female members. Also, I'd never before worked in a multi-national environment. But again I would rely upon grandmother's wise advice of "treating others as I would wish to be treated". Following this rule I would serve through the end of my tour here without ever experiencing an unmanageable situation.

At the end of my first partial workday on the job, I proceeded to our base dining hall. I looked about in search of any familiar faces, but regrettably— I saw none. So after eating I proceeded directly to my dormitory room, where I began unpacking and arranging my personal belongings. My first act was that of securing the Elm. While here, I would always keep this device locked away inside my foot locker. I would not trust leaving its container candle exposed to inspectors and passers-by.

I had earlier during in-processing, enrolled in a course of Arabic, so now with nothing else to do I began my review of this material. At the time of enrollment in this course I'd had no idea of the benefits to be gained by having taken this action. But since social activity in this area was virtually non-existent, I would spend the majority of my off-duty time here by studying Arabic. Two full weeks had dragged past, and we'd reached mid-May. By this time I had familiarized myself with my duties and responsibilities and felt comfortable in my new position. In some strange sense, I sort of liked it here. Our office building was situated less than twenty yards from the sandy beaches of the Mediterranean Sea. This close proximity allowed base personnel to relax and swim during lunch period on a daily basis. I would never again find such a unique work environment. Unfortunately, I still had not learned to swim, so I stayed away from the water. I simply would not risk another near-death experience, such as I'd had back in Japan three years earlier. So for the rest of the month of May, I focused upon studying Arabic, while expanding my knowledge of my new position, and solidifying professional relationships with supervisors, co-workers, and subordinates.

Now the month of June 1961 had arrived, bringing with it constant daily temperatures ranging above 115 degrees. It was at this time I noticed that the men all dressed in unusual attire. Each wore a full-length woolen top coat. "How can this be?" I asked myself. Finally, when I could suppress my curiosity no longer, I asked one local national, "Why do you wear heavy woolen clothing during summer months"? Using his limited command of the English language, he answered, "If we no wear thick wool in summer—, we burn"! Now I understood— these woolen garments acted as insulation from the tremendous heat of this region!

Until now I've spoken exclusively of males, but this was simply because I had seen no Libyan females. The local culture prohibited the employment of local national women on base, so there were only males employed here. For this reason, the use of European women was practiced on this huge U. S. airbase in North Africa. These cultural differences required great amounts consideration and respect of me, but I adapted and adjusted quickly.

Just before quitting hour on Friday afternoon (first week of June), I received a very special long distance telephone call. As I sat at my desk while reviewing accounting reports, my phone rang. I promptly answered this call, "Base Laundry & Dry Cleaning, Airman Van York speaking". "Hey Jake, how are you?" came the familiar and authoritative voice of none other than my Tactical Commander, Major James. "I'm fine sir," I answered. "Great— have you adjusted to the heat?" he asked. "I think I may be working on that for another eighteen months sir," I answered. "I'm sure you can handle it." he chuckled. "Sir, I really appreciate your helping me with this assignment." I said. "Think nothing of it," he responded. He then added, "You can be of great assistance to me while you're there in good old Tripoli". "Whatever you need sir, just give me a call," I replied. "I'll do that Jake, and have yourself a great weekend." he concluded. Before I could answer, the major was gone.

One week later, I received another call from Major "J". His call again began in the usual casual manner. Something in his voice though had told me that this was a serious and more official call. After his usual warm greeting, the major asked, "Jake, do you think you could handle a little special reconnaissance duty tomorrow evening for me"? Without an inkling of what I was getting myself into, I answered "Of course sir, no problem". "Great, I'll schedule a briefing for you tomorrow on base at 2:00PM sharp." The major then provided me with the location of my special meeting. This concluded the content of our brief communication.

At exactly 2:00 the next afternoon, I met with two fairly young American men who introduced themselves to me by first names only. Judging by hair style alone, I surmised that the younger of these two was in all probability a military officer. After six years of military service, I had learned to detect and distinguish certain mannerisms of both officer and enlisted personnel. I am certain that the senior of these two was civilian, although connected to our government. I would later discover that they were human resources of Major James. Their current target was a terrorist group visiting Libya.

Then after the exchange of a few pleasantries they arrived at the focal point of our meeting. According to their briefing, Washington's Military Strategic Planning Division (Major J's office) had uncovered a critical plot of major proportion, in which certain emerging terrorist groups had commenced the targeted bombings of military facilities throughout North Africa and the Middle East regions. My role in this major secret operation was that of verifying the validity of this information. But I was only a lowly airman first class, administrative specialist— so how was it possible that I might succeed in such a sensitive endeavor? I'm certain that these were the thoughts of my two briefers. Before I proceed further though, please allow me to properly appraise you of this particular situation and time period.

This was during a time period when radical Islamic anti-American sentiment was in its infancy stages. Internet and cellular technology was non-existent. Therefore, most highly sensitive communicative activity was conducted on a face-to-face basis. Accordingly, my briefers had provided me with photographs along with the time and place of my reconnaissance operation. We concluded our meeting, and I returned to my room to inspect the Elm listening device, my miniature voice recorder, and my personally designed audio antenna. I found the Elm to have been undamaged while in transit to Tripoli. Also, my recorder had retained full operational functionality. Now I was ready for these terrorists!

At 7:45PM, I arrived at my selected observation point. It so happened these fellows would conduct their affairs in open space on the east Mediterranean shore of Tripoli. Cautiously, I inserted the Elm into my left ear and then performed necessary distance calibration. I then prepared my recorder for receipt of their full meeting session. This small group had situated themselves well within listening range of the Elm, so my hand crafted antenna was not needed. As they began their verbal exchange, I received their conversation loud and clear. They spoke Arabic, and I did not understand a single word they had spoken. Nevertheless, I successfully recorded their entire meeting session. Two hours later, I presented my recording to my two mysterious visitors as per instruction. They then informed me that they would depart this very evening, returning to Washington, D. C., and would deliver this recorded information to their superior (Major James) on Monday morning. Each thanked me for my efforts before hurriedly departing from my room. I would eventually discover that the recording I'd made revealed a malicious plot whereby this group would

soon have placed concealed explosive devices at various locations on Wheelus Airbase prior to their actual attack! I
would also discover that commando team Alpha 7, lead by
my old friend Bill Houser, had subsequently (during pre-
dawn hours) visited the terrorists' training site! I learned
that their visit had lasted for only three minutes; during
which time, this group of twelve terrorists was completely
terminated! The initial plan of these terrorists had been
thwarted! Unfortunately, many other such incidents would
follow, for these were the beginning stages of today's global
terrorism activity!

This was the extent of excitement I would experience
during the remainder of this unbearably hot summer in
Tripoli. My only form of recreation was that of attending
movies. It was during this period that I attended a sufficient
number of movies to totally compensate for all that I had
missed as a lonely teenager. Ironically, the beautiful beaches
of the Mediterranean were at my fingertips— but I still had
not learned to swim! Occasionally I would sit at some spot
on these beach sands while watching others as they thoroughly enjoyed the cooling waters.

At long last, the month of September arrived, ushering
in slightly cooler temperatures that averaged 100 degrees
daily. During this period I received a total of three courtesy
calls from Major "J". During each call, he commended me
for the outstanding job I'd recently performed for him. It
seemed my involvement had aided to such a degree, I was
granted the remainder of summer free of any reconnaissance duty!

It was during the first week of September that I entered an on-base talent contest. I took first place in the

male vocalist category by singing the famous classic "Canadian Sunset". Now I do not wish to appear as bragging, but I really wowed the audience! As a result, I was immediately invited to join a newly formed on-base vocal group. I gladly accepted the group's offer, and soon I found myself rehearsing three to four nights weekly. Our group contained seven band members, accompanied by five vocalists. I was number five.

Our leader was an accomplished pianist, and a total perfectionist! He was well versed in the field of music, and accepted only the highest standards of musical performance. We quickly mastered a long list of the most popular songs of groups such as The Temptations and others, although we were quite versatile and talented. Thus within our first three months, we had compiled an eclectic selection of tunes intended for public performance. We gave our first performance at our Base Recreation Center on Thanksgiving Day of November 1961. We were an immediate smash hit! For the next several months, we performed weekly on base (for pay) at our airman's club, non-commissioned officer's club, and even our prestigious officer's club. Soon, we were invited to perform at a number of fancy Italian nightclubs in the downtown Tripoli area. At this point, we envisioned commercial stardom in our future! Meanwhile, we continued rehearsing and performing (free of charge) at our on-base recreation renter.

During one such session at intermission, we were approached by a young airman first class whom I shall refer to only as "Will". Will worked at our recreation center as a recreation specialist and was always present during our performances. He eventually asked, "Hey guys, may I sit in for you during your next intermission"? It so happened that Will was a talented comedian. Our group agreed we would allow his performance. At next intermission we introduced him, (along with his special sidekick), to the audience. Will was an instant success! Thereafter, he performed with us on a regular basis (while gaining experience). Months later Will would exit the military and actually achieve his well-deserved stardom! As of this writing, you can see Will and sidekick as they perform in Las Vegas and an unlimited number of other famous night spots around the world.

In mid-November, my fiancée and I set a wedding date of January 14, 1962. I planned to spend Christmas, my birthday, and New Year's Day with my parents. This would be my very first holiday season with them in nearly nine years. I then planned to travel to California, where I would marry my beloved Chris. Regretfully, this latter portion of my plan would never materialize. During the first week of December 1961, I applied for thirty days leave to the United States. To my great dismay, my leave was denied! Not only was this disappointing to Chris and me, it was deeply embarrassing to Chris and her entire family, because she'd already sent out invitations! I felt so badly about this situation, I soon reached the point of borderline depression! By mid-December my state of depression further escalated. Then, in a state of total desperation I placed a call to Major James. He instantly sensed lowered morale in my words. "What's wrong, Jake?" he asked. I explained my situation. When I'd concluded, he commented, "Keep your head up Jake, I'll get right on this". I thanked him, and we wished each other "happy holidays".

Even in my present state of mind I succeeded in

completing the first twelve-month volume of my Arabic course. Meanwhile, I anxiously awaited some news regarding the status of my previously disapproved leave application. Finally, at 1030AM on Friday December 22, 1961 my supervisor approached me. "Jake, your leave has been approved, and you've been granted forty-five days" he said. He continued, "There's a military flight leaving at 2:30 this afternoon, so if you hurry you can make this flight". He promptly released me from duty so that I might prepare for my travel. Then within the next three hour period, I had lunch, purchased gifts for mom and dad, and packed my belongings (including the Elm). I reached the passenger terminal with ample check-in time. As I sat waiting to board my flight, I reflected upon recent events. Evidently, Major "J" had ordered from Washington, D. C. that my squadron commander approve my leave.

That afternoon we took off from Wheelus airbase (Tripoli) bound for Charleston, South Carolina via C-135 jet aircraft. Three hours later we stopped briefly at Lajes, Azores. Nearly seven hours later we landed in the continental United States. I stepped from the plane, nearly freezing immediately! I had never before heard of Charleston being snow-bound. This was in fact a blizzard, and visibility was near zero. Also, ground temperature appeared to be just slightly above freezing level. After several minutes of braving the strong winds, I reached the passenger terminal. Imagine my shock and disappointment upon discovering we had landed at Dover AFB, Delaware, instead of Charleston! As a kid growing up, I'd often dreamed of visiting this region of our country, but never under present conditions.

Feeling dejected and again bordering upon depression,

I approached the middle-aged lady who stood at the ticket counter. "Ma'am, my flight was bound for Charleston AFB, I don't know how I wound up here in Delaware." I said. "Your plane was diverted for reasons of special cargo," she responded. Unfortunately, her answer did not resolve my current problem! "I need to be in South Carolina by tomorrow— can you help me?" I asked. "All flights in this area are grounded until after Christmas." she answered. I knew that bus or train transportation would not reach my home by Christmas, so I found myself in a real predicament! I considered the irony of my current situation: I had crossed the Atlantic Ocean but was unable to complete my travel.

In desperation I placed another call to Major James in nearby Washington, D. C. "Sir, I really hate to make a complete nuisance of myself, but I'm stuck here on Dover AFB, and can't get home by Christmas time." I said. "What a bummer," commented the major, adding "Let me see what I can do to help you. "If you don't hear from me in one hour, call me back." he said. Within minutes I was paged by Dover passenger service. I promptly approached the ticket counter and the very same lady I had recently talked with. This time she was much more courteous and helpful! "Young man, you must know some people in very high places." she said. "What do you mean?" I asked. She surprised me by saying "There is one presidential aircraft leaving here within the hour, bound for Key West, Florida— would you like a lift to that location"? I knew that by traveling to Key West, I would end up farther away from home than I currently was here at Dover. However, I had never before seen Florida so this was my chance to do so. Plus, I would extricate myself from this snow-bound place of Dover, DE. "I'll take it!" I blurted. The ticket agent then advised me, "This plane does not carry passengers, so I've been instructed to list you on the manifest as a crew member". "It must be nice, knowing someone." she concluded. "It certainly is ma'am," I answered. Just ten minutes later, I boarded a plush twenty-four passenger Lear jet!

Minutes later we were airborne and heading southward. Our flight to Key West lasted just over one hour and thirty minutes. While in flight though, I witnessed a string of fantastic scenery along our route, and upon landing I discovered a seemingly completely different world! Here, was there snow on the ground, and temperatures were quite mild. In fact, there was even a slight balmy breeze. I thanked the pilot and flight crew for having saved my life! Next, I hailed a taxi and rushed to the downtown bus station.

That afternoon I climbed aboard a large Greyhound, bound for my hometown. For the next few hours preceding darkness, I marveled at my surroundings. At around 10:00PM I fell soundly asleep for the remainder of the night. I arrived home during early afternoon on Christmas Eve. After one more very short cab ride, I gave my parents the greatest and most pleasing surprise of their entire lives! This would be my very first time as an adult in spending the holidays with my wonderful parents.

After hugging, hugging, and more hugging, I took my very first winter time bath while indoors at home, and in a genuine bathtub. Now, and after twenty four years, I felt as would have any normal human being— truly wonderful! After bathing I invited mom and dad into town for a little shopping spree, which was something the three of us had never before done as a family. Now even though dad had totally lost his vision, he remained active. So he and mom dressed casually before heading into town. I learned that he and mom had kept my car mostly parked inside their garage, to protect it from the elements. Thus, it was still in like-new condition and currently with low mileage. They had also held onto the Buick I'd given them four years earlier. It also was in excellent condition. Then for old times' sake, I chose to drive the Buick on this cold winter evening. During our short drive into town, I suggested inviting my Aunt Emma along. Mom and dad thought this was a great idea. So we drove to my aunt's house, where I also greatly surprised her. Although it had only been nine months since my aunt and I had seen each other, she was still overjoyed at seeing me. She informed us that several of her children would join her for Christmas, but still she joined us for shopping.

Fortunately, I had brought sufficient cash funds with which to support pre-Christmas shopping, so as we walked from store to store, I made several purchases for my parents and aunt. We'd finished our shopping and were preparing to return my aunt to her home when I heard the sound of a once familiar female voice. As I turned in the direction of this voice, I found myself face-to-face with the still beautiful and most unforgettable Catherine Cunnings! "Jake, is it really you?" she asked as uncertainty sounded in her warm voice. Truthfully though, it was I who received the greatest thrill. "Catherine!" I stammered. "I can't believe you're standing here before me"! Quickly we hugged each other, while respectfully maintaining our composure. I certainly could not allow my parents to even slightly suspect that there were feelings between Catherine and me. I learned that she was on foot and heading home. This gave me the excuse I needed to rediscover her address. "Since you are walking around out here in these freezing temperatures, allow me to give you a lift home," I offered, and she accepted.

"Why thank you, Jake" she answered. I soon discovered that Catherine had returned to teaching at home, and lived on the north side of town. I also discovered that she currently lived with just her mother. As I dropped Catherine off at her place, she thanked me for the ride. But as she wished us each a "Merry Christmas" she pressed a tiny strip of paper into my hand. Without comment I carefully tucked this paper into the pocket of my topcoat. I then returned my aunt to her home before heading for ours. Upon reentering mom and dad's new home, I found myself pleasantly surprised to find that it had maintained its automatically set temperature while we were away shopping. "This is really nice," I said to them, adding "I'm so happy that you both finally have yourselves a nice home and comfortable life— you deserve it".

After our evening meal I went to my room to arrange my clothing. As I did this, I thought of my beloved fiancée, Chris. I wanted so badly to telephone her and reaffirm my love for her. I also longed for the opportunity to hold her in my arms. Then reality set upon me. Suddenly I realized I could not (even once) telephone Chris, for she thought that I was stuck in Tripoli at this time. I felt very badly about this unfortunate turn of events, although I'd found myself helpless. Now I realize, the vast majority of you will view me as a dog of sorts. Nevertheless, I'd spent the past nine months in Tripoli while having been forced into sexual abstinence. Hence, as a young and virile male who'd not yet reached the age of twenty-five, I would voluntarily abstain no longer! I fully accept here any criticism you may level upon me for my obvious lack of discretion.

I dressed in proper attire in anticipation of an elegant evening. I then drove to the Lantern, where I proceeded to the nearby phone booth to call Catherine. By the second ring, she picked up the receiver. "This is Jake, are you free?" I asked. "It so happens that I am free Jake, but why do you ask?" replied Catherine. "Because for six long years— I've been dying to ask you out," I said. She then confided, "Well, I was praying that you would call, so I've already dressed for you". "Wonderful, I'll be there in fifteen minutes," I said. After hanging up I would not risk entering the Lantern from fear that I might meet friends who were visiting home for Christmas. Instead, I drove directly to Catherine's home. She'd heard my car as I entered her driveway, and poked her lovely head through her front door. For a brief moment she appeared a bit bewildered, but then I turned on my interior lights, which allowed her to see me. Under the faint lighting of her porch, I could see the bright, warm smile that covered her face as she rushed down the steps and toward me. I stepped from the car and we nearly collided as a result of our heightened state of emotions! Now don't get me wrong here— I loved Chris dearly— but to date, absolutely no other woman could completely erase Catherine from my mind and heart. She had remained irresistible to me! Back then, guys held open doors for their lady, and also held the chair in which their lady would sit. I find these courtesies truly define "the good old days"!

Accordingly, after a lengthy embrace there in the semi-darkness, I held the door of my fine Bonneville as Catherine seated herself. "How many cars do you have, Jake?" she asked as she shifted her body, making herself comfortable in the car's right front bucket seat. "I gave this one to my mother because I felt that she deserved a much newer car," I answered. "I must tell you— you're a wonderful son Jake," said Catherine. She continued "I hope that someday I might have a son like you – but until then, I'll just settle for having you as my lover"! Her brazen words served to quickly reignite the flames that had smoldered inside my body for the past eight years! I immediately pulled to the curb and then took her into my waiting arms! She instantly melted against me! Six long years had passed since I'd held Catherine close, and this feeling was truly indescribable!

We drove to a small city located just thirty minutes from our hometown. Once there, we stopped at a dimly lighted nightclub for dancing and drinks. The realization of finally being with this indescribably beautiful lady had lifted me to a state of near delirium! I simply could not believe my great reverse luck.— Namely, by having missed out on being with my lovely Chris, I had hit the jackpot in Catherine! After just one hour of nightclub activity, we each realized just how greatly we desired each other. So without even commenting upon the subject, I drove her to a quality facility providing temporary living accommodations. Once inside our room, she immediately flung herself upon me! Then within minutes, and for the next several hours, we remained totally oblivious to our surroundings – and to the rest of the world. But in case you're waiting for lurid details of our lovemaking sessions, I shall regretfully disappoint you. I willfully enact this restraint purely out of respect and admiration for this wonderful and beautiful young lady. Simply stated, she commanded this level of self-respect! I returned Catherine to her home shortly after 2:00AM on Christmas morning, fully aware that I'd already received the ultimate of gifts!

I then drove directly home, where I climbed into my cozy bed to begin dreaming of Catherine. I would spend the next ten days of the Christmas holiday season in the presence of this lovely lady. Even as school resumed she would spend her free time with me. Our days and evenings together passed fleetingly. Throughout my vacation, I thought of my dear Chris each day. I soon found that even with Catherine in my life, I truly missed my wonderful Chris. I might also mention here that even with my currently heavy social schedule, I still spent a great amount of my time with my parents.

All too soon the month of January 1962 had ended, and regretfully so had my leave time. So on Thursday, January 4th I once again bade farewell to my loving parents. I then rode by bus to Charleston AFB, from which I would return to Tripoli. This time, leaving my parents had not hurt so very deeply, as I expected to return home in just nine more months. Unfortunately, even this wish would not materialize.

After having ridden for just over three hours, I arrived at the airbase just outside the city of Charleston shortly past the hour of 4:00PM. Once there I proceeded directly to the check-in counter for flight booking. The clerk promptly asked to see my travel orders along with my immunization record. I handed him my travel orders but immediately realized that in my great haste to depart Tripoli, I had overlooked bringing along my immunization record! This meant that I would not be allowed to board the flight to Tripoli. "I must leave today, so what do I need to do to correct this problem?" I asked the clerk. "I'm sorry to tell you this, but you must retake each of your required immunizations right now." he answered. His words nearly floored me! Unfortunately, there was no alternative or exception to this policy. I was in luck, as there was a medical unit just feet away from the check-in counter. The medical specialist informed me that I would be simultaneously administered a total of nine immunizations! My jaw dropped upon hearing this. I then braced myself, as I imagined becoming a living and breathing pin cushion. I must say here— some of those shots hurt like the dickens! After completing this requirement, I painfully returned to the check-in counter for processing.

Two hours later, we took off bound for Tripoli. This would be quite a long flight for me because of extreme soreness in each of my arms. Sleep did not come quickly or easily, but finally I fell into deep slumber. I would sleep through this entire flight. We landed back in Tripoli at 8:00PM on Friday evening. Then with nothing to do and no place to go, I just sat around watching TV for the next several hours. While sitting there, I recalled the wonderful days with my parents. And of course, I recalled my many unforgettable evenings with my dear Catherine!

My weekend had passed slowly for me, but now I'd returned to my daily work routine. I decided against enrolling in additional courses in Arabic, thus freeing up my evenings for song rehearsals. At closing hour of my first day back on duty, I placed a call to Major "J" thanking him sincerely for his assistance in approving my leave, and in arranging my flight from Dover, DE to Key West, FL. "Don't mention it, Jake, just glad I was able to help you," he said. His tone of voice quickly shifted, as he added, "But now I could use a little help from you". "Name it sir," I replied. "I'm quite curious about the currently evolving political situation there in your area." replied the major. "So, I need you to lend your ear to what's being discussed there— both publicly and privately". he said. "Do you feel you can handle this for me?" he asked. "I'll do my absolute best, sir," I answered. "Great, I'm depending upon you," he said. I understood the major's request (and objectives), so now I would provide him with information necessary to formulate contingency plans for the future security of our military forces here in North Africa! These plans to which I refer, would provide for the rapid evacuation of military aircraft, equipment, and dependents from Wheelus Airbase in the event of a sudden and unfavorable regime change! I would not fail in this endeavor!

Subsequently, mid-morning on February 17, 1962, I found myself seated at a small coffee shop located in that portion of Tripoli, known as The Old City. This area constituted the center of operations within this desert nation. While there, I 'read from my pocket novel' as I casually sipped upon overheated and super-strength Libyan coffee. I also listened to various small groups of men as they discussed general concerns and national politics. By now my command of Arabic language was satisfactory, but not sufficient. Nevertheless, I understood much of what was said. Unfortunately though, I'd not understood all. But not to worry, for I had recorded the majority of that which I'd overheard. After one hour I left this particular coffee shop and then immediately relocated to a different shop on the far side of the city. From my new vantage point, I resumed the acquisition of such verbal communication which I deemed pertinent to the strategic planning purposes of Major James. I would ensure that he received this information directly from me, at the beginning of his workday on each Monday. I would accomplish these transmissions by means of my recently conceived personal transmission system (of which I shall not elaborate here). However, this system to which I refer would completely eliminate the need for courier or mail service— and would prove much faster and considerably more reliable! Hence, my new (unofficial) information acquisition program had commenced! I would follow this special routine for the remainder of my tour here at Tripoli.

During the course of my numerous future visits into this city, I would eventually overhear the profound comments of one ambitious and aspiring young local personality: "My brothers, the day I become leader of our country, I will allow the Americans just twenty-four hours in which to exit our great country". "And on that great day, all that which they are unable to carry away with them, will become ours"! "We will keep for ourselves much of their equipment and a great number of their airplanes"! The speaker's comments elicited loud and continuous cheering! Unfortunately, his threatening words had not gone unnoticed by us!

Meanwhile, that previously nonexistent social aspect of my life here would soon take form. I discovered that during my recent vacation period in the U. S., our band leader had secured several bookings in local Italian nightclubs. I also learned that we would make our first such appearance here on Friday night of March 2nd. This allowed us more than ample time in which to expand our already expansive repertoire of R&B. Now with even greater reason for seeking perfection, we promptly intensified the depth of our rehearsals. We would accept nothing less in performance than our absolute best! Thusly, whenever we stepped onto the stage, our audiences were assured of nothing less than consistently great performances!

On the night of our first show, we performed a total of twelve current and popular R&B tunes, after which we performed another three encore. We had stepped onto the stage without having consumed even one ounce of alcohol, and we had naturally never used drugs of any form. Hence, our performances were given strictly from our hearts and souls. This first performance opened the doors of entertainment for us! As a result of this great opportunity, we commenced weekly nightclub performances in downtown Tripoli. On Tuesday and Thursday nights we would give performances at both the on-base non-commissioned officers and officers clubs respectfully.

We rapidly gained popularity on and around our military base, and in the city of Tripoli itself. Soon we found ourselves regularly receiving social invitations at the off-base homes of both American and other assigned allied forces. So over the ensuing six-month period, each member of our eleven-man group truly enjoyed the good life. Parties were frequently given in our honor. As guests of these parties, we would invariably perform several tunes.

Now as one might suspect of such occasions, we received many unsolicited sexual advances. Accordingly, the vast majority of our band and vocal group eagerly accepted and exploited these offers from dependent wives. I might clarify here that no Libyans ever attended any of these affairs and as such only American and European wives were involved in this adulterous behavior. I might also add— not even once did I ever partake in these gatherings for sexual pleasure. I attended the parties and enjoyed myself immensely. However, here I would not repeat the pattern of social behavior in which I had engaged while stationed back in Reno. Here, for reasons of self-preservation, I would completely abstain from sex!

Several months of enjoyment had passed and we had entered the unusually hot month of July. By this time I had submitted nearly twenty confidential reports to my Tactical Commander, Major James. As feedback I was informed that each of my reports contained information of great interest to the major. But now I found myself nearing the completion of this duty tour. So in acting out of respect, I advised the major of my desire to return to Japan once more. This was the mutual wish of each member of our musical group— to visit Japan!

When I informed the major of my wishes, his comments were "Jake, you've already seen Japan— so why don't you try Greece for a change"? "Greece, sir— why would I want to go to Greece?" I asked. The major responded, "Greece is a really great place, and I believe you would like it", he replied. "Plus from there, you can periodically visit the Middle East for me." he said. Well, truthfully speaking, I had absolutely no desire to visit the Middle East! However, I agreed for the major's sake, that I would apply for: (1) Japan and, (2) Greece— feeling that this would enhance my chances of being returned to Japan. Two months passed before the return of my reassignment request. During early August I was summoned to our personnel office, where I was notified that my new assignment had arrived. With my heart racing, I quickly opened the envelope— only to see the words ATHENS, GREECE!

Now to say that this assignment notification was a great disappointment would constitute a major understatement! I was nearly floored by this news. I hastened to contact the members of our musical group, and was further disappointed to discover that they each had received assignments to Japan! "*What a waste*", I thought as I recalled how each of us had adjusted our rotation date, so as to travel as a group to Japan. I was totally devastated in realizing that my friends would all be in Japan, but I would be all alone in Greece!

We had entered the hottest and most unbearable months here in Tripoli. But simply knowing this tour of duty would soon end, greatly helped in easing the misery caused by these extremely high temperatures. On September 23rd we gave our final nightclub performance. Our military replacement personnel arrived and already reported for duty, which allowed us one full week of leisure time on Wheelus Airbase. I must say, we partied like crazy during our final week in this country. Early on Monday, October 1st I stood alone at the base passenger terminal as I (almost tearfully) watched my ten friends climb aboard their flight bound for bases in Japan. As another chapter in my life neared its end, I finally realized this had been a unique learning experience for me. Now though, the time had come for me to venture into unchartered territory!

Chapter 9

Grandeur of Greece #1

After traveling by military aircraft for nearly three hours, I landed in a strange land, which I instantly recognized as the one true paradise! I had landed at the commercial airport situated just four miles east of the city of Athens. This airport location was now my new duty station. Here, accommodations and all else would be vastly different from any that I'd previously known. First there was no airbase at this location; consequently, there were no on-base dining facilities or dormitories. Here in Athens, all assigned military personnel resided off-base in private rental quarters. Also, these personnel prepared and consumed their meals within their residences. But this presented a significant problem for me, as in addition to not having yet learned to swim— I had also not learned to cook! In fact, my culinary skills were so very poor,— I could not have properly boiled water! I quickly resigned myself to the unmistakable fact that in coming months, I would lose quite a bit of much-needed weight.

Now instead of being escorted to some on-base dormitory, I was promptly driven to a nearby hotel of high quality. Once there I was provided a swank room (minus roommate), which I really appreciated. I was then advised I would remain here until I found permanent living quarters. I quickly unpacked my belongings (except the Elm), which I left locked securely inside my suitcase. Next, I grabbed a quick shower before heading out into the exciting streets of Athens, for a most unforgettable evening!

Let us pause for a moment as we perform a few mathematical computations. At the time, my current military take-home pay was only $180 per month. The room I'd been assigned, cost $30 per day. This meant that in just six days I would have expended one full month's pay! However, I would soon discover that during my authorized stay of sixty days in this room, my daily income would be $100. I figured my food would cost no more than $10 per day; thus, I would spend $1,200 per month on food and lodging. I was astonished by having discovered I would profit $1,800 for each of the coming two months— totaling $3,600. This huge sum equated to more than two years military pay! But adding to my newfound 'pain and suffering' was that — this money was tax-free income! Suddenly my thoughts of this being paradise were confirmed! With my morale now greatly elevated, I stepped from my fine hotel and onto the streets of Athens. Within hours I discovered that this magnificent city hosted more than three hundred restaurants, nightclubs, bars, and theaters. What more could I have wished for? After visiting several of these fancy facilities, I returned to my private room for the remainder of the evening.

The next morning I arose timely in preparing to greet my first full day here in Athens. I was pleased to find that military bus service to and from the installation was readily available. After dressing, I treated myself to my very first continental breakfast. Afterwards, I stepped onto the city streets where I hailed a passing bus. I instantly noticed that temperatures here in Greece were considerably milder than those back in Tripoli.

After a short and scenic ride we arrived at the single gate of this small military installation, then known only as Athenai Airport. This location was so very small it contained less than fifteen buildings. I would soon discover that less than fifteen hundred military personnel were assigned here. I was quite pleasantly surprised to find that troop morale here consistently remained at exceptionally high levels. I should not have been surprised by this though, for these airmen had realized that they were in paradise! Each enlisted person received in excess of $500 in tax-free monthly income; of which, any prudent airman could easily have saved at least $250 monthly while living well and enjoying life.

I checked into my organization. This was a postal detachment that operated with just thirty-six personnel (including four officers). At my orientation I was once again disappointed at having been informed I would immediately undergo reclassification as an Air Force postal specialist. This action necessitated that I be formally retrained from my current field of administration. I also discovered that I would be assigned shift duty, and would work for thirty-six hours per week. My shifts would consist of three twelve-hour days consecutively I would work Monday through Wednesday, with subsequently four days off (for example). I knew for certain that I would thoroughly enjoy having four full days off each week, so I willingly accepted this assignment. Now I suddenly found myself in a unique position, in that I was assigned outside the jurisdiction of the base commander here. This meant I would not be subjected to military formations or extra duties after hours! I would really enjoy this added freedom.

At the end of my two-hour in-processing period, I was given the remainder of the week as off-duty time. Therefore, from Tuesday at noontime until Monday morning (7:00AM) I was free to explore Athens and its surrounding areas. What I had not realized was that, my Tactical Commander (Major James) in Washington had personally coordinated this particular work schedule for me! I would soon find that the period of four days was sufficient to support my frequent deployment into various Middle Eastern regions!

My new base boasted a highly frequented cafeteria, which was a life saver to me. By noon time I had developed quite an appetite, so I headed directly to this facility. The food was excellent (both American and Greek dishes) and since I'd eaten only American food for most of my life, I would now try Greek food for awhile. As I sat enjoying my delicious meal and thinking of my friends in Japan, I entered into a state of near shock! Suddenly standing before me was my dear friend Bill LeGrande of Tachikawa and Reno, respectively! I quickly arose from my seat, and we instantly entered into a long hugging session. "I'd heard you were in Greenland, Bill," I excitedly exclaimed! "I was, Jake, but I'm here now," Bill said. "How long have you been here?" I asked. "Got here three months ago," he answered. I invited him to sit, which he immediately accepted. I then said, "I thought that you and your team were assigned western hemisphere responsibility— what happened?" I asked. "Well, awhile back the members of our two teams took a vote concerning rotation. As it turned out, each of the guys voted for rotation. So since our vote was unanimous, we approached the major with our request, and this is the result." said Bill. "That's really great— so where is my good friend Bill Houser?" I asked. "He and Team "Alpha" are now headquartered at Seattle." Bill replied. "So are all your guys here in Athens?" I asked. "They're all stationed in Italy, but we can assemble and deploy in just three hours," Bill answered. "That's really wonderful." I said.

As Bill and I sat chatting, two more familiar faces entered the cafeteria, and each instantly spotted me. Upon receiving their food trays, they joined Bill and me at our table. These were airmen I'd known in Tripoli, and we were on very friendly terms. The four of us then sat laughing, joking, and chatting together. During the course of our conversation, one fellow, (Dave), offered me the accommodations of his rental residence, which I appreciated. Now of course I had a very nice hotel room in which to stay, but a house would be even nicer. I felt I would enjoy greater freedom of movement and added accommodation at Dave's place, so on a part-time basis only, I accepted his kind offer.

Dave's place was only two blocks from my hotel, so I could easily walk to and from either location. So since I had been given the remainder of this week as off-duty time, I opted to remain at Dave's home for the next five days. This choice commenced a five-day period of virtually non-stop partying! I quickly found that my friend Dave and his roommate Ray were two guys who really loved to party!

And as such, as they had worked through the remainder of the week, I received continuous visits from numerous cute and very nice young ladies. This influx would begin each morning at around 9:00 by the frequent ringing of Dave's doorbell. As each young lady arrived, she would ask, "Is Dave here"? I would immediately respond that he wasn't, but the young lady would enter anyway. Soon we would find ourselves dancing, sipping wine, and cuddling— before moving into my bedroom. Oddly though, these ladies seemed to have arranged a schedule of visitation between themselves, as no two were ever present during the same time period! In the evenings after my friends had finished work, we would cruise the streets of Athens' suburbs, using Dave's late model Cadillac or Bill's late model Lincoln. This was my general welcoming program to Greece, and by the end of the week I'd enjoyed myself tremendously!

With the past five days having blissfully passed, I reported for duty. During these first three days of work, I was truly surprised to find the general morale of the airmen assigned here was, so very high. Slowly though I realized that the social environment coupled with excellent pay was the main reason for this positive atmosphere. I noticed also many of the airmen here owned fancy new cars such as BMW, Porsche, and Mercedes-Benz. Never before had I seen this many luxury vehicles owned by ordinary GIs! I would later discover that although a small number of these GIs had purchased their vehicles with military income, quite a few had done so through other means!

My first three days at work seemingly flashed past, and now I found myself off-duty for another four days (with lots of spending cash). *"What a life?"* I thought as I recalled my ten close friends who were currently 'suffering' in Japan. Sure, they would enjoy a wonderful social life, but not the extra pay and exciting party life I enjoyed here in Greece. In time I would discover that this was one of the prime vacation spots for government officials, diplomats, and many military members and families. One particular reason for this was— that this installation contained and operated no airplanes. Though it is quite difficult for anyone to imagine finding any Air Force installation minus airplanes! As a result, the mission of this local facility was greatly relaxed. But making matters even better, was the fact that Greek society generally favored American presence and considered us friends.

Having pleasurably experienced my first week here in Greece, I returned to work for my next three days. However, in contrast to the many previous weeks of my lifetime, this would truly begin "The first day of the rest of my life"! Up to this point I'd previously visited a number of clubs, bars, and airmen's homes. But on the evening of Thursday, (October 11th), we visited the home of another of Dave's friends. Over recent years I had learned a few card games such as blackjack and poker. We had come to this residence to play blackjack (which was part of the local routine). On this particular evening, I dressed casually but impressively. We arrived at our host's home whereupon we conversed briefly while listening to music and sipping drinks.

At about 8:00PM we began playing "GI blackjack" with five players at our table. In this type of game the deal rotates from player to player, with high card commencing the game. This game differs from Nevada blackjack, in that the dealer takes pushes. This means that if the dealer and every player at the table ends up holding equal points, the dealer wins the pot. Granted this seems a bit unfair, but everyone has an equal chance at dealing. I soon noticed that there were two other visitors seated in an adjoining room— (the fiancée of our host, along with a younger sister). We'd played blackjack for only a short while, when I was blessed with a glimpse of our host's future sister-in-law. She was stunningly attractive! For a brief moment my heart fluttered, but I succeeded in maintaining composure. Suddenly this lovely young lady vanished from sight. We continued playing cards, although my concentration was greatly diminished by the apparent illusion which I'd just witnessed! Our game continued momentarily.

Our dealer had just dealt our current round of cards. I peeked at mine and was pleasantly surprised to find that I held one queen of hearts and one king of spades! Our dealer had shown one jack of diamonds, but also held one concealed card. I knew that my hand of (twenty) was quite strong, so I did not consider a hit. This was the point where my world turned upside down! Suddenly my illusion reappeared near the door-way of the adjoining room. She appeared to have been studying me. At this moment I instantly became totally distracted! In short, I lost it! When our dealer asked if I wanted a hit, I answered, "Hit me"! Oddly, I had completely forgotten that I held the nearly unbeatable point of twenty! The dealer plucked a card from the deck, placing before me an ace! Instantly my mind regained awareness, causing me to recall the cards which I held. The dealer then flipped over the ten of diamonds! This gave him wins over each player, but a loss to me! I realized that had I not taken a hit, I too would have lost! I then also realized that had this lovely young lady not appeared before me, I would not have inadvertently taken this hit— thereby resulting in a loss! From this evening forward, I would discreetly view this young lady as my very own personal good luck charm! I would very soon discover that her name was Lora. She seemed interested in me, as I was in her. Unfortunately, Lora spoke no English and I spoke no Greek. But even under these odd circumstances, some powerful (but unseen) force was obviously at work here! Moments after our very brief encounter, Lora and sister bade us good night (in Greek) before returning to their small apartment. After her departure, I found that I could not erase her from my memory. I had to see her again!

For the next four days of my off-duty time, I thought only of Lora, while conjuring up ingenious techniques with which to draw her closer to me. Then during these evening hours I would nightly find myself walking all alone in darkness and heavy rainfall— simply for the chance of seeing her. As she appeared before me, my heart rate invariably quickened its pace! Now in case I have not made clear my point, THIS WAS TRUE LOVE— and the kind of love with the power to completely erase all others! Fortunately, as I experienced these wonderfully uncontrollable feelings— so did Lora. Eventually, time would reveal that the two of us would spend our entire lives together in continuous happiness!

I fully realized that I truly wanted Lora in my life; however, our total inability to communicate posed a problem of major proportion! *"How shall I eliminate this great obstacle?"* I asked myself. Then after much deliberation I visited our Base Education Office, where I obtained limited Greek language study materials. I also enrolled in a two-week crash course in spoken Greek. Next, I created my personal program of Greek language study. In so doing, I established the goal of learning ten new Greek words each day, including both definition and grammar. Additionally, I would seek the assistance of our six Greek employees in tutoring me in this language. I soon discovered that I possessed the mental capacity for absorbing and retaining the words I studied.

Beginning Friday evening, I was fortunate to have the opportunity to escort Lora to movies and nightclubs on each of the three weekend evenings. But though we were together, verbal communication was nearly non-existent. Nevertheless, we used sign language in lieu of words. I found this method of communication strange, difficult, and even a bit novel. Somehow though, we enjoyed these very precious moments together. I continued studying the Greek language on a daily basis (including weekends). So after only one month here in this country I had acquired a vocabulary of three hundred commonly spoken Greek words. At this point I began feeling sort of good about myself, although I would not relax my study program. Things were going well between Lora and me, and we continually drew closer.

Until now things had gone really well for me here in Greece. I had given a courtesy phone call to Major James in Washington, during which I thanked him for guiding me to this assignment. During our conversation he informed me that I would soon receive a new pocket recorder, along with a set of Repeated TDY Orders. On the morning of November 8th I received this package. My recorder was a much newer model than the one I'd previously used. Also my TDY orders were pre-funded for travel throughout our current fiscal year. But what interested me most was, these orders stipulated Variations of Itinerary! These two separate provisions facilitated TDY travel to any point on the globe— and at any given time! Now without having been informed of such, I remain confident that Major James had already coordinated with my local commander regarding any future travel which I might perform. The very next afternoon at work, I was summoned to my local commander's office and advised, "Airman Van York, I'm sending you to Tehran for a period of thirty days – you leave on Monday, November twelfth". My first thoughts were of Lora, and I wondered if she' would remember me after thirty days. I was advised to proceed to our immunization clinic for screening. At the clinic I was given three immunizations pertinent to my region of travel. But upon return to work, I was advised that my TDY destination had been changed to Iraklion, Crete (which made me feel much better). One hour later via telephone, I received further confidential instructions from Major James. "Sorry to bounce you around this way Jake, but there've been a few recent changes in plans." he said. "You will proceed to Iraklion as ordered. However, once you arrive there you'll be met by one of my liaisons. He will then escort you directly to a waiting plane. Once you're airborne you'll then be given final instructions." he concluded.

After work that evening I was lucky to have met Lora while on her way home from work. Now even though she was very young in age, she was quite perceptive. She immediately noticed that I appeared somewhat troubled. So in straining my limited Greek vocabulary, I explained to her that I cared for her deeply— but would be away for one full month. She indicated that she'd understood my message and would await my return.

I arrived on the great and expansive island of Crete on November 12th. I was met by a young captain who had been given my description by Major James. He promptly identified himself before escorting me to my next waiting plane. Then after remaining airborne for nearly four hours, we arrived at our destination. Up to this point I had not been briefed as to my destination or mission. I realized though that we had landed at some far away military desert location. This time I was met by one young Army sergeant, who promptly took me to my temporary on-base living quarters. Once we reached my room the sergeant informed me "You will be met here at nine o'clock this morning by one of our DOD civilians, who will then brief you on your mission". Make sure you're ready to go at that time." he said. I assured him I would be ready to leave.

At 7:00AM I arrived at the on-base dining hall. I'd already discovered that this was an Army base, thus so I did not search for familiar faces. After eating I returned to my room and waited. At the appointed hour there came a faint knock upon my door. I opened the door to find one American male, dressed in a dark business suit. He identified himself while presenting to me his credentials. He then asked to see my identification. Having satisfied himself of my identity, this gentleman began his briefing.

I discovered that although this was not Iran, I was in fact standing upon the soil of another prominent Middle Eastern nation. In the course of my briefing I learned that

I would perform reconnaissance upon suspected members of an established terrorist organization. It had been revealed by an informant that this group was in the initial planning stages of a massive attack against our U. S. military forces operating in the Middle East. My specific role was that of monitoring a secret meeting by this group, which was scheduled for 1:00PM in this city's downtown area. Finally, I understood the reasons for the cancellation of my Tehran trip.

At precisely 12:00 noon, I stepped from the late model black Ford sedan, driven by my liaison officer. The local temperature here hovered around ninety degrees. I had dressed casually as an ordinary American tourist. I even carried my recently purchased Japanese camera strapped across my left shoulder. Had any person paid close attention, he or she might have noticed the tiny and inconspicuous 'hearing aid' I wore snugly tucked into my right ear. I casually strolled up and down this designated street, 'window-shopping' as I walked. Occasionally I would stop to peer inside some shop's show-window. I never stepped inside any of these shops though, as I needed to remain outside on the street. As on all previous occasions, I'd been shown photographs of my targets. So now all that was needed were samples of their voices. Cellular communication was non-existent during his time period, so greater planning was always necessary. Accordingly, I had positioned myself one city block east of this expected meeting place. I had also pre-calibrated the Elm to this exact distance. At 12:30PM I saw four young men walking in the direction of the anticipated meeting location. As they neared their destination, I recognized them as my targets, and received their voices clearly. I then adjusted the angle of my head ever so slightly in tracking these fellows up four flights of stairs. I could even hear them as they huffed and puffed their way up to the top floor. At that point they entered a room or office and were warmly greeted by a man who was already inside this building. I began my recording process! I quickly found my recorder to be invaluable because even though these fellows were speaking in Arabic, I understood little of what they said. Although, during their meeting I did distinctly overhear the name of one very special U.S. ship mentioned— one of our U. S. Navy's most sophisticated and advanced aircraft carriers! As their leader continued talking, I continued listening and recording their words. Over the course of this meeting, I picked up a few other words like "soon," "deadly," and "missiles"! This suggested that these guys were quite possibly planning a heavy missile attack on this aforementioned vessel! Their meeting concluded at 1:45PM, so I chose to wait around to witness their departure. Within five minutes these four exited their building, heading in my direction. I had heard them though as they'd descended the stairs, and started casually walking in their direction. Minutes later we passed each other on this street, without them even noticing my presence.

As previously planned, I walked the short distance to a nearby sidewalk café, where I was met by my liaison officer. I'd wisely taken the precaution of removing the Elm from my ear before joining him. My liaison was shocked as I presented him with my recorded tape. "How in the world did you accomplish this, Van York?" he asked. I jokingly said "I'd be happy to explain sir, but you don't possess the proper level of clearance". We each had ourselves a little laugh at my words of wit. He then said "You really should consider teaching your skills in military special ops training courses". "Sir, this is a gift which I was born with, so it can't be learned in classrooms or in the field." I replied. "You've done a truly great job here, and I thank you so much," said the gentleman as he firmly shook my hand before escorting me to my waiting flight.

I arrived back on Crete shortly before 8:00PM of this very same day. The following morning, I found myself busily sorting and delivering letters and parcels to the families of airmen and officers assigned to Iraklion Air Station, Crete. Now this was only Wednesday morning, but it had already been quite exciting for me! I would remain here at Iraklion for the next thirty days. Shortly before quitting hour, I received my customary congratulatory phone call from Major James in Washington. "Great job Jake— you've just prevented a planned terrorist attack against one of our carriers!" he exclaimed. "Thank you sir," I meekly answered before ending our call. I then had a great meal at our local dining hall, though I saw no one here that I recognized. Next, I showered and then toured this small but well-kept base here at Iraklion. I marveled at the many significant changes and improvements in my still young life. I also gave considerable thought to my wonderful new love— Lora!

After what seemed as decades, I returned to Athens on Friday afternoon. I reported directly to my duty section, to find my shift ending for the week. This meant I would now enjoy the next four days as off-duty time. My top priority was to seek out Lora to determine if she remembered me. So after dining on base I boarded the shuttle bus and headed downtown to my waiting hotel room. Once there,

I secured the Elm listening device and recording equipment before showering. That evening, I stepped onto the semi-crowded streets of wonderful Athens. I would now walk the three-quarter mile distance to the home of my new friend Jim, who was engaged to Lora's older sister Andrea. I made a slight detour to see Bill LeGrande but was informed by his landlady that he had departed TDY (Temporary Duty) nearly two weeks earlier. I was quite disappointed by this news, for I had really looked forward to seeing my good friend.

Along my route to Jim's house, I encountered one middle-aged couple who were walking in my direction. As we passed each other, they each greeted me. And since I'd grown accustomed from childhood to always greet passersby, I warmly returned their greeting (in limited Greek). Now although they had greeted me in English, I wanted to impress them by responding in Greek. Evidently I succeeded, for upon hearing my response, the middle-aged gentleman stopped in his tracks and asked, in English, "Are you seeking a home for rental"? "I shall soon be searching for a home," I replied. "Good, then may we show you our home?" he asked. "Is it nearby?" I asked. "Yes, it is close by," he said. "Fine, I would like to see your home, sir." I replied. He seemed quite pleased and, turned briefly to seek agreement from his wife. At this point they reversed direction and began escorting me to their rental home.

With the exception of street lighting, semi-darkness was around us as we reached this home. Still, I was quite impressed by what I'd seen so far. This was a two-story building of moderate size with a very nice fenced front yard. Upon entering this house, I was even more impressed.

It was quite spacious, with two bedrooms, dining room, kitchen, and bathroom. Its walls were of stone and its floors of highly polished marble— such as I had not seen before. As I looked about this place, I considered the standard extra $500 in future monthly income I would receive, but quickly concluded that this amount would be insufficient to defray the rental expense of this house. At this point the gentleman's wife finally spoke, "Do you like the house?" she asked. "It's very nice," I answered. "How much are you asking as rent?" I asked. The husband said, "Fifty-five dollars each month".

I simply couldn't believe my ears, although I remained 'poker-faced'. I responded a bit impetuously with "I'll take it". I should have negotiated the asking price, but at twenty-five, I had never before engaged in this practice of price bargaining. I would later find that I could have easily gotten this house for just $50 per month. But what the heck— this meager sum amounted to only ten percent of my additional income. So in my manner of thinking, I had already received a substantial bargain even at this price. Plus, if I had wanted I could have easily sub-let one bedroom for $25 monthly. We shook hands in confirming our agreement, and this couple accepted this form of contractual agreement. We also agreed we would officially sign the necessary documents come Monday afternoon.

When I arrived at my friend Jim's place, anxiously hoping that Lora might be present, I was quite disappointed at finding she had not yet arrived, but I concealed these feelings. We sat listening to music and chatting. But when Jim asked about my recent TDY trip, I selectively told him only of Iraklion. Soon Lora arrived, once again causing rapid heart palpitations within my chest cavity. I struggled to overcome this rare and exhilarating condition, and at least succeeded in displaying some degree of outward calm. As soon as Lora saw me, she rushed to greet me. Then in my current Greek vocabulary of just over three hundred words, I engaged in limited (but effective) communication with this lovely young lady. I amazed Lora with my rapidly acquired command of this language. Soon we found ourselves laughing and joking together. This had quickly become one extremely happy reunion for us both!

We stepped out onto the streets of Athens for an evening of incessant partying! First we visited a partially hidden beach-front restaurant, where I experienced my very first shrimp with lobster combination dinner. Next, we walked (while constantly holding hands) to a number of American house parties. I quickly noticed that it seemed as though each host had sought to surpass every party currently in progress. Most noteworthy though was the fact that,— other than alcohol, absolutely no drugs were present at any of these parties! This particular evening would remain prominent within my memory throughout the remainder of my life. This would prove only the beginning of an unending series of such events. It goes without saying— our lifelong love affair had undoubtedly begun!

The following week I moved from the hotel and into my cozy rental home. The place was fully furnished, requiring only that I purchase linens, cooking and dining utensils, and a few other miscellaneous items. Lora's apartment was only two blocks away, which allowed for frequent visits. During those first days in my new 'luxury' living quarters, she would stop by often, in assisting me with arranging and decorating the place. In fact, it was Lora herself who did the majority of pre-move-in housecleaning. By Christmas time we were prepared to begin a week partying at my new place, for oddly there first came Christmas, second my birthday (December 27th), and third Lora's birthday (December 28th), followed closely by New Year's Day. I still find it unbelievable that Lora's birthday falls on the heels of my own!

Having joyfully celebrated the holiday period, we then entered the month of January 1963. Incidentally, you may have noticed by now that I have not mentioned my fiancée, (Chris). I assure you this was purely unintentional. Sure I still remembered this truly wonderful young lady, but upon the totally unexpected appearance of Lora, something unexplainable occurred within me. Presently, (although unwittingly), Lora had already completely obliterated any and all feelings I had previously held for: Jeanne, Carol, Catherine, and even the wonderful and lovely Chris! Thus at this juncture, I painfully wrote to Chris, informing her that I would not return anytime soon. I figured that once Chris received my disturbing and disappointing letter, she would quickly forget me. However, time would reveal that I had erred greatly in my assumption. Meanwhile, this indescribable relationship between Lora and me flourished. By the end of March I'd completed my entry level training into the postal career field. But even more importantly, I had successfully added another three hundred words to my Greek vocabulary! Now Lora and I truly had begun understanding each other— so we continued partying as our love grew stronger.

On Monday, April 1st I returned to duty to complete

my three-day shift. Then after a morning of mail processing, I headed for the cafeteria. As I walked along I was joined by my close friend Bill LeGrande, who had just returned from four months TDY in the Middle East. I quickly learned that he and his team had deployed to the very same location I'd visited in November. This time Bill made an exception by confiding in me that their mission had been a major success! I learned that his team had removed and relocated a large number of key terrorists from that region. I was also quite pleased to hear that my prior visit had made this operation successful. Later during the afternoon I learned my Tactical Commander, Major James, had been promoted to lieutenant colonel! I also learned that my friends Bill Houser and Bill LeGrande had each also received promotion to the grade of technical sergeant! These men were highly deserving of their promotions, , and I was very happy for each of them.

Over the next three months I concentrated heavily on the study of my skill level-5 of my postal career field correspondence course. I concurrently continued my study of the Greek language. Also, it goes without saying— I continued that fantastic social aspect of my life with Lora! During this time period, I purchased another automobile. This was not a new car, but one that had been maintained in excellent condition. So now, Lora and I were even more fortunate by realizing the benefits derived from vehicle ownership. Now, instead of busses and taxi cabs, we cruised about in my very own car.

Lora and I were virtually inseparable, and life was simply great. Our flourishing relationship was briefly interrupted though by a follow-up return trip into the Middle

East region I'd visited only months earlier. This time my trip was much more casual and relaxed. This time there was no liaison officer to meet me. I had received my instructions from Lt. Col. James by telephone, thus upon arrival I simply presented my Repeated TDY Orders to Base Military Police Head- quarters. I was directed to my on-base living quarters, which were comfortable though definitely not of five-star quality. I soon found that being here at this time of year reminded me very much of my former days back in Tripoli. Simply stated, local temperatures were sizzling hot! Nevertheless, each morning, afternoon, and evening I visited parks and coffee shops— (as a source of relaxation). I photographed a great number of historical sites. And, without elaborating, I made a number of voice recordings! Otherwise my leisure trip was uneventful. I was never challenged by any person (or persons). In fact, on the surface it appeared as though my presence here had again gone completely unnoticed. Moreover, If the heat had not been so unbearable, I might have considered this trip pleasant. Upon return to Athens, I would make the particulars of this 'vacation known to my tactical commander. I would also subsequently discover that this had certainly not been a wasted trip, as even more newly organized terrorist groups would soon be neutralized!

I arrived back in Athens, where I found that Lora had anxiously awaited my return. We quickly resumed our 'whirlwind' love affair, which was facilitated by my ability to communicate with Lora in her native language. During my most recent TDY, I realized how very much I cared for this wonderful young lady. But even so, I went to great effort in concealing these unbelievably strong feelings from her. After two weeks of this— and only when I could resist no longer— I knelt upon my left knee, and I asked Lora to marry me. My proposal came as a great surprise to her; although, her eager acceptance came as an even greater surprise to me! This occurred on Sunday evening of June 30th 1963. The following day I rushed to our tiny base, where I proudly purchased a very attractive engagement ring! When I placed this ring onto Lora's finger, she vowed to never leave me. As of this writing (fifty years later), her vow remains true. Our wedding would be held just four months later, signaling the beginning of our joyous and life-long relationship!

Summer had begun, bringing with it beautiful clear days of moderately high temperatures. My personal weekly routine continued unchanged, although my close friend Bill along with his special ops team had returned to the Middle East for another two months. This left Lora and me free to party nightly with her sister and fiancé, Jim. We frequented the beautiful sandy beaches of Athens on weekends and went to house parties, restaurants, and nightclubs as a foursome. Needless to say, I truly enjoyed this summer of 1963 in Athens!

Now, I admit that I've focused primarily upon the social aspect of my life here in Greece. However, during each of our thirty-six hour work weeks— we really worked! This particular mail terminal operation handled mail, (in bulk) for all the western world! Tons upon tons of mail were processed here each day of the week. There were no holidays observed here within this terminal operation. This was also where all classified and high-value items (such as large amounts of cash) were received, stored, and dispatched.

We were afforded considerable flexibility and freedom while performing our duties, and so long as we did not blatantly violate governing rules and regulations, we enjoyed freedom of movement. There was no punch clock, but this never caused problems of any sort.

Having said this, one warm Saturday evening during mid-August, I took one of our metro van vehicles to the commercial side of the airport. This was a routine trip to get the mail directly from an inbound commercial flight. Since I had become assistant shift leader, I required no other person along as monitor. By 9:30PM, I had off-loaded my mail cargo and secured it inside my van. At this hour the sun had disappeared, requiring lighting from airport lights. This plane I'd off-loaded had parked at the east end of this runway, which was nearly one mile past the control tower and passenger terminal. I sat for nearly fifteen minutes as I watched this plane taxi across to the next parallel runway, in preparation for takeoff. Soon it was airborne, (which I found quite exciting). I started up my van and then commenced my low-speed drive alongside the runway toward the exit gate. I had driven for less than a quarter mile when I suddenly noticed what appeared to have been some small object lying upon the grassy median between runways. This object was dark in color, blending with the green grass and surrounding darkness. As I reached this object, I stopped for a closer look and instantly recognized this container as a DIPLOMATIC POUCH! This was highly unusual, as no such pouch should ever be left unguarded! I could only think of one explanation for such an occurrence— our couriers had somehow accidentally dropped this pouch from their vehicle. Cautiously I picked it up for closer inspection.

Ordinarily such pouches contained bold TOP SECRET markings on all six sides. However, this pouch contained no markings whatsoever. Now after having served nearly eleven months here with this organization, I'd become quite familiar with applicable governing directives. I knew beyond a doubt that such unmarked pouches contained great amounts of cash; thus, depending upon the denomination of bills inside, there could've been up to one million dollars inside this pouch! I cautiously looked all about, (even peering into the darkness) but saw no one nearby. So there I stood, all alone in semi-darkness with no one aware of this current situation— AND HOLDING ONTO POSSIBLY AS MUCH AS ONE MILLION IN CASH! Now I ask each of you readers "What would you have done in such a situation"? I'm confident that only a few of you will have even the slightest idea of what you might have done!

Oddly, I remained calm. My hands did not shake or perspire, nor did my heart rate accelerate. I quickly secured this pouch inside my van before driving directly to our organizational courier station. I approached the two-inch thick reinforced steel door. I then rang the buzzer and waited. Momentarily, the officer in charge, (2nd Lieutenant J. Sachs), peeked through the door's security window. "Sir, did you lose something?" I asked. With both anxiety and excitement in his voice the lieutenant asked, "Did you find it"? "I did," I answered. Upon hearing this, the lieutenant uttered a great sigh of relief as he hurriedly opened the door of the courier station. "Give it to me," he ordered (but in begging fashion). "Check it closely," I said, handing him the sealed pouch. The lieutenant then issued a long series of "thank yous" before returning back inside the courier station. I then drove next door to our mail terminal, and promptly off-loaded my mail cargo. I would never again hear mention of this incident.

I am certain that no report (neither verbal nor written) was ever submitted regarding the loss of this pouch. Had there been an incident report submitted, a number of actions would have occurred. First, the career of my detachment commander would have ended for failure to control operations within his organization! Second, Lt. Sachs' career would have also ended! Third, the two airmen who had lost this pouch would have been court-martialed prior to immediate separation from military service! Fourth, the families of all those involved would have suffered needlessly! Prior to this incident I had always given great consideration as to what action I might take under such rare circumstances. Well, on that very special evening I received my answer. I have never since regretted having turned in this money! Eight years later in upstate New York, I would again meet and become very close friends with the (now technical sergeant) responsible for the loss of this high-value pouch. Over time, Lora and I would spend a lot of time with him and his wife. Even our three baby daughters would become friends. This was my only needed form of thanks, as all had ended well!

During the next two months I completed my five-level career development course in postal. I also added a significant number of new Greek words to my vocabulary, and returned to an intense program of billiards training. Meanwhile, Lora and I enthusiastically prepared for our rapidly approaching wedding date. This time though, I looked forward to this very special day. In fact, at least four persons highly anticipated this very special occasion, for this would be a double wedding!

At the beginning of October, I moved into an even nicer home in my neighborhood. I made this to provide the best possible living conditions for my dear Lora once we were married. My newly rented house was of more recent construction, and was of better quality and condition. Thus once we were married, Lora and I would better appreciate our daily lives together. Finally, the all-important date of October 26th 1963 arrived! My soon to be brother-in-law and I had made plans for an elaborate and lavish reception immediately following our wedding. We purchased a total of thirty (forty ounce) bottles of high-quality alcohol, along with twelve cases of costly American-brand beer. Our beer would be kept in Jim's bathtub and packed in ice. We also bought an abundance of groceries for sandwiches and a wide variety of snacks. We even purchased several cases of beverage soda for our once-in-a-lifetime event.

An hour before the ceremony, the four of us arrived at the church where our wedding would be performed. At 8:00PM, our wedding ceremony began— and would extend for two hours. The wedding was conducted according to Greek custom and culture— thus the long duration. Immediately afterward, we were driven to our homes where we changed into casual clothing for the reception. By 11:00PM, nearly all the guests (150 people) had arrived. Our wonderful evening of festivities had begun— and would last until early Sunday morning! There was lots of great music, much food, and a considerable amount of alcohol consumption! No one cared about roadside police conducting alcohol tests, for there would be none. Hence, we all thoroughly enjoyed ourselves through the entire evening. At 7:30 Sunday morning, I took Lora by her dainty little hand and walked her across the street to our new home! Once there, we gave thanks to our Lord before engaging in that which newlyweds invariably resort to! At this point things were quite intimate, and I feel these expressions of love should remain unspoken. I will say here though— this was a very special and unforgettable Sunday for both Lora and me!

The spectacular city of Athens and its surrounding areas are the perfect honeymoon locations! As such, this was exactly where we spent ours. For the next seven full days, Lora and I enjoyed our new life together! We visited sites we had not seen before. We even spent two of my off-duty days touring nearby Greek islands. While there we traveled about on foot while visiting a number of movie theaters and very fine restaurants. And although I still had not learned to swim, we even spent a few warm October days at nearby beaches. Having this very special young lady as my wife was nearly overwhelming, and I must say, this new experience was one I would forever remember!

On Monday November 4th 1963, I returned to duty as a happily married young man! Upon arrival I was summoned upstairs to the office of my local detachment commander. I figured he might have wished to congratulate me regarding my recent wedding. As it turned out he congratulated me, but there was more. I discovered that although I had only recently become a fully qualified postal specialist, I was now being offered a new and very special job. On official manning documents, this position was listed as postal specialist. However, this function actually entailed accounting and administrative duties. For the past three years it had been occupied by an airman first class (E-4) same as myself, who would soon separate from military service. I eagerly accepted this position, as I had never really cared for working twelve-hour night shifts. I was then instructed to report downstairs to the technical sergeant (E-6) who would become my new supervisor. I complied with instructions as ordered.

I immediately replaced the outgoing airman, affording him ample time in which to out-process. Here I would work Mondays through Fridays, but only during daytime hours. This posed no problem though as my local detachment commander was aware of the fact that I possessed a set of Repeated TDY orders. Thus in the event I was deployed, my supervisor would perform this duty temporarily in my absence.

This new job involved the daily calculating, recording, and reporting of mail manifests from commercial airline carriers. My job while back in Libya also had involved working with numbers, but not to this extent. I'd already been made aware of the fact that my predecessor was highly regarded by all personnel within our detachment. Regardless though, this sentiment would have absolutely no affect upon the manner in which I performed here. Therefore, I quickly familiarized myself with applicable directives and procedures relative to my new position. I then dedicated my efforts toward producing quality performance!

Over the first two weeks in this work, I occasionally noticed my supervisor as he curiously scrutinized my work routine. Soon these odd looks from him began taking their toll upon me, so I asked, "Sergeant Smith, is there something wrong"? He assured me that nothing was wrong, so I continued tabulating figures throughout each day. My supervisor continued giving me strange looks. Finally, when I could take his glances no longer, I said, "Sarge, it would help me a lot if you would simply tell me what's bothering you". My supervisor then answered, "Well, back when Airman Josephs was here doing this job, he would take several breaks each morning, but still finish his work by 2:00 each afternoon." This slightly annoyed me, but I had also made this very same observation of Airman Josephs. I recalled having envied him on several occasions and thinking, *"Gee, I sure wish I had a job like that"*. The significance of my supervisor's comments though was this— he'd seen me as slow in my work; and therefore, incompetent in this position! I could not allow this opinion to persist, so I asked "Would you like to conduct a time-test between yourself and me"? "No, I can easily see that you are working hard and steadily each day— I'm just wondering why this is taking you so long." he answered. "I would much rather that we conducted the test," I said. Still, my supervisor declined. I was then left alone to do my work, although I was concerned over the possibility of being rated inefficient come performance evaluation day. Over the coming months I even attempted accelerating the pace of my work. However, I quickly discovered that in seeking increased speed, I sacrificed accuracy. This slowed my production rate. I then resolved that above all else, I would maintain accuracy!

On the social front, the already strong feelings which Lora and I held for each other grew even stronger. We continued our lifestyle of greatly enjoying life when not working. We celebrated Thanksgiving, which was soon followed by Christmas, our birthdays, and the New Year. These were the most wonderful holidays of my life to date. Making this even more appreciable was the fact that I had not been selected for any further TDYs during this period.

On April 18th 1964, Lora and I were blessed by the birth of our very first child— a beautiful (but quite small) baby girl, whom we named Mari! Both Lora and I took great pleasure in loving and protecting this wonderful baby girl. It seemed that everywhere we traveled the locals would stop to admire her! I need not tell you just how happy and proud their attention made Lora and me. Incidentally, this very special child would throughout our lives bring us joy, happiness, and, great pride by rapidly becoming, a loving, compassionate, sensitive, and highly productive human being!

But let us now return to the military aspect of my life. Beginning Monday June 3rd our unit underwent its first day of annual inspection by postal authorities of the Air Force Inspector General's evaluation team. Suddenly all military activity here entered into a heightened state of readiness. As a result of their presence, tension within our organization quickly escalated! This hand-picked team of officers and non-commissioned officers were elite in their own right. These were the guys vested with the power to make or break any officer's military career! They also exercised indirect control over the careers of all enlisted personnel.

Two members of this team (one captain plus one master sergeant) were tasked to inspect our organization's voluminous batches of mail manifests. Upon request I promptly gathered all manifests of the past eighteen months. I then returned to tabulating current day manifests, as these two inspectors began their tedious task of reconciling mail manifests with monthly expense reports prepared by me or my predecessor, the illustrious Airman Josephs. By the end of their second day of records inspection, their attitudes and reactions suddenly took a serious down turn! They surprised me by stopping their work and moving outside our building. Through the Plexiglas of my office cubicle, I could clearly see them as they discussed what seemed a very serious issue. After about five minutes, they walked upstairs to the office of our detachment commander. Soon, I too was summoned upstairs. My commander appeared quite agitated, but invited me to sit. I didn't know what to make of this new development, but I silently took a vacant nearby seat. My commander held the grade of captain, and so did the lead inspector of my work center. However, the captain of the IG Team was more highly regarded by virtue of his position. It was he who explained to me my problem. "Airman Van York, there seems to be some major discrepancies in your monthly expenditure reports!" he began. His announcement both shocked and alarmed me! "Could you give me some specifics, sir?" I asked. "Each of your reports are far off the mark— compared to those of Airman Josephs." he answered. "Might I ask, sir, have you compared any of my reports to the figures contained in the mail manifests?" I said. "That's our next step," stated the captain, adding, "We'll need you to remain with us for a couple of hours while we run our computations though." said the captain. Naturally, I could not disagree, so I stood by in observer status as these two resumed their work. My supervisor also volunteered to remain on duty while this special audit was performed.

EXTRAORDINARY EXPERIENCES OF JAKE VANYORK

The inspectors selected the month of May 1964 as their first audit, sharing this workload equally between themselves. At the end of three hours, they completed that month's audit. Surprisingly, neither found a single error! This visibly perplexed them, for they were certain that the existing errors were contained specifically in my reports. But this was okay by me, for after all— the brilliant Airman Josephs never made mistakes! At 8:00PM the inspectors decided to end their day's work. After all, they also had very much looked forward to evenings of socializing in downtown Athens.

The following morning, the inspectors assigned a team of six officers and non-commissioned officers the task of auditing our detachment's accounting reports covering the past two-year period! Their audit surprisingly revealed no discrepancies in any of the reports which I had prepared. By contrast, each monthly report prepared by Airman Josephs contained numerous major discrepancies! When they had concluded their two-year audit, their findings revealed numerous overcharges, totaling more than $1,200,000! This was money that had erroneously been paid to national and international commercial airline companies from the pockets of U. S. taxpayers! The inspectors were stunned beyond belief! Our poor detachment commander was the most stunned of all, for this had all occurred during his watch! Simply stated— this was his responsibility. Now if you find yourself asking "How was this possible?" – here's the answer.

It was generally assumed that Airman Josephs was highly intelligent, competent, and responsible in the performance of his assigned duties. Beneath the surface of this masquerade though was an individual who simply loathed this type of work, and would resort to even unethical methods in avoiding same. Consequently, as Airman Josephs gained knowledge and confidence in that position, he began taking shortcuts. More specifically, he began falsifying accounting reports by fabricating figures! Hence, the majority of reports he submitted were generated through the use of estimation, instead of tabulation. He knew that if he under-estimated, airline companies would have screamed 'bloody murder'! Thus, during the latter two-year period of his assignment, he consistently over-estimated in reporting monthly mail tonnage transported. This was the reason why my supervisor had on numerous occasions given me those curious looks of doubt. Shortly after his first several months in this assignment, Airman Josephs became lax in his work habits, (although no one had noticed). So, he began fabricating nearly one hundred percent of his accounting reports. This was how he'd found the free time to sit around sipping coffee (or whatever) for at least two hours of each work day. I, on the other hand, had consistently tabulated each weight figure contained on each mail manifest. Moreover, this position required full-time production— rather than just five hours per day! Finally, my supervisor understood, and fully appreciated my dedicated work contribution.

These events which I've just related to you constituted dereliction of duty by Airman Josephs, and were punishable by military court-martial! However, he had already separated from military service, which made court-martial consideration unlikely. The Inspector General team concluded their visit and returned to their permanent station in Frankfurt, Germany. I was not privy to their written report of this visit, although I feel certain that it was not at all complimentary to our poor detachment commander. From this day forward though, I was given cart blanche within our unit. But even so, I continued my professional duty performance.

Now since I was a newlywed and serving in a one-deep position, my Tactical Commander Lt. Col. James in Washington advised me that every effort would be made in releasing me from short-notice reconnaissance duty travel into Middle Eastern regions. So now I would relax here in beautiful Athens for the remaining fifteen months of my tour. I had successfully completed all career-related courses of study. I had also attained an adequate level of competency in the Greek language. So now, it was once again party time for Lora and me!

Lora's mother had joined us for an extended visit to helping care for our baby daughter Mari, which was a great help to us both. So on July 1st 1964, after a brief moment of hesitation and sadness, Lora and I climbed into our automobile and drove northward. This four-week vacation would become our official honeymoon. During our trip we would tour all of northern Greece along with the countries of Italy and Switzerland. I had always yearned to see the world, and had already seen much of it; however, this vacation would remain in our minds throughout our lifetime. Over the next four weeks we visited many villages and small towns in both Italy and Switzerland, although, we visited every major city in each country. At the very end, having toured such magnificent locations as Rome, Venice, and Geneva, we settled on Milan and Zurich as our favorites. We would return to these two locations in celebration of our 50th wedding anniversary!

On August 1st, I returned to military duty and resumed my accounting activities. This time, however, those frequent looks I'd previously received from my supervisor had completely disappeared. No longer did he (and others here) question my abilities. In fact, both he and our detachment commander were so greatly relieved, they each granted me full freedom of movement within our organization! This meant I could leave the confines of our unit as often as I chose without requesting permission or answering to any superior. I greatly appreciated this rare form of recognition, but of course I would never abuse this special privilege. Nevertheless, my remaining fifteen months here in Athens virtually flew past!

All too soon we had entered the month of January 1965, meaning Lora and I would leave Athens in just ten months. (My— how time flies when we're having fun)! Six months later our postal inspectors paid us another surprise visit! This time they were primarily interested in auditing my accounting reports. So when the captain (team chief) asked me to fetch the past twelve months of records, I promptly complied. I presented to him twelve one cubic ft boxes containing my reports. This time though, I would not be requested to remain after normal duty hours as they performed their audit! Once again the chief inspector assigned six military persons the task of auditing my records. After four long days and nights of tedious tabulation of figures, the IG team completed their task. They then summoned me to our commander's upstairs office, where we would be briefed regarding their findings. This most recent audit revealed that I had erred— but only in the amount of .02 cents, which warranted commendation! The team chief then lauded me for outstanding performance of duty, which naturally made me quite pleased. Both my commander and supervisor followed suit, having been considerably more pleased than even I was. At this point the IG team chief really stunned me by saying, "Airman Van York, pick yourself an assignment"! Then in being a bit uncertain as to his meaning, I hesitated before answering. Sensing my uncertainty, he quickly added, "You can have the assignment of your choice—anywhere in the entire Air Force"! "Thank you very much sir," I answered (still a bit uncertain). I repeated his statement intent in the form of a question, asking, "Anywhere I'd like to go sir"? "Anywhere" he answered. "Well, I would really like an assignment to Copenhagen." I replied. "I'll coordinate your request and advise you on this before we leave tomorrow," answered the captain. "Thank you so much sir" I meekly replied. This concluded our briefing. Back inside our office cubicle my supervisor commented, "Jake, the offer you've just received is unprecedented"! "I've never before heard such an offer in my twenty-four years of military service." he said.

Now, of course I was extremely happy at having received such a rare opportunity. However, my fantastic offer was unfortunately short lived. Next day at work the IG team chief approached me saying, "Airman Van York, I have great news for you"! "Copenhagen will be available to you on October 1ˢᵗ 1966, which means you will be required to extend here in Athens for an additional year." he said. It was at this point in my career that I made my absolutely greatest blunder ever! I answered the captain by saying "Sir, I thank you so very much, but on second thought— I think I'd better take myself back to the States instead". "Are you sure about your decision?" asked the captain. I reluctantly answered, "I'm sure sir". "Well, it's your call," he responded. The next week I forecasted for stateside assignment, (an act for which I would forever kick myself)!

On August 31st, I received my stateside assignment to Dayton, Ohio. Just three days later, my friend Bill LeGrande (along with his entire special ops team) received permanent reassignment orders to an undisclosed location within the Middle East. I never inquired as to the exact location, and was never informed. I would never again see my dear friend. One year later I would be informed by (then Colonel) James that my friend, along with two members of his team, had been killed while executing an insurgent extraction!

On October 30th, following our two-hour airport rooftop farewell party, one large TWA Boeing 707 aircraft took-off, bound for the great city of New York. We traveled as first class passengers and were treated by airline cabin crew almost as VIP travelers (the good old days). Lora and I each carried sixty-five pounds of luggage, along with two special containers, each containing 200 ounces of high-quality whiskey. Upon arrival in New York city, we would spend the following two weeks as tourists. We would then travel into the great state of New Jersey, where we would spend another full week. While there I would purchase for myself and family a newer automobile. Throughout our eight-hour flight, our cute little daughter of eighteen months, Mari entertained the flight crew and passengers by talking to them. She would stand upright in her seat and then wave to nearby passengers, saying, "Hi, my name is Mari"! Passengers just loved her! Finally at 6:00PM we arrived in New York. Greece had just become a great dream of the past!

Chapter 10

Operation Ohio

Having spent the past four weeks enjoying our vacation, My wife, young child, and I arrived at the sprawling and prestigious airbase commonly known as Wright-Patterson AFB, located just outside Dayton, Ohio. As might have been expected, a layer of light snowfall had already accumulated. Neither my young wife nor child had ever witnessed such a marvelous sight, so they were simply fascinated by this strange but wonderfully beautiful snow. Local temperature was considerably lower than Greece, but I had anticipated such weather conditions so we were adequately dressed for winter. This was a totally new experience for me. It was an even greater experience for my young wife of just two years. I had never before completed an assignment rotation as a married person, so I was nearly overwhelmed by this new experience. Normally, I would have in-processed onto the base as a single airman, where I would have been assigned a dormitory room on base. However, this time I was assigned off-base living quarters. Once we arrived at our apartment complex, we were quite pleased by the size and overall condition of our cozy two-bedroom unfurnished apartment. Here though,

I would be required to buy a complete set of new furniture. Luckily, I would not commence my new assignment for five more days, which allowed ample time for us to familiarize ourselves with our surroundings and buy new furniture and food items. I even took time out for a short visit to my new work location, which was a large consolidated mail room operation providing mail services to airmen of our base.

We had spent the past three days at a rather frenzied pace; so, by Saturday morning we had received our new furniture and arranged our apartment to our satisfaction. I found myself wishfully thinking of visiting some nearby nightclub for a pleasant evening in the city of Dayton. But then reality struck me and I quickly realized I now had myself a young wife and an infant child to care for. This meant we would probably not visit any clubs for quite some time! I wistfully longed for even a semblance of the social experiences I had enjoyed over the past ten years, but we would now spend our evenings quietly at home while watching television and enjoying such shows as *I Spy, Mod Squad,* and *The Rifleman.*

Finally, Monday morning, December 6th, arrived. I arose, dressed for military duty, hugged and kissed my wife and baby daughter, and hurried off toward the base for in-processing. This took two full days. On Wednesday morning, I reported for duty at the Consolidated Mail Room. As in Reno and Tripoli, my supervisor was a civilian (only younger than the previous two individuals). My new supervisor's name was Bob Salyer, a friendly person who was easy to get along with. We quickly became what I'd then considered as friends. My job was routinely simple, since here I would not supervise as I'd done years earlier back at Harlingen.

Ordinarily, it takes time to learn a new job; but since I was already a fully qualified postal specialist with extensive prior mail room experience, no familiarization period was necessary. It was as though I had worked here for years. I soon discovered that my personal qualifications had greatly impressed my supervisor. I also learned that his respect for my knowledge caused him to grant me greater flexibility in performing my assigned duties. By the end of my first week in my new position, I'd gained considerable status in our organization. My second level supervisor was also a civilian, but one of much higher grade. I also immediately gained his respect and admiration. So at the end of my first week of duty, I felt quite comfortable in my new environment.

As my first duty day here neared its end, I received a familiar phone call on Friday afternoon. The esteemed caller was my tactical commander, Colonel A. T. James of Washington, D.C. My supervisor had answered the phone and was clearly impressed by the status of this high-ranking officer! He considered this call completely out of the ordinary, as colonels never, ever telephoned lowly airmen! He peered curiously at me while handing me the phone and saying, "Col. James of Hq USAF".

We exchanged pleasantries, and the colonel began his briefing. "Jake, I have great plans for you at Wright-Patterson. I have drafted a Special Ops plan which I've dubbed Operation Ohio. This involves your deployment into South Vietnam, several times during the next twelve-month period. In conducting this secret operation, you will perform three separate thirty-day TDYs to that location. "Do you think you can handle such an extremely dangerous assignment?" asked the colonel. "Can do, sir," I answered. "Great, your first deployment shall commence four months from now, which will be during the entire month of March next year, so let's begin making plans, shall we?" he said. The colonel then advised me of the details of these missions. "Jake, I'm confident that you have fully grasped the magnitude of this operation, so I won't comment further except to say— make absolutely certain you have your personal affairs in order! "I will need a complete list of those items you consider essential to conducting these missions." he advised. "Sir, I'll have my list prepared and ready for you by the middle of next week," I said. "That's great, Jake. Have yourself a great week." – "Out". As I cradled the telephone, my supervisor asked, "What was that all about"? "Oh, I've just been advised that I'll be away TDY during March, July, and October of next year," I answered. "At least we've been informed well in advance— so we can plan for your absences," said my new supervisor.

At home over the weekend, I would carefully create a list of those items I would need for these extremely dangerous deployments into the dense jungle territories of Vietnam! I knew full well that on each of these deployments, I would operate alone and unsanctioned by my government while penetrating the heart of Viet Cong territory. Ah, but there's more to this than meets the eye. Namely, I was a member of the U.S. Air Force (not Marines or Army), which means I was not a member of our military's ground fighting forces! Under no circumstances should I ever have found myself in the midst of any ground combat environment.

And compounding this already sensitive situation was the fact that I was never fully combat trained. Heck, I was just an ordinary administrative/postal specialist. However, I would perform no typing or mail handling services there in the jungles of Vietnam!

At home on Saturday while my wonderful young wife prepared our meal, I concentrated upon compiling a viable list of equipment I felt I would need relative to personal safety and survival while on deployment: (See below).

QUANTITY/ NOMENCLATURE /UNIT OF ISSUE

1 pack ammunition rounds, .45 cal; 15 arrows, 24 aluminum shaft; 1 each crossbow, 12" shaft; 2 each canteens; 1 each first aid kit; 2 pair goggles, night vision; 1 each handgun, .45 cal automatic; 1 each hunting knife; 1 each machete, 15" blade; 1 each mesh screen, 20 sq ft; 1 each nylon (fabric) 20 sq ft; 1 each recorder, pocket size w/tapes (12) each; 1 each shovel, portable; 1 each signal communicator; 1 each walking cane///////////Last Item//////////////.

I would forward this list on Monday via official mail to the Washington office of Colonel James. With this requirement completed, I turned my attention to my young family. Later that afternoon I took them for a drive through the countryside. Lora was a bit disappointed by the absence of sandy beaches and scenic mountains, which made me feel somewhat guilty over having brought her here. I consoled her by saying, "Don't worry, I'm sure we'll only be here for a short while". My words seemed to have cheered her up (at least slightly). At this point we both realized just how lonely and vulnerable we felt by having come to Ohio. We also realized that only the love we felt for each other would sustain us. We then spent our weekend by visiting the base and driving about town.

Soon six long weeks had passed and Lora and I found ourselves excitedly planning our very first Christmas together in the United States. We visited several stores, where we purchased a number of gifts for ourselves and our baby daughter Mari. I really wanted to drive home and spend some time with mom and dad so they could meet their baby granddaughter and young daughter-in-law. Unfortunately, road conditions during this time of year were simply too severe to consider such a drive. Hence, Christmas arrived only to find my family and me lovingly snuggled together inside our cozy apartment. Although my parents were not present, we three had ourselves a wonderful Christmas. Two days later we celebrated my birthday, followed immediately by Lora's. Then came our festivities for New Year's Day. Overall, we had a great time together, although Mari had comprehended none of this.

We had now entered the year 1966. At work things had consistently gone smoothly, with no reportable incidents of concern. Regretfully though I had recently become acutely aware of the shortage of personal cash. The move from Greece to Ohio had been quite costly for me as I had just purchased an automobile and household furnishings. Compounding my problem was the fact that my military pay had just suffered a sixty percent reduction! Now my monthly income had been reduced to normal levels. Sadly, those huge extra allowances I had received while serving in Greece had completely disappeared! In alleviating this financial shortfall I could have sought part-time employment, but this would have required working evenings. Since we now had a small child to protect, and Lora understood very little English, I opted not to seek such work. "*What to do?*" I thought! At this point I recalled that my skills in pocket billiards had vastly improved during recent years, so I decided I would become a pool hustler (of sorts)! Each evening after work I would play billiards for two hours. At the end of my first week, I realized I had found the nearly perfect solution. The one hazard requiring my constant attention appeared in the form of other, (more experienced), hustlers! Once I had developed my very own technique for avoiding such pitfalls, I was on my way to success! Soon I found myself once again capable of taking my dear wife shopping, while not experiencing extreme panic upon receipt of the tab. Thus, I continued mixing billiards with work!

Near the end of January I received an official parcel—most of the items I had requested from Colonel "J". I had not expected shipment of the handgun/ammunition, or the twelve chemically laced arrowheads. The colonel had already advised me that I would receive these items from one particular individual upon my arrival in Vietnam. The crossbow and three practice arrows were present and not damaged (which was one of my main concerns). All other requested items were present and in excellent working condition. The fabric for my two tents required construction. I would take this fabric to my local parachute shop for measuring, trimming, and sewing. At the parachute shop

I was advised that these two items would be designed to my specifications, and ready for pick-up by mid-February. I would keep the remaining items stored inside my garage until deployment.

During the next ten days I diligently practiced my previously acquired archery skills while using the crossbow. After one week I felt I'd gained the level of competency required for use of the crossbow in combat situations! Might I point out here that I did not anticipate encountering actual combat. I planned to use this bow only in the event that some sort of stealth attack by me was needed. Time would prove this to have been a wise decision on my part.

The days flew past, but I still had not informed my dear wife of my rapidly approaching TDY deployment. I simply did not want to reveal this upcoming situation to my wife. Finally, when I could wait no longer I briefed her, not telling the whole truth. I said to her "My dear, beginning the first of March I'm going to have to leave you for a thirty-day TDY to California". At first she thought I was joking, but when she realized that I was serious, she nearly fainted right there on the spot! "How will I survive here with a baby while you're gone, Jake?" she asked, teary-eyed. I felt so very badly over this situation, I could think of no suitable response. I tried consoling her by saying, "We'll buy every-thing you might need before I leave, so things will be easier for you. I sensed that my words had been of little comfort to her, as she then ran upstairs and fell onto our bed and began sobbing uncontrollably! At that moment I experienced a sadness of the magnitude I'd not felt since that unbearable day on which I joined the military. But had I actually told Lora, "Honey, I'm going to Vietnam for thirty days", she might not have survived such news! So in reality, I felt better in lying to her.

During the last week of February, Lora and I made the final preparations for my departure. Needless to say,— this was a very sad time for the both of us. Then four days later I watched in severe emotional pain, as my dear little Lora stood while holding our young baby daughter in her arms, as through the screen of our front door— she waved "bye" to me. As I affectionately waved back to my dear wife and child, I found myself suddenly unable to speak. Luckily (at least for me) the military vehicle in which I rode quickly rounded the nearby corner, whisking me away from view of my loving young family. My driver then drove me directly to our base passenger terminal, where I was immediately hustled onto a waiting military flight bound for Travis AFB, California.

After slightly more than three hours of flight, we reached this huge California airbase. I'd been pre-briefed that I would exchange flights at this location. A glance at my watch revealed the time as 1:30PM. This meant I would remain here for a period of only one hour, as my special charter flight was scheduled for take-off at 2:30. I promptly proceeded directly to the check-in area, where I presented my newly funded Repeated TDY Orders to the ticket clerk. After a brief review of my credentials and immunization record, I proceeded to my waiting flight.

Once I had boarded the chartered C-135 jet aircraft, I settled back in my seat in preparation of this long flight directly to DaNang airbase in (then) South Vietnam. Surprisingly I managed to sleep through much of our flight. Then just after 8:00AM on the morning of March second, we landed on the main runway of that well-known military installation of DaNang AB, Vietnam. As I stepped from the plane I immediately noticed that temperatures here were much milder than those back in Ohio. With my two duffle bags of clothing and equipment, I proceeded directly to the inside of the large passenger terminal.

There I was met by a young captain who looked as youthful as I was, only I was a lowly airman first class. On the surface, my relatively low grade might have been an indication that—somewhere during my career— I had really goofed up! Such was not the case though, as I had always strived for excellence in the performance of my military duties. The captain had received my description from Colonel "J", so he instantly recognized me. He promptly approached while grasping my hand and introducing himself. With introductions behind us, he commented, "Come, airman, let me get you to your living quarters". We rode in his open-aired jeep for only a short distance, whereupon he announced, "This is it". We parked and entered the building. I was quite surprised to find one rather large and insulated room had been prepared for my stay here. In this room was not only a television, but also a private telephone. As the captain looked about, he said, "Airman, I don't know how you rate— but only our wing commander and fire chief are afforded phones in their rooms". I did not respond, as I simply couldn't think of a suitable reply. The captain then opened a mid-sized cardboard box which he'd brought along. From this box he removed one handgun (.45 cal automatic) with ammunition, plus twelve special arrowheads. Next, from a second packet he removed six regular-type hand grenades. Lastly, he removed from a third package, one portable tape player/recorder and four (thirty-minute pre-recorded tapes). When I inquired about the tapes, the captain stated, "These are intended to help you in learning the local language". "Do you have any questions"? "No sir, the items you've just given me will serve just fine." I said. Lastly, the captain presented me with a map of the base which highlighted the base dining hall and our combat operations command post. Colonel James had already provided me with the name of the lieutenant colonel who currently served as deputy director of this Combat Operations Center. From this point forward, I would deal only with him. This officer would be my sole contact for the next twenty-nine days.

With the captain having departed my room, I busied myself unpacking, arranging, and securing my belongings. Soon it was lunch time, so I locked my weaponry inside my utility locker before rushing to the dining hall. This time I would not search this facility for familiar faces, for I would find no time here for socializing. After lunch I proceeded to our command post in the hope of meeting with my contact/support officer. I was in luck as he had not yet taken lunch. We greeted and conversed briefly before the deputy director dropped a bombshell on me! "Well, Airman Van York, are you ready for your first night of jungle duty?" he asked. "Tonight, sir?" I asked. "Why not, do you have anything better to do?" he responded. Then for lack of a better answer, I replied, "Sure sir, I'm ready". "Great, then we'll see you back here at 1800 hours sharp," he officially ordered. I excused myself and went directly back to my room.

EXTRAORDINARY EXPERIENCES OF JAKE VAN YORK

It was 1:00PM and I longed to speak to my dear wife. The telephone sat invitingly upon the nearby steel desk. So with fingers slightly trembling, I dialed my home phone number back stateside in Ohio. On the third ring my beloved wife answered, "Hello"? "Hi my love, how are you?" I asked (in Greek). "Jake, we're fine, how are you?" came Lora's reply, also in Greek. I assured her that I was well and doing fine. Lora sighed in relief and I tried convincing her that I would soon return.

Now at 7:00 after having slept for four hours, I'd washed up, eaten, and was jungle based! But contrary to other military personnel, I was the only Air Force member to be saddled with such a dangerous mission! And to make matters even worse, I was all alone out here in soon-to- be complete darkness! I was approximately twenty-four kilometers north of the base at DaNang. Having arrived here by heavily armed helicopter gunship, I requested that I be deposited in an area that was filled with craters caused by bombing raids from our awesome Air Force B-52 bombers.

During this season and at this time of evening, total darkness was rapidly settling in upon me. Before lowering me onto the ground, my chopper had strafed for five minutes with lethal .50 caliber machine gun fire. By so doing, the chopper crew felt that any Viet Cong in this area would surely have been killed by our attack. Thus, feeling slightly confident that this location had been rendered relatively free of enemy forces, I scampered about while busily erecting my camouflaged 7'x7' tent. I quickly located the perfect sized bomb crater in which to pitch my tent. Luckily I finished the job before darkness arrived. Although this was my very first visit to this region of the world, I fully realized that this was the optimum season for one to be present in these jungles. I had read and heard a number of horror stories depicting the dangerous situation here because of mosquitoes, snakes, and other crawling reptiles. But since this region was just emerging from winter, I knew such life-threatening hazards would not yet be present. Then with the erecting of my tent completed, I settled inside for the evening. Five minutes later darkness was all around me.

For national precautionary measures, my uniform consisted of plain (unmarked) camouflaged jungle fatigues. I wore no name tags, rank insignia, or indicators of nationality. As an added precaution, I tucked the legs of my fatigues into the tops of my combat boots. I also wore a scarf tied tightly around my neck and made certain I had securely fastened all buttons and zippers of my uniform and fatigue jacket. I'd had the foresight to specify that each of my two tents be completely sealed around and across their bottom side. Finally, I was ready for commencement of this uniquely dangerous military duty (the detection and verification of actual Viet Cong presence)! This included immediate reporting of my findings directly to the deputy director of our command post. I inserted the Elm into my left ear. Once each hour throughout the night I would conduct a complete 360-degree audio scan from ground zero out to a distance of two and one-half miles. I would repeat this process hourly throughout the night.

At this point you may wonder why this was necessary. In the first several years of U. S. military presence in Vietnam, our combatants were publicly labeled as only advisors. It did not matter that many of these 'advisors' were

losing their lives on a daily basis. As time passed even greater numbers of our military forces were either captured or
killed in the line of duty. (Might I point out here that I remain confident that death was preferable to capture)!

Over time this conflict escalated, bringing an even
greater number of deaths to our U.S. forces. Large numbers of Viet Cong (VC) fighters also lost their lives primarily as a result of our B-52 bombers! But then matters took
a turn through the ingenuity and resourcefulness of the
"VC". Consequently, as this war raged on, more and more
bombs rained down, resulting in increasingly greater ex-
penditures from our defense budget. During this very same
time period, the reported numbers of U.S. casualties failed
to reflect proportionate losses to Viet Cong forces, because
the "VC" had recently resorted to the ingenious tactic of
dispatching small herds of farm goats as decoys and precursors to their incursions! Thus, as our infra-red equipped
bombers detected heat-sourced images on their viewing
scanners, they released large quantities of highly expensive
explosive ordinance upon their targets— only to net a few
dozen farm animals! This was as the "VC" lurked nearby in
the safety of their numerous underground excavated tun-
nel systems. Only when they were alerted by their highly-
trained forward scouts by use of the "ALL CLEAR" signal,
did they venture out to resume their destructive activity
against their American and South Vietnamese human targets! As a result of the Viet Cong's newly developed combat
strategy, this war had rapidly become unbearably expensive
to our United States government.

Meanwhile, at his elaborate strategic planning unit
back in Washington, D. C., the esteemed Colonel "J" had

devoted an extensive number of man-hours toward the resolution of this most serious problem. Specifically, the colonel had been tasked to devise a method whereby men could be distinguished from goats by our high-flying recon-naissance aircraft patrolling the area. Unfortunately, after great deliberation and extensive research, no such method was conceived. Then in an act of sheer desperation, Colo-nel James decided upon employing my personal scout- ing skills in this region. This was the means through which I currently sat alone in darkness, here in these dense and dangerous Vietnamese jungles!

At 7:15PM, I initiated my first local area scan. As I po-sitioned my upper body for maximum comfort and mo-bility, I quickly realized that my heartbeat had significant-ly increased! I considered this normal though, for after all— I had never before undertaken such a task. I aimed the Elm due north, slowly extending my listening range from ground-zero to a point which stood two and one-half miles away. I repeated this process until I had covered a radius two and one-half miles in all directions, which took me twenty minutes for completion. At the end of my first hourly scan I was quite relieved that I had not detected any indication of humans (or goats) in the area of my audible range. Might I mention here that in performing this sensi-tive task, I focused upon the recognition of human and/ or animal sounds. Particularly, I listened for the sound of voices, a sneeze or cough, the snap of a twig, or that distinct sound of a flip-top cigarette lighter! I also listened for the abrupt cessation of animal sounds— the aborted chirping of locusts or croaking of frogs, etc. Satisfied, I relaxed in silence inside my tent for the next forty minutes. Over the

next five hours I performed another five complete scans—
all with negative results. After each scan I would close my
eyes and relax for forty minutes. I felt that by so doing,
I just might complete my twelve-hour shift here without
experiencing undue exhaustion.

As I relaxed there in the quiet of the evening, I did so
without even a clue as to the scary and deeply embarrassing
event which was about to unfold. At 12:55AM, as I readied
myself to conduct my seventh scan of the evening, I
suddenly became alarmed by a truly strange sound which
caused me to abort my 1:00AM area scan. This sound was
rather faint (although I sensed it was nearby). I found it
eerie and disconcerting! As I sat listening to the spoken
words, I was struck with this thought: "Damn it, *Jake, you've
allowed the VC to sneak up on your position—you've had it*"!
Those frightening words to which I refer were: "Fu-k you,
fu-k you, fu-k you"! At this point I was certain that I had
somehow allowed myself to become surrounded by Viet
Cong forces! I was also equally certain that I would soon
be captured and dragged away to some "VC" prison camp
where I would be severely tortured until death! Quickly, I
loaded the .45, and then jacked a round into its chamber!
Next, I placed three grenades at my side! Now I lay in
wait, expecting at any moment to hear enemy footsteps
surrounding me! Fortunately those footsteps never came.
To my great regret though, those highly disturbing "F You's"
persisted for nearly another hour. For the next five hours I
lay there nearly petrified, but convinced I was going to give
these bastards the battle of their miserable lives! Luckily for
me this greatly dreaded battle never materialized. Finally,
those frightening "F You's" ceased— though I remained

convinced that the Viet Cong had lain in wait close by! This event effectively ended my reconnaissance duty for the evening, and I sat for the remainder of the night in combat-ready mode!

Shorty before 6:00AM I detected the welcomed whirring sound of an approaching helicopter gunship. I noted that the chopper had not fired upon my position, or the surrounding area. This suggested that sometime during the night, the "VC" must have abandoned their efforts to attack my well-concealed position. Then after quickly retrieving my gear and me, the chopper safely dropped me off at command post operations, where I stored my equipment until next evening. I then proceeded directly to our dining hall, where I had myself a hearty breakfast before returning to my room.

Immediately upon returning to my room, I used the telephone which I'd been provided for its sole intended purpose, (to brief Colonel "J" back in Washington). He seemed to be in a cheerful mood, as he asked "Hey Jake, how was the 'fishing' last night?" (referring to "VC" detection). We were now partially speaking code and would make no mention of VC. By conducting our conversations in this manner, neither the colonel's peers nor his staff would suspect the true nature of my calls. Might I remind you— the colonel currently operated without the knowledge or authority of our United States government! I replied, "Fishing was lousy sir, didn't get a single bite". "Bummer," he responded. Now although I had informed him of my failure, I did not detect any disappointment or frustration in the colonel's voice. I continued "Sir, I strongly believe though that I may have been spotted by a forward scout of the 'fish' late last night," (meaning the "VC").

"Why do you say this, Jake?" inquired the colonel. "Well sir, at around 1:00AM I distinctly heard a somewhat feeble voice, cursing at me and repeatedly saying "Fu-k you"— but I never saw anyone"! At this point the colonel chuckled quite loudly, saying, "Gosh Jake, I completely forgot to warn you about those darned geckos"! "Geckos sir?" I asked, somewhat confused. "They're a species of large lizard commonly found there in your region" answered the colonel. He continued, "They're a mean bunch of bastards though, so you'd better watch out for them"!

I was nearly as embarrassed as I'd been eleven years earlier during my very first airplane ride when I had frantically summoned the two airline stewardesses, advising them of a (non-existing) fire on board our aircraft. Now I realized that I'd wasted nearly half of the previous evening by hiding inside the confines of some old bomb crater! I resolved then and there— I WOULD NOT MAKE SUCH A MISTAKE AGAIN! I graciously thanked Colonel James for the invaluable information which he had provided me regarding the Geckos. Then in ending our conversation, the colonel said, "Keep your chin up Jake, I'm sure you'll snag yourself a whole mess of 'fish' real soon". I would soon discover just how accurate my colonel had been in his prediction! After providing my first such briefing to the colonel, I showered and hopped into bed for the majority of the day.

At 4:00PM I was awakened by the sound of my alarm clock. I arose, washed up, and grabbed a quick shower. Next, I telephoned (only briefly) my dear and lonely wife back in Ohio. Upon discovering that she and our baby daughter were faring well, I ended our call and then proceeded to our nearby dining hall for my evening meal. I would eat well during this hour, as for the next twenty-seven days, I would not enjoy the luxury of noon meals.

Two hours later, I once again found myself boarding another helicopter gunship and heading into the jungle for round two of my extremely unusual fight here. This time though instead of heading due north, the chopper assumed a heading of northeast. However, we flew for approximately the same duration of time. The chopper soon began circling an area covered by dense underbrush, and again our gunners sprayed this area with heavy machine gun fire! Once our pilot was satisfied it was safe to land, he momentarily lowered the craft onto the ground.

As we approached this area I'd visually inspected the surface inasmuch as possible for any visible evidence of enemy presence. My careful inspection had revealed no such evidence. So, after quickly hopping down from the chopper and onto the ground, I moved hastily about, searching for a suitable crater in which to erect my specially designed tent. This time I used my modified (sharpened tip) walking cane to test the ground directly before me prior to stepping upon it. I'd noticed that several surface areas here were lightly covered by patches of weeds and grass, and Colonel "J" had advised me of the possibility of ground excavations which contained numerous vertically positioned bamboo shoots. Each shoot contained a sharpened tip that had been cut at a ninety-degree angle. Thus, any person who fell into one of these artificially covered pits was certain to suffer a long and excruciatingly painful death! This was but one type of the Viet Cong's many booby traps. I'd taken only three steps toward my selected crater when, the sharpened tip of my walking cane easily punched through the surface! I immediately took one step backward, as I began brushing away the patches of grass before me. Imagine my shocking discovery! Here at my very feet was a gaping hole in the ground that contained more than one dozen of those deadly bamboo shoots! I made certain that I had sufficiently uncovered this pit before moving on to my nearby bomb crater.

Once I had safely reached my selected crater (only a few feet away), I quickly went about lowering my equipment and erecting my tent. I preferred spending my nights of duty here in these craters for two specific reasons: First, these craters allowed me to countersink my tent to the point where only the upper half of my head and face were visible. This rendered detection of my presence extremely difficult. Second, in the unlikely event that it became necessary that I direct a bombing raid upon my position, I would stand a much greater chance of survival by flattening my body against the crater's surface.

No sooner than I'd erected my tent did I begin my first audio scan of the evening. As on the evening prior I scanned all directions, beginning at my immediate position and extending to a distance of two and one-half miles. I would routinely perform one complete audio scan each hour, on the hour. By the hour of midnight I still had not detected any "VC" presence. During the course of my 1:00AM scan, my gecko friends revisited and commenced their eerie chants! At one point I found myself greatly tempted to return these geckos' complimentary phrases in kind! But I quickly discarded this most unwise thought and continued my work in complete silence.

Near the end of this particular scan I detected what I

instantly recognized as the tinkling sound of small bells. Having lived the vast majority of my adolescent years in rural areas, I quickly realized that this sound most likely represented one or more herds of goats passing through an area approximately two miles from my present location. I continued tracking the faint sound of the tinkling bells for another five minutes. By this time I had determined that unless this herd changed its course, the animals would pass in close proximity to my concealed position!

Standard operating procedure dictated that I use my tiny signaling device to alert my command post and advise the officer-in-charge of my discovery. In so doing, I would confirm to the officer that this current movement consisted of only a herd (or herds) of goats! The command post OIC would then alert one of the several B-52 bombers that were patrolling these skies at altitudes high above. Meanwhile, I would continue my present scanning activity until such time as I detected human movement!

Nearly forty-five minutes after the animal herd cleared my area, I detected the unmistakable sound of a flip-top cigarette lighter. Within seconds I picked up several more such sounds! I immediately notified the command post OIC, who in turn notified those destructive B-52 bombers! I was advised to maintain my current position, while pressing the heels of my hands tightly against my ears. With my heart rate rapidly accelerating, I followed closely the instructions I'd been given! As I lay there quietly upon my side, my mind raced, and passing through it were many unpleasant (even outright scary) thoughts. I was fully aware of the B-52s' capabilities regarding precision bombing, though one particular thought plagued me the very most. *"What if one (or more) of these bombs happen to stray from their intended target"?* Unfortunately, I knew that I would just have to ride this one out! Within minutes a series of devastating explosions commenced! The ground around me shook violently as the walls of the crater in which I sat began crumbling, allowing mounds of dirt to settle around the outer edges of my small tent. I continued lying there with my ears covered and my eyes tightly closed! Fifteen minutes later, all was once again silent. One minute after the barrage had ended, my signaler suddenly lit up displaying a single fifteen-second pulse. This was a query from my command post OIC concerning my condition. I immediately answered back with one fifteen-second single pulse of my own indicating "ALL IS WELL". At this point, I immediately resumed my scans. Over the next twenty-six days, I would detect and report a total of twenty- two incursions by the Viet Cong! I would also sit through and survive each of these incidents without sustaining even a single scratch!

Back on base next morning I placed my customary phone call to Colonel "J". He had already received a detailed Incident Report of last night's bombing raid. He had also just received a tentative casualty assessment. I immediately sensed that he was particularly pleased on this brisk spring morning . "Way to go, Jake!" he exclaimed quite excitedly, adding "I knew you would come through for me"! "I just got a little lucky sir," I responded, feigning modesty. "Lucky or not— keep up the great work!" he exclaimed. Then after a few brief comments concerning sports activity, we ended our call. I would sleep through the next seven hours.

The remainder of my first TDY to this region was spent

repetitiously. Each night I received nightly visits from my gecko friends. Also, for the next twenty-two consecutive nights the Viet Cong would often use herded animals as precursors to their nightly raids. However, during each of their attacks, those poor goats were allowed to pass unharmed. Unfortunately, the "VC" enjoyed no such protection! For the remainder of the month, large numbers of Viet Cong were killed; but most significantly, our government had wasted less of its defense budget on bombing false targets! Needless to say, my Tactical Commander (Colonel "J") was highly pleased!

At 6:00PM on March 31st, instead of returning to the jungles, I boarded another chartered flight heading for good old Travis AFB, CA! After sixteen hours flying time, we arrived at our initial destination. Luckily for me I would spend the next four hours awaiting my flight to Ohio. Meanwhile, I visited an on-base gift shop where I purchased a few clothes for my dear wife, Lora. I then purposefully left the receipt inside the bag as proof that I, had in fact, visited California. Shortly before 6:00PM the next day, I once again held my wonderful wife and baby daughter in my arms. This was a joyous reunion! We would spend the next two days shopping, sight-seeing, and relaxing together. Then on the third day I found myself once again back inside the mailroom, sorting and pitching mail. When my supervisor asked me "How was California, Jake?" I merely answered, "It was fine, Rob— but I worked most of the time". At the day's end, I immediately resumed my early evening billiard games!

Two weeks later I would make a major (temporary) change in my current routine. I drove alone down to South

Carolina to bring mom and dad to Ohio for a short visit. This trip would also serve as a sightseeing opportunity for my parents and me, for in all his lifetime dad had only traveled through the states of North Carolina and Virginia. Even worse, mom had only known two locations in her entire lifetime, the town in which she was born and raised, plus the town in which she currently lived— (which I found very sad). Thus, this trip would prove quite a treat, (especially for mom).

Returning to Ohio, we drove through the Smokey Mountains of North Carolina, in addition to the state of Kentucky. This was also a first time route of travel for yours truly. My parents really enjoyed our twelve-hour drive. But I believe I can say with complete confidence, they enjoyed their four-week stay with their daughter-in-law, grand-daughter, and me even more! Sadly though, time passed much too quickly. It was soon time for me to return my beloved parents to their home in South Carolina.

Just two short weeks later I found myself boarding another specially chartered flight and once again heading for the jungles of Vietnam! At least this time the pain caused by my departure had slightly diminished. It seems that this time both Lora and I had mentally better prepared ourselves. Of course, I told Lora that the destination of this trip was the same as the previous. Granted, I was deceitful in making this statement to my wife; however, I actually would travel to the exact same location as before.

Upon arrival at DaNang Air Base I was escorted to the very same room that I had previously occupied. My liaison officer and deputy operations officer were also the same. Such consistency would serve to make my present visit a

bit more relaxed. Upon meeting with the deputy ops officer (DO), I again let him talk me into deploying on the first
evening of my arrival. So at 6:00PM, I boarded a chopper
bound for the same general location I had previously scout-
ed. While flying along at treetop level, I recalled my recent
briefing from Colonel "J", in which he had said, "Jake, we
want to force these "VC" to believe that we've established
an invisible 'hot zone' around DaNang! I believe this will
cause them to divert their attention elsewhere. And when
they do, we'll be waiting for them!" he concluded.

In preparation for landing, my chopper pilot again
issued the order to strafe the area, which was immediately
carried out. When it was deemed safe to land, the pilot
briefly did so. I darted from the chopper while bent low
to the ground and scampering in zigzag pattern. I'd already
noted that the surface of this immediate area bore no signs
of underground booby traps, so I did not use my modified
cane. I quickly located an adequate crater from which I
would set up my command post. At 6:15PM as usual, I
initiated my first area scan. As expected I failed to detect
any Viet Cong activity. Then each hour thereafter I would
conduct my 360-degree scan. During my 2:00AM scan, I
detected the soft sounds of rustling of underbrush. For the
next five minutes I focused upon this area, and at one point
I distinctly detected the sound of a small twig snapping.
"Someone is out there", I thought. I noted that these sounds
emanated from a distance of just one and a half miles away.
I immediately contacted my command post, knowing that
they would investigate through coordination with the B-52s.
Five minutes later I received a series of three one-second
pulses via my signaling device. This confirmed that attack

by the B-52s was imminent! I knew the drill quite well by now, so I hunkered down as I waited for those deadly bombs to rain down on the enemy's position! My wait was short! Soon numerous bright flashes of light, closely followed by continuous loud explosions, saturated an area only one mile from my current position! This attack lasted for at least fifteen minutes, but when it ended I again found I was unharmed. Subsequent area scans throughout the remainder of the night revealed no enemy presence. I felt these bombs must have accurately found their targets, since I had detected not a single moan or groan after the attack ended. Conversation with Colonel James the following morning would confirm my suspicions. At 6:00AM, my chopper retrieved me from this treacherous region of Vietnam jungle. After securing my equipment I placed a call to Colonel "J", who said, "Hey Jake, we hit ourselves a jackpot last night"! "If we continue catching them, there soon won't be any left." he added. Unfortunately, we would not always be rewarded by such success.

Next evening at my usual hour I resumed area scanning, but in an altered state. The area to which I had today been deployed miraculously contained no bomb craters, forcing me to pitch my tent above ground and in dense underbrush. It was now summer, so mosquitoes were everywhere and the snakes had begun crawling about. It would be an understatement to say— this was definitely not my favorite time of year! I had just completed my first scan of the evening and had settled in to relax a bit. But there would be no relaxation for me at this time! As I peered out through the eye-level twelve-inch square window of my mesh screen tent, I noticed the reeds of tall grass as they

danced back and forth in weaving motion! Having spent
the majority of my adolescence on snake-infested farms, I
was quite familiar the causes of such erratic grass and weed
movement. I knew beyond a doubt that some awfully large
snake was present in this immediate area! I sat quietly as I
attempted to hold my breath as the unseen snake began its
pass just ten feet directly in front of my tent! I remained
completely silent and unmoving, but I believe this snake
must have sensed the presence of my now rapidly beating heart! Suddenly the reeds of the tall grass ceased their
movement! I remained completely quiet and still. But even
though I'd taken these extra precautions, the weaving of the
grass resumed. Only this time the direction of the weaving
had changed— and was now moving in my direction! Now
although I'd often faced (and killed) countless numbers of
deadly snakes as a teenager, never before had I faced such
a dire situation! However, under no circumstance would
I allow myself to panic (even though I'd not yet caught a
glimpse of this reptile). Cautiously, I prepared myself to
meet (head-on) this ominous threat! I remained sitting upright, though I'd positioned my hands and braced myself.
As the weaving grass slowly inched closer to my seated position, my heart rate quickened but I maintained my posture. Suddenly there loomed before me the raised, hooded
head of what I instantly recognized as a king cobra! This
cobra had raised its head to a level that equaled that of my
own, indicating its length to have been at least twelve feet.
I sat there as though petrified! I was certain that the cobra
would strike, but unsure when it would do so. I was also
uncertain as to the trajectory its venomous fangs would
follow! I had calculated though that its huge hooded head

would arc downward, potentially striking my chest area. But regardless of whether or not I had erred in my calculations, this deadly snake would strike at any moment!

I then recalled the intensive defense training, which as a teenager, I'd received from dear old Mr. Lim back home. Of the many lessons I'd learned from this kindly old gentleman, I would apply the one I deemed most appropriate for this situation. I would strike first! Now this is not to suggest that I would foolishly attempt to out-speed this king cobra. Instead I would provoke this snake's deadly strike! Only seconds had passed since the cobra had challenged me, although I knew beyond a doubt that my time had expired! So with my hands each held firmly at shoulder level— I ABRUPTLY PROPELLED MYSELF BACKWARD AND ONTO THE GROUND! Instantly upon sensing my motion, the cobra unleashed its deadly attack upon me! Fortunately, I had calculated correctly, so as the cobra initiated its strike—IT LITERALLY LOST ITS HEAD!

As I had so abruptly lunged backward, I'd thrust my hands forward! But to avoid confusion here, my hands had firmly held onto my razor-sharp machete! Thus, as this cobra had struck at me, its raised upper body was instantly severed just inches below its large hooded head! The body of this now harmless snake violently thrashed about just inches in front of me, but its head lay on the floor of my tent! At first I just couldn't force myself to touch this snake's head, although I would need to actually pick it up in order to toss it out. Only recollections of the courageous actions of my friend Cadet Callen, (Matamoros) provided me with the fortitude needed to eject this most unwelcomed snake head! With the recent several minutes of excitement now behind me, I resumed my 7:00PM scan in timely fashion. Fortunately, I found myself still emotionally fit to perform my duties. I soon realized, I'd even survived this dreaded experience without the need for a change of underwear!

Beginning the third night of this current TDY, and for the next twenty-one evenings here, I would detect and report a total of twenty-one actual Viet Cong incursions. Oddly during twenty of these attacks, herded goats had preceded "VC" presence. But what baffled the "VC" to near immobilization was the fact that not a single animal had been bombed by patrolling aircraft. Conversely, on each of their attempts within my scouting range, they suffered insurmountable casualties. This particular TDY would prove the most successful to date!

On Friday, Jul 2nd I arrived back on the base of Wright-Patterson, where I was affectionately greeted by my waiting wife along with our adorable baby daughter. I had arrived just in time for 4th of July celebrations. It goes without saying this quickly became a wonderful occasion for the three of us. For the next two and a half months my precious family and I greatly enjoyed our time together. During weekday evenings (after billiards), I would take them sightseeing, shopping, or to an occasional movie theater. All too soon though our period of joyous activities reached its unexpected and abrupt end!

For several months I had been advised that I would on October 1st commence my third deployment to Vietnam. This scheduled deployment had been unexpectedly advanced in response to significantly increased Viet Cong activity in that region. My new departure date was changed to September 1966 , which benefited Lora and me because

October 26th was our third wedding anniversary. At least now, I would return shortly before this important date. For the next week Lora and I made all the necessary preparations for sustaining both her and our dear daughter, Mari as Lora had not yet learned to drive.

Soon I found myself in Vietnam for the third time in only six months! Both my liaison officer and deputy director of operations had been replaced by new personnel. Each had recently been thoroughly briefed concerning my missions here, so these personnel changes presented no problems for me. Our current operating routine would remain unchanged. Even my rather comfortable on-base room was the same. This time though I was not pressured to enter the jungles on my first day, and I was quite pleased to have this short break. I would spend at least a couple of my first evening's hours phoning and consoling my precious and lonely wife. After talking to Lora, I walked about the base for awhile before retiring. I then slept for most of the following day.

At 6:00PM on September 21st, I once again reported to flight operations for immediate deployment. Upon landing at my operations site, I quickly realized that this particular TDY would be markedly different weather-wise. This area had entered monsoon season, bringing with it great amounts of rainfall to the region. Consequently, those bomb craters in which I preferred pitching my tent, were all half filled with murky water. And since the many snakes had not yet hibernated, there was a strong possibility that these craters would be filled with snakes. This meant that during each of my nights here, I would remain above ground. I quickly selected a suitable site for the night's stay and settled in for the next twelve hours. I would tolerate visits and insults from my gecko friends; but, I would keep my fingers crossed that no snakes would come my way!

I conducted my area audio scans, and each met with negative results— with the exception of geckos chanting, locusts chirping, and frogs croaking. The evening was still early though, so I did not expect any visits from the "VC" at these early evening hours. Still, I performed my scans diligently to prevent the possibility of sneak attacks. At 3:00AM I commenced my next scan, but in sweeping the area I sensed that something was slightly abnormal here. For the next several minutes I continued scanning— but with similar results. Then it struck me! As I had conducted my scans, I'd detected not a single animal sound at my outer northeasterly listening range! There was no chirping or croaking. It was then that I realized— animal sounds existed elsewhere within my listening range. Now as a teenager, I'd acquired many of the skills of the great Indian scouts. As such I'd learned that the sudden absence of regularly heard animal sounds was a strong indicator of human presence! Then, acting strictly upon the absence of previously detected sound, I signaled my command post operations center while advising them of possible Viet Cong presence! Shortly, I was signaled to prepare for attack! Within minutes the B-52s launched the heaviest bombing run I had ever before witnessed! The explosions were continuous and deafening, and even the horizon to my north east was continuously lit up! With no crater to protect me, I lay prone with eyes closed and hands pressed against my ears! Finally those awful explosions subsided. Only the density of this jungle area protected me from injury. Just seconds later I received my personal condition inquiry via my miniature signal device. I immediately signaled back that I was unharmed. Over the next three hours I performed a series of continuous area scans to confirm that no other Viet Cong forces were nearby. My (unconfirmed) reporting had been a complete success!

Next morning as I placed my customary call to Colonel "J", I found him ecstatic! "Jake, this time you've even out-done yourself!" exclaimed the colonel. He continued "My initial report shows over two hundred fifty casualties from this morning's raid. "If this continues Jake, we're certain to win this darned war." he excitedly added. "I'm pleased to hear this sir," I answered. I failed to mention that I had submitted my initial report in the absence of actual proof. Fortunately I had chosen to follow intuition in sounding my alert. I would later discover that patrolling bomber air-craft had already detected numerous heat-sourced images on their infra-red scanners, but were awaiting my confir-mation.

The next two weeks would pass with equal success! By now my new deputy director of combat operations was simply amazed at my success rate. Namely in my areas of operation, over the past fifteen-day period, no bombs had fallen on false targets! More important though was the great increase in enemy casualty figures. Unfortunately the same could not be said of other regions of this coun-try. Regretfully, I was only one warrior among thousands. So although attacks in my areas of responsibility had been relatively brought under control, other areas had suffered dramatically. Fortunately, my duty contributions had been duly noted by my Tactical Commander, Colonel James.

Eventually I entered the fourth and final week of this visit. Both raindrops and heavy bombs had continuously fallen from the skies above. Still I had remained unscathed. Finally just three nights prior to my departure, activity in this region intensified. As I recall, the date was Oct 10th. As usual I'd been dropped here at 6:10PM. I'd begun my area scans after having properly arranged my equipment and weaponry. Now I'd just finished my 3:00AM scan and was relaxing while lying on the floor of my tent. As I peered out into the darkness, I noticed something a bit odd about an old tree standing nearby. I recalled that just moments earlier this stubby tree had apparently contained a slight protrusion at a point approximately five feet above its trunk. Presently though, there appeared no such extension or bulge! At first I thought that my mind had been playing tricks on me. Luckily though, my scout's natural instincts took control of my thoughts. I knew I had to be really careful here.

I had camouflaged my mesh screen tent well, although a trained Viet Cong scout just might have suspected my presence here. For the next fifteen minutes, I lay there perfectly quiet and motionless. Moments later my suspicions were confirmed, as this odd protrusion suddenly reappeared at the exact position as before! Now, I knew beyond a doubt that someone was hiding behind this old tree! Over these past fifteen minutes I'd done my contingency planning and assessment, so I knew that my options were limited. First, I could not run, fearing I might stumble into one of the many bamboo pits in this area. Second, I could not fire the .45 or toss any grenades, as the loud noises would have surely attracted Viet Cong forces. Third, although I had retained my knife-throwing skills, I would not attempt it in total darkness. This left me only one option— the crossbow! Thus, I quietly prepared a single poisoned-tip arrow. Next, I cautiously unzipped the front side of my tent, providing a clear and unobstructed path for my arrow. I then lay in prone position in anticipation of my uninvited guest's arrival. My wait was not long, for before another ten minutes had elapsed, the protrusion of this tree took full form! From my flattened position I could clearly distinguish the mid-sized form of a man as he inched forward in crouched position. He was silhouetted against the skyline, so I could clearly see and recognize the AK-47 automatic rifle he held in firing position. I instantly concluded that this was a Viet Cong forward scout (which was not to infer that this fellow was not extremely dangerous)! Slowly, this "VC" fighter crept forward. I sensed that he had not yet determined that a human being lay in wait for him. As I observed his stealthy advance, I made no sound or movement. Then when he'd reached a point only twenty feet from my position— I released my arrow, striking him at the center of his chest! His body instantly contorted, as he vainly struggled to fire his weapon! His efforts though were fruitless, as the spontaneous toxic chemicals had already entered his bloodstream! Quietly, the "VC" insurgent pitched forward onto the ground! During this brief ordeal he had made no sound at all, so for the next several minutes I would be safe from attack by the main body of Viet Cong fighters. For the very first time in performing this special duty, I briefly ventured from the confines of my small tent. This "VC" was now lying face-down, so I rolled his body over to retrieve my arrow's shaft. I then quickly covered his inert form with a number of light branches. Might I explain here that I'd not used a lethal arrowhead for this particular job. I had actually chosen not to kill this fellow, even though he was an enemy, and would not have hesitated to kill me. Instead I'd followed the procedure frequently employed by my late friend (Bill LeGrande). I had only partially (but permanently) paralyzed this Viet Cong fighter! My decision had ensured that this person would never again wage war against our military forces— FOR NOW, HE HAD BE-COME JUST A VEGETABLE!

Having eliminated this threat and secured the area, I promptly returned to my tent. Once back inside I signaled my command post, alerting them of Viet Cong presence. Now of course I had not verified my report, but since a forward scout had been dispatched, there was no doubt that the main body of fighters were somewhere nearby, (probably hiding out inside one of their many underground tunnels). I felt certain that these fellows were in fact under-ground, since none of my recent scans had detected their presence. It was now 3:40AM, meaning I would remain here for another two hours twenty minutes. To be perfectly candid, I really wanted to evacuate this area immediately! Accordingly, I signaled my command post requesting im-mediate extraction! Within one minute I received a reply denying my urgent request!

Feeling a bit uncomfortable in my current situation, I initiated continuous area scanning! I felt that I would be physically capable of maintaining this stepped-up pace of activity since I'd just survived my recent bout of excite-ment. Just minutes later I detected voices, accompanied by movement through underbrush. I was quite alarmed by the fact that these rustling sounds were emanating from a distance of just one mile away! Once again, I signaled my command post indicating "VC" presence in this area! This time, I was advised to prepare for immediate extraction! I promptly began storing my weaponry and tent! Minutes later, I heard the distinct sound of a helicopter speeding toward me from a southerly direction! The chopper was homing in on me using the wave output from my signal device. In just three short minutes I found myself hurriedly climbing aboard this helicopter gunship! No sooner than we'd cleared the immediate area did the bombs begin a series of continuous explosions north of our present position! I was extremely happy I'd been picked up in time to escape this deadly bombing raid! As we sped southward toward our base, a familiar voice spoke to me: "Hot damn, Jake, now we're even"! I instantly recognized this voice as that of (now Lt Colonel) VINCENT CALLEN! Ignoring rank, I excitedly responded, "Vince, is it really you"? "It's really me Jake," answered my friend. As soon as Vince had set the chopper on its landing pad,— the hugs began, followed by an early morning beer. Vince and I quickly brought each other up to date regarding the eight years since he had saved me from drowning in that Tachikawa swimming pool. This was the second time he had saved my life, by removing me from the danger of the B-52's deadly bombs! Oddly, our new deputy director of operations had ordered that I not be picked up, fearing the unnecessary loss of additional lives and equipment. But although the deputy director was his immediate superior, Vince had elected to ignore his boss's order on his first duty day here at DaNang. No other officer would have had the courage to risk such a dangerous mission when beginning a new tour of duty!

During my usual early morning out-briefing of the deputy director of combat operations, he sincerely apologized for his lack of courage in having ordered that I not be rescued. I accepted his explanation while knowing fully well that the military career of this particular officer would advance no further! My subsequent briefing to Colonel James would ensure the validity of my statement. During my briefing with the colonel, I received a long string of verbal accolades. In ending our conversation, he stated, "I am forever indebted to you, Jake"! Those memorable words would serve as full compensation for the three TDY tours I had spent here in the jungles of Vietnam! There would be no promotion, or any other form of recognition given me for this most unusual service to my country. Now many of you might have difficulty understanding this statement, but in explanation, I WAS NEVER OFFICIALLY IN VIETNAM! Accordingly, there is no record of my contribution in that country. These were the terms under which I performed my reconnaissance duties, and as a patriot— I ACCEPTED THESE TERMS. Earnestly speaking though, the only form of compensation I sought was— the loving companionship of my wonderful wife and child!

I spent my final two nights by relaxing on the base at DaNang. Of course much of this time was spent together with my long time friend Vince Callen. *"What a way to end my tour here in Vietnam"*, I thought as Vince and I sat in the privacy of my room while sipping cold beer and reminiscing over old times. A total of thirty years would pass before I would once again see my friend, Vincent Callen.

On October 11, 1966 I once again arrived at my doorsteps back in Ohio. And as during my previous two trips I carried a few gifts for my loving wife and child. Of course we instantly began our joyous celebration of my return! Two days later I found myself back inside our mail room and handling mail. No one questioned my most recent absence, so it was as though I had not even been away. I wasted no time in returning to the billiard tables. Three days later my wife informed me that she was quite possibly again with child. A subsequent visit to the doctor's office revealed that she was in her first trimester of pregnancy. We were then advised that we should expect the birth of our second child during early April of the following year. Lora and I were both very happy over this recent bit of news, so we went about making preparations in anticipation of our second child's arrival!

The time passed rather quickly, and soon we celebrated Thanksgiving Day together in the midst of heavy snowfall. As the month of December approached, Lora and I anxiously looked forward to celebrating Christmas and our birthdays. Sadly, our high level of excitement was short lived. On December 1st, I was notified of assignment to Tan San Knut Airbase, Vietnam, reporting date of January 1st 1967. This disturbing news really tested our morale during the days leading up to Christmas! I did not want to be separated from my family during the Christmas season. *"What luck"*, I thought as I prepared to break this news to my dear wife. Upon hearing this, Lora was completely dumbfounded! She'd understood that this time, I would be away for twelve long months. We both knew that since Lora did not drive or even speak English, caring for two babies would be impossible. I cheered her up by telling her, "Lora, this will be the perfect time for you and the children to spend the year in Greece with your mother". My words had made her feel slightly better. Now I definitely did not relish the thought of being separated from my young family for such a long period. Heck, my children would not have recognized me upon my return! At this point, that feeling of stomach sickness I'd often experienced as a teenager, returned to haunt me. I was in a desperate and untenable situation! I needed to be with my family— at least during the next several months. Although I constantly reminded myself that "The mission comes first"!

Somehow though, Lora and I managed to hold things together. Naturally, our two-year old daughter (Mari) didn't have a clue as to what was transpiring. For the next three weeks I would go to work while feeling sick inside. Concentration had become extremely difficult for me. Even those skills I had acquired in billiards had deserted me! By December 30th I had completed my immunizations and prepared for the departure of myself and family. However, at 2:00PM of that very same day, I was summoned to the office of my local squadron commander. Once there, he presented me with an electronic message, stating that my pending assignment to Vietnam had been cancelled effective immediately! I couldn't believe my eyes— so I read the message again, and again! As I stood there in my commander's office, I found that concealing my great joy was a near impossibility! I took this message along as I reversed my recent out-processing actions. Next, I rushed home, where I presented to Lora the wonderful news! She was genuinely overjoyed, even though this meant that she would not at this time return to Greece. We really celebrated New Year's Day!

I returned to work on January 2nd and resumed my daily routine. This new year had begun wonderfully for Lora and me. With each passing day, I gave considerable thought to my cancelled assignment. I found it strange that no reasons for cancellation had been provided. But throughout this time, I expected a replacement assignment to arrive at any moment. I found the anticipation of such an event completely nerve racking! When I could stand the pressure no longer, I placed a call to Colonel "J". When I explained my problem, the colonel calmly replied, "Relax Jake, I'm sure you won't be returning to Vietnam at anytime in the near future". Before I could speak, he added, "I could really use your help in matters involving Eastern Europe— so that's where you'll be headed next." he said. "If I should end up with an assignment to Europe, I should be able to take my family— right, sir?" I inquired. "Roger that," he responded, adding, "Your new reporting date will be May 31, 1967, so consider this as confidential advance notice." he said. I stood nearly speechless as I thanked him.

The great news I'd subsequently given my wife may have come as too much of a shock for her. I say this because two weeks later she unexpectedly entered labor! Then on January 19th 1967, she prematurely gave birth to a miniature baby daughter of only two and one-half pounds! For a number of reasons we called this our miracle child! In her own unique way, she was equally as adorable as our first child (Mari). We would name her Paraskivi (Friday in Greek). Now this child, (Friday), was so very small in size, she was kept the hospital's incubator for the first two full weeks of her life. During this period she began growing and gaining weight, causing her numerous prematurity wrinkles to rapidly disappear. At long last, we were allowed to bring our infant home. Might I remind you, this was in the dead of winter when more than three feet of snow covered the ground. But with special attention and lots of tender loving care from Lora and me, Friday's condition improved rapidly. Soon it became evident that our adorable little Mari appreciated and loved her new baby sister! In coming years these two would grow up lovingly together! And throughout their lives Mari and Paraskivi would serve as both companion and protector to each other! The months passed quickly, and on May 25th 1967, my young family and I found ourselves happily traveling across the vast Atlantic Ocean, heading to our new European destination!

Chapter 11

Hahn–The Hunsruck

After having traveled for nearly nine hours, my family and I arrived at that great (but busy) commercial airport known as Frankfurt International. This was our very first time of walking upon German soil. Special arrangements had been made for my new supervisor (and wife) to meet and escort us to our new military installation. Fortunately for us, my new supervisor had previously been provided our family's description, so he recognized us even as we walked among the large numbers of airport passengers. After the formalities, I loaded our suitcases (minus one) into a Chevy station wagon in which we would travel. Then for the next two hours, we wound our way northward up through the scenic Hunsruck mountains. During the first half of our drive, we saw no signs of human life— only expansive forestry. Finally we arrived upon one great plateau, which contained several small villages. We had seen no towns or cities— only these villages. We continued driving for several more minutes before reaching the airbase at which I would be assigned. We then drove directly to the on-base post office, which was my new duty location. While briefly there we were introduced to the assistant supervisor and new work crew, consisting of one NCO plus seven airmen. I would soon discover that this was a closely knit group of young men. I discovered that these guys (all male) considered themselves as family (which I found commendable).

Shortly afterwards, my supervisor drove us to a nearby small hotel where we would reside for the next several days. My family and I then had lunch before relaxing for a couple of hours. We were then escorted through the two nearby villages in search of reasonable (but decent) rental apartments. After hours of searching, we finally located a suitable place to live. We moved into our new residence just ten days later. We would spend the next several days cleaning and arranging furnishings, etc. In our leisure time we walked about this neat little village in which we'd settled. In walking about this area, I carried our little Mari in my arms, as Lora pushed young Paraskivi about in her new baby carriage. Both Lora and I found it quite lonely here because we knew no one. Still, we realized that our togetherness would sustain us during these first difficult days.

At 7:30AM on June 5th June 1967, I was picked up by a coworker and driven to our duty section for my first day of duty. I reluctantly left my young wife Lora to care for our two babies while alone and unassisted. There were no telephones with which she could call me in the event of an emergency. I found this lack of communication quite unsettling, as I would not see my family for nine long hours. Still, this was unquestionably a vast improvement over the jungles of Vietnam! Thus, I would accept our new environment without complaint.

Upon reporting to duty I was given an in-briefing by my highly impressive supervisor. Here in this organization, there was no squadron commander or first sergeant in my chain of command. My current supervisor served as incumbent of both these positions. This sole master sergeant was vested with authority and responsibility for all functions of our small unit. I especially appreciated the fact that neither the wing commander nor any squadron commander here held any administrative or operational control over me. It was as though the members of my unit were seen as guests here at Hahn airbase. As such we performed no base details, nor did we participate in any military formations. In summary, all that was required of us was that we timely report to work—and then do our assigned job! I really liked my new organization! Of course, my position within the secret organization of (now Brigadier General) James would remain unaffected by this assignment. In fact, during my in-briefing my current supervisor informed me of his recent briefing from the general. He also advised me that my connection to the general would pose no problems for me here in my new organization. All this, but still no promotion! Although, there was hope for me here, as this organization usually received a small number of promotions each year— and I was now in the FULLY QUALIFIED category. This meant as of October 1st, 1967 I fully expected that I would finally receive my long overdue promotion!

Over the next two months I worked my butt off in learning my new job here in this post office! Remember, a total of twelve years had passed since I'd worked in a post office in Harlingen, Texas. Also, at Harlingen my duties were of the apprentice level— thereby routine in nature. Here though, I would perform the full line of postal duties including stamp sales, money orders, international mail services, etc. Hence, there were no similarities between my work back at Harlingen and my work here at Hahn. At home each evening I would entertain my young family by treating them to walks around our village and occasional restaurant visits. Regretfully I had not yet resumed my billiards activity, so money remained quite scarce for us. Still, I never lost sleep over the need to pay the rent. Thus, our days together as a family passed rather enjoyably.

I had served efficiently at this location for only two short months, when I was summoned unexpectedly to my supervisor's office. With an expression of disappointment his face, my supervisor stated, "Jake, I want you to immediately turn in your fixed credit account— you're taking over, as of this moment, the position of postal finance supervisor"! I stood there in shock and total disbelief! "How can this happen?" I asked. "It seems my assistant Sergeant Holder has had some problems in maintaining our unit's financial account, so he has been relieved of duty ," answered my supervisor. "I've checked your military record and find you to be the senior and most qualified— so you're it." said my supervisor. I would soon discover that the Assistant NCOIC (SSgt Holder) had embezzled funds from our operating account, which was strictly forbidden within military organizations!

Now since my arrival here two months earlier, I'd performed a wide variety of postal duties, and I had learned these duties well. But even so, I was somewhat apprehensive over the added responsibility that had been placed upon me. Nevertheless, I thanked my supervisor for placing his trust and confidence in me as I prepared to assume this new position. My predecessor had been just minutes earlier apprehended by local military authorities and physically removed from the premises, which created a great void in our operational capability. My job, (although I had never before done this) was to continue operations as usual, thereby sustaining mission capability. This was not as simple as it might sound, for inherent in this new position were a number of factors and considerations. First and foremost, I'd instantly become the immediate supervisor of all assigned airmen! Three of these airmen were of equal grade to me. One of these three happened to be a highly intelligent and capable individual who was well-respected among his peers. Accordingly, he had naturally assumed that in the event of an incident such as this, he would assume this most critical position. So naturally he was quite bitter and confrontational. In time, I would resolve this unpleasant situation. Second, not only did I assume responsibility for our unit's financial operations, I also assumed responsibility for all assigned equipment and supplies. Added to this was the fact that I would still occasionally be called upon by General "J". Notwithstanding though, I was determined to do my absolute best in each of these capacities.

Now at the very beginning of my tenure in this new position, I'd met with a few obstacles. The main thorn in my side was my lead peer, whose name was Barney. It seemed that Barney had inwardly decided to personally challenge my every move and decision. In coming months this fellow would cause me to nearly develop ulcers. Compounding this situation was my very strong desire to not goof things up. This served to slightly slow my rate of production (reminiscent of my beginning accounting days earlier in Athens). Nearly one week into my new assignment, my supervisor called me into his office, asking, "What's the matter, Jake, can't you do this job"? Upon hearing those awful words, I was somewhat shattered! His comments really concerned me, for I simply would not allow myself to fail! I responded by calmly replying, "I can— and will do this job, Sergeant Sessions". He did not respond, but merely returned to an official task he'd been working on. I considered that moment to be my wakeup call! But instead of panicking, I maintained my sense of calm and successfully increased the speed at which I performed certain functions, such as handling large sums of money. In doing this I recalled my days back in Reno where I'd been forced to work as a cashier. I also recalled my days in Tripoli where for eighteen months I had successfully served as cash sales supervisor. Lastly, I recalled my successful two year period as an 'accountant' in Athens. That night as my wife slept, I lay awake reviewing those greatly challenging days of my life. I decided then and there, "I've never failed before, and I definitely shall not fail now"! The next day I returned to work with new confidence in my abilities. From that day forward my work became quite elementary!

On the morning of October 1st, I was again summoned to my supervisor's office. This time he seemed quite pleased as he said, "Jake, I'd like to commend you firsthand on the outstanding job you've done here so far". Then with his right hand, he shook mine— while with his left, he handed me a brand new pair of staff sergeant's stripes! There are no words that would adequately describe that moment in my life! My promotion would become effective on December 1st, 1967. But prior to this date I would visit an undisclosed location bordering Eastern Europe.

Meanwhile, I continued being confronted by Barney and his cohort/co-worker Matt. It seemed these two had conspired to jointly break me! But that which they failed to realize was— I HAD OFTEN BEEN TESTED! Although, without elaborating, I shall simply say that Matt and I would soon become close friends. But even more important, Barney and I would become life-long, close friends. Meanwhile I would continue dealing with them in my own unique way of patiently accepting their challenges!

On Friday of November 3rd, I received my very first call from my Tactical Commander, General James, advising me of the need for an upcoming trip north-eastward. He was keenly interested in ascertaining the general consensus of citizens currently residing in those areas which were then referred to as "behind the Iron Curtain". At the end of the general's briefing, he asked, "Do you feel comfortable with this new role, Jake"? I answered, "Sir, after Vietnam— I can handle almost anything"! "Those are exactly the words I want to hear," responded the general.

After we had ended our call and I'd returned to my duties, I considered my new assignment! I fully realized that my new role was accompanied by a certain level of danger; although, nowhere near that which I had faced in the jungles of Vietnam. I'd already been informed by the general that I would depart on Friday, November 10th. For this trip though I would carry no weapons, for none would be needed. However, for obvious reasons I would need a larger tape recorder. Thus, after work I stopped by our on-base thrift shop in search of a recorder. I was in luck and found the perfect machine— a lightweight portable recorder which was capable of handling seven-inch tape reels. Later at home I tested this recorder and was pleased to find that it contained no mechanical defects. I had spent $40 for this used tape recorder. The very next day I purchased eight reels of one-hour tape. I was now logistically prepared for this upcoming covert assignment.

By this time we had met and become friends with our next-door neighbors, and it so happened my neighbor's wife had gotten along extremely well with my wife. Consequently she had begun helping Lora in caring for our two small children. She had even begun informally assisting Lora in learning English. In coming years this lady's friendship and invaluable aid would vastly improve Lora's level of confidence. Soon my departure date arrived! This date fell on an American holiday, so there was no disruption of my military postal duties. This time as I prepared to drive away, neither my young wife nor I felt despair as we had previously. "I'll see you in two days," I said to her as I held her tenderly in my arms. She answered (in Greek), "I shall anxiously await your return, my love". I then walked to our car and immediately drove away, heading for the nearby train station. Incidentally, we'd received our car via ocean carrier just two months earlier, which helped us immensely in going about our daily lives— such as shopping and traveling to and from work.

At 9:00AM I arrived at the Koblenz train station, where I purchased my ticket before boarding my train. Now in the interest of confidentiality, I shall not disclose the specific location to which I traveled. However, I will at least say— I arrived at my destination shortly after 2:30PM of the very same day. I'd been provided a short list of inexpensive hotels in the immediate area, which helped me locate a suitable place for my brief stay. After a short ride by taxi cab, I reached one small out-of-the way hotel somewhere on the east side of town. By reasons of its close proximity to Eastern Europe, this particular location was well-suited for my purposes. After receiving my room key, I placed my single small suitcase (recorder enclosed) into my tiny corner room. I then proceeded to the hotel's dining room, where I had a light snack.

After eating I returned to my room, where I set up my recorder (with microphone). For this task, I would position and aim my previously acquired six-feet extended automobile antenna. Over the years I had discovered that by following this procedure, I would maximize audio reception. At exactly 6:00PM I begin my first audio scan of this minuscule area located within this eastern bloc region. I would replace recorded tapes hourly, recording continuously for the next four hours. This was the optimum time for the recording of conversations (including those occurring via telephone). My first hour of scans netted four conversations between mostly married couples who had just returned to their homes from their day's work. Regretfully, I'd not understood a single word of what was spoken. Nevertheless, I continued scanning and recording continuously for the next three hours. By 10:00 PM I had completed four hours of recorded information, although I did not know if any was of value.

Shortly after 10:00, I peeked out through my window, immediately noticing that the ground was completely covered by (still falling) heavy snowfall. Then with full knowledge that I would not be venturing outside on this extremely cold night, I secured my equipment before proceeding to the hotel's downstairs bar. I noticed an attractive young couple who appeared European, sitting at the far corner of the room. For some reason the young lady at this table seemed to be quite nervous! She often fidgeted, and her facial expressions indicated that she was experiencing great anxiety. I'd always considered myself a highly curious person— even as a young kid growing up. So now I was quite eager to discover what was transpiring between these two. I recalled that I had also brought along my pocket-sized recorder, so I quietly arose and then casually strolled from the bar room area. As soon as I'd removed myself from this couple's line of vision, I raced up the three flights of stairs to my room! I then grabbed the Elm along with the recorder and its two attachment wires. Next, I carefully attached my wires as I had previously done. Lastly, I adjusted the Elm's calibration ring to ground zero audio range. This allowed me to detect and record sounds emanating from distances of up to approximately fifty feet. Then as I left my room I removed my cigarettes from the left side pocket of my heavy winter jacket. As I returned to my table inside the bar area, I placed my cigarette pack upon the table before me. I had taken these measures that I might create the impression of having retrieved my smokes (just in case this couple had been watching me).

With the Elm firmly in place inside my left ear, I then positioned myself at a ninety-degree right- angle from this visiting young couple. I then began discreetly recording their words. They appeared not to have noticed me. Then just five minutes later, they were joined by two well-dressed, middle-aged men who were apparently of Latin American ancestry. I pretended not to notice as the young couple stood while warmly greeting their guests. Immediately upon seating themselves, the elder gentleman spoke (in English) asking, "So you have in your possession those items we previously discussed"? "We have them all," answered the young man of the first couple to arrive. "Excellent," responded the elder man. The nervous young lady then said, "They're yours— provided you're willing to meet our asking price". The elder responded "But your price is a bit high— don't you think"? "We believe our price to be quite fair," the lady sharply responded. At this point there came a brief pause in communications. The elder gentleman then spoke again. "We're prepared to pay you the sum of two hundred thousand U. S. dollars, but not more". The young man of the first couple again spoke up, saying "Two hundred twenty-five thousand, and we have ourselves a deal". Another brief pause ensued. Finally, the elder spoke saying, "This will be extremely difficult, but we agree to your terms".

Only then did this young lady appear to have relaxed a bit. The four then agreed upon November 30th as the date on which this transaction would be completed. Unfortunately for them, they had also revealed the hour and location of their next meeting. Throughout this transaction I sat quietly and nonchalantly watching the bar's wall-mounted television. I was totally astounded by what I had just overheard! I would later learn from General "J" that this recording revealed details of the sale and purchase of a large number of stolen military weapons, which were intended for use in a planned coup inside one certain Latin American country! Luckily for our side, those weapons would never be used for their intended purpose. This small core group of four, along with numerous others, would soon find themselves incarcerated for long periods of time!

Throughout the night I slept soundly beneath the thick warm comforter inside my room. Next morning, I arose, washed up (including hot shower), and then located the hotel's dining room. After a hearty breakfast of sausages and eggs, I stepped outside onto the (still) snow-covered streets for a bit of sight-seeing. I made a mental note of my hotel's location so that I would not become lost. This area boasted an abundance of plant life, which I found quite interesting. But that which caught my attention most of all, was the consistently formed and brilliantly displayed architecture of this city's building structures. As I moved about admiring these many magnificent structures, I thought, *"Jake, you've always wanted to see the world— well, now you're really seeing it"!*

After an afternoon of leisure, I was once again inside my room in preparation of another round of recording. Again today, I completely failed to understand any of the languages I overheard. Although regardless of my language inefficiency, I continued recording for another four hours. Upon completion I decided I would pay another visit to the hotel's bar. This time the place was packed and the band was playing, which rendered my particular type of recording virtually impossible! But this was fine by me because I had completed today's recording assignment.

The following morning (Sunday), I arose and began my day. After breakfast I paid my hotel bill and then headed for the nearest train station. One hour later I found myself speeding homeward to my precious family. The return drive from Koblenz took me only forty-five minutes. My wife and children were as thrilled at seeing me, as I was at seeing them. Of course, I made sure I had brought back small gifts for each. We would spend the remainder of the early evening by dining and visiting with friends we'd met since arriving here.

On Monday I returned to my officially assigned duties at the base post office. One of my first tasks of the day was to package and mail the nine recordings to General 'J" back in Washington, D.C. I found this quite an easy task, since I worked directly inside the post office. Later in the day as our assigned workers discussed their weekend, I simply listened to them speak (as I'd done back in my early high school days back at home). Soon that most memorable date of December 1st, 1967 arrived! This was the day of my long overdue promotion to the grade of staff sergeant (E-5)! For this most special of occasions, I wore an all-new uniform (including socks, shoes, and underwear)! Obviously, this was an awfully proud day for yours truly! No longer would I feel embarrassment over the fact that at age thirty-one, and with thirteen years, six months military service— I ONLY WORE THREE STRIPES! I would have reached the grade of E-5 at least six years earlier, were it not for that single conspiratorial performance evaluation in Reno! It had taken five long years for this evaluation (through attrition) to filter itself from my military records. Subsequently, it took an additional five years in which to accumulate a series of five or more evaluations with the ratings of OUTSTANDING! There you have it— five years plus five years equaled ten years' time in grade as an E-4! Now my trial period had ended! There would be no more days of austere living by my family and me as a result of that unjustified performance evaluation! With my overdue promotion, there came an immediate 100% increase in my military pay! Finally, my wife and I could breathe a bit without the concern for penny-pinching. At long last, we'd at least partially arrived!

The arrival of my promotion slightly exacerbated relations between Barney and me. Conversely, Matt had apparently resigned himself to the fact that I was now the sole E-5 in the house! Soon he and I were paling around together. Also, the fact that I had always gotten along well with all other assigned airmen (and supervisor) tended to undermine Barney's position. Slowly, I then began noticing a mild easing of his previous sarcasm and hostility. From this point forward, relations between us rapidly improved. More than forty-five years later, Barney and I would still consider ourselves close friends.

The following three weeks passed fleetingly. Soon my family and I found ourselves celebrating Christmas, followed by our birthdays and New Year's Day. January brought along a brief period of more celebration! On January 19th, we would celebrate the very first birthday of our younger daughter Paraskivi! This dear child had miraculously survived her first twelve months of life, and this in itself was strong reason for celebration! We finally had entered into a new year and a new lifestyle. At last, the pressures of semi-austere living, and those of my partially hostile work environment, had completely dissipated. These significant changes served to make the remainder of this three-year tour truly enjoyable!

As the seasons changed, this brought warmer temperatures to the surrounding areas. Now that I had realized a recent doubling of monthly income, we began venturing out and really enjoying our tour here in Europe. Together we traveled to many of Germany's major fine cities such as Frankfurt, Wiesbaden, Mainz, Cologne, and Koblenz, during our weekends. We even ventured farther, visiting such places as Luxembourg, Belgium, and France. These were all places which were totally new to me, and had I not joined the military, it is unlikely that I would have ever visited any of them. This extensive amount of travel caused our summer to seemingly pass within the "blink of an eye". When we weren't traveling, I was busy at work. At the very same time my dear wife Lora had busied herself at increasing her knowledge of the English language. And I must say— during our three-year stay at Hahn, my wife made great progress. So generally speaking, life for us had suddenly become— simply great!

Concurrently with our travels about Germany and other nearby countries, I conducted two additional reconnaissance missions. In March and June 1968, I returned to the very same location I'd visited just months earlier. While there I repeated the procedures I had previously employed (scanning the very same locations at identical hours). Much of the information I had obtained during my first visit here had been of particular interest to General James, and he had expressed his desire for follow-up missions. Surprisingly, each of these missions revealed highly sensitive information concerning secret plans for defection to the west of a small number of east European engineers and scientists! The general and his staff of intelligence experts would utilize this information in bringing about the successful defection and relocation of these individuals. Each mission had been a success!

Both my dear wife and I had expended great amounts of physical and mental energy since our arrival here twelve months earlier. This entire period had been especially taxing upon my young wife. And at times, I'd even mildly considered pulling out my hair. Then I thought *"Why not take the wife and children down to Greece for some enjoyment and relaxation"*. When I voiced my thoughts to Lora, her eyes instantly lit up! "What a great idea, Jake!" she exclaimed! And since neither of our young daughters voiced any opposition, we made our plans for summer vacation.

Our car, which I'd purchased while en route to Ohio, remained in excellent condition. So after installing a new set of tires, we were ready for our trip. I had already been advised by General James that I would not at anytime soon be re-deployed. My unit NCOIC approved my leave without hesitation. Thus, I temporarily appointed my friend (currently Sergeant) Barney as replacement during my thirty-day absence. So on Friday, June 28th we began our nearly twenty-hour high-speed drive from Hahn, Germany to Athens, Greece. As the sole driver, I drove through the entire night, stopping only for gasoline or rest rooms. Lora had prepared snacks for us and special food for little Paraskivi. At 2:00PM of the next afternoon, we sat a beachfront Greek restaurant while enjoying our delicious meals. This had been a long and tiring drive, though we were lucky in having completed our trip without accident or incident. We would spend the next twenty-five days visiting Lora's mom and sisters. Naturally, much of this time would be spent enjoying these beautiful beaches of Greece. Of course, I would always remain in the very shallow water! At the end of our vacation, we said farewell to Lora's family and then began our return trip to Hahn. During our return trip I drove more casually, allowing ourselves to reach Hahn next afternoon. On the following Monday morning, I returned to work. This had been a great vacation for us.

Now summer had come and gone, and we'd entered the first week of October, 1968. This was the date when semiannual promotions were announced. As a result of escalated fighting in Vietnam, there had been a major increase in the number of personnel serving within the United States Air Force and other branches of military service. Consequently the number of Air Force promotions had greatly increased. Three members of my unit were benefactors of this special promotion cycle. Both Barney and Matt received E-5 promotion, along with another airman whose name was Alvin. Now, as a staff sergeant, I supervised not only the remaining assigned airmen, but also three NCOs holding the same grade as myself. Remarkably, I successfully accomplished this challenging feat without the occurrence of even a single minor incident!

October 1st was also of great importance to yours truly. It was on this date that I moved my small family from our off-base rental apartment into on-base military housing. This move afforded us living quarters of much higher quality, and more spacious. But the most important consideration was that— we were provided these living quarters at just half the cost of our previous off-base residence! Ultimately, I realized an additional one hundred fifty dollars of extra spending cash. With this extra income my family and I would really enjoy the remaining twenty months of our tour at Hahn. Thus, socializing and entertainment became our favorite pastimes. Over coming months we met increasing numbers of truly great friends. And now that Lora and I had a bit of extra spending money, we raised our social activities to another level. We had great fun with a large number of families. Even our two young daughters quickly developed close friends of their own. We even traveled to such places far away as Paris, enjoying every minute. The following summer we would return to Greece for another wonderful thirty days. Months seemingly whizzed past, and soon this very special tour regrettably reached its end. Our three-year stay at Hahn, Germany would remain in our memories throughout our entire lives!

Chapter 12

Mountains of Minot

Before proceeding further, please allow me to elaborate upon the title of this chapter. Actually, no mountains exist near the city of Minot. And don't quote me here, but I'm quite certain that no mountains exist anywhere within the state of North Dakota. If one ventures southward into South Dakota, one might find mountains. This term which I've chosen merely refers to the seemingly limitless number of mountainous mounds of heavy snowfall which is visible for much of each year in this region.

My family and I arrived in the small city of Minot at the optimum time of year. This was after having spent one full month visiting each of the eastern and Midwestern states from New Jersey to North Dakota. We arrived in Minot near noon of July 30th, 1970. This was that brief window in time when one could travel the highways of North Dakota minus the hazards caused by snowfall and ice. We had just left the Hunsruck Mountains of Germany where there were frequently highly adverse weather conditions. I would soon discover that those weather conditions I'd previously experienced— paled in comparison to these. I shall never forget a brief exchange, during which one airman asked the other, "Bob, when does summer start around here"? "Around mid-July, Tom." replied Bob. "Well, when does it end, Bob?" asked Tom. "Around mid-July, Tom." answered Bob. Now this may seem like a joke to many of you, but Bob had answered Tom strictly based upon his own past personal experiences. As I stood there listening to these two guys talk, I said, "But it's near the end of July now Bob, and it's still a bright sunny day". Bob's answer to me was "Well, you just wait for a couple of more hours"! He had not greatly exaggerated! In just a few short weeks, I awoke one morning and then tried to peer out from my front window. I was unable to see outside though because snow had covered the entire front side of our two-story on-base living quarters! It took me more than one full hour just to clear away the heavy snow from around my garage door. This was my welcome to the city of Minot!

The base of Minot held responsibility for conducting highly critical bombing raids in those regions conducting hostile aggression against the United States. In conducting these raids they flew those awesome and highly destructive high-altitude B-52 bombers, which I've previously mentioned. The pilots and crew members of these aircraft were some of the very guys who had conducted bombing raids over Vietnam during each of my three visits there. In short, this was one very prestigious military installation! Minot also served as home to a large number of underground ballistic missile sites. So generally speaking, this was an assignment which many airmen would have literally begged for!

My duty assignment was within a squadron of more than 450 men and women who supported the flying mission of this base. The personnel of my particular squadron both flew and maintained these long-range bomber air-craft. The vast number of assigned enlisted members here were jet engine mechanics. These were the guys who en-sured that each plane was constantly flight-ready! Now in this instance the term "flight-ready" infers combat-ready, mainly because their sole mission was that of aerial combat. So at any hour of any day or night, these aircraft (along with pilot and flight crew) remained on the alert for travel on a "no-notice" basis to points anywhere on the globe. Most impressive was the fact that this major organization had never lost an aircraft!

One week after arrival here, I reported for work at my new duty location. My assignment was that of Non-Commissioned Officer In Charge of Unit Administration (NCOIC, Admin). My title sounded most impressive. Ah, but this was a major problem for me because I had been absent from the administrative career field since July 1961 (nine years earlier). During this lengthy time period, the administrative field had been completely revolutionized! Thus, all my previously acquired knowledge of this field had become obsolete! I knew absolutely nothing about my new position! This was completely unacceptable by Air Force standards, for I was supposed to be the expert here— the supervisor! My first three days in this new po-sition were totally traumatic for me! But I would not fail here. Therefore, in my desperate attempt to simplify my situation, I approached the lieutenant colonel commanding officer (also my supervisor), discreetly seeking guidance. "Sir, what exactly do you want me to do here?" I asked. The colonel calmly replied, "Sergeant Van York, I simply want you to supervise my administrative operations". Heck, I already knew this much! He hadn't given me any specifics whatsoever, but now that I was a staff sergeant, I simply could not have said to him, "But sir, I'm totally unfamiliar with the administrative field". Such a statement would have ended my military career for certain!

I thanked the colonel for his input before returning immediately to my duty section. I'd felt quite competent regarding the managerial aspect of this position. However, I fully realized that I was totally incompetent in those technical aspects of my field! This meant I could make job assignments to my subordinates; however, I was incapable of judging their finished products according to current Air Force standards. It seems that no one here (including subordinates) suspected my career-related deficiency. So in resolving this highly critical situation, I quickly rounded up all governing directives relating to my career field. Then as my staff went about completing job assignments which I had given them, I discreetly reviewed this extensive volume of regulations and manuals. I even remained each evening in my office long after all others had departed. At the end of two weeks, I'd successfully completed a sufficient number of directives to consider myself competent in my new position!

Compounding matters here though was the fact that I had never before worked with or around female military personnel. Here, I suddenly found myself as not only supervisor of a number of men, but also a sizeable number of female personnel. Unfortunately I had not uncovered any directives that delineated supervisory responsibilities regarding women. Therefore, I resorted to my dear grandmother's philosophy of treating others as I would hope to be treated. But I went one step further, by treating these female members as if they were my sisters. I quickly realized that this policy of consistency and respect was highly effective! Thus, within my first sixty days here I had molded my office staff into one harmonious and highly efficient group of workers. At the end of my second month, I received from my commander verbal commendation for the rapid but vast improvement in administrative document processing. Still though, I continued diligently reviewing directives— with particular emphasis being placed on newly issued directives. This would become my method of supervising throughout the remainder of my military career!

Months seemingly passed slowly for my family and me, but finally Thanksgiving Day arrived. For this Thanksgiving Day, we received two special guests. Luckily, while in Germany Lora had learned to properly prepare a turkey. Her newly acquired culinary skills made for a very delicious meal. Our guests were none other than my new friend Barney and wife from Hahn. They had recently arrived at an Air Force base at Grand Forks, North Dakota. We enjoyed our meal together. Suddenly, both Barney and I broke out in raucous laughter! When our wives inquired "What we two found so funny?" we each gave the same answer (but without choreography). Our answer was "Who would have thought that we two would have become friends"? That weekend Barney and his wife returned to Grand Forks. They would again visit us years later in Athens, Greece.

Back at the office three days later, activity at work resumed smoothly and without a glitch. It would continue this way for the remainder of my twelve-month stay here at Minot. I had become so well-known around the base,

I even received an invitation to work at one of the base's many ballistic missile silos. This offer had come with the assurance of guaranteed timely promotion to the grade of technical sergeant (for which I was now eligible). But after much deliberation I declined the offer for personal reasons. Namely, such an assignment would have required that I conduct my work in some silo far below the surface. Each shift consisted of two weeks in duration. Now, we had two young children and my wife had not learned to drive. (She didn't drive—I didn't swim)— what a combination)! Anyway, I simply did not feel comfortable in abandoning my young family for such extended periods. Consequently, I would remain at my current assignment for the duration of my stay at Minot.

Christmas was just around the corner. And although Lora and I would spend this Christmas with just our two young children, we were quite satisfied with this arrangement. I had held the grade of staff sergeant now for just over three years, in which time I'd managed to significantly improve our family's financial situation. So two weeks prior to Christmas, I loaded my wife and children into our car (of five years) and then headed into the little city of Minot. I had not told Lora the intent of our visit, for I wanted to surprise her. We drove directly to a Chevrolet car dealership. Naturally Lora knew nothing of cars, so I chose a new car for us. I picked out a beautiful new powder blue Chevrolet Monte Carlo. Both Lora and the children lauded my choice, which was a very special car, and the very first of its kind.

This car had artificial black leather upholstery, along with simulated wood-grained instrument paneling. Its styling was unusually sleek and impressive. But the most outstanding feature of this car was the fact that it housed a powerful (but energy saving) V-8 engine! This was my early Christmas gift to my wonderful young wife and children. This was also the very first totally new car I had ever purchased! I would drive this car for a total of fifteen years, and during this entire time the Monte Carlo would prove itself as the absolutely best American automobile I would ever own! In short, this car provided me and my family with fifteen years of trouble-free driving enjoyment.

Soon Christmas arrived, followed by our birthdays. Luckily, my personal finances were such that I was able to provide my family with a number of gifts for this most special occasion. On this special day, weather conditions were such that venturing outside the walls of our home was absolutely unadvisable. But this did not matter to us for we were comfortably warm inside our home. But most important of all—WE WERE TOGETHER FOR THE HOLIDAYS!

With the holiday celebrations behind us, I returned to work—as Lora resumed her routine of caring for our children. Incidentally, little Mari had commenced school just four months earlier, which had significantly altered Lora's routine in caring for the children. But even with no assistance and little experience, she managed these demanding tasks quite expertly. I say this because neither Lora nor I'd had any prior experience in living and working in sub-arctic temperatures (minus sixty-five degrees). If outside without adequate thermal clothing, any persons here would freeze in less than sixty seconds! My dear wife managed to successfully care for our children even under these adverse weather conditions!

At this point in my life I had smoked cigarettes daily for the past seventeen consecutive years. It so happened that in early January 1971, I'd taken Lora to our local on-base hospital for a medical examination. As Lora was in the doctor's office, I sat in the hospital's reception area. While waiting there I happened to pick up a pamphlet listing the many hazards of cigarette smoking, and when I had finished this article I decided that I would stop smoking. I had unsuccessfully attempted doing so on numerous prior occasions. Each time, within just two weeks I returned to smoking— but at an accelerated rate! I sincerely wanted to quit, but as so many others had done— I failed miserably! But I was determined I would succeed in this most difficult endeavor. Simply stated, I had a strong desire to stop smoking— but not the discipline with which to achieve my objective. This time things would be different, for I would establish for myself a simple method for success. This would consist of a two-step process. First, I realized mental preparation was essential to success. Second, consistency in discipline was equally essential. Therefore, I told myself, *"Jake, you have in your desk one full carton of cigarettes plus an additional six packs. So when you finish the six packs, you'll have only one single carton remaining. However, when your final carton is finished, you will have smoked your very last cigarette! When you've run out of cigarettes—you will purchase no more, and neither will you bum cigarettes from others"!* I fully realized that my cigarette stash would expire within two short weeks. This meant that I had two weeks in which to condition my mental faculties for a life of not smoking. In nearing the end of my two-week probationary period, as I opened a cigarette pack, I observed that only one pack remained. I made a mental note to myself that my smoking days were almost over". The very next afternoon I opened my final pack, saying, "Well Jake, this is it— NO MORE"! My friends, I'm proud to say to you— my personal program for quitting smoking worked beautifully! As of January 31st 1971, my days of cigarette smoking were permanently behind me. Forty-one years later, I would remain free from cigarette smoking! I've written these particular words for you in hoping that they just might be of some value.

My miraculous success in finally having quit smoking did not materialize at low cost. Over the next six months, I would constantly find myself longing for even a single puff of cigarette smoke. After this critical period had passed though, I gradually began losing my strong desire for a cigarette. During this period I found myself frequently tempted to literally beg for just one cigarette (even from total strangers)! This longing sensation was particularly prevalent while consuming alcohol at social events. On numerous occasions I had at least temporarily considered abandoning my program of abstinence. However, only a strong sense of discipline aided me in retaining my great resolve. Months later I was completely cured!

Meanwhile I had consistently conducted myself professionally while on duty. I made certain that I displayed absolutely no indications of physical or mental irritation toward my peers, superiors, or subordinates. Most of all, I made certain that I never vented my feelings of frustration toward my dear wife or young children. Simultaneously during this time period, I had privately initiated a desperate search for reassignment to another location having a warmer climate. So by mid-February 1971, I had secured for myself and family a special assignment in Clovis, New Mexico. Upon receiving this assignment, I was quite happy. I immediately called Lora to inform her that we would very soon be leaving this ultra-cold region known as North Dakota. My wife was also thrilled by this news! However, when I briefed my commander of my pending reassignment, he said, "Jake, you're much better off here at Minot". Upon hearing his words I fought to conceal my great disappointment. For the next several days I sought any and all persons who had previously served at the Clovis site. I received the same general consensus from other military members. Reluctantly, I then submitted my request for release from this assignment. In early March, I received my notice of release from same.

I had, in the interim, located another special assignment as an Air Force Recruiter at Berkeley, California, and I wasted no time in applying for it. By mid-March 1971, I received official notification of selection for the Berkeley assignment. Again, I told my wife that we would be leaving. Again, she expressed great happiness at hearing this news. But behind the scenes, some maneuvering had occurred, for just two weeks later I was also released from this assignment at Berkeley. I was devastated! But worst of all, I would need to inform my wife. Surprisingly, she accepted this great disappointment, saying, "We'll be okay, Jake". At this point though, I had my doubts.

It was mid-April, but there were still sizeable mounds of snow on the ground. It was during this time that there was a potentially grave incident involving one of our base's KC-135 refueling jets. I happened to noticed large numbers of people scurrying from our building and toward the flight line runways. "What's happening?" I asked of someone in passing. "One of our jets is about to crash!" exclaimed the sergeant as he brushed past me. At this point I forgot all about work and raced behind the crowd ahead of me! Many people had gathered at the flight line runways to witness this life-threatening event. I checked the skies in all directions, but saw no plane. I asked the person standing next to me "What exactly is the problem with our plane"? "Its landing gear is frozen and won't deploy." he answered. This meant there was a strong possibility that upon touchdown this plane would likely burst into flames, instantly disintegrating! *"This is awful,"* I thought as I quietly stood there. During this era the foaming of runways was in its early stages of use, so there was no guarantee that foaming would prove successful. But our courageous wing commander had ordered this emergency action. Meanwhile, the pilot and his efficient crew had circled our base, dumping fuel. This was clearly a potentially disastrous situation, but even worse— I KNEW THESE GUYS!

Now the fire trucks were in the final stages of spreading several feet of special-purpose foam onto the runway. All the while, I continuously scanned the skies for any sighting of our troubled tanker jet. As I looked westward, I spotted what appeared as just a tiny speck in the sky. As this object drew closer, its outline became more discernible. Someone in the crowd yelled, "Here they come"! Up to this point I had remained quite calm. But now I suddenly realized,— my recent state of calmness had just been replaced by those darned 'butterflies'! I stood among more than one thousand people, all of whom were anxiously awaiting the safe return of their friends and loved ones aboard this distressed aircraft. Now that the runway had been completely prepared, our plane gradually grew larger in appearance, while maintaining its steady inbound course toward the runway. *"This is it"*, I thought. Lower and lower this plane dropped. Finally, it touched down upon the heavily foamed runway! I feel certain that the hearts of everyone here momentarily stopped beating as this large plane held steady, skimming along the runway. Within seconds the pilot reversed its four powerful jet engines! Still, he held the plane on its course. Gradually, this large aircraft began slowing, while still maintaining its course. Then after what seemed like an eternity, the plane finally came to a complete stop. "They're safe, they're safe!" yelled the crowd. I yelled right along with them! This great pilot had maintained total professionalism throughout this nerve-wracking ordeal! More importantly, he had saved his crew and himself, while fully protecting his aircraft. He had accomplished this amazing feat without causing injury to his crew, or damage to his aircraft. This, my friends, was the true example of greatness!

Back at the office and all across the base, this incident became the topic of discussion for months afterward. But with this now just a memory, each of us returned to our duties. Just two weeks later I received a call from my Tactical Commander, General James, advising me of my upcoming reassignment to an airbase in northern Thailand. Naturally this was welcomed news! When I inquired of the general the possibility of assignment cancellation, he quickly responded, "Not a chance Jake, this one is for sure".

At home that evening I gave my wife the good news— for the third time! She was guardedly thrilled, responding,

"We'll wait and see". Incidentally, her English had improved considerably. Now that the weather had warmed somewhat, my family and I would thoroughly enjoy our remaining two months here at Minot. In our nice (still) new car we traveled through much of this expansive state, eventually even reaching Canada. So in retrospect, we had spent a peaceful and enlightening eleven-plus months here in Minot.

Chapter 13

Towers of Thailand

After having relocated my family to southern
California, I arrived at my base in northern Thailand shortly after noon hour on July 7th 1971. This was near the beginning of monsoon season, and heavy rainfall had already
commenced. Five long years had passed since I'd last visited
DaNang, Vietnam, but I'd spent those five years in much
colder regions such as Ohio, Germany, and more recently
North Dakota. Also, my most recent twelve-month assignment was spent in a region of extremely low humidity.
Here though, there was extremely high humidity during
periods of the summer. This sudden change in temperature
and humidity drastically lowered my energy level at a time
when I could least afford it. Luckily, I'd once again been assigned living quarters comparable to those I had occupied
while in Vietnam. Hence, my new single occupancy room
was spacious and quite comfortable. It also contained ample insulation, air-conditioning, and one special-purpose
telephone!

After completing two days of in-processing and orientation, I reported for duty at my new unit. I had been
assigned to the 56th Combat Support Group, a sizeable

organization of just under three hundred male military personnel. Here, there were no women. The current commander of this organization held the grade of captain, and was a young man of medium build. Over time I would find this young officer quite competent in his position as commander. Usually each commander runs his (or her) organization with the assistance of their first sergeant. However, at the time of my arrival here, my unit had no first sergeant assigned. Consequently, I was assigned as NCOIC, Unit Administration/First Sergeant (Acting). So in addition to managing all assigned administrative functions for my unit, I would also fill in as first sergeant. My predecessor (a staff sergeant) had escaped this added responsibility, as he'd been in the process of returning stateside.

My duty hours were established as Monday through Saturday, from 7:00AM until 7:00PM. This dual function I now served was further compounded by a phone call from General James. After we'd gotten through our greetings, the general casually stated, "Jake, while you're there at Nakon Phanom, I'd like you to do a little nightly reconnaissance work for me— are you up to it"? "Exactly what is it that you want me to do, sir?" I asked. "Over the past several months there've been a great number of attacks leveled against your base by the "VC" he responded. "I'd like for you to see if you can get a handle on their local operations, so that we might be able to put a stop to this." he added. I responded somewhat naively, "But sir, this is Thailand— there should not be any "VC" in this region". "Oh, but there are!" answered the general. "Okay sir, I'll get right on this" I replied. "Great, then I'll need you to patrol the base's perimeter between the hours of 10:PM and 2:00AM each night until we bring these attacks under control." he ordered. "I will do this sir, but local security police personnel are already patrolling this base," I said. "I know this Jake, but your efforts might just produce a little something extra," stated the general. "Okay sir, I'll commence tonight then," I said. "Great, I've already briefed your commander and he's agreed to grant you flexible working hours at the office, which will allow you ample time for rest and relaxation" stated the general. He then asked "Are we clear on what I want you to do"? "I understand that you want me to locate the source of these attacks and report them immediately to our local security police personnel," I answered. "That's precisely what I'm asking," said General "J". "Use the special telephone in your room to keep me informed, okay?" he concluded. "Will do, sir" I replied.

When I approached my local squadron commander about my recent discussion with the general, he responded "Sergeant Van York, I appreciate the fact that you wish to brief me regarding this confidential operation; however, this is outside my area of responsibility— so I would rather not know about this". "That's fine sir," I said, adding "I ask your permission to take off for a few hours each afternoon, in preparation of my nightly duty". "You have my full concurrence," answered the commander.

Later that afternoon, while at the dining hall I mentioned the topic of recent Viet Cong attacks against the base to the three other NCOs sitting at my table. I was surprised to discover their willingness to discuss this sensitive issue. One NCO jokingly said, "If you want evidence of these attacks, all you need to do is look up at our water towers". When I asked what he meant, he said "Whenever you look up at these towers, you will notice that each has a great amount of patchwork". Another chimed in saying, "Those patches were caused by AK-47 automatic rifles". The third NCO spoke up, "These "VC" have also attacked this base a number of times using rockets and mortars"!

I found these revelations quite alarming. After our meal I borrowed our squadron's bicycle to personally inspect each of our water towers. I noticed that our north tower contained numerous patches! Conversely, I discovered that our south tower had noticeably fewer patches. Follow-up revealed that both towers had been erected during approximately the same time period. This suggested that for some reason, the north side of our base had come under attack more often than its south side. No towers stood at this base's east and west sides, and I discovered little evidence of attacks on either of these two sides. I would therefore conduct the majority of my audio scans by primarily focusing upon our base's north side!

After completing my inspections, I located the operations officer of our security police unit. "Come in, sergeant, you must be Van York," said the somewhat muscular captain currently serving as ops officer. Extending his hand toward me, he said, "I've heard a number of good comments about you and your abilities". "Thank you sir," I said, accepting the large comfortable leather chair at the corner of his desk. "Sir, I'm here to coordinate with you my upcoming nightly patrols— I'll be starting tonight." I said. The officer listened intently as I presented my patrol routine and schedule. When I'd finished briefing him, he immediately shook my hand once again, saying "Most impressive, I wish you great success in this operation". I thanked the captain and as I turned to leave his office, I briefly paused at the door, saying "Sir, I hope none of your personnel takes any shots at me while I'm conducting my patrols". The captain chuckled, saying. "Don't worry, I'll make certain that they all know you're here".

Upon returning to my room I carefully removed the Elm from its resting place of the past eighteen months. Then after ensuring its condition, I unpacked my minia-ture recorder and proceeded to check for any mechanical defects. Lastly, I unpacked my special antenna along with my two electrical connector wires. At precisely 10:00PM of that very evening, I positioned myself at the base of a telephone pole approximately one hundred yards from the center of our base's north fence. This particular location would become my secondary (nighttime) duty station. I am not complaining though, for this site was a far cry better than any I'd visited during my three previous TDYs in Viet-nam. At least here I felt safe from attack by the Viet Cong. I also had selected an area that was free of vegetation, so the likelihood of any visits from snakes was minimal. And, here I would not be plagued by my gecko friends! By having positioned myself in a cleared area, I would enjoy improved audio reception. But the greatest advantage was that of a tension-free work environment. Here I felt safe and com-pletely relaxed.

I would perform audio sweeps of this region beginning at a point northeast of the base, followed by sweeps north and then sweeps northwest. I would repeat this process for thirty minutes. Then I would move to the south side of the base, where I would perform area scans for fifteen-minute durations. This would become standard procedure. Just ten minutes into my initial area scan, I detected male voices that sounded as though they were discussing some issue of serious nature. I instantly began recording, and oddly, I understood some of what was spoken. I wondered how I could understand the Thai language, but then I quickly realized that these guys were speaking Vietnamese! I do not know just how much of this session I had missed, but I recorded four separate fifteen-minute tapes while sitting there, at which point their secret meeting concluded. I distinctly understood that this group was in the planning stages of a mortar attack upon our base, which was to occur near the end of this month! For the remaining three hours of my shift, I patrolled our base, scanning nearby areas. While doing so I recorded two additional tapes; both of which were in Thai. I had not understood either of these recordings, but I would nevertheless submit them for local and Washington (General J's) review. At the end of my four-hour shift I returned to my comfortable room, where I immediately prepared for bed.

Five hours later (7:00AM) I reported for my first nearly full day of work at my duty section. My commander was quite happy to see me for two reasons. First, I had safely made it through the night before. Second, I was punctual in arriving at work. My section was minimally staffed, as fewer workers were needed since each person worked at least sixty hours per week. My first task was to prioritize the day's work, and then issue work assignments and instructions. Next, I began sifting through the stacks of documents in my in-basket. I was instantly reminded of a period fifteen years earlier back at Harlingen AFB with Staff Sergeant Joe "G", who had concealed sacks of letter mail. Fortunately, this was an administrative unit and not a mail unit, but I was once again shocked by discovering unprocessed administrative documents that had sat upon this desk for as far back as ten months earlier. Oddly, like in Harlingen, the offender here was also a staff sergeant named Joe! But this is where the similarities ended, for this latter Joe (my predecessor) was not handicapped by our English language. Joe "L" had simply chosen to reduce his workload by fifty percent by processing only top priority administrative documents. All routine documents were untouched upon his desk for months! Surprisingly, no one seemed to have noticed this condition.

Since SSgt Joe "L" had already departed the base, I would not have harmed his career by reporting this offense. However, had I done this there would have ensued an investigation into this matter. And since the commander was ultimately responsible here, his military career would been negatively impacted. More specifically, this incident quite possibly may have ended my commander's career. So I quietly resolved this problem with-out seeking assistance. I would ensure though that I would not allow any such recurrence during my stay here at Naknon Phanom Airbase!

For the next ninety days I managed (as 1st Sgt) the health, morale, and welfare of all enlisted personnel of our squadron. Concurrently during this period, as NCOIC I retrained assigned administrative personnel, thereby improving their efficiency. During this period I conducted my nightly reconnaissance missions, and identified three separate groups of Viet Cong insurgents along with a small number of sympathizers. During my first ninety days here, not only were these groups identified— they, along with their many sympathizers, were arrested and confined! With the confinement of these insurgents, some provided valuable information pertinent to current and future Viet Cong operations. With this information now in the hands of General "J", I was temporarily released from nightly reconnaissance duty. The information which was received and analyzed by the general and his staff greatly reduced our military's operating costs within four regions of South East Asia!

During this same period, I took several actions toward improving living conditions for enlisted personnel of our squadron. First, working with small groups of volunteers, we removed the numerous walkways within our squadron area. These crude walkways had been constructed using a material commonly known as PCP. This material was originally intended for use as temporary emergency landing strips for small to mid-size U. S. aircraft. The problem was, this material was only one quarter inch thick, and rested directly upon the ground. Making matters worse, it was pure black. Now imagine the great amount of accumulated rainfall resting upon the surface during monsoon season. These are the times when the deadly venomous snakes are usually present. Now further imagine yourself here at NKP, casually strolling along some PCP walkway within our squadron area— when zap, (you've just been bitten by a venomous viper)! You feel the searing pain as it shoots up your leg, rushing to your heart! Sadly, your chances of survival are less than fifty percent! You failed to notice the snake for three reasons. First, darkness was all around you. Second, the PCP was black— blending with the darkness. Third, the deadly snake was either black (or dark gray)—

blending with the PCP material. These deadly reptiles enjoyed lying upon the PCP walkways, as they provided a source of heat.

As a corrective measure, my group of volunteers and I called upon my brick masonry skills (from high school days) to replace the PCP with light-colored genuine concrete, which was professionally installed. We had taken the precaution of raising our new walkways to a height of eight inches. Thus, in case of flooding, these surfaces usually remained above water level. Additionally, the unusually bright color of the concrete we used created great contrast between itself and any dark-colored snake which may have been crawling or resting upon the surface. But since these newly installed walkways contained little (or no) inner heat, the snakes naturally avoided them. This single project immediately reduced our unit's snakebite rate by more than seventy-five percent!

During mid-October, my unit was assigned a genuine first sergeant in the grade of master sergeant (E-7). This instantly reduced my previously untenable workload to reasonable levels. Now I was finally left with just my normal administrative duties to manage. This allowed me to commence my overdue study program of the Thai language. This time though I reduced my daily quota to just three words per day. In so doing, I significantly increased my ability to retain what I had studied. Over coming months I progressed well in the language of Tai.

Soon we were approaching Thanksgiving Day, which was a particularly lonely occasion for me. Compounding matters, there followed closely afterward Christmas, our birthdays, New Year's Day, (Paraskivi's) birthday. I braced myself though, and somehow I succeeded in surviving this very special festive period while away from my dear and loving family. With the holiday season having passed, I devoted my full attention to my military duties and my study of Thai language. Soon the month of February 1972 arrived, bringing with it a sense of improved morale. I realized that with just a little more patience, I would soon return to my wife and children. At this point the weeks and months seemingly increased the rate of speed at which they passed.

At long last, we entered the month of May—which brought with it warming temperatures. But this month would prove different from any we'd previously experienced. Regretfully, this would be the month during which a number of evil-minded persons would conspire to end the lives of my beloved family! I'd often heard tales of bad luck occurring on Friday 13th. Such an incident occurred involving my family, (but on Saturday 13th). I'd recently had a premonition that something might not have been quite right with my family, so I called my wife. Immediately upon answering my call, Lora exclaimed, "Jake, someone tried to kill us last night"! Her statement shocked me deeply, so I quickly asked, "What happened"? In Lora's excited state , she resorted to speaking Greek, telling me that someone had purposefully tampered with the gas line leading into their trailer unit! I found her words unbelievably alarming! Fortunately, Lora had been awake and alert. She had heard noises outside her bedroom window, and had arisen from bed without awakening the children. Soon she smelled gas, so she quickly grabbed the kids before rushing to a nearby relative's home! Police and one gas company technician were called to the scene. The police checked for both fingerprints and footprints, while completing their report. The technician safely repaired the gas line. The police tried reassuring Lora by telling her that they would commence additional patrols in her area. I feigned composure though as Lora provided me with the disturbing details of this incident. I suggested that she immediately remove our older daughter (Mari) from school and return to Greece for a visit with her mother during the remainder of my tour in Thailand. Lora felt that this was a wonderful idea, so she accepted my suggestion and then made rapid preparations for a temporary return to Greece. The following month I would also begin making my plans for return to the United States. On July 17th 1972, having been nominated for the prestigious Air Force Bronze Star Medal, I proudly ended my twelve-month tour of duty in Thailand.

Chapter 14

Placement at Plattsburgh

On the morning of July 19th 1972, I once again arrived at that major transportation base known as Travis AFB, California. There was no one here awaiting my arrival, causing me to feel a brief loneliness inside. I quickly recovered though, for I fully realized that my dear wife and children would have loved to have been here to greet me. By noon, I'd retrieved my (still nearly new) Monte Carlo from storage. This car had just reached the 9,000-mile point on its odometer. I couldn't wait to test its speed across the spacious plains of Utah, which was directly in my route to mom and dad's home in South Carolina. I hadn't seen my aging parents since 1966, and it was now 1972 (six very long years) , so naturally, I very much looked forward to seeing them. And knowing that my wife and children were safely enjoying life with my mother-in-law, both relaxed me and lifted my spirits.

After four days of rigorous high-speed driving, I reached the home of my parents. Again this time I had not informed them of my visit, so they were totally overjoyed! For the next three weeks mom, dad, and I truly enjoyed each other's company. We frequently visited with my sweet

Aunt Emma, and other friends of the family. But with each passing day, I longed for the day when I would once again embrace my dear wife and my two wonderful young daughters. *"What irony?"*, I thought as I realized that— when with my wife and children, I longed for my parents. But now that I was finally with my parents, I longed for my wife and children. Alas, I could not "have my cake— and eat it too". My weeks at home passed much too quickly, and soon it was time for my parents and I to once again say "farewell" to each other.

On the afternoon of August 10th I headed north toward the great state of New York. I found this drive both exciting and interesting, for I had never before taken this route. Within just four hours, I'd reached the great city of Washington, D.C. I decided I would stop here and possibly spend the evening, since driving straight through to Plattsburgh was unnecessary. So after securing a comfortable room at one of the nation's leading motel chains, I settled in for the evening. I placed a call to the general's D. C. office, but he had left his office for the day. I would not attempt calling his home, so I simply lounged in my quiet and peaceful room for the remainder of the evening.

On Friday morning, I commenced the remaining mileage of my trip. Approximately three hours later, I passed through New York City. After four more hours I located that expansive military installation known as Plattsburgh AFB, New York. Once on the base I signed into my unit before securing temporary on-base living quarters. I would not occupy dormitory facilities, as I would soon be joined by wife and children. Afterward I visited our local noncommissioned officers club (NCO Club) for dinner. I had spent a relaxing, but lonely weekend here on this base, although I did venture into the downtown area of this pristine and peaceful little city of Plattsburgh. I quickly found this location a great area for family recreational activities. With the weekend passed, I entered my first week of duty here in my new assignment. My first three days were spent completing in-processing onto this base.

On August 10th I initially reported to my new organizational duty section. After introductions and light conversation with office staff, I was escorted to the office of my new commanding officer. I was pleased to find that this commander was a personable officer in the grade of lieutenant colonel. He was also an experienced command pilot of both fighter jets and bomber aircraft such as the B-52. For some reason he seemed to have placed his trust in me even though I had not yet begun work. At Plattsburgh, I was assigned as NCOIC, Technical Administration, which was considerably different from my Minot and Nakhon Phanom (NKP) assignments, although, the mission of Minot was nearly identical to that of Plattsburgh. My specific function was to monitor personnel and aircraft deployments, and keep my commander informed of their status. So here in my new position, I was considered key personnel. The tracking program, for which I was solely responsible, was vital to this squadron's global bombing mission. Therefore, even the slightest of error in my statistics quite possibly might have resulted in a failed bombing mission! Such a key position demanded that I not take leave or proceed on temporary duty (TDY). This restriction brought about an immediate and adverse effect upon my capability for performing TDYs for General James. During my first several weeks, I concentrated upon perfecting my duty operating procedures. I had already been advised that these records, which I manually maintained, were subject to review by my commander on a no-notice basis. This meant that my deployment figures must remain current and completely accurate at all times. Consequently, I dedicated myself completely to the effective management of this highly sensitive program!

On August 21st I received shipment of our household goods, which had remained in storage during my assignment in Thailand. Each evening after duty I worked feverishly in preparing our newly assigned on-base living quarters for the arrival of my family just one week later. Our new place was already cleaned, but in my strong desire for pleasing and impressing my young wife, I completely cleaned the apartment for a second time. Finally, after arranging furniture and unpacking our clothing— our new home was ready for my family!

At last, on August 28th I was granted the afternoon off to meet my family at Kennedy Airport. On this very special day, my 'butterflies' chose to visit me once again, for I would be able to embrace my dear wife and my two wonderful young daughters! Also, I would again visit this famous location known as New York City! I arrived at this world famous airport, feeling as if I hadn't seen my family in years, although only thirteen months had passed. Finally, my long-awaited moment arrived, as my lovely wife and two equally adorable daughters appeared before me. Our reunion was a most memorable occasion! The joy I now felt, more than compensated for the unbearable sadness I experienced in leaving my family one year earlier. After clearing customs, I loaded their luggage inside the trunk of our car before heading northward to our new home in upstate New York. With my family back at my side, the next three months passed blissfully. Each evening after work I would take them for drives around the city of Plattsburgh and surrounding areas. On weekends we would visit the great and beautiful city of Montreal, Canada. We even found time for short visits to a great number of scenic locations throughout those very beautiful Adirondack Mountains. I would forever remember those days we spent in the Plattsburgh area.

On September 5th, our little daughter Mari started school in on-base educational facilities. Unfortunately, the forced one-year separation of our tightly knit family had taken a slight toll upon Mari, causing her to falter during her first days of school here at Plattsburgh. Hence, the school's teaching staff were of the opinion that Mari was not capable of performing at the third grade level. They therefore arbitrarily returned our daughter into second grade, which was highly disturbing to Lora, and totally unacceptable to me. So, after several visits to the principal of the Plattsburgh's school, I convinced her to return Mari back to her rightful third grade. At the end of school year, Mari would complete third grade with honors!

Summer had ended and Thanksgiving was rapidly approaching. Continuous heavy snowfall had turned the trees and ground surfaces into a virtual dream world of snow and ice. Now although Minot had accumulated 'mountains' of snowfall (which was in fact beautiful), Minot stood upon level plains (with no trees). In contrast, Plattsburg stood in mountainous terrain, and contained countless numbers of beautiful large trees. This major difference was my reason for considering the Plattsburgh region as a dream world.

Meanwhile, while in Thailand I had taken the mandatory written examinations for promotion to technical sergeant (E-6). At that time, I felt confident that I had performed well on each test. However, on October 2nd, I was greatly disappointed by the fact that of a total 190 possible test score points, I had missed promotion by only 1.36. Ah, but I had been nominated for the Air Force Bronze Star Medal upon rotation from Thailand, which was worth five whole points within our promotion system. I knew that this medal should have been awarded prior to the promotion cut-off date. Therefore, I should have received this missed promotion! "What to do?" I thought. Then I remembered that while studying Air Force regulations at Minot, I had stumbled across a directive that prescribed procedures for correction of Air Force personnel records. I had never before seen or heard of this particular directive. So the following day at work, I researched this regulation and discovered that there was hope for my situation after all. Thus, I initiated tracer action regarding my Bronze Star Medal nomination. Weeks later, I learned that my nomination was never forwarded to proper issuing headquarters, located in the Philippines. This revelation was quite disturbing to me. Further investigation of this matter resulted in the following comments by the issuing headquarters: "This office is not in receipt of said award nomination for SSgt Jake Van York. However, if such nomination had been received by this office, it would have been approved by 31 August 1972". This information was forwarded to my current commander via electronic message. With this written document in hand,

I requested re-submission of my Bronze Star nomination. Several months would pass before resolution of this issue.

In the meantime my family and I celebrated Thanksgiving and the Christmas holiday period. And of course, we also celebrated our birthdays, culminating with the birthday of Paraskivi, (our younger daughter). During this festive period I'd pleased my family with a variety of gifts and pleasure trips. Needless to say, this holiday season would prove to be one of our very best. At this time I assured my dear wife that we would spend each of our future holiday seasons together as a family unit. Over the years I would keep this promise.

The months passed quickly for us, and soon we'd entered the month of March 1973. Then on March 1st I received retroactive award of my third Air Force Commendation Medal. My Bronze Star nomination had been downgraded to just a Commendation Medal. Incidentally, this Commendation Medal held a value of three (3) points toward promotion. This meant that unofficially, I was now a technical sergeant; albeit, without accompanying pay and benefits! Few members serving in the military had ever heard of or experienced a situation such as mine! At this juncture, I submitted my case to the Air Force Records Correction Board for their appropriate action, which would require another six months in processing. Meanwhile, on April 5th 1973, I was again administered our Air Force's annual promotion examinations. This time around, I felt I'd done really well. Unfortunately, results of this current promotion cycle would not be released until October 1st.

Over the past two years I'd diligently applied myself by studying current applicable Air Force directives. Hence while at work during mid-April, I accidentally stumbled upon one newly issued regulation that prescribed revised enlisted personnel assignment policy. As I read and digested this directive, I eventually arrived at a chapter that allowed me to apply for immediate reassignment to certain overseas areas. I reread this information several times, each time arriving at the same conclusion. Specifically, I was eligible for reassignment under these new provisions. I wasted no time in preparing my special application. That very afternoon after securing my commander's favorable endorsement, I presented my application to the flight surgeon of our base. This person held the grade of full colonel (O-6), and was responsible for reviewing and forwarding my application to our military personnel headquarters in San Antonio Texas.

Upon reviewing my application request, the colonel peered solemnly at me, saying, "Sergeant, this simply won't fly," which was military jargon meaning ("this won't be approved)". I was momentarily taken aback by this colonel's blunt statement! At this point, I knew that he expected that I would simply thank him and then leave his office— never to return. But I would not be so easily deterred! So I said to the colonel, "Sir, I fully respect both your rank and your position; however, I also ask that you respect mine". I continued "Sir, I've carefully reviewed the current governing directive applicable to my request, so I respectfully ask that you forward it". Then without hesitation, the colonel stated, "Sergeant, I'll go you one even better – why don't we just call Randolph AFB right now"? I was surprised by his forthright suggestion, for such a response was truly unexpected. I replied somewhat meekly, "If you would do this sir, I'd be deeply indebted to you".

The colonel then called out to his secretary, "Sally, get me Colonel Thomason on the phone. Within just two minutes the Air Force Personnel Director responded. Our flight surgeon then read (over the phone) the contents of my reassignment application, then sat listening attentively. After a few minutes, he said, "Okay, Jim, I'm going to also include your comments in my endorsement". The flight surgeon abruptly turned to me saying, "Congratulations sergeant, Colonel Thomason of MPC has just now approved your request for reassignment"! I couldn't believe my ears! The event I had just witnessed was unprecedented! I thanked the colonel graciously before promptly leaving his large and highly impressive office. Back at work, I promptly briefed my local commander, and he expressed both patience and understanding of my situation, saying "We're really going to miss you around here, Jake".

At home that evening I broke the wonderful news to my wife. "Lora, my dear— pack your things, you're going home soon!" I said. At first Lora was quite confused by my comments. "Jake, I've just returned from home, so how can this be?" she curiously inquired. "We're being reassigned to Greece!" I gleefully exclaimed. "But we've just recently arrived here," said my wife. "And we're now leaving again," I answered. Now as you may have expected, we really celebrated on that evening! We even went out to a very fine restaurant.

On April 30th, I received my official reassignment orders. I then began making arrangements for shipment of our car and household goods. For the next forty-five days I continued the daily monitoring and reporting of assigned aircraft and personnel. I also continued my constant review of newly issued and revised Air Force regulations and manuals. Finally, I considered myself a true expert within my current field of administration. Our household goods were scheduled for pick-up on the morning of July 16th. I had been given the day off to witness the packing and pick-up of our belongings. It so happened that the movers were scheduled for arrival at 9:00AM, and they arrived promptly. But then there came an unusual and extremely disappointing turn in events. At the very moment of our movers' arrival, our home telephone rang! There followed one of the very worst moments of my young life! The caller was my squadron commander, informing me of the cancellation of my pending assignment! For the next several minutes I stood quietly in utter disbelief! I was reluctant to inform our movers that their work here had been terminated. I was even more reluctant to inform my poor wife that we would not be going to Greece as I had promised. But after bracing myself, I made both notifications. The movers were not happy, which was understandable. My poor wife was totally heartbroken! I tried consoling her, but to no avail. By noon she had calmed a bit, so I returned to work.

For the next two full weeks I dedicated myself whole-heartedly toward the performance of my assigned military duties, in an effort to overcome my recent disappointment. Then on Wednesday morning (August 1st) I received a second message from the Air Force Personnel Center (MPC) in Texas. Miraculously, my previously cancelled Greece assignment had mysteriously been reinstated! However, within the reinstatement there was one stipulation. Namely, I must arrive in Athens no later than August 31st 1973!

This constituted an unreasonably inadequate preparation period, which would be next to impossible! Still, I was determined that my family and I would meet this strict deadline! I apologetically informed my commander of the reinstated short-notice assignment. I even assisted him in selecting and appointing my replacement from within our squadron. I'd taken the precaution of training a replacement for myself, which was a very wise move. My commander was pleased with my personnel choice.

Now I quickly rearranged for pick-up and shipment of our car and household goods. Then on August 10th my family and I climbed into our car, heading south for a visit with my wonderful parents. This time though, I had notified them in advance of our arrival. My parents were completely overjoyed at seeing their son, daughter-in-law, and their two lovely young grand- daughters! We spent a wonderful ten days together while visiting my Aunt Emma and other close family friends. Then on the evening of August 27th, we briefly returned to Plattsburgh. The very next morning, I took the liberty of placing a call to my recently promoted Tactical Commander, (Major General) Austin T. James. Today I found the general in high spirits! Before I could even begin speaking, he said, "Hey Jake, I see you've got your reinstatement of assignment— I'm pleased". "How did you know, sir?" I asked. "Oh, I keep up with all that's important," he answered. "By the way Jake, while you're there in Athens you'll be strategically located, for I would very much like you to visit a few nearby countries— for a little sightseeing". I understood his meaning, so I promptly replied, "No problem, sir". "Great, then call me as soon as you're there," he said.

On the evening of August 30th, my family and I were unbelievably seated together aboard one very large Boeing 707 aircraft, heading to our fantasy land, (Athens, Greece)!

Chapter 15

Grandeur of Greece #2

On August 31st 1973, I entered our Inbound Assignments section here at the re-designated Hellenikon AB (formerly Athenai Airport, Greece). Normally the base personnel office would have received notification of my pending arrival. However, my reassignment was of such short notice, even our base personnel office had not yet received this information. This instantly created a bit of confusion within our personnel office. Namely, current established military procedure specified that there must be a personnel folder with my reassignment information. Unfortunately, no such folder could be located. Consequently, there existed no official authority for signing me in onto this base. But complicating matters even further, I was informed that there was no position vacancy within my specialty. This constituted a total departure from standard Air Force assignment policy! So at this point, the young captain serving as chief of personnel advised me, "Wait here sergeant, while I confer with the boss (Director of Personnel)". He then took a copy of my reassignment orders the personnel director's office. He immediately returned, saying, "Sergeant, our DP would like to see you in his office immediately".

I promptly proceeded down the long hallway toward the DP's office. Then as per protocol, I knocked once before entering. The Director (DP) invited me inside. "Take a seat Sergeant, and welcome to our little base," the DP said as we shook hands. He then presented me with a 9"x11" thin, (unopened) manila envelope, stamped "URGENT" using red ink! Also, it was addressed ATTN: SSgt J. Van York— EYES ONLY. Such endorsements were usually reserved for the transmission of high-priority information! I quickly opened the envelope. Inside was a brief typewritten (unsigned) note. Also enclosed were copies of recently published Repeated TDY Orders, stipulating "Variations of Itinerary Authorized". The personnel director sat quietly as I read this note, which read, "Report to passenger terminal at 0900 hrs, 1 Sep 73 for 12-hour deployment". I had been forewarned of such contingencies, so this message did not come as a surprise. I then said to the personnel director, "Sir, I've been directed by a special Washington D.C office to perform a twelve-hour TDY, starting tomorrow morning". "Well, it so happens that tomorrow falls on the weekend, so report back here at 0730 hours, Monday morning." he replied, adding, "This will give me time to find a job for you". I thanked the DP and then promptly departed the military personnel office. While returning to my family, I reflected upon recent events. I finally ascertained the reasons for my short-notice reinstatement of assignment! Someone had intervened, after discovering the earlier cancellation of my assignment to this location! That someone would have only been General James himself! Finally, things had begun making a little sense!

Having misled my wife by telling her that I needed

to work, the following morning I arrived sharply at 0845 hours at our local passenger terminal. I had been provided the name and rank of the officer to whom I'd been ordered to report. I was dressed in casual civilian attire, so I was certain this officer would not recognize me, which meant that I must seek him out. So in seeking the expedient way of doing this, I had him paged via intercom. Within minutes I was approached by a fairly young officer of moderate size and build. He was also dressed in civilian attire, but he identified himself simply as "Major Jones". He greeted me by saying, "Sergeant Van York, I'll be accompanying you to our destination". "Where are we headed, sir?" I asked. "That information is classified, sergeant," replied the major.

At 0850 hours, we boarded our midsized military jet aircraft and were advised to prepare for immediate take-off. Just ten minutes later we were airborne. After clearing the immediate area our pilot assumed an easterly heading. On the aircraft were approximately one dozen other military personnel, each of whom was quite young, and all appeared to be in top physical condition. Oddly, no one spoke during our entire three-hour flight. I surmised that these fellows were most likely some special forces (black ops) team, although I made no inquiry or comment.

We reached our Middle Eastern destination at 12:15 PM. Our plane parked at the far end of the runway, some distance from the military passenger terminal. Awaiting our arrival were two vehicles, (one Air Force crew bus and one unmarked black sedan). Both our plane's crew and the team of young men boarded the crew bus; however, the major and I were escorted to the unmarked sedan. We were then driven to a highly fortified and heavily guarded concrete structure on base. Once there we were briefed by a young civilian gentleman who introduced himself as Bob Smith (although I strongly suspected this was not his real name). In his briefing to the major and me, Mr. Smith stated "Gentlemen, over the past several months we've noticed a definite increase in terrorist activity throughout the Middle East and parts of North Africa! We've also identified several newly emerging terrorist groups within this region. This is the reason for your presence here today, Sergeant Van York. We have strong reason to believe that there shall be held locally today, a high-level gathering of the leaders of these groups! Unfortunately, we're unable to place any of our resources within close proximity of today's meeting place. Our government really needs someone with special talents to infiltrate and record the proceedings of today's special meeting". Smith then looked directly at me, as he somewhat desperately asked, "Sergeant Van York, do you think you might be able to help us out here today"? Now truthfully speaking, I was quite flattered by his most desperate appeal. "Where and when will this meeting commence, sir?" I inquired. "On the outskirts of this city, starting at 1400 hours today according to our source," replied our Mr. Smith. "How close can you get me to this meeting's location?" I asked. "Therein lies our problem— I can only get you within one mile from this site." he replied. "Sir, in order for me to adequately assess this situation, I ask that we ride out and survey the area in question." I responded. "That much I can do— so let's take a ride," answered Mr. Smith. I excused myself to prepare for my upcoming task. I had already confirmed that the Elm and my pocket recorder were fully operational. I then wrapped my reception antenna along with my two connector audio cables, inside a newspaper which I'd brought along just for such an occasion. I had brought along twelve short-length audio tapes and one pocket novel, which I had placed inside a brown paper bag. Finally I was ready for this most sensitive of covert operations!

After nearly twenty minutes, we arrived at a point of this city where the density of taller buildings had slightly diminished. "Sergeant, this is the closest I can safely bring you," said Mr. Smith. "Can you point me in the direction of this special gathering?" I asked. "It's to be held inside one four-level building two kilometers up this street and to your left" said Smith. Having noticed that we'd just passed a small city park, I said "Sir, drop me off right here". Both men were obviously perplexed by my seemingly unusual request. Smith even voiced his concern by asking, "Sergeant, how do you expect to listen in on this meeting from this great distance"? I simply smiled, while saying "Trade secret, sir". "I hope this works," he said.

As I dismounted from the vehicle, the major said, "Sergeant, you'll probably be here for at least two hours, so we'll check on you again at 1600 hours sharp". "Wish me luck," I said as they drove away down this crowded street. Once the major and civilian were out of sight, I walked the short distance to the nearby park. My next step was to prepare both the Elm and my pocket recorder for operation. Next, I sat back with legs crossed as I lowered my face toward my new pocket novel. To the average passerby I would have appeared as just some dumb American sitting upon a park bench, attempting to read from some story book. But

I wasn't actually reading, for my eyes were trained upon this busy street directly before me. Luckily I had come here fully prepared, so sunglasses hid my eyes. Up to this point though, I had observed nothing out of the ordinary. I'd not seen a single distinctive vehicle passing in the direction of my targeted building. I figured that possibly some invited guests were already inside the home of their host; so, I decided I would perform a second scan of the site of today's scheduled meeting.

My three-minute scan detected no voice communications from within this building. At this point I began feeling that quite possibly this had been completely wasted effort. *"Maybe I should've stayed back in Athens with my family"*, I thought. But my thoughts were suddenly interrupted by the hurried passing of two late model European luxury automobiles. Each car appeared to have contained a driver and three passengers. I considered this significant! Casually, I arose and strolled out to the street. As I reached the sidewalk, I was just in time to observe these two vehicles as they executed left turns from the street. Then just as casually, I returned to my park bench seat and resumed 'reading' from my novel. I began recording just in time to hear the exchange of the customary Arabic greeting between members of this small group. Minutes later, the group's host began speaking. Unfortunately, I failed to understand the dialect he used. Luckily, I had brought along an adequate number of tapes for recording the comments of this very special high-level group of terrorists leaders! Thus, after having recorded a total of eight fifteen-minute tapes, the group's meeting was concluded. They remained at this residence, discussing a wide variety of less important issues, so I continued recording their comments for another thirty minutes, at which time they entered their vehicles and left. As they passed me, I remained seated with my head lowered. Luckily the major and Mr. Smith were a bit late in returning for me.

Back inside our vehicle I presented my two operational superiors with the ten tapes I had just recorded. "You might need an interpreter for these," I said. Both men were equally taken aback by the inexplicable feat I had just accomplished! Mr. Smith excitedly exclaimed, "Sergeant Van York, either you're a magician or a true genius, I don't know which"! Major Jones was a bit more controlled in his response, saying, "Either way, what you've done here today is truly great work, sergeant"! I sensed that each man viewed my reconnaissance success as a stepping stone for their next promotion! *"If only I were so lucky"*, I thought. The men then drove me directly to another waiting plane. By 5:00PM I was airborne and heading back toward Athens!

When I entered our suite that evening, my loving wife asked, "Did you work very hard today, Jake"? "It wasn't too bad," I answered (with a shrug). Then after a quick soothing shower, we ventured out into the exciting busy streets of Athens. This had been quite a day for me (both here in Athens and wherever else it was that I had gone)! My family and I really enjoyed the remainder of this wonderful weekend here in beautiful Athens!

Following the holiday of Monday (September 3rd) , I commenced initial in-processing onto the American airbase here at Athens. During my brief absence the Director of Personnel (DP) had secured for me a supervisory administrative position, (but through unusual means). He had removed an incumbent staff sergeant from his current position, thereby creating this position for me. Now many of my readers may say "Jake, this was unfair to that poor sergeant"! However, I would answer by saying as unfair as it seemed, the DP's action was more than fair. This poor staff sergeant was on the verge of being court-martialed for dereliction of duty! Therefore, by removing him from his current position, our DP had salvaged his military career. (Incidentally, I discovered this bit of sensitive information only after the fact).

My new assignment was that of NCOIC, Unit Administration. I had just begun my fourth consecutive administrative assignment. Here though, my commander/supervisor held only the grade of captain. But I say to you quite candidly— this was the absolutely meanest captain I would ever encounter in my twenty-eight year military career! This officer's personality was so very forceful, he even had intimidated a number of superior officers here on this base. He simply loved reprimanding and berating other military personnel (regardless of their rank)! During my first few weeks here in my new assignment, I 'walked very lightly', wondering when might this 'lion of an officer' pounce upon me! Miraculously though, I would work harmoniously with this commander for nearly two years, and during this entire period there would never arise an occasion where this officer would speak harshly to me. Though, on many occasions I would personally witness his verbal berating of our very own first sergeant (E-7). Our days passed quickly, as I strived for consistently professional duty performance. Even the efficiency and morale of my office staff had noticeably improved. As a result of this major improvement in attitudes, the administrative workload of our organization was drastically reduced during my first ninety days here! Finally our commander began smiling and even interacting jokingly with our first sergeant and administrative staff. When I approached him over this, he responded "Jake, I have you to thank"!

On October 1st 1973, just one month after my arrival here in Athens, I was greeted one afternoon with a pleasant surprise. Reminiscent of my first days in Japan years earlier, upon returning from lunch my commander presented me with a brand-new set of (E-6) technical sergeant stripes! It goes without saying this was another memorable moment for me! "Congratulations, technical sergeant, you've earned these," he said. Then with our first sergeant standing by, the commander led our unit in applause.

That very afternoon I returned to our local credit union, where I increased my recently established savings account from $300 to $400 monthly. In coming years this would prove to be the most prudent move I had taken to date. As a result of this action I would eventually depart from Athens, having legitimately accumulated a cash savings account valued at over $30,000! This was during the year 1973, when prices were reasonable. At today's economic rates, this amount of cash would have equaled approximately $200,000— (not too shabby for a former poor dirt farmer)!

This was just phase one of this dual-phased process. Luckily, just one month later my former request for Correction of Military Records was completed. Thus, I was once again promoted to the grade of technical sergeant— but with a retroactive date of rank of October 1, 1972!

This meant that I now had more than one year of time-in-grade toward promotion to the grade of master sergeant (E-7), which was quite significant! But there's more, for this action authorized thirteen months of unpaid technical sergeant (E-6) retroactive pay and benefits! Moreover, this action provided a meaningful, positive effect upon the great injustice that had been perpetrated against me years earlier back at Stead AFB in Reno, Nevada!

Major General James back in Washington had been keeping track of my progress (or lack thereof). So late on Friday afternoon of October 5th, the general called to congratulate me on my recent well-deserved promotion. He also offered his congratulations regarding my recent Middle Eastern visit. I was then informed the information I'd miraculously obtained revealed matters of grave concern to our nation! Luckily my visit was timely, thus creating an opportunity for thwarting a great number of terrorist attacks against our great nation. Then after once again congratulating me on promotion, the general commented, "Take the rest of the year off, Jake— I shouldn't be needing your services for at least another three to four months." During our conversation I learned that the twelve young men who had accompanied me into the Middle East, were in fact Air Force Commandoes— sent to intercede in, and eliminate this terrorist plot!

Now that I'd been temporarily released from reconnaissance duties, I focused on my family and my new job. Thus far I had encountered no problems whatsoever in the workplace, as administrative processing of documents flowed smoothly. In my off-duty time I treated my wife and young daughters to the many pleasures provided by living in Greece. And now that we no longer needed to lose sleep over the lack of spending money, we began really enjoying our lives together.

Both Thanksgiving Day and the Christmas holiday season (including our birthdays) had come and gone. By now my family and I had become quite comfortable in our present environment here in Greece. Our precious little Mari and Paraskivi were progressing well in the fourth and first grades (respectively). Lora and I had made new friends and were enjoying a great social life, frequenting nightclubs, restaurants, and theaters. Simply stated— life was just great!

The year 1973 had been a wonderful year for my family and me; and, at this point it seemed as though 1974 would be equally as great. We often took the children out to restaurants and movie theaters, and we were really enjoying ourselves together. But then came one very sad day in my personal life. I had taken my family to our on-base movie theater, as they had wished to view a highly popular movie that was being shown here. But as we approached the ticket window, the ticket clerk refused us entry. It so happened that he was the very same individual whom I'd replaced upon my arrival here. This staff sergeant and I had maintained daily contact after his reassignment to another unit. We'd even become casual friends, so he easily recognized me. I suppose this poor fellow did not know just how he should handle this situation. So, instead of selling us tickets for the movie, he simply sat silently while sadly looking at me. Then when I inquired as to what the problem was, the sergeant commented, "You need to go and see your commander". The tone of his voice, coupled with the expression on his face, strongly suggested that something was seriously wrong (possibly with my parents). I then requested movie tickets for my wife and children, telling them, "I'll be right back". Thus, as they'd entered the movie theater, I went directly to my commander's office. Even though it was past regular duty hours, I found my commander still at work. Then with a solemn expression upon his face, he said, "I regret having to break this sad news to you, but your father has passed away". This news deeply saddened me, although over recent years I had anticipated receiving such news at any moment. I thanked my commander before immediately applying for emergency leave.

I did not want to disturb my family while they were enjoying their movie, so I waited outside for them to exit the theater. Lora had met dad on two separate occasions, and had become quite attached to him. So the news of his demise deeply saddened her also. I realized that the children needed to remain in school, and Lora's presence here was needed by them. So in the interest of expediency, I proceeded alone to support my devastated mother. After dad's funeral I remained with mom for another three full weeks, comforting her and helping in administering to dad's personal affairs. I found it noteworthy that although he had endured austerity through most of his life, he had left no debt whatsoever for mom to repay! Also, he had left a fairly new home along with a new car— both of which were completely paid for! These personal accomplishments served as evidence of the greatness of my wonderful father.

Having assured myself that mom would survive this devastating loss, I returned to Greece on the afternoon of March 29th. As might have been expected, I found my family anxiously awaiting my return. I was quite surprised to find that Lora had begun teaching herself to drive our car, which I'd left parked at home. I was even more surprised to discover that there were no scratches or dents contained on the car! Naturally, I commended my dear wife.

On Saturday morning of April 13th, I returned once more into the Middle East. This time though I traveled alone, as my destination was known to me. My mission was similar to that of my most recent visit, although with different targets. I conducted my operation, which again involved the gathering of sensitive information during a two-hour period that very same evening. As on previous missions, I succeeded in acquiring the information my tactical commander had sought. Over the next six-month period I would return to this region on two more occasions. I would also visit one familiar region of North Africa on two separate occasions. I find it prudent that I do not elaborate on these particular visits, as the current (October 2012) political situation within these regions have become so highly volatile! Therefore, I shall wisely refrain from further comment relating to reconnaissance within these two regions! The following day I returned to my waiting family.

Soon my family and I found ourselves again enjoying the warm and sunny summer months here in beautiful Greece. So with money no longer a problem, I took my wife and daughters on a one-month vacation to the beautiful Greek islands. While there we partied on the beaches of the islands each day of the week. During evening hours we visited a great number of cafés and restaurants around these islands. This was our most memorable vacation to date!

On September 3rd, I returned to work only to discover

that I had been assigned two additional male military personnel. I would quickly learn that these two were quite notorious! The elder of the two was a technical sergeant named Chummy Vee. The younger individual was a twenty-one year old senior airman (E-4) whose name was Ricky Oddman. Both Chummy and Ricky had been removed from their positions as base security personnel! I soon learned that these two had been placed under investigation by our Air Force investigative services agency. They were also under suspicion of conducting (black marketeering) activity. But what would much later disturb me most was the fact that these two fellows had been placed under my supervision for the purpose of spying on me! This meant that I also had been placed under investigation! I would eventually discover the reason for this was the fact that I had opened a substantial savings account of $400 per month while holding the grade of only technical sergeant (E-6). Heck, if these investigators had asked, I could easily have shown them how it was possible for a technical sergeant to legitimately save $400 per month! The investigators had known that this savings account (in itself) did not serve as evidence of wrong-doing on my part. Hence I'd been allowed to remain in my current position. During this time period, neither I nor my squadron commander had been alerted regarding the initiation of this investigation.

I always treated both Chummy and Ricky with compassion and respect while supervising them. But the fact that my unit's function was that of administration meant these two fellows were at a distinct disadvantage since neither possessed administrative training or skills. Still, I succeeded in identifying meaningful work for each man. Then with the passing of time the three of us began socializing together. This was the desired tactic of our base investigative service unit. Over time I would discover that I had unknowingly fallen victim of this strategy. Meanwhile, at work each day we performed our assigned duties professionally. Our off-duty time though was an entirely different story. Nearly each weeknight found Chummy, Ricky, and me, along with our wives, partying at various nightclubs around the city of Athens. At the time I had thought that we were truly friends— (how naïve of me)!

Soon we once more celebrated Thanksgiving Day, which Lora had fashioned into one truly festive event. The holiday season of the following month became even more festive! By now we had entered the year 1975, which history would prove as catastrophic for many U. S. military personnel and families assigned here at Athens. I refer specifically to the still current confidential ongoing military investigation. In early April, my squadron commander received the results of this investigation. This report revealed that Technical Sergeant Vee (Chummy) had over a period of just three years, amassed a small fortune in the amount of $250,000 through his dealings in black market activities! And, he had personally recruited more than twenty-five young airmen who'd purchased items through our base exchange service and commissary facilities for resale purposes. The items ranged from cigarettes and whiskey to clothing and stereo equipment. At some point though, greed entered the picture, causing Chummy and his group to expand their already elaborate operation. Soon they were no longer purchasing only from Athens facilities, but also through overseas mail order catalogs! The whole of these purchases were passed on to Chummy for resale (at 250 a percent mark-up)! Chummy had also bribed local sales clerks and customs personnel.

Here's the way this worked! First, as airmen purchased cigarettes and whiskey, they were required to produce their military ration card (for purchase of rationed items). Cashiers were then required to stamp the card of the buying airman. However, Chummy had also recruited a large number of these cashiers for his operation, who only pretended to have stamped the airman's ration card! Officially, all airmen were authorized the monthly purchase of six cartons of cigarettes, along with five forty-ounce bottles of alcohol. Each carton and bottle would bring more than twice its purchase price on the black market! But with Chummy's ring of crooked cashiers and customs agents, there was no limit to the volume of alcohol and cigarettes bought and resold! The purchasing airmen realized a 100 percent profit from their illegal purchases! Concurrently, Chummy realized more than a 150 percent profit on these collective purchases! Ah, but these were only the small-ticket items!

The other facet of Chummy's operation involved the local and mail-order purchase of audio receivers, tape decks, turntables, diamond rings, watches, and cameras! Each of these items netted a 150 percent profit for Chummy, as his selected customs agents (also for profit) promptly removed and destroyed the customs purchase records from the customs folder of the purchasing airman. It goes without saying that everyone in Chummy's group realized substantial sums of tax-free income! Now in case you are wondering how I happened to discover these facts, as the NCOIC of Administration, I processed the court-martial documents upon Chummy and his group! Naturally, local Greek authorities assumed legal responsibility for their customs agents and cashiers.

Ricky's case was negligible when compared to Chummy's and certain others. Ricky was highly intelligent, and a person who lived in a dream world! So while he appeared perfectly normal to the average person, he had inwardly convinced himself that he had an identical twin brother. He had also convinced himself that he was wealthy! I might also mention here that Ricky was a handsome and exceptionally charming young man, which caused the vast majority of women (regardless of age) to eagerly throw themselves at his feet! He stood six feet tall, with a muscular weight of 210 pounds. I had even often found myself mildly wishing that I might have had a son resembling Ricky. Luckily, he had not joined Chummy's group, instead choosing to work solo. So with his charming features and personality, he realized an unbelievable amount of tax-free income! He had befriended at least one female cashier in each of our base's six major retail outlets! Thusly, while exploiting the availability of these cashiers, he would make several daily purchases of small but expensive items. He had already established buyers for his merchandise, so the instant he'd purchased a number of items, they were immediately released to his buyers. This way, in the event of an investigative raid upon his residence, no merchandise would ever be found!

Near the end of the investigation of Ricky's case, he was called in for a Polygraph examination. Unbelievably, having been asked a series of questions regarding his black-market activities, Ricky defeated the machine! I would later discover that when asked these questions, he had mentally transformed himself into his non-existent twin brother, causing the Polygraph machine to erroneously interpret his answers! No cashiers could be linked to him in this operation, so Ricky was eventually freed of all charges! Ricky now lives in the Far East while operating his very own popular nightclub!

Since I'm on a roll here, I shall continue by telling you about the case of Lady X. This person happened to have been included in this very same wide-spread investigation! Lady X was the dependent wife of one non-commissioned officer within my organization. She had escaped detection during this extensive base-wide investigation— which is not to suggest that she was not involved. Hence, while Chummy and many others had preoccupied themselves with raiding base retail outlets and mail-order services, Lady X had not engaged in any of these practices! And to make matters even more difficult for investigators, customs folder entries of this lady were within normal limits. Added to this was the fact that no cashier had implicated Lady X in any black market activities! So she considered herself 'home free'! Only through a twist of fate was it discovered that Lady X was in fact the key figure in this current massive black marketing operation! It was discovered that she had purposely established a personal relationship with one high-level manager of the Port Authority near Athens. But during a rift between these two, things became a bit ugly and she was subsequently reported to local authorities— who conducted their own investigation. They discovered that Lady X had once during each month, arrived at the port via a five-ton covered truck. Investigators soon discovered that once a month this truck arrived at certain ships (while empty). But in each instance, this same truck had departed the port (fully loaded)!

It was later found that this loaded truck usually carried American-made appliances; namely ten refrigerators, ten washers, and ten dryers. These items were simply loaded onto the truck and hauled away to some waiting buyer! The cargo manifests of these ships were then manipulated or destroyed. No one had ever complained about this illegal operation. But with her arrest (and release on bail), Lady X faced several years jail time along with a huge monetary fine! Oddly, during her trial this lady was released from court proceedings for reasons of technicalities during arrest. At this point, Lady X was immediately expelled from this country and ordered to never return to her homeland of Greece!

She then left her husband (who served the remainder of his tour in-country) as she returned to the United States. I would later discover that she proceeded directly to the great state of California, where she established residence near Los Angeles. Also, once there she executed the purchase of two new and (quite expensive) homes, and I would find that she had paid the full purchase price of each in cash! Next, she drove into the city and bought a fancy new European sports car! After three months, her husband joined his highly resourceful wife— where they lived happily ever-after!

Finally, there was the case of Technical Sergeant L. This NCO completely escaped this thorough base-wide black market investigation! He had always conducted himself professionally while on duty, and gentlemanly while off-duty. Consequently TSgt. L was highly regarded by all who knew him. But TSgt. L was a loner! He was always alone whenever seen moving about the base, and he was never seen visiting any of the many fine off-base establishments. But even when considering these idiosyncrasies, everyone liked this quiet fellow. This was but one of several reasons why investigators had completely overlooked him. Oddly, he did not even own a car. Sergeant L also happened to be a member of my organization, and as such he'd occasionally visited my office for various reasons. We would invariably engage in casual and friendly conversation, and I liked this sergeant quite a bit. Finally, at the beginning of June 1975 Technical Sergeant L attended his bon voyage party atop our commercial airport's main terminal. A great number of individuals (including myself) were in attendance. Sergeant L arrived dressed in civilian attire, which was customary. He had dressed fashionably but conservatively, causing many women to notice him. There was cake along with alcoholic and non-alcoholic beverages—something for everyone. Everyone had a grand time at the farewell party of dear Technical Sergeant L!

Just three days later, I discovered that this NCO had departed from the airport carrying the sum of $50,000 cash. He had enclosed this money inside manila envelopes disguised as military documents! "How was this possible?" one might ask. It seems Sergeant L had over the past three years made authorized purchases of a variety of items through base retail outlets. However, unlike those who'd dealt in black marketeering activities, Sergeant L had sold none of the items he'd purchased over recent years. Quite to the contrary, he had stored all of his purchases inside one nearby abandoned (but secured) storage shed. He wisely had much earlier identified potential buyers for his accumulated merchandise. This sergeant had planned his scheme so well, neither of his buyers was acquainted with the other. Then just one month prior to his scheduled departure from Greece, Sergeant L separately made contact with each of his 'would-be' buyers. I discovered that on two separate occasions he had taken one single buyer to view his merchandise and had then negotiated a purchase price of $25,000 for his complete inventory. Just four hours later, Sergeant L then repeated this process with the second 'would-be' buyer. He had just negotiated a total purchase price of $50,000 for items costing him only $10,000! One month later, on the day prior to his departure from Greece, Sergeant L collected full payment in U. S. currency, with the understanding that he would meet with buyer #1 at 10:00 the following morning transfer these goods. Amazingly, he had subsequently made these same arrangements with buyer #2! At 10:00 the following morning, both buyers arrived at the very same location—only minutes apart. Each man wondered why the other was present, although neither spoke. At 10:30 Sergeant L had still not arrived! At this point the two men began tactfully querying the other as to the reason for his presence. But since each fellow suspected the other of being an undercover policeman, they avoided revealing the true nature of their visit. Finally, at 11:00, when these two strangers could no longer endure the suspense of the moment, they weakened and began divulging bits of information to each other. Imagine their astonishment and anger upon discovering that they'd each been duped! But retaliation was not possible, for at that very moment, Technical Sergeant L was airborne and heading for the United States of America! It is my understanding that Technical Sergeant L retired at an undisclosed location somewhere in South East Asia AND IS LIVING THE GOOD LIFE!

I shall now discuss with you the case of (yours truly). Months earlier I had purchased an audio receiver for my Koumparos (Greek God Father) as a gift during a special personal occasion. I received no monetary compensation for my simple gesture of gratitude. But in so doing, I had violated one little known Air Force policy requiring that I first be granted permission for such an act of generosity. At the time of this purchase I had strictly followed all existing procedural requirements. Therefore, I had initially intended on paying the full amount of customs taxes at the time of my rotation from Greece, which was standard procedure. But the discovery of my (then) sizeable monthly savings deductions had attracted the attention of investigators! They dispatched two airmen (already under investigation) to meet with me. So one afternoon as I sat at my desk processing paperwork, these two villains arrived at the door of my office, summoning me outside. I promptly left my desk, proceeding to the point where they stood. As I approached them the older of the two commented, "Jake, we just left the office of OSI Special Investigations. While we were there we happened to see a list of people who are under investigation. We wanted to make you aware that your name is on that list"! I responded, "Well, they can investigate me as much as they'd like, for there's only one item in my customs folder that I can't account for". This revelation was a huge mistake, as each of these two crooks was wearing a wire!

One week later, I was summoned to the office of our Office of Special Investigations (OSI) for an interview. Two officers began their seemingly informal interview by asking simple questions such as "How's that mean old squadron commander of yours doing these days"? But gradually, the interview advanced to more serious topics, such as "Sergeant Van York, since your arrival here, have you engaged in any form of black market activity"? I gave them my truthful answer of "No"! Near the end of our interview, the lead investigator said, "Would you object to our visiting your home to conduct an inventory of your purchases"? I could not object as this would have served as a clear indication of guilt. Accordingly, I responded "Sir, I have no objection". At this point the lead investigator commented "Fine, then let's go".

We proceeded immediately to my residence, where we found my poor wife busily cleaning our home. I was more embarrassed than concerned over this intrusion. The investigators had brought along a copy of my customs folder in an effort to facilitate their inventory. Their efforts focused upon only one item, which was the audio receiver I had previously mentioned to their two villainous spies! Upon verification that one item was in fact missing, the investigators promptly concluded their inventory.

For the next three months I heard nothing more from the investigators. During this entire period, my 'mean' commander was patient with me, and never even once appeared irate. I was even allowed to take my family to my wife's home island for a thirty-day leave. As usual we immensely enjoyed our summer vacation. Each day found us on various fine beaches. Likewise, each evening found us frequenting cafés, restaurants, and ice cream parlors. Throughout this entire period though, thoughts of my interview with OSI personnel plagued my mind. *"What if I'm demoted over this nonsensical incident? "Jake, you've worked for too many years to suddenly lose your stripes and career over this"*!

By mid-October my case was received by my commander. For this minor offense I was fined the sum of $400, which was prorated over a two-month period. I had just lost one full month's savings because of my intended act of generosity! But this was acceptable since my rank and career were no longer in jeopardy! At this point the nightly partying escalated to an even higher level, but with strong justification. I personally found myself celebrating the fact that this investigation was concluded— and I had survived! So for the remainder of the year 1975, my wife and I along with friends truly enjoyed our lives together!

The year 1976 would prove itself as peaceful and pleasant. On January 1st, my esteemed Tactical Commander, General James was promoted to the highly respected grade of lieutenant general! Promotion to such a level was unprecedented for any officer of non-flying status; however, General "J" had defied previously existing standards by attaining this rare grade level. I would often thereafter find myself wondering if my contributions in the area of reconnaissance had to any extent, enhanced the general's chances of promotion. Either way, he deserved this high degree of recognition and respect!

Meanwhile I would spend this year focusing upon completion of Senior Non-Commissioned Officer's Academy. Of course though, I would always find ample time for socializing with my dear wife and friends. So between work, studying, and partying, this year of 1976 had become one very busy year for me. Thus, before I had even realized that eight long months had passed, we'd entered into the month of September. I had completed my Air Force Academy course by correspondence. Now I found myself feverishly studying for my upcoming promotion test to the coveted grade of master sergeant! So for the following three months I prepared myself for this most rigid of tests. At the beginning of December I was administered this promotion examination. At the end of my test period, I felt quite confident with my test performance. Soon thereafter, we celebrated the holiday season, which was again a wonderful occasion for my family and me.

In January of 1977, I received a new commander in the grade of only first lieutenant. This was an extremely intelligent officer who had medically failed to meet the rigid standards required of officers on flying status. He had a mild personality, and was less confrontational in interacting with others. From the very beginning he and I got along well together, with never a challenge from him.

At the beginning of April promotions were announced. I was somewhat disappointed that I had not been selected for promotion. But just days later I received my promotion status report, indicating that I should receive promotion during the next (B-Cycle). I waited patiently, partying nightly and vacationing during the summer. Finally on October 3rd, promotions were again announced. This time the listing actually contained my name! *"Hot Ziggity"!* I thought as I quietly stood while reading this all-important promotion listing. I had finally (nearly) arrived! On November 1, 1977, I pinned on my impressive master sergeant stripes!

For the remainder of the month, I floated about on 'cloud nine'! I could not believe my great fortune! This promotion immediately resulted in another significant pay increase. So now my family and I were really positioned to enjoy life together. The shame of my past ten-year period of non-promotion had finally been erased. I soon found myself fully prepared for retiring happily in the highly respectable grade of master sergeant!

The year 1978 ushered in more of the same with respect to social activities. Incidentally, I failed to mention that during the spring of 1976, because of my outstanding duty performance, I had been afforded the opportunity to extend my previous three-year tour of duty. At the time of this generous offer, I recalled the great blunder I'd committed while stationed here in 1965. I refer to my refusal to extend for one year here in Athens, in exchange for a three-year follow-on assignment in Copenhagen, Denmark. I would not make such a blunder again! So I gladly accepted this offer of another three years here in Greece. Thus, the great party continued!

Finally we'd entered the month of May 1978. As I sat at my desk reviewing monthly reports for accuracy, I received a phone call. The caller was the secretary of Lt. Gen. James. She advised me that the general would briefly be in my area at noon of the following day to meet with me. She also assured me that this was purely a social visit. She had called ahead to confirm that I would be present. "Ma'am, please inform the general that I will definitely be here," I said. Afterwards, I sat reflecting upon what had just occurred. I was truly flattered by the fact that such a high-ranking officer would take time from his busy schedule— just to visit with me!

At noon of the following day as I sat inside my office, one of my office staff loudly announced, "Section— Attention"! I knew immediately that my visitor, General James, had arrived! I arose and then proceeded toward the reception area of our cluster of offices. But as I did so, I was somewhat startled to behold two gleaming columns of silver stars! These six stars were on the general's collar. Just as I raised my hand to salute, the general quickly grasped my hand in a firm hand shake. "Jake, how are you?,— you old son of a gun!" he exclaimed. "I'm doing just great, sir— How are you?" I asked. We then moved to my office as my staff looked on, fascinated by what they had just witnessed. "I've only got a few minutes, so I'll be brief," said the general. He then handed me two mid-sized glossy wooden containers, saying, "These are for you—thought you might like them". I thanked him wholeheartedly for my precious gifts. Then after a bit of casual conversation, the general stated, "I've gotta be running now Jake, so until next time— keep your chin up"! "I'll do just that, general," I replied. General James then took one backward step before snapping to 'attention'. I matched his movements, and we saluted each other. This great man then spun about on his heels before immediately departing my office!

My office staff stood silently in awe! Back inside my office, I opened my two containers. One contained two chromed, pearl-handled, Colt .45 automatic handguns. The smaller box held a highly polished miniature crossbow, along with six small arrows. Closer inspection revealed each of these weapons to be fully functional. I would cherish these very special gifts for the remainder of my life! I feel I should clarify here that I harbor no misconceptions regarding my relationship with General James. I am fully aware of the fact that we were not friends— or even associates. In fact, were it not for my possession of the tiny Elm device, the general and I might never have become acquainted!

The remainder of 1978 passed pleasurably. Our daughters were no longer babies, which allowed Lora and me to raise the level of our social activities. Accordingly, we found our-selves out and about, totally enjoying an unlimited number of social venues in and around this beautiful city of Athens. But even though we'd stepped-up our social activities, we still frequently took our two young daughters on excursions, sight-seeing, and dining affairs. These would eventually become known as the truly "good old days"!

Now we'd finally entered the final year of our six-year tour/vacation here in wonderful Greece. Though my entire family and I had reluctantly accepted this reality, it was difficult coming to terms with the fact that this was the year in which we would leave this beautiful country. Finally, my wife and I began making preparations for our departure. In March of 1979, I submitted my forecast application for reassignment to the great state of California (my intended retirement location). One month later though I was disappointed by having been informed that there were no vacancies within my career field in California at this particular time; and, two days later I received notification of assignment to Lowry AFB, Colorado. Now admittedly, Lowry was a fantastic assignment! Regretfully though, my family and I'd had our fill of assignments to regions with extremely frigid temperatures.

As such, I wrote a personal letter to the Commandant of Military Personnel Center (MPC) in Texas, requesting reconsideration. In my letter, I outlined the numerous fallacies within our Air Force personnel assignment system. My letter did the trick, for Just two weeks later I received a reply from the Commandant (also a general officer) informing me of assignment to Vandenberg AFB, Lompoc, California. This pleased me very much, as I viewed Vandenberg as a great assignment location— the site that houses our Air Force Ballistic Missile Testing Program. Hence, this was considered as a highly prestigious assignment, so my family and I were quite happy over this!

Just two weeks later, I was alarmed by a phone call from our local military personnel office. The young sergeant calling said, "Sergeant Van York, you must know someone in high places—because you've got an assignment change". *"Oh no"*, I thought— *"Now we won't be going to California"!* Grudgingly, I inquired of the sergeant, "Where am I going now"? Imagine my great surprise as the sergeant responded, "You're now going to March AFB, which is in Riverside, California"!

I was even more pleased because March was both prestigious and historical. More importantly, this was a centralized location. From Riverside my family and I could frequently travel to places such as Los Angeles, San Diego, Palm Springs, and even Las Vegas. These were but a few of the many great nearby locations available to us. Finally, at 11:00AM on Tuesday July 31st 1979, my family and I ended our six-year vacation in paradise by boarding one huge 747 Jumbo Jet, bound for JFK International Airport in New York. Those six wonderful years would forever remain in the memories of my loving wife, our two wonderful daughters, and me!

Chapter 16

Residence at Riverside

Upon landing and clearing customs at Kennedy Airport, my family and I immediately traveled south to Bayonne, New Jersey, where we picked up our waiting car. After locating a suitable motel, we settled in for an evening of much-needed relaxation. The following morning after breakfast we drove onto Interstate 95 south, heading for my mother's home. During this long drive I continuously exceeded posted speed limits, as I was anxious to see her. Shortly before dusk we arrived at mom's home. She had not known the exact date of our arrival, but was aware of our pending brief visit.

As we entered our driveway that evening, mom rushed out to greet us. A total of six long years had passed since this very lonely lady had seen her family. Fortunately, this period of near solitude had not adversely affected her mental capacity, and I immediately realized that she was keenly alert. Over the next three weeks, mom and my family became reacquainted. At the time mom had last seen our children, little Mari was only ten and Paraskivi seven. Needless to say, we had lots of catching up to do. We visited family friends and Aunt Emma on several occasions during our stay. We even attended church during a couple of Sundays!

Regrettably though, our visit ended much too soon, and we found ourselves once again packing suitcases for the long drive to California. On the morning of August 27th we said our farewells before once again driving onto the interstate and heading southwest. We'd had a wonderful visit with mom, but sadly it had reached its end. We passed through Georgia and then Tennessee—and onward. We were nearing the end of the absolutely hottest month of the year, August, but our vehicle (the same Monte Carlo from North Dakota) had no air-conditioning! Now imagine driving across the Texas Panhandle and through the deserts of New Mexico and Arizona— with a wife and two daughters— without air-conditioning! At the time temperatures within this region ranged above 110 degrees. We were nearly cooked by the time we reached San Bernardino! Even under these torrid conditions, our two young daughters never complained of discomfort. These were obviously two wonderful girls! After two days of constant high-speed driving, we reached the state of Arkansas, where we would spend the night in some motel. The following morning we awoke to discover that our car had been broken into, and many of our possessions had been taken! The local police indicated that such incidents were commonplace in this area. Luckily, the doors of our car had not been damaged, as the thieves had used professional equipment and techniques.

We then immediately departed this area, and I silently vowed to never again return! I was quite irate over having been vandalized, so I drove the remainder of our trip, only making a few rest stops. We finally reached our destination and did not experience any other incidents along our route. We had driven the Monte Carlo since the summer of 1970— and though we were ending the summer of the year 1979, we'd never experienced a single problem with this car!

Having spent the night in San Bernardino, we navigated our way to Riverside, just nine miles away. Then after searching the countryside for one full hour, we finally reached that historical military installation known as March Air Force Base. I had already been briefed that this base was quite similar in mission responsibility as Minot and Plattsburgh, so I was quite impressed. Then after securing my family in temporary quarters, I promptly reported to my new unit.

After briefly meeting with the first sergeant, I was escorted to the office of my squadron commander (my new supervisor). Although I must admit, I was a bit surprised to find that this officer only held the grade of captain. I found it significant though that my commander worked directly for our base commander (colonel, 06), who in turn worked for our wing commander (also colonel, 06). During my in-briefing with my new commander, I was pleased (even amazed) to discover that a new duty position had been created specifically for me! I was then informed that my official duty title would be that of Superintendant, Organizational Administration, and that I would simultaneously serve not one, but two bosses! I knew such an organizational structure would comprise a major deviation from standard operating procedure. Prior to this day I had extensively studied both leadership and management, and

I'd learned no individual is capable of effectively serving more than one boss concurrently. Therefore, based upon this premise, I was destined to fail in my new assignment! At this point I was tempted to protest, although I accepted this assignment without further comment, fully realizing that over the next twelve months, every ounce of managerial skill I possessed would be squeezed from my very being!

Upon entering my new and unique position, I was surprised to find that my supervisory role consisted of managing all administrative and human resource management programs of two nonrelated organizations, with manpower totaling 725 military personnel. This assignment would normally have been overwhelming for anyone! Nevertheless, I would assume my new duties within just three days. Fortunately each of my two immediate bosses held the grade of only captain, and each consistently conducted themselves in a professional manner. However, there's more to this, for I was also indirectly responsible to their bosses (base commander and wing commander, respectively). But what none of these officers knew was that I'd already made plans for retirement, to become effective just one year later. At the time I definitely did not anticipate remaining on duty for another full three years!

At this point I was tempted to provide the lengthy details of this newly implemented combined organizational operation to General James. However, I strongly believed that had I done so, other units also might have been tempted to install similar structures and procedures. Although I would exceed expectations in my new assignment, I did not wish such challenging responsibility to be placed upon any human being. Accordingly, I shall omit details while merely stating, over the three-year duration of this duty, I would successfully disprove this aspect of management theory! One year into this unique assignment, I would be rewarded by promotion to the highly coveted grade of senior master sergeant! Ultimately, upon retirement I would be recognized through the award of one final prestigious medal!

Meanwhile, two weeks into this assignment I stumbled upon another longtime friend, also named Bill. I shall refer to this fellow as Bill M. It so happened, Bill M had just recently retired from the Air Force, and he had entered the business of financial planning and insurance. Surprisingly, he wasted no time in inviting me (along with several others) to join him in this lucrative industry. After carefully considering my friend's offer, I enthusiastically accepted. But in preparation of entering into this totally nonrelated career, I was required to undergo extensive training prior to taking the state's qualification examination. Thusly, over the next sixty-day period I devoted a great amount of effort toward learning my new job while at the very same time familiarizing myself with the intricate details of an insurance and financial planning career.

Then just two months later while on my second attempt, I successfully passed the California state's exam for licensed agents. With the receipt of my agent's license I pursued the studies of financial planning. Soon I found myself raking in the cash! Luckily, my friend Bill "M" had quickly secured a very generous producer's contract with one of our nation's (then) leading financial firms. At this point I figured I was finally prepared to reenter civilian life, although I had not known that the Air Force would, at a later date, provide me an alternative. I felt confident that I'd entered into a viable source of supplemental income upon retirement from the United States Air Force.

I chose to continue driving my aging Monte Carlo, as I had previously been advised that in seeking to purchase a home, I should present myself as debt-free if possible. From the day of our arrival here at March Air Force Base, my wife and I had been searching for a new home. Then finally we located one pre-owned home that had been well maintained and would accommodate our needs. Thus, we moved into our very own home on December 1st 1979. This was a huge step for us; hence, our entire family was happy over this purchase. Then finally after nine long years, we drove into the beautiful city of Riverside, where we purchased a fancy new Buick. So at this point, we had ourselves a decent home, a nice new car, and a stable and ever-increasing income. So it goes without saying— we had another truly great holiday season (preceded by birthdays of course)! Thus far, our time in and around Riverside had been quite pleasant.

I had remained in frequent contact with General James back in D.C. During one such telephone call, he advised me of his rapidly approaching retirement. He was planning his new career as chief executive officer of one of our nation's major aerospace defense firms. He also said that I would be granted at least one full year's release from reconnaissance duties. I thanked the general sincerely, for although I had thoroughly enjoyed such exciting duty, I realized that I could use a vacation!

Time kept moving forward, and now it was April 1980.

At this time, even though I fully intended to submit my retirement application, I allowed my dual commanders to talk me into taking the promotion examination for possible promotion to senior master sergeant. I came away with the strong feeling that I had performed quite well on this managerial examination. Then just three months later, I would receive verbal confirmation from my base commander that I had in fact been selected for promotion to the highly coveted grade of senior master sergeant (E-8)!

Unfortunately, concurrently with my promotion notification, I found myself facing a condition commonly referred to as dichotomy. Specifically, as I was elated over the notification of this significant promotion, I'd received a separate phone call notifying me of my dear mother's impending death! I immediately and completely removed all promotion consideration from my thoughts as I hurriedly prepared to board the very next commercial flight heading for South Carolina.

I finally arrived at mom's small brick home. A neighbor had been informed of my possible arrival, so she invited me to dine with her family. Naturally I accepted. I then quickly rushed through my meal before climbing into mom's car and driving somewhat maniacally to the capital city of Columbia. But once there (without GPS) I roamed about this city in search of the famous Richland Memorial Hospital. I was highly impressed by the professionalism of this hospital's staff, along with the immaculate condition of the hospital itself. But upon meeting mom's doctor, I became even more impressed! I discovered that a team of several doctors had participated in mother's surgical procedure. Unfortunately, the surgery had not been completely successful.

Even before visiting mom's room, I'd been briefed by her lead surgeon of these concerns. In short, it was generally felt that she would not leave this hospital alive. Fortunately, they did not know mom! Now although she was near death and heavily sedated, I immediately detected that mom was thrilled by my presence. I held her feeble hands as I sat at her bedside, desperately attempting to comfort and console her, but naturally she was much too weak to respond noticeably to my words and gestures. Finally, at 10:00PM I was ushered from her comfortable hospital room.

The following morning I returned to the hospital to find mom slightly improved. I remained with her throughout the entire day, having my lunch in the hospital's spacious cafeteria. Each day I would feign cheerfulness as I strived to return my wonderful mother to a stable condition. For the next two weeks I visited mom, spending full days with her. I would tell her short stories about my family and experiences in traveling about this world. During this time I was not aware that mom's doctors had not expected her to survive her cancer surgery. Miraculously though, with each passing day she grew a bit stronger, clinging to her belief that our Lord would not abandon her during this period of tribulation.

Finally after just two short weeks, mom had recovered sufficiently to be released from hospitalization. She was transported via ambulance to her home, where she daily continued improving. Unfortunately, I still had never learned to properly prepare meals. In noting this, mom herself began cooking each day for the two of us. Naturally, I did the washing and housekeeping chores. Eventually, I asked, "Mom, how will you survive once I've left"?

She then answered, "Well, son, He has brought me this far, so I'm trusting in Him to take me through the rest of my journey".

I extended a personal invitation that mom come to live with us in our new California home, and after much deliberation, she accepted my offer. During this one-week period, I'd returned mom to Richland Memorial for three separate physical exams. On Monday of the fourth week we visited her doctor once more. At the end of our visit he and I held a private briefing, during which time he revealed to me that in his professional opinion, she would survive less than three more years. I was devastated by this revelation! Nevertheless, her panel of doctors issued their approval for her to travel to California.

Having finally secured mom's medical release, we made rushed preparations for our rapidly approaching date of departure. First, we gave away the vast majority of her belongings to family, friends, and charitable organizations such as the American Red Cross. I then contacted a former classmate who had become a realtor and with mom's permission, I regretfully placed her cherished home on the market. Within just one hour her house had sold! The only condition attached to this transaction was that mom was asked to provide the necessary financing. Fortunately, I had already become quite familiar with the intricacies of financial planning and advised her that she would benefit financially by complying with this request. Without protesting she accepted my advice, whereupon we concluded this transaction within hours of our initial listing.

Three days later, I packed mom's spacious Chevrolet Caprice with her most precious belongings inside its very large trunk. I also placed a number of pillows across the car's rear seat and along the inner sides of its rear seat compartment. Neighbors and family friends stood looking on in utter disbelief as I loaded the car. They simply could not believe that they would never again see this wonderful lady (their dear friend)! Finally, after a very emotional farewell I secured mom upon the wide rear seat of her car before sadly driving away. At this point, my foremost concern was that this poor lady had never lived outside the state of South Carolina in her entire lifetime! *"How will my mother fare out in California"?* I asked myself. As I drove along I continuously talked to her, frequently checking on her via the car's rearview mirror. This would be quite a long trip, and mom's serious health condition would further compound matters. However, I was both relaxed and comfortable— for this time we were afforded air-conditioning! Finally, on the evening of June 26th we safely arrived at our home at the outskirts of Riverside.

I had much earlier advised my loving wife of my plans to relocate mom into our home, having been fully aware of the potential for personality problems between these two ladies. Fortunately, Lora instantly welcomed my mom into our modest home. The very next day I located the most highly recommended oncologist within southern California. Luckily he had an open appointment on the morning of the coming Wednesday. So after returning to work on Monday and Tuesday, I took Wednesday morning off and escorted mom to her doctor's appointment. Lora joined us for moral support and assistance. I was immediately impressed by our oncologist, who upon examining mom and ordering blood work quickly established a treatment program comprised of chemotherapy. Our new doctor commenced mom's treatment on the following Monday morning. Then for the next eighteen months she suffered as she endured this debilitating treatment!

Meanwhile, at work I'd become quite adept at managing comprehensive administration programs for two very large military organizations. Then just two months after my return to duty, each of my organizations underwent major annual inspection by our Air Force Inspector General's team of specialists. But after three days of systematically reviewing all available records of these two major organizations, they had uncovered only minimal discrepancies. As a result, each of these organizations received inspection ratings of EXCELLENT. I had already been informed that recent ratings had resulted in the issuance of only SATISFACTORY ratings; thus, this had been a significant improvement in combat readiness! These ratings served to solidify my standing with each of my two bosses, and their bosses (wing commander and base commander, respectively). Suddenly I became known as the local authority of administrative programs. Consequently, I was then granted greater freedom of movement, allowing me to function virtually free of supervision. I truly enjoyed my newfound freedom! With my newly attained status, I soon found myself enjoying life considerably more than usual. Each weekend I would take my family (including mom) into nearby cities such as Los Angeles, Palm Springs, and San Diego. Several evenings each week we would visit Riverside, San Bernardino, and numerous other cities of close proximity. I soon realized that by having been reassigned from Lompoc to Riverside, we had greatly benefited in terms of access to other major cities. Time for my extended family and me marched forward, and soon the date of November 1ˢᵗ had arrived. This was my actual promotion effective date to senior master sergeant! I find it quite difficult to adequately describe my feelings of elation!

Generally speaking, everything in our lives was going just great— with the exception of mom's slowly deteriorating condition. Simply stated, my dear mom was not improving! At this point I contacted her doctor seeking advice relative to the discontinuance of her unbearable treatment. Early into our conversation he shocked me by commenting, "Jake, I thought you were calling to tell me that your mother had just passed away"! I was stunned, so I inquired, "Doctor, since you feel that my mother might die at any moment, then why do you require that she continue this treatment"? The doctor then casually commented, "Your mother has my approval to cease her treatment at any time she so desires". I thanked the doctor for his candid observation before promptly ending my phone call. At this point I realized that this competent doctor had expected that my mother might die at any given moment. I then thought *"Why should mom suffer this treatment in vain'?* That evening at home as we sat chatting together, I casually asked, "Sis, how do you feel about taking your medical treatment"? "Son, I don't believe I'm getting any better at all." mom replied. "Well, I talked to your doctor this afternoon and he says if you would like to stop your treatment, then you may do so." I said. Instantly, mom's eyes lit up! This was the very first time I'd seen any display of happiness by her since arriving here in California. From this day forward, she would undergo no further chemotherapy! Then just one month later we noticed dramatic improvement in her appearance and demeanor! She had regained much of her hair and physical strength, and her skin tone had been rejuvenated! One year later, mom had seemingly returned to normal. She would continue living happily for another seven long years, surviving on faith alone! (NOTE: DO NOT ATTEMPT THESE DRASTIC MEASURES, BASED UPON THESE COMMENTS)! I am not suggesting (even for a moment) that any of my readers choose to follow this example. I have merely presented this case because this was exactly the way it happened. Ironically, as mom's condition improved she began expressing her strong desires that she be allowed to return to her hometown in South Carolina. I would occasionally ask, "Sis, since you're here in California with your only family, why do you wish so very badly to return home to South Carolina"? She would smile and answer, "Son, out here— I never get to see anybody I know." I fully understood her plight, for I recalled how during my earlier years, I had always searched for some familiar face upon reporting onto a new base. But now that I had my wonderful family with me, I no longer felt such great loneliness; consequently, I no longer searched for familiar faces.

With mom having apparently recovered, morale within my family quickly and noticeably improved. Conditions at work remained consistently pleasant, paralleling conditions within my household. With the rapidly passing months, we soon entered the month of January 1982. At this time I submitted my application for retirement from the military. Over the coming months I stepped up my efforts in job hunting activities, focusing primarily upon the Aerospace Defense Industry. In conducting my job searches, I visited every defense corporation within southern California. "But Jake, what about your insurance and financial planning career?" you might ask. Well, it so happened that the more I delved into these fields, the more I realized that I should also seek a regular day job. Hence, my many job searches. I would retain my approved license for this type of work, while using this career to merely supplement my regular income. In time I would discover that I had made the proper decision.

Meanwhile I continued job hunting, but with a number of potential base closures pending, defense firms had begun reducing their hiring practices. This meant my chances of securing meaningful employment were rapidly becoming more and more limited! On August 31st, I shed my military uniform and then proceeded on sixty days' terminal leave. My actual effective date of retirement was established as November 1, 1982. During my two-month period of terminal leave I had continued my job search. One month later I received an interview with one of our nation's leading aerospace defense corporations! After the first and second interviews, I was called back for a third time. This third interview invitation provided me with strong hopes for a job offer, as it was quite often during this final interview that job offers were made. Shortly before 2:00PM on the date of my final interview, I approached the receptionist's desk of the firm at which I sought employment. On each occasion I had ensured that I was well-groomed and well-dressed (although conservatively). After two prior interviews this receptionist remembered me. "Good afternoon, Mr. Van York. Mr. Smith will be with you momentarily." she said. I politely thanked the receptionist before turning away to take my seat. Then after approximately fifteen minutes of waiting, a middle-aged gentleman of medium build and height approached my seated position. "Mr. Van York?" he asked. Yes sir," I smilingly responded. "Please come with me," replied my interviewer". We then proceeded for some distance down a very long corridor, before arriving at this gentleman's spacious and well-decorated office. "Please be seated," he said. "I've carefully reviewed your qualifications, and quite frankly— I'm very impressed." he stated. He then arose and walked to where I sat, extending his hand as he said, "Welcome to Dockwell International"!

His surprising comments nearly floored me; although, I outwardly maintained composure. As I thanked my interviewer, he continued. "I'm assigning you to our B-1 Bomber project"! Those words thrilled me beyond belief! My interviewer instructed me to pick up a folder containing forms to be completed from the receptionist up front. I thanked him courteously before immediately proceeding to the receptionist's desk. "Congratulations Mr. Van York," commented the receptionist as she handed me the folder. I also cordially thanked her before proceeding directly to my car. During my short walk, I was tempted to perform a little dance step in celebration of having just been hired into such an important position. I maintained self-restraint though until after such time as I'd reentered my vehicle. I then uncontrollably voiced a series of loud "woops"! I simply could not believe my great fortune! Now for those of you who are not familiar with the term "B-1 Bomber," this was the successor of our Air Force's awesome B-52 Bomber. It is also the predecessor of our current B-2 Stealth Bomber. My reasons for such great elation stemmed from the fact that I would be directly involved in the production of this very special aircraft! After leaving the aerospace facility, I rushed home to relay this wonderful news to my wife and family. Then for the next three hours I busied myself in completing the batch of forms I had been given. Later in the evening Lora and I drove into the city of Riverside, where we celebrated my new job offer. We would continue celebrating throughout the weekend. It goes without saying that this was a truly great moment in our lives!

The weekend finally passed, and at 9:00AM Monday morning (September 27th) I returned the thick batch of completed forms to Dockwell's Human Resource Office. Imagine my great dismay and disappointment upon being notified that as a result of current and ongoing funding reductions in our government's defense budget, the Dockwell firm had just today suspended its hiring program! The word "devastation" in no way describes the disappointment I felt at that moment. But even worse, I would soon face my wife with this unbearable news. Surprisingly, Lora understood my predicament and consoled me. Unfortunately, I was so totally dejected, I completely terminated my search for employment!

I returned to school, taking nighttime college courses in pursuit of my eventual degree. I had already completed a number of college courses while serving in the military, so I would end up spending only the next three years attending night school. For the next twelve months I would work as a security guard, a janitor, and an insurance agent/financial planner in addition to attending evening college courses.

One year later while attending one of my classes, I was

casually offered an entry-level civil service position on Norton Air Force Base located at nearby San Bernardino. The very next morning I took the ten-mile drive up to Norton AFB. Upon arrival there I completed formal application for this position. Just three days later, on November 1st 1983 I eagerly began work on Norton AFB, as an administrator within the United States Department of Defense! I quickly discovered that the actual work I would perform was quite interesting. I was fortunate in that I had been at least temporarily released from reconnaissance duties for the first year of this assignment. Consequently, during this period my little acoustic device (the Elm) would remain sealed inside its holding candle. This allowed me to fully concentrate on my regularly assigned duties of administration. As a result, over the following two years, I received rapid promotions through GS-6 and GS-7, culminating with a substantial promotion to grade of WS-4 (equivalent GS-10). My retirement and civilian income rapidly increased to more than $40,000 per year. Additionally, I continued receiving a certain amount of income from my insurance/financial planning business. In short, I would not find the need for concern over a lack of spending cash. At this juncture, I felt that I'd arrived!

Incidentally, one sunny Sunday afternoon during the month of June 1984, Lora and I placed my dear mother onto a jumbo jet headed for South Carolina. This would become mom's first and only airplane travel during her entire lifetime, although she would complete this trip all alone and unassisted. She would luckily enjoy a safe and trouble-free flight back to her home state, where she would resume her life— living both comfortably and happily (on faith) over the next five years! Might I mention here that the respectable manner in which my parents had lived their lives, netted them a great number of trustworthy friends. It would be these very same friends who would care for and assist mom until the very end!

Well my friends, it is a widely known fact that all things in life eventually reach an ending. Accordingly, so has my candid story of my earlier days on this planet. Although, I must say here that I have truly enjoyed visiting with you in this manner. In conclusion, I leave each of you with this very special prayer and wish. I sincerely wish for you continued love, happiness, peace, and prosperity! Now until next time, this has been:

Yours Truly,
Jake Van York

P. S. During the years 1985 through 1989, I (and the Elm) would again deploy into regions of North Africa and the Middle East on six separate occasions. Following the successful completion of these covert operations, the Elm would rest until June 2006, at which time I would honor this most magnificent device with a proper burial at sea— within the depths of the crystalline waters of the vast Pacific Ocean!